I0716489

SIGILS & SUSHI

SIGILS & SUSHI
BOOK ONE

NIA QUINN

Robot Dinosaur Press

Published by
Robot Dinosaur Press

https://robotdinosaurpress.com/
Robot Dinosaur Press is a trademark of Chipped Cup Collective

Author Photo: Cali Walters

KDP32028290

ISBN: 978-1-958696-27-9 (paperback)
ISBN: 978-1-958696-25-5 (ebook)

First paperback edition September 2023

SIGILS & SUSHI

To those who can laugh even on their worst days.

AUTHOR'S NOTE

No cats or dogs were harmed in the making of this book.

For a list of potentially triggering content present
or alluded to in this book, please flip to the list at the end of the
book, or view an updated list at:

niaquinn.com/triggerwarnings-sigils/

FANGED FIENDS & MAGICAL MISHAPS

I'm the weirdo who makes friends with crows and collects little demons who just want to retire in peace, damn it.

I'm the crazy girl who pored over medieval-sword-replica catalogs until I was old enough to afford one—best use of a lemonade stand ever.

I'm the witch who never could quite get a grasp on how to work magic properly, but uses it anyway.

Enter my current problem, stage right.

My job is checking in rental cars—sounds pretty boring, I know. But when your town is the headquarters for the Harmonic Council, all sorts of interesting supernatural customers fly in and need a set of fancy wheels.

And the stuff they leave behind in their cars at 6 a.m. on a Monday morning?

That's worth getting out of bed before the crack of dawn for.

The cars come to me first. The clients toss me their keys, I enter their mileage and gas level into my gizmo, and check for any damage. The shop guys are supposed to be the ones who clean the cars, but I always do a courtesy clean before they waltz up. Not like a deep-clean or anything, just grabbing any obvious trash or larger items—empty cups, fast-food bags, Beats headphones, a dragonfly pin that commands the loyalty of a pixie.

Super nice of me, I know.

It's not like it's stealing—people buy this junk knowing they're going to leave it behind. Mostly. At least three customers a day hand me a camping chair, a bottle of booze, or a wrapped muffin from their hotel, because they don't want to deal with it. It doesn't fit in their carry-on, so they don't want it.

Ah, to be rich. Or at least not edging the poverty line like I am.

So, there I was, popping the trunk of this black BMW, when some bitty beastie jumped out at me, fangs first. I try not to use magic aside from my sigils—which are foolproof, thank Finéa—but when some fiend with more teeth than skin wants to stake a claim on your nose, you don't worry so much about misfires.

I swatted a hand down, sparking with magenta magic like a downed power line at a rave, and Fangy crashed to the asphalt . . . as did the bumper of the BMW.

Crud on crackers.

After a frantic glance around to make sure no one had witnessed me beating up a poor innocent $60,000 car, I raised my voice to carry down the lot. "What the hell? I think this guy got rear-ended and just hoped we wouldn't notice!"

It wasn't like it'd do him any harm—my scanner gizmo said that Mr. Sutula had rental insurance, which I highly advise getting if you ever rent a car. You never know when a deer or a golem is going to end up on the hood of your Mercedes.

You also never know when you'll end up within three blocks of me. Better to play it safe.

A newly cleaned Lexus zipped into the nearest open space, and Bert hopped out, heading my way. "This the one you're yelling about, Immy?" He jerked his chin at the BMW, inscrutable behind his dark sporty sunglasses.

But I'm Bert's favorite—he's the one I give all the customers' extra booze to, so even if he knows my story is a total crock, he'll let it be.

"That's it, yeah. See the bumper?" I pointed, like it wasn't completely obvious.

"Here, grab that end."

I crouched down and hefted one end while he lifted the other, holding it in place against the car. "A little higher . . . there." Something sizzled along the edge of the plastic, and after a moment Bert let go. I backed up cautiously, and the bumper held. Bert's a quarter svartalf or something—I don't ask questions. He gets the job done. "That'll hold till I can work on it later."

"Thanks." I ran a hand through my curly pixie cut.

"This one ready to go back?"

"Yeah, just watch out for toothy little monsters. One jumped out at me. Hopefully it doesn't have any friends."

"Got it." He jogged over to my booth and pulled a modified ping-pong paddle off the wall.

"Hey, that's—"

Bert climbed in the car, and it purred to life, and in a flash he was gone, cruising down the lot.

"—mine."

I pulled the next couple cars up to fill the gap, then got to scanning barcodes and checking mileage again.

I was on hands and knees, inspecting a scratch above a wheel well on a bright yellow Camaro, when stinging pain lanced through my ankle and I jerked forward, banging my head on the car door. I growled, scrambled around, and kicked my leg viciously, trying to dislodge the new toothy bane of my existence.

What the hell *was* this thing?

One last fierce kick, and a little blue streak flew over the next row of cars, followed by a metallic clang.

I held my breath, listening. Sirens and songbirds, had I at *least* managed to knock it out?

The lot was silent, with only the faint splash-and-clunk of the car wash in the distance.

I got to my feet cautiously, and snuck around the neighboring car to take a good look at my quarry.

Nothing. The asphalt was bare of fanged disasters, unconscious or otherwise.

I glanced around warily, hands held out in a lame karate-chop stance. If Bert was going to make a habit of stealing my anti-monster tools, I really needed to start bringing my sword to work.

A shadow twitched under the nearest car, followed by the most sinister chittering I've ever heard. I know, 'chittering' and 'sinister' don't usually go together—just take my word for it.

I froze. Maybe it had a terrible sense of smell and sight . . . *and* hearing, and only attacked based on movement?

Yeah, right.

Well, I had an extra layer of protection that no one else knew about—if I could activate it soon enough to make a difference. I slowly raised my right arm and focused on the tattoo on my wrist—a rib cage intertwined with poppies.

The ink began flowing under my skin.

Don't ask me how I discovered I can do this. Okay, *fine*. I was that moron who got their boyfriend's name tattooed on my wrist. We were happily ever after, after all.

Until about three weeks later, when I found out he was banging some Lamian girl.

I glared daggers at that tattoo for about two days before it *moved*. A bit of practice, a few years later, and here I am—unable to reliably do a single piece of magic aside from shifting ink around under my skin.

It's a cool party trick, and sure as heck saves on the budget for new tats. The hard part is convincing a reputable tattoo artist to just keep packing ink willy-nilly as I basically blow it out. Look, I *know* it's not supposed to work that way. The last guy fainted, so I dropped a twenty and pointed him out to the buff receptionist on my way out.

Most people draw sigils in a more traditional way—pen on paper, chalk on pavement, Sharpie on the back of their hand—though I've seen a couple rich supers come through the car rental who had sigils tattooed bold as brass on their biceps. Clearly they weren't worried about getting mugged for the designs. I'd snapped pics real quick, but the sigils were pretty weak sauce—no one wants to run around giving out freebie imprisonment sigils or anything.

You *can* draw sigils on your phone, for safekeeping or practice or whatever, as long as you don't charge them—one hearty zap of magic and you've got an eight-hundred-dollar brick riding around in your pocket instead of an iPhone. The Apple wizards are great at enchanting their tech with leash spells and theft-deterrent hexes, but there's no getting around the fact that delicate chips and wires just don't play well with concentrated bursts of magic.

The ink on my wrist blew out into a messy halo, and then, eyebrows knitted in concentration, I channeled it inward one line at a time, forming my stealth sigil.

A car zipped down the aisle, and I stopped, clasping my wrist not-so-surreptitiously with the other hand.

Aaron, a skinny kid with red hair, parked a clean Toyota Sienna in one of the bays, water drops still shimmering in the sun, then jogged over and ducked into the last car left in my lanes. I waved, and he flashed the lights before zooming back to the shop.

After a quick glance around, I focused on my ink again. Just a little more, and—there. The sigil was complete. I double-checked it against my memory to make sure I wasn't about to knock the roof off the booth or something stupid, then touched a finger to the symbol, infusing it with a zip of my magenta magic.

A frisson of energy snapped up around me and diffused out to about twenty feet, leaving behind a subtle prickle on my skin. It didn't even set off any car alarms.

Score one for me.

My stealth sigil is pretty handy, as sigils go, which is why it's one of only two I have memorized. As far as I can tell, it muffles my sound and scent, and, according to my friend Damarion, dissipates my heat signature and puts the kibosh on any tracking spells in my general vicinity. It doesn't do anything for visibility, but if whatever you're hiding from already has eyes on you, you're probably screwed anyway.

I'd just have to hope Fangy wasn't lurking in a wheel well, waiting for me to turn my back. There were distractions aplenty across the lot—the racket of the car wash and vacuums, birds and pixies picking dead bugs and worse off car grilles, chewing gum sprites rolling along looking for shoes to victimize. With any luck, something had distracted the wee beastie for a minute.

I slipped into my booth and thunked out the first-aid kit, crackling open an ancient bandage wrapper and gluing the cloth strip across my sigil. That thing was probably never coming back off. Then I scooted the top book off my stack of ratty paperbacks, kicking back in my wheelless no-longer-rolly chair.

I glanced at the cover: *Minimum Wage Magic* by Rachel Aaron. Nice—I'd been looking forward to this one.

Half this job is waiting for the next car to come in, and I am abso-freaking-lutely delighted to spend company time and money on getting through my TBR pile.

I was on page twenty-seven when a customer rolled into one of my lanes in a bright red Chrysler. Sighing, I looked around for a bookmark, ripped the cardboard top off a new tissue box, and stuck it in the book. Whatever works, right?

By the time I got out of my booth, the classy silver-blonde woman was already halfway to the airport door, her black blazer blowing in the wind, and another car was pulling up behind hers.

Scan, mileage, damage check, and I was on to the second car, whose driver looked unsure about what to do.

"Good morning," I chirped, plastering a customer-service smile on my face. "Go ahead and get unloaded, and I'll take care of the car."

The guy looked like some kind of fae—pale green skin, leaves twining through his hair, not to mention a small purple lizard just chilling up there. He retracted thin vines that had curled around the steering wheel, turned the car off, and pocketed the keys. I waited for him to get out of the car before putting out a hand.

"I'll just need the car keys, sir." He fumbled in his pocket and held them out sheepishly. "Thanks." I noted down the car's info while he got *three* carry-ons out of the trunk and headed toward the airport, the bags tipping off their wheels and nearly tripping him every five seconds.

"Sheesh."

I checked the trunk, but it was clean. Back seat—nothing. Front seat, empty. The little flip-down compartment under the radio?

A fifty-dollar bill.

I squinted through the windshield to verify the frazzled guy was nowhere in sight. He was long gone, which made the cash fair game.

Cha-ching.

I pulled out my phone and sent a text to my friend Samaire.

Immy: You up for sushi tonight?

A minute later, a reply popped up.

Samaire: Sure, I go on at 8, does 6 work for you?

I sent a thumbs-up followed by every sushi emoji I could scrounge up, and a heart-eyes smiley for good measure. Every day I got to eat something other than microwave chimichangas was a fabulous day.

More cars rolled in, and I started to sweat. It wasn't usually this busy on a Tuesday, not after the 6 a.m. rush, anyway.

Bert tried to make off with the red Chrysler, and I pointed an accusatory finger at him. "You! Eager beaver! Not that one, I haven't cleared it yet."

Bert shrugged and hooked a thumb at the Mazda behind it. I nodded absently and got back to work.

The cars kept piling up, customers hurrying to gather their carry-ons and make their flights.

"Leave your keys on the windshield, and you can go!" I called.

Most of them already knew the drill and were halfway to the airport entrance, but a couple customers slapped their keys down—don't worry, the glass is all spelled with no-chip enchantments—and scurried after the others.

One car remained occupied, and I stood on tiptoe to see what was going on.

Oh crap.

The Centaurmobile was back, and he'd pulled into the wrong lane.

CENTAURS & SNICKERDOODLES

I strode down the line of cars and rapped on the window. "Just a moment, sir, and I'll get these cars out of your way."

If the genius had just pulled into the outer lane like he was supposed to, he'd have plenty of room to get out of the car. But no, he'd ignored the 'standard vehicles only' signs painted on the asphalt and squeezed into the inner lane, wedging himself between the overhang and the other cars, with no room to disembark.

I skimmed the keys off the windshield of the adjacent car and hopped in. Keeping one foot out with the door ajar, I whipped the Hyundai out of the tight line of cars and backed it up, punching in the mileage and doing a damage check real quick before flagging down one of the shop guys to take it back.

The Centaurmobile was already cracked open Delorean-style, and out he came, one hoof at a time. I never got tired of watching centaurs extricate themselves from those death traps.

The centaur looked down on me from his ridiculous height, wearing a poorly tailored multipiece suit that covered the bulk of him. Gauging his expression, I slowly replaced the business card of a good tailor I'd been sliding out of my back pocket.

No need to risk an early death at the hooves of a peeved centaur.

"You haven't asked me why I don't just gallop about," he noted.

Seriously? "Last I checked, centaurs can't go seventy on the freeway," I said.

He nodded approvingly and trotted off. Weirdo.

Sure, there are plenty of ignoramuses who don't put their brain in gear when it comes to magical beings, but to go around interrogating anyone who *doesn't* make faulty assumptions? That's a great way to end up on the Asshole Alert subreddit.

Three more cars stalked down the lot, making a beeline for my lanes.

Man, there must be some conference that just wrapped up, with all the attendees eager to get home. I jogged down to make sure the drivers knew what to do, and started clearing cars.

Two more pulled up right as "I Like Food" by Descendants blared from my phone, signaling it was lunchtime. My stomach grumbled in synchronicity. I palmed my phone, silenced the alarm, and shot off a text to my manager.

Immy: Hey, do you mind spelling me for lunch? It's that time.

My phone buzzed a second later. *Omw.*

I helped some little old lady with black claws get her carry-on off the backseat, just about giving myself a hernia in the process. What was in this thing, bricks of gold-pressed latinum? I hoped it fit under her seat, because no way was she hoisting it into an overhead bin.

She peered at me dubiously, slit pupils narrowing. "You're not giving off any heat."

"I know."

She smiled. "Smart girl, not giving away your secrets. Keep it up."

Grandma Claws was cheerfully rolling the carry-on away when my manager, Keisha, shuffled up. Keisha is four-foot-six, fat, and has long purple hair. She's an absolute delight and brooks no nonsense. Also, she brings a fresh batch of cookies to work every day. Today was apparently snickerdoodle day.

"Dessert," she said, shoving a plastic-wrapped snickerdoodle at me. I took the cookie with one hand, and tugged the strap of my scanner over my head with the other, handing it over.

"I have everything after the Chevy checked in, but they just keep coming." I nodded at another vehicle cruising into place at the end of the right lane.

"Bet you one of your books I'll have 'em all cleared out before you're back on shift. You got any beach romances in there?"

"Uh . . ." I mentally perused the box of finished books I kept under the booth counter. "How about a beach romance with a bit of kraken horror thrown in?"

"I'll take it. Enjoy your lunch, kiddo." She cinched the strap on the scanner so it wasn't slapping against her knee, then strode off, disappearing between the cars.

Back in the booth, I unearthed *Kisses & Killer Krakens* from the cardboard box and put it on the counter. I set a timer for thirty minutes on my phone, then yanked half a microwave pizza out of the mini fridge—the kind that basically turns into congealed cheese on soggy-yet-hard flatbread, with cornmeal that's probably actually sawdust. I buzzed it in the microwave for a minute and picked up my copy of *Minimum Wage Magic* again.

Ding! I teased out the orange-grease-stained paper plate and started nibbling at the pizza hanging off the edge of the plate. The last thing I needed was a neon-orange thumbprint on one of the pages. Sure, my books were ratty, but I draw the line at *gross*.

Once I'd polished off the pizza, I swished around a good slug of water to take care of any remaining sawdust between my teeth, and scooted

Keisha's cookie over. I reverently pulled the plastic wrap away from the snickerdoodle one corner at a time. Cookie in one hand, book in the other, I thoroughly enjoyed the rest of my lunch break.

Bring-a-ling-a-ling! My phone chattered at me, letting me know relaxation time was over. I hit the power button to silence it, and glanced up. Keisha had cleared most of the cars, but the first three right outside my booth still lingered. One of the shop guys had pulled up, and she was talking to him through the driver's window, her expression less than pleased.

Were we looking at the next great pixie purge? The last time, the flying miscreants had dumped peanut-butter-flavored IncrediBubbles into the car wash solution. How they'd gotten their fiendish little hands on such a huge quantity, I couldn't even begin to guess. We really should just get a cat for the shop, but it's hard to find a feline who doesn't mind hanging around torrential downpours of soapy water day in and day out.

I dumped the plate and plastic wrap in the trash and grabbed the kraken book before heading over.

"What's up?" I leaned against the hood of the Audi, looking between Bert and Keisha.

"You didn't get the emergency alert from the Harmonic Council?" Keisha frowned.

"I don't think so . . ." I slipped my phone out of my pocket. Huh. It must've come in at the same time as my back-to-work alert.

Sure as sugar, there it was: *HARMONIC COUNCIL EMERGENCY ALERT - A dragon storm is approaching from the northwest. Be advised of severe weather, including rain, hail, lightning, shed scales, flooding, and micro tornadoes later this evening. Seek shelter indoors where possible.*

Saskia Springs handles any run-of-the-mill alerts—half banshees with dementia wandering around wailing in the middle of the night, malfunctioning golems, spree killers, that sort of thing. The Harmonic Council only chimes in for the big stuff.

A dragon storm is middling on the scale of big stuff. If you're sensible, you'll probably be fine. If you're not . . . Well, they'll probably find your lightning-riddled corpse floating in a sewer a week later.

"You're off lunch?" Keisha asked. I nodded. "Great, then get these last cars cleared. Bert, bring the guys up, and we'll start anchoring the cars and putting up the rubber buffers."

Magic often goes haywire in a dragon storm, but hook up a hefty chain between a car frame and the massive eye bolt embedded in every parking space, and at least the cars won't float away when the floodwaters hit. The rubber buffers are to help keep the cars from bashing into each other, though we always get some dings and dents regardless.

"Aye, aye, Captain." I handed her the book and scarpered off before she could protest. She was a stickler for winning bets fair and square, but it wasn't like I needed the book anymore.

I cleared the furthest back of the three cars first, pocketing a couple quarters from inside the center console and a pair of mirrored sunglasses from the holder above the windshield.

Alex, our only shop gal, dumped the first load of buffers out the back of a hatchback after parking it, then ambled over to me.

"Can I steal this one?"

I dropped the keys in her hand. "Sure thing. New undercut?"

She scuffed a hand along the buzzed hair below her messy bun, shaved to resemble rolling waves. "Yeah. You like?"

"Looks awesome."

She smiled and ducked into the car, revving the engine before whisking it away.

The second car was empty, and I thought the third was too, until something glinted at me from between the front seats.

In the bottom of the cup holder nestled a shiny trinket that looked like it should be under glass.

On a pedestal.

In a vault.

Surrounded by lasers and tripwire spells.

I peered closer. It was about the size of a donut hole; a creepy oblong black void encircled by something like one of those chintzy time-turners you could buy from the Warner Brothers catalogs fifteen years ago.

Please let it be a whiz-kid toy for the magically precocious toddler in your life, and not a black hole contained only by delicate gold bands and a lick of magic.

I reached out and grabbed it.

Yeah, I know, maybe not the smartest move. But I have a tendency to grab first, ask questions later, and the worst it's gotten me so far is glowing blue fingers for a week.

The whatchamacallit was heavier than it looked, which skewed my suspicions over to the black hole side of things.

I was tempted to chew on one of the bands to see if it was real gold— it sure looked like it—but I hear putting random magical artifacts in your mouth can be detrimental to your health. Never mind putting *black holes* in your mouth.

A nervous laugh escaped me.

I didn't want to know what this thing was worth on the black market, because then I'd want to keep it. And no way did it look like the sort of thing you wanted hanging around long-term.

Aw, what the hell. I pulled out my phone and took a photo, then did an incognito image search. The results popped up—the aforementioned time-turners, wicker balls that were supposed to be rabbit chew toys, wicker balls that were supposed to be decorative, some sort of astrolabe—but nothing that looked like the whackadoodle thing I was holding.

At least it didn't seem to be giving off any kind of magic. That was one point in its favor.

A car turned into the lot in the distance, heading my way. I scanned the barcode on the Chrysler, saving its profile so I could come back to it later. Unhooking the clasp of my parakeet-pendant necklace, I looped the chain through one of the gold bands of the orb of sinisterness. Keep your friends close, keep your creepy artifacts closer, right?

Like hell was I putting something this valuable in lost and found. Besides, if it was going to kill me, it would've done it already.

The car whipped into a space instead of my lanes—just Bert bringing the next load of buffers. Sweet. I'd get the last of these cars squared away real quick, then look up whoever rented the Chrysler and let them know they forgot something that they just might want back. If I was lucky, they'd still be in the airport, and could mosey on over here and take it off my hands.

I stroked the interlocking bands, the metal colder than it should be. A shiver ran through me.

Right. Back to work.

Only two more cars pulled into line before I had everything taken care of. I plopped down in my booth and brought up the Chrysler's record on my scanner. Customer: Nardi Seabrook. I scrunched my nose. What a name. There—her phone number. I punched in the numbers and waited.

No rings. No answer. No voicemail recording, even. After a moment, a beep came through the speaker. Wait, was that the voicemail beep?

"I—uh—Hi, this is Immy. Imogen. Immy. Whatever. I found an item left behind in your rental car that you probably want back." Ugh, that sounded like the start to a lame ransom demand or something. "So, uh"—I checked the scanner again—"Nardi, if you'd like to collect it, just give me a call." I repeated my number twice, then hung up. Hopefully that was her voicemail? I'd never heard one without a recorded message before the beep. Better try to contact her another way to be safe.

I shot off a quick email to the address listed on the scanner, then glanced at the clunky corded blue phone in the corner of the booth, labeled 'Official Use Only.' No one had ever said I *couldn't* use it, and I *was* official—I worked here, after all.

I grabbed the receiver. If they didn't want me paging people in the airport on a whim, then they really shouldn't have put Big Blue in here with me.

The cord crackled as I pulled the phone toward me, the plastic coil about twenty years past its expiration date. I brushed desiccated plastic crumbs off my polo shirt with a grimace. Tucking the blue monstrosity between my ear and shoulder, I held up the scanner with one hand to read the woman's name, cleared my throat, and thumbed the silver button on the cradle.

In my most computerlike voice, I droned, "Nardi Seabrook, please return to the outdoor rental-car booth immediately. Nardi Seabrook, please return to the outdoor rental-car booth immediately. Thank you." It came out way more nasal than I'd expected. Oh well. I released the button with a snick, and put the phone back on its cradle, shedding more plastic dandruff.

I turned the volume on my phone way up, so I'd for sure hear any incoming calls or email notifications, then went to deal with the new car rolling up to my booth. Before I knew it, it was 1:50 p.m. and this Nardi Seabrook woman hadn't tried to contact me in any way. She had to be in the air by now, and I'd probably get a frantic call in three to five hours when she landed wherever and found my messages.

I held up my necklace, letting the bauble twirl idly at the end of the chain. What was I going to do with this thing? Our lost and found was basically just a shoebox under the check-in counter, accessible by any snoop wandering through the airport. This woman had my name, phone number, and email now—if I left her property there overnight and it was gone in the morning, I'd be on the hook for it when she showed back up. Not happening.

I flopped my head back against the unforgivably low headrest on my broken chair. The safest place I had for weird magic gizmos was in Bracchius's care, which meant it was coming home with me.

Fabulous.

"Hey, hey! Guess who's done for the day!"

I rolled my eyes at Julian's overenthusiasm. If at least it was on his own behalf, I could understand. Why he was so chipper about *my* work day ending, I'd never be able to wrap my mind around.

"That would be me," I said, grabbing my belongings from where they'd gotten scattered around the booth during the day.

Julian ducked into the booth, grinning. He's six foot seven and built like a wraith; his black polo shirt is always at least half-untucked because nobody designs company uniforms with Bigfoot in mind.

Something chittered, and I froze. I'd almost forgotten about Fangy; clearly my sigil had been effective so far. Julian was too big to miss, though, and the little fiend was probably sneaking up behind him right now. I looked up at Julian to warn him, and my jaw dropped a little.

No way.

HOME SWEET DEMON

Fangy wasn't about to attack Julian. Fangy was freakin' *riding* Julian.

"Oh yeah, I found this little cutie digging around in the trash by the door," Julian said, nuzzling my nemesis under the chin with one oversized finger. The beastie was perched on his shoulder like a parrot, or those teacup griffins that were all the rage last year.

"Whaddya think, new company mascot?" He booped it with his nose, and the attacker-of-ankles skittered around in a little circle before curling up on his shoulder contentedly.

I glared at it. Really? *I* get needle-sharp fangs to the leg, and it can't be bothered to give Julian even a little nose nip?

Un. Fair.

A slither-thump drew my attention outside again—just Aaron, with the next load of buffers. He perked up when he caught sight of Julian and his passenger.

"Whoa, what's that?" He kept a respectful distance as he peered at Fangy. Smart kid.

Julian stroked Fangy's forehead with a finger. "I dunno. Looks like a cross between a miniature wyvern and a feefal, don't ya think?" He nodded at the buffers flopped unceremoniously across the asphalt. "What are those for?"

"Oh, the buffers? They're to keep the cars from banging into each other during the dragon storm."

Julian grinned. "Man, dragon storms sound so cool! This will be the first one since I moved here, are they awesome? Do you think they'll let us off work early?"

I left them chatting, clocked out, and slipped into the bathroom to strip out of my itchy black polo shirt. Rootling around in my bag, I pulled out my white tank and blue plaid not-actually-a-flannel, and got changed. A quick mirror check told me my hair was a disaster, so I finger-combed my waves into some semblance of order.

The artifact hung gleaming on my necklace, the black center stark against the white of my tank. I pursed my lips. Too obvious. I tugged my tank neckline forward, the necklace dropping inside, cold against my skin.

There. Much better. Didn't need anyone ripping it off my neck on the subway, after all.

Clunking my sneaker up on the counter, I tugged my jeans up and checked my ankle. A tiny oval of red pinpricks showed where Fangy had done its worst. No oozing, no pus, no sinister dark line creeping up one of my blood vessels.

Good. I wasn't sure if my worker's comp covered toxic animal bites.

I spooled out a scratchy paper towel and doused it with soap and water, then swiped it over the tiny bite a couple times just to be safe. It didn't even sting—hopefully I was in the clear.

Speaking of which, I didn't need my sigil any longer. I ripped off the bandage—now *that* stung, yowza—and ditched it in the trash on top of what looked like a wad of hair.

Gross.

Concentrating, I reformed the ink on my wrist into my floral rib cage tattoo. My skin was still sticky with bandage residue, even after scrubbing it with some more soap and water. Ugh.

Slinging my bag over my shoulder, I headed into the airport and made my way downstairs to the subway station. Dead air hit me in the face, warm and musty, carrying the scent of weed and orrax. I sneezed. Finéa, that was strong. Must have been a whole troupe of fauns down here earlier.

The clamor of an oncoming train echoed off the walls, and I stepped up to the yellow safety line. The train rushed in, blowing grit in my face as I squeezed my eyes shut. It rattled and hissed to a halt, a set of doors a couple feet to my left clacking open. I waited a millisecond for anyone getting off before stepping forward, only to nearly face-plant into a huge furry black beast. It turned to face me, slavering jaws open to reveal row upon row of serrated teeth, red eyes gleaming in the flickering half-light of the train.

I might've squeaked. I was definitely rooted to the spot.

"Oh, I'm sorry," Nightmare Beast said in a hushed feminine voice. "We're packed pretty tight in here, why don't you just slip under my arm, and we can share a pole."

Wide-eyed, I eased under her shaggy arm and latched on to the dirty pole for support as the doors wheezed shut, and leaned into the acceleration as the train pulled out of the station.

"Thanks."

"Not a problem, dear." One of her tree-trunk arms swung down, holding out a bitty white square. I took it—a wet wipe, pristine in its paper packaging. "For later," she explained. "I really wish they'd get around to casting those automated sanitizing spells on the subway already. It's not *that* expensive to maintain."

I nodded politely, she smiled a terrifying smile, and we settled into the stagnant silence of strangers.

She was right; the train car was packed, far more than usual for this time of day. Every seat was filled, breaking the sacred commuter tradition of always leaving an empty buffer seat—the better to identify creeps. A horde of pixies flittered near the ceiling, and I gave them my best don't-mess-with-me glare.

All the extra traffic must be because of the forecasted dragon storm—businesses would much rather let their employees ride out the storm at home than risk the fallout if anything went wrong at the office. A few hours of productivity and profit weren't worth the potential hassle and insurance claims.

I got off at the Glenbrook station, climbed up to street level, and made good use of the wet wipe as I walked the few blocks to my place, the sun starting to disappear behind clouds rolling over the horizon.

Crows congregated by the curb, a couple hopping around, but most solemnly observing something in their midst. I scrunched my nose at the clump of disarrayed feathers sticking up from the patched asphalt.

"Are you guys holding another murder investigation?" Several of the crows fixed their black eyes on me. "Because I can help you out with this one—vehicular crowslaughter. Sorry, guys."

I did a quick scan, and the crows I could recognize were still alive and squawking—Russell, Jekyll, Darth, and Flirt. Predictably, Flirt fluttered over and did a little dance around me as I walked up to my ground-floor apartment.

"Yeah, yeah, I'm working on it."

I unlocked the front door and dug out a scoop of kibble from the bucket just inside.

"Here you go."

The crows launched in my direction as I tossed the kibble in a wide arc across the broken sidewalk, the brown bits skittering across the concrete. Within a moment, the sidewalk was obscured by black wings, and delighted squabbling caws filled the air. I headed back inside and dumped my bag on the cluttered table.

My apartment only has two tiny windows out front, which are overhung by the balcony of the dude who lives above me, so most of the place is pretty gloomy—just the way my demon roommates like it.

"Bracchius! Kor! There's a dragon storm on the way. I'll be out later, so you'll need to batten down the hatches so we don't get flooded like last year."

Cold, wet demons make for miserable roommates.

It's not exactly your traditional roommate arrangement, but I can't afford this place on my own, and they don't leave dirty dishes in the sink or soggy hairballs in the shower drain, so it could be worse.

Bracchius is an under-the-bed demon, though I kicked him out from under mine a couple months back, using the justification that people sleep on couches too, so the living room sofa was a perfectly acceptable domicile. He's better than a spider—hold on, stick with me here—because he keeps the place bug-free, and creeps me out less.

Yup, I said it. The demon is less creepy than the huge friggin' spiders that I don't have to deal with anymore. Cue evil laughter.

Kor lives in the bathroom mirror, though he makes regular excursions. That said, I try not to use the bathroom at night wherever possible. Glowing red eyes in your mirror in the dark are terrifying even when you really should be expecting them. He at least has the decency to fog up and muffle the mirror when I'm in the bathroom for, well, bathroomy things. Apparently humans are gross.

You really don't want to owe a demon a favor, and they don't particularly want to owe you one either. But they *love* being owed. So my demons and I are constantly playing a game of chicken—they owe me rent for letting them stay, which they gladly fork over, but then I have to figure out if whatever oddball trinket they've given me is secretly the least favorite brooch of Cleopatra, worth such a fortune that *I'd* then be in *their* debt, rather than our scores being evenly settled.

Well, Kor does this, anyway. Bracchius is too much of a softy, for a demon. He's got eighty-four months of rent paid in advance. Who knows if my landlord will even still own the building that far out.

"Guys, you hear me?" I called.

Bracchius's dorky voice issued from under the couch. "Yes, Immy. We'll do the usual."

Whereas I'd have to spend a couple hours nailing plywood over my windows, Kor and Bracchius had demon magic at their disposal. Storm wards over the windows and doors? Check. Containment spell around the cracks in the foundation? Check. And it was all part of our contract, so I didn't even have to worry about compensating them for it.

"Thanks, Bracchius." I raised my voice so Kor was sure to hear. "And if the power goes out, don't open the fridge! I don't want the food going bad."

Speaking of food . . .

I turned to my tiny kitchen, only to find crimson smeared all over the fridge door like a gory ransom note.

Not *again.*

The red streaks on my fridge spelled out crude letters that read "Immy—buy more Crunchy XXTRA Flamin' Hot Cheetos."

Complete with the apostrophe.

"*Please* tell me that's ketchup," I moaned.

Bracchius piped up again. "It's not."

"Ugh, what did he kill this time?" The splattered crow outside came to mind, but unless Kor had learned how to hot-wire a car, it seemed unlikely.

"I honestly haven't the faintest idea. There aren't any corpses on the premises."

I ripped a generous handful of paper towels off the roll and attacked Kor's shopping list with a vengeance. "I swear . . . if I find . . . bloody feathers in the toilet . . . again . . ."

After inundating the fridge with half a bottle of Windex, I went at it with another round of paper towels, threw the whole mess in the trash, and washed my hands for way longer than was probably necessary.

"I'm doing more than raising the rent this time," I muttered. "Clearly only something more heavy-handed will make an impact on that demon's skull."

"Demons don't have—"

"I don't care," I snapped.

"Good luck," Bracchius said weakly.

On my way back through the living room, I snagged the two couch cushions off Bracchius's sofa, wedging them strategically in the hallway behind me to block it off, before ducking into my bedroom.

I grabbed a bundle of dried sage—ethically sourced and purchased from my favorite Native witch, thank you very much—and lit the edges with my lighter, slipping the sage into the black-sand-filled copper bowl I keep on my dresser. Fragrant smoke began pooling in the bowl, slowly drifting over the lip and rolling away.

Biting my lip to suppress a grin, I flopped back on the bed and kicked my bare feet up against the wall. Then I pulled up Pentagram to scroll through #MiniDragons reels. They're cute, all right? I especially can't resist those tiny blue-speckled black dragons that play in the bioluminescent surf, though apparently they're a pain in the ass to get on video.

A demonic cough echoed from the bathroom across the hall.

I gave it another few seconds.

"What the— Is that *sage?!* IMMY!" Kor's Balrog-deep voice was punctuated by hacking coughs. "Sage is against our"—wheeze—"contract!"

Rental contract, that is, not demon contract. Although, when you're renting to a demon, there's probably not much of a difference.

"So's smearing blood all over my poor innocent fridge!"

"*Our* fridge."

"Definitely my fridge. Nothing in the contract stipulates that you are granted use of the fridge."

Kor spluttered, which swiftly turned into another series of coughs so severe, I almost wondered if he would come up with a hairball.

"This argument is not over," he growled. "I just need to . . . get something, out of my domain. I will return."

The coughing died out as he retreated deeper into the mirror, presumably. I sighed and dropped my feet from the wall. I'd kinda hoped the sage could penetrate further into his hidey-hole, but I was pretty sure I'd made my point regardless.

I had a while still before dinner with Samaire, so I did some stormproofing in case Bracchius and Kor's precautions failed. Books on the bottom shelves got nestled securely in the bathtub behind the shower curtain; my sheathed sword wrapped in plastic bags and placed across the over-the-door clothes hooks on my closet door. I put mixing bowls under each ceiling can light, and a beat-up roasting pan left by the previous tenant under the stove hood.

My phone went off, and I pulled it out—a video call from Damarion, my sort-of next-door neighbor. If you can really call a guy something that blasé when he lives in a house twenty times fancier than yours.

I definitely didn't expect to become friends with a vampire, never mind one who looks twice my age. But Damarion is one of a kind. I mean, don't get me wrong. He's good-looking for a fifty-going-on-five-hundred-year-old. He keeps his silver hair styled long on the top and short on the sides, with a just-there beard. I don't know if he shaves every day, or if vampire hair just doesn't grow anymore . . . I've never thought to ask.

He talks and acts like anybody does these days, but he's never been able to part with the three-piece suit—and his suits, unlike the centaur's, are immaculate.

I answered the call, and sure enough, he was wearing a grey number with a lavender silk vest.

"Immy, do you get off work at two tomorrow?" he asked.

"Just like every day I work, yeah."

"Fabulous. Would you be willing to accompany me to Vein & Vice tomorrow at three thirty? My supply is running low."

"You could just have it delivered, you know."

"Of course, Immy, I'm not dense. But it's supposed to be such nice weather, and I have a new pair of wingtip Oxfords that I need to break in. I'll bring the backpack you like."

Why he always insisted *I* accompany him as he schlepped fresh blood from the blood bank back to his place, I'd never understand. I got the general principle—the masses of rabid vampire fanatics perpetually lined up outside Vein & Vice and its sister establishments were less likely to hound him with offers of slave contracts and fresh feeds if he was already accompanied by a human. But still.

He'd clearly been a pickpocket at one point in his storied history, because every time I got home after another of our blood runs, I'd find a crisp one-hundred-dollar bill in my back pocket. I'd put up a token protest the first couple of times, but he'd never taken no for an answer, and frankly, I could use the cash.

"I'll add it to my calendar." I literally did, right there and then, because otherwise I was guaranteed to forget.

"Wonderful. I'll see you then."

My phone screamed out a harsh alarm as he ended the call, and I nearly dropped the freaking thing. The adrenaline shot my heart rate through the roof as I fumbled to read the message—the exact same message from the Harmonic Council that had come through a couple of hours ago.

Ugh. Couldn't they at least give an actual update? Like how far out the storm was? These generic warnings were less useful than a Blockbuster membership card.

After hauling all those books around, I was smelling distinctly ripe. Unfortunately, my shower was full to the brim with said books, so I set the mystery gizmo on the counter and freshened up with a soapy cloth, then washed my hair in the sink. By the time I'd done my hair, picked out multiple outfits and finally settled on one, *and* redone my makeup, it was practically time to leave for the restaurant. I swung the whirligig on its chain, considering.

I'd been planning on leaving it here with Bracchius, but the negotiations for that could run long, depending on what he wanted in exchange. And Samaire might just be able to tell me something about it; she got a lot more prolonged exposure to the magical elite than I did.

I stuffed the strange bauble into my clutch beside the fifty dollar bill, my phone, and my dagger—things could get crazy in a dragon storm—and waltzed out the door.

AT LEAST IT'S NOT A BLACK HOLE

"Do you have a reservation?" The hostess glanced from me to her ledger and back.

"Probably, I don't know, but that's my party—right there." I pointed at Samaire, who was sitting at the crowded bar, defending an empty chair with her purse. Samaire is half-Pakistani, and just enough siren to give her an alluring voice and gold feathers in her dark hair. She waved her chopsticks at me.

"Oh, perfect. Let me just take you over."

"No need, I think I can make it thirty feet by myself, but thanks."

I clacked across the hardwood floor in my heels, and slid onto the stool next to Samaire as she retrieved her purse. I set my clutch down on the black marble bartop, and tugged on my outfit to make sure it hadn't ridden too high.

The edamame was too far away for my liking, so I snagged the lip of the bowl and dragged it over. Samaire plucked out a pod as the bowl skated by.

"There's a dragon storm coming, and you're wearing *that*?" she said, eyeballing my classy romper.

"You're not exactly kitted out yourself," I said, and popped some edamame out of its pod.

To be fair, she was wearing a sweater and faux-leather leggings, but it wasn't like she was toting a raincoat or umbrella either. Not that any of the above would do much against a dragon storm.

She tugged on the sleeve of her sweater. "Yeah, well, I found a new sigil on Sigileaks that's supposed to protect you from the elements."

"Supposed to?"

"Fingers crossed?" She grinned. "Honestly, I'm hoping we can just ride it out here, and it'll blow over by eight."

"Optimist. You ever heard of a dragon storm that lasted less than two hours?"

A flutter of paper caught my eye.

"Ladies." A waiter stood across the bar from us, holding out two menus. "Go ahead and make your selections whenever you're ready."

"Thanks." I slipped my menu in front of me to peruse. What would be the best bang for my buck? I double tapped the toro sashimi with one finger, the subtle glow of the paper confirming I'd selected it. For sure some unagi nigiri, hotate, uni, and . . .

I bit my lip. The tip definitely wasn't coming out of that fifty dollars.

What the hell, if the rest of the meal was effectively free, I couldn't exactly complain about having to fork over my own money for a tip.

I added one more item, then double-checked to make sure I hadn't accidentally selected anything crazy expensive with an errant touch—the last thing I needed was a two-hundred-dollar charge for omakase. Nope, all good. I traced the sigil across the bottom of the menu with one finger, and it lit up, sending my order to the kitchen.

Samaire was still hovering over her menu.

"What're you getting?"

"That's the problem," she groaned. "It all looks too good."

Pretty much half her menu was glowing, and her fingers danced across the paper, deselecting several items. I peered over to see what she'd kept. A 'happy spoon' oyster, seaweed salad, gyoza, toro, miso soup—

"Damn, I should've ordered some miso." I hadn't even looked at the hot dishes.

Samaire tapped the miso, adding another bowl.

"You don't have to—"

"Girl, it's miso, it's like a buck. Chill."

"Thanks."

"Besides, you're already eating my edamame."

I snorted. "That's complimentary."

She smiled mischievously, then sent her order in as well. The waiter returned to collect the no-longer-glowing menus, and I wriggled, trying to get comfortable on the stool. It had a weird hole near the back edge, and the footrest was just out of reach, which sucked. This stool was probably designed for a minotaur or something.

A scrawny guy squeezed behind our seats, brushing against us. His head was shaved, every inch covered in tattooed sigils—though I doubted he could do the same trick I can. I've never met anyone with my particular magical oddity.

I didn't even bother peering more closely at his sigils. A display like that was pure ego; meant to be impressive, but if the sigils were any good, he wouldn't be parading them about.

I rolled my eyes. "You see that guy?"

"Yeah. He must think he's hot stuff." Samaire played with one of the golden feathers in her hair. "It's not like the number of sigils you have is some sort of status symbol. I've got nineteen, and I'm just a nightclub singer."

"And how many of those are actually useful?" I asked. "And by useful I don't mean temporarily changing your eye color. Or zesting every lemon within fifteen feet."

"But I like the zesting-lemons one! Have you ever tried to zest a lemon by hand? It's a pain in the ass."

I huffed out a laugh. Sure, I download every new sigil that gets posted on Sigileaks, and save them for future reference. But they're party tricks at best. The real sigils—the useful sigils—are guarded better than state secrets. Locked behind paywalls that only the über-rich can afford to break down.

Every now and then some fool gets lucky and manages to create a useful sigil from scratch. But the trial and error required means you're more likely to burn down your house and turn your cat into a sentient ball of slime than ever get anywhere with it. Believe me, I know. My jerk of an ex-boyfriend was one of those fools.

I have him to thank for my stealth sigil, sort of—I drew it, he just got lucky enough to give me some helpful suggestions—and nothing else. My other useful sigil is a family heirloom, although a secret one. I hadn't had occasion to use it yet, and honestly, I hoped I never would.

Sigils are like the arcane geometry of the universe. Most everybody has a little spark of magic, one or two tricks or talents. But sigils are something else. You know how bees make perfect hexagons for their honeycombs, pyrite forms in cubes, and fractals are littered all through nature? Sigils are like that. Patterns that are an echo of the universe. Except no one's figured out a way to calculate their forms. It's all just guesswork, luck, and ancient history.

Intricate *maddening* guesswork.

A waiter brought out our two bowls of miso. I eagerly dove into mine, savoring the hot umami flavor, and finished before Samaire. It'd be a minute or two before they brought the next plates, so I popped open my clutch.

"I wanted to ask you something . . ." I started.

Samaire slurped down the last of her soup, earning a glare from the woman sitting on her other side. "Shoot."

"I, uh, found something at work that I was hoping you could help me identify." I pried the mysterious orb out of my clutch, and set it on the bartop between us.

The moment it touched the marble, it shimmered, a dark sheen coruscating across the surface of the black void at its center. The marble was suddenly ten degrees colder beneath my fingers. I yanked them back as frost crackled out along the bartop.

That couldn't be good.

I leaned forward and hurriedly exhaled over the marble, trying to thaw the frost traceries before anyone noticed.

"Here," Samaire said, snatching the folded black cloth napkin to her left, shaking it out, and settling it over the bar in front of me—artifact, frost crystals, and all. It looked odd with the lump in the middle, but certainly less eye-catching than magical ice crackling out from a bizarre artifact.

I glanced around, but no one seemed to have noticed.

"Do you think it's still doing that under there?" I whispered.

Samaire gave me a flat look and lifted one corner of the napkin.

Right, duh. I wasn't thinking straight. I peered under the edge of the cloth. The frost was gone.

"Ladies," came a voice from behind me, and I dropped the napkin in panic. The waiter stood patiently at my shoulder, holding our next dishes.

"Oh, sorry." I shoved the napkin—and its contents—to the side, making room for the plates. He set them down with a clink.

"Enjoy."

Samaire picked up the Chinese soup spoon resting on her otherwise empty plate. The spoon held an oyster, some tobiko, and other garnishes. She studied it as the waiter walked away, then gave me the side-eye.

"What have you gotten yourself into this time?"

"I haven't—that's not fair, I—"

Samaire pointedly slurped down the contents of her spoon, never breaking eye contact.

"Look, I found it in a car at work, and it seemed too valuable to trust to the lost and found box."

"So, wait—you stole this?"

I picked up my pair of obsidian chopsticks and looked down at my plate of two hotate nigiri. "More like I'm making sure no one *else* steals it while I try to find the owner."

"Let me have another look."

I carefully pulled back the cloth napkin, on tenterhooks as I waited for the artifact to do something else sinister. It sat innocently in the black folds, the soft lighting of the restaurant glinting off the gold bands.

Samaire leaned in to get a closer look, her nose almost on the table.

"You ever seen anything like it?" I asked, then took the opportunity to pop one of my hotate nigiri in my mouth. The scallop practically melted against my tongue, blending deliciously with the rice. Yum.

"Can't say I have," she muttered, shifting to look at it from another angle.

"You could pick it up," I suggested.

"Have you?"

"Yeah, how else do you think I got it here?"

She glanced at my fingers suspiciously, as though checking for magical lesions or signs of the manticore plague.

"I swear, that frost was the only weird thing it's done, otherwise it's just acted like an inert bauble."

Samaire sat back up. "The fact that I don't feel any magic coming off it worries me. It's obviously magical, so it must have a seriously strong containment spell on it—and a pricey one, to not give off its own magic. So, what's it containing that's worth that much money and effort?"

My gaze fastened on the creepy black core at the center of the artifact.

"Black hole?" I ventured, leaning back a little further on my stool.

Samaire rolled her eyes. "Don't be ridiculous. No one's bothered to mess with those since that incident in Szczecin with the Servants of the Night Ravens."

"Right." I'd honestly forgotten about that—it had happened *years* ago. Only so much news and history you can hold in your head at once. "What do you think, then?"

She cautiously picked it up and studied it in the dim lighting. "No idea. Could be a dozen things—a dark coalescence, a revenant seed, a void creature egg or embryo, some witch's amped-up black mirror, a demon core, sentient Ebonian coffee—"

I tried to keep up with her, typing on my phone, but she held out a hand.

"Immy, it's not worth writing all that down, I'm just spitballing. And besides, you're giving this back, right? What's it matter what it is, as long as it doesn't morph you into a wraithling between now and when you get rid of it?"

"Uh, excuse me, seventy-five percent of what you just 'spitballed' sounded awfully horrifying," I said.

"Yeah, but it's contained." She spun the orb between her fingers. "Like, *contained* contained. Here." She leaned back, glancing along the bar, then slid off her stool and approached a camazotz a couple stools down, the creature's black wings folded neatly behind them and wisps of shadow swirling about them.

"What are you *doing*?" I stage-whispered after her.

She tapped the camazotz on the shoulder. "Excuse me, zi'ra. Sorry to bother you, but my friend and I are having a bit of a disagreement. Can you tell me if you feel any magic coming off this cheap bauble? She thinks it might be dangerous."

Camazotz were renowned for their sensitivity to magic, although not necessarily for their kindness toward random strangers interrupting their meals. I held my breath as the camazotz stared up at Samaire, unblinking, one batlike ear flicked in her direction while the other faced the bar.

"Let me see, as you've seen," they croaked, holding out a hand that was ninety percent thin claws.

I exhaled. Why had I been worried? Samaire might only be part siren, but I've never seen anyone turn her down; her voice is just enchanting enough, even when she's not singing.

Samaire held up the artifact, and the camazotz delicately took it between their claw tips. One of the shadow wisps flowed around the object, obscuring it for a moment before swishing back to circle the camazotz's body.

"I cannot sense the magic of the contained, only the magic of the container," they rasped, returning the bauble. "The contained might be dangerous as your friend believes, but the container renders it harmless. It is interesting, as I'm sure you find it interesting. Thank you, and you're welcome."

The camazotz bowed in their seat, and swiveled to face the bar again.

Samaire shuffled back over. "See? You should be fine until you can get rid of it."

"Give that back." I plucked it from her fingers and shoved it in my clutch. Realizing my other hotate nigiri was still on my plate, I grabbed it with my chopsticks and wolfed it down, faster than I'd really intended. Moments after I'd finished, our waiter swooped by and whisked away the empty plates.

I was so absorbed watching the gold-and-green miniature dragon behind the bar sear some ahi tuna that I didn't notice the seat beside me become available. I *did* notice when a new patron nabbed it, jostling me as he scrambled up onto the stool.

"Pardon me," he said. The kappa finally got himself situated; seated, he was half my height, with webbed hands and a soft turtlelike shell. I surreptitiously peered down into his skull pond—the depression at the top of his long head. How he'd managed to climb up onto the stool without spilling any water was beyond me, but his head was perfectly level, with not even a drop trickling down the side. A tiny gold-edged waterlily floated on the surface of his pond, and blue goldfish were swimming around in there.

I've always been tempted to drop a penny in a skull pond, but I've never quite felt brazen enough to do it.

The kappa raised one pebbly arm, and the gal behind the bar tending the miniature dragon perked up. "The dragon storm is about to hit," the kappa rumbled. "Do you have adequate protections in place?"

"Of course, Councillor." The woman smiled. "Thank you for choosing us as your refuge from the storm."

I did a double take at the kappa. This guy was on the Harmonic Council? I didn't envy him, poor sap, or anyone else on the council. On the one hand, they have to figure out things like how to get the pixies— who might as well all share the same juvenile brain—to stop luring delivery golems into oncoming traffic.

On the other hand, they have to thwart pegasus terrorists when they plan to bomb seven major airports because airplanes are 'unholy' and 'make a mockery of the divine nature of flight.'

Yup, I was working that day. Fun times.

'Councillor' has taken on a whole new meaning since the Harmonic Council was established. It's not enough to be a bureaucrat or a small-town politician, like you see with some councils. You've got to be pretty much half diplomat, half Lara Croft.

The kappa smiled back. "Can never be too careful. You have my usual?"

"Sure do. One large dandelion salad and fifteen-piece sashimi coming right up."

She slapped a fresh batch of ahi steaks down for the tiny gold-and-green dragon to sear, and disappeared into the back kitchen.

Samaire nudged me. "Girl, are you going to eat that, or what?"

I looked down, surprised to see a new plate with my uni nigiri waiting. "Oh, thanks, I—"

My answer was drowned out by a devastating roar, two tones overlaying each other, immediately joined by the rattle and tinkle of all the glass and silverware in the restaurant. Lightning flashed through the windows, and as it faded, an explosion of rolling thunder followed, ushering in the beat of pounding rain on the roof.

The dragon storm had arrived.

THE HEEBIE-JEEBIES

Something slammed against the closest window, and I jumped, whirling on my stool to look. Whatever it was had already blown away, and the glass looked undamaged.

The kappa councillor looked up at me with a placid smile as I faced forward again, his head somehow still perfectly level. "Not even one of the storm dragons could crack that glass," he assured me. "I helped spell it last year."

"Oh, great." The kappa turned his attention toward the salad being placed in front of him.

"What did he say?" Samaire whispered between thunder blasts.

"The glass won't break."

"It better not."

I decided to ignore the staccato of clacks and bangs as street detritus tumbled against the windows. It wasn't hard—the drum and roars of the storm nearly drowned it out anyway.

My uni nigiri was waiting for me, after all.

I plucked up my chopsticks and tucked the first morsel in my mouth. The creaminess of the uni contrasted with the tiny pop of tobiko as they burst in my mouth, and I smiled.

"So I told you about my . . . gadget." I nudged my clutch with an elbow. "What's new with you?"

Samaire glanced up from typing on her phone. "Sorry, that was my boss."

"Do you have to go in?" I hadn't been keeping track of the time, but it had to be getting closer to eight o'clock.

"Nope!" She grinned. "He said not to come in. There are like three customers in the whole place, and they're not tippers."

I wished I could miss an entire day of work and not be worried about the bills. It was good, though—nobody should have to go out in this weather.

"As for what's new . . ." Samaire let her head flop back dramatically. "They want to do 'variety week' next week. I hate it so much."

"Variety week?"

"I have to sing in a different style every night. But it's not like Barbra

Streisand on Monday, Aven Glimmersong on Tuesday, and Britney Spears on Wednesday. It's like *opera* on Monday, *rap* on Tuesday, and screamo redcap *death* metal on Wednesday."

I winced.

"Yeah, that face is what my throat is going to be doing in a few days."

My clutch twitched on the bartop, and I slammed a hand down on it in panic. What was the artifact doing *now*? It vibrated again—just my phone. My heart slowly returned to its place in my chest.

I flicked open the clutch and pulled out my phone. It wasn't a number I recognized. Usually I would let it go through to voicemail, but I had left my number in that message for Nadine what's-her-face—Nardi. Nardi something. If it was her, I wouldn't have to worry about the whirligig any longer. Better get it.

"Hello?" There was a brief pause after I answered. Damn, it was probably a stupid automated golem call. Just as I was lowering the phone to end the call, a deep voice came over the line.

"Is this Immy?"

"Speaking," I said hesitantly. "Is this Nardi?" The being on the other end sounded like a barrel-chested troglodyte, but you never know.

"I hear you have the Calamandrian artifact."

Not Nardi, then. No way would the owner of the 'Calamandrian artifact' ask about it like that, not to mention dodge my question. But who else would know I'd made that call? My palms started to sweat.

"No, not me," I lied. "Just calling on behalf of Saskia Skies Car Rental." I caught Samaire's concerned look and pressed my lips together, glancing from my clutch to her and back again. She leaned in to my phone, and I scooted a little closer.

"Can you get me in touch with Nardi?" I tried after a few seconds of dead air.

The dial tone blared in my ear.

"So much for that," Samaire said as I set my phone down. "That was someone about the you-know-what?"

"Yeah," I said a bit shakily. "But I don't think it was the person I left a voicemail for."

"Weird."

I ate my next couple of dishes absentmindedly as I searched for 'Calamandrian' on my phone. I tried a few different spellings, one of which returned literally no results. 'Calamandrian' only returned four—the same street name mentioned twice, and two references to a random old Italian dictionary.

One more dish clinked in front of me, interrupting my frustration. They'd saved the best for last—the toro.

I set down my phone. This deserved my full attention.

I grabbed the first piece of sashimi with my chopsticks and folded it into my mouth, closing my eyes. The buttery silkiness dissolved against my tongue, the subtle savory taste perfect.

"You look like you're enjoying that," Samaire said, her tone wry.

I waited until the mouthful was gone before responding. "Duh. It's toro."

The final piece was even better. I closed my eyes again so I wouldn't have to see Samaire's smirk.

"She's having a mouth-gasm," she stage-whispered, and my eyes snapped open. She was trading smiles with the mini-dragon minder.

I stuck out my tongue at Samaire, and she laughed.

Another monstrous crash of the storm hit the building, and suddenly Samaire leaned in and kissed me, teasing my lips, lingering a moment before pulling away a few inches. One of her golden feathers stirred in the breeze from the AC, brushing my bare shoulder.

"If you wanted to taste the toro that badly, you could've ordered some yourself." I raised an eyebrow, but maintained our intimate tableau. There was a reason she was doing this. "Besides, I thought I wasn't your type."

"You're not," she murmured, letting a smile grace her lips, eyes on the bartop. "There's a guy over there watching us—which one of us, I'm not sure. Looks like trouble."

"And you thought us kissing would deter him?"

She shrugged. "Did you bring your sword?"

"No."

"Kisses can be weapons, too." She reclaimed her chopsticks and sat back, picking at the forgotten bowl of edamame. "Your lips are chapped, by the way."

I rubbed my lips together—she was right. I dug in my bag for a lip balm, found one, and popped off the cap. As I swiped the peach balm on, I casually glanced in the direction she'd been looking. A hulking guy in dripping wet clothes stood near the door, ignoring the hostess's efforts to engage him.

I got the crawly feeling on the back of my neck that he'd been staring at me until the instant I'd looked his way, which lined up with what Samaire had said.

Goose bumps rippled over my skin. Was he connected to the guy on the phone? Had they somehow put a tracking spell on the call? Were they after the artifact, whatever it was?

"Girl, you look like a selkie on the edge of a panic attack," Samaire whispered. "Do you recognize him?"

I shook my head, gathering up my belongings with shaky hands. "But first that weird call, then this—what if they put a tracer on the call? I made it sound like the artifact was at work, but what if they didn't believe me?"

"I don't—" Samaire moued her lips. "Well, better paranoid than sorry."

All this was giving me the heebie-jeebies, and I just wanted to get out of here pronto. I got the attention of the girl behind the bar as I fumbled the battery out of my phone. "You're not connected to the tunnels, are you?"

"Sorry, no. But the closest subway station is only a block away." She glanced at the windows, which were still awash with driving rain.

Samaire touched my elbow. "I'll distract the guy at the door. Act like you're heading for the bathroom, but be ready to slip out."

I nodded and slid off the stool, making my way toward the bathrooms, angling toward the door at the last second as Samaire full-on tripped smack in front of Sinister Guy, sending edamame husks flying everywhere as she tumbled to the ground and yelped at top volume.

I opened the door and stepped into the storm.

Emerging into the dragon storm was like stepping under a waterfall at night. There were no individual raindrops, just an instant cold deluge that slicked my hair and clothes against my skin, at least until a blast of wind slammed the torrent against me from another direction, and I stumbled against the wall of the building as a dragon roared high overhead.

I was ankle-deep in a current of murky water, and couldn't see more than a couple feet ahead of me before the world disappeared in dark grey chaos. Probably better to stay close to the wall anyway, especially with the strong tug of the water at my heels. I just had to make it the short distance to the subway entrance.

Not trusting myself to hang on to my clutch, I looped the strap around my arm and wedged the bag in my armpit, clamping down on it firmly, then grazed both hands against the gritty concrete wall to guide me north to the subway station a block away.

Detritus brushed against my ankles in the water as I moved along, and I grimaced, trying not to think of what could be floating in the stormwater.

My fingers suddenly encountered open air as the wall of the building disappeared around a corner, and I stopped, squinting against the downpour to survey the street before me. Lights from cars should still be visible, right? Assuming anyone was moronic enough to try and drive around in this.

I stepped off the curb, plunging deeper into the water, and lost my footing for a moment as the current swept me off my feet. Why had I thought this was a good idea, again? Banging into a parked car, I managed to get enough of a grip on the hood to stop and find the asphalt under my feet. Lightning blitzed across the sky as I exhaled a shaky breath, illuminating my surroundings enough for me to catch sight of the subway station sign on the opposite corner. Now I just had to get there.

Bracing myself against the car, I took another minute to catch my breath as the wind pounded the rain against me from three different directions. I waded forward into the street, one heavy step at a time.

I was halfway across when a flipping *boat* veered down the road, spotlight blinding me momentarily as I thrashed through the water to get out of its way—it wasn't stopping, not with this current, and the last thing I needed was to be plowed down by a five-hundred-pound hunk of wood and fiberglass.

I just cleared it before it swept by, and then my legs were out from under me again, knees scraping against the asphalt. Splashing face-first into the gross water, I held my breath and flailed around until my grasping hands caught on something solid, and I tugged myself to my feet.

Panicked, I slapped a hand to my shoulder, checking to make sure my clutch hadn't washed away in the tumult. The strap had saved me— the clutch was bobbing on the choppy surface of the water, but the loop was still around my arm. I secured it again, and patted the errant bike rack I'd caught on in thanks.

I struck forward, only a few feet from the other side of the street. Sidewalk and shallower water, here I come.

I actually made it, to my surprise and delight. My trembling legs heaved me up onto the curb, grey water sluicing down them as the storm lulled for half a second. A sharp sting sliced across my calf, and I yanked my leg up with a yelp. A bright line of red bloomed on my skin amidst the beading water. Balancing on one foot, I plunged a hand into the water to find the culprit—better to keep it from doing any more damage.

Something sharp tumbled between my fingers, and I felt around, hoping it wouldn't slice my fingers before I caught it. There. It was slippery, but I snagged it and pulled my hand up to examine my catch.

A shimmery dragon scale winked up from my palm, its surface roiling with blues and greys like ink thunderclouding in water. As long as its dragon still lived, the colors would continue to shift, a surging camouflage against the storm.

The wind buffeted me again, and I almost dropped the scale. Hopping haphazardly on my uninjured leg, I shifted under the overhang of the building before me, ducking into the doorway of the darkened storefront to slip the scale into my clutch and snap it closed. Finding scales in a dragon storm wasn't unheard of, but they were valuable enough to make it worth hanging on to.

The overhang gave sufficient shelter for me to take a breather, staring out into the ferocity of the storm. The subway station was mere feet away, though the railing around the stairs made it a longer trip unless I wanted to vault the rail and drop fifteen feet onto the stairs.

Not in these shoes.

I considered the line of blood on my leg, which I'd kept out of the stormwater so far, not quite ready to subject myself to possible blood poisoning from whatever ick was pervading the murky water. Did I have anything in my clutch I could wrap it up with before dousing it again?

The roar of dragons and thunder quieted for a moment, and an isolated splash from my right had me glancing the way I'd come.

A hulking dark form battled the current in the middle of the street I'd just crossed. The sinister man from the restaurant? I didn't wait to find out, plunging my injured leg back into the water. Blood poisoning, I could do something about. A giant scary guy stalking me in a storm, not so much.

I waded forward till I caught the railing of the station entrance, and used it to guide me to the top of the stairs. Water cascaded down the concrete steps, which descended into darkness.

Had the power gone out? The subway was supposed to be stormproof, but the view wasn't encouraging. I flicked my eyes up to the huge form just visible through the downpour, still headed my way.

I gulped, and took the first step down into the dark.

BLOWING MY STALKER A RASPBERRY

I held on tight to the handrail as I descended the steps to the subway station, the stairs a miniature waterfall with the water rushing down them. The storm light was meager, aside from the occasional lightning strike, and the deeper I went below street level, the darker it became. I considered sparking up my magic, but with my luck I'd probably end up electrocuting myself.

One more step, and my foot splashed into pooled water. Was I at the bottom? It was impossible to tell. I quested forward with my other foot, and found another step down. And another.

The water had collected at the bottom of the stairwell; how deep, I didn't know. I stopped when the water reached my waist, hesitant to go any further. Was the whole station flooded? There should be spells in place to prevent that, but this didn't look promising.

A scrape at the top of the stairs had me wheeling—a dark figure loomed above, silhouetted against the storm-stricken sky. Mr. Tall, Dark, and Stalkery.

I lunged forward, deeper into the standing water, the fabric of my romper floating around me. At least there wasn't a current here. The water hit chin level, and I sucked in a gasp of air before submerging and swimming forward. I tried opening my eyes briefly, but the murky water was difficult to see through, and stung my eyes something fierce.

A few clumsy strokes forward through the water, and the tips of my fingers tingled against something. I clawed a hand forward, and it breached open air, suddenly chilly as the water began to evaporate from my skin. A little further, and—

I collapsed out of the wall of water onto smooth tile, not quite managing to keep my feet and coming down hard on my knees.

Youch.

Instead of stormwater, I was surrounded by dry air, and the glaring light of cheap, bare bulbs. I glanced back at the spell holding the water—and the light—back. Neat trick, if perhaps a bit flawed. There had to be a way to keep commuters from risking drowning just to get to the train, right? Granted, dragon storms usually only lasted a few hours, but still. I didn't make a habit of traveling during them, so this could be business as usual.

A train waited in front of me, mostly empty. I took a squelching step forward, just as a muffled voice came over the speakers to stand clear of the doors. I rushed forward and slipped through the doors half a second before they hissed shut, a puddle forming at my feet as I shivered in the cool underground air in my sopping wet clothes. Grabbing a pole and turning to the window, I spotted my stalker bursting out of the wet barrier as the train slid away into the darkness of the tunnel.

I couldn't help sticking out my tongue at him as I swished by.

If he had a way to track me, I couldn't go straight home. I had to figure out how he'd found me, and make sure it wouldn't happen again. Which meant checking to see if he could find me again—preferably somewhere public, crowded, and with multiple exits.

Good luck with that in the middle of this storm . . .

First I had to find out where this train was going, though.

I wrung out my curls and used them to mop my face as best I could, then peered up at the scrolling message board. We were headed for the Garden City District, the opposite direction of my place, and home to most of the city's fae—at least the nature-based species.

Slinging an arm around the pole, I popped open my clutch, which was surprisingly dry inside; a few drops of water, sure, but I'd expected it to be swimming. The artifact looked none the worse for wear, though I wouldn't be able to tell if my phone had survived my adventure until I put the battery back in. If they'd tracked it from that call, though . . . I wasn't chancing it.

I stroked a finger over one of the gold rings of the artifact. If it was really what all this was about—and I wasn't just being paranoid—it had to be worth even more than I'd thought. But . . . there was still the issue of how anyone could know I had it, aside from the owner. What if Stalker Dude had been sent by her? Was he just some innocent guy who'd come to pick it up for her, and here I was, leading him on a merry chase for no good reason?

No—any rational person would've just called or emailed me back and arranged for a time and place to meet, not made sinister phone calls and sent anonymous henchmen after me in weather like *this*. Something hinky was definitely going on.

I snapped the clutch closed again, not wanting to draw attention from any of my fellow traingoers. Three stops until Meraki Market in Garden City, and then I could lose myself in the crowds and test out my theory.

To keep myself from fidgeting, I studied an old lady who was sleeping with abandon a few seats away. She clearly didn't worry about pickpockets—one hand clasped her purse, while the other caressed an

Eldevarian Haymaker E7 shoved through a belt loop of her long jeans skirt. That little stick would give you a magical wallop like an ogre's backhand with the slightest touch. Granny wasn't messing around.

Granny was also watching me back, one eye shut, the other just slit open. I started, and she winked before resuming her façade.

Note to self: don't underestimate grannies on the subway.

I missed the announcement for the Meraki Market stop, but the sudden inertia as the train decelerated clued me in. I wrestled my way out the door against the inflow of new passengers; this station was much livelier than where I'd boarded.

The stairs opened up directly in the middle of Meraki Market, the city's largest indoor market, spanning three city blocks and at least six levels, half of which were underground, and several of which were only rumors, or extant in this realm for a mere two days every seven years. It was organized in a way unique to the fae—supposedly organic and logical to their way of thinking, but complete and cluttered chaos to anyone else, me included. The walkways weren't straight, the vendors weren't grouped into any sort of categories, and if you were lucky, the one you wanted wasn't suspended from the ceiling and only accessible by a rickety perforated-metal staircase bolted to the wall with one rusty bolt.

Luckily, today I wasn't after anything except a rat maze to get lost in, and Meraki Market was perfect for that.

I stepped forward into the jumble of the market, ready to set a trap for my pursuer.

It was harder to hear the storm in here, if only because the clamor of the market was somehow even louder than the dragons rampaging above. The occasional roar got through, but the bells and beeps of commerce, the sizzle of frying food, and the chatter of a hundred languages ping-ponged throughout the huge space.

I strode past a shopfront with disco balls made from undine scales and shattered glass golems, ducked under draped scarves woven from glowing deva silk, and lingered by an Indian-Salamandrine fusion curry stall, my mouth watering. The sushi had been more than enough to eat, but *damn* that smelled amazing.

This area was too narrow and closed off to be of any use to me—what I needed was an open area where multiple halls and walkways converged. Somewhere I could see my stalker coming, and disappear down a crowded corridor.

The atrium on the top level would be perfect.

I followed a winding path between stalls to the stairs, where a guy in a suit was trying to budge a teenage asphalt titan sleeping in the stairwell. At least, I hoped she was sleeping.

"Will you just . . . move!" He huffed, then caught sight of me. He looked a bit sheepish, his tie flipped over. "The closest stairs are fifteen minutes away!"

"You're gonna be getting some exercise either way," I said, before sticking my clutch between my teeth.

There was a shallow gap between the titan and the top of the stairwell, so I got a grip on the nearest handhold and clambered up a gravelly black leg.

"You act like that's easy . . ." the dude grumbled.

I responded with an elegant "Mmphle" and kept climbing. The kid had a yellow median stripe down her side, and she was definitely still breathing—just taking an infamous titan nap. I don't judge—being that huge has got to be exhausting, especially when you're a teenager. Party all night, sleep in inconvenient places all day. I'd done worse when I was her age.

I shimmied through the gap between her shoulder and the ceiling, then scrabbled down the other side. Dusting the asphalt grit off my hands, I climbed the remaining steps.

One flight, two flights, three . . . The stairs opened up beneath the bright span of the paneled glass atrium ceiling, sweeping overhead like an ironwork sky holding back the storm. Fist-sized hail bounced against the glass, clearly no match for the market's storm wards, adding a drumming rhythm to the background cacophony. I gulped. Good thing I'd gotten off the street when I did.

While the center of the huge ceiling was clear glass, swaths of panels at the edges boasted a myriad of colors. The section of glass directly overhead was tinted magenta, signaling the light was specially filtered for troglofae. Sure enough, a stall in front of me was tended by an axolotlae—translucent white skin, no eyes, teal frills coming off their neck. I made a point not to study the organs on display through their cave-evolved flesh.

They were selling boba tea, of all things.

"Care for a tea?" the axolotlae burbled, probably heat-sensing me gawping.

"I—" I was about to turn them down when I spotted their more unusual offerings. The poison dart frog boba was tempting for defensive tea-bombing, but if I missed my stalker and hit a random passerby . . . Well, let's not go there.

They did have somnubus milk tea, though, and the price was right. I'd feel less guilty about a little sleepy-time overspill. Maybe the titan had some of this before she conked out. No—she'd need a cup the size of a fire hydrant to knock her out. I shook off the thought.

"A somnubus milk tea, please."

"Add boba, pudding, pixie dust, or jelee?"

"No thanks."

"Green straw or pink?"

"Pink." I rolled my eyes at myself—it wasn't like I was going to drink it.

"Five dollars, please."

I snapped open my clutch and rootled around. There, at the bottom, a crisp bill—

A fifty-dollar bill.

My eyes widened. Sirens and *songbirds*, I hadn't paid at the restaurant. I'd gotten so freaked out I'd just booked it without even thinking of the bill.

Had Samaire ended up paying for me? I should text her, except, right, my phone. Ugh, I'd have to *seriously* make it up to her.

"Is a fifty okay?"

The axolotlae stuck out a webbed appendage, and I forked the money over.

Change and tasty-looking stalker deterrent in hand, I made my way to the center of the atrium, the hub of Meraki Market.

I wasn't worried about the crowds; my pursuer was tall enough that he'd tower over nearly everyone here. I'd spot him long before he could spot me. What I did need to worry about was scoping out several exit strategies. He could come from any direction, and I didn't want to duck into a doorway only to discover it dead-ended in a broken toilet.

Standing at the center of the tiled plaza at the heart of the atrium, I let the crowds orbit me, watching the flow of traffic, the people who slipped into obscured nooks and crannies. There—a half-form hyena shifter emerging from a beaded curtain. To my left—two kids sneaking into an open vent. By the bookshop—a wooden panel that flickered as an enraenra walked directly through the illusion, her dark form wreathed in blue mist.

I stepped back into the flow of the crowd and let it carry me to my destination. The beaded curtain obscured a closet-sized shop with shelves covered with bones. No other exits made it a no-go. The vent was too small for me, thank Finéa—shuffling through a vent while toting slightly toxic tea wasn't high on my list. The illusory panel led to a narrow corridor filled with plumes of colored smoke. I held my breath to be safe and pushed forward, the smoke swirling around me, mixing into new colors. I didn't see anyone else in here with me, but the smoke had to be comming from somewhere. The air cleared momentarily, and I glanced up. A pair of dark eyes glistened near the ceiling, and I almost stumbled as I hurried on. At last I reached the other end, with a door that let out on another starburst of shops and walkways.

One exit strategy down, a couple more to go.

I circled back to the plaza and analyzed the stream of shoppers again. The music playing through the amplification spell overhead paused, replaced by a droning voice. *"Shoppers are reminded that consumption of sentient beings in public is not tolerated."* It repeated once more before the music resumed, and I pursed my lips. People really should know better.

A woman with more curls than body accordioned open a bifold door set back between two storefronts and strode into the darkness beyond it. Presto. I slipped behind a snallygaster—their gigantic feathered wings neatly tucked back against their peach scales as they ambled along—and rode their wake toward the door, exiting the bustle of beings with minimal fuss. The bifold door had closed again, but slid aside easily on oiled rollers. A staircase spiraled down before me, lit up in flickers like a silent rave was going on below. Bizarre.

I glanced behind me before committing to the stairs, and there over the shoulders of the crowd loomed a familiar form, eyes fastened on mine as my heart rate increased.

Mr. Tall, Dark, and Stalkery had caught up with me.

OUT OF THE FRYING PAN AND INTO THE SILENCE

He'd found me again, despite my phone being a batteryless brick in my clutch, which meant he had to be tracing the stupid bauble I was carting around.

Ugh, why had I ever thought palming it was a good idea?

I tore my gaze away from his and clattered down the spiral staircase, my defensive drink sloshing in my hand. Should I ditch the artifact? He presumably wanted *it*, not me, so if I tossed it his way and bolted, I should be in the clear. But everything about it screamed that it was valuable, magical, dangerous.

And I didn't love the idea of blithely handing something like that off to a dude who was clearly not on Team White Hat.

The staircase just kept going, the scatter of strobing neon on the walls growing brighter, though I still couldn't hear any music to accompany it. What kind of fae rave doesn't have a bass beat or siren synth?

A clang reverberated from above, the iron railing beneath my fingers carrying the tremor as my pursuer's heavy footfalls drummed down the steps over my head. I picked up the pace, cursing my still-damp shoes. My feet would be one big blister by the time I got home—if I ever got home.

I needed a moment to concentrate, to form my sigil and see if that cut off the tracking he had on the gizmo in my clutch.

The bottom of the stairs was in sight. Hopefully whatever was down here would help me out.

I hit ground level—or whichever level this was—in the middle of a huge dim room sparkling with the flash of colored lights from all directions, like a strobe light and a disco ball had a whole litter of dazzling kids, and this was their nursery.

Various beings lounged throughout the room, snacks or drinks in hand, seated or standing, alone and in clusters, but absolutely silent. I clicked my tongue to assure myself my ears were still connected to my noggin.

Every being in the room slowly turned to examine me, their

expressions neutral, their motions starting and ceasing at precisely the same moment, shifting back into immobility with all eyes focused on me as the claustrophobic silence persisted.

I waded into the room, wary as the black pit, trying to keep everyone in my sights as I made some space between me and the staircase. It felt incredibly urgent to move slowly, gracefully, silently, and I didn't dare blink.

My hindbrain was screaming that I was a minnow surrounded by piranhas, and the wrong movement would jounce them from peaceful placidity to a feeding frenzy. I tried to ignore it—these beings looked almost human, with only subtle differences, and certainly not like they'd strip the flesh from my bones at the slightest opportunity—but the uncanny way they'd moved in unison and the profound silence set my entire soul on edge.

Was there another exit, or did I have to retreat to the staircase and take my chances with Big, Loud, and Creepy? He didn't seem so alarming now, to be honest.

I scanned the room, avoiding eye contact, which was difficult as the fifty-some beings were all still staring fixedly at me. There, a door that almost blended into the wall, half a dozen paces away. All I had to do was make it there without incurring something horrifying.

My peach fuzz signaled my nerves were ready for takeoff, Captain.

Eyes wide open and beginning to burn, breath held as my heart pounded and panic-sweat beaded on my skin, I glided across the room in a slow-motion ballet, rolling heel to toe to keep my shoes silent, holding my arms out to avoid any scuff of fabric on fabric, keeping the drink in my hand level to prevent the tiniest slosh. Five steps, four steps, three . . .

A rattle echoed from the staircase as my pursuer thudded into view. I kept him in my peripheral vision, not daring to snap my head in his direction to watch his lumbering approach. Two steps, one . . .

I let my free hand drift to the door handle, slowly levering it down as synchronized streaks of motion stirred the air behind me. A grunt from across the room as I swung the door out, one foot sliding into the space beyond. A gurgle as I pirouetted through the doorway, facing the room I'd just left as I eased the door closed. As a spray of blood spattered the ceiling amidst the colored lights, above the circle of silent beings, who were no longer still, or human-looking.

Then the white surface of the door replaced my view of the room, and I released the handle with shaking fingers.

No lock on the handle.

I whirled and assessed the area—a narrow hallway, running left and right in semidarkness. A breeze brushed my cheek, and I turned right, rushing down the corridor, silence no longer the priority.

A minute later, the hall ended in a single door barely muffling a cacophony on its other side, air whistling through the gap at the bottom, and my shoes slapped in the puddle forming at its base. I flung the door open without hesitation.

Rain peppered my face, cold and fresh, and the wind tugged at my sleeves. Lights from cars and buildings glared through the damp, and people filled the sidewalk, the ferocity of the dragon storm spent. The dragons had moved on, the storm clouds deflating in their wake, and society was back to bustling through the sodden city.

I shivered. On the one hand, I didn't think my pursuer was a problem anymore. On the other . . . I wouldn't be coming back to Meraki Market anytime soon.

I sipped my drink, needing something routine to steady my nerves. The tea hit my tongue, tasting like soft dreams and warm covers, and I sipped deeper before I could stop myself, swallowing a fraction of a second before my eyes widened in horror.

How much somnubus venom was too much? I dropped the cup, the venom splattering across my shoes and the asphalt at the entrance of the alley, and scrambled for my clutch, popping it open and collecting the pieces of my phone with trembling hands. If I could text someone before the venom took effect, then at least I'd know help was on the way.

I slotted the battery back into place as the clamor of traffic muffled around me, my vision blurring. I gripped the power button for dear life as the door I'd escaped through became intimately acquainted with my face, and something gathered me up and cradled me within its embrace, cool against my skin but soothing. Light flared from my phone screen as darkness overtook me, my eyes too heavy to keep open.

DONE WITH DAMSEL-IN-DISTRESSING

I surfaced from the dregs of sleep, unusually cold and uncomfortable, not yet willing to open my eyes. Had the heat gone out? Were there cookie crumbs in the bed again? Totally my own fault, but still annoying. I stirred to brush the crumbs out from under me, only to find a rough surface cold with damp, grit sticking to my palm.

What the—

My eyes opened, practically glued shut. Gross. The darkness and distant light resolved into a blurry alley, with me haphazardly snoozing in the dreck. Everything flooded back: my pursuer, the silent room, the hall, the alley . . . the drink.

I tried to curse at myself, but my mouth was parched and gummy, and only a croak emerged. Certifiable genius, that's what I was. Who else would slurp down the poison they'd just purchased to fend off the bad guys?

Smearing at my face to remove the gunk of alley-nap from my eyes, I shifted to sit up, and suddenly cool hands were on mine, an indistinct figure hovering over me, too close to make out more than a jacket.

"Samaire?" I'd gotten my phone out to text her as I was crashing—I'd managed to text her, right? I leaned back to make sure it was her, and the hands became rough, scrabbling at my half-closed fist, the cloy of bad cologne settling on me.

A jolt of electric cold shot up my arm, and the last of the fog from my snoozefest cleared my mind pronto. I jerked back, kicking out at the weirdo who was groping at my fingers. He stumbled back a step with a grunt. What the wyvern did he want, my phone? I clenched my fist tighter, except I wasn't holding my phone—my fingers were hooked through delicate metal rings in a sphere.

The artifact.

"Just give me that shiny toy, and it'll be like I was never even here." His voice was equal parts soothing and putrid as he closed on me, backing me further into the alley, away from the social safety of the street.

"Won't work, pretty sure the ghost of your cologne will haunt this alley forever." Was this guy friends with the former Mr. Tall, Dark, and Stalkery? How else would he know about the artifact? Some random bum shaking people down wouldn't fixate on a bauble he couldn't even fully see in my fist.

How long had I been drooling in the alley, for them to send a replacement thug? I didn't have the bandwidth to worry about the nebulous 'them' in that thought yet—I could worry about that when I wasn't cornered in a dark alley by Mr. Grabby Cheap Cologne.

"You know what happened to your predecessor, right?" I threw on a grin, hoping to unnerve the guy. "Why you haven't heard from him?"

"Doesn't matter," he growled, advancing and almost stepping on my phone, its bright screen glaring up from the asphalt. "I'm better'n him anyway."

The blue light of my phone glinted off metal in the shadow of his jacket cuff—a knife. Perfect. Since drowning him in the dregs of the somnubus venom congealing on the alley floor wasn't exactly an option, I'd have to come up with something more creative.

They say that if some asshole is trying to rape you, you're supposed to scream "Fire!" because people actually give a crap if their property is about to burn down—they don't give a crap about you. I'm lucky enough I've never been in that situation, but I figure if some thug is mugging you for a probably priceless artifact, the theory's the same, right?

So when this guy flicked the knife out in front of him, I started hollering.

"Alligator!" I bellowed, pumping a healthy dose of hysteria into my voice. "There's a friggin' alligator over here, come look! Oh geez, dude, stay back—oh, it's got his leg. That's no good."

The guy with the knife looked around nervously, like he was worried there actually was some invisible alligator I could see, that he couldn't.

"ALLIGATOR!" I screamed at the top of my lungs, and he flinched.

Heads started poking around the corner from the street, and I grinned fiercely. Screw fires—everybody wants to see a rogue alligator wandering around the Pacific Northwest.

"Back off, psycho," I hissed at my would-be attacker. "We've got witnesses now."

He put up his hands, knife-free. "You're the psycho," he muttered.

Probably true, but I liked my kind of psycho.

I skirted around him, scooping up my phone and the nearby clutch, and booked it for the street and the onlookers, thumbing over my shoulder. "Seriously, somebody should call Redcap Creature Control, that thing'll take your leg off if you're not careful. Huge toothy monster. Must've come up from the sewers. The guy it got is definitely a goner." They peered deeper into the darkness of the alley, and I slipped into the crowd, adrenaline still pumping as I stuffed my phone and the artifact back inside my battered clutch.

How many more of these bozos did they have hanging around to send after me in the middle of the night? It was a good thing the city was always bustling, what with half its inhabitants being nocturnal. I needed to make tracks for home, and as soon as I crossed the threshold, I was duct-taping my sword sheath to the front door and never leaving without it again.

After all, what's the point of owning a pokey death weapon if you don't lug it around to poke lowlifes with?

But at this rate, would I even make it home? Getting this tracker off my back was my first priority. I just needed to find somewhere secluded where I could take a breather and form my sigil. Hopefully it would dispel whatever spell had latched on to the artifact.

I ducked into an ATM kiosk, the light overhead buzzing and wavering—the fluorosprites inside were probably having an orgy, horny little dastards—but bright enough to see what I was doing.

Focusing on the tattoo on my wrist, I willed the ink to shift, to scatter and reform. The black lines blew out, hazy at the edges, and sluggishly swirled into a mess of an inkblot. 'Kay, now tighten, separate . . .

My temples pounded, and my vision swam, and the ink stayed stubbornly put in a Rorschach test that reminded me of Bracchius.

Pushing past the headache, I tried again, and the ink diffused slightly, doing the exact opposite of what I wanted. I gritted my teeth and mentally screamed at it, bearing down with my will, and . . . nothing.

Ravens and revenants. What was this, a somnubus hangover? I'd never had occasion to find out what those were like, but what else could it be?

Ugh, I'd have to do this the risky way. I fished out my phone and woke it up, the battery down to seven percent—I'd have to hurry. Pulling up my sketching app, I plugged away at the screen with a clumsy finger, drawing the intricate lines, erasing the oopsies, and trying again. Finally I had it right, at two percent battery remaining. I bit my lip.

Now came the tricky part.

I dangled a single spark of my magenta magic from the tip of my finger, centering it over the sigil, and drew in a deep breath through my nose.

One percent. Now or never.

I lowered my finger.

The spark sizzled into the sigil and radiated out, the screen morphing into a burst of colored static and winking out to black.

No. No no, no, *no*.

I pressed the home button once, twice. I mashed the power button. Please, please, please.

The screen stayed stubbornly dark, raindrops beading on the glass.

Ramming my bricked phone back into my clutch, I jabbed myself with something sharp. What the—

My finger was bleeding from a short slice. I peered into the jumble inside my clutch, not willing to risk my fingers until I had an idea what was lurking down there. Phone, stupid bauble, random bills and change from the axolotlae . . . a glint of light off something smooth and metallic, obscured by the cheap lining. I scrabbled the coins aside and shoved my nose half inside the bag.

The lining was torn, and the shiny thing had slipped through the tear and nestled between the lining and the shell of my clutch. If I could just squeeze my finger through the hole . . .

I grazed another sharp edge but managed to latch on to it without opening an artery or anything. As soon as I had it between my fingers, I knew what it was.

Schnauzers and shadowmakers.

My flipping *dagger*. The one I'd been smart enough to grab before heading out for dinner, and then completely forgotten about because it was out of sight, literally out of mind.

Sometimes ADHD is a real drag.

I ground my teeth. I could've turned my would-be mugger into a pincushion, if only my brain had cooperated for once.

Although, the look on his face when I was screaming about alligators was pretty worth it, and I'd gotten out of that scrape anyway.

I ran my tongue over my teeth and smiled. I wasn't exactly Silvana the Slicer when it came to knives, but at least I could make the next stalker sorry.

Better not to tempt any of the Fates, though—I glanced around for the closest subway entrance. None in sight, just the neon glow of signs for scale-polishing salons, bruja bodegas, and crystallariums.

Leaving the shelter of the ATM, I rejoined the bustling stream of foot traffic. Getting to Bracchius was my best chance—better than staying out in the open with borked magic, a useless phone, and the troublemaking trinket. The dagger gave me a fighting chance, but who knows who they'd send after me next.

A flashing sign for the Decadance nightclub caught my eye.

Wait, was I—

I hurried around the corner just ahead. Yes, I was. My tattoo shop was on the next block.

Could I kill two pixies with one stone? Ruby could tattoo my sigil faster than I could get home on the subway, and I'd been wanting a white tattoo for ages—all the better not to draw attention to any sigils I formed.

Could I afford it? No. Could I afford *not* to do it?

Not really.

Metallic Stymphalian feathers chimed together overhead as I entered Ruby's. The dark walls were plastered with posters of tattoo designs, and how different colors looked on skin, scales, and hide.

Ruby stepped out from the back, her garnet hair in an updo with short bangs, her eyes a slightly brighter shade of red.

"Hi, Immy." She glanced at a twenty-four-hour clock on the wall—the kind nocturnal beings prefer to use. "Isn't it past your bedtime?"

A yawn ripped through me out of nowhere, my jaw cracking with it, and I avoided looking closely enough to read the time—I really didn't want to know how little sleep I was getting tonight.

"Yeah, I . . ." My voice came out like gravel, and I cleared my throat.

"Girl, you sound like you need to hydrate." Ruby disappeared and returned a moment later with a bottle of water. "Here. On the house."

I cracked the lid and lifted the bottle to my lips, only to twitch as the label filled my field of view.

"This is Pure Bliss! I can't take this." My raspy words were barely intelligible. "Do you know how expensive this stuff is?"

Pure Bliss is the gold-plated Rolls Royce of bottled water, purified by unicorn horn by the Reinhuf herd, who have made beaucoup bucks off the whole enterprise—enough to buy up a quarter of the Midwest for an elite unicorn sanctuary slash resort slash snobbiary.

Ruby gently pushed the bottle back toward me. "Please, take it. One of our customers used a literal pallet of it to pay for a tat, and we're all sick of drinking it."

I eyed the bottle. If I'd be doing her a favor . . .

Raising the bottle to my lips, I let a trickle of water slip through. It hit cold and clear, fruity and somehow effervescent, despite the lack of carbonation. I tipped my head back and guzzled, my parched body demanding every last drop. My last drink had been at the restaurant, and that had been *how* many hours ago?

Nope, not doing the math, bad math. Those numbers would just depress me.

I set the empty bottle down on Ruby's front counter with a crackle. "Thanks. I really needed that."

She smirked. "I couldn't tell. So, you here for a tat, or what?"

A pastel sheen hung over my vision, tinting the room like a marshmallow rainbow. "Yeah, uh . . ." I blinked to clear it, but nothing changed. Damn unicorns.

I snapped open my clutch and upended it on the counter, the artifact rolling a few inches and the dagger sticking in the beat-up countertop at an awkward angle. I winced. "Sorry."

I shoved the loose bills and change across to Ruby, who seemed remarkably unconcerned about the dagger. "Look, I don't have much cash on me, and you know my credit isn't any good, but what I want you to tattoo is a valuable sigil. I gotta give you the design to tattoo it—it'll be my collateral until I can pay you. And I *will* pay you. Just . . . just don't sell the design to anyone, or I'm going to be seriously pissed off."

A black corona flashed out from the artifact, like a dark-magic bang snap, and I stared at it warily.

"Neat party trick."

I nodded slowly. Did this thing just not like being outside my clutch? Or could it hear me? I— Nope, not going to worry about it right now. I scooped it up and returned it to my clutch, unstuck the dagger from the counter, and chucked it in as well.

Ruby held out a pen. "Draw your sigil for me?"

I grabbed the pen and popped off the cap, hovering over the paper Ruby had gotten out. Could I just draw the sigil on myself with the pen? It'd be faster than a tattoo, and I wouldn't have to share the design.

No, it was still raining outside, and the ink would smudge lickety-split. I needed a sigil that would last longer than five minutes.

I put pen to paper and sketched the sigil. Ruby looked it over and nodded. "Easy enough."

"Oh, and I want it in white ink. Forgot to mention that, I think."

"White ink? You know that looks nothing like the photos you see online, right? Most of those Instagram shots are of gel pens or chalk markers. White ink turns out like a paler version of your skin color, and gets more difficult to see over time."

"Yeah, I know, that's exactly what I want."

Ruby smiled. "Perfect, then. I love an informed client. Come on to the back, and I'll get you taken care of."

She held back the dark curtain that divided the shop, and I slipped through, fully ready to shake my stalkers off my back.

WHEELIN' AND DEMON DEALIN'

The first prick of the needles bit into the skin of my left wrist, and I gritted my teeth. It wasn't bad, but focusing on something else was helpful. I zeroed in on the opaque white ink pooling on my skin before Ruby wiped it away, gliding the machine along.

Buzz, wipe, buzz. The sigil formed line by line, a pale highlight under my skin, partly masked by the pink flush blooming around the pierced skin.

Ruby was totally in the zone, the very tip of her tongue sticking out between her lips in concentration, her vibrant red eyes focused on the needles. I'd never been rude enough to ask what she was—there are a lot of beings with red eyes that can pass for human—though I'd pretty much ruled out vampire.

The buzz of the needle cut out, and Ruby gave the tattoo another wipe-down. She leaned in, her breath warming my skin as she inspected the sigil and compared it to my drawing. A couple touchups here and there, and she sat back, a satisfied smile dancing on her lips.

"There we go. Take a look, and let me know if it's anything less than perfect."

I gave the sigil a thorough twice-over, making sure the lines connected in the right places, curved at the right angles. It was flawless.

"You nailed it, Ruby."

She grinned. "I know. Let me just get you finished up, and you'll be good to go."

One more wipe-down, and she swiveled on her stool and sorted through her aftercare kit, pulling out a large bandage and a bottle of ointment.

"One sec." I glanced around, not wanting to filthy up the freshly cleaned tattoo with my grimy fingers. I snagged a clean finger cot from her kit, rolled it on, then sucked in and released a deep breath.

Brushing the finger over the tattoo stung, but I ignored it and infused the sigil with just a speck of my magic, the magenta sparks racing along the lines until they brimmed over.

My skin prickled, and the air shivered as the protection snapped into place. Ruby's eyes widened a fraction as they flicked around the room, but the purpose of the magic wasn't obvious from the outside.

Ruby shrugged and moved in with fresh gloves and the bottle of ointment. "Curiosity killed the charybdis, as they say."

I hummed to myself as she smoothed the cool ointment over my skin, soothing the sting.

"Let me know how this feels. It's a new formula I'm trying out—shea butter and caladrius albumen."

The redness on my wrist was fading. "It already feels like I've had a couple days of healing."

"Good." She placed the breathable clear bandage with precision. "Leave this on for twenty-four hours, then apply a dab of the lotion every twelve until it's gone." She held out a plastic bottle the size of her thumbnail. "A little goes a *long* way."

"Thanks." I palmed the bottle.

"Whoa, what happened there?" She jerked her chin at my other tattoo, which was still a blownout mess. "Don't like seeing my work look like that."

"Yeah, uh, had a magical mishap. Hopefully I can fix it after I've gotten some sleep."

Ruby gave me a stern look. "If not, you come on back here."

"Yes, ma'am."

"Cheeky."

"Always."

She smiled and snapped a flame into existence, lighting the corner of the sigil I'd drawn. When the paper was half-burnt, she set it in the sink. "Guess I won't be putting this one in my book." She passed me a receipt for how much I still owed her, and I winced. Definitely no more sushi for me for a couple months.

Ruby's work was worth it, though.

"I'll pay you as soon as I can, pixie promise." My IOUs were racking up: Ruby, Samaire—

Samaire. Sirens and songbirds.

I crumpled the receipt in amongst the collection in my clutch, along with the tiny bottle. "Can I borrow your phone? Just to send a text. Mine's smashed."

"Sure thing."

Samaire's number is one of the few that's actually cemented in my brain. I hunt-and-pecked a short message letting her know I hadn't drowned, been kidnapped, or murdered—yet. If I ever got my phone fixed, there'd probably be a flurry of messages from her, getting increasingly panicked as the hours went by and I didn't respond.

A chime binged in almost immediately.

Samaire: I'm going to kill you next time I see you!! SO glad you're okay <3 <3 <3 I'll need the $50 for sushi before rent's due next week, sorry :/ Talk soon

I deleted the message and passed the phone back to Ruby. "Thanks." My jaw cracked with a rip-roaring yawn. Either the effects of the somnubus venom were lingering, or my late—*late*—night was catching up with me. "Gotta run, but I'll be in touch."

"I know. Good luck, girl."

The train pulled in just as I hit the subway platform, and I fought heavy eyelids all the way home. Stumbling up to my apartment, I narrowly avoided tripping over a bedraggled crow, his feathers sticking up in all directions.

"Storm got you too, huh?" I crouched and offered a hand. The crow eyed me for a minute before giving in and hopping over with a resigned squawk.

I eased the cockeyed feathers back into place one by one. The last was loose, and I held it up for the crow to see.

"This one abandoned ship, I'm afraid. Mind if I keep it?"

The crow spread his wings and pumped them a couple times, cawing, then tucked them back in and started tidying himself with his beak.

"I'll take that as an 'all yours.'" I creaked back to my feet, my thigh muscles telling me I was a moron for gallivanting around all night long. "Tell your friends I can sort them out tomorrow if they're in the same shape you were."

He squawked again, and hopped away down the walk.

I fished for my key but paused as Bracchius's voice carried through the thin wall.

"We have struck a bargain with her. I really cannot have you devouring her oatmeal."

What on— I crept to the lit window and peered into the kitchen.

A blobby black miasma rolled along the kitchen floor—one of the few forms I'd seen Bracchius assume. I eyeballed the canister of oatmeal on the counter, but no one else was in the kitchen.

"You will need to report back to Andamantos for reassignment. Git!"

Git? What, was Bracchius watching old Westerns while I was out? Little weirdo. And who in tarnation was he talking to?

His voice lowered to a mutter. "As if I didn't have enough to worry about with Kor and Sparkles. Cursed pantry moths."

There was no way I'd heard that right. I found my key and fumbled the door open.

Bracchius hovered innocently half an inch off the kitchen floor, the flickering red in his depths letting me know he'd turned to face me.

"Bracchius? Who are you talking to?"

His form swirled subtly. "No one. Myself."

I narrowed my eyes, glancing between him and the oatmeal canister. The swirling intensified.

Launching myself across the kitchen, I snatched up the canister and popped the lid off, tilting the can to inspect the oats. Nothing sinister greeted me. I pawed through the oats, and just found . . . more oats.

I weighed the canister in my hand. "Were there moths in this oatmeal?"

Swirl, swirl. "What? No. Definitely not. Why would there be?" He scoffed. "Moths—preposterous!"

The gears churned in my brain as I put the pieces together. "Bracchius . . . are pantry moths minions of the Dark Ones?" I couldn't quite believe I was stringing those words together.

Bracchius's voice got squeakier. "Minions? Pantry moths? Whatever would make you think something so absolutely impossible? Highly improbable."

"Mmhmm."

I took pity on the poor demon and set the canister down. My damp clothes had gotten a rainy refresh on the walk here from the subway station, and I was sick and tired of them clinging to my skin, making me jump with each cold contact.

"Don't go anywhere—I've got something to talk to you about. I'll be right back."

The demons' stormproofing must've worked—I didn't squelch on any patches of sopping carpet on my way to the bathroom, and the ceiling was free of any new water stains.

I stripped out of my wet clothes and slung them over the shower bar after rescuing my books from the tub, then rummaged through my pile of this week's clothes on my broken-backed desk chair and picked out a pair of sweats and a T-shirt that passed the sniff test.

Ruffling a towel through my short curls to get the worst of the wet out, I called it good. Bracchius wouldn't care if my head looked like a mangy poodle.

I plopped down on Bracchius's sofa in the living room, and he levitated into place on the pedestal centered on the coffee table. His favorite place to hang out is under the sofa—where he hoards away who knows what, I'm honestly afraid to look—but when I wanted a face-to-face convo, he'd grudgingly oblige.

The pedestal had been one of Kor's demands. He was too high-and-mighty to deign to touch the sofa cushion, or the coffee table, or . . . anything, really. He'd insisted on a throne worthy of his august darkness, and the ornate silver pedestal satisfied his requirements.

It gave me the warm fuzzies—okay, maniacal glee—knowing he was really resting his august shadowy butt on a clearance-sale three-wick candle pillar from Bath & Body Works.

Heh.

Bracchius liked using it too, if only because it made him feel special.

"What's that on your arm?" he asked.

I lifted my arm, showing off the clear bandage Ruby had applied. "I got a new tattoo."

Bracchius's form went oval, hovering over the pedestal slightly as he peered at my arm. "What, a *white*-ink tattoo? What's wrong with black? I like black. You like black. Don't you?" He deflated. "It's the color of darkness, like me."

Oh crap. I rushed to reassure him. "I do like black, and I really like you. You're perfect just the way you are, Bracchius."

He swelled back up to his normal chubby black miasmal self. Crisis averted.

I traced a finger over the design. "I got the tattoo in white ink so that I can use my sigils more subtly."

It didn't matter if Bracchius saw the sigil—demons don't give a rat's ass about such "low" magic, apparently. Kor had dissolved into a fit of horrifyingly creepy giggles the first time I'd gotten defensive about my sigils in front of them.

"Why don't you just use black in a more discreet location? Like the tattoo over your rib—"

His voice cut off with a squeak, and his form condensed defensively.

My demons had been gossiping.

Again.

I blew an errant curl out of my face. "Tell Kor to keep his eyes to himself when I'm in the bathroom."

Bracchius perked back up. "I will. But Immy—look, you know I hate defending him, but—it wasn't intentional. In fact, if it's any consolation, he said his eyes burned like the fires of Rokonor at the sight of your hideous form, and he was forced to return to the shadowmurk before he felt any better."

"Yes," I deadpanned. "That makes me feel *so* much better."

"So . . ." Bracchius obviously wanted an answer about my tattoo, but was afraid to bring it up again.

"I need to see the ink to shift it, and ripping my shirt off in public doesn't work so hot if I want to be discreet."

"Oh, right, humans and their modesty. Very strange. You don't see demons running around with shirts and toe rings and . . . and *sequin* scarves."

He lingered longingly over those last words.

Hmm. I'd have to add a sequin scarf to his Ascension Day gift list.

In black, of course.

Bracchius rolled from side to side. "So, *why* do you need to use your sigils more subtly?"

"So I can keep them going longer without worrying about hiding them."

"Because . . . ?"

"Because I need to keep this artifact from being tracked."

"Artifact?"

I upended my clutch on the table beside him, scattering the contents everywhere, then held up the irksome ball for his viewing pleasure.

He shifted, elongating to peer at the orb from various angles. "Hmm . . . hrm . . . Interesting . . ."

I fought a yawn as the hemming and hawing continued.

Bracchius cleared his whatever-demons-have-instead-of-a-throat. "Well, that sigil you're using will stop a basic tracking spell, but that 'artifact' could still be scried for."

I jolted upright. "Damn it, really?"

"I'm afraid so."

"If I give it to you for safekeeping, does that stop them from being able to scry?"

"Yes, subsuming it within my essence will keep it perfectly safe."

My brain screeched to a halt. "Subsuming it . . . within . . . your essence?"

"Yes."

"Is *that* what you do with the things I give you?" I curled my lip. "Scratch that, I don't want to know how your digestive system works."

Bracchius harrumphed. "How you could *possibly* imagine that the sublime demon form has *anything* so disgusting in common with humans . . ." He shuddered. "No, my form is free of anything resembling the horrifying slime and muck that resides within your flesh suit." Said form swirled turbulently. "No offense."

"I—" I blinked. Nope.

Just nope.

He gave the bauble another once-over. "What is it, anyway?"

"I have no idea."

"I could find out for you."

I snorted. "Oh yeah? And what would that cost me?"

Bracchius bobbed with anticipation. "Well, Enthilia just put out the Deal of the Day challenge on Pentagram—taking a mortal's conscience, but not their guilt."

"Hard pass. What's the prize for that one?"

Bracchius sighed wistfully. "The demon who collects the most consciences gets a trip to Suspiria's secret tar springs."

"T—*Tar* springs?" Yikes.

"Oh, Immy, they're reputed to be utter bliss—just imagine, hot black tar bubbling up just above a magma pocket, roiling and steaming. Apparently, she's even got it set up so the tar oozes down endless terraces of rimstone pools . . . Just *beautiful*."

As awful as that sounded, all the talking of bubbles and pools made me realize I had to pee—pronto. "Yup, demons are weird." I slapped my thighs and stood up to scurry to the bathroom.

"Humans are weirder!" Bracchius said petulantly, his voice trailing after me. "Wait, Immy! What about your artifact? Don't you want me to keep it safe?"

I hollered from the bathroom. "At the cost of my conscience, hold the guilt?"

He mumbled something I couldn't hear. I flipped off Kor's mirror on my way out a minute later.

"What was that?" I plopped back on the sofa.

"I said no . . . I knew you'd never go for that." Bracchius's tone was oddly anxious.

I tilted my head. "Then what? Something worse?"

"Not exactly . . ."

If he'd been anything but a demon, I would've said he was scuffing his shoes.

"You know . . . you know Sparkles?"

I nodded solemnly. Sparkles is Bracchius's favorite stuffed animal—stuffed unicorn, to be precise, shimmering white with a mane, tail, and horn colored like rainbow galaxies.

His next words were a whisper. "Kor stole Sparkles and took her through the mirror. Can you get her back for me?"

A SUCKER FOR PUPPY EYES

"Into the mirror?" Poor Bracchius. Kidnapping someone's stuffed animal is the lowest of the low. "Why in the three hells did Kor take her?"

"He said . . . he said"—Bracchius lowered his voice, imitating Kor—"'consorting with fluffy simulacra is beneath your dignity, and you need to learn to cope with reality without such infantile crutches.'"

"That jerkwad!"

"So you'll do it? You'll get Sparkles back for me?"

Bracchius peered up at me with hope shimmering in his little ebon form. Maybe I shouldn't have sounded so sympathetic.

When Kor moved in, I asked for access to his mirror domain as part of the roommate agreement. No way did I want some hellhole being operated out of my apartment without even being able to tell what was going on in there.

Kor put up one heck of a fuss about it, but eventually gave in—me graffitiing his mirror with shaving cream liturgies and poems about rosy-cheeked cherubs might've had something to do with wearing him down.

He admitted that denying me access would create quite the loophole in the contract—he could just hide in the mirror and never have to pay the rent.

Me simply smashing the mirror—or chucking it out into the snow for the tanukis to have a heyday with—never occurred to him as a possibility.

Dunderhead.

Demons are wily, but they're also fundamentally incapable of believing anyone else could possibly be even wilier. They assume you'll play by their rules, or try to *betray* them by their rules, so chaotic messes like me come as a bit of a revelation.

Bracchius has started to cotton on, but Kor seems to have a denser demon skull. Maybe he'll figure it out this time.

Not that I'd be smashing any mirrors today. That wouldn't help Sparkles one bit.

I really had to do this, didn't I? Needing Bracchius to safeguard the artifact was one aspect, but I was also a hopeless sucker for his demon-equivalent of sad puppy eyes, which were latched on to me like a tractor beam right now.

Damn, but he could look pathetic when he wanted to.

"I, uh—"

No, I needed to think this through before agreeing to anything. Despite working access to Kor's mirror into our contract, I'd never actually ventured in.

Sure, I'd poke my head in there from time to time—I mean, who isn't going to sneak a peek at a demon's walk-in closet slash super secret subbasement slash private lair, given the chance? Not to mention that shoving your head through a supposed-to-be-solid object is a serious trip.

My curls got a little crispy the first time. I stocked up on massive bottles of heat protectant after that.

My main takeaways were that it was hot, dark, and smelled like the backside of a kelpie after eating too many gummy worms. You couldn't really tell much more than that.

If there was any way to avoid having to tromp around in there, I'd take it. Knowing the universe, though, I'd better plan on the worst-case scenario. Which meant diving head-first into the stinky demon domain.

I finally gave in and looked at the time.

Rack and ruin.

Did I even *have* time to save Sparkles and make it to work? Never mind get even a minute of shut-eye?

"If you don't want to . . ." Bracchius said in his most despondent voice.

"No, it's fine. I'll rescue Sparkles from that dastard."

"What is it, then?"

I slumped, eyeballing the traitorous clock. "I'm not going to get any sleep."

Bracchius swiveled between me and the clock. "What? Why not?"

"Because if I rescue Sparkles now, there won't be any time left to sleep."

Bracchius scoffed. "Oh, right—'time.' Ridiculous. You can't seriously think we apply such absurd constructs to our domains."

My brain ticked over for a minute as I processed that.

"Are you saying . . . time doesn't pass inside Kor's mirror?"

"Obviously."

I narrowed my eyes, dangerously close to letting them shut the rest of the way. "So if I leave now, it'll still be now when I come back?"

"It's always 'now,' Immy. What a question."

"I mean—" How to phrase this to a being that just didn't grok time . . . I pointed at the digital oven clock. "You see those numbers change sometimes, right?"

"Of course."

"So those numbers won't change while I'm in the mirror?"

"Ah, yes. That's right."

I chewed at my lip. Huh. Theoretically, I could rescue Sparkles, return her to Bracchius's metaphorical bosom, and nip back inside the mirror for a long snooze.

As tempting as limitless sleep outside the bounds of time sounded, though, I'd have to make that call after seeing just what kinds of horrors Kor kept in there.

I couldn't count on that working out, and my phone was still fried, so my alarm was out of commission too. But we hadn't finished negotiating yet.

"Bracchius, in exchange for attempting Sparkles's rescue, I want two things."

"Attempting?"

"Yes. Two things."

"Okay . . ."

"One, that you guard that artifact for the foreseeable future."

He must've been even more desperate about Sparkles than I'd thought. He glommed off the pedestal and straight onto the artifact, 'subsuming it within his essence,' as he'd so delightfully put it.

"Done. And two?"

"When I come back, I'm probably gonna pass out pretty much immediately. Problem is, I won't be able to wake up on time for work by myself. Can you wake me up at four forty-five?"

That'd be cutting it close, but any earlier than that, and I'd probably murder the first person—demon—to disturb me.

"Four forty-five? What does that even mean?" Bracchius pulsed, still sheltering the artifact like a mother cockatrice with her eggs. "Why fleshbound beings insist on not only making up this imaginary concept, but also dividing it up and inventing even more things to track it, I'll never understand."

His time-superiority was starting to get on my nerves. "Don't demons make, like, ten-year contracts? You know, ten years of bliss and riches, then eternal servitude?"

"Sure, we'll play make-believe with you. We try to keep our contractors happy."

A suspicion snuck up on me, and I sat forward. "Do demons actually know when the ten years is up?"

Bracchius's form became a bit more turbulent. "Er, well, of course we do, mmhmm, yup. Just because we don't need your made-up nonsense, doesn't mean it isn't a perfectly understandable concept, simplistic, childish, really—"

I decided to stop torturing the poor demon. "Great, that's a relief." I pointed again at the digital clock on the stove. "If I come back and fall asleep in the apartment, when those numbers change to zero four four five, come wake me up."

I paused. If demons couldn't tell time, maybe their concept of numbers was just as shaky. "I don't need to draw the numbers for you, do I?"

Bracchius huffed. "Well, I never—I am insulted, Immy. Insulted. I can read numbers, not only in your barbaric language, but also in Mermish, and Camazotz, and Krkrchchung, and—"

"Okay, okay, I get it. Sorry. But you'll wake me up?"

"If you return Sparkles to me, I will rouse you from your rehearsal of death, yes."

Drama queen.

"Deal."

Now I just had to kit up to wrest a sparkly unicorn plushie from the sinister clutches of my asshat demon roommate.

I was definitely taking my sword this time.

First things first: if I could talk sense into Kor, I wouldn't even have to go into the mirror. Granted, if I asked him for Sparkles and he said no, he'd know my next steps would be to go get Sparkles myself, and if he was determined enough to keep her away from Bracchius, I would be in for a world of trouble inside his domain.

I chewed on my lip, considering. Was there some way I could suss out his mood without raising his suspicions?

Bracchius bobbed anxiously on the table. I patted the couch cushion. "Why don't you go under your sofa? And if you overhear anything I'm about to say to Kor, ignore it. I'm going to lie my socks off to get Sparkles back."

"All right." Bracchius plopped off the table and rolled under the couch, the skirt flapping back into place in his wake. I glanced at the table, which was artifact free.

Nope, not going to imagine the bizarre inner landscape of a demon. After all, I had a stuffed unicorn to rescue.

I rummaged in the junk closet in the hallway, excavating tattered boxes and tangled clothes hangers. Somewhere in here . . .

There it was. I hauled out a grimy old terrarium that had once been the home of an ill-fated turtle named A'Tuin. Better known as my first roommate.

The contents clanked as I set it down. First layer—haphazardly folded tissue paper I'd saved with good intentions. Into a gap in the closet Tetris it went, with a defeated crinkle. Second layer—a shoebox of batteries, at least one of which was oozing sinister substances. I gingerly lifted it with two fingers and shiffed it down the hallway a couple feet. Those would need to go to the hydra delicatessen ASAP.

Third layer—there we go, the heat lamp. I upended the rest of the junk onto the closet pile, and lugged the tank and lamp into the bathroom. Kor wasn't anywhere in sight, so I set to work.

Sitting crisscross applesauce, I squeezed an unopened double pack of toilet paper out from under the bathroom sink and tossed it in the tub, then heaved the tank inside the dark, empty space. Perfect fit. I swung the cabinet door closed to test, then back open.

Now, was the heat lamp cord long enough? I crawled to my knees and stretched over the sink to the outlet, preferring to balance precariously on one knee and risk toppling over than to just give in and stand up. What can I say? I'm a dork that way.

I slotted the plug into the outlet, and the heat lamp flared to life, already warming in my hand. Wriggle the cord past the faucet, don't knock over the toothbrush cup, hook it around the drawer, and . . . there. It stretched just far enough to fasten the lamp to the top lip of the terrarium.

The glaring orange light really emphasized how gross the tank was, though. If I could at least put something in the bottom to make it more appealing . . .

I scavenged through the closet again, looking for anything likely, and came up with two distinct possibilities—a bag of ratty black fleece scraps, and lava rocks I'd totally stolen from someone's landscaping ages ago. But what would a demon rather lounge on?

"Hey, Bracchius." I flopped on my stomach behind the sofa, lifting the dusty skirt a scant inch to reveal the gloom beyond. "What wins out for a demon nap? Black fleece or lava rocks?"

"Oh, lava rocks, definitely. The scrape of their porous surface against our true form . . . There's nothing like it. And if you relax enough that your form actually sinks down into those teeny pockets—"

I scrambled to my feet with said rocks. "Thanks, I don't need to hear any more."

"I can't believe you're making a nap spot for me, Immy, that is so kind. After the stress of being without Sparkles, I haven't known what to do with myself."

Oh, crap. I dropped back to my elbows and whispered under the sofa. "Uh, actually, it's for Kor—at least for right now. I need it to help get Sparkles back. But once that's done, I'll boot him out, don't worry. It'll be all yours, and there should even be room for Sparkles."

His voice wavered. "I understand. I—I think I'll just close my eyes until Sparkles is back safe."

"Okay." Poor guy. I might need to rework our roommate agreement to keep Kor from torturing him anymore.

I cracked another vicious yawn as I got off the floor again. Right. Couldn't dawdle, or I'd get fired tomorrow for passing out on the job.

Hurrying back into the bathroom, I rolled the lava rocks into the terrarium, then rummaged for the first aid fanny pack buried at the back of one of the drawers. I dumped out the pill packets and about half the bandages, and buckled it around my hips.

Now, what to pack?

Sword, right. In my bedroom, I lowered the plastic-wrapped sword off the back-of-the-door clothes rack, slid it out, and slung the sheath strap over my shoulder. The grip was wrapped in thin leather, but the core was the same metal as the sword—and it got awfully hot in Kor's domain, based on what I'd seen. Would the leather be enough to protect my hands?

Better play it safe.

I darted into the kitchen, snatched up the oven mitt, and wrapped it around the haft. Too bulky.

I snagged a nearly empty roll of duct tape from the odds-and-ends drawer along with a heavy-duty pair of scissors.

"Farewell, trusty oven mitt. Your sacrifice is appreciated."

I brutalized the mitt with the scissors, cutting out a smaller rectangle of the layered fabric. Fold that around the sword haft, and apply a healthy helping of duct tape, and . . . Voilà. A sword suitable for venturing into Mordor.

'Kay, what else?

Well, I was going to melt in these sweats, for starters. I changed into loose shorty-shorts and a tank, ankle socks and sneakers with good tread. I guzzled down a tall glass of water, then hooked a full Nalgene bottle to my sheath strap.

Snacks would be smart. I stuffed the fanny pack almost to bursting with Grandma's Cookies packets and gummy dragons. A few more odds and ends—a half-full mini spray bottle, a tin of Altoids, bobby pins, nail clippers, one of those reusable grocery bags that stuffs down super tiny— and I called it good.

No, wait. A neon-yellow-and-orange hunk of plastic called to me from the bottom of the closet. I unearthed the old Nerf gun, checked it for foam darts, and added it to the chaos.

I dumped my supplies on the toilet seat and draped the shower curtain over everything, then doused my hair with heat protectant and smeared moisturizer everywhere.

All right, time to lie my ass off.

I knocked on the mirror.

THROUGH THE LOOKING GLASS (RELUCTANTLY)

My little knock boomed, echoing as though the mirror hid the entrance to a huge cavern instead of a patch of damp-buckled paint on the wall.

To be fair, I'm pretty sure Kor's domain is a lot bigger than a cavern.

I crossed my arms, waiting for Kor to kick his ass in gear and come answer the "door."

Kor's mirror is a clunky Victorian affair. Oval glass, ornate frame with curlicues and whatsits, covered in what was probably gold leaf before it got tarnished by the fires of the three hells, or the breath of a sulfur dragon—take your pick.

It also weighed at least a hundred pounds. Believe me, I know. I was the bonehead who cheerily agreed to install it, and then spent half an hour lugging it across the apartment travois-style on a grungy bedsheet.

Kor still hasn't noticed the curlicue I broke off on the baseboard heater. Gold paint markers for the win.

The surface of the mirror swirled, darkening to an inky whirlpool as Kor finally made an appearance.

"Oh, it is you," he rumbled.

I forced myself not to roll my eyes. Kor seems to think avoiding contractions makes him sound high-and-mightier, but get him excited enough—or pissed off enough—and he's spewing them all over the place.

"Yup, it's me."

"Immy, you appear to be . . . sticky."

As far as I could figure, Kor understood nothing about the human body, and I took great delight in freaking him out about it as often as possible.

"Oh, this?" I smeared a hand over the moisturizer coating my skin like frosting. "Yeah, just had a shower, and gotta make sure to glue all my skin down now so it doesn't slough off."

The black surface of the mirror shuddered, sending ripples skittering. "Never mind. What is it that you want?"

"I just heard about the trick you played on Bracchius, and . . ." I gave him a second to sweat—not that demons sweat. I don't think. "I swear I laughed for an hour straight. That's amazing! That dumb unicorn always got on my nerves too."

I kept my wince at my words totally internal. Kor had to buy this, even if it made me feel like a callous dirtbag.

"Really?" Kor sounded smug. "I misjudged you, Immaline, I was certain that you would be peeved at minimum. You have always seemed to get along better with Bracchius than with me."

How many times did I have to tell him my full name *wasn't* Immaline? I gritted my teeth—I needed him to think I was on his side right now, and harping on about my name wouldn't help.

"Oh, well, I *have* known him longer." I waved a hand dismissively. "But I love a good practical joke! What do you think you'll do with the toy?"

"I have not quite decided yet—there are simply too many delightful options. Tell me, what sounds better: letting it slowly turn to ash in a pool of magma, or be devoured by maggots?"

I swallowed. "Gee, that's a tough choice. You don't plan to return it, then? I think that's a good call."

"Why, thank you. No, it never even crossed my mind to return that infantile construction of fluff. Bracchius may be retired, but that is no excuse to sully the reputation of all demonkind with such tomfoolery. He is better off without it, and it will be amusing to watch its destruction."

A hint of a whimper sounded from the living room, and I cleared my throat. Hopefully Kor's hearing wasn't as good as mine. "Well, I've been working on a project to show my appreciation for, uh, services rendered." I swung open the cabinet door, revealing the terrarium. "Come take a look."

Kor oozed out of the mirror, dripping down to form a chaotic ball of evil in midair. He drifted over to peer under the sink.

"So, I've set up this"—don't say tank, make this sound appealing—"miniature demon lounge so you can bask in heat and darkness. The lamp heats the stones until you're ready to relax, then is shut off. I insist you try it out, as a token of my appreciation." I smiled, batting my eyelashes at him.

Kor shifted left a few inches, then right, studying the tank.

Come on, come on, come onnn.

"I appreciate the gesture, Immaline, amateurish as your efforts are," he said dubiously, and inched closer to the tank. A frisson ran through him. "Although . . . Are those igneous stones? Perhaps I could indulge for a moment."

He descended into the terrarium and relaxed into an opaque black liquid that filled the bottom of the tank, hiding the rocks from view. "Ah, yes, that is somewhat satisfying." Runnels of black spiderwebbed their way up the glass walls of the tank a couple inches. "Hmmmm."

Yeesh, I didn't want to know what *that* was about. I clicked off the heat lamp, dousing the tank in shadows. "Those stones'll hold the heat for a while, and with the door closed, you'll have almost complete darkness. I'll just tidy up in here and get out of your way, yeah?"

"Indeed, that would be ideal, Immaline. Much appreciated."

I swung the door softly shut, whipped the shower curtain off my stuff, and geared up as quietly as possible. Bulging fanny pack, sword, water bottle, Nerf gun—all good. I squared my shoulders and faced the mirror, stepping up onto the plastic toilet lid, which squeaked a complaint.

Then I dredged up a spark of my magic, letting it dangle at the tip of my finger. After our squabble over the roommate agreement, Kor had keyed the mirror to recognize my magic, allowing me passage at its touch.

The magenta spark sizzled across the surface, replacing the solid glass with a molten silver that gave beneath my finger, warm and slippery. I recoiled instinctively, then huffed out a breath.

Here goes nothing.

I gripped the hilt of my sword and took the plunge, curls first.

I landed on my butt, of course, in pitch blackness. I reached for my— Ravens and revenants.

I didn't have a flashlight. How had I forgotten a *flashlight*?

I almost turned back right then, but if I went back through the mirror, I would for sure tumble off the toilet with a maximum of noise, drawing Kor's attention. I'd lose my chance to get Sparkles, and Bracchius would be a miserable puddle of a demon for the foreseeable future.

The room was silent except for a constant, ominous rumbling that seemed to come from all directions. The air was stale and hotter than asphalt in the dead of summer. Once my eyes adjusted, faint green pinpricks of light became visible in the darkness.

The glowing eyes of a hundred tiny sentries?

I'd always gotten the impression Kor didn't hang out alone in here— what was the fun in having your own domain if you didn't get to lord it over lesser beings, after all?—but the sheer number of green eyes watching me had me rethinking this plan.

A sudden hiss and roar made me jump back, ready to pull my sword. Jinkies, what kinds of monsters did Kor keep in here?

My hand brushed my fanny pack, and I froze. What if—? I'd crammed a bunch of stuff in there, but I hadn't taken out half the first aid materials. I clawed it open and wriggled my fingers down past the snacks, bandages, aspirin—there, something cold to the touch, cylindrical.

I pried it out, grinning. A penlight. Now, if the battery would just work . . . A weak beam of light flickered to life. It only let me see about a square foot of my surroundings, but hey. Better than nothing.

Flashing it around, I tried to figure out how many bugaboos were lurking in the dark. The light glinted off a massive eye, as big as my chest, embedded in a smooth white eye socket that looked hard, plasticky.

I flinched, clicking off the penlight, and stumbled back from the behemoth. Could it see in the dark—or smell me? Was I toast? I unsheathed my sword as quietly as possible and held it ready.

Not that it would do much good against the hard exoskeleton of a polymerae. I hadn't known any of the polymerae grew to be *that* size. I was used to the bitty ones—bottlecap bats, foot-long saurs with red plates like broken taillight shards. And drifters . . . Drifters tumbled along like plastic bags in the breeze, ready for some fool to snatch them out of the air and lose a hand.

I crouched, waiting for the giant beast to come after me.

Nothing shifted in the dark.

Nothing swallowed me whole.

I chanced turning the penlight back on—I had to get a better look at this thing. Maybe it was dead? That would be just like Kor, decorating his demon pad with the corpse of some leviathan.

Sweeping the wimpy light ahead of me, I eased forward. There was the eye, glassy and blank. The eye socket, the . . . buttons?

I squinted, hurrying forward.

No.

Nope.

I refused to believe it. Tricks of the light were one thing, but—

I sighed.

It was a damn *clothes dryer*.

I swiveled, the flicker of my penlight revealing a tidy row of rumbling washers and dryers, green lights marking the mode they were set to.

And here I was, brandishing a sword at the scary demon laundromat.

I choked on a possibly slightly hysterical laugh, tempted to bang my head against the washer a couple times. Looming leviathan, my ass.

Why in the three hells did Kor have a *laundromat* as the entrance to his domain? I just— I—

I ground my teeth as the real heart of the matter hit me.

Kor had a whole freaking laundromat right here, just through the mirror, and I'd been hauling my ass, hamper, and a billion quarters fifteen minutes across town for *months*.

And he'd never said a word.

I was actually going to kill him.

A high-pitched wail behind me put me back on high alert. Not even the crappiest broken-down washer or dryer could make a noise like that.

I wiped my sweaty face and hands with my tank before redoubling my grip on the sword.

The wail repeated, and I slunk toward it, rolling heel to toe on the linoleum floor, penlight beam skipping off the fronts of the machines.

A third wail. There, a top-loading washer just ahead of me. I gripped the penlight with my teeth, raised my sword, and flung open the metal lid of the washer with a clang, ready to skewer whatever dread beastie was lurking inside.

A veritable whirlpool of water filled the machine. I moved my head, and the beam of light caught a scraggly demonling swirling around inside, screeching.

Demonlings—the subservient second cousins to the Dark Ones—always made me think of those wriggly, shriveled souls in Ursula's lair in *The Little Mermaid*. The art had probably been modeled on them, to be honest. I was tempted to burst out in a rendition of "Poor, Unfortunate Souls," but managed to keep a lid on it.

It was for the best—my singing voice wasn't much better than the demonling's wailing.

The demonling disappeared down the eye of the whirlpool before bursting back out of the water with another round of caterwauling. Was this Kor's idea of torture? Maybe if I helped this guy out, he could lead me to Sparkles.

"Uh, do you need help?"

The demonling's squeaky voice was barely audible over the sloshing. "Are you kidding? I never get to play in here when Kor's around. Leave me alone!"

The washer top slammed back into place, almost catching my fingers. Rude. I rapped on the lid, the bang echoing, then eased it upward an inch.

"Tell me what I need to know, and I won't rat you out to Kor."

The wailing cut off, and I waited.

"I'm listening!" the demonling squeaked.

"I'm looking for something that Kor stole." Better keep it simple, demonlings' brains were basically popcorn. "A tiny fat horse of many colors."

A three-fingered misshapen hand appeared on the lip of the washer, and a pair of sunken eyes gleamed in the penumbra of the light beam.

The demonling's voice was hushed. "You seek the Dread Fluff?"

I sputtered, then pressed my lips together for a sec. When I continued, there was only the slightest tremor in my grave voice. "Indeed. I seek the Dread Fluff. Can you help me?"

The demonling looked me over—sword, Nerf gun, fanny pack in disarray—and nodded.

"I can help you, Lady Knight."

A BIG BALL OF FUN

Lady Knight, eh? I could deal with that.

I nodded seriously at the little squirt. "I'm Lady Immy. What is your name, my vassal?" Might as well make him feel special, right?

"Cucumber, Lady Immy." His voice quavered. Clearly I was fearsome, or awesome, or the-size-of-a-freaking-treesome in his overly large eyes.

I hitched up my makeshift fanny pack, averting a shorty-shorts wedgie. "*Cucumber?*" Demonlings always had the weirdest names.

"That's right, Lady Knight!" He climbed out of the washer with some difficulty, flopping on the neighboring machine, panting. I eased the lid closed once he was through the gap.

"All right, Cucumber, gimme the rundown. Where's the Dread Fluff, and how do we get there?" No way Sparkles was tumbling around in one of the dryers here—Kor was too devious for that, and my life was never that easy.

"Master Kor locked the Dread Fluff away in the Baleful Tower, where its sinister power cannot influence any of our kind." Cucumber shivered. "It is a terrifying beast, milady. It can remain so still that it appears dead, and the moment you let your guard down—"

Cucumber shrieked, and I jumped out of my skin, almost whacking myself in the face with the Nerf gun.

"—it gets you." He craned his malformed head up at me. "Do you plan to challenge it in combat?"

"Something like that," I muttered. *Baleful*, really? That was the best Kor could come up with? He was like those cheesy B-movie villains who reveal their harebrained schemes at every given opportunity.

"Where's this Baleful Tower?" The last word died in a croak. I unscrewed the Nalgene and chugged some water—warm, gross. My tank top was soaked through by now, or I'd've wiped off the sweat running down my face too.

"At the other end of this dazzling domain, milady. You will be able to see all the sights along the way."

Not exactly my priority. Hopefully this 'dazzling domain' wasn't as big as it sounded, or I'd pass out before we ever got to the Baleful Tower. I sized up the little guy. He didn't precisely have legs—his bottom half was more like a snail's foot, only without the slime. He wasn't going anywhere fast.

I scratched my head. "May I, uh, find you suitable transportation for such a great distance?"

"Certainly, Lady Knight."

I plucked him off the washer, his saggy grey skin soft and leathery under my fingers, and plopped him on my shoulder. The sensation of him suctioning onto my bare skin for stability was . . . cringeworthy.

What else was I supposed to do, though? I needed my hands free, and no way was he riding in my hair. I suppressed a full-body spasm.

"And the Dread Fluff . . . It's guarded?"

"Oh, of course, milady!" Cucumber's shrill voice wasn't any better next to my ear. I winced and judiciously rearranged some curls on that side, hoping for more soundproofing. "Otherwise it would escape in a flash and wreak havoc across the domain."

"Of course." It wasn't like I hadn't planned ahead, but a girl could dream, right? "What kinds of guards?"

"Imps, milady."

I did a mental fist-pump. Score one for me—imps had been my guess, and I'd packed accordingly.

"And a typhon."

My mental fist plummeted. "A *typhon*?"

"Afraid so, milady. But surely it is a minor matter to a battle-hardened warrior such as yourself." The pipsqueak eyed my accoutrements with wide eyes.

Imps I could handle any day. Typhons, though . . . Yeesh. Squish together every nasty bit of any being you can think of, and you'll probably have something pretty close to a typhon. They have the body of a supersized boa, the razor-clawed arms of a slicer, the hooked wings of a bone dragon. Oh, and the jaw strength of a snapping turtle, only with a viper's venomous fangs.

Basically, a big ball of fun.

I licked my lips. "Where is the typhon?"

"At the top of the tower, guarding the Dread Fluff's cell, milady."

Could be worse. I could come up with a strategy to handle the typhon along the way—or run for the hills if I drew a blank. For now, though, I needed to prep for the imps.

I dug out the tin of Altoids and the little mister bottle, unscrewing the cap. "Here, hold this."

I passed the bottle up to the demonling, who almost toppled off my shoulder with the added weight as he took it. I had to use both hands to pry open the Altoids tin, and I scooped up half the mints inside before closing the tin and shoving it back in my fanny pack.

"Thanks." I relieved him of the bottle and poured the mints in with one hand, twisting the cap back on as they sizzled in the liquid inside. A quick shake of the bottle created a fizz that was audible even through the glass, and I smirked.

"Is that what I think it is, Lady Knight?" Cucumber hunched down on my shoulder.

"As long as you're on my side, you don't have to worry about it."

I unloaded the Nerf darts and gave each one a healthy spritz from the bottle before shunting them back into the plastic gun. Cucumber coughed and leaned back, out of my peripheral vision.

"You okay?"

"Yes, milady." He coughed again, pitifully. "While repellant, your concoction is not as devastating to my kind as to the imps."

"Fabulous." It was time to get this party on the road. "Where to, Cucumber?"

A shriveled, wobbly arm the size of an ambitious toothpick appeared next to my face. "That way, Lady Knight."

I shone my penlight thataway, revealing a door with a panic bar. A burnt-out exit sign dangled from some wires overhead.

"All right, Cucumber, let's go."

I slipped forward through the darkness, scanning the ground with my penlight to keep from tripping over anything. I opened the door of the laundromat, expecting light to flood in, but it was almost as dark outside.

Duh. If there was one thing demons liked, it was darkness.

There was no moon, obviously, but there was a faint hint of light coming from somewhere. I clicked off the penlight and gave my eyes a moment to adjust.

The landscape was partially obscured by billowing black smoke. No, fog—it didn't smell like a barbecue out here.

Red lightning crackled through the fog, providing just enough light to make out silhouettes—hills? buildings? boulders? slavering beasts waiting to chomp down on me?

Guess I'd find out.

"Is the lightning dangerous?" I whispered.

Cucumber kept his shrill voice quieter too, thank Finéa. "Only to humans, Lady Knight. The flickerblood will boil their brains and scorch their bones to ash."

Perfect. Juuuust perfect.

I tapped my short fingernails on the Nerf gun, the plasticky clack the only sound in the darkness. Could I buy Bracchius a replacement for Sparkles? What were the chances Build-A-Beastie still sold the exact same plushie two years down the road?

Even if they did, I'd have to smudge it up exactly the same way—Cheeto dust ingrained on the tush, chocolate stains around the mouth, blood on the tip of the horn—

Don't ask.

Or could I just say I'd washed it?

An unholy racket erupted behind me, inside the laundromat, like a typhoon had just touched down.

"Kor," Cucumber hissed in my ear. "He's back!"

Kor? *Crud.*

I made a mad dash forward, Cucumber flapping in the breeze, clinging to my shoulder for dear life.

"What is Kor doing?" I huffed, giving a wide berth to the patches of death fog. "Tearing the place down?"

"No, that's—the por—tal!" Cucumber wailed, his voice jolting with each of my footfalls.

Breadcrumbs and barghasts, had *I* made that much noise coming in, too? "Is there something wrong with it? Does it always sound that way?"

I slowed down, hopefully out of sight of any enraged demons bursting out of the laundromat.

"Only when Master Kor arrives." Cucumber righted himself on my shoulder. "He likes us to be prepared to lavish attention on him."

Of course.

"So that's not his 'I'm pissed and coming to wreck you' alarm?"

"No . . . Lady Knight, does the master not know you wish to challenge the Dread Fluff to mortal combat?"

"Not so much."

He perked up. "Ooh, it will be such a surprise!"

I snorted. "That's the idea."

Something chittered in the gloom, obscured by the black fog.

"Imp?"

"Yes, my lady."

I locked and loaded the Nerf gun—okay, it was already good to go, but I liked the drama of snapping around a couple of the moving parts— and aimed into the darkness, edging around the nearest bloom of red lightning as I scanned for the imp.

"I thought you said the Baleful Tower was a long way away."

"Indeed, my lady, but Kor's guards are spread throughout the domain."

Figures.

A duller shift of red flashed my way, not the flickerblood but a beefy runt with four wings, serrated horns, and the subtle gleam of far too many rows of black teeth.

I took aim, and popped the imp right in the forehead with a foam dart, which clung instead of bouncing off.

"Good aim, my lady!" Cucumber squeaked.

The dart sizzled against the imp's skin, barely audible before the bloodcurdling screams started.

Altoids, one—imps, zero.

I dashed past as the imp dissolved into a steaming black puddle that gave me flashbacks to an ill-fated pan of brownies I—and my now nonfunctional oven—still mourned. I didn't feel so bad about the imp. They'll eat *anything*, and I'd make a tasty mouthful for sure.

Flickerblood lanced in front of me, and I leaned back in a ridiculous jogging limbo-arch, giving Cucumber a fabulous view of the cracked ground as I barely dodged the horrifying lightning inches from my nose, my vision swimming scarlet. I almost toppled all the way back, but falteringly kept my feet beneath me, highly motivated by not wanting my brain boiled.

"I'd—advise—more cau—tion, my lady."

"No joke." I stumbled into a clearing amidst the dark fog and took a breather, hands on knees, as Cucumber wheezed on my shoulder. It wasn't like the little guy was doing the running—he had his own sweaty palanquin, for crying out loud.

"You got asthma or something?" If only I'd thought to pack a mini inhaler for minions.

"Just hysteria, my lady."

I huffed out a laugh, and then the fog began closing in around us.

"Which way to the Baleful Tower, Cuke?"

Cucumber pointed, and I slipped between the inky clouds. I'd gotten lucky with that last imp—it had warned me it was coming. I couldn't depend on them all being that dumb.

I tucked the Nerf gun under my arm and started picking at the edge of the duct tape I'd wound around the oven mitt. If I could just rip off a couple inches . . .

The *kkrrhh* of the tape pulling back was the loudest thing in the sweltering darkness, and probably a fantastic homing signal for anything watching for intruders. My still-active sigil wouldn't do me much good when I was making *that* much racket.

I tore a sticky strip off, and taped the penlight to the barrel of the Nerf gun, the light beaming forward like the world's worst laser sight.

It'd do.

Then I kept quiet, as Cucumber directed me through the darkness with a wavering finger.

"The imps do not seem to notice you," he whispered. "You are stealthy indeed, Lady Immy."

I nodded, probably whapping the poor guy in the face with my gooey curls.

The first sign of trouble was a minuscule squeak from Cucumber as he tensed, suctioning tighter to my shoulder.

I was totally going to have a huge demonling hickey on my shoulder tomorrow.

Yick.

"What's up, Cucumber?"

His voice notched up half an octave. "My lady, I do not wish to alarm you, but a shadelurk is coming this way, and I think it best that you *run for both of our lives!*"

I'd never heard of a shadelurk, but my heart started racing thanks to his frantic tone. I didn't book it, though, keeping the same pace. "Won't running make us more obvious? I have a spell going that disperses my body heat, sound, and scent, so we should be good unless we act like lunatics, right?"

"Maybe."

I picked up the pace a bit and veered right, still quiet.

"That's not the way to the Baleful Tower!"

"I know. Is the shadelurk still coming our way?"

"Yes, it has shifted to follow us, my lady."

"How far away?" I couldn't see more than a dozen feet past my face without the intermittent glow from the flickerblood, but demonlings had darksight.

The shadelurk probably did too.

"Perhaps a mile."

And it was following us. I slid my sword out of the sheath an inch, making sure nothing would block a smooth draw. I got the feeling minty-fresh foam darts wouldn't faze this particular beastie.

"Tell me about shadelurks."

Cucumber shuddered. "They are stealthy, so stealthy. It is when you can see them that you are in the least danger."

"The *least—*" Great, so it was only gonna get worse from here. "Sorry, keep going."

"It stalks its prey, studying it, creeping ever closer, until it is ready to attack. Then it latches on to a shadow and enters it, moving through shadow paths until it reaches its prey, ambushing the prey from their own shadow. Once the shadelurk has devoured you, it will sink into a comatose state for several days, but . . ."

But by then you were dead anyway.

Lovely.

"Can it be attacked in shadow?"

"Only by another shadowwalker."

Which I was not. "You don't happen to b—"

"I'm afraid not, my lady."

Not that the pipsqueak could probably do much damage even if he was. About the biggest thing he could wield would be a plastic cocktail sword.

"Will we be safe from it at the Baleful Tower?"

"There is more light there. It would be harder for the shadelurk to attack."

Light, right. I could sweep my Nerf gun around me to try to cut off the monster, if it came to that. In the meantime, I loped toward the tower, chugging my quickly disappearing water and trying to ignore the threatening cramp in my leg.

Clearly I needed to get a gym membership at MagmaFit, bulk up with the salamanders and lava titans.

"I believe we lost the shadelurk, and the tower is within sight, Lady Immy."

"Awesome," I panted, still following his raised finger. Now I just had to figure out how to deal with a typhon in two minutes flat.

Bracchius was going to owe me *big* time.

Cucumber did his impression of a manhandled guinea pig again. "*Run!* It must've traveled through shadow—the shadelurk is only thirty feet away!"

I booked it, flourishing my modified Nerf gun like a glow stick at the craziest rave you've ever been to.

A little square of light called to me in the distance—a barred window on the door of the Baleful Tower. I churned toward it at top speed, my overworked legs heavy like cement. If cement could burn like hellfire and scream like tortured souls, that is.

I lunged for the door handle, which was surprisingly modern for a rough-hewn medieval tower of evil.

I shoved down on the latch, ready to barrel through and slam the door in the shadelurk's almost certainly creepy face.

Instead I smashed into the solid wood door at top speed, probably squishing Cucumber to a pulp.

The door stood firm as I spammed the latch like the B-button on a Game Boy Color.

Locked.

SLIME & SPARKLES

I had a flashback to the moment I'd clicked on a haircut-at-home reaction video instead of the lockpicking series put out by BrownieBasics—their middle-of-the-night surprise remodel videos were gold. But noo, I'd been lured by the siren call of some poor girl's botched bangs instead of watching something actually *useful.*

It would be seriously embarrassing if *that* was the decision that killed me.

I fumbled my arm through the barred window as Cucumber wailed, *"I deserve better than to be eaten aliiiiiive!"*

"Not. Helping." At least I hadn't crushed him to death. I flailed around, trying to find a deadbolt, a bar, a doorknob, anything, but my fingers just met rough wood.

Cucumber's panicked monologue devolved into a drawn-out scream right in my ear.

"Screw it." I extricated my arm, stepped back, and walloped the door with a torrent of my magic, the magenta flare ballooning from my hands like the fireball when Crazy Ed tried deep-frying a phoenix in cryostasis on a livestream.

The door exploded, somehow instantly transmuted into slime, spattering us both from head to toe with thick, cold jellylike sludge.

Piranhas and *pixies.*

There's a reason I avoid using my magic. Everybody else's is fine, but of course *my* magic has to be the cross between a sputtering engine and a freaking chaos bomb.

I scraped the gunk out of my eyes with one hand as I lunged forward blindly through the muck, swinging the Nerf gun–penlight combo behind me with the other and praying to every god, devil, and eldritch horror that I was moving fast enough to avoid the shadelurk—like hells was I going to look back to check.

I broke free of the slimy remnants of the door, dashed to the spiral staircase, and launched up the stairs two at a time, legs screaming.

"Go go *go!*" Cucumber's voice was gurglier than before. Poor little guy was probably half-drowned in slime.

We rocketed up the stairs, the shadelurk on our tail, and I almost smashed face-first into *another* door. I screeched in frustration and maybe a little existential terror, and wrenched the scorching metal doorknob, expecting another roadblock, but the knob turned, and we fell into the room.

I scrambled to turn around on slippery shoes, nearly biffing it, and slammed the door on an empty staircase. Had Cucumber's imagination gone wild, or was the shadelurk still hiding in shadow somewhere on the stairs? This door was solid, without even a gap at the bottom—hopefully I wouldn't have to find out.

Until we needed to leave, that is.

Crap.

A huff of hot breath stirred my curls—quite the feat, considering they were glued down by heat protectant, sweat, *and* slime at this point—and shivers raced along my arms and the back of my neck.

"*Cucumber?*" I whispered. "The typhon is right behind us, isn't it."

His voice was a tickle in my ear. "I'm afraid so, my lady."

Hand on oven-mitted hilt, I ripped my sword out of its sheath and whipped around, slashing in a broad arc, my blade meeting only air.

The typhon wasn't as close as I'd feared. He was just really. Freaking. BIG.

We stood—well, slithered, on the typhon's part—in a circular room, barred cells curving along the walls, with an open area between them and the door. A dozen torches in sconces on the walls lit up the room quite well.

The typhon loomed over me, maybe fifteen feet away, the hooked bone claws of his black wings brushing the ceiling, his massive serpentine body reared up like a cobra about to strike, but he wasn't moving yet.

Had I surprised him? I did have a demonling on my shoulder; maybe he thought I was one of the bad guys.

Although I *was* brandishing a sword at him, so that likelihood was shrinking by the second. I lowered the sword, hoping I could still play this off as a 'coming to check on the prisoners' thing and book it with the plushie.

He cocked his weirdo scaled head at me, red eyes glowing. His fingers were each a giant claw, sharp as a scythe, and his oversized jaw parted to show needle-sharp teeth.

Oh, and his hair was made up of pit vipers.

Just a bundle of delight all round.

Each cell behind him was occupied, and I scanned the prisoners as the typhon sized me up. A necrowraith, with its rotted tendrils stirring on the air; a chupacabra, black fangs bared; a lou carcolh, its spined snail shell taking up most of the cell, eyestalks poking out between the bars; and—was that a *black widow* arachnofae?

Yeesh.

Every creature looked sinister, evil, like the stuff of nightmares, until you came to the little blue, pink, and purple stuffed unicorn staring with flat black embroidered eyes through the bars of the cage right behind the typhon.

"The *Dread Fluff*." Cucumber quaked on my shoulder, more terror in his voice now than when he'd first described the shadelurk.

Man alive. The thing was only a *foot* long, how anyone could be—

Oh. Sparkles, tiny though she might be, was actually *bigger* than Cucumber.

That explained a few things.

I patted Cucumber carefully on his slimy head. "Don't worry. I won't let it hurt you."

Wiping my hand off on the warm stone wall, I kinda wished I had an itty bitty weapon for Cucumber too—it might bolster his confidence.

Next time.

Yeah, right.

Sparkles herself looked unharmed—no scorch marks, no acid burns, and the stuffing hadn't been ripped out of her. Her velvety golden horn shimmered in the torchlight.

The world's tiniest manacles connected each of the plushie's hooves, and I almost lost it.

It— I just—

Geez *Louise*, Kor. That demon needed a therapist.

Another whirlwind of hot, fetid breath washed over me as the typhon exhaled, and I wrinkled my nose.

Time to make my move.

"Heya." I waved one hand—the one with the sword, oops—and smiled. "Just here to check on our . . ." What would Kor call them? Distinguished guests? Unworthy vermin?

"Prisoners of war," Cucumber breathed in my ear.

"Prisoners of war." I womanfully avoided rolling my eyes, and pointed toward Sparkles. "By order of Master Kor."

The typhon surveyed me with narrowed glowing red eyes, the pit vipers wreathing his head bobbing and weaving, hissing and muttering unintelligible words in turn.

His voice was a slow rumble underlaid with a hiss, his forked tongue tasting the air as he spoke. "You do not ssserve Massster Kor, witch."

I sighed. Guess this wasn't going to be easy after all.

Such is life.

"Ready, Cucumber?" I muttered sotto voce.

"*Eep!*" A tiny cough assaulted my ear. "I mean, yes, Lady Immy."

I couldn't help myself. I took a dramatic stance with my sword in one hand, Nerf gun braced against my shoulder with the other, and called out, "My name is Immy Cordell. You stole my friend's stuffed unicorn. Prepare to die!"

CLASH OF THE TERRORS

The typhon roared, head reared back, each of the writhing snake heads hissing and flashing fangs in turn. I ducked to one side during the dramatic display, getting a few feet closer to Sparkles.

Razor claws slashed at me as the roar died out, and I jerked my sword up, catching a claw on the blade. My sword didn't shear through it, though—the wicked black claw screeched along the blade, kicking up sparks, and I flinched back, disengaging. The last thing I needed was a spark to the eye.

Another arm sliced my way, and I swung my sword, the blade biting deep into the wrist and sticking as the claws danced inches from my face. The typhon grunted, and ripped his arm free of the sword, almost taking it with him, but I clung to the oven-mitt hilt, my sweaty grip better on the fabric than it would've been without, thank Finéa.

Green blood oozed from the typhon's wound—probably just a scratch in his book, even though I'd hit bone—and dripped to the wood floor, sizzling and sending up a trail of acrid smoke.

I coughed, while Cucumber blew out the wimpiest breath ever, trying to dispel the smoke. That stuff *had* to be toxic.

The typhon paused, sizing me up again.

I quirked an eyebrow. "Didn't expect me to be competent?"

"You will need to be much more than merely competent to bessst the likesss of a typhon, *witch*."

He shifted, his gargantuan snake tail uncurling beneath him, and I caught the flash of something smoother than scales in the midst of the coils.

Gargoyles and *glitter*.

A gleaming black stinger rose at the end of the typhon's tail, a drop of ruby liquid dangling from the needle tip. He raised it beside him, so I faced his claws and teeth on the right, and the stinger on the left.

No way could I jump between without getting sliced, diced, or skewered.

If I could deal with the stinger, though . . .

I feinted toward the typhon's torso with a "Ha!" and a raised sword, then spun on my forward foot as he moved to counter, and slashed at the tip of his tail, hoping to lop off the stinger.

His tail jerked back, stinger shuddering before lancing toward me like a whipcrack. I smacked it aside with my sword, but the damned thing was heavy as lead, and I only deflected it far enough to keep the stinger from piercing my shoulder—the side of the stinger smashed into my shoulder instead.

Thankfully *not* the shoulder Cucumber occupied, but still, it hurt like a *mother*.

I shook that arm out, my fingers numb and my shoulder screaming, but the typhon didn't give me a second to recover.

He whipped his stinger toward me again, and lunged forward at the same time, claws first. I dove to the right, and his claws sliced into the *same* shoulder, raking a fresh trail of blood across my skin as I gritted my teeth against a scream.

I landed hard near the door—probably getting a zillion splinters in my leg thanks to the rough wood floor—and stumbled back to my feet, slinging my sword around to stave off a follow-up attack.

My sword slashed into the typhon's arm at a shallow angle, shaving off a decent chunk of skin and muscle, and the typhon growled, ripping his arm away.

I pressed my advantage, hammering furious blows into his wounded arm, and the typhon slithered back, bowing his torso away and twisting so the sturdier scales on his back took my strikes while he nursed his wound.

His stinger flicked toward me again, but I didn't bother deflecting it. It missed, crashing into the wall instead, before pulling back.

I rained a few more pointless blows on the typhon's toughened scales, contemplating the wings out of my reach above. I *was* competent, but the typhon had the definite advantage. As long as he faced away from me, he could only attack—with terrible aim—with his stinger, and my blows would be useless.

As soon as he faced me once more, I'd be in trouble again, barely holding my own, and probably not for much longer.

And then I had an idea worthy of a trickster fox.

I slashed toward his wings, his tail, his face—chaotic attacks that would keep him guessing for a sec, keep him on the defense while he healed or whatever he was doing back there.

Then I bolted for the door to the stairs.

I whipped the door open, coming face to face with the waiting shadelurk. A towering black form, semitranslucent, with glowing white orbs for eyes, loomed on the landing, swaying back at my sudden appearance. Cold rolled off it, and palpable dread.

"*Oh no,*" Cucumber whispered.

It wouldn't be startled for long. The torches behind me ensured my shadow fell across the shadelurk, and I bent my legs, ready to run.

The shadelurk recovered from its surprise, a ghastly rent that had to be its mouth curving up in a sinister grin. It collapsed in on itself, rushing toward the floor like a black waterfall.

Before it got halfway to the floorboards, I booked it straight for the typhon, who faced me again. I raised my sword like an oversized ice pick, and the typhon slithered back a few inches, red eyes wide.

A clawed hand raked up, but too slow. At full speed, I slammed my sword into the thinner scales above my head, praying the blade wouldn't just slice down through the typhon's dense musculature, and yanked, catapulting myself up toward his massive shoulders—and the nest of snakes that served as his hair.

I hit his shoulder in a belly flop, my breath bursting out in one big huff and my ribs pissed off, to say the least. The snakes recoiled, and I scrambled up, batting at them with the Nerf gun—thunk, thunk—as I heaved myself the rest of the way over the typhon's shoulder and wing to Cucumber's running commentary: "Take *that*, foul serpents! Back! *Away!* You are not worthy to be crushed under Lady Immy's boot—sneaker!"

We toppled down the backside of the typhon in a nose-dive, the stinger at the end of his tail bobbing directly in our path. I bashed it aside with the Nerf gun, then tucked and rolled at the last possible second, shielding Cucumber with one hand as we jounced over a couple huge coils of the typhon's body and ground to a halt on the rough wood planks of the floor in front of Sparkles's cage, my shoulder pulsing with agony.

Launching clumsily to my feet, I ripped the closest torch out of its sconce, backed against the bars of the cage, and waved the torch in front of me, disconnecting my shadow from the typhon's.

Everything was still for a moment, the typhon hunched over the sword impaled in his torso, me panting and gripping the torch with a shaking hand, and Cucumber muttering under his breath. "Goood Dread Fluff, yes, stay right there, don't mind me and the lady knight, we have no sinister designs on your welfare, none at allll, please don't eat me."

And then the screaming started.

I say screams, but it was more like the enraged bellow of a titan bear being torn apart by a cloud of piranha sprites.

Maybe I watch too many nature documentaries, but still.

The typhon's agonized roar shook the room, and I almost dropped my torch.

The massive coils of his body writhed and twisted, his wings beating frenetically against the walls and ceiling, like a moth at the flame. Translucent darkness rolled along his scales, coating him inch by inch until he was suffused with shadow.

He stilled a moment, then went *nuts*.

A gibbering series of throat-rending screams filled the room as one of his muscular coils slammed into the wall, crumbling stone. A wing knocked a torch from its sconce, leaving it smoldering on the wooden floorboards, and his stinger missed us by inches, lodging between the bars of the cell to our left as the typhon bucked desperately against the shadelurk's attack.

I yanked on the door of Sparkles's cell, but it was locked. Cucumber and I huddled in a ball at the base of the door, hoping not to get crushed, scooting back from the growing fire just feet away. The little guy had a death grip on my curls.

The screams were replaced by a horrible wet crunching and tearing as the typhon twitched into stillness.

"You said the shadelurk goes comatose after eating, right?" I whispered.

"Indeed, Lady Immy. After a meal *that* large, it might be weeks."

"Great. Let's get out of here!"

I clambered back to my feet, my shoulder royally pissed at me, and faced Sparkles. The bars were too close for me to squeeze between, but the stuffed unicorn was much smaller—and squishier—than me. I replaced my torch and reached between the bars with my good arm.

The arm Cucumber was riding.

"Ahhh! Stop, nooo, please don't feed me to the Dread Fluff, Lady Immy, I am too darksome to be sacrificed as bait!!"

The demonling unsuctioned from my shoulder with a slorrrp and freaking *climbed into* my curls, taking refuge from the horrifying plushie of evil.

I snagged Sparkles and drew her back through the bars, the tinkle of fairy bells coming from her fiber-filled tummy. "Cucumber, get *out* of my hair! I'm not feeding you to anyone!"

My curls stopped quivering with his mad scramble, and his keening protests died out.

"The Dread Fluff . . . It isn't attacking you?"

"Yeah, uh—"

His voice became awestruck. "You are mighty with the sword *and* with magic, Lady Immy, if you are able to sedate such a fearsome beast so effortlessly! It is truly an honor to fight by your side."

He'd really mostly just *panicked* by my side, but I let it slide. Especially since he deigned to disentangle himself from my hair—he lowered onto my shoulder with a soft *splut*.

"Thanks, buddy."

I looked around for my Nerf gun, but it was just neon orange plastic shards at this point. Farewell, staunch weapon. Hopefully we wouldn't run into too many imps on the way back.

I'd been avoiding checking out the remains of the typhon, but it was time to retrieve my sword—if I even could. Did shadelurks devour inanimate objects, too?

I swallowed and turned around.

A misshapen shadow-tinged mound lay at my feet, awful bubbling noises rising from it as it quaked and quivered. The shadelurk was still at work, evidently.

I dug out a roll of medical tape from my fanny pack and secured Sparkles to my sheath, not wanting to spare a hand to keep hold of her. Retrieving the torch, I inched closer to the fallen typhon, and extended a foot.

Poke.

Nudge.

No shadows engulfed me, and my shoe didn't melt off or anything.

"'Kay, let's see . . ." I circled the bubbling mass.

There, under the shattered wreck of a wing, my sword's hilt was just visible. In the middle of the sprawling corpse, of course.

"All right, Cucumber, hold on."

Little hands fastened onto my neck, and I eased forward onto the shadow-steeped remains. One step, two . . .

I grimaced. The corpse was spongy beneath my feet, and I sank into it a bit. Yech. But my sword was worth treading across half-eaten corpses—I could always burn my sneakers later.

Crouching, I lifted the wing. The shadow-skin of the shadelurk was stretched over the sword as well, giving it a dimling sheen.

I heaved the wing aside and gave the hilt a good yank, but the shadow-skin just stretched outward, my sword trapped within.

Rude.

I lowered the torch until the shadow-skin sizzled beneath it. A screech pierced the air, and the darkness retreated from the hilt, revealing my duct-tape-and-oven-mitt MacGyver.

Getting a firm grip, I tugged, and the sword slid free of the typhon's corpse, sticky with green blood.

Gross.

I wiped it off as best I could on the rest of the corpse, leaving green streaks on the shadow-skin. It was the shadelurk's problem now, not that it probably minded—this was dinner, after all.

Sheathing my not-totally-covered-in-dreck sword, I stepped back across the monstrous corpse, headed toward the door.

Jumping off the corpse, I patted myself down. Sword, check. Sparkles, check. Cucumber, check. Even my water bottle had survived the battle.

Cucumber bobbed on my shoulder. "A successful venture, Lady Immy! You outwitted the typhon, evaded the shadelurk, subdued the Dread Fluff, *and* leave Master Kor's other enemies to burn in ignominy!"

The tiniest evil cackle drifted up from him, and I swear he rubbed his hands together.

I looked back. Flames flickered across a quarter of the floor now. The other prisoners stared at me from their cells, eyes wide—those that had them, anyway.

The necrowraith's grey tendrils reached through the bars, desperately stirring on the scorching air.

The black widow arachnofae skittered up the wall into the furthest corner from the fire.

The lou carcolh slowly retreated into its shell, eyestalks disappearing last.

The chupacabra whimpered, cowering at the back of its cell, looking just like a terrified dog.

Part of the floor fell away with a crash, sparks dancing into the air.

"Ah, crap."

I was going to have to save the freaking *monsters*, wasn't I?

SAVING THE FREAKING MONSTERS

I beat away the sparks that drifted my direction, while Cucumber went overkill on the huffing and puffing; his little lungs would've lost out to a party blower.

"Lady Immy, we must leave before we are consumed by flame!" He stretched toward the still-open door, but I took a step toward the cells.

I didn't want the monsters inside to burn to death, but letting them out probably wasn't the smartest thing either—Oracle knows what they'd do if I freed them.

But if I could put out the fire . . . they'd still be alive, and I wouldn't have to worry about anything else.

Like getting my soul gnawed on.

I eyed the necrowraith.

Right, definitely putting out the fire.

I reached for my water bottle, but it was more than half-empty, and honestly, even full, it wouldn't've stood a chance of putting the fire out. I chewed at my lip, looking around.

Stone walls. Iron bars. Wooden floor. More torches in sconces on the walls. Nothing handy, like a heap of sandbags or a convenient water barrel. Was Kor not keeping his prisoners hydrated?

Heathen.

The ceiling was obscured by smoke, but what would be up there, anyway? No way Kor would perch a water tank on top of his tower of doom.

A sharp tug on my hair brought my attention back to Cucumber. "Youch! What was that for?" I rubbed my scalp, scowling.

"Lady Immy, I know the beasts are alarming, but we can't stand here and stare at them! We must leave!"

"About that . . ."

My magic had actually done me a solid earlier with the door. Maybe I'd get lucky again?

I raised my hands, letting my magic spark at each fingertip, before unleashing it in a roaring wave toward the flames.

Put it out, put it out, put it out . . .

The magenta glow crashed into the flames, which shrank like the oxygen was being cut off.

My eyes widened as the magic swept over the rest of the fire, subduing it, if not snuffing it out.

Had it worked?

In my magic's wake, the diminished flames looked . . . different.

I squinted.

New colors flickered amidst the orange of the flames, teals and pinks and purples licking their way up until the fire was its own chaotic rainbow.

Pretty. If that was the only side effect, then I'd be—

Harpies and *hairballs*.

The flames nearest the tower wall rose, crackling hungrily to life as they found new fuel.

As they bit into freaking *stone*.

What— How—

"That shouldn't be possible, right?" I muttered to Cucumber as the fire somehow began consuming the massive boulders that made up the tower walls.

"I do not believe so, Lady Immy," he piped. "An impressive creation! Master Kor will be honored that you saw fit to immolate his enemies with a new breed of fire! I shall call it . . . chaos flames!"

Fabulous.

At least he hadn't named them after *me*. I was notorious enough as it was.

I rubbed at the back of my neck. Putting the fire out was clearly off the table, so that left unleashing the monsters. Lockpicking was still out, and after the newly dubbed chaos flames, I didn't want to see what would happen if I sloshed my magic around cells with such already-fearsome beings inside.

A keening shriek behind me drowned out the crackle of flames, and I whirled. The typhon's corpse twitched as the shadow-skin rolled off it, acrid black smoke trailing from the edge nearest the fire.

I backed the hell up as the shadelurk flopped off the typhon's remains to the floorboards at my feet, not regaining its humanoid form, but shuffling desperately in a lump toward the arrow slit in the wall beside me. A few tortured flops later, it disappeared through the gap and into the perpetual night.

I glared down at Cucumber. "Comatose, eh?"

"Your chaos flames are powerful indeed, Lady Immy!"

I sighed, but my eyes landed on what was left of the typhon: desiccated limbs, shredded wings, scales flaking like mica.

He had been the monsters' jailer . . . Had he locked them in?

More importantly, would he have been able to let them out?

I hadn't seen him toting anything during our fight, but you never knew. Would he keep the keys to the cells on his person? They didn't seem to be anywhere else.

Unless his massive python body had pockets for spare change, they didn't seem to be on him, either.

I pursed my lips, then froze.

Something glinted amidst the nest of dead snakes that had served as his hair.

Crouching, I crept closer. There, hidden under the flaccid corpses of a few of the snakes, was a ring of keys. I unsheathed my sword and slid the tip through the ring, not wanting to chance my fingers if any of those suckers were just playing dead. I wiggled the ring out, the keys jangling, and hoisted my sword as I backed away from the typhon as the flames licked closer.

Every monster stood—or oozed, or hovered—at the bars of their cells, eyes glued to the key ring. I slipped it off my sword, and waved it in their direction.

Cucumber clutched at my neck again. "Lady Immy, what are you *doing*? Do you intend to challenge *all* Master Kor's enemies to mortal combat?"

"Something like that."

I sized up each of the monsters, all carnivores—or soulvores, in the necrowraith's case.

"All right, listen up." I shook the key ring. "You saw what I did to the typhon. If I get you guys out of here, there will be no backstabbing, no attacks of opportunity." I glanced at the lou carcolh's swaying eyestalks. "No devouring of sentient beings. You make one wrong move toward me or my friend here"—I jerked a thumb at Cucumber, almost taking out one of his minuscule eyes—"and you won't live to regret it. Got it?"

The chupacabra's tail wagged, and the necrowraith inclined its void-filled hood. The eyestalks of the lou carcolh withdrew and extended in slow motion, which I hoped was its version of a nod, and not the giant snail assessing how much meat was on my bones.

"Agreed." The arachnofae's voice was silky, feminine, dangerous.

I let my gaze linger on each of them, chaos flames crackling at my back. "And you all owe me. Big time."

Another round of hopefully yeses.

It'd have to do.

The necrowraith was nearest the flames. I strode over, fumbling with the key ring, and shoved the first key in the lock, the metal scorching in my hands.

Second key.

Third.

Fourth was the charm, and I shook my head. Clearly the universe was bending all her laws for me today.

I swung the heavy iron door open, and the necrowraith floated out of the cell. I raised an eyebrow, daring it to attack, but it simply drifted past me toward the door.

Moving from right to left, I released each monster from their cell as the far wall of the tower began to crumble beneath the flames.

The monsters didn't leave; they waited at the door as if expecting me to give them next steps. What was I, their freaking life coach?

I ran a hand through my curls—well, I jammed my fingers into the sticky helmet hair that was my curls now, and wrenched my hand free before I could accidentally scalp myself.

The chupacabra quivered like a chihuahua in February, big sad eyes locked on mine.

Well, crud.

What the hell was I going to do with them now?

MY MONSTER POSSE

First thing was getting the monsters out of this death trap, and me with them. I checked to make sure Sparkles was still firmly taped to my sheath, and stalked over.

"Seriously, guys, no sense of self-preservation, huh?"

I shooed them ahead of me toward the stairs as Cucumber sulked on my shoulder—I'd have to vanquish some more imps to make up for the disappointing lack of mortal combat challenges.

Gotta give the demonlings what they want, right?

The black widow arachnofae took the hint and skittered down the spiral staircase.

Next went the lou carcolh—it better be faster than it looked, or we'd all be literal toast. Giant snails—*any* snails—weren't exactly known for their speed.

Once it oozed to the top of the stairs, though, it retreated into its spiny shell and teetered off the edge, rolling down like a wrecking ball gone rogue. The tower shuddered with each impact of its massive shell against the walls.

The lou carcolh must be one tough cookie.

I swallowed. If there were smashed spider guts at the bottom of the stairs now, I was throwing in the towel.

A girl can only take so much in one day.

The necrowraith drifted above the steps, its shifting tendrils tickling the chupacabra below, but the little beastie didn't keel over soulless, so I guess they were buds.

Fire flickered at my back, and I closed the door behind me before following the necrowraith down, giving those tendrils plenty of room.

We might be best buds, too, but I wasn't gonna count on it.

The once-door-now-slime still covered the ground floor, with a deep furrow through it where the lou carcolh had barreled past.

No spider guts, thankfully.

The chupacabra and I trudged through the remaining couple inches of slime, while the necrowraith remained slime-free. I totally didn't glare at it.

These shoes would never recover from this rescue mission.

Out the open doorway, we all backed the hells away from the tower, which was spitting multicolored flames from the top.

I assessed my monstrous posse, none of whom were streaking off into the night. In fact, the lou carcolh oozed back in our direction from where it'd rolled to a stop.

"All right, what gives? If you're expecting me to take you to some lavish paradise, you're outta luck. Your options are here"—I gestured grandly at the darkness punctuated only by the red crackle of flickerblood—"and the real world. Well, the normal world. The Not-Kor's-Domain world. So, you sticking around here, or what?"

The arachnofae scuttled nervously to one side. "If you know how to exit this domain, I will gladly follow you."

The chupacabra wagged his tail hopefully, and the other two gave what passed for their approval too, apparently.

They all wanted to go home—well, to Saskia Springs. Who knew where they'd started out from.

And there was only one way there, as far as I knew.

Through the mirror in my freaking bathroom.

I eyed the gigantic snail. Maybe I hadn't thought this all the way through. Could the lou carcolh even fit through the mirror?

Did I really want a horde of monsters traipsing through my bathroom?

Were my storm-soaked bra and undies still drip-drying over the shower rod?

Yessiree.

I scratched at my helmet hair, almost taking Cucumber out. "Sorry."

"You intend to release them from Master Kor's realm, Lady Immy?"

"Would you rather they hang out at your laundromat?"

"Erm . . . Well, no."

"Then yeah, seems like."

Cucumber heaved a mighty high-pitched sigh on my shoulder. "Lady Immy, as proud as I am to have aided you in your fearsome endeavors, you must never tell Master Kor that we are acquainted. That I had anything to do with the events of this night. He would pickle me in merbrine and feed me to the primordial gloom."

"That doesn't sound so bad," I teased.

"It has *teeth*!"

"Okay, that's worse. Deal. I wouldn't rat you out even if it got Kor to be less annoying."

"Thank you, Lady Knight."

"You're welcome."

I turned back to my posse, wiping the sweat from my—well—everywhere. "So here's how it's gonna go. It's a bit of a hike to the exit. There's a bunch of imps and who-knows-whats between here and there, ready to sucker punch us, and I lost my best weapon for dealing with them up there." I pointed at the supersized Roman candle above our heads.

Damn, I'd forgotten the penlight up there too—at least we could see by the fire for now.

I pointed at my monsters. "So it's up to you guys to keep them off our backs, okay?"

The necrowraith's tendrils stirred menacingly, the arachnofae's mandibled mouth spread in a far-too-wide smile, and the chupacabra growled.

The lou carcolh bobbed its eyestalks again. Seriously, though, how much damage could it actually do? Sure, if you got close enough, it could devour you—slowly—or impale you with its spiked shell, but stay out of range and you'd be fine.

The others would have to do the heavy lifting.

I pursed my lips. Had my speech made me sound too helpless? I didn't want these monsters to think I was easy pickings—who knows how they expressed gratitude in each of their cultures.

For all I knew, it just meant they'd be kind enough to rip my head off *before* sucking out my intestines, instead of after.

I patted my sword hilt, setting off the tinkle of fairy bells inside Sparkles's butt. "I've still got my sword, so I can help out too. I just won't be good for long-range attacks. And watch out for the flickerblood." I nodded at a nearby patch of black fog laced with the red lightning, then looked down at Cucumber. "What'd you say it'd do? Boil your brains?"

"And scorch your bones to ash!" he piped. "But it will only harm you, the Fanged Hound, and the Sinister Snail. The others are immune to its touch."

I stifled a snort at his dramatic epithets. Seriously, he'd put *two* syllables in 'fanged,' like he was one beat short in a line of bad poetry.

Guzzling down half my remaining water, I flopped an arm in the general direction of the laundromat. "Forth, Eorlingas!"

And my monsters and I strode, slithered, and spidered into the darkness.

Without my penlight, it really *was* dark. The occasional lance of flickerblood was only enough to keep me from wandering into a crackly red death sentence, not enough to avoid rabbit holes—well, whatever-hell-creature-burrowed-in-the-dirt-in-a-demon-domain holes, that is.

Cucumber's whispered directions in my ear were all that kept me in the vicinity of my monster posse. I considered hitching a ride on the lou carcolh's shell, but those spikes weren't real conveniently placed.

It might not love the idea anyway.

The chitter of an imp had me grasping my oven-mitt sword hilt again, scanning for any variation in the darkness. A dull glimmer of red to my left—

The lou carcolh beside me seized up like it was about to stroke out, made a horrendous retching sound, and a glowing virulent-pink streak shot through the air in the direction of the imp.

Sizzle.

Shriek.

Silence.

I gulped, eyes wide, and inched away from the lou carcolh. I didn't even know what that flying pink glob was, but no way did I want to risk pissing the giant snail off.

"Lou carcolhs spit acid." The whisper in my ear came from the opposite side from Cucumber, feminine and sultry. I flinched back, head whipping around to the arachnofae at my side, her fanged face much too close for comfort.

"G-Good to know."

The next two imps might as well have been field mice instead of vicious carnivores—the arachnofae devoured one whole, and a touch of the necrowraith's tendrils turned the other into a withered husk crumbling in our wake.

Thank Finéa these horrors were on my side.

I stumbled in the darkness, my adrenaline long since gone, my shoulder and scrapes and splinters screaming, only able to keep my eyes half open as I trudged toward the distant laundromat.

Mermaids and madrigals, I was exhausted. I'd been up this long before, but never on a day when I'd also been chased by stalkers, fought through a dragon storm, and challenged a freaking typhon to mortal combat—and won.

And it wasn't over yet.

I might've whimpered, just a little.

My feet left the ground, and I jammed my arms forward to keep me from face-planting, but the ground was moving further away, not closer . . .

Vertigo swirled in my head as I tried to make sense of what was happening, limbs flailing.

And then I spotted a chitinous black leg. Two.

Cradling me.

I blinked up at the black widow arachnofae, who'd scooped me up with two limbs while she skittered forward on the rest. I drifted along remarkably smoothly, perfectly supported, with no jounces or even rocking to indicate I was being carried like a spider babe.

"Rest, fierce one, if only for a moment. The demonling will direct us, yes?"

An only-moderately-terrified "Indeed, O Sinister One!" piped from my shoulder.

Could I sleep in the not-arms of a giant spider?

My fluttering eyelids said yes.

"Lady Immy?"

The tiny whisper tickled my ear, and I groaned back to consciousness, feeling like I'd been hit by a bus, or a street leviathan, or two buses being *thrown* by a street leviathan—

Let's just say it sucked.

I opened my eyes, then tried again, because it was dark either way.

Right. Kor's domain. Sparkles. Monsters.

Taking a nap cuddled up to an arachnofae.

No biggie.

"My lady, the portal is just over this next hill," Cucumber squeaked. "We must plan before we approach."

I flapped a hand bonelessly and tried to sit up. The arachnofae lowered me to the ground, and my nap legs almost betrayed me, but her spidery limbs held me in place until I steadied.

I smiled up at her hesitantly. "Uh, thanks. For the nap."

"You are most welcome. I could hardly allow my rescuer to be trampled underfoot. It is only the smallest of steps in repaying my debt to you."

Flickerblood lanced twenty feet away, illuminating our little group of monsters huddled around me. It was lighter over here, though—I could still see once the flickerblood faded.

I cleared my throat. "So, plans?"

Cucumber shifted on my shoulder. "Indeed, Lady Immy. Master Kor is likely to be nearby, and he will need to be distracted so you can pass safely through the portal."

Resentment tinged his voice near the end of that—he clearly still wasn't thrilled about me kidnapping all Kor's prisoners.

The little guy really had been a champ through all this. I'd have to make it up to him somehow. Maybe some prismatic bubble bath or undine shimmer dust to spice up his future washer-whirlpool rides?

Speaking of the portal . . .

I eyed the massive lou carcolh. Time to spill the beans. "I'm not even sure you'll all fit through the portal, to be honest."

Cucumber scoffed. "My lady, it is a *portal*, not a hole in the wall. *Anything* can fit through it."

I studied him skeptically. He hadn't seen the mirror on the other side.

Or my bathroom, for that matter.

Ugh, my *bathroom*. I looked down at myself: stinking, sweating, dehydrated, covered in gunk and slime and blood and gross. Oh, yeah, and wounds. Having to take a shower before work would be enough of a time sink without having to remove a million splinters from my legs and slather antiseptic from head to toe.

"Any chance you've got some tweezers and a first aid kit stashed in that laundromat?" I glanced over at Cucumber.

"I do not, my lady, but I have something better!"

I raised a dubious eyebrow. Unless he had a caladrius he could whip out of his ass, I couldn't imagine what better options there'd be in a hellhole like Kor's domain.

"Cover your ears, my lady."

"Really?"

"Yes!"

I clamped my hands over my helmet hair, and Cucumber whistled, a bizarre monotone whistle in a very regular pattern, only slightly less deafening thanks to my hands.

I lowered them cautiously. "What was that for?"

"The negentropes."

"The nega-what-nows?"

Cucumber gave me a grandmotherly pat on the cheek. "They'll take care of you."

That didn't sound sinister at all.

"Take care of me how, exactly?"

"You'll see."

I narrowed my eyes, craning my neck to get a better look at the little squirt. "Not good enough. Spill."

"Here they come."

A shifting cloud of *something* sped our way, like a murmuration of starlings, except itty bitty and . . . geometric. The dark specks that made up the cloud swirled constantly, forming complex fractals one second, and the next a dodeca-trixa-hedro-poly-codone—

Okay, so I might've failed geometry.

Moving on.

The cloud swept toward us, and I cringed back as I realized it wasn't going to stop.

Tiny black icks swarmed around us, and the cloud froze, suspended in midair with me at the epicenter.

"Cucumber?" I muttered out of the corner of my mouth. Another pat on the cheek was my only answer.

Great.

A million black specks hurtled toward me like iron filings to a magnet, and I held my breath along with a panicked squeak as they shimmered across my skin, through my hair, under my freaking *clothes*, tickling and pricking and rustling my curls and—*ow*! What were they *doing*, spelunking in the slashes on my shoulder?

I squeezed my eyes shut and clamped my lips together, praying to an assortment of eldritch horrors that they'd at least leave those alone.

When this was over, I'd be giving Cucumber a hell of a lot more than a stern look, the little dastard.

Hot air brushed over my skin, and I realized the black icks had gone. I pried open one eyelid, then the other when I confirmed the coast was clear. The bizarre cloud floated before us again, rotating through shapes and patterns, pulsed once, and whizzed over to the chupacabra next.

"I— What— That—" I ran my hands across my chest and arms in a panic, not quite managing to suppress a shudder. Everything seemed to be intact . . .

My hands stilled.

Wait . . .

I gave myself a more thorough examination, pulling my tank away from my skin, running hands through my hair, craning around to see the slashes I'd sustained in the fight with the typhon.

I *was* intact. Like, completely.

My wounds were half-healed, my curls were bouncy, my splinters were gone, and even my freaking clothes seemed to be clean.

And Cucumber was snickering on my shoulder.

I pursed my lips and plucked him off with a *slorp*, settling him on the palm of my hand and raising him to eye level.

"Is that the demon domain version of a suds 'n' style?"

Cucumber flopped over giggling, almost toppling from my hand. I rolled my eyes.

He straightened. "I apologize, my lady, it was faster not to explain, and . . . and . . ."

"Yeah, I get it, hilarious."

I couldn't really hold it against him, though. I was sparkling clean, which meant I didn't have to lose precious sleep to scrub my skin and hair into oblivion in the shower before work.

And was that . . .? I sniffed my armpit, my shoulder still twinging with the movement.

I smelled like freaking peaches and marshmallows.

A yawn that could've swallowed Atlantis ripped through me, my jaw audibly cracking, moisture beading at the corners of my eyes.

Guess there was one thing Cucumber's friends hadn't fixed.

"All right, next steps." I jerked a thumb at the now clean monsters looming over my shoulder. "How do we distract Kor and get the gang through the portal?"

Cucumber leaned in close, almost bopping my nose, and whispered. "I tell Master Kor the truth."

A PRETTY RAD PLAN

"I'm sorry, *what*?" I jerked my hand away from my face, Cucumber wobbling with the sudden motion. After all that, was he gonna give us up to Kor?

Not that I was exactly worried about myself—Kor and I had a contract, after all—but my new monster buds would be a whole nother story.

Cucumber steadied himself and rolled his ghoulish eyes at me. "I'll tell him the *truth*, Lady Immy. That a fierce crusader entered his domain and defeated the typhon, freeing all the captives in the Baleful Tower."

I narrowed my eyes. "Naming no names?"

"How would I know the name of such a mighty warrior? I am but a lowly demonling."

Kor would figure it out in a jiffy—who else would be clambering through his mirror? Even if his domain had other entrances I didn't know about, when he saw that Sparkles was gone, he'd know. No sane person would bother rescuing a stuffed animal.

Heh.

I frowned. The tower was up in flames, though. He wouldn't be able to tell who'd escaped and who'd burned to a crisp.

So maybe there was a chance this wouldn't lead back to me?

A girl could dream.

Nah, no chance. I'd be giving Sparkles back to Bracchius, and unless he hid the unicorn within his *essence*—I wrinkled my nose—for the rest of time, Kor would clue in pronto.

Ah well.

I could handle Kor.

"That's a pretty rad plan, Cucumber. So you'll report to Kor, he'll zip over to the tower to check things out, and we'll sneak through the portal back to my place?"

"Indeed, Lady Immy."

There was one major flaw that I could see. "How do we get you into the laundromat with Kor, without him seeing us?"

Cucumber huffed, crossing his puny arms. "I am perfectly capable of doing things on my own, you know. Put me down."

I lowered my hand, then paused. "Guess this is goodbye, huh?" I had to say, I would miss the little guy a teensy bit—he had spunk, and had helped me out when he didn't have to.

Cucumber hooked a minuscule thumb over his shoulder. "Actually, could you leave me at the top of the hill, Lady Immy?"

"Sure thing." My last word dissolved into a yawn as I lifted Cucumber back up, and his eyes widened like he thought I was about to swallow him whole. I clacked my teeth together. "Sorry, just tired."

Just about to transcend to a new state of consciousness, more like— enlightened freaking hallucinatory fatigue.

I froze, glancing between the various terrifying monsters who were just palling around with me. Was I even awake right now? This would make a lot more sense as a bizarre dream.

Heck, I could still be drooling back in that alley, grinding asphalt- textured nap creases into my cheek as somnubus venom puddled around me.

Nah, my dreams were *way* less weird than this.

I shrugged it off and trekked to the top of the little hill, peeping over the edge at the laundromat below. This was a different side of the building than we'd left through, with only a blank wall facing us. "Here?"

"Perfect."

I set Cucumber down. I'd have to come back and say hi sometime— after all, I was one hundred percent co-opting that laundromat for my own sinister laundering purposes. Plus, I owed him those bath suds or whatever as a thank you.

"It has been a pleasure assisting you, Lady Immy." Cucumber stuck out one shrivelly hand, and I shook it solemnly between thumb and forefinger, hoping I wasn't crushing his tiny little bones.

Pretty sure he'd screech if that were the case—he wasn't exactly restrained in the vocalization department.

He looked up at me sternly. "Stay here until you see Master Kor leave, and he's out of sight. You'll need to hurry inside, and enter the portal one at a time."

I nodded. "Oh, what's it look like on this side?"

"A swirling vortex of the crushed hopes and dreams of all beings, milady."

I stared Cucumber down until he cracked a smile, tittering.

"A huge black portal, Lady Immy. You cannot miss it."

Underwhelming—I'd been half expecting this side's portal to be a giganto Washer of Doom, soapy maw gaping.

"Thanks, Cucumber." I patted his head. "Don't drown in any washers while I'm gone, yeah?"

He scoffed. "Drown? Hardly, milady. Safe travels, and dark dreams!"

The dorky demonling flopped over on his side, tucking in his arms and rolling down the hill like a kid about to be yelled at for grass stains. A shrill 'wheeee!' echoed up behind him, and I stifled a laugh.

A hissing wheeze beside me had me jerking to my right, where I bonked into a spider leg. My monsters had joined me: the chupacabra flopped on my left, tail wagging, and Madame Arachnofae on my right. The necrowraith stirred in the darkness just past the chupacabra. The lou carcolh loomed over me from behind, its eyestalks bobbing above my head.

Hopefully it didn't make a habit of drooling that sizzling pink acid.

I put a finger to my lips as Cucumber rolled to a stop near the wall of the laundromat, heaved to his slug-foot, and splutted awkwardly around the corner toward the door.

How in blazes was the little guy gonna get the me-sized door open on his own? I squinted as he stopped short of the door, faced the wall, and dove headfirst into what had to be a doggy door.

Demonling door.

Well, there you go.

It flapped back and forth a couple times, then settled back to stillness. Only the crackle of the flickerblood and the hush of our breathing disturbed the silence.

Until a huge crash echoed from the laundromat, followed by the door bursting open and slamming back against the wall, the knob embedding in the concrete with a crunch.

Yikes.

Cucumber must've reported in record time. He'd be okay, right? Kor wouldn't—? No.

Kor emerged, a seething mass of black and red, muttering extremely creative curses under his breath. I pouted—I didn't have anywhere to write them down, and I'd never remember.

I'd just have to get him blood-boilingly mad some other time.

Kor bolted away from the building, making a beeline for the Baleful Tower in the far distance.

Damn, there was actually a teeny blue-green ember glowing against the darkness in that direction. Was the tower *still* burning? I'd've thought those flames would've chewed it all up by now.

Unless the ground was just as tasty to my new chaos flames?

Welp.

I stood up, not eager to find out if Kor's whole domain would be going up in smoke next. The monsters followed suit. "Guess we'd better book it."

We hurried down the hillside, and slipped inside the laundromat. Well, the lou carcolh *scraped* inside, its spined shell leaving some nasty gouges in the doorjamb, but that was Kor's problem, not mine. He'd done enough of a number on the door himself that it really didn't make matters worse.

The stifling scent of detergent and hot dryer sheets assaulted my nose, making me cough.

"Cucumber?" I whispered, thinking of the giant crash a minute ago. "You okay?" If Kor had squashed him under a washer, I'd—

"Here, Lady Immy!" he piped, and I breathed a sigh of relief. I followed the sound of his voice through the dim interior, and found him squelching over to the wall I must've fallen through on my way in hours ago.

Not that this portion could really be called a wall.

Cucumber hadn't exaggerated with his description, joke or not. An inky vortex funneled into the wall from floor to ceiling, a chill blooming off it that was welcome in the oppressive heat. I'd been getting sweaty again despite the negen-whatsits' cleanup.

Goose bumps prickled along my arms and legs, and I narrowed my eyes. Was this freaking portal the reason the electrical bill had been going up?

I was *so* sticking Kor with the surcharge.

"Lady Immy, you must hurry! Master Kor can travel much more quickly than we did, and might be back any moment!"

Right, save scary monsters from pompous demon lord. I could worry about the electrical bill later.

I gathered my monsters around me.

"Okay, guys, here's how it's gonna go. I'll go through first, to make sure the way's clear." Really, I just wanted to fling my wet undies out of sight before these fearsome beasties came waltzing through, but they didn't need to know that. "Chupacabra, you'll go next."

I felt bad that I hadn't asked their names, but we could handle that once we were out of Kor's domain. The chupacabra's name was probably a whuffled bark-snarl I couldn't replicate anyway.

"Necrowraith, you third, then you, madam." I nodded at the arachnofae, then the lou carcolh. "And you'll take up the rear."

It was the biggest, and I was still worried it wouldn't fit. I didn't wanna strand it, but leaving it at Kor's mercy was better than all of them getting stuck if it went first.

And I could always go back if it didn't come through—hopefully not impaling myself on a shell spike along the way.

"It'll be tight quarters on the other side, so exit through the nearby door as soon as possible to make room. I'll stay close in case of any problems."

My monsters each nodded, bobbed, or yipped, and I took a deep breath.

"Here goes nothing."

And I stepped into the swirling portal.

TRIALS & TUBULATIONS

Of course, I didn't stick the landing.

My foot slipped off the top of the toilet tank, and I tumbled down, banging my shin on the toilet-paper holder, and my elbow on the corner of the counter.

I splayed in an aching heap on the bathroom floor—yech, I really needed to clean down here more often—and stared up at the mirror.

The mirror had . . . become bigger. Huh.

I heaved myself back to my feet, whipped the still-dripping unmentionables off the shower rod, and crammed them into the hamper, fishing out a towel to drape over the lot.

Turning from the hamper, I twitched—I wasn't alone.

Bracchius was bobbing in the open bathroom door like a lotto ball, fixated on my hip, where Sparkles was taped to my scabbard. I lunged forward and scooped Bracchius up with both hands, prompting a squawk of indignation, and bustled into the living room, plopping him on the sofa before he could free himself.

"I— Immy— What—?"

"Don't want you to get trampled by my new pals. I'll explain in a sec."

I darted back to the bathroom, where a massive spider leg was poking out of the rippling mirror, questing for a surface to land on.

I limboed beneath it and scrambled into the tub, one foot slipping with a squeak on the trail of water left by my sopping clothes. The suction cup soap caddy saved me from an ignominious death-by-bathtub.

The arachnofae's black limb touched down on the toilet lid, and two more punctured the mirror, finding the counter and tub rim respectively. I blinked—the mirror was even bigger, its ornate frame scraping the ceiling.

Her head breached the silvery surface next, and she spidered her way into my bathroom, taking up pretty much the whole room, one leg braced against the tile wall above my head. I slid lower in the tub.

"What happened to going fourth?" Opening my mouth was enough to set off a massive yawn.

"The chupacabra was hesitant, and the necrowraith was loath to abandon it."

She stuck one leg back through the mirror—giving the all clear?—and then pulled back, glancing at me with all eight eyes.

I pointed at the bathroom door, and she skittered thataway. I called after her belatedly. "Stay in the hall!"

Couldn't give Bracchius *too* much of a heart attack.

Ethereal wisps drifted through the mirror's surface, and I hunched at the far end of the tub. The rest of the necrowraith followed, settling slowly over the toilet.

Carrying the chupacabra in its arms.

The bitty beastie wore a doggy grin, black tongue lolling.

Talk about the royal treatment.

They really *must* be best buds.

I jabbed a finger toward the door again, my eyes blurring with exhaustion for a moment, and they joined the arachnofae. Hopefully Bracchius had stayed put on the sofa like a good little demon.

All that was left was the lou carcolh. I eyed the already-huge frame. Could it get any bigger without busting the ceiling?

I prepared for a popcorn-ceiling shower, tugging the curtain over preemptively.

Two eyestalks oozed through the mirror, which *did* get bigger.

It freaking *warped*, the top curving onto the ceiling a la Salvador Dali and his goopy clocks.

And then there was a giant snail sliming its way across my toilet.

That was gonna be a delight to clean up later.

I clung to the tub wall, not wanting to lose an eye to the shell spike gliding past my face.

My doorframe suffered a similar fate to the laundromat's, wood crunching and splinters flying. The shower curtain came in handy after all.

I crawled out of the tub and tiptoed along the narrow strip of linoleum not covered in shimmery snail slime. My sneakers stuck a couple times, but I yanked them free.

My carpet was gonna be a nightmare, though.

Closing the bathroom door behind me, I wedged one of my trashed sneakers in the bottom gap. That wouldn't stop Kor for long, but it might buy us a minute if he buzzed back here at top speed.

I wrestled my way past the monsters assembled in the hall and poked my head around the corner. Bracchius was peeping over the back of the sofa, a couple of the arachnofae's legs in plain sight.

He'd waited long enough.

I held my hands out toward my posse. "Wait here one sec, I'll be right back."

Carefully unwinding the tape from my sheath and Sparkles, I trooped over to Bracchius. Once tape-free, I held out Sparkles over the back of the sofa, tiny bells tinkling.

Bracchius gently stretched out a couple pseudo arms and pulled Sparkles into his embrace, muttering sweet nothings and sinking back into the cushions. Blobby bits of him wrapped around Sparkles from different directions in a demon hug, like inky Playfoam enveloping a Happy Meal toy.

His voice went mushy. "I'm never gonna let you out of my sight again, oh no I'm not. You'll be safe here with me forever and ever, and if Kor ever comes within cursing distance of you again, I'll shred him with the rays of a sun phoenix and dissolve his remains with unicorn blood. Oh yes I will. Uh-huh."

Watching Bracchius's reunion with Sparkles almost made me want to track down an azure animafae to bring the plushie to life, but even pint-sized unicorns could be real assholes, and Bracchius was obviously content with things as they were.

Very content.

I left him to his goo-goo-gahing, and hurried back to my monsters. "All right, let me get you guys oriented, and you can take off before—"

The necrowraith raised one creepy finger to my lips, shushing me immediately. Wide-eyed, I glanced between it and the others.

"We insist on a proper round of introductions before we part ways," the arachnofae explained. "We must know to whom we owe our debt of gratitude, and you who to call upon for repayment."

I rubbed the back of my head. "I don't really n—"

The chupacabra hissed from his perch in the necrowraith's arms, and the arachnofae's many-eyed fanged face got real close to mine. "We will pay our debts."

Gulp. "Okay, sure. I'm, uh, Immy. Immy Cordell."

The arachnofae backed up, bending a few legs to give me a deep bow. "A pleasure. My name is Noss Ra Kri."

The chupacabra barked something like "Arghbargle," and the necrowraith intoned a gravelly, echoing "SHARN."

Finally, the lou carcolh burbled a surprisingly intelligible "Kindred Smudge."

I inclined my head to each in turn—practically nodding off—then opened my mouth, but the arachnofae beat me to it.

"While I have no way to repay you at present, I am greatly in your debt, as are we all, and that debt will be repaid."

There was a chorus of nodding heads and a yip from the chupacabra.

"Great, yeah, thanks." I waited a second for any other unexpected formalities, then got back to the point. "So we're in Saskia Springs. You know where that is?" Who knew where they'd come from—Kor hadn't always lived in my apartment, and they could've been trapped in that mirror for dragon's years.

"Indeed."

Perfect. Noss Ra Kri could get the others up to speed, then, once they were out in the wide world.

I opened the front door and pointed down the street. "The closest subway station is five blocks that way, and you can get most anywhere in the city from there. You, uh . . ."

They didn't exactly look like they carried pocket change or metro cards. I bit my lip, then caught sight of my battered clutch on the table. I rifled through the dumped-out contents for the change from my fifty, and held it out to the arachnofae. Easy come, easy go.

Sigh.

"Here."

Her spider feet weren't really designed for snatching cash, though. I suppressed a wince as the necrowraith's unearthly hand stretched out, folding the bills into its palm, and not taking my soul with them.

I released a breath, which of course turned into a yawn, my eyes watering.

"Our debt increases." Noss Ra Kri smiled—at least, I think that's what that arrangement of mandibles and fangs was meant to be. "I wish you well, Immy Cordell, and will seek you out when I have recompense worth the debt owed."

She gave another deep bow, then skittered out into the predawn night.

The necrowraith nodded solemnly and followed her, still cradling the chupacabra in its arms.

The lou carcolh didn't budge, though.

"Do you . . ." Need a map? Extra cash? Help getting unglued from my carpet? ". . . need something?"

It stared at me for a moment, and then a periscoping limb slowly extended from its soft flesh.

Wait, this thing had secret *arms?*

The arm unfurled, strands of slime stretching and sagging, until a blobby tip emerged, tapping against my hand.

I pulled back, but it tapped again. Gritting my teeth, I held my hand out, palm up.

And something heavy—and gooey—dropped into it.

Gosh darn it, I'd just been cleaned up by magical nanobugs or whatnot, and here I was getting all gross again.

The lou carcolh retracted its surprise limb, a slime string stretching between it and the object in my hand, which took up my whole palm. I peered closer, careful to keep my nose slime-free, though my hand was a goner.

It looked like a giant pearl, only heavy as a brick. Beneath the clear slime, the dark blue sphere shimmered, almost holographic.

Pleeease let this not be a lou carcolh egg. Did they lay eggs? Who knew. Regardless, I was the last person anyone should trust with their offspring, born or unborn.

Though, if this was repayment for me breaking it out of Kor's domain, it had to be pretty important. Or valuable.

And there were way too many fairy tales and modern-day agreements littered with clauses about handing over your firstborn.

Whose deepest desire was having to deal with someone else's rugrat?

Always seemed like a bonkers stipulation to me. If I was passing out favors like someone's fairy godmother, I wanted something a heck of a lot nicer than a mewling kid or faun or nugget in return.

I sized up the pseudo pearl reluctantly. "Uh . . . thank you?" Nope, I had to ask. "Is this your . . ." How to put it? Egg? Child? Reproductive Byproduct? Snail minion? ". . . your spawn?"

The soft flesh of the lou carcolh quaked, a *slurp-slurp* coming from somewhere within the massive beast.

Was that . . . laughter?

The lou carcolh laughed itself all the way out the door, leaving behind one last slime trail.

So was it laughing because the question was ridiculous, or because I'd guessed right, and it reveled in my misfortune?

I shredded a paper towel off the roll in the kitchen and plopped the mystery sphere onto it, wiping the gooey remnants from my hand onto another towel that went straight in the trash.

Now I had two freaking magical orbs of unknown purpose.

Bully for me.

My vision blurred as I ripped out another jaw-unhinging yawn. I probably looked like a snake about to devour its prey.

The lou carcolh's gift could wait till tomorrow. I was gonna get some shut-eye, or so help me.

I contemplated my bedroom, but odds weren't good that I'd even make it that far.

Bracchius was still blissed out on the sofa with Sparkles, but it wasn't like the two of them took up much room. He'd migrate back under the sofa eventually anyway.

I staggered over to the sofa, shedding my various accoutrements—sheath, fanny pack, one sneaker. "Budge over."

The words might not've been intelligible, but Bracchius budged. I slumped onto the sofa cushion, teetered over, and nestled my head on the plush armrest.

Bracchius's voice came from somewhere near my tucked-up toes. "What's this green stain?"

I cracked one eyelid, peering at a green smudge on Sparkles's white butt. "Probably typhon blood." I closed my peepers again.

"Typhon—"

I waited blearily for a follow-up, but Bracchius kept quiet.

Which was my cue for lights out.

"Immy? Immy. It's time to wake up. C'mon."

A persistent nudge against my spine finally roused me, unfortunately. I felt almost disembodied, I was so dead.

I rolled onto my back, not ready to unglue my eyes just yet, and a muffled yelp beneath me gave me pause. Had I invited someone back to my place last night? No way.

A subtle *pop* preceded a muttered string of curses.

Bracchius.

Why was I sleeping on top of Bracchius?

For that matter, why was my bed so uncomfortable?

I flailed an arm out, punching something squishy.

"For sprinkles' sake!"

What an undemonly epithet.

I finally unstuck one eye. Bracchius hovered above me, a bit more turbulent than usual.

Oops.

I groaned out, "Did I just punch you in the fa—body? Whatever?"

"Uh-huh."

"My bad."

"It's time to get up."

"Whyyy."

"You have to go to work."

"Ugh." I gave in and opened my eyes, staring at a dark popcorn ceiling behind a broken ceiling fan. Why was I sleeping on the sofa?

"How much sleep did I get?"

"Practically none."

That explained the death-warmed-over feeling.

Snippets of the night before began trickling back to me, each one a fresh jolt of horror. I propped myself up and stared Bracchius down.

"Did I—"

"Yup."

"The monsters?"

"Oh yes."

"Sparkles?"

"In a safe place."

I creaked around, spine protesting, to peer at the Mini Cooper–sized snail trail winding across the carpet.

Hot damn. I plastered on a smile. "Are you grateful enough to hire out some brownies?"

Bracchius hummed. "Maybe. Did you really fight a typhon?"

"And a shadelurker."

"Brownies it is."

I'd also unleashed the Monster Mash on the city. Damarion would know how much trouble I was in.

I patted around on the coffee table for my phone, then my hand stilled. Right. My phone was toast.

Crud.

Bracchius hovered above a thermos further down the table. "I thought this might help. You know, with the lack of sleep."

"Perfect." I snatched up the thermos, did a quick tongue test to keep from scalding myself, and downed a couple glugs of the delicious coff—

Not coffee.

I eyed the thermos suspiciously and licked my teeth, trying to figure out the taste.

"Do you need to call someone? I'd be delighted to let you borrow my phone."

"Thanks, but I don't have any of the numbers memorized." I took another sip. It was pretty good, but nowhere on the coffee spectrum flavorwise. Alertness was already creeping over my consciousness, though. "What *is* this?"

"LivingDead DreamStopper. It should get you pepped up any minute! And no problem, I have them all stored in my contacts."

LivingDead? My eyes widened midsip. "Wait, isn't this stuff illegal?"

Bracchius bobbed cheerfully. "Only if someone can prove you're using it, and it's undetectable in the human body by any known tests."

"Is it gonna kill me?"

"Probably not."

Eh. I already felt like death. Could it really get worse?

I chugged another couple gulps.

Then the rest of what he'd said percolated into my brain. I narrowed my eyes. "You . . . have all *my* contacts stored in *your* phone?"

Bracchius stopped bobbing. "Erm . . . Yes?"

We traded a charged glance, mine dire, his like Wile E. Coyote just before the boulder lands.

Then I sighed.

"You know what, I don't even care anymore. Hand it over." I made grabby hands.

Bracchius pulled a phone from his inky depths, unlocked it, and held it out. I examined it for any lingering demon residue, but it seemed to be clear.

I tapped on his contacts, and sure enough, all the names looked familiar. I cast him another bristly glance, and I swear a little "eep" squeaked out of him.

There, Damarion.

He hadn't slept since 1785 or thereabouts, so I knew he'd be awake.

I dialed.

"Good morning." Damarion's suave voice blared out on speakerphone at a volume I was not mentally prepared for, and I smashed down on the button.

"Quick question. So, I just unleashed a necrowraith, a chupacabra, a black widow arachnofae, and a lou carcolh on the city. Think that'll come back to bite me?"

"Sounds like an eventful morning. I didn't think you were a morning person."

"I'm not." Unfortunately, my job didn't take that into account.

Nor did stalker lunatics, or demon roommates.

"As far as problems . . . Perhaps just don't inform anyone else of your culpability."

I quirked my lips. "Good point."

"Rampaging monsters aside, are we still on for this afternoon?"

I was feeling startlingly awake now, but my vision was also tingeing lavender. I side-eyed the nearly empty thermos. "If I survive that long."

"Wonderful. I look forward to it."

I ended the call. "Bracchius, does LivingDead have any side effects?"

"It's very rare, but there have been reports of, uh, levitation, olfactory hallucinations, hair loss, toe mutations—"

He rattled off a bunch more as I resigned myself to the fact that today would probably be just as delightful as yesterday.

Woe is me.

It suddenly struck me how peaceful the apartment was. Monster-damaged, sure. About to be littered with my LivingDead-mutated corpse, almost definitely.

But quiet.

Too quiet.

Too Kor-free.

The hellion should've been nipping on my heels as I unleashed the monsters into the night. And yet, I'd gotten a sound hour or two of sleep, uninterrupted by screaming matches or unrighteous demon fury.

I set down my toxic pick-me-up and studied the plushie-loving blob of darkness before me.

"Bracchius . . ." I cocked my head. "Where's Kor?"

FACING MY NOT-INNER DEMONS

"Kor?" Bracchius did a good job of sounding oblivious.

"Uh, yeah. The big meanie who stole Sparkles and locked her in a jail cell guarded by a typhon? Remember?" I'd never get tired of reminding Bracchius about the typhon. He owed me a heck of a lot more than stimulants and a brownie cleanup crew.

"Oh . . . That. Well . . . I might have sealed him in the bathroom."

"*Sealed?*" That wasn't sinister at all. I tried to stand, but plopped back down as every muscle in my body roared its protest at such inhumane treatment.

Right. I hadn't exactly kicked back and been a couch potato last night. This morning.

Sob.

My second try, I eased up slowly, face scrunched as I pretended my thighs weren't halfway between agony and jelly.

I teetered on my feet, but my legs didn't give out beneath me.

Good first step.

Now that I was upright, my body reported that it hadn't sweated out *all* the water I'd chugged on my merry adventure in Kor's domain, but it sure did need to get rid of the rest post-haste.

I rounded on Bracchius, stiffly. "What exactly does 'sealed' mean? So help me, if I can't get in there—"

"I can unseal it!" Bracchius zipped toward the bathroom, looking alarmed. I staggered after him, lunging over the wide trail of shiny dried snail slime.

The bathroom door was shut, a red glow pulsing between it and the splintered doorjamb. Please let that be Bracchius's magic, and not a hellfire Kor had set in the bathroom.

Not like I'd be getting my deposit back whenever I abandoned this dump, anyway, though.

Bracchius hovered nervously by the door.

I pointed at the crimson glimmer. "That's your seal?"

"Yes."

"And it kept Kor in there all night?"

"Well, I can't say for sure—he could've gone back to his domain, but—"

"But he didn't come careening out of the bathroom while I was asleep? This kept him trapped on the other side?"

Bracchius gave me a whole-body nod in midair.

I twisted and tugged on the knob experimentally. The door didn't shift a millimeter.

I stared Bracchius down.

"Why in the three hells did I not know you can do this? Do you know how many times this would've come in handy?"

"I know."

"Then why did you never tell me?" Wasn't he on my side? I'd thought we were buds.

Bracchius drifted down a bit, edging toward the wall sheepishly. "I, er . . ."

I crossed my arms, trying to ignore my bladder.

Bracchius blurted it out in a rush. "It's, uh, fun watching you two duke it out most of the time."

My eyes narrowed, but I had to admit I had fun torturing Kor too, sometimes. He was just so easy to rile up, and he one hundred percent deserved it.

I jerked my chin at the door. "And this time is different how?"

Bracchius took on a grim aspect. "This time, it was personal."

Fair enough.

"Well?" I flapped a hand at the glowing door. "You gonna unseal it?"

An ominous thud came from the other side.

Bracchius cleared his throat. "We could, uh, just leave it, you know."

"Not unless you want to watch me peeing in the kitchen sink in ten seconds." Not that I could probably even get up on the counter right now, with my body this pissed off.

"Eurgh!" Bracchius shuddered. "I don't need to know any more about your horrifying mortal bodily functions than I already do, thanks. Blech."

I jabbed a thumb at the door, and his disgust one-eightied to apprehension.

"You *really* want me to unseal it?"

"YES!"

Bracchius zoomed along all four edges of the door, the red glow fading in his wake. Kor's voice was immediately audible, spewing a tirade of curses at top volume.

Sealing *and* soundproofing, huh? I'd have to remember that.

The sheer decibel level of spite being hurled made me pause. Maybe the kitchen sink *was* a viable option?

Nope. Screw the consequences—I *had* to pee.

I took a deep breath and opened the door.

Maybe a bit overenthusiastically.

It swung inward, almost taking Kor out right there, smacking his roiling form out of the air and into the sink like a flyswatter on steroids.

Kor's curses morphed into stuttering incoherent rage, his spherical body more crimson than black.

I lumbered over to the toilet. "Out."

Kor didn't seem to hear me as he emerged from the sink, swelling like a balloon, still flinging a steady stream of ragey nonsense.

I flipped up the snail-sticky toilet lid and stabbed one arm toward the doorway. "Out!"

Kor paused in his advance, swiveled minutely toward the toilet, then back toward me, and bolted, muttering something about filthy mortal habits. The door slammed behind him.

After taking care of business, I surveyed myself in the mirror. I looked surprisingly alive, thanks mostly to Cucumber's flying geometric whatsits.

I fumigated my curls with some dry shampoo, hacking a couple coughs as the chemicals settled, then brushed my not-so-pearly whites.

Hey, not everybody can afford whitening treatments, especially at the prices the unicorn conglomerates charge.

The clear bandage Ruby had smoothed over my new tattoo seemed none the worse for everything I'd put it through in the depressingly few hours since.

A bit scuffed, sure. But no scorch marks, slime, blood, or other gook, so I'd call it good. My slightly pink sigil tattoo was healing up nicely.

I couldn't feel the telltale buzz of its effect anymore. Going through an interdimensional portal twice—not to mention flirting with whatever magics my chaos flames had given off—had probably shut 'er down.

My other tattoo was still a blownout disaster. I focused on the ink, and managed to tidy it up a tiny bit, but then a headache drilled right between my eyes.

It could wait.

I eyed my ADHD meds, but decided I'd better not mess with the LivingDead cocktail churning through my system. I might catch fire or transmogrify into a pterodactyl or a chicken or something.

A few minutes later, I was as ready to face the day as I was gonna get.

And to face Kor.

I emerged to find Kor buzzing around the apartment like a remote control helicopter in the hands of a three-year-old.

As soon as he saw me, he screeched to a halt on his flight path.

"Immy— You— My *typhon*! How—?"

Clearly the extra minutes hadn't helped with the forming-sentences thing. I looked him dead in the not-eyes, one eyebrow raised. "I was simply retrieving stolen property. Don't pick fights you can't win."

"But—"

"And I'm not buying you Cheetos for a month."

Kor shrieked in frustration and barreled into the bathroom. I poked my head through the door as he plunged into the mirror, which glowed red-hot before slowly cooling again.

"Rent's due in a week!" I hollered after him, just because I could.

I waltzed back into the living room, grinning. Maybe today wouldn't be so bad after all.

Bracchius was in the kitchen, studying a wad of paper towels on the counter. I squinted as I went for the fridge.

Right—the gooey orb the lou carcolh had spit out at me. I gave a tentative poke at the paper towels, which had stiffened into a papier-mâché-like crust as the slime congealed. The sphere was probably entombed in there for good now.

Ah well. Not like I even knew what it was, anyway.

Bracchius spun on the counter, tilting back to look at me as I fished a bag of stale English muffins off the top of the fridge.

"Immy . . . why is there a dusk pearl in our kitchen? Are you *trying* to get us killed?"

I gave him a dubious look. "Get us killed? Wha—" No, I'd loop back to that in a sec. "You seriously didn't see the giant armored snail slithering across the living room a few hours ago?"

Bracchius stared, then peeked past me at the desiccating slime trail on the carpet. "So *that's* where that came from?"

Wow, he must've been *mega* absorbed in Sparkles to miss that.

"Uh, yeah. Never mind." I set the English muffins on the opposite end of the counter from the so-called dusk pearl. It couldn't be *that* dangerous, if Bracchius was cozying up to it instead of backing away in alarm. "What's a dusk pearl?"

"This . . ." Bracchius nudged the paper towel with his pudgy tummy. "Really, Immy, I thought the LivingDead would've helped with your morning brain by now."

I rolled my eyes. "I meant, what *is* a dusk pearl? Why is it dangerous?"

"Ohh. You've really never heard of one? Huh. Well, it's not *inherently* dangerous—I don't think, anyway." Bracchius peered at it from a couple different angles. "But it's quite valuable, and if anyone knew we had it, they might kill us for it."

I blinked. "Seriously?" Leaving my stale muffin forlorn on the counter, I pried back the stiff paper towel and held the dusk pearl up to the light. If it was that valuable . . . "We could just sell it, right?" Not having to worry about the expenses of life for a little while would be the bee's knees.

"Ehhh . . ." Bracchius wibble-wobbled from side to side. "Depends if you could find a reputable dealer. It's not like you can take it to a pawn shop or a corvidae bartery or something. And a dealer might not want to mess with it either. Dusk pearls are notorious for being mayhem magnets."

I knew the feeling. I rummaged in the fridge for the congealed package of plasticky cheese slices. "Guess I'll worry about it later, then."

"Worry about it la— Immy, you can't just leave it on the counter!" Bracchius whipped around toward the window. "Anyone could walk by and see it, and if you're gone at work, who'll defend me from crazed homicidal burglars?"

I was reasonably certain he could fend off any number of crazed burglars just fine on his own, but it was easier not to argue. I yanked open my junk drawer and nestled the pearl between my rubber band ball and the tangled mess of twist ties, then shoved some Bubble Wrap over it.

I popped a couple bubbles for good measure.

What? Show me the person who can resist Bubble Wrap, and I'll show you a cyborg.

"There. It's safe from Peeping Trolls, and no burglar ever bothered with a junk drawer."

"I suppose it'll do." He extended a blobby arm and scooted the drawer closed.

Speaking of valuable doodads tucked away for safekeeping . . .

"You still got that artifact sphere thing?"

"Of course."

"And no mysterious knocks on the door? Phone calls?" Scratch that, they could call my number all they liked. It wouldn't do them any good.

"Immy, I *told* you it would be safe with me. Besides, it's only been a few hours."

Right. That.

The LivingDead was doing a great job of masking my fatigue, but it was definitely still lurking under the surface. Work today was gonna be fuuun.

I didn't have much time to finish getting ready, or I'd be late. I peeled back the plastic sleeve of the no-way-this-is-actually-cheese, and slapped the orange square on the English muffin. Frozen sausage patty in the microwave, mini griddle plugged in, and I scooped an egg out of the fridge door.

The egg felt a bit bottom-heavy—probably on its last legs. Eh, I wasn't picky. I cracked the egg into the griddle and went to throw on some clean clothes.

Breakfast sandwich assembled, I wolfed it down while I scrounged around for what I needed for work. I grabbed my Mary Poppins–sized bag and pulled out my work polo from yesterday.

I gave it the sniff test—good enough—and shoved it back in the bag. I'd done enough of these recently that it was probably getting close to laundry time, and now I even had a laundromat that wouldn't eat my quarters.

Hopefully.

Granted, Kor might feed my laundry to his imps or something, but I could always kick back with a book in there and guard it. Better than schlepping it five blocks to the subway, then another three to the Spin City laundromat, and ignoring the advances of a maenad cherub two machines over.

I considered my sneakers, one by the sofa, the other by the bathroom door, the soles sticky and slightly melted—probably thanks to my chaos flames. Or the typhon's blood? Maybe I'd stepped in a stray glob of lou carcolh spit.

Who knew.

I gingerly held one sneaker up. "Think the brownies stand a chance with these?"

Bracchius looked it over doubtfully on his way back to the sofa. "Nope."

Ah well. I chucked it in the kitchen trash, sending the revolving lid into a lazy spin. The other one followed a second later. At least I still had my work kicks.

I dropped my bag on the coffee table and plopped myself on the sofa, only to jerk aside as something jabbed me in the butt.

"What in the—"

I stuffed a hand between the sofa cushions and sniggled out the culprit: the tiny pair of plastic manacles Kor had wrestled Sparkles's squishy hooves into.

Bracchius must've taken them off while I drooled into the armrest.

Probably best not to retraumatize Bracchius, but these could come in handy . . . A quick trip to my room, and they were stashed at the back of my closet.

You never know when some miniature miscreant is gonna show up in your room and make trouble.

Again.

The purple tinge over my vision was getting stronger, with a few pops of glitter added in. It reminded me of the Pure Bliss.

I picked up the mostly empty thermos. "Is this manufactured by unicorns?"

Bracchius peeped out from under the sofa. "The LivingDead? I believe it's made by Nalustrak night terrors, but unicorn water might be the base."

There you go.

"I put a second thermos by the door, too. For later." His voice got more muffled as he slipped back under the sofa skirt.

"Oh, thanks."

I shoved that in my bag, then surveyed the contents. Anything I was forgetting? Wallet, keys, work shirt, water bottle, thermos, chapstick . . .

Lunch.

I bounced back up off the sofa, probably giving Bracchius a mini earthquake—not that he'd ever complained—and tugged open the freezer door.

There was an ice-encrusted box crunched into the back corner of the freezer behind the Ziploc bags of random leftovers and realistically-expired-before-I-froze-it meat. I chiseled it out with my ice cream scoop, revealing the flimsy green and beige paperboard box of a ninety-nine-cent chicken pot pie.

Better than nothing. I crammed it into my bag and headed for the door.

"Have a nice day at work!" Bracchius called.

"Have a better day poking around the house with Sparkles!" I tossed back as I unlocked the door.

I stepped onto the concrete stoop, pulling the stubborn door shut behind me with a good heave.

Jangling my keys back into my bag, I took another step into the predawn darkness.

And something crunched beneath my shoe.

LOST & FOUND OUT

What the—? I stepped back, hoping I hadn't just pulverized a shadowmouse or something. A small piece of metal glinted in the moonlight against the concrete. I plucked it up carefully, and scoffed.

An iron Stymphalian feather, left by my crows.

These things were a dime a dozen—after all, there was a Stymphalian nest on the roof of the derelict Jack in the Box a few blocks over, not to mention dozens more all over the city. But it was shiny, and that was the most important criteria for the crows.

I was lucky it hadn't sliced straight through my sneaker, razor sharp as it was. It'd make mincemeat of my purse if I tucked it in there, but I didn't want to rummage for my keys in my cavernous bag, or drop the feather again either. Stepping on it later with worse consequences to my poor feet would be bad enough, but offending the crows was another level of nope altogether.

You *don't* mess with crows.

In case they were watching from the trees, I hugged the feather semiclose, minding the sharp edges, and called out, "Oh, how pretty!" Then I jabbed the pointy end into the door like a makeshift dart.

What? My front door already looked like it had held up to a couple of orc sieges: battering ram, kamikaze Urukhai, and all. Another tiny ding wasn't gonna hurt it any.

Ugh, but I needed to feed the crows.

I fumbled a hand around inside my bag, burrowing to the bottom where my keys inevitably settle, and yanked them out by the beaded salamander attached with a wonky O-ring.

Door open, I gave the feather a wide berth as I slapped a hand down on the three-legged credenza held up by the wall and sheer luck, grabbing the kibble tub.

"Forget something?" Bracchius asked.

"Crows."

"Ah." He paused. "I've never tried kibble, is it any good?"

"They sure seem to think so." The day I would come home to find Bracchius equator-deep in kibble, crunching it down and assessing the flavor, would be a good day. Even if he liked the kibble.

Better if he didn't.

I stifled a chuckle and pried the plastic lid off, then shuffled a generous helping onto the stoop, the rattle of kibble bits on the concrete prompting a chorus of caws from the trees across the street. I shoved the tub home and swung the door shut, narrowly avoiding taking out an eye with the feather—I'd have to figure out a better place for that later.

"Sorry, in a rush!" I hollered as the crows flapped my way. They usually got to eat on the broken walkway through my yard, but today I was running late. I didn't think they'd mind hopping around on the porch.

The stars overhead were difficult to see with the city lights blooming against the sky, but the devas made up for them, like little fairy lights swirling in the darkness.

Granted, actual stars don't usually flash lime green, pink, and purple to the oonz-oonz-oonz of the car driving down the street with its bass beat blaring.

Starting work even *before* the crack of dawn isn't my favorite, but I guess it could be worse. It is kinda peaceful this early, with the city subdued in that window of too-late-to-be-partying and too-early-to-roll-out-of-bed.

Dawn wasn't *that* far away.

I slurped down some more LivingDead as I trekked the few blocks to Glenbrook station, hurrying my steps the closer I got. The train was always late, but it didn't hurt to play it safe.

The LivingDead kept changing flavor every few sips; this time, I got a mouthful of liquid Lucky Charms.

At least I hadn't hit any Bertie Bott's flavors yet. I repressed a shudder.

The subway station sign glowed in the predawn twilight two blocks ahead, and I reached for my pocket to check the time.

Right. My phone had passed on to the great electronic graveyard in the sky. How the heck was I gonna afford replacing it? I already owed Samaire for covering dinner last night, and Ruby for the tattoo, plus rent was coming up . . .

Maybe I could chum up to a technofae artificer and ask a favor.

The dusk pearl at the back of my junk drawer was looking mighty attractive. How hard could it be to find a "reputable dealer," as Bracchius put it? It would solve a lot of problems.

"Cotton Eye Joe" started looping in my head a block out from the station. Ugh, why? Sometimes I woke up with a song stuck in my head—dream soundtrack, anyone?—but I didn't remember any line-dancing dreams during my woefully brief snooze.

The song kept going, and I womanfully resisted sliding to the left. Wait, was this a mashup with "Cha Cha Slide"?

Welcome to my brain, y'all.

Then my toes started tingling, and lightheadedness washed over me, my steps becoming bouncier, like gravity decided to give me a bit of a break today.

Seriously?

I screwed the lid back onto the thermos of LivingDead and shoved it decidedly into my purse.

Last time I trust Bracchius with illicit substances.

Although . . . With a running start, and a hop, skip, and a jump, I tested out my new astronaut-floatiness, and couldn't hold back a grin as I drifted along.

As side effects went, it could be worse—at least my toes hadn't mutated.

Yet.

Hopefully.

I hit the top of the stairs into the station, and started down. Perfect, the train was waiting, doors open. I was just in time.

Annnd the doors were closing.

A woodwose twenty feet ahead of me shimmied through the doors into the closest car, morning glories, charging cables, and crime scene tape woven through her fur—urban camouflage, I guess? I stretched out a hand as I hammered down the stairs, curls flying in my own breeze.

"Hold the doors!"

The subway doors were designed to back the hell off if something got stuck between them—one Mongolian death worm nearly vivisected on the platform had been enough for the city to implement some "please don't squish me" spells.

But the woodwose was either deaf or a dick, and the doors wheezed closed two seconds before I screeched to a halt in front of them.

Pixies and potholes.

I was gonna be late to work, and I couldn't even call in to overexplain my excuses.

I bounced up the steps from the subway to the main airport level at top speed, twenty minutes late, shoulder-checking some poor electronymph when my LivingDead-induced antigravity got a little too boisterous.

"Sorry!" Static crackled across my skin, and my curls frizzed out a bit as I flew past her toward the rental concourse, fully expecting a reprimand or at least surly looks from my coworkers for showing up late.

The Saskia Skies rental counter was aflutter with activity—super bizarre for six-something in the morning—and no one even glanced my way as I skated up.

I'd thought *I* was wired, but my still-floaty steps couldn't compare to the morning check-in guy, Doak, running around like a chicken with his head cut off.

Maybe a bit gauche, since Doak was a chicken shifter, but I couldn't help myself.

What?

I snuck into the bathroom to change into my work polo, and when I emerged, Keisha had joined Doak with a security guy. The counter was in disarray—papers everywhere, computer monitors off-kilter, debris scattered across the floor behind it.

"There you are." She shoved my clunky scanner my way, and I grabbed it. "Scan in the cars that came in overnight, and then I want you back in here pronto. Also, your scanner's only half-charged, so you might need to plug it in again when you get the chance."

"What happened?" I eyeballed a splintered keyboard tray dangling beneath the counter by one screw.

"Someone trashed the counter." Keisha tipped a rolly chair upright. "Not sure they found whatever they were looking for. Not like we keep cash overnight."

I blanched, eyes flicking to the cubby that housed the lost and found box. All that was left was a smattering of cardboard scraps tossed around like confetti.

Had this happened before my stalker found me at the restaurant last night? Or after I'd given the mysterious orb to Bracchius for safekeeping?

Thank goodness they couldn't track it to my place.

Might be safer to ditch the thing, but what if it was dangerous? Wouldn't that be playing right into the bad guys' hands? They had to want it for something, and I doubted it was good.

Keisha nudged me. "What are you waiting for? We need those cars checked in and out of the way."

"Right, sorry, got distracted." I headed off to dump my stuff in my booth.

Outside, I scanned my way through the line of cars that'd been dropped off in the night, checking mileage, wrangling keys, and keeping an eye out for dings and dents.

The asphalt was littered with storm detritus—leaves, pebbled glass, the occasional washer or screw, grit dried in waves as the water receded. I stepped over a lone bicycle wheel that must've washed up from who-knows-where.

It would be *so* fun cleaning all this up later.

I couldn't muster up the motivation to scrounge around in trunks or under seats for goodies left behind—what if I found something else hazardous to my health? One bad-guy magnet was enough, thanks.

I did scoop up a pristine Milky Way Dark Magic on a passenger seat, though.

Girl's gotta eat, right?

Alex waved as she and Bert jogged up. "Morning! The ones at the back ready to go?"

"Yup." I only had the few cars closest to the booth left to check in.

Bert handed me my modified Ping-Pong paddle with a grunt. I swiped it, glaring. "You owe me, leaving me defenseless against that tiny toothy monstrosity!"

Bert scratched his head. "Can't be that bad. Julian took it home."

Of course he had. At least I didn't have to worry about it anymore.

Unless . . . "The next bring-your-pet-to-work day's a while off, yeah?"

Bert chuckled, ducking into a silver Kia Kitsune.

"That's not an answer!" I shook a fist at him as he buzzed down the lot to the car wash.

A few more minutes, and the cars were cleared, with no new ones on the horizon. I slipped back inside.

"All done. You needed help here?"

Keisha, still tidying the counter with Doak, grabbed her tablet and turned to me. "Nah, but we need to start on de-stormproofing the lot. Come on."

Back outside we went.

"These are the cars slated to go out in the next few hours." Keisha jabbed her tablet screen, and little red lights flared above a dozen bays down the rows of cars. "Let's clear those first, and then we can start on the rest."

I sighed, contemplating the dirty buffers destined for the shop, and rotated my battered shoulder. Manual labor for the win.

Alex pulled up in one of the few pickup trucks on the lot—most of our customers are tourists or business folk, not locals wanting to haul a charybdis tank they found on Craigslist for a steal. I pointed to the closest lit-up bay, and she parked the truck beside it.

A handful of scrapes and pinched fingers later, we'd denuded the first batch of cars, the truck bed overflowing with buffers. Alex climbed into the cab, her face red, her short hair sweaty. I didn't look any better.

She revved the engine. "Be right back. Unfortunately." She grinned ruefully and took off.

I didn't bother getting up from the asphalt where I'd unhooked the last eyebolt. Time for a breather.

"Cookie?"

I twitched, snapping my eyes open. A plate of peanut butter cookies swam in front of my face, Keisha smiling on the other side.

"Heck yeah." I reached out, my shoulder protesting my dastardly behavior—how dare I want a sugary morsel of deliciousness?

Keisha whipped the plate away just as I was grazing the surface of a plastic-wrapped cookie. "Wait, you're not allergic to peanuts, are you?"

"Nope."

"Oh good." The plate drifted back under my nose, and I grabbed up a homemade peanut butter cookie complete with a crosshatch in the soft center.

I started unpicking the plastic wrap. "That would suck, to miss out on the daily cookie because of an allergy."

"Oh, you wouldn't miss out. I've got a box of double-fudge that I made separate."

I swallowed, my salivary glands insisting I get my hands on one of those too. "Think you'll run out?"

Keisha grinned. "Assuming our whole shop team isn't allergic, I maybe could spare one for you when you head out."

I gave a triumphant fist pump.

Keisha's smile faded. "When you're done, come on back inside again. There's a guy who needs to speak with you. I'll cover you while you're in there."

"A guy?" I sat up, licking the last crumbs from my lips. "That's specific. Someone I know?"

"No, he's an investigator with Gravis-Witherspoon."

An investigator? Gravis-Witherspoon was some highfalutin insurance company, wasn't it? Maybe Saskia Skies used them. I clambered to my feet and brushed the grit off my pants. "He's here because the counter got tossed?"

Keisha waved dismissively. "No, airport security's looking into that. This is about some incident yesterday, I'm really not sure what. Did anything happen that you didn't tell me about?"

My heart stopped for half a second. Something unusual that had happened yesterday, worth an impromptu visit from an insurance investigator?

Like maybe my sticky fingers snagging a probably priceless artifact out of someone's car?

I gulped.

Redcaps and rutabagas, how much trouble was I in?

QUESTIONS & QUAGMIRES

I hooked my shaky fingers through my belt loops. "Uh, no, nothing I can think of." I beamed a hopefully convincing smile. "Same old, same old."

Keisha bobbed her head once. "Well, let me know what he says, yeah? He just had me pull up some security footage, but it all looked normal to me. No ghouls hefting storage tubes of smuggled artwork or void diamonds or anything."

"Sure thing." My eyes flicked up at the nearest security camera. How long had I gawked at the artifact in full view of the cameras, before pocketing it?

No, it would be fine—I'd paged and called and emailed the owner, after all. There'd be a record of at least the phone call and email. The guy was probably just here to collect the artifact and ensure I hadn't scuffed it up too bad.

Or fed it to my demon.

That might be a bit awkward to explain.

"Well? You going or not?" Keisha tossed back her purple hair and held out a hand.

"Right, yeah." I unslung my scanner from my shoulder and passed it over. "See ya."

Hopefully.

Was it really that likely they'd cart me off? As long as they gave me a chance to explain things, I should be in the clear.

I headed inside, using my jeans to wipe the sweat off my palms. Here went nothing.

The automatic door ushered me in with a whoosh, and I scanned the small rental concourse. Our counter was almost back to its original state, albeit with a bag of trash waiting to go out, complete with a couple chicken feathers clinging to the plastic.

Doak must've gotten extra flustered.

He was checking someone in—back in his human form—and a few people formed a line with carry-ons and suitcases. The other rental counters were moderately busy too, and no one really stood out as not belonging . . .

There.

Almost hidden by the counter, a guy in his early thirties was perched on one of the bench seats against the wall, scribbling on a tablet. He had a suit like most of the business people loitering around, but his lack of a carry-on was a dead giveaway.

Nobody gets on a plane without some kind of bag to stash their munchies or noise-cancelling headphones in.

Well, except marsupiafae, but the rest of us don't have handy-dandy stomach pouches.

He glanced up at me right as I was gawping at him, and he stood with a smile.

A smile? That was a good sign.

Actually, he looked pretty nonthreatening overall. He was tall, slim, with tanned skin and acorn brown hair. A pair of hipster glasses framed his greenish-hazel eyes.

"Immy Cordell?" He walked toward me, one hand out. "I'm Fitz Greymoore, with Gravis-Witherspoon."

My anxiety had me blurting the first thing that popped into my head as I shook his hand.

"Fitz? What, like Fitzwilliam Darcy?"

His smile deepened, bringing out a dimple and the laugh lines at the corners of his eyes. "Except I don't make today's equivalent of ten thousand pounds a year."

I squinted up at him, then stole his tablet and did a quick search.

Damn, that really was what Darcy made in the book.

I poked him in the arm, creasing the navy blue suit fabric—you never know when some bored fae will dream you up a hallucination. But he was solid, and warm. I pulled back.

"Huh. You're real."

He chuckled a tad nervously as I handed him back the tablet. I *was* acting like a mildly crazy person. "I hope so. Otherwise I'll be really bummed about all the hours I've wasted running reports at work."

"You're not bummed about that already?" I smirked.

"Well . . . maybe." He ducked his head.

He didn't have a British accent, but his voice was soft and deep, soothing to listen to in a rumble-your-chest kind of way.

I didn't have any more good comebacks, and our banter stalled. "So, uh, Keisha said you needed me for something?"

My fingers might've been crossed behind my back.

"Yes, I just have a couple questions. If you'll come this way." He waved toward the door behind the counter that led to Saskia Skies' little office.

I hurried after him, and the last dregs of the LivingDead DreamStopper must've decided to kick in all at once, because I bounced alarmingly high, arms flailing for balance, and nearly crashed into poor Fitz on the way down.

Eyes wide, he grabbed my arm and steadied me until I found my footing. "Are you always this light on your feet in the morning?"

I gave an awkward laugh. "Not so much. My roommate made my . . . coffee this morning, and it's a little peppier than I'm used to. Hoping that wears off soon."

He held open the door. "Let me know if we need to tie a string around you to keep you from floating off."

I bit my lip, trying not to smile. "Deal." How was he so charming? If he was here to get me in trouble, it was really gonna ruin my whole day.

We stepped inside the office, and he gestured toward a bank of monitors with black-and-white security footage pulled up on a loop, the people on the screen walking for ten or fifteen seconds before jolting back to the beginning again.

The only sign of me was two sneakers propped up on the desk inside the booth, and the top half of the book I'd been reading, just visible through the window. As the footage played, both disappeared from view, and right before it looped, my curly mop poked out of the door.

And then the video stuttered back to the beginning.

No grand-theft artifact in sight.

Phew.

Fitz rattled a rolly stool over in front of the screens and patted the seat helpfully, the torn faux leather catching on his fingers. He tugged them free with a little shake, and I sat as he cleared his throat.

"I already spoke with your manager, and reviewed the security footage. Do you remember this woman?" Fitz tapped one of the screens with a finger, and I zeroed in on the grainy grey figure.

She climbed out of a Chrysler—no telling what color—and pulled a carry-on out the passenger-side door. Her hair looked white on the screen, the elegant long bob flapping in the mild breeze.

I did remember her, vaguely. She'd been halfway to the airport entrance by the time I scrambled out of my booth to check in her car.

"Yeah, I saw her yesterday."

Fitz leaned in. "Anything unusual about her?"

"Not that I noticed." I shrugged. "She was in a hurry, but so's everybody. Sorry. What's special about her?"

He glanced away. "We just need to find her, that's all. Nothing out of the ordinary."

Riiight.

He stepped away from the screen as I spun back and forth on the stool. "Did she speak to you at all, or interact in any way?"

"No, I only saw her from a distance, as she was walking toward the airport. I never even saw her face till just now."

Fitz pursed his lips, then sighed. "Well, if you see her again, I need to know. Let me give you my card—"

He tugged a sleek black rectangle out of his inner suit pocket and held it out between two fingers. *Fitz Greymoore, Insurance Investigator, Gravis-Witherspoon.* A phone number and email were the only other details. I tucked it away in my back jeans pocket.

"That's it, then? Nothing else?" It seemed like he didn't have any idea about my artifact snatching, and I was perfectly happy to keep it that way.

"There is one other thing you can help me with."

"Yeah?"

Fitz gave a sheepish smile. "I'm new to Saskia Springs . . . Is there anywhere you'd recommend for dinner?"

I blinked. That hadn't been on my list of potential follow-ups, but at least it was an easy question.

"Oh, sure." I eyeballed him again. He didn't look like the picky, prissy type, and his suit was nice enough that he probably wasn't pinching pennies like me. "Anything you don't eat?"

"Not much." With a flick, he reset the monitors to play the live camera feed.

I kicked around on the stool as I contemplated. "Hmm . . . There's this great ramen place over on Callahan. The entrance looks like a beat-up back alley security door, but it's legit. You can't go wrong with anything on the menu, honestly."

"Sounds great. What's your favorite of theirs?"

"Ooh, tough choice." I thought for a minute, starting to salivate— good thing my lunch break was coming up, even if it was only a chicken pot pie the size of a postage stamp. "Probably their bao buns. The pork belly is to die for."

He fiddled around with a map on his tablet, zooming in and out, trying to find the building.

"Here." I stole the tablet and swiped over to the restaurant, which was tucked between a smallfolk shoe store and an actuary. "That's the place."

"Thanks. I'm notorious for never being able to find things." He shut off the tablet and paused, drumming his fingers on the glass screen. "I don't suppose you'd be willing to come along . . . ?"

I screeched to a halt in my stool-swiveling.

Had Mr. Tall, Funny, and Not Mr. Darcy just asked me out on a *date*?

PRESENT PALOOZA

Was he asking me out? No way. I had to look like death warmed over, or at least like I was on crack, between the lack of sleep and whatever the LivingDead was doing to me.

"Uh, no, I don't really do the dating thing." Not since Tucker.

"Oh, sorry, that's not what I meant." Fitz scuffed a hand along the back of his head. "Not that you're not— I mean, not that I wouldn't want—"

My smile broadened as he dug himself further into his awkward hole.

He stopped, sucking in a deep breath. "Can we start over?"

I nodded, amused.

He held out his hand again, and I shook it. "Hi, I'm Fitz. I need a tour guide, and I can pay in ramen. Does that work for you?"

I tapped my chin with a finger. "Hmm . . . payment in ramen, huh? What if I want those bao buns? Or takoyaki?"

"Good point. Payment in dinners, then."

"Dinners, plural?" I raised an eyebrow. "Dunno if you want to commit to that, I might be a terrible tour guide."

"All right, start with *one* dinner. You drive a hard bargain."

I muffled a laugh. "I can do one dinner."

"Tonight?"

"Well, I already have plans tonight . . ." Damarion's blood runs were usually pretty short, but there'd been a couple that had dragged on for hours, and I didn't want to leave him in the lurch to play tour guide.

I expected Fitz to do the typical guy thing of trying to wheedle me out of my plans, or getting offended, thinking I was making excuses.

Instead, he just nodded. "Tomorrow?"

I blinked. "Tomorrow works."

"Super. Eight o'clock?"

I grimaced. "I get up at four in the morning for work, so that would definitely keep me out past my bedtime." And after the night I'd had last night—well, this morning, blergh—it would for sure take me at least a couple days to recover. I fought a yawn just thinking about it.

"No problem. What time would work best for you? I can do anytime after five."

"Six?"

"Perfect."

While he made a note on his tablet, I pulled out his business card and went to send him a text. Exceeept my phone was back at my place, bricked.

There *was* an email listed on his business card . . .

I swiveled to the computer beside the security monitors, which was awake and unlocked, and I logged into my email real quick.

"What are you doing?"

"One sec." Tip of my tongue between my teeth, I typed out an email:

Your tour of Saskia Springs is scheduled for 6 p.m. tomorrow evening. Please remember to bring your fanny pack, and secure your belongings against hobgoblin pickpockets.

I signed it and sent it off into the ether. This way, if he got completely lost, he could at least blow up my computer with frantic emails. Not that that would do him much good, but it was better than nothing.

Maybe I could con Bracchius into letting me borrow his phone?

Fitz's phone chimed in his pocket, and he pulled it out. A second later he glanced up at me with a smile in his eyes. "Got your confirmation email. Good to know about the fanny pack, thanks."

I bowed grandiloquently from my stool, which spun beneath me and almost dumped me on the floor face-first. I coughed. "Glad to help."

"No phone?"

"Busted it yesterday."

"Oof, sorry."

"Thanks." I got up off the stool. "I'd better get back to work."

He ushered me to the door, but stayed in the office himself. "I've got to scrub through the footage a few more times. I'll see you tomorrow?"

"Unless I get run over by a minotaur first!" I only half joked. It had been that sort of week.

I headed back out to the rental lot, tiredness seeping into my bones. That last jolt of antigravity must've been the final drop of LivingDead working its way out of my system—I definitely wasn't feeling light on my feet any longer. I slogged up to Keisha, who was just wrapping up a damage check on a newly returned car.

"Mmback." I held out a hand for the scanner.

She faced me and folded her arms. "What'd that insurance guy do, suck the life right out of you? Are you okay?"

I shrugged. "Had a rough night. Iz catching up with me."

"What kind of rough night?"

I launched into a rambly retelling of all the nonsense of the last eighteen hours or so, and only got about halfway through it before Keisha cut me off.

"Go home."

"What?" I blinked rapidly, clearing the blurriness of a yawn from my eyes.

"Go. Home. You're asleep on your feet, and the last thing I need is to scrape your corpse off the pavement when you stumble in front of the wrong car. I'll see if Julian can come in early, otherwise I'll cover your shift myself."

"You don't have t—"

"No, but I'm gonna. Do you *wanna* become pixie food? No? Then get out of here! Get some rest."

I didn't argue. You're supposed to do what your manager says, right? And I was beat.

Moving like a sloth, I got my things together and somehow managed to trade my work polo for the normal-people clothes in my bag.

The subway ride home was like a dream, probably because I was asleep on my feet for half of it, one arm hooked firmly around a pole to keep me from toppling.

Pretty sure the kerfluffle snuggling up to my toes for a few minutes wasn't a hallucination, though.

Trudging the several blocks to my place in the cool air woke me up a bit, at least enough so I didn't drift off the sidewalk. The crows cawed along my route, but I waved them off with a floppy arm.

"Later, guys, sorry. You'll have to deal."

It took me longer than it should have to locate my keys, then locate the *right* key, but I got there eventually. I opened the door and did a double take.

Had I somehow walked into someone else's place by mistake? I wouldn't put it past me.

I ducked my head back out to check the apartment number, which was correct. Huh. I peered inside again.

Everything was immaculate, cleaner than it had been in, well, ever. Heck, it hadn't looked this good when I moved in.

The carpet could've been brand new, fluffy and five shades lighter than it had been, with no traffic patterns worn into it—or snail slime gluing it down. More light flooded through the small windows, and the kitchen positively sparkled. Even the turquoise doormat beneath my feet was dirt-free, bright as the day Damarion had given it to me.

"You're home!" Bracchius blooped out from under the sofa, the skirt draping across his head as he emerged. He drifted up and settled on a sofa cushion, bouncing excitedly.

Yup, the brownies had really done a bang-up job, but amidst the glamour of cleanliness, one thing stuck out.

The coffee table looked like the present table at a five-year-old's birthday party, every inch of the surface absolutely jam-packed with gift bags and wrapped boxes, tissue paper and curly ribbons abounding.

"Uh . . . Bracchius?" I surveyed the present palooza with suspicion. "Did I forget someone's birthday?"

What *was* the date, anyway? I glanced at the mini-dragon-themed calendar on the wall.

It wasn't a major holiday. Bracchius's birthday is October 13th, the same as National M&M Day—don't get me started on the ball pit's worth of shimmer M&M's I had to swim through in the living room last year. I mean, it was my own fault, but still.

My birthday's September 16th, and I *really* didn't think Bracchius would be throwing a surprise party of any kind for Kor the day after he kidnapped Sparkles, which left . . . no one.

So what was with the presents?

Bracchius bobbed closer as I dumped my bag and kicked off my shoes. "I didn't have time this morning to properly thank you for rescuing Sparkles, so I spent some time today putting together an appropriate thank you." He beamed.

"This . . . This is all for *me*?" I plopped on the floor in front of the table, criss-cross applesauce.

"Well, there's still one coming." He bounced up onto the sofa and elongated, peering toward the window. "I didn't expect you home for a few more hours."

I swallowed a yawn. "Yeah, Keisha sent me home early to get some more sleep."

"Oh . . ." Bracchius deflated slightly. "You can open these after your nap, if you want. You must be tired."

"No way, I'm opening these now." I snatched up the first present, a Girl-Scout-cookie-sized box wrapped in gold paper. "If that's okay, that is?"

Bracchius resumed his perky spherical shape. "Yes! Go ahead."

I am not a deliberative gift opener. I know there are people out there who carefully peel back the Scotch tape so it doesn't ruin the wrapping paper, fold the paper up neatly to reuse later, and make a tidy pile of bows and ribbons.

Not me. When it comes to presents, I'm like a three-year-old playing Godzilla, Destroyer of Decorations.

I tore into the first present, and a few seconds later, a pile of shredded wrapping paper littered my lap. The box in my hands was plastered with photos of the unicorn Lego set inside, and highlighted the play features: 'Movable legs!' 'Change the color of the mane and tail!' 'Unicorn horn shoots real rainbows when you tap the sigil on its tummy!'

Grinning, I shook the box, rattling all the tiny plastic pieces inside. "You gonna help me when I build this?"

The red flickers within Bracchius went wild. "Yes!! Really, you want me to help? Thank you! Ooh, I can't wait." He spun a full 360 on the sofa cushion, and I laughed.

"No, thank *you*." I set the box down, and realized Bracchius's own unicorn was uncharacteristically absent. He usually kept Sparkles within arm's reach.

"Did Kor give you any trouble while I was at work?"

"Nope! He hasn't come back since you chewed him out this morning."

Probably plotting his revenge. It was definitely time for another talk about roommate boundaries and acceptable behavior.

Not that it would stick, if the last three times were any indication.

"Then where's Sparkles?"

"Oh, I had to hide her—the brownies wanted to give her a makeover."

"Haven't they left?"

"Noo, they're still patching up the bathroom."

Now that he mentioned it, I could hear the whine of what might be a miniature electric drill coming from that direction. I leaned right to peer down the hallway.

"Don't look! They'll never finish if they think you're spying on them!"

"Right, sorry." I refocused on the presents.

"Open this one next!" He extended a blobby little appendage toward a gift bag on his side of the table.

I grabbed the purple handles and plucked out the tissue paper as the bag swung toward me. A fruity scent wafted up from inside, along with a plasticky crinkle as I shoved my hand in.

"Peach gummy rings!" I held up the bag like a prize before tearing into the corner and shaking the sugar-coated rings onto the table. I popped one in my mouth. "It's a good thing Kor *isn't* here—he might get jealous."

"Not of those, he wouldn't. He only likes the charcoal-chili flavor."

Yech.

"I meant in general." I swept a hand to encompass the gifts and massacred wrapping. "Have you *ever* given him a gift?"

"Him?? Why would I ever give that insufferable, self-centered, nasty . . ." Bracchius trailed off and stared at the presents for a minute. "Do . . . Do you think that's why he's so mean?"

I offered Bracchius a gummy ring, but he swiveled slightly and drew back. More for me.

Chewing, I considered his question. "Because you've never given him a present? No. But bullies sometimes get that way because nobody's really ever nice to them—or mostly mean. Being nice probably won't work miracles, but it might help."

I could stand to listen to my own advice, but sometimes Kor was just so, *so* freaking aggravating.

Bracchius's red flickers swirled thoughtfully. "I suppose I could try doing something nice for him. *One* thing."

"That's all a girl can ask. Which present next?"

He rolled onto the table and pointed out a square box with a pink glitter bow on top. "Might as well get that one over with."

I glanced at him curiously, but he didn't elaborate. I yanked off the top and upended the box onto a shimmery silver piece of crumpled tissue paper, revealing what could only be described as a hodgepodge.

"This is . . . interesting."

Bracchius twitched in a demon shrug. "When the crows found out what I was up to, they wanted to chip in."

I looked at the veritable treasure trove of crow goodies—bottle caps, a molted pixie wing, mica-flecked pebbles, a couple aluminum wyvern scales, street sweeper bristles. Was that a *pegasus* feather?

This was at least a week's worth of collecting by the whole murder, an extremely generous gesture.

"They care this much about you and Sparkles?"

Bracchius toyed with the pixie wing with one blobby appendage. "Nah, I think they just want to make sure you never stop feeding them."

That made *much* more sense.

Another yawn reared its ugly head, this one refusing to be quashed.

"Okay, there's one more I want you to open before you go to sleep!" Bracchius hopped over to a tiny gift that could fit in my palm. "Please?"

I smiled. "Like I'd say no to opening another present."

He shuffled aside, and I picked up the bitty package. A few rips later, I held a block of sticky notes in my hand, the paper a pretty pastel gradient.

My jaw dropped, and I whipped my hand up to see the block better.

The bottom-right corner of the sticky note was decorated with a little chibi illustration of Bracchius hugging Sparkles, complete with pink blushie marks on Bracchius's cheeks.

I riffled the corner of the block, confirming the custom illustration was printed on every single note, and giggled. "This is adorable!"

If Bracchius could've blushed in real life, he would've been.

Heck if I know, though—maybe demons blush black.

He bobbed happily on the table. "You always seem to need sticky notes to remind yourself of things, so I thought this might help."

I glanced at the wall above my rickety desk, which was graffitied in sticky notes with passwords, reminders, and random factoids.

"You're not wrong. These are perfect, thanks!"

I held out my fist, and Bracchius poked out an appendage to give me a mini fist bump.

Just as I was flipping through the sticky notes again, the doorbell rang.

Well, I say rang, but it was more like the strangled gasp of someone who accidentally inhaled a chime sprite on their morning jog.

Apparently that was one thing the brownies hadn't fixed.

Yet.

Bracchius plopped off the table. "Ooh, your last gift must be here! Close your eyes!"

"Really?"

"Yes!"

"All right, all right."

I rolled my eyes as I covered them with my fingers, trying not to imagine what other kind of crazy gift Bracchius would've special ordered.

If there was a real live unicorn at the door, I was calling it quits.

DEMON DELIVERY

The door creaked open, but I kept my hands firmly planted over my eyes.

"Bracchius Doommonger?" the delivery gal asked.

"That's me!"

I stifled a snort. I never could take his last name seriously, but apparently his folks'd had high hopes.

"Sign here."

"Oh. Just a second."

Bracchius's blobby form probably wasn't the best for scribbling signatures. Would he change shape to sign for the package?

I couldn't help it. I peeked.

A chubby black cherub fluttered his wings four feet off the ground at my open front door, wielding an outsize pen in his bitty hand.

Actually, 'cherub' was too angelic of a term for a demon. What *did* you call a demonic cherub?

A beelzebub?

Bracchius scrawled something on the delivery girl's tablet, then made grabby hands for the small package tucked under her arm. She checked the signature, then handed the box over.

"Have a nice day!"

I flung my hands over my face as Bracchius turned my way, package in cherub-hand, shortly followed by a clunk on the table.

"Okay, you can look!"

Cracking another yawn, I lowered my hands. Bracchius was back to normal, and the same innocuous brown box sat on the table amidst the wrapping wreckage.

Why had he wanted me to close my eyes if there wasn't anything spoilery to see?

Little drama demon.

"Open it!"

I looked at the heavy-duty packaging tape entombing the cardboard. "You got a utility knife on you?"

"Oh. Nope."

I scrambled back up off the floor and tugged open the sticky drawer of the credenza, grabbing a knife. The package was open in no time flat.

Within a nest of crumpled kraft paper lay a sleek, featureless black box. Hmm. I lifted the box out and slid off the outer shell.

A glossy black phone gleamed up at me from a dark pillowy cushion.

"Wha—? Bracchius, this is too much. A new *phone*?"

And unlike the phone I'd bricked last night, this wasn't a five-year-old fewest-possible-frills iPhone, either. I didn't dare contemplate how much this high-class sliver of technology had cost.

"It's actually not too much." Bracchius sounded awfully self-satisfied. "I called the Mercenary Guild and asked how much they charge for defeating a typhon and a shadelurk. After reassuring the panicked receptionist that there *wasn't* a rampaging typhon loose in the city, and admitting that I didn't know what a shadelurk was either, she told me the going rate for a typhon takedown. And that number was bigger than the cost of everything on this table, including the phone."

Well, I couldn't really argue with that.

The phone lit up when I lifted it off its luxe cushion. Already charged? Nice. I flipped it over to check the brand, but it was so fancy, they hadn't even bothered putting a logo on it.

I touched my thumb to the screen out of habit to unlock it. Duh, that wasn't going to wo—

It unlocked.

To my thumbprint.

A brand-new phone.

I peered at it suspiciously. The wallpaper and app icons were the same as my dead phone. I opened the messages app, and all my old conversations popped up.

"But . . . this just arrived. How did you get it set up already? My apps, my texts . . ." I tapped another app. "My *photos*?"

"What do you *mean*, how did I—" Bracchius puffed up a little. "I'm a *demon*, Immy!"

He was right. As long as other demons weren't involved, Bracchius could pull off pretty much any damn thing he wanted to.

Including cloning my phone into a new mystery phone in a warehouse on the other side of the city somewhere.

Hey, no complaints.

I slid my fingers over the velvety surface. "What is it, anyway?"

Bracchius tilted back. "It's . . . a phone, Immy."

I sputtered. "I know *that*! What brand is it?"

"Oh, it's an Obsidian. You really need to be more specific when you ask questions, you know."

"You really need to assume I'm not an ignorant pinecone, you know," I shot back.

"Pinecone?"

I swatted a hand in his direction. "Whatever."

Another yawn overtook me, and I went hunting for the alarm on the phone. It was exactly where I'd expected. I set it for an hour before I needed to meet up with Damarion.

"Thank you, Bracchius, really. These gifts are wonderful, especially the phone. I'll have to open the rest later, but right now I seriously need to crash."

"You're welcome! Do you need me to wake you again?"

"Nah." I shook the phone. "This'll take care of it."

"Oh, right. It also has some other features you should know about . . ."

He paused as a yawn befitting a Morpheusan assaulted me.

". . . but we can go over those later."

I gave him an awkward double thumbs-up, still clutching the phone, and traipsed down the hallway, past the whine and buzz of brownie industry coming from the bathroom. I opened the door to my bedroom.

Tumbling onto the mussed sheets, I sank my head into my pillow and was a goner within a minute.

The trill of my alarm pulled me from a dream about a hippogriff parade, and I scrubbed a hand across my face, trying to decide how alive I felt.

Actually, not too bad.

I sat up, kicking the tangled sheets off my legs, and blinked in the afternoon light. Right, it was still today. Just a nap, not a whole night's sleep.

Bracchius peeked around the doorframe. "Awake?"

I waved a floppy arm. "Think so."

The movement brought my thoroughly messed-up tattoo within view, and I cradled my wrist in my other hand. With any luck, the somnubus venom from last night had completely cleared my system by now.

Tip of my tongue between my lips, I concentrated on the blownout ink. A push here, a pull there . . . The ink responded the way I wanted, and moments later I'd reformed my tattoo into its usual rib cage with poppies.

Sweet.

No more somnubus venom for me, that was for sure.

Bracchius rolled a little further into the room. "The brownies left while you were sleeping. Bathroom's all fixed."

Good thing, too. I would've totally forgotten about them and probably gotten halfway to scandalizing them before I realized they were there.

I started getting ready, and dug out the tiny bottle of weird lotion Ruby had given me for my newest tattoo before I could forget it, setting it on the bathroom counter. The bandage should stay on for another eight or nine hours, but I checked it to make sure the tattoo looked okay.

A bit pink still, but considering what I'd put it through in the last however-many hours, it was healing up like a champ.

A text came in from Damarion on my shiny new phone. I grinned, stroking the soft surface again. Ugh, I probably looked obsessed. I shot back a text that yes, I would meet him at his place in thirty minutes.

I munched on some peach gummies as I contemplated more substantial food—no way would I make it through the next few hours on just these. The fridge was getting depressingly empty; I'd have to go grocery shopping pronto.

In the meantime, I stuffed my face with a Baby Bel cheese that'd rolled to the back of the fridge, chugged down the last dregs of orange juice, and shook one remaining granola bar out of a box on top of the fridge.

Make that *very* pronto.

I was unwrapping another present on the coffee table when Bracchius scooted out from under the sofa, Sparkles in tow this time.

"There's our favorite unicorn!" I patted Sparkles on the head as Bracchius heaved her up onto the sofa beside me.

Then I froze.

Something shimmery was dangling out of Bracchius's, well . . .

Demonly derriere.

MY, WHAT SHARP TEETH YOU HAVE

Hand still hovering over Sparkles's fuzzy head, I cleared my throat.

Bracchius bounced a little, fixated on the gift I'd been tearing into. "Well, open it already!"

The motion jiggled the silvery substance hanging out of his butt—a fine chain.

Horrified realization dawned just as a tiny ceramic parakeet pendant slid out of Bracchius's dark form to dangle at the end of the chain flopped off the edge of the sofa cushion.

"Bracchius . . . You've got a little something . . ." I pointed, my nose wrinkled.

"Hmm?" Bracchius swiveled, dragging my poor beleaguered parakeet across the cushion behind him as he went.

"Stop!" I reached for it, then hesitated an inch away. Did I really want to touch it?

Bracchius caught sight of it, and the red flickers inside him bloomed closer to the surface in what had to be a demon blush. He quickly hopped over, hiding the chain and pendant beneath him, and probably resubsuming it.

"So *that's* what was itching . . . How embarrassing, sorry. Can we forget about that? Please?"

I nodded absently, my thoughts on a more concerning track. If Bracchius couldn't tell when something he'd subsumed was dangling half out of him, how effective could hiding it with him really be?

If the artifact peeked out, even for a minute, would it be trackable again? How long would it need to be exposed for the baddies to pick up on it, to zero in on my apartment?

Heck, if they'd found my address in the ransacked paperwork at the rental counter, they might be waiting for the slightest indication that I had it here, and then *wham*—they'd tear this place apart just as viciously.

Or maybe more, since this place had way fewer prying eyes than the airport.

"Is there any chance the artifact poked out like that?"

"No, that I'd definitely notice. This necklace is just so small and fiddly . . . Does it need to stay attached? Is that important?"

I shook my head. "I forgot to take the artifact off the necklace before I gave it to you, that's all." Truth be told, I'd forgotten about the necklace entirely. It must've gotten tangled up in the rings of the artifact after I took it off.

"Then let me just give it back to you. Problem solved!"

I leaned back on reflex, not really wanting to touch something that had been floating around Bracchius's insides if I didn't have to. "That's okay."

"I've already unclasped it, just hold out your hand."

He'd unclasped it *inside* him? Was that the demon version of tying a cherry stem into a knot with your tongue?

I cringed back further, and Bracchius tilted slightly to one side. "What's the matter?"

"Nothing."

"It's obviously something. 'Fess up."

I almost smiled at his order—he'd definitely picked up some of my speech patterns since moving in.

"I, um, ah . . . I'm not sure I'm comfortable handling something that you just"—I mulled over my word choice. Pooped out? Regurgitated? Evicted from his substance?—"expelled."

Bracchius puffed up again. Poor demon. I really was putting him through a whiplash of emotions today.

"I'm an extremely sanitary being, thank you very much. Haven't you heard of cleansing fires?"

I narrowed my eyes. "Isn't that a religious thing? Like holy fire?"

He scoffed. "Like there isn't such a thing as *un*holy fire."

I pointed at the parakeet once again dangling unceremoniously out of his butt. "If that went through an unholy fire, wouldn't it be charcoal?"

Bracchius hopped off the necklace, leaving it lying on the sofa cushion. "Okay, fine, no fire involved, but I'm still twenty-seven-hundred times more sanitary than you are! You wear this thing around your neck, where it collects sweat and salts and"—a shudder raced across him—"dead *skin*, and who knows what else. Inside me, it only collects a refreshing demonly aura."

"You live on the floor, buster—where all that dead skin ends up. How is that any better?"

"Nice try. That's just dust, and it doesn't adhere to me unless I choose to let it. Which I *don't*."

I paused, mouth open. Did he really not know?

Did I want to be the one to disillusion him?

One hundred percent.

"Bracchius . . . what exactly do you think dust is made of?"

He swiveled side to side. "I dunno . . . uh . . . pixie dust, rock and dirt bits, pollen, unicorn glitter?"

I bent and shoved a hand under the sofa skirt, swiping a finger in the under-the-couch dust, and sat back up.

Huh. There *was* actually a bit of glitter.

I really needed to get a Roomba.

Well, win it in a sweepstakes, more like, but still.

I held my dusty finger under his metaphorical nose. "Outside, sure. But inside, it's mostly dead skin." I ruffled my curls with the other hand, releasing a subtle shower of loose hairs and a few flakes. "*My* dead skin."

Bracchius stared at my finger, perfectly still, for about thirty seconds before he proceeded to yick out of existence.

I waited for the existential whimpers and wails to quiet, the dramatic pancaking and shriveling and hiding behind throw pillows to subside. At long last, he stopped twitching, just visible behind the furthest pillow.

I couldn't resist. "There's dust back there too, y'know."

Five minutes later, he'd seemingly come to terms with it, though his blobby form drifted half an inch above the sofa—above the dust.

Figuring if dust freaked him out that much, his insides probably couldn't be *that* bad, I scooped up the necklace and clasped it around my neck, the little parakeet resting just above the collar of my T-shirt.

"Well, I've gotta go meet Damarion. Do yourself a favor, and don't look up eyelash mites while I'm gone."

"Eyelash—"

I slung my bag over my shoulder and rushed out the door before I could witness another midimmortality crisis. Hey, at least I hadn't pointed out how dusty Sparkles must be.

I'm not *that* mean.

I walked the couple blocks to Damarion's place—all it takes to move from a crummy neighborhood to a ritzy one, in this part of town. The houses got bigger, the paint fresher; the potholes vanished, and the parked cars glistened.

A lot fewer chewing gum sprites, too.

Damarion's place was three stories tall, the driveway flanked by palm trees—not exactly native this far north, but he could afford the warming spells. A balcony curved out from the second story, catching the afternoon sun.

I strode up the clean stone walkway to the massive front door, and tapped the sigil on the center panel with a spark of my magic. Magenta flared along the sigil's lines, and a resounding *boom* echoed through the house three times, more dramatic than any physical knocker ever invented.

Damarion's doorman swung the door inward on silent hinges and gave me a half bow. "Miss Immy."

"Mr. Greco." I inclined my head with a smile, then raised my voice. "You ready to go, Da—"

I pulled up short.

Damarion was nowhere to be seen. Instead, a regal woman in her sixties or seventies commanded a velvet armchair, her pose perfect, her aura arresting—in a hairs-standing-up-on-the-back-of-your-neck kinda way.

Her white-blonde hair was immaculately coiffed, complementing her silver eyes.

She finished patting a cloth napkin against her lips and lowered it, a bright red stain stark against the white fabric. A smile graced her face, revealing sharp, pointy teeth.

"Why, don't you look positively delicious."

"Be nice, Cynna." Damarion clattered down the marble stairs, tying his tie. His silver hair was immaculate, styled long on the top and short on the sides, his just-there beard the same length as always.

I breathed a sigh of relief as he joined us. I didn't *think* the woman was going to eat me, but really, you never know.

"I *am* being nice. Are you telling me 'delicious' is no longer an acceptable compliment?"

"I'm not sure it ever was, my dear."

"The Archduke of Hambly was quite taken by it right before I hoisted him on a spit." She patted her silver-blonde updo delicately. "It's a shame one can't get away with such things any longer. Villainy was quite fun before it all became tax evasion and drug-running and defrauding the elderly. Amateurs. No one knows how to put a proper scare into people these days."

She bared her pointy teeth in an elegant, dazzling grin, her silver eyes boring into mine. "Do they, darling?"

I scrambled for an appropriate response, but she turned to Damarion before I thought of anything.

"Oh my, do you think I'm alarming your little lamb here? I'd hate for her heart to burst from terror."

Damarion snorted. "Hardly. You might find Immy has a different reaction to idle threats than most, Cynna. Take that as a warning."

"Mmm, I like her already." She held up a hand toward me, limp at the wrist, her long nails a shimmery black. "Please, let's introduce ourselves properly."

I stepped closer, ready to shove my wallet between her sharp teeth in a flash if needed, and took her hand, gently pressing her fingers to my lips. She must be older than she looked, if this was her default greeting.

"I'm Immy." I dipped slightly, an awkward curtsy in jeans.

"Cynna. Charmed. Not many would dare to touch me, even at my invitation." She glanced back at Damarion. "Brave, this one."

More like uninformed.

I started racking my brain for all the various beings that matched her characteristics, not that I knew much about her yet. Probably immortal, pointy teeth, silver eyes, bit bloodthirsty . . .

"She is that." Damarion gave me a less toothy smile.

A smear of white sunblock clung to his chin, and I reached up, rubbing it in with a thumb.

Damarion quirked an eyebrow.

"Sunscreen."

"Ah, my thanks. Ready to go?"

I adjusted my purse on my shoulder. "The backpacks?"

Damarion bounced the heel of his hand off his forehead. "Of course. I was distracted by my guest. One moment."

He bounded back up the stairs.

Cynna leaned forward in her chair. "He hasn't told me about you, darling. He doesn't take feedmates or bloodlings, so you are . . . ?"

I shrugged. "Just a friend."

"A rare honor, to be the friend of someone such as Damarion." She settled back against the teal velvet, eyeing me lazily. "But then, the same might be said of you, I suspect."

"There's just something about me?" I quipped.

That jaguar smile returned. "Something, yes. Tell me, would you take offense if I were to court you as a friend?"

I blinked. What was I, a girl in a regency romance? "Court me . . . as a *friend*?"

"That is indeed what I proposed."

Did I dare say no to the toothy lady? Not that I really wanted to—she seemed pretty kickass. Eh, what the heck.

"Sure. Court away."

Her eyes gleamed as Damarion hurried back down the stairs, two empty backpacks looped over his shoulder.

My backpack was a delightful clash of neon oranges and pinks warring with lemon lime; aqua raced along the seams and accented the zipper pulls. It was loud, proud, and didn't even make my back hurt when it was full of blood bags.

Damarion's bag, on the other hand, was sleek leather in browns and blacks. Sophisticated, if a bit boring. But it did the job.

"Anything before I go, Cynna?"

"I'm sure your Mr. Greco here can take care of me quite well in your absence. Enjoy your little jaunt."

"I daresay we will."

Eyes narrowed, I nodded to Cynna. "Looking forward to our courtship." Hopefully it didn't entail her taking bites out of me. Or leaving a carcass on my doorstep for my 'enjoyment.'

"As do I. You will make a scintillating addition to my coterie."

Damarion ushered me out the door as I slung the bright backpack over my shoulder. His first few steps outside were exaggerated, his polished shoes catching the light. They were wingtip Oxfords, brown and black to match his backpack. And no, I'm not really a shoe person. But you couldn't spend time with Damarion and not pick up a few things.

I indulged him. "Oh, are those the new shoes you wanted to break in? They're . . ." He'd be insulted by 'nice,' and 'bodacious' seemed over the top. ". . . pretty spiffy."

His gait returned to normal. "Thank you! I quite enjoy them."

Compliment paid, I steered the conversation in the direction I really wanted to go. I pointed over my shoulder at the house, and Cynna. "What is she?"

Damarion shrugged. "She's Cynna."

"So, you have no idea."

"Nope. Terrifying, though. I make it my highest priority to stay on her good side."

"She wants to court me. As a friend."

"So I noticed. It was wise of you to accept. She's a redoubtable ally, in both senses of the word."

Guess I'd see what came of it. "How long's she staying with you?"

"Until she leaves."

I huffed a laugh. "That kind of houseguest, eh?"

"Perennially."

We left his neighborhood, headed the opposite direction of mine, toward the Emendelmiria pedestrian district, which was full of little shops, restaurants, cafés, and parks. The sun soaked into my skin, and Damarion's cardamom cologne tinged the air—he made a habit of mixing it into his sunblock, to avoid that poolside scent.

A couple blocks from Vein & Vice, we passed Santiago's Street Eats, a mile-long permanent food truck pod—and dragon hoard. I plucked at Damarion's sleeve. "On the way back, can we . . . ?"

He chuckled. "Why you feel the need to ask every time is beyond me. I already had it on my agenda, but we'll need to make another short stop first."

I raised an eyebrow, but he didn't enlighten me. Ah well. If he was feeding me, I was willing to put up with a mystery errand.

On Vicente Way, we found the first signs of vampire groupies—the main reason I was keeping Damarion company. Nobody would mistake *me* for a vampire, and my presence at his side was—usually—enough to deter all the fanatics and kinksters who'd otherwise fling themselves at his feet, begging to be made a bloodling or just sucked dry entirely.

I shuddered. Sure, vampires could be sexy, but who wanted to become a shriveled husk on the side of the road?

Not me.

As we approached, the few fanatics lying in wait were replaced by an organized line for Vein & Vice—beings willing to donate blood through official channels, rather than ambush any vampire in the neighborhood.

Think of the ridiculous lines at midnight of opening day for Lord of the Rings or the Marvel movies, the lines that go out the door and around the block. Add fake plastic—or veneer—fangs, blood drop tattoos, and goth makeup, and you've got the line for Vein & Vice.

Well, the line for hopeful donators, that is. Vampires—and handy-dandy vamp assistants—get to use the express lane.

In other words, we could walk right in.

First, we had to make it past the groupie gauntlet around the door, though. I grabbed Damarion's arm and led him into the morass of ripped fishnet stockings, crimson lipstick, and 'Bite Me' T-shirts.

VEIN & VICE

I swatted an errant tail aside as we wove between the groupies at the head of the line. "All this for a glorified blood bank."

Damarion kept a fixed smile on his face as he muttered between his teeth. "Don't call it that in front of the patrons, Immy. You'll ruin the mystique. Do you really think our fans would show up in these numbers if this looked like one of your concrete-slab plasma centers?"

He was right. Vein & Vice had absolutely zilch in common with your run-of-the-mill plasma center or Red Cross donation setup. It was like 'velvet baroque sitting room' meets 'high-class dominatrix dungeon.'

The crowd stirred as we wrestled our way through. "Is that a vamp?"

"Mmm, I'd let him taste me any d—"

I jostled around a suspiciously-normal-looking hulk of a guy on his cell phone, who gave me flashbacks to my stalker the night before. A bouncer, maybe?

He rumbled, "Got it," before sliding his phone into his pocket.

A girl decked out in black from head to toe—except for her teased hot-pink hair—caught sight of Damarion. A grin spread across her face, and she squeezed through the crowd in our direction. I swung Damarion ahead of me, thwarting her efforts to get close.

Unfortunately, I almost shoved him face-first into a delivery golem leaving Vein & Vice. He skirted the golem smoothly, barely a hair ruffled, and glanced at me over his shoulder.

"I appreciate the enthusiasm, Immy, but perhaps a helping of restraint to go with it?" He reached for the door.

Something pinched the back of my arm, and I swatted at it. Mosquito? Pixie?

My hand came away pest-free, but a speck of blood dotted my palm. I whirled around, but no obvious fliers hovered nearby, and nobody looked like they'd just stuck a needle—or a fang—in me, so I let it go. Probably an overzealous mosquito.

After all, the groupies were here to be fed *on*, not to do any feeding themselves.

Damarion held the door for me, and cool air enveloped me, welcome after the sweaty bustle of the crowd. I stepped into darkness, and gave my eyes a moment to adjust.

Mood lighting highlighted certain areas of the room while leaving the rest in shadow: On the left, black velvet thrones where volunteer donors were seated after approval, their blood drawn by conventional medical means. A more opulent crimson throne on the right, where a randomly chosen groupie was honored with a live feeding—what most of the mob outside was hoping for, even though their chances were slim.

A lounge area hosted recovering patrons sipping at complimentary drinks, snacking at a grazing table, flirting with the vampire servers. Doors at the back led to private rooms, where patrons with deep pockets could purchase more deluxe experiences.

Another bouncer ushered us to one of several hostesses arrayed at the entrance, each dressed elegantly, sexily, with flawless makeup and bloodred lips.

"Damarion, nice to see you again. Here to procure the usual, or for something more special?"

"Just the usual."

My attention drifted as they moved into small talk. The next hostess over was entering a donor's information on her tablet.

"Species?"

"Plain Jane human, ma'am."

"Blood type?"

"O-negative."

Damarion brushed my shoulder as he leaned in. "Don't tell them, but we pass all the O-negative blood along to the hospitals. Stuff's got no flavor, and you humans need it more than we do."

"Really?"

He nodded.

We followed the hostess to a sunken lounge area near the back, more exclusive than where the bulk of the donors were milling. A black nightclub-style sofa wrapped around a low glass table with an untouched charcuterie board.

It wouldn't stay untouched for long, now that I'd spotted it.

"Anastasia will be with you momentarily." The hostess dipped her head and returned to the front.

Damarion took a seat, setting his backpack down. I sank onto the plush sofa beside him, eyeing the cheese and ditching my bag as well. "So, what blood type tastes the best?"

"Oh, it's about so much more than type, Immy. Age of the donor, vintage of the blood, lipid ratios, and a dozen other things."

I shook my head. "You missed your calling as a blood sommelier."

"Me?" He chuckled. "I have no interest in telling anyone else what to drink. But I know my own tastes."

"So, ignoring all that other nonsense, what's your favorite type?"

"A-plus."

I scoffed. "Figures."

I'd never gotten an A-plus in *anything*, including blood. At least Damarion wouldn't be vamping me anytime soon—not that I'd ever thought that was a concern.

Scooting forward, I snagged a few crackers from the charcuterie board and helped myself to a smattering of cheeses. Mmm, and some grapes.

They were so crisp, they crunched when I bit into them.

There was a natural ebb and flow as patrons moved from their dark thrones to the main lounge area, and fresh donors took their seats. Each vampire attendant lavished attention on their throne's new occupant while needles and vials were switched out behind them, and the small black tables sterilized.

I swallowed my second bite of cracker with goat cheese. "They must pay well, to get so many vampires to work here."

Damarion followed my gaze. "Most of the attendants aren't actually vampires. You can make a lot in tips, playing the part."

Huh. Their fanged smiles looked real enough.

I snagged another couple crackers and smeared them with cheese.

"You'll spoil your appetite for the food trucks."

"Nah, I'm like a bottomless pit."

A door clicked shut behind us, and I turned. The woman approaching had skin almost as dark as the room's velvet, her lipstick a stark contrast. Her sumptuous curves belonged to an era of oil paintings and palanquins; she looked like a queen, and it was safe to say she'd be worshipped like one here.

Anastasia smiled, revealing her fangs. "Damarion, it's been too long. We might have to limit your order quantities, to keep you visiting more often. And Immy, yes?"

She remembered me from last time—good memory.

"That's me."

Anastasia gestured behind her to a slim younger man carrying a tray with three wineglasses, the bowls rivaling a brandy snifter. A blood snifter?

No way they'd call it anything so inelegant.

Anastasia pulled out a tablet as the waiter set the tray on the table in front of us. A scant half-inch of blood coated the bottom of each glass.

"Please, feel free to sample our latest special varieties. Limited stock, and quite an unusual treat. We have panther shifter, a doppelgänger blend, and lastly, cherub."

The waiter indicated each glass as she spoke, the blood in each a different shade: deep crimson, shocking red, and the last almost pink.

"Thank you, Anastasia." Damarion didn't bother looking at the glasses. "I'll have my usual order of the Sinful Serum blend. And the same quantity as before, unless you are serious about luring me back in sooner." His eyes crinkled.

"I suppose we will manage without you for another few months." Anastasia sighed, but her smile never left her. "Just give your bags to Juan, and I'll get it taken care of. Please enjoy yourselves in the meantime."

We handed over our empty backpacks, and Juan slung them over one forearm like a butler with a polishing cloth. Anastasia and Damarion chatted a moment more, while I contemplated the glasses on the tray.

Panther shifter blood, eh? Damarion might not be feeling adventuresome, but that had nothing to do with me.

I cradled the first glass in my hands and swirled the blood delicately, letting the aroma drift upward.

Hey, I can be sophisticated when I wanna be.

The tang of copper, ammonia, and musk assaulted me, and I coughed.

Damarion smirked beside me. "The bouquet not to your taste?"

"Don't think so, no." My voice came out a bit strangled. "The others any better?"

"Only one way to find out."

I scowled at him, hoping he'd crack, but his smirk just softened to an amused smile. He knew my curiosity was killing me.

"Go on."

"Ugh, fine."

I set the first glass down and grabbed the second. Swirl, lift, sniff.

This one wasn't as bad. Meaning it didn't immediately repel me—not that I'd be chugging the stuff anytime soon.

Rust, salt, and something fresh, like spring water.

"This one's the doppelgänger, right?"

"Correct."

Next time I saw one—not that it was easy to tell—I'd have to compliment them on the bouquet of their blood.

Or was that too morbid?

The last glass smelled sweet, like burnt sugar and rose petals overlaying metal warmed by the sun.

"What is this, vampire dessert wine?"

"Something like that."

"But you don't like it."

Damarion shrugged. "Why chase the pricier blends that come and go? There's nothing worse than having a craving for a rare variety when it's impossible to come by. I prefer my regular blend."

A sharp voice cut into our conversation. "Ah yes, that *does* sound like the Damarion we all know and love *so* dearly. Daring to break out of the mold is simply a step too far, isn't it?"

I jerked my head up at the newcomer descending into the sunken lounge. The man was startlingly tall, in his seventies or eighties, and dressed to the nines. Granted, the latter was true of everyone in the room except the groupies. And me.

Guess I was ruining the ambiance a bit.

Damarion glared up at him. "Ambrose. Such an unaccustomed pleasure."

The two hadn't broken eye contact since Ambrose had first spoken, and the rising tension was palpable. I gently set down the glass, afraid to break the spell of hateful silence.

Though, if the ruby gleam in Ambrose's eye was anything to go by, all the hells were about to break loose, regardless.

FRIENDS & NEMESES

Ambrose halted on the other side of the low glass table. "Rather like stepping on a rusty nail, I find. Only less invigorating."

Damarion gazed up at Ambrose through half-lidded eyes. "Does that happen to you often? Sounds like you might need to splurge on a pair of shoes worth more than ten dollars."

Ambrose's crimson gaze flicked over to me, almost watchful. "If you knew what this scoundrel has done in his past, you would not so closely associate with him. I'm certain you are deserving of worthier company." He stepped around the table, offering his arm. "Would you join me? I can offer you far more than this backstabber can."

"Not on your life." I scooted further back on the dark velvet sofa.

His eyes shuttered. "Have it your way, then."

A door just past Ambrose opened, letting an attendant into the lounge area, and revealing just a sliver of the private room she'd come from: red and black decor, dim lighting, and a muscled arm wrapped in black rope and secured to the wall.

Annoying Ambrose was definitely on my menu, so I leaned in to Damarion and pointed as the door swung shut. "How much does *that* cost?"

"More than you could afford, so don't get your hopes up."

I scoffed. "I wasn't asking for me!"

It's not like I'm a prude. I'd just . . . rather be the one in charge.

Damarion smiled, doing a good job of ignoring Ambrose himself. "Just curious, I know."

The high-and-mighty vamp might as well have had steam billowing out of his ears. Unfortunately, the same attendant rushed over and spoiled all our efforts at ignoring him.

"Lord Ambrose, we weren't expecting you. Let me take you to the private lounge, and we will have your room ready in just a moment."

Ambrose cast a resentful look over his shoulder as she led him away, but it was directed at me, not Damarion. Weird. Was he really that bothered by me turning down his pathetic offer?

I'da thunk vampires were a little more unflappable than that.

Damarion usually was.

I shook it off and got down to the business of grilling Damarion, facing him cross-legged on the sofa. "So what in the three hells was all that about?"

He waited until Ambrose had been whisked out of sight, then flopped his head back against the sofa. "An old . . . acquaintance. Doesn't like me much."

"No, really." I rolled my eyes. "Come on, spill."

Damarion sighed. "We knew each other before we were turned."

Wow. That was *way* back at the grey dawn of time.

"And?"

"And when I became what I am"—he waved a limp hand along his body—"he asked me to turn him. I refused."

"Well, yeah, who would wanna spend eternity with that jerk?"

"It wasn't that. We were actually on good terms, almost friends, back then. Before."

I tilted my head. "Then why not?"

Damarion shrugged, jostling his still-flopped head. "I thought it was a curse. At that time, the cons were definitely more prominent than the pros. There were no blood banks"—I smirked at his use of the term he'd scolded me for just a little while ago—"no fridges, no sunscreen. In many places, vampires were even hunted. I didn't want to curse him as well."

"But he wanted immortality."

"And he got it, later on. But by then, he was bitter, and we certainly were no longer friends."

"So that's what, a five-hundred-year grudge? Hasn't the guy ever heard of 'forgive and forget'? He got what he wanted, after all. If you ignore the few extra wrinkles."

Damarion leaned over. "And significantly sparser hair."

I burst out laughing and gave him a playful shove. "Stop! Poor guy."

"I suppose."

I reached around the goblets of blood and helped myself to some more of the charcuterie goodies. The closest attendant was explaining the virtues of a vampire venom tattoo to the groupie on her black throne as she drew their blood.

"It's completely invisible except under black light. The venom itself has an anti-inflammatory and sterilizing effect, so you don't need to worry about infection or laborious aftercare."

Damn. Maybe I should have gotten one of those instead of the white ink tattoo. It hadn't even crossed my mind.

The attendant pointed to a second sunken lounge lit with black lights. "Those chosen for the crimson throne will often socialize there. The lights allow you to see the venom. When we're finished here, please take a look."

I knew all about the crimson-throne tattoos, having gotten an eyeful on past visits with Damarion. When the lucky winner was done being fed on, they were granted the additional privilege of an exclusive tattoo to mark the occasion: a pair of fangs, with a single blood drop. An extra blood drop was added if you were ever picked again.

And yeah, groupies were constantly whipping out their tattoos—and egos—to one-up each other.

I poked Damarion's knee, and he opened his eyes, looking hopeful. They didn't usually take this long to bring out his blood.

"Nobody here yet, sorry. How much does a vampire venom tattoo run?"

He closed his eyes again. "I believe it's anywhere from three to ten thousand dollars, depending on the complexity."

Neeever mind. Just a smidge out of my budget—only a teensy bit.

Plus, I'd have to be packing a portable black light in my pocket at all times in order to manipulate the ink.

And we all know how good I am at hanging on to important things.

A door snicked closed, and Anastasia drifted our way, followed by the same dude with our backpacks—which looked considerably heavier. I elbowed Damarion, and he sat up.

"Thank you so much for your patience, Damarion, Immy. It is always an adventure running a business such as this." She bestowed a fang-tipped smile upon us.

The waiter slash bellhop guy held out my raucously colored backpack, and I nearly dropped it. Did these things get heavier each time? Kelpies and caterwauls, this thing was like a sack of cinderblocks.

I stashed it between my feet and massaged my still-recovering-from-typhon-bashing shoulder.

Damarion took his own backpack with much more grace. "It's never a hardship to wait in such accommodating surroundings. You've billed the usual account?"

"Of course, Damarion. If there's anything else you need before you leave, please let me know. And, as always, stay as long as you wish."

Anastasia inclined her head and swept the lackey along in her wake.

Damarion slid toward me. "Shoulder troubling you?"

I dropped my hand. "Yeah. I busted it up pretty good last night."

How was that only last night? I needed a serious vacation.

"Let me see."

Damarion gently shifted my arm around, testing my range of motion and taking note of my winces. He'd been a doctor at some point—1720s? 1940s? 2002? Heck if I knew—so he at least had some idea what he was doing.

"That's a bad bruise. I don't think it's sprained, though, and definitely not fractured. If it's too bothersome, you might seek the services of a caladrian masseuse."

Ha. Like I could afford that.

What I *could* do was grit my teeth and bear it.

He released my arm and gave me a sympathetic glance. "I know a good one, if—"

"Nah, I'll be fine. I'll just take it easy for a few days."

"Please do. Shall we go?"

"What, you're not even gonna check your bag?" I unzipped my backpack. Inside was a rich black velvet drawstring bag just smaller than the backpack. I teased open the top, revealing two cut-faeglass decanters filled with ruby liquid, cushioned by a foam divider. The matching stoppers were sealed with marbled black and crimson wax.

A red-foil-stamped card dangled from one of the drawstrings. The side opposite the logo read: *Best stored chilled. Best served at room temperature.*

Cold radiated from the laptop compartment of the backpack, and I peeked inside. Even the friggin' ice pack was branded—the black plastic embossed with red foil for the Vein & Vice logo. That was new.

I left it up to Damarion to make sure the blood itself was the right kind.

"Inspected to your satisfaction?" Damarion stood, easily shouldering his bag.

"Yeah, whatever." I slung the backpack over my non-pissed-off shoulder, and almost toppled like the Leaning Tower of Pisa. Damarion held out a cautious hand, but I righted myself and hefted the bag higher on my shoulder. "All good."

The attendants helped part the sea of groupies on our way out—after all, if the merchandise broke on the premises thanks to their own patrons, they'd be on the hook to replace it. They really oughta have a secret exit, not that it would stay that way for long.

We emerged into the sunshine, and I squinted my eyes shut until the world wasn't a blaring white. Damarion tugged me along till we were free of the crowd.

"You said you had some kinda errand to run?"

"Not precisely an errand, but yes." He pulled a sleek grey tube out of his vest pocket and unscrewed the cap, then dabbed a little extra sunscreen across his face and neck. "Do you know where Ouroboros Yoga Studio is?"

"Don't tell me you've taken up Pilates. Actually, don't tell me you're trying to sign *me* up for Pilates." I made a cross with my forefingers and held them toward him, mock warding him off. The backpack slid down my shoulder, and I snatched at the strap before it could go too far.

Damarion fiddled with his phone. "You'll see."

That wasn't ominous at all.

"Ah, here it is." He tucked away his phone and started down the street. "This way."

Pilates, here we hopefully don't come.

I took comfort in the fact that we at least wouldn't be doing Pilates *today*. Not with Damarion strutting around in his fancy suit.

That didn't mean he didn't have designs on my future, though.

Damarion paused at a corner, glancing between his phone and a nearby building. "There it is!" He waved for me to follow him.

Like I wasn't already.

I blew a curl out of my face and grudgingly kept playing baby duckling. There was food at the end of this detour, after all.

The Ouroboros Yoga Studio was one of those highfalutin modern buildings of glass and wood, with an artistically slanted roof with massive spaced beams. At night, you'd be able to see everything happening on all three floors through the glass front wall. Right now, it was just an overbright reflection of the street.

"After you." Damarion swept open the door and ushered me inside.

Fragrant whispers of sandalwood, chalk, and sweat filled the lobby, which was decorated with plants. An elevator waited ahead, and wide stairs headed both directions.

"This way." Damarion started down the stairs.

What kind of weird-ass classes did they hold in the *basement* of a yoga studio? Troglofae hip-hop?

The backpack of blood was already getting heavy on my shoulders, and I regretted agreeing to this detour. Not that my shoulders wouldn't be equally pissed off when we trekked over to Street Eats, but there at least I'd have nummy food to distract me.

We hit the bottom of the stairway in a dim hallway. Voices echoed from further ahead—young voices. Like, elementary-school young.

I peered suspiciously up at Damarion. Were we sneaking up on a kindergarten kickboxing class or something?

It could be some of the smaller denizens of Saskia Springs—hobgoblins, brownies, satyrs—but they tended to sound different.

Damarion held out a restraining hand as we approached an open doorway, lights on inside. I slowed, but peeked my head around the doorframe to get a look.

Human kids sat in a circle of chairs, feet mostly dangling above the floorboards. Weird that there weren't *any* kids of other species—had we stumbled upon a human-supremacy preschool?

Also weird that there weren't any adults in the room.

And that most of these kids were wearing seriously non-kid-friendly outfits. I mean, a tiny Victorian dress that laced up the front, really?

Someone's mom enjoyed playing dress-up a little too much.

One of the kids was mid-yammer. "And then not only did they refuse to let me see it, they kicked me out of the museum! Insisting I was 'too young' to be on the premises unaccompanied! What chutzpah."

A five-year-old girl with auburn hair nodded seriously. "It's always a trial when museums refuse to recognize the claims of rightful owners. I believe Gerry has a legal contact who can help you with paperwork to submit through official channels. Gerry, would you stand?"

A little boy with brown skin and curly black hair hopped down from his metal folding chair and waved. "Come find me after the meeting, Clark."

What in the?

I stepped closer to Damarion. "Exactly *why* are we here?"

"To pick up Cynna's sister, Aster. She is also staying with me at present." He pointed at a girl facing away from us, her white-blonde hair a perfect match to Cynna's.

She couldn't be older than eight.

She and Cynna were sisters? How was the eight-year-old the sister of a—best guess—six-hundred-year-old? Were they half-sisters? Maybe their father was even longer-lived than Cynna.

"That's Cynna's little sister?"

Damarion shook his head with a smile. "Aster is Cynna's *older* sister."

I gaped like an aquafae—the fishy kind, that is. Merpeople usually have the sense to keep their mouths closed.

The screech of chairs kept my brain from going off Tangent Cliff. The kids were folding their chairs, dragging them over to stand in rows against the wall. Some of the older kids took pity on the younger ones struggling not to get crushed by chairs nearly twice their size. A couple pillaged donut boxes laid out on tables at the back of the room.

My eyes widened as a little Asian girl clambered up on a stool and pumped out a generous cup of coffee from a carafe before going on her merry way. She flashed me a pointy-toothed smile as she toddled by.

I turned on Damarion, eyes narrowed. "Is this . . . a mini vampire support group?"

He chortled. "Yes, but don't let them hear you call them that! They've got enough grievances as it is."

A throat cleared behind me, and way down. I put on my best don't-hate-the-lady-who-just-called-you-mini smile and faced Aster.

She was *adorable*. Rosy cheeks, reddish brown eyes, a snub nose, and silvery freckles. Put pigtails on her, and you'd have the next Mini-Miss USA.

I winced internally—there I go again.

"Hi!" Despite my best efforts, my voice came out like I was talking to a puppy. Crud.

Aster craned her neck to meet Damarion's eyes. "Is this a friend of yours?"

"Aster, this is Immy." The little vampire girl's eyes widened. "Immy, this is Aster."

"*You're* Immy?" Aster beamed. "Damarion's told me so much about you!"

Great, she didn't hate me. Now if I could just keep myself from talking like a sugar-snorting grandma, we should be good.

"That's me." I ran my tongue over my teeth. "I'm afraid to ask what he's told you, though."

Aster giggled. "All the juicy stuff, of course."

I glared daggers at Damarion. "Just how many people are you regaling with my secrets?"

"I wouldn't call them *secrets* . . ."

Aster tugged at my arm. "I wouldn't be mad if I were you. He makes you seem pretty cool."

I elbowed him anyway. "Cut it out. Cynna, now Aster . . . I don't need even *more* immortal beings wanting me to be their playmate."

Aster's face fell.

"Oh no no no no." I hovered my hands over her shoulders. "I didn't mean you. I just worry that the next person who comes along might want to play cat to my mouse, and I've got enough to deal with."

I was worried enough about Cynna's threatened 'courting,' but Aster didn't need to know that.

"Okay."

I crouched in front of her. "I'm serious. I'm really not a lie-to-your-face kinda girl, unless you're trying to kill me—then all bets are off. You're not gonna try and kill me, right?"

"Not anytime soon." The tips of her fangs showed in a mischievous grin.

I rolled my eyes. Between her and Cynna, I didn't stand a chance. "Guess I'd better stay on your good side."

We headed up the stairs and out of the building. Damarion took a step in the direction of the food trucks, then paused.

"Immy was hoping to visit Santiago's. Is that all right with you, or would you rather I take you home first?"

I licked my lips. "It's really okay, we don't have t—"

But Aster bounced on her toes. "Do you know if there's still that truck that we ate at last time? The one with the blood caviar?"

Damarion cocked his head. "I believe it's still part of Santiago's hoard, yes."

"Yay! Let's go." Aster took off, and we followed.

It didn't take much effort for me to catch up. "So, you're older than Cynna, but you talk like, well, someone young. Modern. Hip. Whatever." I cringed. "No offense."

Aster giggled, then pointed at her head. "Child brain. I'm still *really* good at picking up on everything around me."

"Don't get her started on how many languages she speaks," Damarion muttered.

"You're just jealous because I outstripped you years ago, and you can't keep up, old man." Aster winked up at me.

Damarion thwapped a hand to his chest, faux wilting. "You wound me, child. I may never recover."

A few blocks over, we turned the corner onto Greenscale Street. Food trucks lined both curbs for as far as the eye could see—well, my eye, anyway. A griffin could see further, no problemo.

The sizzle of food, chatter of the crowd, and whirr of blenders at the nearby juice truck brought the street to life. The scent of chilis and fresh strawberries washed over me, and my stomach growled. Where to head first?

Aster surveyed the teeming crowd, then plucked at my wrist. "Would you mind holding my hand? Don't wanna get lost in there, and Damarion's hands are scratchy."

Damarion stiffened. "They are not!"

"Are too. Maybe you should use more moisturizer."

I smirked as I offered my hand. "Struggles of being a height-challenged vamp?"

"Struggles of being a height-challenged *anything*." She sighed and clasped on.

We'd only made it past the first two trucks—Pulped and Cannoli Imagine—when wind buffeted us from above and behind, nearly knocking me flat. Aster clung to my legs as I turned.

A shadow enveloped us, cooling my sun-warmed skin, and I peered up.

At the silhouette of a massive dragon coming right for us.

SANTIAGO'S STREET EATS

Aster squeaked and ducked behind my legs, but I hefted her onto one hip and hurried out of the way, Damarion following suit.

The green dragon flapped his wings above us, sending dust and discarded paper napkins flying. My curls decided this was a good time to completely block my vision, but I managed to keep my feet amidst the bustle as the crowd parted, people crushing together to create a landing zone for the dragon.

At least the giant glittery fae wing in my face was clean.

Not sure I could say the same about the gremlin who'd hopped on my shoe to avoid being trampled, though.

With one more buffeting flap, the dragon touched down on the asphalt, wings held awkwardly above our heads for just a moment before they vanished with a shimmer and the scent of fennel.

Air rushed into the suddenly unoccupied space, and Santiago stood in the center of the open asphalt in human form. He was short, with a lithe muscularity, and wavy brown hair tied at the nape of his neck.

He grinned magnanimously, white teeth stark against his light brown skin, and held out his arms. "Such a delight to see so many admirers of my hoard! Please, continue to enjoy your evening!"

Everybody shuffled back into the street as he walked to the nearest food truck. The gremlin loosened her grip on my shin and disappeared into the crowd with a "Thanks!"

I set Aster down sheepishly, raking my curls into place. "Sorry for the, uh, indignity?" Centuries-old vamps probably didn't appreciate being yanked around like little kids, no matter how much they looked like one.

She smoothed her dress, which had hitched up a bit with my manhandling—girlhandling? Whatever. She smiled up at me. "I appreciate not being crushed by a dragon more than I mind being grabbed. Especially since you were only being nice."

"Awesome." My stomach grumbled again, and Aster took my hand.

"Let's get you something to eat!" She glanced over her shoulder. "Coming, Damarion?"

Aster in tow, I made a beeline straight for Picante, but got distracted by a new truck I'd never seen before: Totine. I squeezed Aster's hand.

"Do you wanna go to your blood truck with Damarion while I check this place out?"

She shook her head, her loose white-blonde curls bouncing. "That one's further down anyway, and I like exploring."

I peered at the menu as we stood in line. Their specialty was poutine, but with tater tots instead of french fries. They had half a dozen options: classic, buffalo, hangover . . .

A blue-and-purple parrot strutted along the counter and squawked down at me, "What'll it be?"

"Classic, please." Can't go wrong with that, right?

"Small, medium, or large?" The parrot gestured a wing at three take-out boxes taped to the truck just above the window.

I glanced at Damarion, who shrugged. He was paying, but I didn't want to go *too* overboard. "Medium."

The parrot screeched my order into the depths of the truck. "That'll be ten dollars."

Damarion stepped forward and paid. The parrot caught my eyes over his shoulder. "Name?"

"Immy."

It set a talon on a stack of flat-pack take-out boxes, and blue magic zapped into the sigil printed on the box. The parrot hopped back as the box popped into shape. "Two minutes!"

The three of us scooted over to wait. The juice truck next door had almost the whole side of the truck folded down, displaying a zillion different fresh fruits and veggies. A willowy green fae woman reached out, swiping a thumb over a small blemish on a starfruit and glamouring it away. She caught me staring, and winked before shuffling down to a new customer.

"Immy!" the parrot squawked.

I grabbed the steaming take-out box and some chopsticks from the counter. Unfolding the top, I stuck my nose in, breathing in the savory aroma, before greedily shoveling in a mouthful of tater tots, cheese curds, and gravy.

Yum.

I offered the box to Aster. "Wanna try?"

"Yes please!"

I glanced from my gravy-coated chopsticks to the line at the truck window. "You a germophobe?"

Most vamps weren't—when you can down raw blood and trust your super-duper immune system to KO whatever weird diseases are floating around in there, a little incidental spit-swapping is pretty low on the threat-meter. But you never know what someone will get squicked out by.

She rolled her eyes and commandeered my chopsticks, helping herself to a bite. "Tasty!"

I raised an eyebrow at Damarion, but he just smirked and shook his head. Purist.

Next up was Sanguinsation. Aster got a little paper cone of blood caviar—pea-sized glistening ruby-red globules that burst in your mouth like fruit boba, only way more macabre.

Well, not *my* mouth. Her mouth. I'm only so adventuresome.

She did manage to convince Damarion to try one, though. His expression morphed from grudging resignation to pleasant surprise.

The line at my go-to—Picante—was longer, and Damarion wandered off, leaving a credit card with me. Aster tugged on my hand as we waited.

"I didn't want to ask in front of Damarion, but . . ." She picked at the edge of her paper cone. "Well, he's a bit more highbrow, and there are places in the city I'd really like to go, that aren't . . ."

I smiled. "That aren't really his style?"

"Exactly. And I can't go by myself, because . . ." She looked down at her child's body and shrugged. "Would you be willing to go with me sometime?"

They probably wouldn't even let her shop at the grocery store by herself, never mind let her into the city's nightlife scene. No wonder the mini vamps had a support group.

I resisted the urge to ruffle her hair. "Sure! As long as it's not like a brain bar or something, that's not really my thing."

Her nose wrinkled. "No, I was thinking Comet, the club."

"Ooh, nice. Samaire and I have been wanting to go there again now that they've remodeled." I pursed my lips, not sure if this was supposed to be a one-on-one invitation. "Samaire's one of my friends, she's part siren. Would you mind her coming with us?"

"That would be great!" Aster beamed. "I've always wanted a girl gang."

I laughed, and she ducked her head with a giggle as we moved up to the counter.

"Immy! Been a while. The usual?" Rajaki glanced down at Aster. "And anything for ya little friend?"

She twisted her lips but shook her head.

"Yup, the usual." I swiped the pen from behind Rajaki's ear with only a startled protest from him, and I scrawled out a note on a napkin: *Don't call my friend little. Apologize?*

He scuffed a hand along the back of his head as his tan skin flushed the tiniest bit. He peered down at Aster. "Sorry for calling ya little. I'm Rajaki. You?"

"Aster. And that's okay, I get that all the time."

"Which is probably why it's so annoying, huh?" He fumbled in the pocket of his apron, and passed me a wrinkled card. "Ice cream on me, yeah? For both ya. At Rollin', right down there." He pointed down the street, then raised a brow at Aster. "Assuming ya like ice cream."

She nodded vigorously, and I handed her the coupon as I paid with Damarion's card. Plate of street tacos in hand, I approached the salsa dispenser and stared dubiously at the sigil marking each kind—salsa roja, pineapple-jalapeño, avocado-tomatillo. With my luck these last twenty-four hours, I'd create a blockwide salsa-splosion rather than dispense cute little squirts.

Aster cocked her head. "Don't know what you want?"

"I do. I've just been having some . . . magical issues lately."

She hovered a hand over the sigils. "Which one?"

"Pineapple."

I held my tacos under the nozzle, and Aster zapped the sigil with a spark of silver magic. A perfect drizzle of salsa dropped onto my taco, and we repeated for each one. "Thanks."

Three bites in, I noticed a pink bloom on Aster's cheek. "Oh crap. You got sunblock with you?"

Aster's eyes widened as she shook her head.

"Hold this." I shoved my folded plate into her hands and heaved her up onto one hip again, hurrying into the busy street. "Damarion!" Where was that blasted vampire? "Damarion!"

A suit-jacketed arm lifted above the crowd, and I jogged toward it.

Damarion frowned as I set Aster in the cover of his shadow. "What's the matter?"

"Sunblock." I made grabby hands.

He pulled out his tube. I snatched it and unscrewed the fiddly cap with my teeth, then crouched in front of Aster. I smeared a healthy dose across her reddening cheek, working it in. Over her shoulder, I caught sight of a tall, blocky guy a dozen feet away.

The supposed bouncer from Vein & Vice.

Our eyes met, and he flicked his away, shifting out of sight in the crowd.

Demons and demagogues. I *was* being followed.

A-freaking-gain.

My thumb slowed on Aster's cheek, and I pulled my attention back to her. Make sure the cute little vampire doesn't get third-degree burns, *then* worry about the hulking stalker.

"Anywhere else?" I circled my finger.

Aster turned slowly, clutching my taco plate as I checked her arms, legs, the back of her neck. I dabbed sunblock a few more places to be safe.

"What did you see?" she whispered, returning the tacos.

"An annoying jerkface." I stood—more difficult than usual with a zillion pounds of blood riding my back—and handed Damarion the sunblock.

He tucked it into his breast pocket, shifting his backpack strap. "Someone you know?"

"Not exactly." I scanned the crowd, but my lurker kept out of sight. "That guy from outside Vein & Vice."

Damarion looked supremely unconcerned. "The bouncer?"

I pursed my lips. "If he even *was* a bouncer. People keep stalking me."

He could have easily followed me here from the blood bank, but how would he have known to pick up my trail *there*? Without the artifact or my old phone on me, these losers shouldn't have any way to track me.

My heart skipped. They *shouldn't* have any way to track me . . . unless they knew where I lived.

This dude could have followed me from home to Damarion's, then Vein & Vice. The ransacked rental counter flashed through my mind. When they hadn't found the artifact in lost and found, what was there to stop them from rifling through personnel files?

I shot off a text one-handed to Keisha: Any chance those bozos got employee info from the counter?

She didn't respond right away, so I slipped my phone back in my pocket.

"Immy, if he's a bouncer at Vein & Vice, surely this is a natural place for him to eat lunch. It's highly unlikely he's following us. Do you even see him anymore?"

"No . . ." That wasn't gonna keep me from watching the crowds like a griffin, though.

Damarion sighed. "Either way, you'll be fine with us. When we're done, I'll see you safely to your door, yes?"

Aster tugged my hand. "Nobody's getting past me!"

I couldn't help but smile. It was *seriously* hard to remember the little vamp was like twenty-seven times my age. "Thanks, yeah."

The tang of pineapple salsa hit my nose, and I glanced at my practically untouched tacos. Might as well enjoy 'em if Fake Bouncer Guy wasn't ready to shake me down yet.

I picked up the half-eaten taco, folding the bitty double tortilla to keep the toppings from doing a lemming off Taco Cliff. Then I jammed it in my mouth.

My eyes closed as the almost-citrus burst of pineapple blended with the heat of jalapeño, mellowed out by the savory slow-cooked beef falling apart in my mouth.

Mmm mm mm-mm mmm.

I opened my eyes to grab the next taco. Jerkface Stalker stared at me from across the crowd, and I growled.

"Guard these with your unlife." I handed the tacos back to Aster, then slung off the backpack of blood and shoved it at Damarion. "Here."

"What are you—"

"Be right back."

I ducked into the crowd and speed-walked in his direction, annoying some tourists but managing not to knock anybody's food out of their hands. Jerkface saw me coming, and made a lame effort to act like he hadn't noticed and didn't care, casually strolling away.

But I was faster, and didn't give a flying furball what the crowds thought of me.

He turned away as I caught up, pretending to read the menu at WaffleBus, but I stepped in front of him. He spun again; I followed. Finally, he gazed down at me without trying to sniggle away. "What?"

I planted my hands on my hips. "I know what you're doing, and what you're after." His eyes narrowed. "I don't have it anymore, I gave it to the authorities."

His lashes fluttered, one-two.

Gotcha.

Realistically, I probably *should* give the stupid bauble to the authorities, but it's easier to buy someone in power than to get past my stubbornness, especially when you've been doing a *seriously* fantastic job of pissing me off.

"See?" I turned out my front jeans pockets, spilling lint and pennies to the pavement. I lifted my pant cuffs, revealing three inches of unshaven ankles. I patted myself down. Ran my fingers through my curls. Spun around twice, arms raised.

By the time I was shaking out each shoe, he looked like he regretted his choice of stalking a crazy lady across town.

I stepped back into my shoes and jabbed a finger in his face. "Following me isn't gonna get you what you want, so just leave me alone."

He held his hands up and backed up a step.

A tug at my elbow brought me around to face Damarion, who was cringing—at my behavior or the neon backpack clashing with his suit, I wasn't sure.

"My deepest apologies, sir." He kept pulling me away, Aster just behind him.

I could've dug in my heels, but I'd made my point. I freed my arm and took a few steps away. When I glanced back, Stalker Dude was gone again.

Damarion huffed and held out my backpack when we found an open place to stand. "Have you lost your mind? What good do you think that will have done?"

I shouldered the bag—*ouch*—and snagged my tacos from Aster. "Well, I feel better. Plus, if he's with the guys who've been following me, there's the slightest chance they might leave me alone now, if he believed me."

"And if he's *not* with them?"

I swallowed. "Then he'll just think he's fallen afoul of the local crazy woman, and good thing, too—I've got a rep to maintain."

Aster giggled. "Ooh, you and Cynna *are* gonna get along!"

Damarion frowned. "On the off chance he is with them, and *didn't* believe you, should I escort you home now?"

"No." I took Aster's hand. "*We* have a coupon for free rolled ice cream, and we're not going to let some jerk keep us from using it. Come on, Aster."

We trooped over to Rollin' and got in line. This food truck had an open front so passersby could watch the spectacle of the ice cream being made—and get lured in, obvi.

The lady taking orders whisked up ingredients in a huge bowl: flavored creams, chocolate sauce, fruit drizzles, sprinkles, you name it. After twenty seconds, she poured the sugary concoction on a steel plate embedded in the counter, and smoothed it out whisper-thin with a spatula.

Beside her waited a miniature snow wasset, like a cute white weasel with pupilless ice-blue eyes and frost riming its whiskers. Its long tufty tail flicked as it watched the cream being spread.

The moment the lady lifted her spatula, the snow wasset unleashed its wintry breath on the steel plate, the plume of chill air freezing the cream instantly.

Job well done, the snow wasset rolled playfully onto its back as the lady scraped the ice cream into perfect spirals and nestled them in a paper cup.

Aster's eyes widened. "It's so cuute!"

"And we're about to get up close and personal with its royal cuteness." I winked. "Just try not to get frostbite, 'kay?"

We stepped up and ordered with our coupon. Triple chocolate cream for me, with brownie bites and dark chocolate swirl. Aster went for lychee cream with ruby chocolate sprinkles.

The snow wasset's tail flicked against Aster's nose as it froze her ice cream, and she sneezed, but managed to look delighted as she did.

Ice cream cups in hand, spoons in mouth, we turned to Damarion.

He raised a brow. "*Now* should we head back?"

I pulled the spoon out of my mouth. "Why not. Lead the way!"

The spoon made for a good saber to command the charge. Damarion rolled his eyes.

We stopped at his place first to drop off the blood, and Aster—with whispered promises of nightlife excursions in the near future. Damarion and I ambled toward my place as I licked the last of the chocolatey goodness from the bottom of the cup, definitely smearing it all over my face.

I absolutely did not give a whatever.

Crows cawed in the distance as my place came into sight, sounding like somebody had ruined their day, poor corvids. They'd probably be descending on my lawn later for compensation.

I removed my face from the cup. "I'll be good to go from here."

Damarion slowed to a halt, hands in his pockets.

"Oh, your card." I retrieved his credit card from my back pocket. He wouldn't have cared—or even noticed—if I'd kept it for a month, but better not to be tempted.

"Right, thank you." He slipped it away. "Are you sure you'll be all right?"

I glanced around at the obvious lack of sinister henchmen, and the scant half block between us and my front door. "Yep."

We hugged, then each moseyed toward home.

I stepped onto the crumbling walk to my front door, and paused. The lawn looked even scruffier than usual, with dirt clods and torn yellow grass scattered here and there.

I marched closer. "If those freaking firemoles are back—"

I screeched to a halt.

A lone sneaker decorated the dying lawn to one side. And . . .

Were those *teeth*? I peered closer.

Scary monster teeth protruded from the dirt in a couple places, like they belonged to something belowground. Blood flecked the ivory surface.

I crept to the door, which looked freshly battered. For once, I knocked instead of just unlocking it and waltzing in.

The door muffled Bracchius's voice, but I could still make it out. "Back for another round, *eh*? You haven't had *enough*?! Well, I'll show y—"

The peephole darkened.

"Oh, Immy!" The locked clunked, and the door opened. "Thank goodness you're home!"

I stared down at my blobby little demon as he hovered in the doorway.

"What in the three hells happened to our yard?" I hooked a thumb over my shoulder, just as a sinister burble erupted behind me.

CHROMASLAYER

I spun, frantically searching for whatever mutant lawn monster was emerging to eat me, but the yard was still empty, unchanged.

There was a mud puddle I hadn't noticed, though.

Bracchius piped up. "Oh, I haven't had a chance to tidy up yet, sorry!"

A bubble of air belched from the depths of the mud puddle. Only, the surface didn't ripple like water or mud . . . It shifted like wet sand.

Quicksand.

I whirled back toward Bracchius. "Tidy up from *what*, exactly? Did you host the annual Deadly Demon Obstacle-Course Championships while I was gone?"

Bracchius scoffed. "No, silly. Those get televised, and this place is nowhere near camera ready."

"It sure isn't *now*."

Bracchius muttered, "Never was, never will be."

I grabbed his blobby demon self, eliciting a startled squawk, and raised the sass bucket to eye level. "What. Happened."

"Oh, that. I bravely defended our home against evil brigands, obviously."

I raised both eyebrows as he floated out of my grip and back to the ground. "Brigands?"

It was too much of a coincidence to *be* a coincidence.

My stalkers knew where I lived now.

"You know, assailants. Intruders. Assassins. Trespassers. Burglars. Bad guys."

"I know what the word means." I rolled my eyes. "But there was more than one?"

"A whole bunch, but that didn't matter! I valiantly fought them off, tooth and nail! Well, tooth and substance. Their lame infiltration methods were *no* match for my defenses and counterattacks, none at all! You shoulda seen me, I was amazing!"

"I bet." Speaking of teeth . . .

I jerked my head toward the yard; lone shoe, mystery teeth, quicksand, and all. "And that explains the yard how?"

"Oh, that's some of what I used to attack the bad guys. They tried their best to get past me, with stealth and magic and knives and even a battering golem, but I outwitted them at every turn, using my darksome skills and—"

The quicksand burbled again, and I tuned Bracchius out. How did you *attack* someone with quicksand?

Unless . . .

My eyes widened.

Reapers and renegades.

There were two wolves inside me: one wanted to go poking around in the quicksand with a giant grabber tool, and the other wanted to stay way the heck away.

Maybe I should hire out a magma wyvern to pave that over. Stick a fire pit on top, or a patio set.

No, something more permanent. Water feature? Unicorn statue?

Bracchius would love *that*.

The landlord wouldn't mind me adding a little value to the property, right? To make up for the potential corpse that nooo one ever needed to know about?

Bracchius was still talking. ". . . the quicksand, yard fiends, some curses and hellfireballs. Oh, and the giant skeleton."

I turned very slowly to look at him. I'd be revisiting 'yard fiends' in a minute, but . . . "The giant skeleton?"

"That's what I said, yup."

"*What* giant skeleton?"

"Oh. This one." He ducked back inside from where he'd been hovering by the door.

I followed him into the apartment, and sure enough, in the corner of the room sat a giant multicolor humanoid skeleton, its head almost brushing the ceiling, and its legs extending to the sofa.

Several questions tried to burst out at once: Where had it come from? How had it fit through the door? How had a fake rainbow skeleton scared off grown men?

But the one I settled on was: "What is it *made* out of?"

"Laffy Taffy."

Yup, I needed to sit down.

I plopped on the couch, gazing openmouthed at the presumably sticky monstrosity taking up half my apartment. Was it glued to the carpet? What happened when it got hot tomorrow? I didn't have AC, or a sigil for AC.

My phone buzzed, interrupting my now-I-can-never-move doom spiral. I pulled it out.

A hundred-dollar bill fluttered out with it.

Damarion, the sneaky dastard.

I swiped the bill up off the floor and laid it on the coffee table. This puppy was destined for paying back Samaire for dinner, and paying down the cost of my tattoo from Ruby, and rent, and corpse-obscuring landscape improvements, and—

Yeah, this wasn't gonna get me very far.

Ugh.

My phone vibrated again. Right, notification. I woke it to find a junk email, and a text from Keisha.

It's possible they were able to access employee information.

No.

Freaking.

Kidding.

I shut my phone off with a sigh, then kicked the skeleton's foot, my sneaker adhering slightly. Ick. "This isn't staying."

The red flickers in Bracchius's depths went wild. "But I used up my whole stash to make it!"

I just stared at him.

"And it really brightens up the living room."

"It *takes* up the whole living room."

Bracchius peered up at it. "Okay, fair. I'll find a new home for ChromaSlayer."

It probably said something about our relationship that I didn't even blink at the name. I was too busy thanking Finéa that ChromaSlayer would be out of my hair ASAP.

I ran a hand over my curls, shuddering at the thought of it getting *in* my hair.

No bueno.

So ChromaSlayer had helped chase off the bad guys, but had it been in time? Other than the giant skeleton, the room seemed unscathed, but I had to make sure.

"Did the bad guys get inside? They didn't take the artifact from you, did they?" I looked my demon up and down—a very short trip— but he looked fine.

Not sure what a manhandled demon would look like, though.

Bracchius huffed, and extruded a couple of tiny arms, just to cross them. "What kind of sorry excuse for a demon do you think I am? Of course they didn't make it inside! Between the crows and me, they didn't stand a chance!"

"Wait, the crows?" Was that what all the ruckus had been about when I'd been walking home?

"Yeah, they showed up a few minutes into the fight, and helped me out. Not that I needed it, of course. But *sprinkles*, they're vicious. They were still trying to peck the bad guys' eyes out as they ran down the block!"

Heh.

I'd need to get a special treat for the crows as a thank you. Not to mention Bracchius.

Right, I needed to go to the grocery store anyway. Forgot.

That sparked an idea, though . . .

I eyed Bracchius speculatively. "Can you lower any wards you and Kor have put on the house? Against intruders, I mean. Not like the storm wards, or the fire wards, or— well, anything except burglar wards, basically."

A pulse rippled across Bracchius's black surface. "What? Why would I do that? Then they could just walk right in if I wasn't paying attention!"

"Exactly."

Bracchius rocked back, looking up at me. "But . . . Oh, you've come up with one of your plans, haven't you?"

I smiled mischievously.

Bracchius bobbed up onto the shiny pedestal of Bath-and-Body-Works-ness on the coffee table, clearly eager for me to spill the beans.

I scooted forward on the sofa. "How would you feel about coming to the grocery store with me?"

"Fine, but— Immy, don't get distracted! You were about to tell me your sinister plot."

"I'm working on it."

"Oh. The grocery store?"

"Yup. Now lemme talk, will ya?"

Bracchius formed another arm nubbin and traced it across his glossy black surface, left to right, then dramatically flopped the bitty arm to one side.

I narrowed my eyes. "Did you just zip your lips and throw away the key?"

He nodded, mute.

"It's a little hard to parse when you don't have lips, buddy."

Bracchius pulsed impatiently.

"Sorry, okay. So, we both go to the grocery store, leaving the apartment unguarded for the bad guys to search. When they don't find what they're looking for, maybe they'll believe me that I don't have it anymore."

He rocked back. "You told them I have it?"

"No." I filled him in on my lies at Santiago's Street Eats. "So, we let them break in and see what's what." I pursed my lips. "Maybe we should even leave the door unlocked?"

"What if my attacks chased them off forever?"

I'd cheer, that's what. But . . . "They've been on my tail for twenty-four hours. I doubt they'd give up that easily. Er, I mean, not that your defense wasn't"—comically overdone and also somewhat terrifying?—"enough to scare off the fiercest of villains, but they seem pretty determined."

Bracchius bobbed seriously, then stilled. "But Immy, what if *regular* thieves show up instead? I can't lose Sp—" He vanished in a puff of deep purple glitter, teleporting off somewhere.

Why couldn't *my* magic do things like that?

And then he popped back into place on the pedestal, with Sparkles getting a piggyback ride. Demonback ride?

Nope, *that* sounded NC-17, and I didn't think Bracchius's cute blobby self had ever stirred anyone into the throes of passion.

Not that I knew what demons were attracted to—not humans, certainly. Did Bracchius have a love life? Did he *want* one? Were there demon dating apps? Should I set him up a profile?

"Immy?"

I zoned back in, blinking as my mind dragged itself out of the abyss it'd fallen down. "Sorry, got distracted."

"Can I bring Sparkles with me to the store? I don't want her to get stolen again, or—or ripped apart because they think something's hidden inside her, or . . ."

And *I* didn't want to go on another death-defying unicorn-plushie-retrieval quest if I could help it. "Of course."

He squeezed Sparkles tight to his chest—face—whatever area. "Thanks. So, do you want to leave?"

"Uh, lemme run to the bathroom first."

"Say no more—please."

A couple minutes later, I was washing my hands in the bathroom sink when Kor's mirror darkened, the reflection replaced by a midnight whirlpool.

Ugh, now? Could I still make a run for it?

I sighed, straightened my back, and finished rinsing off the suds as Kor erupted through the mirror. He looked slightly singed, sooty streaks marring his inky surface.

Annnd, of course, he rounded on me.

"What foul bane did you wreak upon my domain, Immaline? You burned half of it down! Do you have any idea how many different ways I had to try to put those flames out?? I had to use cockatrice dust, Immy! *Cockatrice dust!* Do you know how expensive that is?!"

I crossed my arms. "And here I thought demons *liked* flames. Man, what a wuss."

They'd been that impossible to put out, huh? My chaos flames might just come in handy. Could you patent fire?

That was assuming I could even reproduce it.

Kor puffed up. "I will wreak such revenge upon you and Bracchius that you will never—"

I planted a hand in Kor's spongy black hopefully-face. He shut up immediately, a jolt running through him beneath my fingers.

"Kor, I'm going to say this once, and once only. You listening?"

He rocked up and down slightly, and I pulled my hand away.

"Do whatever you want to me—I can handle it just fine—but if you are anything but a cherub of delight toward Bracchius in the future, I'll send far worse than chaos flames your way."

"What could be worse than—"

"Do you really want to find out?" I snapped. "Because you should know me well enough by now to realize I'm awfully good at causing mayhem."

Kor gulped, audibly.

"So no more tormenting Bracchius. In fact, if he needs a snack, you'll get it for him, with a whole damn chocolate bar on the side."

"Demons don't like cho—"

"If he wants a spa day, then you'll whip out the cucumber slices and hot rocks. Heck, if he wants a real live *unicorn*, I expect it to be on the doorstep the next morning."

I really hoped Bracchius wasn't listening in, because there was no way a unicorn was fitting inside this apartment. Not to mention the whole thing with aiding and abetting—or at least encouraging—a kidnapping.

"Is that clear?"

Kor nodded timidly. "Puppies and rainbows, got it."

"I really want to like you, Kor, but I don't. When you first moved in, I was happy to give you a chance, since you needed some help. But all you've done since is become meaner and more of a bully, and I'm not putting up with it any longer. If I were you, I'd go hunker down in your laundromat for a while and think about whether you want to have any friends, ever, or if a domain full of cackling imps is all you need out of life."

Kor shrank in on himself a bit.

"Bracchius was so excited when you decided to move in, because he really wanted a demon buddy to vent to and hang out with. Now you're his least favorite being on the planet, and that's on you. Bracchius is incredibly easy to get along with, and yet somehow you managed to make him your enemy. And frankly, he deserves better."

I took a deep breath, having ranted on longer than expected. "So shape up, or ship out, I guess," I finished lamely.

Kor stayed quiet, the red flickers inside him tingeing more toward purple.

"I know how he can help!" Bracchius's voice echoed through the closed door.

How much had he heard? Enough, clearly.

Crud.

There was gonna be a unicorn on the doorstep in the morning, wasn't there.

I swung open the door. "How's that?"

Bracchius drifted up to join Kor on the counter. "Immy has to get groceries, and she needs me to defend her."

I stifled a chuckle at the half-truth.

Bracchius continued. "Some thieves tried to break in earlier, and I had to chase them off. We're going to let them break in while we're gone, as part of Immy's plan, but you could watch them, secretly, so they don't steal all Immy's stuff, or burn down the building or anything."

Why hadn't I thought of that?

'Cause I wasn't used to the idea that Kor could be cooperative, that's why.

I threw the demon a bone. "If you're up for it . . . I guess I could pick up a bag of Cheetos for you."

Kor twitched. "Crunchy XXTRA Flamin' Hot Cheetos?"

"Yup."

"I'll do it. I believe a little brigand-blasting is exactly what I need right now."

"Well, don't blast them unless they get up to trouble. And they might not come back, anyway." Didn't want to get his hopes up.

Kor puffed up again. "If they do not return, I will summon a hellhound and track them down, and wreak such vengeance upon them as they have never—"

I tuned him out, having already heard the 'wreaking' spiel once this evening. Maybe I could get him a word-of-the-day calendar, broaden his vocab a bit. Did they make a wannabe-villain version?

"Great, so you monitor the house, and we'll head out."

We left him plotting and planning and trying to decide where to hide if any baddies showed their faces. I grabbed my wheeled fold-up canvas tote thing, a couple reusable bags, and my purse while Bracchius got Sparkles situated. I surreptitiously glanced at Bracchius's posterior, making sure no sign of the artifact was visible.

Good to go—only demon derriere showing.

"Ready, Immy?"

"Ready, O Dark One and Staunch Unicorn Sidekick." I opened the door. "Lead the way."

MUNCHIES & MYCOFAE

Bracchius fidgeted with one of Sparkles's legs. "Well, I don't actually know where we're going."

"Oh, right." I shut the door behind us, *not* locking it.

"Right?"

He veered right across the pitted yard, and I scrambled after him.

"No, not— Just follow me, unless you want to ride in this disaster." I shook the wheeled tote and waved him left toward the sidewalk, narrowly avoiding the quicksand puddle. "And get rid of this soon, too, yeah?"

"Oops, of course. I forgot. Don't want anyone else to fall in."

I could blithely pretend I'd never heard the word 'else,' right?

More sinister burbling erupted from the quicksand, like the belch of a satisfied sand creature.

Maybe not.

The red flickers at Bracchius's core pulsed, and the sand settled down, losing its liquid sheen. A moment later, it matched the ratty look of the rest of the yard. "There. Good to go."

"Thanks." I think.

The reason for the sorry state of the yard—well, *sorrier*, anyway—reminded me. "Have you had a chance to dig up any more about that gizmo?" I waved in the general direction of his butt.

"Not yet." Bracchius squished down a bit. "I was so glad to get Sparkles back, and it hasn't been very long, and then those brigands attacked, and—"

I held up a hand. "You're right, you've been pretty busy. Just wanted to check."

The bad guys knew enough about it to want it, so there had to be *some* information out there. Whether we could get our hands on it was another matter.

"I will ask around, Immy. Don't worry."

My phone buzzed as we headed down the sidewalk toward the subway. I retrieved it from the abyssal depths of my purse.

Keisha: Everything all right?

I typed back real quick: Yeah, fine.

I had it handled, after all.

Hopefully.

Not like Keisha could do anything about this mess, even if I *didn't* have it handled.

Bracchius floated alongside me, Sparkles bouncing cheerily on his head.

Body.

Whatever.

He glanced up at me as I tucked the phone away. "Is your new phone okay?"

"Yeah, it's great!" I smiled down at him. "I still can't believe you bought this for me."

"Well, I could hardly leave you phoneless, could I? Not when something terrible might happen, and I need to get ahold of you."

Bracchius didn't call me often, but when he did, it was almost always a dire crisis, at least from his perspective.

I was honestly surprised he hadn't blown up my phone when Kor had taken Sparkles.

Then again, maybe he had. Between taking the battery out of my old phone last night, and frying it with my magic, I'd been incommunicado for quite a while. There might be a whole host of panicked voicemails on there, lost forever.

I mean, I could probably still access them if I *really* wanted to, but who dials into their voicemail anymore? Not me.

Bracchius continued. "With your nap earlier, I didn't get a chance to tell you about how your phone works."

"Uh, just like any other phone? Call or text people, take pictures, use the Internet?"

"Not that stuff. The *cool* stuff. Like how it's made of tungsten and faeglass, so even if a leviathan steps on it, it'll be fine. And it uses mycofae nano organics as computer chips, so it won't get fried by magic either."

I fished the phone back out and looked it over. There was *fungus* growing in here?

Hey, as long as it didn't decide to get adventuresome and start growing on me too, I was all for magicproof tech.

My estimation of the absurd cost of this thing tripled, though, and I hopped online to order Bracchius that sequin scarf I'd been thinking about. But black or pastel rainbow? I eyed Sparkles bobbing on his head.

Both. Definitely both.

Bracchius held forth a while longer on the astonishing virtues of my new phone, including anti-tracking magic worked directly into the hardware, and an app to store and charge sigils—though I wasn't sure I'd trust it.

At this rate, I wouldn't be surprised if there was a miniature flamethrower installed beside the camera.

We took the subway one station over to Chaingage, and emerged a block from Save & Savor. The three-story supermarket even had its own parking lot, though the competition for spots was fierce.

As barebones as the kitchen was right now, my arm would probably fall off trying to haul my groceries around in a wimpy little shopping basket, so I headed to the chaotic lineup of carts sized for everything from gremlins to grizzly shifters and wrestled one out.

It wouldn't be any fun dragging all the groceries home, either, but at least it wasn't *that* far.

Delivery sounds great if you've never tried it. But when you're paying a ten-buck delivery fee, only to get barghast kibble instead of bowtie pasta, and ketchup instead of kimchi, *and* they decide those are reasonable substitutions, so they won't refund you . . .

Yeah. I get my own groceries.

I dumped my purse in the cart and folded down the kiddie seat over top. Bracchius cheerfully drifted up and settled onto the blue plastic seat advertising Mandro's Tar Bars. He placed Sparkles beside him and buckled the unicorn in.

"I know, it's not that comfortable, but this way you don't fall and end up in all that horrifying dead skin coating the ground."

I stifled a snicker. I'd have to check the floor when I got home. I'd been too distracted by the giant skeleton when I'd walked in to notice whether the apartment as a whole looked any different, but it was a safe bet the floor might be a tad cleaner now.

If I told my demons enough horror stories, could I get them to do the dishes and clear up the water stains in the shower too?

Only one way to find out.

Getting them to scrub the toilet was probably a pipe dream, sadly.

The automatic doors swished open as I wheeled the cart into the store. Bracchius swiveled to take in the colorful explosion of food in every direction, trembling with excitement.

What? He doesn't get out much.

He spun back to face me. "Can we go to the candy department?!"

I huffed a laugh. "They don't have a whole department, but yes, we can go to the candy aisle. Eventually."

Produce first, though. If I used up most of my budget on the healthy stuff, it'd be easier to keep Bracchius from swimming in a sea of candy. I was lucky *I* was full, or I'd also be picking up twenty-seven different things just because they made my mouth water right that second.

I rolled the cart past the pallets of field grass and flowers, getting stuck behind a unicorn complaining about the color of the poppies.

Prissy ponies.

Bracchius, of course, tilted Sparkles's plush head to admire her larger, livelier cousin. If he'd had eyeballs, they'd have been the size of Saskia Springs' potholes.

I grabbed a discount bag of 'ugly' fruit, and spoiled myself with one avocado. Bananas were on sale, so those went in the cart too. Bread, tortillas, peanut butter.

The candy aisle made for a good shortcut to the milk, so I indulged Bracchius a little early.

Halfway down the aisle, Bracchius started bouncing on the kiddie seat, making a racket as the plastic slapped against the wire frame.

"Ooh, Immy, can we get some of that?" He extruded a little arm to point at . . .

The DemonDelight. Of course.

I pulled a bag off the shelf and deposited it in his eager appendages. "Just save the packaging if you finish it, yeah?"

He tore into the bag. "I will!"

Right, had to get Cheetos for Kor too, and something for the crows. Nipping into the next aisle, I snagged an XXL bag of Cheetos—his preferred variety, obviously.

Once Bracchius was enjoying his DemonDelight, he scooted closer to Sparkles, leaning in to her snout. "Is there anything you want, Sparkles?" He nodded a couple times as though listening to her speak. "Immy, Sparkles says she wants Rainbow Turds!"

Back down the snack aisle it is.

Marshmallowy Rainbow Turds collected, we rolled on past the juices and various bottled animal blood to the milk. Specialty shifter milks, camazotz milk . . . There, cow milk.

In the bulk section, I squeezed past a rock troll dispensing granite pebbles and parked myself at the quinoa bin. Her kid kicked his heels in the cart, pointing at the amethyst chips.

"Mooom, can we please get some? I promise I won't eat it all at once like last time!"

"Just a little, and be patient."

At the mondo escalator to the second floor—the meat department—I waited for a kelpie to clomp onto the moving six-by-four-foot step, a trail of murky water in her wake.

Must be fresh from the pond.

I rammed the cart onto the next step, and we chugged upward. In the lunchmeat section, I scrounged up a reduced-price package of bologna expiring tomorrow. The crows would eat it all in one fell swoop anyway, so why not get it cheaper?

A kobold was salivating over the prosciutto just out of reach, so I nabbed the package and passed it down. "Thanks!" they squeaked, and scurried off.

The Rainbow Turds and DemonDelight had mostly disappeared by the time we hit the checkout. I teased both packages out of Bracchius's grasp and set them on the conveyor with my groceries and reusable bags.

The checkout golem rang me up, and I gave it my card. "Oh, and can you break this?" I handed over the hundred-dollar bill. "Two fifties, please."

The automatic doors swept open, letting in the refreshing scent of car exhaust, and I glanced over as the golem gave my card and change back.

Three hefty dudes stepped in, heads on a swivel. One's gaze snagged on me—the guy I'd chewed out at Santiago's.

Werewolves and *watermelons*.

Not only had my stalkers chased me down, this time they were ganging up on me.

FOOD FIGHT

The two new guys were a minotaur and a concrete ogre, big and brawny and almost certainly mean. The dude I'd chewed out held a weird device like the love child of a TV remote and a dowsing rod.

As he nudged the other two and nodded toward me, I asked Bracchius sotto voce, "Can you tell what he's holding?"

Bracchius elongated and peered thataway, then snapped back into his orb shape with a reverberating jiggle. "Redcap blood tracker."

I slapped the back of my arm, remembering the pinch of the, quote, unquote 'bug bite' outside Vein & Vice.

Leeches and *legerdemain*.

We stood in a stalemate, my brain buzzing as the checkout golem loaded my bags into the cart, the bad guys waiting for me to make a move.

I whispered down to Bracchius again. "How do you circumvent a blood tracker?"

"Get new blood?"

I shifted my gaze from the bad guys to stare at him incredulously. "You're kidding, right?"

"No . . ." Bracchius pulled Sparkles closer.

"How's it work?"

"Put a drop of blood inside, and it'll lead you straight to the owner."

"So the blood has to stay in there for it to work?"

"Yup."

Great. So I just had to smash the thing to smithereens, and hope they hadn't set aside half a drop of my blood in case of emergencies.

And make sure no one got a chance to pinprick me again.

Three on one—okay, three on two with Bracchius, but I wasn't counting Sparkles—were rude odds. Nothing I couldn't handle if push came to shove, but why risk it when you can just book it?

This place had to have an employee exit or a loading dock, right?

The checkout golem dumped the last of my groceries into my cart as I stared down the three baddies. "Better hold on to Sparkles."

Bracchius tightened his grip on the unicorn as I shot a crackling bolt of my disastrous pink magic. It arced over the cart and nailed the blood tracker right in the guy's hands.

Good aim for the win.

Magenta embers erupted from it, and the baddies jumped back, the guy who'd been holding it cursing and shaking out his now-empty hands.

I took a firm grip on the cart handle and kick-stomped the metal crossbar at my feet. Jerking the cart into a wheelie, I heaved it around in the narrow lane between the checkout stand and the candy-bar divider.

Reese's Cups rained down, and the woman behind me yelped in surprise and flattened herself against the celeb magazines.

"Coming through!" I pushed off with one foot and jumped onto the crossbar as the cart careened down the short lane.

The other shoppers in line leapt out of the way as we plunged back into the depths of the store and away from the baddies. Sparkles's mane fluttered in the breeze of our passage, and Bracchius held on to her for dear life.

Hopefully they wouldn't risk attacking us in a crowded store. What would they do, anyway? Strip-search me in the protein-bar aisle?

Maybe I should let them. It wasn't like I had the artifact on me, and I doubted any of them would think to reach up Bracchius's butt.

Not that *he'd* let them.

I treated the cart like an unwieldy skateboard—one foot glued to the crossbar, the other giving us repeated pumps of speed as we rocketed down the baking aisle.

Heavy footfalls behind us signaled the trio was giving chase. I kicked off again, propelling the cart past the end of the aisle and almost flattening some poor lepidopterafae, who fluttered out of the way with her oversized moth wings just in time.

"Sorry!"

Bracchius peered around my waist. "Should I lob some magic their way? They didn't like my hellfireballs earlier."

I ducked a quick glance over my shoulder. The concrete ogre was in the lead, but still a ways behind us. They couldn't keep up with our skateboard-style speed, especially with all the intervening shoppers reeling after our reckless passage.

"Better not. Don't want to set the place on fire."

I started scanning the signs on the back wall: deli, dairy, health . . .

Restrooms.

That was our best bet.

At the next aisle cap, I braked with my foot, the rubber sole screeching over the linoleum. I whipped the cart around the corner, ready to pick up speed again, but the scattered islands of the produce section lay before us—no straight shot through to the bathrooms.

Crud.

High-speed maze maneuvers, it is.

The footfalls thudded closer with our decreased speed, and then a magical projectile sailed through the air. Only, not from Bracchius—from the minotaur.

His aim must have sucked, because it sizzled past us into the perfect massive pyramid of navel oranges.

Oranges exploded in every direction, thwacking into me and the other shoppers, tumbling across the floor. One even beaned Bracchius, and he puffed up a few inches in irritation, his red flickers skittering wildly.

Bracchius glared past me. "Are you sure I can't—"

"Not unless you want pineapples raining down on you too."

He grumbled. "I should've brought ChromaSlayer!"

A nearby cougar shifter in half-form rounded on us, growling, rubbing her furry shoulder where she'd probably just been walloped by an orange or three. The kobold from earlier perched on her other shoulder, whispering in her tufted ear and pointing my way.

I wrestled with the cart to give them a wide berth, but with one powerful lunge, the cougar shifter pounced right over the remnants of the orange stand and landed beside us, her eyes fixed on the troublemaking dude behind us.

"These punks bothering you, hun?" she growled.

"Little bit."

"Not for long." Her ears flattened, and she stalked past me. The kobold tossed me a cheery little wave, then went back to clutching the cougar's fur for all they were worth.

I tried to push the cart forward, but the wheels were mired in a sea of oranges.

We could ditch the cart and bolt, but like hells was I going to abandon my groceries because of these asshats. I'd paid for these, and they were coming home with me.

One more forceful jerk of the cart, and the oranges caught flame with a subtle crimson glow, shifting and rolling and then parting like the freaking Red Sea.

I glanced down at Bracchius as I shoved the cart forward along the clear path.

He was scrunched down in concentration, the dim red glow echoed across his own ebony surface.

"Nice going, Moses."

"Thanks."

We escaped the sea of oranges and barreled toward the restroom once more, snarls and shouts erupting behind us.

One of the three dudes must've taken an alternate route, because he bounded at us from the left, a lemon-lime ball of magic growing in one hand.

No innocent bystanders that way, nothing much but cereal boxes . . .

So, in the instant before we shot into the hallway to the restrooms, I shunted a wild stream of my own magenta magic toward him.

Let him have fun with that.

The hallway enclosed us as the cart rattled on at top speed. I almost wished I could've seen the result of my magic, but it was just as likely to have done nothing as to have turned him into a mutant hedgehog or something.

Bracchius pouted. "Hey, I thought you said no magic! No fair!"

"You did some too."

We zipped past the various bathrooms—microfae, human-sized, macrofae—toward the emergency exit at the end.

"Just telekinesis. Yours was offensive!"

"I sure hope so."

I rammed the emergency exit bar on the door with the nose of the cart, and it banged open. We thudded out over the threshold into a grimy dusk-lit alley.

Bracchius glowed red again, and the heavy door slammed behind us with a shriek of metal.

He continued to glow for a moment, and I glanced back. The door was warped in its frame, the edges almost molten.

"Holy crap. That was you?"

"Obviously. Just had to let a little hellfire trickle through at the seams."

"Trickle through from . . . Rokonor?" I cringed.

"Of course, Immy. Where else would you get hellfire from?"

I really didn't like contemplating how skimpy the threshold between our world and the demon paradise was. Sometimes they made it seem like you could just prick the air with a pin, and the flaming, oozing contents of the realm would come bubbling through.

The door shuddered with a heavy thump from the opposite side, and I redoubled my grip on the shopping cart. I was usually a conscientious cart returner—surprising, I know—but today I was A-OK with absconding with Save & Savour's property.

I kicked off, and we coasted down the alley.

Okay, it was more like a bone-jarring rumble across the asphalt, but still. The groceries didn't quite jounce out of the cart, and Bracchius didn't lose Sparkles, and that was all that really mattered.

As we neared the end of the alley, a plastic bag tumbled by in the air, and I leaned away from it.

Litter, or drifter?

Just past it, I stopped the cart for a sec, feeling for a breeze.

There was none.

Drifter.

Better get the freak out of here.

A monumental crash echoed down the alley behind us as I rode the juddering cart. I whirled around. One baddie—the concrete ogre, looking distinctly battered—had busted down the door.

"Bracchius, how are you with wind power?"

He glanced up at me, and I jerked my chin toward the ambling plastic bag.

"Oh!"

The crimson flickers in his depths swirled and brightened, and a sudden gust whipped my curls around.

And sent the drifter smack into the ogre's craggy face.

PROFESSIONAL INGRATES

An unholy gravelly bellow tore from the ogre, his hands shredding at the drifter munching on his face.

"Oof, right to the face." I winced as I shoved the cart back into motion. "I didn't think you were that brutal."

Bracchius shrank, gripping Sparkles. "I . . . might not be that good with wind."

Poor baddie probably didn't deserve that. Concrete ogres were tougher than most beings, though. He might survive.

We wheeled around the corner out of sight, and I handed Bracchius my phone. "Call an ambulance for the dude, would ya? Anonymously?"

Sure, the ogre was a black hat, but I wasn't *completely* heartless.

"Okay." Bracchius accepted the phone and started dialing. When the operator picked up, a voice halfway between Elmo and Darth Vader rumbled out of Bracchius, and I nearly busted my gut trying not to laugh.

Mission accomplished, he gave me back my phone, and I focused on getting us a couple blocks away with multiple twists and turns. Hopefully my magic had pulverized that blood tracker.

Fingers crossed.

Just in case, I double-checked my white-ink sigil tattoo. The lines were all still in the right places, so I dredged up a mini spark of magic and infused it.

Every little bit helps, right?

Not that they couldn't pick us right back up at home . . .

Ugh. Like I had anywhere else to go. Plus, we couldn't schlepp these groceries around town forever.

I worked back toward the closest subway stop. "Bracchius, if they've got more goons waiting at our place, do you have any way to sneak us in? Y'know, invisibility, stopping time, secret demon backdoor?"

"No . . ." He sounded regretful. "We should totally get a secret backdoor, though! Maybe with a slide?"

I huffed out a laugh. "Maybe. Guess we'll just have to hope the bad guys aren't too gung ho, or that Kor is in a smitey mood."

"Kor's *always* in a smitey mood."

"Good point."

I'd probably get murdered if I tried to take the shopping cart on the subway—space is at a premium, and there's always some grumpy mofo ready to take their crappy day out on you—so I pulled up beside the station entrance and started unloading.

Most of the groceries fit in my little rolly fold-up cart, but two bags were left out in the cold. I grabbed the cart handle and reached for the bags with my other hand. I could survive the handles cutting into my fingers for the subway ride home.

"I can take one!" Bracchius drifted down from the kiddie seat, Sparkles in tow.

I pursed my lips, torn between gratitude and skepticism. The latter won out. "No offense, but wouldn't you just be dragging it along the ground?"

"Nope!" He pushed a couple teeny arms out of his sphere form and tied the handles of one bag together. A grunt and a pulse of glowing red magic later, and the bag was balanced on his head, squishing him down a bit. "See?"

"Huh. And it won't slip off?"

He swiveled side to side in a whole-body head shake, Sparkles tucked under one arm. The bag didn't show any signs of toppling.

"Cool. And thanks. You should tag along on more shopping trips." I tugged the canvas rolly cart toward the station. "Let's go."

No one accosted us on the short ride home, and our yard didn't look like it'd taken any additional assaults—demon or otherwise—as we approached.

The door opened as I fumbled for my keys, and Kor peeked out. "Your forgetfulness always astonishes me, Immaline. You left it unlocked, remember?"

Right. "My name's not Immaline, remember?" I grumped before pushing past him. "Anyone take the bait?"

"Yes, they entered not long after you left, and ransacked the place."

I stopped in my tracks, but the living room looked basically the same. One sofa cushion was backwards, and the demons' pedestal was an inch out of place, but that was about it.

Had we gotten the Marie Kondo of home-ransackers?

Kor zipped in front of me as I dumped the groceries in the kitchen, Bracchius helpfully setting his bag on the counter.

"I know you said not to intervene if possible, but would you believe it? One of them tried to take my mirror! Heathens. Ingrates!"

His metaphorical feathers were clearly ruffled, and no wonder— dumb move by Mr. Team Bad Guys, not that he'd probably known he was trying to make off with an entire demon domain, never mind one belonging to a Machiavellian demon.

"Did . . . that one survive?"

"For now. I relegated him to my domain for interrogation." He switched to a disgruntled mutter. "My efforts so far have been in vain, however. These are clearly professionals. But rest assured, I *will* break him. Someday."

I almost asked him where he was keeping prisoners now that his Baleful Tower was presumably toast, but bit my tongue just in time.

He was being somewhat helpful, for once. No need to remind him I'd lit his domain on fire.

"Do you wish to interrogate him as well?" Kor settled next to the carton of eggs as I put away groceries.

"Uh, that's okay, but thanks. If he isn't cracking under your, er, rigorous methods, I can't imagine I'll have any more luck."

I also had *no* desire to know what Kor was doing to the guy. I'd rescued my quota of unfortunate souls from Kor's domain for the month, thank you very much.

"Can you guys put all the wards back up?" If the rest of the baddies were interested in getting their buddy back, I wanted the defenses in place again.

"Already done."

I blinked over at Kor. "Really?"

"Of course. Once they'd completed their search and come up fruitless, I reinstated the protections. Don't want any more riffraff than necessary wandering in and causing trouble."

"Well, thanks. Very helpful of you, Kor." It had probably been more about keeping anyone else from trying to pry his mirror off the wall, but still.

So, what now? They knew I hadn't stashed the artifact here, but obviously didn't believe I'd palmed it off on someone else.

I could ditch the thing down a sewer grate, and all my troubles would be over, but these guys had seriously pissed me off. No way was I rewarding them by giving them exactly what they wanted, screw the consequences.

I mean, they wouldn't really *want* to go sewer-diving for it, but you get the idea.

Since Nardi Seabrook didn't seem to be in any rush to reclaim it from me, my only real option was to do a deep dive and figure out what the hells the artifact was. Once I knew that, I might be able to find someone more official to hand it off to.

Someone who'd have an easier time dealing with a band of ruffians determined to get their grubby paws on it.

But where to go digging?

Sure, most people think the internet contains every piece of knowledge you could ever want, but a zillion books were published before the internet ever came to be, and most of those haven't been digitized yet.

The internet hadn't yielded any results for the name the baddies had used for the artifact, so maybe my next best step was consulting some dusty old tomes.

Eclectica Emporium, here I come.

The Emporium isn't the closest bookstore to my place, but it is one of the biggest. And it's not one of those boring corporate chains, either—thank goodness.

The Eclectica Emporium has personality, to say the least.

It's more like a warren than a shop, endless nooks and crannies and tunnels, and isolated fragments of extra floors that you can't quite figure out how to get to.

And every spare inch crammed with books, mostly used.

Like many businesses in the city, it's open twenty-four seven, but I've only ever seen the one gal behind the counter—Monique. I've never stumbled upon a single soul amongst the shelves aside from other customers, though she does talk about an assistant from time to time.

I closed the fridge. "Wanna go on one last trip with me tonight, Bracchius?"

The little demon heaved the new bunch of bananas onto the banana hook, then rocked back to look at me. "Only if Sparkles can come again!"

I shook my head, smiling. "Duh, Sparkles can come."

"Where we going?"

"The bookstore."

I got the last of the groceries put away and took care of a quick snack and a bathroom break before setting back out into the night with my stalwart demon and his unicorn sidekick.

Now that darkness had rolled in, the subway was filled mostly with nocturnal beings, probably on their way to work: banshees, wraiths, vamps, camazotz, shadowwwalkers.

A dusky blue naga eyed me, then Bracchius, tongue flicking out to taste the air—or our scent. We might just look like tasty morsels to the snakelike carnivore.

I inched away.

The two of us got off at the Rhainaqu subway stop and wound our way deeper into the city, past a hot chocolate café and Glitter, a salon for semi-incorporeal beings. The aeronymph walking out looked quite dashing with metallic blue and green confetti swirling inside her.

We dashed across the street to the bookstore, almost getting flattened by a hulking neon-pink macrofae cab, the driver blaring his horn.

Well, *I* almost got flattened. Bracchius would've been fine, though Sparkles might've come out of the experience a bit squashed, with tire treads imprinted across her butt.

I yanked open the door to the Eclectica Emporium, Stymphalian feathers and wyvern scales tinkling above. The wispy, dry scent of old paper buffeted against me as Bracchius floated in ahead of me.

The place had the warm hush of libraries, only an old lady at the counter breaking the living silence with a whispered conversation with Monique, the owner.

Monique is an older Black woman with frameless glasses, short kinky-coily brown hair, and eyes the color of ink in old paperbacks with the pages falling out. I've never known her to be anything but quiet, calm, and a little mysterious.

I got in line, and Bracchius drifted over to the nearest cram-packed shelf, Sparkles in tow.

The grandma at the counter glanced around. "Do you have *Warlord Arcanist* too? I thought I saw it when I came in, but I forgot to go back and grab it."

Monique smiled. "We do. One moment, and Horley will grab it for you."

Horley? Maybe her elusive assistant?

Movement along a shelf caught my eye, and I gaped.

An octopod slunk along the bookshelves with sinuous grace, tentacles shifting to match the colors of the books behind it, so fluid it was almost invisible.

Now I knew why I'd never noticed it.

One tentacle plucked a book off the shelf, and the octopod slithered along a beam and passed the book down to Monique.

"Thanks, Horley." She continued ringing the customer up.

Octopods—terrestrial second cousins to octopuses—were more common in forests than cities. You were way more likely to run into an octopod on the Olympic Peninsula than a vampire or wolf shifter, to the horror of *Twilight* fans.

Nobody wants an eight-tentacled squish dropping out of a tree to land on their head when they're out looking for lovelorn sparkly vamps.

If this 'Horley' was working in a bookstore, it had to be one of the sentient species. Honestly, when Monique had talked about her little assistant in the past, I'd just figured she was a bit dotty. Guess I owed her a mental apology.

"*Actually, I think you owe her a verbal apology.*" The squeaky words drifted across my mind like a thought, only it wasn't *my* thought.

Wha— I peered at the octopod. "Was that you?"

No answer.

The old lady brushed past me with a huge bag of books, and I stepped up to the counter, jerking a thumb at the octopod. "They're telepathic?"

Monique blinked, one-two, then her eyes darted to her tentacular helper. "Yes. My apologies, I've told him before not to bother the customers. Though there aren't many that can hear him in the first place." She looked me over assessingly.

I raised my hands, all innocence. "Don't ask me. Guess I'm just a special cupcake."

"Cupcakes?" Bracchius drifted over, hopeful.

"Sorry, buddy. Just me—I'm the cupcake." Complete with chaos sprinkles and a weird aftertaste.

"Oh."

Monique's lips pursed as Bracchius settled on the counter beside me. "I have strict rules about demons in my bookshop."

I quirked an eyebrow. "Really?"

Bracchius swiveled between the two of us, gathering Sparkles closer.

Monique scrabbled around under the counter, coming up with a sheaf of papers and a ballpoint pen. "I'll need you to read this over and sign here." She jabbed the pen at a line on the last page.

I leaned on my elbow, scanning the paragraphs. "What's he agreeing to?"

"That he'll be held liable if he goes around incinerating any books about Gandhi, mindfulness, cats, that type of thing. There's a whole list." She leveled Bracchius with a stern glower. "And no ripping out five-hundred-year-old vellum or stealing ancient scrolls so you can have impressive-looking paper to draw up your demon contracts on."

I was tempted to tell her Bracchius was more the type to draw up contracts with rainbow crayons on construction paper, but then she'd probably just add a clause about the children's section.

It was true he wasn't a big fan of cats, though—I'd had to bodily drag him away from the last hissing match.

She held the pen out to Bracchius. "You're perfectly capable of conjuring such materials yourself, so no need to destroy my livelihood, yes?"

"Uh, yes, ma'am." He took the pen with the arm not toting Sparkles. "Is there somewhere for Sparkles to sign too?"

"Sparkles?" Monique glanced up at me disbelievingly.

I smirked. "Not me. The unicorn." I jutted my chin toward the plushie.

Monique's disbelief didn't exactly fade. "You want the . . . unicorn . . . to sign too?"

"Of course. She's my minion, after all."

I swallowed a snort, which did interesting things to my sinuses, like a sneeze that got stuck.

Ack.

"All right." Monique reluctantly dug up a black ink pad from a drawer, and clacked it onto the counter beside the papers. "She can sign with a . . . a hoofprint."

"You don't happen to have gold ink, do you? It would match her hooves better." Bracchius waved one of Sparkles's plush golden hooves.

Monique stared at him. "No, just black."

Bracchius sighed, and dabbed the shimmery gold fabric onto the black ink pad as lightly as possible. He pressed her hoof onto the paper beside the signature line, then tried to smear the rest of the ink off on the back of the agreement.

You'd think of all things, demons would be able to do pretty effective stain-removal magic, but Bracchius hasn't shown any evidence of it so far.

Maybe I could put her through the wash in Kor's domain—Cucumber might know some secret demon detergent.

I was honestly surprised the negentropes hadn't tidied Sparkles up, come to think of it.

Probably should lodge a complaint.

"Ridiculous. That horse can hardly be his minion. It's not even real!"

I flinched, hoping the octopod's scathing comment was for my mental ears only. But Monique frowned, and Bracchius pulsed, turning toward the creature as it slithered across some SF romance novels.

"She is so! And she's not a *horse!*" Bracchius sounded scandalized.

"I beg to differ. I'm telepathic, and there's clearly nothing in her head but fluff and maybe a few dust bunnies."

Bracchius puffed up to nearly twice his usual size, his flickers glowing red-hot, the air warming around us.

Wuh-oh.

DREYELIAN DEVICES

I inched closer to Bracchius, ready to whisk him out of the store if his seething got out of control.

Thankfully we weren't near book-combusting temperatures—yet.

Bracchius bobbed toward the octopod. "That's just because Sparkles's consciousness is so far above yours that you can't even perceive it! If she were a demon, *you* would be a chewing gum sprite." He hugged Sparkles tighter. "Though that might be an insult to chewing gum sprites."

Savage.

I bit my lip to keep from grinning.

The octopod—Horley—fluoresced angrily along his length. Instead of flinging back a witty rejoinder, though, he flared several tentacles and released a cloud of . . . fog?

Hopefully fog.

"Oh, Horley, wait—" Monique lifted a hand, then let it fall to the counter.

White mist drifted outward, obscuring the octopod completely. I prepared myself for a noxious smell, but only a fresh, cool wash of air reached me as the mist expanded.

I was never thinking of foggy forests the same again, that was for sure.

When it dissipated, Horley was gone.

"That's right!" Bracchius waved one of Sparkles's legs at the no-longer-occupied bookcase. "You *should* run and hide, you . . . you insulter, you!"

I poked Bracchius, and he spun as I pointed at the agreement he was supposed to be signing.

"Oh, right." He grabbed the pen off the counter and started scanning the first page.

I half smiled, half grimaced at Monique. "Sorry about whatever that was." I swished a hand at all the nonsense.

Monique sighed, wiping condensation off her glasses with a little cloth. "As sensitive as Horley is, he really shouldn't try to pick as many fights as he does. Thankfully, most of our customers can't hear him." She straightened and smiled. "Now, what can I help you with?"

"Uh, yeah. I'm looking for information on something I can't find online." I lowered my voice. "Have you ever heard the term 'Calamandrian'?"

"Calamandrian . . ." She wetted her lips and gazed past me, eyes unfocused and shifting through her memories. "No, I don't believe so. Do you have more context?"

"Sort of." I scrunched my mouth. Was it worth the risk to show her the artifact? If the bad guys hadn't followed us here, then whipping it out for even a few seconds would probably bring them down on us pronto.

Maybe I could draw it instead.

"Do you have a piece of scrap paper?"

Monique shuffled around some papers beneath her counter and slipped one up onto the surface.

Bracchius had a firm grip on his own pen as he flipped through pages of the agreement Monique had given him, so I looked back up at her. "And a pen?"

She set one branded with the name of the bookstore on the counter with a click, and I got to sketching.

I probably used up half the pen's ink scribbling the black blob in the center, but spent a little more time getting the delicate gold rings right.

Drawing done, I flipped it around and pushed it toward Monique. "Do you know what this is?"

She picked it up, adjusted her glasses, and peered closer. "A Dreyelian device?"

I stared at her blankly. "What?"

"A Dreyelian device," she repeated, then slid the drawing in front of me, pointing at the rings. "These are metal, yes? Interlocking, holding something suspended within?"

"Yeah." I nodded, hope rising inside me. She knew what it was? This Dreyelian thing?

"You'll find what you need in Amber Rabbit Pentacle."

That would've thrown me the first time I walked in, but I was an old hand now.

Monique divided the bookshop as a whole into sections that flowed together like the colors of the rainbow: sage, seafoam, cerulean, cobalt, amethyst, etc.

As long as you knew your color wheel, you wouldn't do too badly.

Of course, within each of those sections there were subsections I hadn't figured out the logic for yet—seemingly random object names like lace and bicycle and persimmon.

Thankfully, an appropriate symbol marked each subsection, though it wasn't a handy neon sign flashing on the wall or anything. You'd find them carved into a banister, woven into a rug, as a knickknack on a shelf.

Today I'd be looking for a rabbit. I crumpled the paper and stepped away from the counter, Bracchius bobbing to follow me. I paused.

The Amber section also included all the books on unicorns, if memory served.

I pointed at Bracchius. "Stay here, would you? Keep an eye out for our . . . friends?"

Bracchius swiveled toward the front door, plopping Sparkles on the counter beside him. "Aye-aye, Immy!"

I wasn't really worried about our stalkers—if I hadn't actually destroyed their blood tracker, they would have found us again by now.

But if Bracchius came within spitting distance of those unicorn books, we'd never get out of here, and I was still planning on getting a decent night's sleep, thank you very much.

Plunging down book-lined halls and bypassing overstuffed rooms, I made my way down the color wheel to Amber, the scant inches of painted wall peeking between books a dead giveaway.

'Kay, now a rabbit . . .

Rain stick propped against a bookshelf, keep going.

Wyvern mobile suspended from the ceiling, nope.

Garland of pinecones strung over a door . . .

I didn't see a rabbit figure or painting anywhere, and the Buttercup section was just ahead. Had I missed it back—

Something hopped across my foot, and I froze.

Too big for a rat, unless it was a cerberat.

Please let it not be a cerberat.

Wincing, I glanced down.

At a soft grey bunny nestled against my shoe, one ear flicked up to monitor me.

"Well, hello there. Aren't you cute?" I crouched and nuzzled one finger across the bunny's head and ears, and he munched contentedly.

All the bookcases in this section were bare of books on the bottom shelf—antirabbit protocol, presumably. Instead, little hidey-holes were cut into the walls here and there, and a half-nibbled grass planter stuck out from under a shelf behind me.

And not a single teensy rabbit turd anywhere.

Impressive.

Either Monique had a brownie on staff full-time, or she'd rummaged up some sort of poop-relocating sigil.

Or . . . just a Roomba.

Mr. Bunny scooted closer, and I stroked his ears again. "Think you can help me find the Pentagram shel— Ope, never mind. Bye!"

The rabbit hopped off across the carpet, disappearing into a mini archway beneath a bookcase.

A bookcase with a square of paper taped to the top edge, inked with heavy black Sharpie: a pentagram.

I laughed and stood. "JK, thanks!"

The bookcase was crammed with books, all about things like artificer's tools and techniques, golem design, magical item transport . . .

There.

One spine read *Dreyelian Design: Theory, Creation, and Use.*

I pried it from between the other books and flipped it open. Diagrams of whirligigs just like mine decorated the pages: some with only a couple rings, others with dozens of complex rings soldered to perpendicular rings inscribed with runes. Gold, silver, copper, platinum, faesteel, and spun crystal.

The smallest the size of a Whopper malted milk ball.

The biggest the size of a city.

All empty, though.

My eyes snagged on a paragraph near the beginning: Dreyelian devices are ideal for transporting volatile magical substances, creations, or beings. See page 73 for intensity grade information.

That tracked with what we'd been thinking—something magical was contained inside the artifact. Well, the Dreyelian device, apparently.

I flipped to page 73, which broke down the designs for different power levels. The column labeled 'Power Grade' went from A to XXX, which stirred vague memories from school, but not enough to be helpful.

Presumably XXX was super mondo scary magic.

They only gave one example here, unfortunately. Want to contain a tiny spark of your own raw magic? You only needed a two-ring device, depicted on the next page.

Flip. This page spread had technical drawings of a dozen designs ranging in complexity. I smoothed a finger over the drawing that looked the most like my artifact: Figure 9b.

Annnd flip back to the previous page, run a finger down the table . . .

There, 9b.

Appropriate for power level . . .

XXX.

I closed my eyes. Of *course.*

FOGGED BY AN OCTOPOD

I remembered going over these in school ages ago, but the specifics had flown the coop long since. Maybe I had it backwards. Maybe XXX was the teensy-weensy, low-grade, nonscary end of the spectrum.

Except they equated A-grade with a minuscule spark of magic . . .

But XXX was at the bottom of the chart, the absolute last entry, so maybe it meant 'miscellaneous'? Like things they couldn't categorize.

There was a chance, right?

Pretty please?

I flipped to the table of contents. Sure, *this* chart didn't give any specifics, but maybe another section of the book did. I swiped a finger down the list of chapters.

Chapter 3: Theory of Materials, Chapter 8: Instituting Containment, Chapter 11: Releasing Containment, Chapter 17: Recommended Uses . . .

Yeah, this puppy was coming home with me.

I shuffled over to Chapter 17, as that seemed like the best bet. After flipping past a few pages so hard I gave myself a paper cut, I found a much bigger table filled with all the goodness I was looking for.

Sucking on my stinging paper cut, I studied the table.

Grade A: minor magical spark. Grade B: pixie. Grade C: fuzzwarg. Grade D: undiluted orrax.

All small-time stuff. Down the list I plunged. Here we go: XXX.

I followed the row over to the appropriate column, and my finger froze on the paper. Instead of listing a being or magical object, the note read:

See Unseen Forces: Nova-Class Beings *by Trillium Slood for more details. While the depicted device should technically be capable of containing most XXX-grade beings, we the authors cannot recommend making the attempt, and its design is included here for educational purposes only.*

Crud.

That didn't look promising for my half-hearted theory of XXX meaning 'miscellaneous.'

It did give me another avenue to explore, though. I just had to find the mentioned book, *Unseen Forces: Nova-Class Beings.*

I clapped the book shut, tucked it under my arm, and scanned the bookshelf in front of me, spine by spine.

If they were 'unseen,' maybe that meant they were invisible, rather than superpowerful? It would explain their being grouped together in one grade, and why the authors didn't recommend trying to stick 'em in their gilded cages—hard to tell if you've succeeded, or just pissed off an invisible being.

My rabbit friend had joined me by the time I reached the bottom shelf. No luck.

I fondled his ears before getting to my feet again. "Sorry, bunners. Gotta dash."

The Dreyelian device book in hand, I wove my way back through the labyrinth of rooms, halls, and shelves to the front of the store, where Bracchius was demonstrating Sparkles's tummy bells for Monique's benefit, shaking the unicorn plushie with vigor.

Was that 'Twinkle Twinkle Little Sprite'?

Monique had a long-suffering look on her face. Bracchius spotted me first. "Immy! Did you find it?"

I shrugged the shoulder clamping the book down. "Yeah, but now I'm looking for another one." I propped my elbows on the counter and gazed sweetly at Monique, who raised an eyebrow above her wire frames.

"What can I help you find?"

"Do you have a book called *Unseen Forces: Nova-Class Beings*?"

Monique tilted her head, and her eyes unfocused as she stared off into the distance.

Bracchius scooted closer to me. "Isn't she going to look it up in her computer or something?"

I nodded at the blatantly computerless counter. "Nope. Just let her do her thing."

"But—"

I shushed him, and he folded his little arms over Sparkles grumpily, the bells in her tummy giving one more jingle.

Monique zoned back in and smirked down at Bracchius. "My magic doesn't play well with technology. I have to keep it all up here." She tapped her finger to her temple.

Bracchius's red flickers erupted into frenzied motion. "Whoa, really?" He gave me the demon equivalent of side-eye. "If humans can have that good of a memory, why is yours so terrible, Immy?"

I gritted my teeth on a smile. "Take it up with the ADHD, Bracchius."

I had great memory for certain things, like sigils and other designs. Once I committed a sigil to memory, I could redraw it line for line, no problemo.

Pesky little things like super important appointments, or where I put my phone down, though, continually eluded me.

Them's the breaks.

Monique cleared her throat, saving me from the awkward moment. "I'm afraid I don't have that one. I could special order it for you, if you like?"

I tugged the first book out from under my arm and flipped it over to the price on the back: $34.95. I sucked in a breath through my teeth.

I could probably just barely wangle taking this one home with me, but to commit to paying for another book definitely at least as expensive, that I wouldn't even know was useful until I had a chance to look through it . . .

"No, that's okay, but thanks. You don't happen to know anything about Nova-class beings, do you? Like, what even qualifies?"

Monique pursed her lips. "Well, I'm far from an expert on the subject, but I know that includes origin dragons, archdemons . . ."

Bracchius rolled forward. "Ooh, those are so cool! What's this about?"

I really didn't want to go into the details in front of Monique. "I'll tell ya later, buddy."

Monique raised a finger. "Oh, and I think dreadnoughts too. And of course all identified deities." She smiled. "Does that help?"

I gulped, and patted Bracchius gingerly, coming to the inescapable conclusion that he had a freaking god shoved up his butt.

One that hopefully couldn't just pop out on a whim and vaporize him.

I definitely need to do a deep dive on that 'Releasing the Kraken' chapter or whatever that had been, just to make sure the artifact's denizen was staying firmly put for the time being.

"That helps *so* much, thank you." My tremulous smile probably wasn't super convincing. "Can I nab this one from you?" I slipped the book onto the counter and pushed it toward her.

"Of course. That'll be thirty-seven ninety-two."

I contemplated the two fifties sitting in my wallet courtesy of the checkout golem, but those were earmarked for Ruby and Samaire. I slid my card across the counter. This would be Next Month Immy's problem.

Last Month Immy was always a real jerk.

Monique tucked the book into a nice paper bag with the Eclectica Emporium logo stamped big across the front, and passed it over.

"Thanks. I'm sure I'll be back at some point. Come on, Bracchius."

He splooped off the counter to hover a few inches off the floor, Sparkles's back hoof merrily dragging along the hardwood.

I hefted the bag in his direction. "Does Sparkles wanna ride in here?"

Bracchius eyed the bag. "Maybe . . . Let me ask."

After a whispered conference with Sparkles, he nestled her delicately inside, front legs and head dangling over the edge of the bag so she'd have a good view.

As I pushed open the door with a jangle, Bracchius behind me, a cloud of cool mist plumed downward, swallowing us whole.

Petty little octopod was *literally* fogging us.

"Oh, you—"

I herded Bracchius out the door with my foot before he could launch a counterassault to Horley's parting shot. The door thumped shut behind us.

"But Immy—"

"You're above such pettiness," I informed Bracchius, hoping I could make it true.

"Oh, yes, of course . . ." He bobbed solemnly. "I'm better than that eight-limbed churl!"

"You sure are."

I led the way back to the subway, wanting to put some distance between the budding archnemeses. Last thing I needed was to foot the bill for replacing the entire shop's worth of crisped—or water-damaged—books.

Bracchius followed me down the subway stairs. "So what was all that about Nova beings?"

How to approach this delicately?

"Well, uh, Bracchius . . ."

There really wasn't a way.

I heaved a deep breath and went for it. "Seems like there's probably one inside the artifact." I flapped a hand at his derriere. "Inside *you*."

The train pulled up, and I rushed to finish before Bracchius could react. "So we've really gotta find a better place for it, pronto, because the last thing I want is you getting supernovaed by a godling or something."

Bracchius scoffed as the train doors opened. "Immy, it's fine, really. I'm a demon, remember? You think I can't handle something like that?"

I blinked down at him. "Uh-huh, right." He seemed confident, but I sure as heck wasn't.

We squeezed between the other commuters onto the train, Bracchius weaving between legs to follow me.

If I hadn't known just how scary whatever was inside him had to be, I would have been a lot more tempted to pop the gizmo open and release its occupant into the wild, hopefully getting the baddies off our tail permanently.

As it was . . .

Yeah. I needed to get that thing out of Bracchius before he went nuclear.

But having it back out meant the baddies could zero right in on it. I was *so* done with stalkers and ambushes.

Which meant I had to figure out something else to do with it.

Did I know anyone who, one, was powerful enough to conceal it from any tracking spells, and two, I could trust with anything this scary?

Not really, no.

But maybe a friend of a friend?

Damarion was my best bet for knowing someone who fit the bill. I shot off a quick text with enough details to get him started—and probably enough to worry him, TBH.

I'd tackle that later.

We got off at our stop and ambled home through the dark streets, unaccosted for once. I guess even bad guys gotta sleep sometime.

I swung open the front door, and a warm sugary smell washed over me. Dumping the book bag beside the door, I whipped around toward the kitchen.

Where Kor was pulling a baking sheet out of the oven.

My nonfunctioning oven.

And the demon was wearing an *apron*.

I had to be hallucinating.

UNICORN BALLAD

Not only was he wearing an apron, but the apron tied around his ovoid waist was a *mini-me copy* of my favorite one.

That, or he'd shrunk it.

Either way, it was preposterous: the words 'Pizza Slut' emblazoned in red sauce splatters across a black apron, pizza slices with arms and legs dancing around the moniker.

Actually looked pretty good on him, had to admit.

My eyes traveled to the baking rack perched on the counter, covered in—

"Are those *cookies*? You're baking . . . cookies."

Was I dreaming? I yanked on a curl to make sure.

Ouch.

Kor tutted. "What else would they be? Really, Immaline, I knew human perception was paltry compared to a demon's, but I didn't think it was *that* outrageously pathetic."

I snapped out of my daze—still the same mean ol' Kor.

Definitely not a dream.

So . . . *why* was he baking cookies? And how was the long-dead oven functioning?

He gripped the fresh-out-of-the-oven baking sheet with one stubby heatproof arm, raising a spatula with the other.

Since my oven wasn't a lump of molten slag, I had to assume no hellfire had been involved in the making of these cookies.

Had he enslaved a miniature dragon for his sinister cookie-baking purposes?

I peered into the still-open oven.

It was empty of anything except metal racks and the standard heating elements, operating like any run-of-the-mill oven should.

"The brownies fixed the oven too," Bracchius supplied helpfully.

Ah. That solved *one* mystery, at least.

I crept closer to the tasty-smelling objects of my suspicion cooling innocently on the wire rack. A few tempting crumbs littered the counter.

Either Kor had decided to get into my good graces but quick, or this was some revenge plot for me almost burning down his domain.

And which was more likely of the two?

Revenge. Definitely revenge.

"Would you like one?" Kor asked sweetly, and I lurched back a step.

Yeah, these were definitely poisoned. Or filled with molten tar, or shards of glass.

Had to be.

"I think I'm good, thanks."

Bracchius bobbed forward at shoulder level and hovered over a cookie, contemplating. "I'll try one."

I held out a hand. "What if they're—"

"Poison?" Bracchius quaked with a snicker. "Most toxic substances can't hurt demons, remember? But still . . ." Bracchius folded his teensy arms. "You eat one first, Kor."

"Very well." Kor scooped up a rather charred cookie directly from the scorching baking sheet and stuffed it inside himself.

The cookie sank into his depths like he was a puffy black marshmallow.

Granted, a marshmallow with homicidal tendencies.

And a bad attitude.

Satisfied, Bracchius grabbed a cookie from the cooling rack and broke off a piece. The glossy surface of his orb form jiggled as he chewed—or whatever the demon equivalent is.

I've never quite been brave enough to ask if they have teeth.

"Not poisonous," he declared. "You wouldn't like these, though, Immy—they're charcoal sriracha flavor."

I repressed a shudder. Sriracha? Good, though maybe not for cookies. Charcoal?

Heck no.

Kor nudged a second cooling rack forward. "I expected so, pitiful human sensitivities being what they are, so I baked a separate batch just for you, Immy. Chocolate-chocolate chip."

He waved magnanimously at the cooling rack, and the admittedly delicious-looking rows of cookies sitting on top.

My mouth watered, but I was still wary. I glanced at Bracchius. "Do you mind?"

"Of course not!" He rolled forward along the counter and crumbled off a piece of chocolate-chocolate chip cookie, popping it into his depths. "Safe for human consumption," he pronounced.

Sweet. I lunged forward and stacked up half a dozen of the cookies into a teetering crumby tower, then scarfed down the first one whole.

So sue me—you'd be famished too, after a frenzied chase through grocery land and all the other antics I'd been up to since Street Eats this afternoon.

The cookie was *divine*—rather ironic, coming from a demon.

I savored the crumbly crunch of the outside and the warm chewy inside suffused with pockets of melty chocolate . . .

Yep. This was the good stuff.

If I didn't watch out, I was gonna have to fend off tiny camerapeople from *Brownie Wars* wanting to document Kor's cooking marvels.

We'd have to keep this our little secret.

I took another bite of the cookie—okay, I smashed another whole one into my face, so what?

Yum.

Had my tirade really had that much of an impact on Kor? Or was this some kind of long con?

I studied him as I munched on the fan-freaking-tastic cookie.

Only time would tell.

My arm complained about the weight of the forgotten bag still clutched in my non-cookie-grubbing hand. Oh.

I hefted the bag onto the only clear square foot of counter, plucking Sparkles out from between the handles and passing 'er over to Bracchius.

The book inside reminded me of how very-much-not-a-great idea it would be for the baddies to lark off with the artifact Bracchius was safeguarding.

And how very much they must want it.

"Can you guys set up some extra wards and protections on the place? Y'know, so the bad guys won't spend the whole night trying to break in and disturbing my beauty sleep?"

Bracchius stole another cookie before saluting me—well, whacking himself in the tummy, but I'd figured that one out after the first five times he'd done it.

"Sure thing, Immy!" He swiveled to Kor. "Whaddya think, noise wards, vibration wards, some extra booby traps?"

Extra booby traps? And here I thought he'd been a good demon and disarmed all the magical landmines peppered across the yard.

Could I at least hope they'd spelled them not to trigger for *me*?

Probably not.

Kor shuffled another batch of cookies onto the swiftly emptying racks. "If you're truly worried, Immy, I . . ." He grumbled to himself, almost inaudibly.

That didn't bode well.

"You what?" Better to get it over with.

"I— You . . . could sleep inside my domain, if that would make you feel better."

My mouth dried out as I stared at him in abject shock, my lips sticking to my teeth. Forget a revenge plot—did he have a brain tumor? Had he been possessed by some semireasonable being?

No, demons *did* the possessing. They couldn't get possessed themselves, could they? Or . . . could one demon possess another? That might make sense.

Oh gosh, was that how they procreated? I—

I clacked my mouth shut and threw my brain back into gear, burying that only mildly horrifying image deep in the recesses of my brain, hopefully never to return.

What was the question?

Right—sleeping in Kor's domain.

The hotter-than-Arizona-in-August domain teeming with hungry imps and who knows what else.

"Uh . . . I don't think that's necessary quite yet. But I really appreciate the offer, Kor. Rain check?"

He bobbed in a nod, seeming relieved. Maybe I could finagle this into permission to use his laundromat.

Not that I'd let a measly little thing like permission hold me back, though.

I snagged a few more cookies and left Kor and Bracchius to their charcoal sriracha ones as they debated wards. Something poked out from behind the couch, and I trudged over to check.

My sword, fanny pack, and a sticky tangle of duct tape.

Riiight, I'd just dumped everything and collapsed last night.

This morning.

Ugh, was that *really* this morning?

I stuffed another cookie in my face to stave off the existential dread. I really should put all this away, and . . . Nooo, I hadn't cleaned my sword either, had I?

Grabbing everything, I slumped onto the sofa. Weirdly, the sword sheath looked brand-new. How—

Hope sparked inside me. Had the negentropes cleaned my sword along with the rest of me? It had been sheathed at the time, but those guys had been itsy-bitsy, so maybe . . .

I pulled out the sword.

No such luck.

The length of the blade was slimed with typhon blood and what could only be half-melted shadowlurk substance.

At least the typhon blood didn't seem to have eaten into the metal.

Yippee skippy.

I dug out the cleaner and some ratty socks, put on an old episode of *Star Trek: Voyager*, and swiftly fell into hyperfocus, eradicating every last speck of grime on my poor sword.

Might as well take care of the fanny pack while I was at it. I unzipped the bag and upended it on the coffee table to sort everything out.

Only, nothing fell out.

Had I packed it *that* tight? I shook it vigorously, and . . . nothing.

Grousing, I flipped it over and peered inside.

Oh no.

A thick semitranslucent layer of green and blue *something* covered the contents. What the—

I poked it cautiously, and it squished beneath my fingertip before recovering its shape, like memory foam or marshmallow or . . .

Or melted gummy dragons.

Sigh.

Could I pry it out? I scrabbled at the gooey congealed seam between fanny pack and gummy disaster, and managed to peel enough back to see the sticky mess beneath.

The Band-Aids, Grandma's peanut butter cookies, and all the rest were entombed within the gelatinous glob. *Why* had I thought bringing candy into Kor's sweltering domain was a good idea?

I dropped the bag in disgust and flopped my head back against the sofa, admiring the old water stain on the ceiling.

Today it looked like a pixie riding a hippo.

The gummy mess had effectively zapped my can-do energy for the evening. A yawn assaulted me, and I looked at the time—bedtime.

I meandered to the bathroom to do the bare minimum with scrubbing off my makeup and brushing my teeth. Midbrush, I snagged against a cable snaking out of the cabinet door.

Weird . . .

I nudged the door open with my foot. The unoccupied terrarium I'd put together to distract Kor stared back at me.

Riiight.

Forgot.

"Bracchius?" Well, it came out more like 'Bwakkiss' around my toothbrush, but he clearly got the picture because he showed up at the bathroom door.

"Yeah?"

I pointed at the terrarium with my big toe. "Haff. At."

The bathroom was silent for a moment, just his red flickers eddying. "What?"

Holding up a finger, I spat not-so-delicately into the sink and took a quick rinse. "Sorry. The terrarium. You can have at it now."

I clicked the heat lamp on demonstratively, and Bracchius scooted closer. "Yeah?"

"Yeah, buddy."

A black streak shot for the tank, and the door thwapped shut behind him as I jumped back with a yelp.

All right, then.

Leaving him to thermal bliss, I made a pit stop in the kitchen to grab my new book and pilfer the last of the chocolate-chocolate chip cookies. Then the plate of cookies and I sauntered off to bed.

Three cookies and ten pages in, my eyelids started to flutter. Just needed to set my alarm and—

My hand scrabbled uselessly at my cluttered nightstand.

No phone.

The prospect of extending so much as a toe from beneath my cozy covers was just not it.

Bracchius was probably a molten puddle at this point, but with Kor as uncharacteristically helpful as he'd been this evening, I figured it was worth a shot. "Kor?"

No response.

I cleared my throat and tried a little louder. "Kor?"

Nada.

I stuck said toe out from under my comforter, frigid air washing over my cover-warm skin, and I yanked it back under lickety-split.

"Bracchius?"

A clunk preceded my bedroom door swinging open. Bracchius—my favorite little demon ever—drifted in, looking . . . a bit more gloopy than normal, like Silly Putty left out in the sun.

"You need something, Immy?"

Bless him, he didn't even sound annoyed.

I peeked over my covers sheepishly. "I forgot my phone in my purse. Would you mind grabbing it? I need to set my alarm."

"Sure!" He disappeared, and I read another page of Dreyelian device operation instructions while I waited.

"Here you go." Bracchius floated over, phone in pseudo limb. "I went ahead and set the alarm already. Same as yesterday, right? Four four five?"

"Uh, yeah. Thanks."

That was a tad later than strictly ideal, but I'd long since mastered the art of getting ready in a raging panic.

Besides, I was probably still sleep-deprived from yesterday's nonsense. Who was I to turn down an extra half hour of shut-eye?

I succumbed to another yawn, almost engulfing Bracchius with my gaping jaw, and he retreated out of teeth's way. "G'night!"

"Night. Thanks again." I plugged in the phone, licked the cookie crumbs off my plate, and hunkered down to read another page or two before conking out.

I clawed my way up from the depths of sleep to some abominable noise blaring beside my ear.

"Sparkly unicorns, racing through the rainbows! Grazing on some poppies and healing all the world!"

Sadly, I'd long since gotten rid of the kind of alarm clock you can beat into submission. Smashing my phone wasn't gonna subdue this chipper racket.

"Twinkly unicorns, prancing through the forest! Shining in the moonlight and—"

I unearthed myself from my tangle of covers and found the glowing screen of my phone, sliding the icon to shut off the damn song before collapsing back against my pillow.

Last time I let Bracchius anywhere near my alarm settings.

"Oh good, you're awake!"

I groaned as light flooded my room from the hall. "Thaz debatable."

Pushing up onto one elbow, I smeared dried drool grit from the corner of my mouth and fumbled around for my water bottle.

Morning dry mouth is no joke.

Blech.

I choked on my water, sputtering—it wasn't just Bracchius invading my room, but Kor too. They bobbed closer as I tried not to hack up a lung.

Something had to be going on. Sure, Bracchius made a habit of following me around every morning, like me sleeping was some sort of missed relationship opportunity, but Kor? I was honestly a bit shocked he even dared cross my threshold.

The sage fumes must've dissipated but good.

I eyed the pair of them. "You, uh, you need something?"

They swiveled toward each other midair, as if trying to decide who should speak first.

Uh-oh.

Either one of them was trouble enough on his own, but if they'd been conniving . . .

I clunked my water bottle down and straightened. "Spill it."

Bracchius took the lead. "Kor and I spent the night poring over your new book, and—"

"My book? The one I fell asleep reading?" I whipped around, confirming the distinct absence of the book, and narrowed my eyes. "You snuck in here and stole it while I was sleeping?"

"Obviously. Anyway, we—"

Kor interrupted. "We've come up with a devious plan, Immaline. Most devious. Would you like to hear it?"

I opened my mouth to disavow any knowledge of their actions, or plotting, or planning, or *anything*, when my phone erupted into the cheery unicorn ballad again.

This morning was off to a rip-roaring start.

ELEGANT PIECE OF SUBTERFUGE

I killed the alarm. "You've come up with a plan . . . together?"

Bracchius piped, "Yep! And it's a good one too!"

I rubbed my eyes. Maybe this was all a dream.

Maybe I'd gotten conked on the head with a can of Chef Bugbeardee back at the grocery store and had dreamed everything since. Bracchius was probably hovering over my limp form to figure out how to wake me back up before the bad guys hauled me off.

Nah, I was too tired for this to be a dream.

I flung the covers off and got to my feet. "Give me two minutes, and then you can tell me all about it."

My two blessed demon-free minutes went toward the couple of bathroom activities I absolutely was not going to put up with company for.

That done, I kicked the door back open, and my demons drifted in.

I shoved my toothbrush inside my mouth and muttered, "Go for it."

Bracchius floated above my jar of Q-tips. "So, you got that book to understand how the artifact works, right? But it also shows how to make—"

Kor jumped in. "How to make our own Dreyelian device, which should be simple enough once we have the appropriate materials. And—"

"And the reason we want it is so—"

"So we can engage in an elegant piece of subterfuge by—"

Bracchius planted himself directly in front of Kor's face. "By making a fake artifact we can let the bad guys steal, and then they won't bug you anymore!"

I gaped at them for a second before spitting in the sink and rinsing.

That was actually a pretty fantastic idea. Except . . .

"But how do we fake the contents? I don't think popping a black marble in there is going to cut it."

I mussed my curls into place with a spritz of dry shampoo and dabbed some concealer on the worst of my dark circles and a couple red spots that would be pimples tomorrow.

Bracchius bobbed closer. "Actually, we were thinking you—"

Kor nudged him aside. "Since *we* will be undertaking the construction of the device itself, it will fall to you, Immaline, to find a suitable dupe for the contents."

Me? I stared at them in disbelief as I swiped on deodorant. "I'm going to be at work all day. You really think I'm just going to randomly stumble across some magical black blob of amazingness as I'm checking in rental cars?"

Bracchius gained the edge as Kor reeled back from my sea-salt-and-flannel deodorant. "That *is* how this whole problem started . . ."

Rude.

"Well, don't count on it. You'd better find something yourselves."

I scratched idly at my arm, only for my nails to glide across a slick patch of definitely-not-skin.

Startled, I glanced down.

Oh, right. The bandage Ruby had put over my tattoo.

When was I supposed to take that off?

Probably yesterday.

Oops.

I scrabbled at the curling edge of the adhesive, which was no longer tacky thanks to all the fluff and dust stuck to it.

It peeled back like a dream, leaving my bare skin and shiny new tattoo behind, the white ink just visible against my skin with a slight pink tinge where it was still healing.

Healing. Right—I was supposed to be using Ruby's tattoo potion or whatever.

I hunted around until I found where I'd dumped the itty-bitty bottle, Kor and Bracchius trailing me like lost ducklings.

Were they waiting for me to pass judgment on their plan? I guess I hadn't really said much yet, other than vetoing the preposterous part they'd expected me to play in it.

"I like it. You guys'll let me know when it's ready?"

"Of course, Immy!"

That would only take them, what, a week?

A week of fending off increasingly dangerous attacks?

Sob.

Swinging by the kitchen, I shoved toast slathered with peanut butter into my mouth, and Bracchius detoured to the remaining charcoal cookies.

I rounded up my far-flung work polos to scrounge up one clean enough to wear today, and groaned.

None of them passed the sniff test.

Time to do laundry.

I only had two minutes until I had to sprint out the door, though, so I fumigated the least-offensive shirt with a bottle of peach-pear body spray and rammed it in the bottom of my purse to marinate in the fragrance.

Hopefully that'd mask the I-already-wore-this-three-times smell.

Snatching my purse, I rounded up all the essentials—water bottle, keys, wallet, phone. Kor and Bracchius were arguing in the kitchen.

"Platinum wire would be by far the superior material—possibly even titanium."

"But silver would be *way* easier to get."

"Bye, guys!"

I unlocked the door, only for Bracchius to zoom past me.

"Immy, wait! We're coming with you."

"What? Why?"

Sure enough, Kor joined us in the predawn darkness just before I could close the door.

"To safeguard you, of course, Immaline."

"Uh-huh. From?"

"From the bad guys, Immy!"

I had my doubts that our nemeses would pry themselves out of bed at the butt-crack of dawn to come hunt me down when they had no trouble finding me at more respectable times of day, but if Bracchius and Kor wanted to tag along, more power to them.

"Fine, but only to the subway, yeah?"

The last thing I needed was them following me all the way to work, and annoying my coworkers—or worse, the boss.

I strode across the yard at top speed. Two days late to work in a row would just be asking for trouble, and I was already cutting it real close.

My phone rang as they picked back up with the bickering. The screen lit with Damarion's name, though it wasn't a video call for once.

"Hiya."

"Ah, good, it sounds like I didn't wake you."

"Nope. What's up?"

"I received your text message, and wanted to glean more details."

"Man, took you awhile to respond. I texted you like twelve hours ago."

"Apologies. When I noticed the message, we were well within your sleeping hours, and I did not wish to disturb you. I was certain by this time you had to be up and about."

I gave him the whole rundown of everything he needed to know, and my hopes he could find someone capable and trustworthy enough to take possession of the artifact—a pretty tall order.

The gist: Bracchius was literally sitting on a demigod or some such trapped in what amounted to a magical ball of paper clips.

I eyeballed Bracchius, who'd just larked off to ride a golem lawnmower as it zoomed across the yard beside us.

Please let Damarion know of someone.

"So you need someone beyond reproach, with top-tier magical skills, who isn't also power-hungry."

"You got it."

"I'm . . . not sure I know anyone who fits all your criteria. But I'm willing to bet Cynna does. I'll ask her and get back to you."

"Thanks."

I hung up just as we reached the subway station.

The totally, one hundred percent steeped in darkness subway station. What the—?

The rest of the block had power, judging by the few house lights of other people crazy enough to get up at this gross time of the morning, so it couldn't be that.

That left only a couple likely options.

Bracchius bobbed at the top of the dark stairs. "Do you think those brigands are lying in wait?"

That was one, but . . .

"None of them looked like they could see in the dark any better than me. I don't think so." Which left . . .

The Dark Coach.

"Why don't you guys lead the way, since you can actually see down there?"

At least the glow-in-the-dark strips on the steps would keep me from breaking my neck on the way down.

Kor and Bracchius could sound the alarm if it wasn't actually the Dark Coach, but it was a good bet that was what was going on.

Not all Saskia Springs residents could tolerate daylight—or any light at all. While many of those hunker down in their subbasement lairs, work from home, and order takeout, not all of them can afford to be twenty-four-seven homebodies. Cavebodies?

Some of them had to, you know, actually get around the city somehow. And driving doesn't work so hot when you can't let any light in through the windshield.

If they can make it to a subway station, they can activate the Dark Coach sigil at the entrance, plunging the station into total darkness after a five-second alert for any commuters already inside.

I clung to the handrail, shuffling down one step at a time. Kor and Bracchius were already invisible in the darkness ahead.

A diffuse glob of red flickers drifted closer, and Bracchius said, "It's just a nightstriker. No dastards. The darkness is nice, though, isn't it? It doesn't ever get this dark in the city."

"Just keep me from tripping over any benches or trash cans, will ya?"

"Okie doke."

My feet slapped across the tile floor at the base of the stairs.

"Ooh, go left. I mean, right—"

I hip-checked something solid and veered right. This was far enough—didn't wanna risk stumbling right off the edge of the platform.

It was only a minute before a rumble and screech announced the oncoming train, every light of the front car extinguished by the sigil to avoid crisping the shadowy creature we shared the darkness with.

Dank air buffeted against me, and the rattle and whine of the train coming to a halt filled the dark station. The hiss of the doors preceded a rustle to my left.

I leaned in to Bracchius—or Kor, it was impossible to tell in here.

"That the nightstriker?"

"Yep."

Ha. It *was* Bracchius.

Rather than plunge an entire train's worth of commuters into darkness at the drop of a hat, every train that ran—theoretically—on the hour was outfitted with three Dark Coaches just behind the engine—more than enough to fill the breadth of the station, and keep the light of the following cars down the tunnel from shining in.

Each Dark Coach had only one door and no windows, completely sealed off from the dreaded lights that would absolutely ruin their passengers' day.

Bracchius shifted beside me. "Okay, she's inside."

Another hiss of the doors, and the train crept forward as the station lights snapped back to full brilliance, searing my poor eyeballs.

Kor and Bracchius screeched at the sudden onslaught of light.

"Come on, guys, you *really* should've expected that."

Kor huffed. "You can't possibly think demons make a habit of riding this infernal contraption, Immy. We have much more sophisticated means of transportation—ones that do not sear one's very soul to the core without so much as a warning!"

"Drama king," I whispered to Bracchius. *He'd* calmed right down after his initial startled 'ack!'

The regular portion of the train pulled into place. The doors opened, and a couple of people disembarked.

Bracchius tried to follow me onto the train, but I waved him off. "I'll be good from here. You two go home and work on your gizmo."

"You sure?"

"Yup."

"Okay. Have a good day at work, Immy!"

The car was empty enough that I could actually take a seat without encroaching on anyone else's territory.

I slouched, my purse clutched in my lap, my head plopped back against the grimy window. The usual assortment of pixies fluttered above, gamboling in playful somersaults and probably plotting their next big prank, knowing pixies.

One spun around a pole like a pocket-size stripper. Another scrawled a blue mustache on a movie poster of Husker Sunburst plastered high on the wall.

I only half dozed off, and thankfully the garbled announcement for the airport station roused me. I peered inside my purse—everything still there—and slid to my feet, joining the small cluster of commuters dragging carry-ons and suitcases.

I was somehow only two minutes late as I bustled to the bathroom and unearthed my work polo from the body-spray stew at the bottom of my purse.

Holding it to my nose, I gave it a good sniff.

Acceptable, I guess.

Hopefully no one would come too close.

Laundry would be way less of a pain in the ass now I knew there was a shiny new—well, dark and creepy—laundromat just through Kor's mirror.

If only I'd remembered to get Cucumber a gift yesterday when we were out shopping already . . .

What would make a good gift, anyway?

I called up Bracchius as I headed outside, the phone ringing.

The stars were obscured by the glare of the parking lot lights, as always. I was tempted to flick the lights off, just for a minute, to watch the few stars visible from within city limits bloom to life.

Bracchius picked up. "Immy? Do you need help? Did you get attacked on the subway?"

I got to work checking in the row of abandoned cars from last night's customers as we talked.

"Nah, I'm fine. Just a quick question. Is Kor around?"

I didn't want to accidentally rat on Cucumber's part in my rampage through Kor's domain. No telling what Kor would do to the slimy little guy.

"No, he's out getting supplies for the fake artifact . . . Was that your question?"

"Nope. What do demonlings like?"

"Demonlings? Uh . . . darkness, dopamine rushes, *Sludge Wars*—"

I interrupted. "No, like, if you had to get one a gift, like marshmallow bubble bath or something."

"Dunno, sulfur-scented bubble bath might be more their style. Or, uh, charcoal-covered slugs, maybe? I never spent much time around demonlings."

"Thanks. Talk later!"

I hung up and stashed my phone in my pocket, hauling a full-size wrecked umbrella out of the backseat of a car—somebody clearly had a bad time during this week's dragon storm.

Into the trash it went.

Bubble bath was probably my best bet for Cucumber. I had no idea where you could buy charcoal-covered slugs, and there was a Bath & Body Works close to the subway line along the way home. They catered to all beings, so hopefully they'd have something demonically appropriate.

I snagged a lonely paperback from a glove box to add to my collection, and pocketed a few Retrocade tokens at the bottom of a cup holder with a smile. Bracchius and I had gone there once, forever ago.

These might be a good excuse to go back—we hadn't done anything fun in a little while.

Bert started whisking away the furthest-back cars as I opened the trunk on a Prius closer to my booth. The moist mineral smell of our famous Saskia Springs smacked me in the face—along with sweat and mildew.

A pair of still-damp swim shorts stared back at me from the floor of the trunk.

Ew.

I slammed the trunk pronto. I'd leave those for the shop guys to dispose of.

So sue me. No way was I getting my hands within a foot of some rando's clammy swim shorts.

One genius had left the radio blaring, and 'Glamour Girl' by Nedra Shine the siren came on as I checked the mileage.

Samaire had a nicer voice, TBH.

Right, Samaire—I still owed her that fifty bucks. Maybe I could swing by the nightclub after work?

Or . . . today was my tour-guide dinner thing with Fitz, wasn't it?

After that, then.

Waking my phone, I winced at the time. Samaire wouldn't be awake for a good long while.

I set a reminder to text her later, and got back to work.

Dawn had come and gone by the time Bert and I cleared my lanes, with a few more harried customers dropping off cars and scrambling to catch their flights.

I'd just kicked back to finish *Minimum Wage Magic* when Keisha appeared in the open doorway of my booth with a wry expression.

"So, you going to a cowboy-themed baby shower for a bouncing baby titan, or what?"

I just stared at her, waiting for her words to make sense. That couldn't possibly be what she'd actually said, right?

But after a full twenty seconds, my brain didn't output anything less nonsensical.

"Uh . . . what?"

"Your delivery arrived." She jerked her chin over her shoulder. "Come on."

Delivery?

Utterly stumped, I dropped my book and followed her inside.

Doak stood smirking beside the biggest basket I'd ever seen—over half my height and stuffed with plaid fabric in a rainbow of colors.

Fabric rolled up into clumsy roses . . . just like those dorky baby-shower-gift onesies that religiously pop up in the Pinterest feed of every woman under a hundred.

Keisha's comment was starting to make sense.

"I, uh, *definitely* didn't order this."

"There's a card." Doak pointed at an envelope nestled amidst the fabric.

I plucked it out and tore it open, my eyes darting straight to the bottom—the sender.

Cynna.

COURTING GIFT

What in all that was unholy?

I scanned back up to the top of the card, and actually read the note.

> For Immy Cordell—
> A gift seemed an appropriate opening gesture. Regrettably, I've as yet been unable to apprehend your enemies. So, instead of a delightful gift of their heads, you will have to make do with this rather pedestrian gift instead.
> For now.
> Happy hunting,
> Cynna

Oh boy. How did she even know where I worked?

Dumb question: Damarion. She probably knew half my life history by now—the half I'd bothered to share with him, anyway.

Keisha leaned in. "You haven't closed your mouth for two whole minutes. Need some water?"

Sticking my tongue out at her, I shoved Cynna's card into my pocket. I yanked the closest flannel 'rose' out of the massive basket, determined to figure out what nonsense Cynna had thought an appropriate gift.

One snap of my wrist unfurled the fabric, leaving me staring at a teal flannel shirt just the size I like to wear—oversized.

Sure, it made me look like a starving artist, but I appreciated the extra snuggle value.

Slinging the shirt over my arm, I stared at the basket. There had to be *fifty* flannel shirts here, in every shade of every color of the rainbow.

Overkill much, Cynna?

I guess she's the 'go big or go home' type.

Speaking of . . . How was *I* going to get this home? Not only could I not carry it, chances were good it wouldn't even fit on the subway.

Keisha must've noticed the flabbergasted look on my face. "How about we stash it in the office for now? Until you figure out what to do with it."

"Seriously? That office is tiny enough as it is. This monstrosity'll take up half the space."

The last thing I needed was my bosses mad at me because I was making their lives miserable with something this ridiculous.

Keisha glanced between me and the gargantuan gift basket. "Are you really sure you want to turn down my incredibly generous offer?"

I snapped to attention. "No! I mean . . . Thanks, boss, I'd love to stuff it in there . . . if someone will help me move it."

We tried to budge it with no success. Even Doak lent a shoulder, but the basket just started to tip with a woody crackle—probably would've worked better if we weren't each a foot apart in height.

Keisha called Bert up on her radio, and he appeared with a couple of the other shop guys and a dolly.

Between the six of us, we heaved the basket onto the dolly and rolled it to the office, where we found our next hiccup—it just barely wouldn't fit through the door.

I chewed my lip as I stared the basket down. "Here." With a well-placed kick, I snapped a section of wicker.

Bert followed suit, and soon enough the basket was crunchy enough to squeeze through the door with a painful crackle, a trail of splinters littering the ground. We wheeled it to the back corner, where it loomed over the rest of the small office.

I'd have to load up with as many flannels as I could every day after work, until I'd shuttled them all home.

Then maybe we could have a work bonfire with the basket scraps out on the lot.

A little fire never hurt anybody, right?

As long as I wasn't in charge of setting it, at least.

The others brushed basket bits off their clothes as I unrolled another flannel, admiring the green, blue, and yellow pattern. I'd have to do a major closet detox to fit even *half* of these in there.

But that was okay—I've been hoarding holey outfits, stretched-out leggings, and pants that don't fit me anymore for ages.

Maybe this would give me the dopamine to finally sort through it all.

"Thanks, guys." I swept the kindling across the linoleum with my sneaker. "I'll clean this up in a sec."

Keisha rescued her long purple hair from where it had caught on some broken wicker. "I think we all deserve a cookie after that. Any takers?"

I might be approaching cookie overload after Kor's batch last night, but who was I to turn down free sugary goodness?

Keisha whipped the plastic wrap off the plate of fresh-baked s'mores cookies, and passed them around.

My eyes rolled back in my head as I munched—bittersweet dark chocolate, caramelized marshmallow, and cookie crumb that somehow tasted graham-crackery.

So what if I looked possessed?

Everybody needs to get possessed by mouthwatering morsels now and then.

When I came back to myself, Doak and the shop guys had left, and Keisha was rewrapping the cookie plate.

"I'll be right back, just gonna grab a broom." I headed toward the door with a cookie-fueled bounce in my step.

"Immy, wait."

I wheeled around at Keisha's concerned tone.

"Is everything okay?"

My brow furrowed. "What, because of the flannels? That's just a not-so-secret admirer, er—"

What *did* you call someone who was courting you for friendship?

"No, not that. You texted me about whether the vandals could've gotten your info. Did someone break in at your place?"

"Oh, that. Not really—I mean, sorta, but . . ." I took a deep breath. "My demon roommates have it handled."

Her dubious expression didn't let up.

"I'm fine, really. Turns out hellfireballs and psycho crows are a pretty good burglar deterrent."

"You must have an . . . interesting living arrangement."

I laughed. "You could say that. Thanks for worrying about me, though."

She waved a hand. "Totally selfish. Can't have my illicit book supplier disappearing on me."

I rolled my eyes. "They're not *illicit* . . ."

"Then maybe you should stop dealing them out of a cardboard box you've got squirreled away in the dark at your feet." Keisha winked. "Sweep up, then I want you back out on the lot, yeah?"

"Okie doke."

I hunted down a broom and dustpan in the nearest janitor's closet, and made quick work of the basket scraps. I unearthed a couple chicken feathers under the edge of a desk in the office, too.

What had Doak been doing shifting in here? I couldn't think of a single thing where his chicken form would be more useful for work than his human one.

Weirdo.

I dumped the trash, shoved the broom back in the closet, and headed outside. The cars had piled back up in my absence, but no biggie. I jogged to the back of the line, warm morning sunshine stroking my face, oil shimmering on the asphalt, and got started checking them in.

Halfway through the backup, my phone rang. I tugged it out: Bracchius.

Craning my neck, I smashed my phone between my ear and shoulder as I turned off an idling car and checked the gas level. "What's up, Bracchius? Kinda in the middle of work here."

His dorky voice chirped over the line. "We're still trying to figure out what to put inside the fake artifact. You didn't find anything yet, did you?"

"Not so much." The closest thing I had to a sinister black blob here was the chunk of asphalt pitted out of a nearby pothole.

"I thought sentient Ebonian coffee might work, but Kor says it would be too unpredictable, so then I—"

He cut off with a rustle, and Kor's deep voice spoke instead. "To save you a ridiculous monologue, Immaline, we've concluded a portion of demon substance would make the most convincing substitute."

I jerked in surprise halfway through slamming a car door, almost catching my fingers. "*Demon* substance? Like, part of one of you guys?"

"Precisely. Now I just need to harvest the appropriate amount, and—"

"Oh, no you don't!" Bracchius huffed in the background, and with a clatter, the line went dead.

Crud on crackers.

I speed-dialed Bracchius in a panic. Pick up, pick up, pick uuup . . .

It rang five times before it connected.

"Bracchius?! Are you okay?"

"I'm— Yipe!" Bracchius's voice rose. "All my substance is staying right here, thank you very much! I've got little enough as it is!"

It was true: Bracchius is smaller than Kor, though not by a whole heck of a lot.

A crackle and boom echoed over the line, and I nearly dropped the phone.

Bracchius crowed, "Yeah, just try that again, why don't you! You've got more to spare than I do, how about we use yours!"

A squawk sounded from further away—Kor, taking his turn on the lam?

I was going to come back to a totally flattened apartment, wasn't I.

Bye-bye, deposit.

I hollered into the phone, trying to be heard over the din of crashes and gleeful taunts. "Couldn't we compromise? You could each give a little—"

Kor's voice went through the full Doppler effect as he presumably barreled past the phone. "Demons don't compromise, Immaline!"

"Would you rather end up a steaming pile of demon goo?" I muttered.

From what I could tell, Bracchius and Kor were actually pretty evenly matched, despite Bracchius's childlike attitude.

A sizzle blew the phone up with static, and then Bracchius returned. "It wouldn't work anyway, Immy. The two pieces wouldn't mix, like oil and water, or unicorn blood and voidling venom."

Crap. Then how could I stop this hellfireball merry-go-round?

Bracchius would chillax if I asked him to, but then he'd just be on the defensive again against Kor. And Kor wasn't exactly in the habit of listening to—

I grinned. Got it.

My fingers tightened on the phone, and I boomed into the mouthpiece, "STOP!"

The poor cervidae getting out of the Nissan twenty feet down froze halfway through a door slam, wide copper eyes fixed on me along with one faun-brown ear.

I waved sheepishly at her, pointed at my phone, and mouthed, "Sorry!"

She gave me a wide, wide berth on her way into the airport, dainty hooves clopping on the asphalt.

I lowered my volume, but not the command in my voice, infusing it with every scrap of Captain Janeway I could muster. "As per section seven, subsection thirteen of our roommate agreement"—I had no idea if those were the right numbers, but hopefully neither did Bracchius and Kor—"I order you to cease and desist all antagonistic interpersonal activities under pain of me adopting a caterwaul!"

Walking, talking bucket of legalese, that's me.

The other end of the line grew eerily silent.

I couldn't blame them—caterwauls are just as awful as they sound. Hence why they made such a delicious threat.

"Bracchius? Kor? You there?"

"Here," Bracchius meeped.

"Good. Hostilities have ceased?"

"Yes, Immy."

"Put me on speaker."

"Okay."

"All right, answer me this: when a piece of your substance separates from you, is it lost forever?"

Kor scoffed in the background. "Lost? What utter nonsense. Unlike humans, demons don't have paltry limbs that can be amputated. Even separated, we are whole."

I ran my tongue over my teeth. "Bracchius, I'm going to need you to expand on that a bit for me, in less pompous terms, please."

Bracchius piped up. "We stay connected to every piece of us, no matter where it is. We can feel it, control it, summon it back."

I rolled my eyes. Then why the big fight?

Morons.

"That means you can stick it back in, right?"

"Yep."

"In that case, Kor . . . It seems like such a meager and temporary sacrifice would be a good show of faith to maintain your roommate status, doncha think?"

Silence.

I waited, checking in the next car in the meantime.

At long last, Kor grumbled, "I sup*pose*." Extra emphasis on the sibilants, like the brat he is.

"Great. Then I expect you'll have this all worked out by the time I come home. Byeee!"

I ended the call and pocketed my phone. No way was I counting on Kor to give up the goods that easily, but it was worth a try. And hopefully any squabbling between now and then would be on the minor end of the scale.

Fifteen minutes later, I'd finished clearing the cars that had piled up during my mediatory phone call. I was now richer by one bottle of iced coffee that I'd pass along to Keisha in thanks for letting me clutter up her office, a rinky-dink cassette-tape-to-headphone-jack converter with a frayed cord, and the shed skin of a Lamia or somesuch.

Not the greatest haul.

Granted, I already had enough to worry about carting back home—those flannels were gonna keep me busy for *days*.

It wasn't long before we hit a dead zone; no customers pulling up, and all the cars cleared. I polished off my paperback, then scrounged up a pen with a little ink left and flipped open the back cover.

Tongue between my teeth, I pressed pen to cardstock and drew.

Drawing's always been soothing to me, something to keep my fingers busy while my brain sorts itself out.

Not that I had anything earth-shattering swirling around up there today, but still.

Sure, I could sketch whatever's around me, but mostly, like today, I draw sigils. Well, potential sigils, anyway.

There's something about the organized chaos of the lines . . . I can tell when a drawing is going wrong, or when a line feels good, though it's still awful tricky to work that intuition into anything usable.

Tech bros have algorithms churning twenty-four seven, trying to compute the next hypervaluable sigil, but it's amazing how rarely sigils get discovered by mathematical means. Good ol'-fashioned human creativity seems to win out more times than not, for whatever reason.

I should know—I've come up with several myself, though my stealth sigil is the only one that's really useful.

It's easy to tell a dud from the real thing. With a viable sigil, any spark of magic will infuse its lines, making them glow.

When all you've got is a barren tangle of lines, the magic won't interact with it.

Zip. Zilch. Nada.

My purple pen glided across the creased white paper, forming arcs and circles and harsh angles. This one was turning out a bit like a wallaby flying past the moon.

I mean, if you squinted *real* hard, that is.

One last line, and the drawing felt right, complete. Score one for me—maybe I actually hadn't messed it up, like I did three-quarters of 'em.

Only one way to find out.

Summoning a dribble of my magenta magic, I lowered my finger to the pseudo wallaby's tail, and let 'er rip.

UPSIDE-DOWN LAND

The freshly drawn lines of the sigil glowed, my magic tracing along each curve and squiggle at a slower pace, like it was finding its way through a labyrinth.

Magic reacted this way to any viable sigil new to the world—one good way to know if I'd accidentally created a duplicate of a sigil already out there, or something truly original.

It was like the magic was exploring the sigil's bounds before fully committing.

I suppressed a little squee. Not only was my off-the-cuff sketch a viable sigil—it was brand-spanking *new.*

As the magic completed the circuit of the sigil, activating it, I tried to tune in to all my senses at once, on the lookout for whatever effect the sigil would have.

No buzz of energy in the air, no—

The world tumbled before me, like I'd been thrown into a cartwheel, only my body wasn't moving, or even experiencing vertigo.

The world stilled . . .

Upside down.

Well, crap.

I held out my arms, trying to orient myself, but my hands reached down from above me. I glanced up at my torso and down at the sky, then slammed my eyes shut before the nausea could gain any more of a hold.

The sigil must be a perception filter, changing my brain's input to register the world upside down.

Hopefully its area of effect didn't extend too far—last thing I needed was a customer totaling their car right into my booth.

Wasn't your brain supposed to automatically adjust to compensate for things like this after a few minutes?

I could ask Siri, only now I had an Obsidian phone . . . What was *their* AI assistant called?

Knowing demons, probably something like Caedamonius Heartripper the Direful.

Maybe Caed for short?

Nah, they'd for sure make you say the whole thing: Hey, Caedamonius Heartripper the Direful, how do I fix my brain?

I'd have to pester Bracchius about the AI.

Had it been three minutes yet?

Granted, the brain-adjusting dealio probably only worked if your eyes were open, so your brain would actually realize things were not status quo.

I crept one eye open, then the other, peering around at the flipped world before me.

It probably wouldn't be so disconcerting if I couldn't see my body—the mismatch between where I felt my limbs and where they appeared was the most stomach-churning part of this experience.

If I could coordinate myself enough to just slap a hand on the sigil and deactivate it, I'd be golden.

The glowing pink sigil was well within arm's reach. Just snake a hand forward, and . . .

I froze. Holy house of mirrors, this was *ridiculous*.

As I moved my right hand, the top-left hand in my field of view shifted down.

Not only was my vision upside down, it was in freaking flipped-selfie mode.

Squinting, I inched my hand toward the sigil, every motion counterintuitive and needing to be corrected like twenty-seven times before I had half a handle on it.

Anyone watching from outside the booth would for sure think I was on LimiNull.

Hand seemingly poised above—below—the sigil, I paused.

Deactivating a sigil was no biggie for basically everyone who didn't have disaster magic, but I fell firmly outside that delightfully normal camp.

I didn't usually bother, since most sigils were either flashers—an instant effect that's over and done with, like opening a door or sending a signal—or their effect was one I *wanted* to run as long as possible, like my stealth sigil.

So, not only was Murphy's law not on my side, but I was out of practice, too.

Here goes nothing.

I lowered—well, lifted, in inverse land—my finger to summon back my magic. In the split-second before I connected with the vibrance of the magenta glow, the world righted itself again as my lame brain finally figured out things were hinky.

Annnd my finger finished its crash course into the sigil before I could yank it back, withdrawing the glimmering magic with some sputtering castoff and returning the sigil to inert lines of ink on paper.

Plus sending my vision topsy-turvy again, since my brain was now compensating for a problem that didn't exist anymore.

I flopped back in my wheelless rolly chair in disgust, gaze fixed on the ceiling. At least *it* looked pretty much the same flipped around.

As long as I could veg here for the few minutes needed for my brain to sort itself out—again—things should be hunky-dory.

That, of course, is when urgent rapping rattled the glass of my booth window.

Finéa, why me?

Eyes half-lidded, I managed to sit up in the chair and swivel toward my accoster, who was waving frantically on the other side of the glass.

A Crusty—well, crustaceafae, if you feel like wrapping your lips around that mouthful.

Upside down, of course.

I held up a 'one moment' finger and closed my eyes fully to stand and shuffle to the door. Doorframe-clinging status attained, I risked opening them again to stare down the blue-carapaced Crusty. "What's up?"

"I'm locked out! My suitcase is in the trunk, and I left the keys in the cup holder, but . . ." Their eyestalks bobbed disconcertingly downward with my reverse vision, like golf balls in pantyhose jostling in the breeze.

I sighed. "But the car locked anyway."

They nodded, sending those eyestalks into further chaos. "And my flight's in less than an hour!"

"Shouldn't be a problem. One sec."

Still gripping the doorframe, I gave my brain a few more seconds in the hopes it'd cooperate before I ventured out into upside-down land.

But no. Everything stayed stubbornly wonky as the Crusty stared at my nonaction, perplexed.

"All right, lead the way."

They turned from the booth and wobbled off. I closed my eyes, stepping forward on a path that would hopefully align with the Crusty's and keep me from face-planting on any car hoods.

Every couple seconds I peeked to make sure I was still on track, only bashing my shin against a half-open car door once.

With my last peek, I screeched to a halt before I could clothesline myself on an eyestalk.

"This one."

First off, I tugged on the driver's door handle to confirm the Crusty's story—you wouldn't believe the depths of moronity I have to deal with on a daily basis.

Thunk. Locked.

I walked my hands along the side of the silver sedan to the trunk, keeping myself upright by sheer force of will. Most cars had a sigil trunk release beside the keyhole, but this one wasn't evident.

Questing around with my fingers, I searched for the roughness of the engraved sigil on every conceivable surface—under the lip, around the license plate, in the light well . . .

No luck.

Fumbling the Acura insignia aside with a *click*, I smiled.

Presto.

If the keys were inside, in range, the sigil should activate. I pressed a spark of magic into the symbol, and the trunk clunked and swung upward.

"There you go."

"Thanks!" The Crusty nearly knocked me over in their haste to retrieve their suitcase and bail for the airport. I leaned back against the car to brace myself, just in time for my vision to tumble around again.

I beamed at the blue sky above, gritty asphalt below. "Now stay put, yeah?"

Maybe I could sell this sigil to the carnival circuit, or some high-security-vault company. Lot harder to crack a safe when everything's upside down and backwards, right?

That was something to worry about later, though. Right now, I had to see if unlocking the rest of this car would be a breeze, or a nightmare.

I climbed into the trunk and felt along the back panel where the seats lived. With any luck, there'd be a release to let me squeeze through into the main compartment of the car and grab the keys.

My fingers met nothing but seamless plastic and felt lining.

One more thorough feel-up bore out the distinct lack of all things releasy.

Time to get creative.

Before I got too adventurous, it was time to check the other three doors. I hadn't exactly wanted to make the full rounds when I was still staggering around like a newborn deer on psychedelics.

Now that up and down were right where they should be, it was the logical first step.

I zipped around the car, yanking on each handle to no avail. The Crusty hadn't been freaking out over nothing.

No windows cracked either, which made this one more level of tricky, but nothing I couldn't handle.

We were approaching lunch, always a slow time on Thursdays, so I should be able to sort this out before too many cars piled up.

I jogged back to my booth and grabbed some tools off the pegboard beside the door: poofy doorstop on a leash, bendy stick, rubber wedger.

Okay, yeah, I'm sure there are supertechnical names for all these things, and I'd probably even heard them all at least once. But is the proper name *really* worth remembering when you can call it a poofy doorstop?

I rest my case.

Arms full of paraphernalia, I trotted back to the Acura and dumped everything across the hood.

Rubber wedger first. The hefty chunk of black rubber was shaped like the love child of a mini crowbar and a wedge of Brie. I sniggled it into the crack at the edge of the driver's door, and leaned into it, prying the locked door a scant half inch outward.

That bought me enough wiggle room to ram in the tip of the poofy doorstop.

A rubber hose connected one end of the doorstop to one of those silicone grenades they pump at the doctor's office whenever they've gotta check your blood pressure with an arm cuff. Only, pumping this one puffed up the doorstop.

I manhandled that puppy like a stress ball on my worst day.

Squash, puff. Squash, puff.

Good old StayPuft on the other end of the hose ballooned, creeping the door further out of its frame, millimeter by millimeter.

That should be enough. I looped the hose over the corner of the door so it wouldn't yank the whole rigamarole out, and grabbed my bendy stick.

I—shocker—bent it in a downward arc, with an extra kink right near the tip, all the better to jab things with, my dear.

Threading the tip through the scant gap between the door's rubber seal and the frame, I cranked my end of the stick up so the tip would head for the armrest.

There were a couple paths to success here: ram the unlock button, or roll down the window. Which one was easier depended entirely on the car.

On this sucker, the window toggle was housed upright in the door panel. No chance of hitting it effectively without some serious contortionist maneuvers.

The unlock button, on the other hand, was smack on the armrest, easy to push from above, though I would need to angle my bendy stick more toward me to unlock the car. Pushing forward would just lock it again.

Tongue between my teeth, I lowered the tip of the rod, aiming for the nearest edge of the button.

My phone blared to life with my lunch alarm. I nearly sent my bendy rod straight through the window with my startled jerk.

Thankfully, it had a blunt end, so all it did was carom off the glass and wind up lodged in the little air vent beside the steering wheel.

It seemed fairly secure there, so I let go and retrieved my phone to silence the alarm. Lunch could wait a few minutes till I'd fixed this.

I gave the rod a good yank to dislodge it from the vent, then finessed it back down toward the armrest. The stick skated across the button, jerking forward and hitting the front portion, and each door of the car clunked as it tried to relock them.

Almost there, just drag the stick back an inch . . .

The tip scraped against the correct portion, but not with enough force.

I rose onto tiptoes, scraping the stick up a couple inches through the gap, then shoved down.

Another clunk as the door unlocked.

Hoo-freaking-rah.

I scrabbled at the door handle, and the door opened, sending all my equipment tumbling to the asphalt.

Oh well, it was rugged. It would survive.

Before any fell wind or 'helpful' busybodies could intervene, I dove into the front seat and snatched up the keys from the cup holder.

Don't worry, I only use my breaking-into-cars powers for good.

So far.

I finished my usual check-in—mileage, gas level, dings and dents—and then shot off a text to Keisha: luuunchtime!

She shuffled out of the building just as my cup of ramen finished microwaving, and I settled down with the noods and the next paperback from my box.

The rest of my workday was same ol', same ol', positively serene by comparison: the rush and lulls of rental returns, untangling a gorgon's hair snakes from a seat belt, cleaning out fast food bags and rogue continental breakfast bananas.

I trashed a wet hair tie, kept the random assortment of coins, and gave Bert the six-pack of Blue Moon hiding in the center console of an F-150.

My phone chimed as I was explaining to a confused stained glass fairy how to strap into one of our avian-friendly vehicles. Poor thing had only driven cars that smooshed her wings before.

One of our actual customer service agents rushed over to demonstrate the six-point strap system, which *I* would just turn into a tangled knot.

I palmed my phone and checked the notification. Right—I needed to text Samaire.

Immy: Can I stop by the club tonight to give you that fifty bucks?

Samaire: 100

My heart lurched in my chest, and my fingers flew across the screen.

Immy: Wait, I owe you 100? From what??

Samaire: Sorry!! I meant, yeah, 100% you can stop by

Immy: *dead of a heart attack*

Samaire: *hug* my bad!! when?

I chewed at my lip. How long would dinner with Fitz take? Definitely at least an hour, and if he wanted to talk about what to do in the city . . .

Immy: Maybe 8? I've got something before

Samaire: Ooooh what's that? <.<

Immy: Dinner

Samaire: You know you gotta give me more than that

Immy: Yeah, yeah, one sec

At minimum, I needed to tell her enough to hunt Fitz down if my body showed up floating in Ponderosa Lake after our not-date.

Not *super* likely, but you never know.

I was wearing the same pants as yesterday, and miraculously, his business card was still chilling in my pocket.

The Gravis-Witherspoon site loaded whip-fast on my phone, and I clicked around until I found the employee headshots. One screenshot later, I was messaging Fitz's photo to Samaire along with a pic of his business card.

Immy: I'm playing tour guide to this guy at 6. If I mysteriously vanish, never to return, he'd be a good place to start looking.

I wasn't actually worried, but not being worried is how you get yourself murdered. Better to be overcautious than end up as nothing but a disembodied foot being licked by a scuttlewisp in an alley.

Samaire: Playing tour guide? Is that some sort of roleplay?

Immy: No, he legit wants someone to help him out. He's new to the city.

Samaire: Huh. Well, hope you have fun!

A plane took off low overhead, rattling loose items around the lot, including the clock on the wall of my booth. I smiled—only ten minutes till the end of my shift.

Aaron zoomed down the lane in a Honda Civic still dripping from the car wash, and parked it in an open space. He jogged over, his red hair nearly glowing in the sun.

"Immy, we've got a problem. Can you head back with me?" He pointed over his shoulder toward the distant shop.

"Sure, what's up?"

"It—" He cringed. "I think you'd better see for yourself."

That didn't sound sinister at all.

Not one bit.

HOW TO MAKE FRIENDS AND INFLUENCE SPRITES

A Mercedes had pulled into my lanes while I was texting Samaire. Aaron opened the passenger door like he wanted to usher me inside.

I scoffed and jogged to the driver's side. "Get in, dork. This lady drives herself."

Aaron laughed and folded himself into the seat before cranking it back for the leg room. I plugged the info I needed into my scanner, then backed the car up and whipped it around toward the shop.

"Oh, right, better text Keisha." I tossed Aaron my unlocked phone.

"Uhh . . . okay. What do you want it to say?" He poised his oversized thumbs above the screen.

"Going AWOL."

He shook his head with a grin, then typed far too long to be following instructions.

"What'd you send?"

He tried to hand it back, but I'd learned long since to keep both hands on the wheel in this lot. Between the dive-bombing pixies, sentient oil flukes, and how crazy half our customers drove, I didn't want to be on the hook for totaling a Mercedes.

Aaron retracted his arm. "I said 'Going AWOL. Aaron needs me at the shop.'"

"Eh, fair enough. Less mysterious, though."

What can I say, I like to keep 'em guessing.

I steered the car in through the open roll-up door into the shop, and parked in one of the six cleaning bays to the left, beside all the detailing gizmos—long-arm vacuum, upholstery shampooer, air pump, what have you.

We both climbed out, and I surveyed the rest of the shop: Three mechanic's bays behind us with multilevel car platforms. Heavy-duty shelving with new tires, belts, oil bottles, windshield-wiper fluid, spare bulbs, resin for rock chips. The whoosh and thwap of the car wash in the adjoining building.

The open break room to one side, complete with Bert scarfing a sandwich, toppings falling out the bottom.

I made the sign of the triptych. "Is that a peanut butter pickle sandwich?"

"Yerp." He downed the last bite and licked an alarming combo of peanut butter and pickle juice from his thumb. "Good, you're here."

Everything looked normal, aside from the monstrosity that was Bert's lunch. My opinion must've shown on my face.

"Hey, don't knock it till you've tried it."

I held up both hands. "Not knocking it. Not trying it, either."

He chuckled and scratched behind the mirrored sunglasses riding the top of his balding head. "I can deal with that."

"So . . ." I waved around at the lack of obvious disasters. "I was expecting a pixie palooza back here. What'd you need me for?"

Aaron's head and shoulders had disappeared into the Mercedes with a vacuum hose, so I assumed he was abdicating responsibility, having delivered me safe and sound.

Bert jerked his chin toward the mechanic's bays. "This."

He whacked the first big green button of three on the wall beside the platform lifts.

It clacked and lit up, but nothing else happened.

I glanced between him and the button. "Looks like a job for an electronics guy."

Not me, in other words. I'm the last person you want around your delicate bits and bobs, unless you *do* actually want them all blown to the three hells.

"Did that first. Electric's working fine. It's the lift. Somethun's stuck." He pointed at the first bay, with an orange Nissan up top.

I raised both eyebrows. "Also not a mechanic."

"But you're little. Bendy."

"Excuse me?" My brows flew off into outer space.

Bert blushed scarlet, scuffing a hand along the back of his head. "I meant . . ." He pointed again. "You could fit up there. To see what's going on."

"Must be Alex's day off?"

"Yup."

"So you want me to climb up in that big moving mechanical contraption and see why it's *not* moving?" Sounded like a prime way to get squished like a bug.

"Basically. Already checked everything obvious and accessible, so it's gotta be out of sight and outta the ordinary."

The second hand of the shop clock passed the official end of my shift. "I'm not getting paid anymore, so you'll owe me big time."

"Yes, ma'am."

"And you won't call me ma'am."

"Yes'm."

I glared at him. "That's really not better."

"Yessirree."

That'd do. "And you'll make sure I don't get ground up in there by accident." I waved a hand at the lift. "Or on purpose." I side-eyed a pixie buzzing by.

"I'll guard these buttons with my life." He took a step closer to the three chunky power boxes.

I pursed my lips, looking the multilevel lift over. "Any theories?"

Bert stepped up beside me and jabbed a finger toward the dim ceiling of the bay. "Could be something chewed through a wire. Or something stuck in one of the pneumatic arms. Maybe a part that rusted through."

He caught my alarmed glance and rushed on. "But that's the least likely—we keep up the maintenance on these. And nothing should be rusty enough to cause you any problems when you're up there."

"Uh-huh."

"Seriously, I only mentioned it on the off chance some ferromites rolled up in here somehow. But I ain't never seen one around here. How about you, Aaron?"

Aaron whacked his head on the ceiling of the Mercedes. "Ow." He ducked out and glanced over the roof. "What did you say, Bert?"

"Ferromites?"

"Here? Nah, I haven't seen any."

I peered in and around the clunky metal pieces of the lift. It didn't seem *too* treacherous.

And brownie points with Bert never hurt.

"All right, I'll do it." I stuck my pinkie out toward Bert. He looked clueless. "Pinkie promise you'll owe me big time for me playing circus monkey up there. Whether I solve your problem or not."

He just stared at me, incredulous.

I waggled my finger. "Come on! It's legally binding between kobolds. Why not us too?"

"Can I just pay you? Seems less risky."

"You got cash on you?"

"No . . ."

"Then a pinkie promise it is."

Bert sighed and hooked fingers with me. I bounced our hands once, and intoned, "So mote it be."

He dropped my hand like a hot brick. "Crap, I knew I was getting myself in trouble."

I grinned devilishly. "What? *Me?* Trouble? Never."

"Course not."

I swiped a pair of fingerless mechanic's gloves from the nearby toolbox and tugged them on. The first platform was within easy reach with a little hop—just higher than the roof of a tall SUV—and I dragged myself up onto the front strut with some scrambling and kicks.

My fingers were already grimy. I wiped them off on my pants. Good thing it was laundry day anyway.

I scanned the various cables, struts, and chains, looking for rust or frayed wires. It could all use a good wipe-down, but nothing obviously broken jumped out at me.

Shimmying along the orange Nissan, I inspected the pneumatic arms too, but everything checked out.

One more level to go.

This time I clambered onto the Nissan's hood before hefting myself up between the struts of the empty top level.

Oof, this was a lot higher than it looked from down there.

I clung to a nearby chain and scooted along the metal grating on my butt, my hands only a tad shaky.

The flitter of tiny shimmering wings caught my eye from the gloom behind one of the struts. No doubt about it, *something* pixious was going on here.

Flying rat dastards.

Not that I have anything against rats, really—regular ones, anyway.

Cerberats, on the other hand . . .

I shook myself. Task at hand, Immy. Task at hand.

The pixie's presence meant I wasn't looking for common-garden rust or frayed cables anymore. I was looking for a prank.

And pranks were my specialty.

I stood with a smirk, stranglehold on the nearest support to keep me upright.

Time to trick the pixie into revealing its mischief.

If there's one thing I've learned about pixies, it's that they can't help snickering when someone is falling afoul of one of their pranks.

Sometimes, that works to your advantage.

Not quite ready to abandon the safety of the support, I propped one fist on my hip and screwed my face up into my best 'I'm stumped' expression.

I muttered to myself loud enough for the pixie to hear every word. "Gosh darn it, I'm just *not* smart enough to figure out what in the three hells is wrong up here!"

Let the game of hot and cold commence.

Trailing my steadying hand against the bay's wall, I shuffled to the left. "Everything looks exactly like it should! Maybe there's something over here?"

Giggles like tiny bells in a glass bowl tinkled across the bay.

Cold.

I about-faced and went right along the bay's opening, fingers grazing the ceiling to help keep my balance.

Even more raucous giggling.

Must be in Siberia.

That made the corner opposite of where I'd started my best bet.

I eased over to the next strut, arms out to either side.

The giggles trailed off.

Getting warmer . . .

I teetered over to the corner and made a show of glancing around so I could sneak a peek at the pixie. Eyes wide, it waited with bated breath, nervous fingers drumming against its cheeks.

Hot potato.

Everything above me looked A-OK, so I crouched and craned my neck around.

An 'eep!' from the pixie had me leaning in to where the rod of the pneumatic arm disappeared inside the cylinder.

The junction was completely glommed over by a clump of chewing gum sprites.

Bingo.

"Found your problem!" I yelled down to Bert.

Vicious whispered pixie curses filled the bay, and I grinned. "Sorry, I don't play fair."

"What is it?" Bert called.

"Just the latest salvo in our endless feud with the local pixies."

Not-whispered human curses filled the shop. "Anything you can fix?"

"Maybe? Gimme a minute."

A grumbled "Not like we're coming up there" floated up from below.

If I somehow got the sprites out, would this whole mechanical rigamarole whirr into action? I chewed at my lip as I tried to remember how it worked from the few times I'd hung around the shop.

The entire lift could retract into the floor, but it never went higher than this, right? They'd load the first car, raise the lift one story, load the second car, same deal. And that was the whole enchilada.

So, worst-case scenario, I'd be descending toward ground level, not getting plastered on the ceiling.

Good enough for me.

I poked a finger into the multicolor mass. Squish, but no stick—they were happy chilling there for the time being. Maybe the pixie had slathered the metal with honey to draw them in, because this sure wasn't primo territory for the little pea-brains.

A lot of them ended up here in the lot due to sheer traffic volume, carried in from the city or off inbound flights. It didn't take 'em long to figure out the parking lot was mostly a barren wasteland—not a lot of crumbs for hungry sprites, especially with the pixies for competition.

So, they'd use their selective stickiness to creep along until an unsuspecting shoe or tire made contact, then hitch a ride to new hunting ground.

And, of course, no matter how much scraping and prying you do, those suckers are never gonna come loose until they're good and ready.

Maybe some input from the guys would help.

"It's a wad of chewing gum sprites!" I called down.

Groans all around. "You sure it's not regular gum?"

"They're breathing." Each little glob pulsed slightly, in and out.

"Well, crud. Guess we'll have to wait till they decide to move on."

I pursed my lips. The smart thing to do would be to split before I spent any more time not getting paid at work, but . . .

I'm not really one for giving up.

Obstinate as a minotaur, as my dad used to say.

Which meant I not only had to convince these sprites there were crumbier pastures elsewhere—I'd have to be their wheels, too.

All aboard the Chewing Gum Express.

"You stuck up there, Immy?" Bert sounded worried.

"Nah, just thinking." I shifted from my painful crouch to criss-cross applesauce, ready to play sprite-whisperer.

"Hey," I breathed over the gooey glob. "Sorry if you're napping or something, but I bet you've finished whatever tasty goodness the pixies left for ya, and you'll be hungry again soon. Not much around here except gravel and motor oil, and I know that's not your jam."

No response. Granted, I'd be knocked out of my socks if I got one.

"So, I was thinking . . . I know a place. Crumbs galore, and not just that—*new* crumbs every day. The real deal. I could give you a lift, if you like?"

One little green wad wiggled, backing out of the dogpile.

I held out a hand, and the sprite plopped into my palm. "There you go! You're the trailblazer, I can tell." I gave it the teensiest of finger pats, and it thrummed happily.

A single sprite was better than nothing, but it wasn't gonna solve our problem. I leaned in.

"What, the rest of you are gonna let Jim here boldly go where no sprite has gone before, all by himself, and get all the good stuff? Nobody's got FOMO?"

A blue sprite started jiggling, then a white one. Pretty soon, my hand was covered with a heap of sticky sprites.

All except one lone holdout.

"You're a tough sell, huh?" I eyed the purple blob. "Guess you'll be king o' the wasteland once all your friends are gone. Get all three of the crumbs to yourself, then get pinched and pulled by pixies on the daily."

Purple trembled, then unlatched and dropped to the pile.

"I knew you were smart. All right, guys, it'll be a bit of a ride, so you gotta hang on till I give you the say-so, yeah?"

Another thrum rippled through the heap, and my hand became harder to move—every scrap of skin stuck to the sprites as they battened down.

Blech.

Now, clamber down, or ride in style on the hopefully working lift?

Such a tough choice.

"Bert!"

"Yeah?"

"Let 'er rip!"

"Uh . . . you sure?"

I grabbed a bar welded firmly to the strut beneath my feet, then hooked my sprite-burdened arm around it for good measure. "Yup!"

A harsh buzz signaled he'd pressed the big green button. With a jerk and a rattle, the lift descended inch by inch, serenading us all with the *beep beep beep* of a garbage truck backing up.

The lift jarred to a halt seven feet up. I waved at Aaron as he ducked beneath me and revved the orange Nissan. Once the car was clear, Bert jabbed the button again. My mob of chewing gum sprites and I drifted safely to the ground.

Well, creaked and clattered, but same diff.

Bert crossed his arms over his belly, looking mildly pleased. "You're a lifesaver, Im, thanks."

"No prob—" I let go of the bar to step forward, and a sharp yank tugged at my hair. "Yow!"

I raised my sprite-free hand to rub my sore scalp, but froze.

Chaos and *chimaeras*.

A tiny purple glob swung from the end of one of my blonde curls, thrumming the day away.

THE MAN CAVE

"You gooey little ball of—"

The purple chewing gum sprite scooted another inch up my curl.

"I mean, you ravishly handsome sprite, you." I gritted my teeth. "There's absolutely zilch up there for you to eat, just FYI. If you wanna miss out on all the goodies your friends are chowing down on, and explore the barren jungle that is my hair, have at."

I stepped forward like I really didn't care, scanning the shop for a pair of scissors.

Heck, even bolt cutters would do.

The last thing I needed was this gummy monstrosity getting contrary and deciding to turn my hair into one giant sticky mess.

Instead of scissors, my gaze fastened on Julian traipsing into the shop, arm buried to the elbow in a bag of potato chips.

I dashed over. "You! Gimme."

"Hey!" His startled look of dismay as I snatched the bag was worthy of the shop's 'Kodak Moments' wall, though it would never beat the photo Alex got of Doak mid-transformation, chicken feet in the air as he slipped on a mop-water puddle, feathers strewn in all directions.

He was fine, honest.

I upended the bag, strewing crumbs all over the sprites glued to my hand. Let the snail-paced feeding frenzy begin.

"See?" I dangled Purple over the morass, my curl bouncing. "You're really missing out, buddy."

Purple didn't budge.

"Ugh." I slumped at one of the break tables and tossed the chip bag toward Julian. He half snatched it out of the air three times before finally getting ahold of it.

"Rude, Immy. Just rude."

I blew him a raspberry. "Survival of the sneakiest."

"That wasn't exactly snea—" He pursed his lips at the talking hand I was giving him.

A faint plop on my shoulder had me craning my neck giraffe-shifter-style.

Purple had deigned to descend from my hair.

"There you go." I raised my sprite-and-crumb-filled hand to my shoulder, but Purple didn't take the bait. "Man, you are stubborn. Guess I can't really talk, though."

I stole a few crumbs from the multicolor horde and sprinkled them in front of Purple.

He rolled forward greedily.

"Told you I make good on my promises. If you want more, you're gonna have to come down when I tell you, 'kay?"

I checked the time. Crud, I'd better get outta here if I wanted to get anything done before tour-guide dinner with Fitz.

First things first. If I didn't get these sprites off my hand, I was guaranteed to forget they were there for at least one split second—long enough to cause all kinds of disasters. I needed a carrier.

I rounded on Bert. "You got any empty clamshells kicking around?"

His eyes narrowed as he considered, then he brightened. "Think so. Back in a jiff."

He rustled through the nearby blue recycle bin, and emerged triumphant.

Tan icing smeared the inside of the lid. "Maple bar?"

"Yup."

I popped open the clamshell with one hand. "All right, my sticky minions, here's the next batch of good stuff. In you go."

One by one, the chewing gum sprites dropped inside with a hollow *plunk* on the plastic. All except Purple, of course.

Eh, he could chill up there for a while. Good way to keep the creepers at bay.

I pinched the clamshell closed and windmilled an arm at the shop as a whole. "Sayonara, suckers. And Bert."

His brows rose. "I'm honored."

"Nah, you were never a sucker."

I stole a car that had been vacuumed out and took the two minutes to run it through the carwash—goosh, thwap, drizzle, whoosh.

Better than hiking back on foot.

I dropped the clamshell in my purse, stepped out of my booth, then backtracked and grabbed an electrified flail off the wall. Today had been remarkably stalker-free, ergo I was sure to be mugged on the way home.

Jumpin' Jemima would deter anyone Purple didn't.

What? Pixies don't go rabid often, but when they do . . .

Gotta be prepared.

Next stop, Keisha's office and my mountain of flannels.

Not wanting to get too overloaded since I'd be swinging by Bath & Body Works *and* the sprites' new home, I tied a few of the flannels around my waist and called it good.

Purple garnered me more concerned looks than usual on the

subway—I really had to start tracking these things so I could beat my own high scores.

Gotta have goals in life, right?

Right.

Now, where to dump the sprites? Somewhere like Santiago's would be ideal, with food scraps getting dropped by the minute. But Santiago took too much pride in his hoard to let the street stay messy long—or to let his customers step on chewing gum sprites—so that wouldn't work for my gang.

I needed somewhere perpetually messy with no pride.

Ah. I knew just the place.

I hopped off at the Brawler's Sprawl station, two blocks from the Man Cave—the local den slash boys' club for carnivorous shifters.

Let's just say it's not great on the nose, even walking by.

I rang the buzzer by the 'Dudes Only' sign, and in short order a hulking bear shifter in half-form lumbered up to the glass door and gawked out.

"You're not a dude."

"Sheer genius, Watson."

He blinked.

"I've got a proposition for ya."

He leered.

"Yeah, not that kind. A business proposition. Can I come in?"

He peered.

Big brains, this one.

"Let her in, Cliff!"

A suave dude sauntered up—some kind of cat shifter, my guess. Lean, sinuous, well-groomed. Tan skin and dark eyes.

I gave him a thumbs-up as I slipped in. "Top-notch bouncer you got here."

He grinned. "Isn't he something? Does what he needs to, that's what's important."

The place lived up to its name, filled with big TVs, leather sofas, dartboards and pool tables, beer-can pyramids and beer-pong tables, empty—and not empty—pizza boxes, punching bags, flickering neon signs, and even a throne made out of beat-up two-by-fours.

A lone pizza box shuffled to one side, three pale tails hanging out.

Cerberat?

I eased back half a step, ready to bolt.

"You said you had a business proposition for us?"

"Sure do." I rummaged in my purse and retrieved the clamshell.

"Chewing gum sprites?" Suave Dude quirked an eyebrow.

"Right on the money."

"Let me stop you right there. This place is messy enough as it is." He wrinkled his nose. "Between you and me, it's impossible to get any of the canine shifters to clean up after themselves. And don't get me started on the bears." He side-eyed the bouncer.

I patted the clamshell. "Well, these won't do much about the cans and pizza boxes, but how would you like the place to be completely crumb-, grease-, and beer-puddle-free?"

He gazed contemplatively at the sprites glooping over and under one another in search of any last shred of potato chip. "They do that, don't they. But I can just see some of our guys going on a rampage when one of these gets stuck to his foot."

I smiled. "I'll let you in on a secret: they only do that when they can't find food and wanna hitch a ride to somewhere new. Step on a happy, well-fed sprite, and no way is it sticking to ya."

Suave Dude rubbed his chin. "Really?"

Didn't need to be a missionary to convert unbelievers. "Watch."

I glanced around for the grossest patch of muck. There, a pile of black olives marinating in a drying beer puddle.

"Geronimo," I whispered as I snapped open the clamshell and flipped it over. My sweet, trusting sprites released their hold on the plastic and plummeted into the unknown.

Well, into the horrifyingly nasty slop below.

Nirvana for a chewing gum sprite, though.

I raised one foot, ready to prove my point—or be glued to the floor of the Man Cave for all of time.

Okay, maybe not *all* of time. But I'd already been in the Man Cave longer than deemed nonhazardous by OSHA, and no way did I want to hobble out of here, on this scummy floor, with only one shoe.

I squished my shoe down on the ecstatic heap of chewing gum sprites gobbling their way through the rotting black olives.

Thank Finéa they were basically indestructible.

My shoe came away sprite-free. It wasn't spared the vile grease of their snack, unfortunately.

I surreptitiously smeared my shoe across a scrap of pizza box beside me, and morphed my grimace into a smile. "See?"

Suave Dude bobbed his head, lips pulled down into an 'I'm impressed' pout. "Would you look at that? Busy little beavers. Ope—" He glanced around, wide-eyed. "Right, it's Dale's day off. Phew. We're good."

"Beaver shifter?" I raised my brows. "I thought this was a carnivore club."

"He's our accountant."

"Ah."

The chewing gum sprites worked their way through the black olives in record time, swelling in size. At this rate, they'd be making like a Kit Kat before day's end.

I waved as the gluttonous globs rolled off in search of their next prey.

"So what do you get out of this arrangement? Do I pay you a finder's fee?" Suave Dude peered at my shoulder. "You've still got one, by the way."

Oh, right. I shuttled two fingers up beside Purple. "Better hurry up before your friends eat all the good stuff."

Purple oozed forward, tickling the hairs on the back of my fingers. "Good sprite."

Suave Dude pointed at a congealing puddle studded with pepperoni.

I skirted a half-empty thirty-pack of beer and sidled Purple up to the gunk. The sprite did its best impression of a high dive right into a shriveling pepperoni slice.

"Bye-bye, bud. Have fun living your best life." I whirled on Suave Dude. "And yes, you do pay me a finder's fee. My usual is two hundred."

"Bucks?" He narrowed his eyes, probably calculating how much he'd save on disgruntled cleaners. "How about one fifty?"

"One eighty, and that's my best offer."

"Done." He obstacle-coursed his way over to the register at the bar.

The first two bills stuck together with some unmentionable substance, and his gaze flicked between them and me before he shuffled further down the stack. He slammed the register and presented me with five crisp bills—four twenties, one hundred.

"Thank you very much." I snatched the cash and squirreled it away.

I'd just turned when he asked, "How do I reach you if I need more sprites?"

I spun back around with dollar signs in my eyes. "Lemme see your phone?"

He passed me his phone, and I added myself to his contacts under 'Chewing Gum Sprite Girl.'

I handed the phone back, and he laughed at the name. "Nice. I'm Felix, by the way."

"Immy. Gotta dash, but good luck!"

"Thanks. We need it."

I might've skipped out the door. My sprite problem solved, *and* two hundred dollars richer? Talk about a good day.

Now I had to get Cucumber a gift, run home and check on Bracchius and Kor, start a load of laundry, get ready for dinner with Fitz, *go* to dinner with Fitz, swing by Samaire's, and Ruby's on the way back, and . . .

Oof. That might be a bit ambitious for one evening.

I shook my curls out of my face as I boarded the subway. Whatever. I'd figure it out.

Worst case, I'd negotiate with Kor for some shut-eye outside the slipstream of time in his smelly domain.

Hmm. My nose wrinkled. Would my clothes pick up that smell? Maybe I'd better do a double dose of detergent to play it safe.

I got off at the Echendia station two stops over. As I approached the glass-fronted Bath & Body Works, I slowed.

The store was dark. I checked the time: 3:27 p.m. They definitely should be open.

I stopped in front of the sheet of paper taped to the door.

"Under quarantine due to spontaneous polymerae generation. If plastics on your person transmute, please bring any nascent beings to the Midden Sanctuary."

Well, that sucked more for them than for me, so I couldn't really complain. It did mean I needed to hurry up and find somewhere else to get Cucumber's gift, though.

Hands on hips, I surveyed the street for anything likely. A ramen place, a dry cleaner's, a flower shop . . .

Somehow I didn't think Cucumber would appreciate a bouquet of peonies. I dug out my phone with a sigh and did a search for 'bubble bath, Echendia.'

There was a Lush ten blocks away, a hydra acid bathhouse five blocks east, and . . . what was this one? Sudscentional?

I clicked on it. Coolio. A little local soap and bath bomb boutique that just opened a few weeks ago. I glanced guiltily back at the Bath & Body Works—I should probably be trying to shop local more often anyway.

And bonus: it was only three blocks from here.

I almost walked right by the place. The front door was nearly crowded out by the two shops to either side hogging all the window real estate.

I shoved the door open with a soothing chime of undine scales and entered a long hallway with another door at the end labeled Sudscentional. Warm light glowed through the frosted glass in the top half of the door.

The door was unlocked, and I stepped inside a welcoming, cozy shop. A mixture of soothing scents instantly washed over me.

They'd taken full advantage of every square inch of the place, with shelves full of bottles, candles, linen-wrapped bath bombs, decorative plants, even a few crystals. One whole wall was decked out with what looked like candy dispensers, but I had a feeling the contents weren't so tasty.

I wandered over, intrigued.

Each dispenser was stuffed with pearlescent shapes: spheres and puffy hearts, seashells, stars, gemstones, you name it. Every type was a different color, and the labels on the front declared the scents.

Rose.

Lavender Peach.

Timothy Hay.

Kelp.

Blood.

Sulfur.

I grinned. I'd definitely be able to find a good gift for Cucumber here. Maybe even something fun for myself, with nearly two hundred bucks burning a hole in my pocket.

The light shifted as movement blocked one of the gold-toned can lights above. I glanced up, worried a pigeon or something had gotten stuck in here.

Definitely not a pigeon.

I swallowed and plunged a hand into my purse for Jumpin' Jemima, just in case.

A fifteen-foot basilisk slithered over webbing strung across the ceiling, headed my way.

DEMONLING DREAMS

The basilisk's head lowered from the ceiling with a sinuous loop of her body. "Welcome to Sudsssscentional. I'm Faina, pleassse let me know if I can help you."

Faina's scales were a stunning blend of purple, blue, and cyan, with a magenta crest like a lotus flower marking her forehead. An iridescent sheen covered her eyes—the brille keeping her gaze from being paralyzing.

Her tail wound down beside her head, the tip pointing at a sign perched between two tubs of bath bombs: *Welcome. Please feel free to ask for a demonstration.*

Demonstration? Shouldn't that be sample, or tester strip?

"Thanks. What kind of demonstration?"

Faina's tongue flicked in my direction. "Human dousssed in an artificial peach-pear ssscent, sssweat, old pizzza and beer, engine oil and indussstrial sssoap, asssociates with a demon—no, two—"

I cut her off before she could get to anything truly embarrassing, like the last time I flossed, or the weird smell in my belly button. "Wow, that's impressive. Maybe you can help me with a weird gift I'm looking for. Bubble bath for a demonling?"

The basilisk descended the rest of the way to the floor before she brought her head to my chin level. "Ahh, yesss. For demonlingsss, glitter, maximum sssudsss, and sstaggering sstink are advisssed. I will create a cussstom blend."

"Oh, that sounds perfect."

She slithered to a shelf of boxy dispensers filled with clear iridescent liquid. Using her tail, she scooted an empty bottle beneath several of the spigots in turn, jabbing each button to dole out a healthy drizzle of gel.

I hovered behind her, careful not to trip on her massive coils. My nose wrinkled at the labels of the ingredients she chose, but she was right on the money for what I needed.

Brimstone.

Wet dog.

Sewer.

Stale cigarette smoke.

Rotten eggs.

Skunk.

Then she stretched up to a higher shelf with powders, glitters, and dyes.

Undine shimmer dust.

Midnight void pigment.

Ruby red glitter.

And finally, one last liquid-soap dispenser filled with a riot of holographic color: prismatic rainbow maxibubbles.

Tail coiled around the bottle's neck, she swirled the concoction until it blended into a glimmering dark whirlpool.

She held the bottle out. "Would you like to sssmell?"

I made like the Leaning Tower of Pisa. "No thanks, I'll trust your judgment."

"I am honored." She set the bottle down, grabbed a silicone cork with her tail and plugged it, then dropped a plastic sheath around the top.

One zap of a heat gun later, I had a snazzy bottle of demonling bubble bath in hand.

I couldn't even smell the nightmare brew through the plastic.

Hot diggety dog.

"Thisss way pleassse." She wound behind the counter and poked at the keyboard one letter at a time. A bitty label printer whirred, and she passed me the shiny new label.

'Sudscentional – Demonling Dreams.'

"Awesome, thanks." I peeled it off the paper and swiped it across the bottle.

Cucumber was gonna love this.

Hopefully.

I paid, turned down a branded paper bag in lieu of cramming the bottle in my purse, and asked for a dozen business cards to hand out.

"Have a Sudssscentional day!"

I grinned. "Thanks, you too."

Out on the street, I heaved my purse strap higher on my shoulder and tightened the four flannels tied around my waist just to be safe.

Home sweet home, here I come.

The train ride home was uneventful; I didn't even get distracted and miss my stop. As I walked down the sidewalk to my place, a whirl of crows gathered overhead, cawing and dropping the occasional pebble on my head.

"Hey! Rude. It's not *my* fault you weren't outside this morning for me to feed you. Gotta show up to get chow, my feathered frenemies."

Flirt darted down to the sidewalk ahead of me. He tried to hop backwards, keeping me in his sights, but mostly succeeded in tripping over his own tail feathers.

"Dorks, the lot of you. No wonder I like you."

Jekyll landed on the roof of a Toyota parked at the curb and shifted into a careful somersault down the windshield, squawking in delight. He fluttered upright on the hood, shaking out his feathers with a triumphant caw.

"Just proving my point, wingnut."

I hurried up to the door as more crows than usual descended on my lawn. They hardly ever brought friends—I'd made it abundantly clear I couldn't afford more kibble than I was already buying, so more crows just meant fewer crunchies for everybody.

The yard, door, and windows looked fine, so we probably hadn't weathered any thug attacks today. Maybe they needed a day off.

I sure did.

After Kor and Bracchius's scuffle on the other end of the phone this morning, I'd better prepare myself for scorch marks on the kitchen cabinets at the minimum, though.

Hopefully the sofa hadn't burned to a pile of ash this time.

With fire wards protecting the walls, ceiling, and floor, the apartment itself would be fine. But the furniture—and all my stuff—was fair game for frying.

I turned the key in the lock and swung open the door.

No active fires.

No obvious scorch marks.

No demons, even.

On the couch table lay the artifact, right out in the open for anyone to see—or scry for.

Unless . . .

Bracchius wouldn't be that careless, right? So could this be the dupe they'd promised to work up? If so, it looked just like the original.

An imperious 'CRAWW!' behind me nearly burst my eardrums. I whirled, foiling Darth's efforts to untie my shoelaces. He hopped back, indignant.

"Yes, food, sorry. Here." I dumped my purse and fumbled open the kibble container before stepping back outside.

I set the lid on the stoop for any crow offerings—the sparkly gift kind, not the poop kind, though there are no guarantees. "Here you go, you big whiners."

The crows fluttered over and around each other as I strewed a couple generous scoops of kibble across the broken walkway. With my 'finder's fee,' maybe I could be nice and grab an extra bag next time.

Oh! I'd almost forgotten the bologna I'd bought them yesterday.

I rootled around in my fridge till I found the packet, then sat on the stoop, waiting for the newcomers to give up on scrounging for any last kibble crumbs and fly off.

Nothing against new crows, but I'd bought the treat for *my* crew.

They were smart enough to sense something was up, too, hopping closer as their friends winged away into the pine trees down the block.

"All right, I've got a special treat just for you guys." Flirt perched on my knee as I tore into the bologna package.

I fed him the first strip, then dropped a handful of shredded lunchmeat in front of me.

The crows' happy warbles were quieter—probably not wanting to attract their new friends, the sneaky shysters.

I checked out the kibble bin lid as they gobbled down the bologna strips. Today's hoard included a ball of foil, a glittery hair tie, and a pop tab.

After the bologna, I'd probably find more goodies on the doormat in the morning.

My favorites had pride of place on my windowsill, but the rest went in the under-the-bed shoe bin I'd gotten after Bracchius moved in under the sofa.

It was almost full—probably needed to open a 'Corvid Curiosities' Etsy shop or something.

The crows cawed their thanks for the already-devoured bologna, and Darth tried to steal my shoelaces one last time before everyone flew off.

When I stepped back inside, the artifact—or pseudo artifact—was gone.

I eyed the murder of jubilant crows settling in the pines. Could one of them have hopped in and stolen it without me noticing?

Not super likely. Mischievous though they be, they're not so hot on stealth factor.

From somewhere deeper in the apartment, Bracchius griped, "Hurry up, Kor, you know I can't stand this form!"

Hmm.

I shut the front door and meandered back to the closed bathroom door, with demonly grumbling issuing from the other side.

Sinister much?

Yanking the door open, I came face-to-face with a whacky tableau. Two stout black-as-night demons in humanoid form on my bathroom floor in—best guess—a game of Twister without the Twister board, both blinking up at me in alarm.

"Oh, Immy, it's just you." Bracchius sagged in relief.

I glanced over my shoulder. "Were you expecting someone else?"

Bracchius shivered. "You never know, these days."

In his humanoid form, he looked like nothing so much as Samwise Gamgee, hobbit extraordinaire, only done up in shades of black with crimson stirring in the depths.

A little potbelly, and teeny black horns curving up out of a curly mop of hair completed the look.

On the other hand, Kor could pass for an avaricious used car salesman straight from the three hells. Still a foot shorter than me, but compared to his usual form, he was massive.

"So much for the conservation of mass," I muttered. Magic bent the laws of physics regularly enough, but demons stomped all over them before setting them on fire.

Kor scoffed. "Conservation of mass? What do you think we do with all the souls we harvest? Wasn't it one of you humans who figured out that whole 'energy equals mass times the seed of blight triangled' or something?"

I blinked down at him, utter disbelief warring with the sputtering giggle bubbling up inside me.

I choked it down, but only just. "Uh, yeah, that was a human. Einstein."

Better not to comment on the 'seed of blight.' The last thing I needed was to try to explain the speed of light to a demon who thought the passage of time was beneath him.

This explained his—and Bracchius's—short stature, though. Most demons in humanoid form were perfectly normal-sized. As I understood it, Kor hadn't exactly been up to snuff in the soul-snatching department.

And obviously Bracchius had . . . *other* priorities.

More wiggling and Twistering ensued, and Kor speared Bracchius with his crimson gaze. "Hold still, would you? I've almost finished."

"Sorry."

I cocked my head. "And you're humanoid because . . . ?"

The tip of Kor's black tongue peeked out between his lips as he concentrated. "This form is one of the best for fine manipulation of fidgety things."

Their hands were out of sight beneath them as they squirmed around. "And exactly *what* are you up to?"

Maybe I didn't want to know.

"We're . . . completing . . . the false artifact."

I eased closer. "But isn't that what was just sitting out there on the coffee table? It looked like it was already finished."

Bracchius piped up. "Well, the Dreyelian device is ready, but we had to test it first."

"Test it?"

Kor heaved an aggrieved sigh, stopped what he was doing, and stared me down. "Yes, Immaline. Since I was unfairly relegated to the indignity of relinquishing a piece of my own dread being for this experiment—"

Never mind that this whole thing had been his idea.

"—and as I am loath to forever lose an integral part of my very essence—"

He was breaking out *all* the big words today, sheesh.

Bracchius cut in. "We tested it first, with one of my bumboozers. The big black one."

"I—I'm sorry, a *bumboozer*?"

"Yeah! You know, the biggest marble that you crash into all the other marbles?"

Oh. "So a shooter?"

"Sure, if you wanna be boring."

Some days I really did.

I covered my face with both hands and sucked in a noisy breath between my fingers before whooshing it out again. "Okay, so you used a marble to test the Dreyelian device."

"Yup. Just in case we made it wrong and it was gonna incinerate the contents or something. Not that demons can be incinerated, but you know what I mean, Immy."

"And?"

"All good."

Kor was back at his writhing on the bathroom floor. "Bracchius, catch it!"

Bracchius joined in, leaving me to watch on in mild fascination and major concern. "And you're wrestling on the floor because?"

"Because the piece of Kor we're using isn't cooperating!" Bracchius squawked.

My eyes narrowed. "Didn't you say you could control it?"

Kor harrumphed. "To a large degree, yes, but it takes its cues from my innermost feelings. And I still do *not* want to have to cram a portion of my substance inside this death trap!"

"You just wanted to make Bracchius do it."

"Exactly."

Better leave them to it, or I'd never get my laundry started before my dinner not-date. I turned just as Bracchius emerged from the pile of ebony limbs.

"Ta-da!" Bracchius beamed. He held up the fake artifact triumphantly.

I leaned in. Was it possible for their version to look more convincing than the original gizmo itself? Interlocking gold bands, pulsing black center, ominous aura . . .

It was a good dupe. A little too good, in fact. I peered closer at the black blob.

There weren't any red flickers inside the substance. "Wait a minute, it's pure black. Is that just because it's so small, that your flickers don't show?"

Kor rolled his eyes. Gotta say, I wasn't really loving the extra dose of sass he could dish with such an expressive form. "My dear Immaline, do you truly not know such an elementary fact?"

I leveled a flat stare at him.

He reined in the attitude a bit. "Do you think we have no control over our own forms?"

"Well, no, you already said you did. So . . ." I connected the dots. "You can choose whether the flickers show up or not?"

Kor tutted. "More than that, Immy. We determine their color, intensity, shape, and pattern. With high emotion or impressive magic use, they may fluctuate somewhat on their own, but otherwise . . ."

"So red is, what, just the gang color for the Dark Ones?"

"Gang—?" Kor devolved into a gargle of disdain.

If they could control all that, I was honestly shocked Bracchius wasn't shimmering with a pastel rainbow of stars and unicorn silhouettes twenty-four seven.

Maybe . . . he'd just never given it a second thought?

I'd have to suggest it—way cooler than same-old, same-old red every freaking day.

Could we turn his tummy into a Lite-Brite board? Ooh, or if he glowed bright enough, would he make a kaleidoscope projection on the walls?

I dialed back the torrent of whacky ideas. "So it's good to go, then? The dupe?"

"Indeed." As soon as the word was out of Kor's mouth, both he and Bracchius splorbed back into their regular rotund forms.

"Thank goodness." Bracchius spasmed, a ripple traveling across his glossy surface. "No offense, Immy, but I really don't know how you put up with . . . that." He waved one stubby arm at me.

"I dunno, gotta say I like having fingers."

Bracchius tugged on the sleeve of one of the flannels tied around my waist. "Immy, you don't usually wear this many clothes, do you?"

"Oh, no. Damarion's friend Cynna"—my friend too, now, I guess— "sent me a whole bunch of flannels as a gift, so these are the ones I brought home today."

It was starting to get a bit toasty under all the layers. I picked at the massive knot as I trooped to my room to sort out my laundry.

Bracchius drifted beside me, sinking closer and closer to the ground. "But . . . you haven't even opened all the gifts *I* got you yet."

Uh-oh.

I whirled, a pair of smelly socks in hand. Bracchius had settled on the mess of sheets on my bed, his orb form slumped into more of a sad potato.

I pasted on a cheery grin. "I know! I'm so excited to see what the rest are, things have just been a little bananas." I folded one of the flannels and dumped it on the bed beside him. "And while these are pretty nice, I don't think *any* gift will ever compare to the new phone you got me. Not to mention all the other lovely gifts."

Bracchius perked up incrementally throughout my speech until he was as close to a perfect sphere as he ever got. "Really? The phone's the best gift you've ever gotten?"

"Absolutely." I wasn't even lying.

"Well, Sparkles is the best gift *I've* ever gotten, so it's only fair."

I glanced back from snatching up stray T-shirts and panties. Sparkles had materialized from somewhere, currently squished fiercely against Bracchius's side.

Definitely no hope of stealing her to throw in the wash now.

"Just wait, though." Bracchius bobbed excitedly. "The phone's nothing. I've got some even better i—"

Kor buzzed in, nearly bowling Bracchius over. "Yes, enough about gifts already, you've spoiled our human too much as it is!"

He zipped from one potential landing zone to another—crumpled covers, cluttered nightstand, stack of books—before reluctantly coming to rest on a fancy plant pot whose plant had long since shriveled into the afterlife.

A sufficient throne acquired, Kor tilted back imperiously. "We need to talk about our plan to divest ourselves of this counterfeit artifact, and foil those ingrates once and for all!"

DEPRIVED OF DEMON ACCOLADES

"A plan?" I raised my eyebrows. "Can't we just, y'know, walk outside and wait for the bad guys to mug us again?"

"Immaline, such a simplistic plan would *never* work. Leave it to me."

I stared at him.

He shifted under my gaze. "What?"

"I'm leaving it to you, Kor. So what's the plan?"

"Oh." He rocked back in surprise. "That was . . . easier than I'd anticipated."

"Good to know I can still surprise you." I plopped in front of the biggest heap of dirty laundry and sorted while he talked.

"Surprise isn't the word I'd use. Horrify, alarm, madden, maybe . . . But I'll admit this instance is more gratifying than most."

Three laundry piles formed in front of me: regular, fancy, and trash. I make life easy on myself by just not owning any whites—who really wants to deal with bleach and pit stains and rogue purple socks ruining your wardrobe anyway?

'Fancy' was all the stuff that probably *shouldn't* go through a washer, but I stuffed it in a delicates bag and called it good.

Hadn't failed me yet.

'Trash' was a new designation. With a zillion flannels destined to clutter up my meager closet, I had to make room. TBH, it was a good opportunity to ditch all the worn-out, shrunken junk I hadn't gotten up the gumption to deal with.

First item to be sacrificed was a pair of leggings with a holey butt. I held them up to the light, confirming their indecent status, and chucked them in the corner.

Kor launched into his brilliant plan. "We should secrete the fake artifact about one of our persons—probably you, Immy, since you present the least challenge to our foes."

"Gee, thanks."

"Then we will venture out into the world at large, flaunting our seeming vulnerability, and allow the enemy to ambush us. I know it will be difficult to hold back from smiting them with our collective might—well, mine mostly—but it is for the most wonderfully sinister of causes, after all."

"Uh-huh."

My work shirts went in the 'regular' pile, anything with lace—mostly panties—in the 'fancy' pile, and I dropped a colorful sequin miniskirt with a no-longer-elastic waistband atop the 'trash.'

Bracchius rolled off the bed and sidled up to the 'trash' pile. "Are you getting rid of this stuff?"

"Yep."

He extended one bitty arm and stroked the sequins, which flipped between pink and purple with each pass. "If you're getting rid of this anyway . . . Could I take it?"

I fought down a smile. "All yours."

A strangled squeak emanated from him as he snatched the miniskirt close, then draped it over Sparkles. "Ohh, Sparkles, this is going to look *fabulous* on you. What do you think, a scarf? Or— No, a pair of footie pajamas!"

He swiveled up to face me, shaking the fabric with one arm. "Do you think it's big enough?"

I was all thumbs when it came to sewing, but the skirt could be a freaking tent for the plushie unicorn. "Pretty sure."

Bracchius wiggled with glee.

Kor cleared his throat-equivalent. "As I was *saying*, we will allow ourselves to be set upon by those incompetent fools, and then comes the hardest part." He surveyed us gravely from his opulent plant pot. "We must appear to fight with our all, to fend them off with earnest desperation, while somehow failing to win."

"Yeah, that's a real head-scratcher."

A couple artistically bleached flannels joined the 'regular' pile. They'd probably still be my faves, but Cynna's shirts would be serious contenders.

"I know, right! I mean . . ." Kor twitched and resumed his imperial tones. "It will be difficult, but I, at least, will not fail. It will be a feat spoken of in demon legend, that I achieved such a devious subterfuge—"

"Don't you mean 'we'?"

Kor grumbled to himself. "Yes, yes, fine. *We'll* be lauded in the halls of the Dark Ones, cursed for our cunning. Except you, Immy, apologies. Demons aren't really into revering the lesser species. You understand."

Poor little ol' me, deprived of lofty demon accolades. How ever would I survive?

"I'll soldier on somehow."

"That's the spirit!" To say his tone was condescending would be the understatement of the millennium.

I scoured my room for any last clothing hiding under the bed or languishing at the bottom of the closet. "Oh, right."

Kor was midsentence when I bustled out to grab my purse, or rather the work shirt crammed beneath my keys and the odiferous bubble bath.

He started back up as soon as I was in sight, but I interrupted. "Kor, it's a magnificent plan. Why don't you go scope out the neighborhood for the bad guys so we know where to find them to set this whole thing in motion?"

"Me? I really don't—"

Kor wasn't one to do extra work unless there was a darn good reason, so I threw in a little ego-stroking. I crossed my fingers behind my back where Bracchius could see, and added, "You're the only one I trust to be sneaky enough not to get caught."

"Oh, well, yes, you're absolutely right about that." Kor puffed up and hovered off the plant pot. "I will accomplish this foul deed posthaste."

"I expect you'll be incredibly thorough. They could be lurking in several groups all throughout the area, after all."

Kor paused halfway out the door, floating near my chin. "True. Do not expect me back for some time, my underlings!" And he was off.

Not even his parting shot could spoil my mood—I was free and clear to sneak into his domain and use his laundromat for my *own* sinister purposes, now.

More sudsy than sinister, but still. Kor wouldn't be thrilled, and that was what mattered.

I flomped the pile of regular laundry into my gargantuan hamper-on-wheels, nestled the bottle of bubble bath on top, and rolled the whole shebang into the hall.

The hall closet surrendered my beat-up bags of detergent and dryer sheets with only a little fuss; they'd sunk further down in the archaeological dig that is my junk closet than I'd realized.

Said bags joined my laundry in the hamper—no way was I trusting whatever demon detergent Kor might have in his domain.

At least not on my very first load.

One quick check to make sure the apartment was indeed Kor-free, and I continued into the bathroom. Standing in front of the toilet, surveying Kor's fancy-dancy mirror, I paused.

Doubt gnawed at my stomach. What if . . . ?

"Bracchius?" I turned to the doorway and peered through to my room.

The little guy bobbed up half a second later, Sparkles in tow—and still festooned with sequins. "What's up, Immy?"

I jerked a thumb over my shoulder. "Kor's mirror. Do you know how it works?"

"Mostly. Why?"

"Does it only stretch to fit living beings? Or does it work for anything going through?"

Currently, the mirror was about one-quarter the size of my hamper—definitely a no-go.

And the last thing I needed was to futilely wrestle this thing up there, topple off the toilet tank, break my neck on the backwards descent, and have my corpse be buried in ignominy under a mountain of smelly laundry.

"Oh!" Bracchius looked between me and the hamper. "No, you should be good. Anything that touches the mirror's surface triggers it, and it'll widen pretty much forever, I think." He chortled. "Pretty sure you could fit a whole titan through it if you wanted!"

"Really?" Visions of the best pranks ever filled my mind. What was the *last* thing Kor would ever want in his domain?

"Well, maybe not. At least while it's in here, anyway." Bracchius swiveled to encompass our tiny bathroom.

"So it's limited by whatever room it's in?"

"I don't *think* so? But you wouldn't be able to get a titan through this door no matter what."

Good point.

"Cool, thanks. Don't tell on me if Kor comes back early?"

Bracchius grasped Sparkles tighter. "Never!"

"You're the best."

Now, how to manage this without killing myself?

I flopped the bath mat over the toilet seat, the grippy backing keeping it from sliding around. I heaved the hamper up onto the seat, then the tank, and stepped up onto the greying mat.

Ew. It could really do with a wash, too. Maybe I'd come back for it.

I zapped the mirror with a spark of my magenta magic so it would work in the first place, the pink sparkles diffusing across the glass. I poked it, and my finger submerged beneath the slippery warm surface.

Okay, now for the real test.

I angled the hamper so one corner touched the oval mirror. Ripples cascaded across the transformed glass, and the mirror's ornate frame inched wider.

So far, so good.

Putting my shoulder into it, I hefted the hamper higher, forcing it deeper into the mirror.

Hey presto—the mirror swelled like a 2D balloon, and the hamper toppled through.

I cringed. Hopefully Cucumber hadn't been casually waltzing—slorping—past on the other side.

Now that I knew we were a go for laundering, I changed into an old swimsuit and drowned myself in heat protectant.

I'd need a shower after this anyway, so might as well keep my curls from catching fire, right?

Barefoot, I snagged the bathmats and took a chance on the newly exposed toilet lid. It hadn't gotten a coating of heat protectant like everything else, so it actually wasn't too slippery.

Okay.

Here goes.

I closed my eyes, and for the second time this week, I plunged into the mirror.

THE STENCH

The stink hit me first, as always, though it probably had nothing on the concoction I'd bought for Cucumber.

The floor hit me second, luckily padded by the mound of laundry I'd scattered all over.

The hamper hit me third. Well, more like I tumbled in an awkward somersault, and my legs flopped across the fallen hamper, but either way I was adding another bruise to my collection.

The fourth thing that hit me was the fact I'd forgotten a water bottle.

And a flashlight.

Genius.

The queen of planning ahead, that's totally me.

A voice chirped out of the darkness. "Lady Immy, you've returned! I had wondered why Master Kor was dumping human-tainted linens through the portal. Not like him at all."

The rumble of the dryers and gush of water was joined by a repeated squelching drawing nearer.

Cucumber was shaking a leg right for me.

Or a suctiony snail's foot, in his case.

"Yup, it's me, Cuke. Good to see you."

Not that I actually could yet.

"It's *Cucumber*, milady. Is your memory not intact after our harrowing quest?"

"Just trying a nickname on for size, Cucumber. I remember just fine."

"I am glad, milady."

The dim green glow of the LEDs on the dryers lit a flash of motion at shin level. Not that I was much above shin level myself just now.

Cucumber hopped into sight, scraggly arms waving to help keep his balance in the air, sunken eyes fixed on me. "Lady Immy, did you succeed in conveying the Dread Fluff to a more formidable prison? I do hope you weren't harmed once I was no longer there to advise you."

A formidable prison?

I thought of Sparkles squished within Bracchius's arms. "Something like that. And no, I, uh, kept the monster docile just long enough."

Cucumber stopped in front of me and shuddered. "You are endowed with more luck and skill than any other I have met, milady. It is an honor to be in your presence once again."

Aw, shucks.

"Well, I've never had a better demonling vassal than you, Cucumber." I scooped my laundry together, stuffing it back into the hamper as I felt for the bubble bath bottle. "I wanted to bring you a gift to thank you for all your help."

"A gift?" His goopy eyes boggled. "There was no need, milady, truly. I am not worthy."

I gave him a stern look. "You're totally worthy, Cucumber. If I say it, it must be true, right?"

"Indeed, Lady Immy. I have never heard you speak an untruth."

Heh.

The little pipsqueak wasn't done. "A very strange trait for an associate of a demon, to be sure, but a forgivable one. Especially when *gifts* are in the offing."

He peered around as my hand finally landed on the plastic bottle.

"The gift isn't the linens, is it?" He drooped.

"No, I'm not *that* mean." I held out the bottle, which was nearly the same size as the demonling.

Whoops. Maybe I should've gotten him a mini ladle to go with it.

"*Demonling Dreams Bubble Bath*." He read the label, then clasped his three-fingered hands and wailed.

I recoiled at the warbling cacophony. Good one, Immy, your gift brought a demonling to the point of shrieking horror.

The wailing crescendoed. "Lady Immy, this is a gift to end all gifts!" He hugged the bottle, not even able to reach all the way around.

So that had been a wail of . . . rapture, then?

Huh.

I unclenched my teeth and smiled. "Glad you like it. You wanna try it out?"

"Oh, very much."

"May I?" I hovered my hand in front of him until he nodded, then I peeled him off the floor with a sticky *smack* and collected the bottle.

One of the top-loading washers was already full of churning water. "How about this one?"

I raised Cucumber to see, and his whole body quivered with his eager nod. "This will be perfect, milady."

Steam rose off the water. "Not too hot?"

"There is no such thing, Lady Immy."

Doh. Right, forgot who I was talking to. Fifth-degree-burn levels of scalding just made for a pleasant soak for demons and demonlings, and this wasn't nearly *that* hot.

I set Cucumber down on the metal edge of the washer and popped open the bottle.

Annnd nearly passed out.

Choke.

Gasp.

Wheeze.

Expire.

Why hadn't I held my nose before opening this? Kelpies and kimchi, but this was putrid.

No offense to kimchi.

My soul eventually returned to my body, but this might just rank among the worst mistakes of my life.

One more clawing hack, and I had recovered enough to see again.

Barely.

Tears streaming down my face notwithstanding.

Cucumber looked lovesick, fawning with clasped hands beside his malformed face. He sucked down a lungful of air through what must be awfully congested sinuses, judging by the snurfling. "Oh, Lady Immy, that aroma is positively hellish! I will be the envy of *all* the other demonlings."

"I'm"—cough—"sure"—gag—"you will."

More to save myself than anything else, I dribbled a healthy gloop's worth into the swirling water and capped the bottle pronto.

The smell did not get better.

Sadly, all my socks and panties were too big to ram up my nostrils.

But—

I dove for the baggie of dryer sheets. Sweet salvation.

I could deal just fine with an artificial *Tropical Breeze* scraping at my scent receptors for the next little while.

No problemo.

When I returned, bubbles were pluming out the top of the washer like a thunderhead forming.

If thunderstorms rained down corpse water, that is.

Cucumber clapped with glee. "Lady Immy, I hope you will not be offended if I partake *immediately*."

I waved him on. "Not at all." Only it came out more like 'Naw ah aww.'

He dove headfirst into the maelstrom, leaving behind a tiny tunnel in the mass of bubbles burgeoning toward the ceiling.

And the wailing recommenced at top volume.

I smiled, the dryer sheets tickling my lips.

Five minutes later, I'd loaded my laundry into a washer at the absolute opposite end of the laundromat, praying to various gods and eldritch horrors that every stitch of clothing I owned wouldn't become permanently imbued with The Stench™.

Please, Flying Spaghetti Monster, Slenderman, and Old Things of Appalachia.

Maybe they'd make up for me not having thought this through.

That done, I went back through the mirror for my delicates and tossed them in the next washer over.

Go big or go home, right?

I mean, I was doing both, but . . . you get the idea.

The washing should be fine to stew in detergent until I could come back later and switch it over. For now, I had more important things to worry about.

I had to get ready for my totally-not-a-date.

THIRD AND FOURTH WHEELS

I emerged from the mirror to find Bracchius hovering in the bathroom doorway.

He drifted closer. "Mission accomplished?"

"Yep. Now you gotta disavow any knowledge of my actions. At least with Kor."

"Done and done!" Bracchius gave me the dorkiest little salute ever.

"Now scram, 'cause I gotta shower." The sweat drenching me was unreal after the roasty-toastiness of Kor's domain. I hadn't even noticed till now, what with the stench stealing all my attention.

"Yeah you do." Bracchius backed up, flapping one arm in my direction. "What did you do, go on a demonling sewage slide? I didn't know Kor had an amusement park in his domain."

Unlike me, Bracchius was *not* allowed in Kor's mirror. "No amusement park, but yeah, I spent some quality time with a demonling."

"That explains it. The brimstone scent is nice, but everything else . . ." Bracchius hacked like a cat with a hairball. "I think I'll go light my rainbow-charcoal-cupcake candle."

Hopefully he wouldn't catch the sofa on fire again.

He skedaddled, and I shut the door to enjoy a hurried shower.

Clean, dry, and curls wrangled, I went hunting for an outfit. All my work shirts might be whirling inside Kor's washer at present, but I still had some regular duds kicking around in my closet.

Not to mention my new flannels.

I kept the outfit caszh and slapped on the bare minimum for makeup. I was just trying not to jab my eye out with my mascara wand when Bracchius peeked back in.

"Kor's back, Immy. Oh, what are you getting all fancified for?"

I stabbed the mascara wand into its tube. "I've got dinner with someone I met at work."

Bracchius swelled up like a balloon. "Immy, have you lost your mind? Going on a date with someone I haven't even *vetted* yet?! How do you know he's worthy of you? How do you know he's not a slimeball like that last guy you dated, you know, uh, Tyrone? Tiberius?"

"Tucker."

"Yes, him. What's this new one's name? Address? Blood type?" He paused. "That's what you humans call it, right?"

"You got it. And I don't know."

"You don't know his *name*??"

I sighed, ruffling a hand through my chaotic curls. "No, his blood type. His name's Fitz. Here." I grabbed Fitz's business card off the counter and flicked it at Bracchius.

It twirled through the air like a throwing star, and sank half an inch into Bracchius's tummy.

"I've been skewered!" He somersaulted backwards in dramatic death throes. "Aghh! It's the end! Tell Sparkles I love her!"

His form oozed outward over the linoleum like the Wicked Witch of the West, and I half expected another cry of '*I'm melting, MELTING!*'

All I got was a gargle—a pretty convincing one, to be fair.

I rolled my eyes. "You really thought *that* could keep me from going out for ramen, huh? I know you're basically indestructible."

Bracchius popped back into his usual pudgy orb, business card clutched in one appendage. "You believed it for at least a second, though, right?"

"Totally. And I was traumatized beyond reason too."

"Of course you were! You'd be sunk without me. But really, Immy, you shouldn't go on a date with a total stranger! What if he's one of the bad guys?"

"One, it's not a date. He wants a tour guide since he's new to the city. Two, one of *the* bad guys, like *our* bad guys, or just *a* bad guy?"

"Either. Both."

"Well, he seemed nice, but I'll be careful anyway. And I doubt he's working for the bad guys, he's from some insurance company that was . . ." I trailed off.

He'd said he was looking for some woman, but what if that was a cover? What if he *was* looking for the artifact, and not on behalf of Gravis-Witherspoon?

What if he was just another bad guy after this gizmo, only he was taking a subtler approach to getting his hands on it?

Woo the girl who's got it, snatch it when she's least expecting?

Maybe I should take the fake to dinner.

Kor barged into the bathroom, grumbling. "No sign of ingrates anywhere within five blocks. I even went so far as to check the roofs and tunnels. They must be forming their own devious plan."

Weird. They'd been stalking me for two days; you'd think they'd have set up ambushes on every street corner in the neighborhood by now.

Was Kor right? They must be getting tired of me slipping through their fingers at this point.

"Well, I need to leave for dinner soon, and I was thinking of taking the fake with me. Any objections?"

Bracchius zipped between me and the door. "Um, yes, objections!"

I planted a hand on either side of His Royal Blobbiness and did a do-si-do to get out of the bathroom.

"Ack, Immy! That's my face!"

"Sorry. What objections?" I started piling things into my purse.

"If you're determined to go, obviously we have to escort you to dinner! You could be attacked on the way, even if this Fitz person isn't out to get you. Which he probably is. So we should keep an eye on him too."

Great, just what I needed: these two weirdos as third and fourth wheels on my not-date.

Could I pass it off as a *double* not-date? They did bicker like an old married couple.

Hmm . . .

Nah, too weird. Fitz had asked for a tour guide, not a sideshow. Besides, Kor would insult the guy all through dinner, and Bracchius would probably quiz him on random unicorn facts till he face-planted in his ramen.

"You can come with me as far as the restaurant, but then you turn around and go home."

"But—"

"Take it or leave it."

Bracchius drifted downward like a falling leaf. "Take it, I guess. But *you'd* better take your sword or something in case your date gets frisky!"

"Not a da-ate." It came out singsong. "And my sword wouldn't fit in my purse." I did still have Jumpin' Jemima in there, though.

"Then carry it over your shoulder like Xena the Warrior Princess!" Bracchius Tasmanian-deviled around me.

I stepped out of the demon tornado. "Doing that in public's not exactly legal."

"Oh. Well, then punch him really hard in the nose if he gets fresh! I hear humans hate that."

"You're not wrong." I glanced around for any last things I might be forgetting. Phone, keys, wallet, weapon . . .

Right. "Where's the fake artifact?"

Kor whirred up off his three-wick-candle pillar. "I have it on my person, Immaline."

I turned to Bracchius. "And you're still guarding the real one?"

"Yup!"

At least it wasn't falling out of his butt anymore.

"Good. Let's not get them mixed up, yeah?"

Kor huffed. "As though that is even remotely possible! You think I can't tell a portion of my own soul from some . . . some . . ."

"Yeah, I dunno what it is either." Other than a freaking terrifying pseudo god, that is.

"But my point still stands! I know which artifact my substance is entombed in without even a *first* thought!"

"Spiffy. Then let's go."

I stepped outside, giving both demons just enough time to zoom through the door—almost colliding in midair—before I slammed it.

I'd put on my Converse to play tour guide—don't want to be leading some dude halfway across the city in heels, no sir. So when I stepped on a stray kibble bit, I only took a nosedive for the grass, rather than spraining my ankle.

The heels of my hands didn't love it, though.

"Oh, Immy, are you okay?" Bracchius swooped in front of me.

"Fine." I picked myself back up and brushed off my stinging hands.

"This is why levitating is vastly superior to bipedal locomotion," Kor sneered.

"Sprinkle some pixie dust on me, and I'll be right there with you."

Kor and Bracchius fell into an argument about pixie dust as we headed to the subway. We'd just missed a train, so I cozied up to the tiled wall and watched the slow trickle of other commuters arriving.

I'd tuned out their argument until one enthusiastic declaration from Bracchius broke through: "Yeah, but it tastes amazing!"

I blinked. "Pixie dust?"

"No, DemonDelight— Actually pixie dust tastes good too, but—"

The clatter of the approaching train drowned out the rest.

Gargoyles and glitter, but the cars were packed for a Thursday night. I guess it was rush hour, but still.

"Come on, guys." I waved to my demons and jogged toward the furthest subway car—the one least likely to make us feel like sardines.

We squeezed through the doors seconds before they ground shut again, and sure enough, this car had all kinds of breathing room as long as you didn't mind standing.

I grabbed a pole, and Bracchius and Kor drifted up to bob alongside the pixies, who should know better than to play pranks on a demon, but eyed my roommates contemplatively anyway.

"They'll crisp you alive and then eat you," I muttered out of the corner of my mouth. Not that Bracchius would, but I wouldn't put it past Kor.

Wide-eyed, the pixies backed way the hells up.

Over the next couple of stops, our car emptied even more, and I manspread across a couple newly vacant seats.

What? It's not like I wouldn't get up if some kid hopped on.

The door to the next car slid open with a racket, and I glanced up.

Right into the gravelly face of the concrete ogre from the attack at the grocery store.

Yeah, *that* ogre. The one Bracchius and I steered a carnivorous drifter into the face of.

Let's just say his stony complexion hadn't held up.

I cringed under his glower. "Uh, hi, big guy."

Kor and Bracchius whirled around, and Bracchius zinged over. "Wait, Immy, that's the concrete ogre from—"

"Save & Savor, yeah."

Kor's confusion was evident. "You met this ogre at a grocery store? How is this relevant?"

"He's one of the bad guys!" Bracchius hissed.

I heaved a sigh. "And he's not alone."

Three other hulking dudes crammed through the door and flanked the ogre. The only witnesses in the car were the pixies—fat lot of use they'd be.

We'd better lose that fake artifact to these bullies pronto, or we'd be mincemeat.

"You know what we're here for," the ogre rumbled. "There's no escaping this time."

He was right. Our only exit was out the back of the speeding train car, right onto the subway rails halfway between stations.

Not exactly prime survival territory.

Kor trumpeted, "You'll never take it from us, you scoundrels!" The fake artifact had conveniently materialized beside him, pressed against his dark body with one blobby arm.

He rocketed straight for the ogre's rubbly face, the red flickers at his center flaring into a fiery gleam.

The others ducked, but the ogre stood his ground—probably wasn't much that could intimidate him after getting half his face eaten off by a drifter.

Kor whipped around the ogre's head, but a stony arm shot up and slapped Kor right across his front. He thwacked to the ground, the fake artifact tumbling away.

"I've got it!" Bracchius dove and scooped it up, the gold bands glistening under the harsh ceiling lights.

Our muscly opponents advanced into the car, a solid wall of testosterone closing us even further in. Bracchius swept up to the ceiling and darted amongst the pixies. "Neener-neener, neener! You can't get me!"

Surprisingly, a few of the pixies were loosening the screws on the hatch at the center of the ceiling. Desperate to escape, or trying to help us out?

Nah, they probably just thought dropping the panel on someone's head would be hilarious.

I eased to one side, far out of panel-of-Damocles range.

Bracchius dodged and weaved between pixies, then ducked as one of the baddies swiped a grasping hand at him.

Two more thugs booked it toward me—to what? Hold me hostage?

Swinging around the pole with one hand, I built up enough momentum to kick the one guy in the chest, slamming him back into the concrete ogre.

The floor would've been a softer landing.

Guy number two kept coming, arms out zombie-style. I grabbed his wrist and yanked, propelling him forward. The tumble wasn't quite enough to deter him, so I snagged his shaggy hair and helped his forehead into the edge of a seat.

Who said those self-defense classes were a waste of time?

Ew, but now I had greasy hair stuck to my hand. About to smack it off, I paused. Never know when I might need to track these bozos down again.

I rubbed my hands together, twisting the few hairs into a teensy rope, and tucked it in my tight-as-two-coats-of-paint front pocket.

Bracchius's attacker hadn't let up, and had my poor demon pinned to the ceiling. Bracchius was busy playing keep-away, the arm holding the dupe lengthening further and further.

"Over here!" I waved.

Bracchius attempted a toss and fumbled the fake artifact masterfully. I did my best volleyball dive to 'grab' it, managing to ping it off my arm and send it in a steep, nearly slow-motion arc toward Kor.

Hopefully these dudes didn't know demons could just telekinetically snatch things in midair, or the jig would be up.

Kor raced backwards, his body tilted to keep the bauble in sight, and oh-so-innocently bowled over one of the baddies, who conked his head on a handrail. All three of them—Kor, baddie, and bauble—sprawled in opposite directions.

Kor's cursing definitely outstripped the baddie's.

I scrabbled across the floor, one 'desperate' arm extended toward the fake artifact as it toodled along the scuffed laminate.

A heavy boot stopped the artifact in its tracks.

"Oh no you don't!" I lunged forward, but stopped short of clasping my fingers around the metal bands of the dupe.

Not gonna get my fingers smashed under a boot today, thanks.

Luckily the ogre hunched and plucked up the fake artifact before he could wonder why I wasn't trying to pry it out from under his boot.

"Tough luck," he growled down at me, and swung his leg back to kick me.

Oh hells no. I shimmied back, not fast enough, but luckily Kor and Bracchius had me covered.

A crimson glow tainted my vision as I was hauled backwards at top speed, not even touching the ground. At the same time, Kor buzzed forward with a hellfireball floating beside him, and the bad guys flinched back.

"Hit it!" one of them yelled.

Silvery sparks erupted, a frisson of magic snapped out, and . . .

The bad guys were gone.

"Come back, you cowards!" Kor yelled, his hellfireball still sputtering beside him.

Damn, was that a *teleportation* sigil? Those things were überexpensive. Like, no way in the three hells could a bunch of thugs like that afford one.

Who were we dealing with here?

Bracchius joined in the hollering as I sat up. "Your father was a fuzzwarg, and your mother smelled of blueberries!"

I snorted. He never got any movie quotes right, but that actually wasn't too far off.

"Okay, you guys, I think we can drop the act. They're long gone."

Kor's hellfireball fizzled out. "But I so wanted to incinerate at least *one* of them."

"Sorry, Kor. Maybe next time. But hey, your devious plan worked."

"How could it fail? It was magnificent, infallible!"

He was gonna be insufferable for *weeks*.

A clang of epic proportions had me wheeling around, looking for a new attacker.

Instead I found a square hole in the ceiling, the metal panel on the floor, and a crowd of pleased-as-punch pixies high-fiving each other.

I swatted a hand in their general direction. "Nice going. You didn't even hit anyone."

Not that I wanted to be brained by flying objects, but that would've been a handy diversion two minutes earlier. The pixies swarmed out the hole, instantly snatched out of sight as the train shot onward.

Bracchius descended to sit beside me on the floor. "Do you need help up?"

"Nah, just chillin'. Thanks for saving me from that one dude."

Bracchius startled me by growling. "He was going to kick you! I wish Kor *had* gotten him with his fireball."

I patted Bracchius consolingly, then we both started skidding across the floor as the train slowed. "I think this is my stop, guys. Why don't you go home and act all frantic, just in case they've got someone watching the apartment."

"We will," Bracchius promised. "Right after we finish escorting you to the restaurant and get a good look at this suspicious Fitz person."

I flopped my head back against the seat and blew a resigned lip-trill.

This was gonna be *so* much fun.

CHAIN SAWS & CANNIBALS

We trooped up the steps from the subway—well, *I* trooped, while Kor and Bracchius drifted along effortlessly, but whatevs.

Gotta say, I was kinda missing the bounciness from the LivingDead Dreamstopper.

Not that it was a good idea to make a habit out of drinking the stuff.

My phone dinged, and I checked it. Fitz had sent me . . . an email?

Right, duh. Now that I had a working phone again, I'd have to give him my number.

Maybe.

And it wouldn't be in a 'give him my number' kinda way. Just a . . . 'here's this in case you need to get in touch.'

Y'know, for tour guide services.

My phone screen darkened, and I woke it back up to read the email.

Fitz Greymoore: Subject: Ramen place

Message: Almost there. Got a little lost, but my phone thinks I'm close now.

I typed back: Cool. See ya soon.

It was nice not being the only one who was fashionably late for once.

Bracchius bobbed beside me. "Was that him? Was he cancelling?"

"No, he's almost there."

"Oh. Maybe he isn't one of the brigands, then."

"Maybe not." I felt better at the thought. If he'd been their alternate strategy for artifact-snatching, surely he would've booked it now that the baddies thought they had it.

He probably really was just a Plain Jane insurance investigator. Temptation knows this wasn't the first time Bracchius had gotten me feeling paranoid for no good reason.

We turned onto Callahan and passed the smallfolk shoe store with itty-bitty workboots and high heels in the window. A three-foot-tall door was cut into the human-sized one to let their hobgoblin, brownie, and kobold customers through more easily.

Next door was Nozomi Nosh, the ramen place we were meeting at—not that you could tell from the street, with its dented security door in the middle of a blank wall.

No sign, no windows, no advertising.

Just the beat-up steel door.

Better wait outside for Fitz.

"All right, you two, skedaddle." I shooed Bracchius and Kor away with both hands, but Bracchius stubbornly scooted closer.

"I'm not leaving until I've vetted this Fitz person!"

Kor floated away. "I'll gladly take my leave of you both."

"Oh no you don't!" Bracchius rounded on him. "We stay until we know Immy's safe. We'll both be looking for a home again if Immy gets killed with a chain saw or trampled by a centaur!"

"Uh . . . He's not a centaur, for one." And most restaurants tended to frown on guests lugging in chain saws.

Yes, most. Since this wasn't 'Carve Your Own Meat' Night at Rawr Ristorante, I figured I was safe.

"Who's not a centaur?" a deep, soft voice asked behind me.

I spun, coming face-to-face with Fitz, his hazel eyes amused behind hipster glasses. Gone was his suit, replaced by jeans and a hooded jacket. "You, actually."

"Is that . . . a problem?" He quirked an eyebrow. "I've never really considered two feet a disadvantage."

"This is him?" Bracchius whispered in my ear.

I pushed him out of my hair. "Yes, this is Fitz. Fitz, these're my roommates, Bracchius and Kor. They were just leaving." I leveled a sizzling glare at them.

Bracchius spiraled around Fitz, examining him from all angles. "Is Fitz short for Fitzorg Soulstealer, the most harrowing demon of the eighteenth century?"

Both Fitz's eyebrows climbed. "No, it's short for Fitzwilliam Greymoore." He coughed and muttered, "The Third."

I smirked. "What's that?"

Bracchius zeroed in on that too, his tone suspicious. "There are three of you? Are you a doppelgänger?"

"Just your garden-variety human." Fitz adjusted his jacket awkwardly.

"Hmm." Bracchius turned to me. "He seems boring enough."

I choked. "So . . . he passes inspection?"

"For now." Bracchius zoomed up to Fitz's face. "Don't even think about hurting my friend, or I'll send hellfire and curses your way. *And* StayStuck glitter." He tilted in a peremptory nod, then darted down the street, Kor trailing in his wake.

Fitz licked his lips. "I don't know whether I should be more worried about the hellfire or the glitter. Your roommates are certainly . . . protective."

I yanked open the heavy steel door, my scraped hands a bit tender after our brawl on the subway. "I know. You'd think I don't even know how to run someone through with a sword, the way Bracchius gets."

Fitz faltered halfway through the door. "A sword?"

"Yup." I left it at that. A little mystery never hurt anybody.

Inside, the place was hopping. I stepped up to the hostess stand and the cherub perched on top. "Dinner for two?"

"Welcome to Nozomi Nosh. Reservation?" The cherub looked up from her tablet expectantly, her grey eyes bright against her brown skin.

"Nope."

"It'll be about a twenty-minute wait."

"No prob."

Fitz was browsing the brochures in a display by the door, his back to me. For the first time, I noticed the black fanny pack riding his butt.

I leaned against the wall beside him. "They said twenty minutes."

"Super. Look, a brochure with the 'Top 10 Tourist Attractions of Saskia Springs'! Think we can hit one after dinner?"

"Probably." My eyes kept trailing over to his fanny pack, and he patted it gleefully.

"See? Got my fanny pack, as ordered. It's got sunglasses and hand wipes and sunscreen . . ."

I straightened, remembering the tongue-in-cheek email I'd sent him yesterday about his 'tour' this evening. "Wait, you didn't think I was seri—"

Fitz was fighting a smile.

"Heh. Good one." This dude did *not* mess around when it came to teasing.

He might be able to give me a run for my money.

I narrowed my eyes. "But really? Sunglasses, sunscreen? It'll be dark after dinner."

"Never know when you'll run into a sun phoenix."

I bit back a smile and shook my head. "Lemme see that brochure. It's probably all tourist traps anyway."

He held out the brochure, but let it fall when I reached for it. "Ouch, are you okay?"

I glanced down at my palm. Not only was it roughed up from my nosedive in the yard earlier, but grit and grime speckled my skin as well—a memento of our subway scuffle, no doubt.

"Oh yeah, I kinda tripped on the way here, but I'm fine. Lemme go wash my hands, though."

He nodded as I pushed off the wall. I slipped past the cherub, who was just seating a group *with* reservations, and followed the short hallway to the bathrooms.

Soft lighting, clean surfaces, and a fresh box of tissues on the counter made it a pretty nice bathroom overall, but there's just no masking that dank public restroom smell.

Wincing, I scrubbed my hands in the sink under the cool stream of water, determined to get every last fleck of grit out. Never know what you'll pick up on the subway, especially with the cerberats and cherubim pigeons that sneak aboard on a daily basis.

I shook my hands off, rustled them around in a scratchy paper towel, and left.

Fitz had taken one of the vacated seats in the waiting area and was reading a book. I clung to the wall, not minding the minute to watch him unnoticed—it wasn't like I knew him yet, and if he was a jerk to the hostess when he didn't think I was around, that would tell me all I needed to know.

I squinted. Was that a Terry Pratchett book?

It was.

He'd packed a fanny pack purely for joke value, but one of the things he'd tucked inside was not only a book, but one of *Terry Pratchett's*?

Maybe he owned them all.

I bit my lip. Maybe he'd let me borrow the ones I hadn't gotten to yet.

Yup, more tour-guiding was definitely in my future.

I strode over before he could catch me lurking. "Back."

He closed the book, one finger for a bookmark. "Better?"

"Much. Good read?"

He smiled as he stuck the tourist pamphlet in the book to hold his page. "The best."

"So, Terry Pra—"

"Ma'am? Sir?" The cherub hostess flittered over. "Your table is ready."

My stomach growled in approval.

I followed the cherub between tight-packed tables, Fitz behind me. She led us to a tiny table against a wall, and slid two menus beside the wrapped silverware.

Just as we sat, my phone buzzed.

"Sorry, one sec." I pulled it out. Rude, yes, but too many catastrophes crop up in my life for me to ignore my phone on the reg.

But this message wasn't exactly a world-shattering disaster.

Bracchius had texted: Fifteen-minute check-in! If you've been poisoned, flayed alive or transmogrified, don't respond.

I sighed. How many more hypothetical death scenarios would Bracchius come up with?

If I didn't message back, he might barge in here in a panic.

I couldn't resist a little sass in my response, though: Don't worry, I've only been broiled so far. Still alive.

Bracchius: Broiled?! Is he a cannibal??

So much for my snark.

Immy: No, just joking. Relax. Go get an hourlong lava bath treatment or something. Pyro Pampering is on your way home.

A few moments passed before Bracchius's next response: That does sound pretty good. You sure you're okay?

Immy: All good here. Flameo, hotman.

I set my phone down right as our poor gargoyle waiter was placing an empty glass in the same spot. Glass and phone collided, and the glass toppled.

"Oh no—" My hand shot out at the same time as Fitz's, but he got there first, snatching the glass a millimeter before it could shatter on the tabletop.

The instant he grabbed it, the faintest shiver of gold magic leapt from his fingers and raced across the glass.

"What the—" I peered closer, but the magic dissipated as fast as it appeared.

Did he not have control of his magic? I mean, not like *I* had control of *mine*, but at least I wasn't zapping it all over the place willy-nilly without even meaning to. "Fitz?"

I glanced up at him for an explanation, and paused.

His eyes were distant, glazed over like he was in a trance. I waved in front of his face.

Nothing.

Huh.

TOUCHY-FEELY THING

I looked from Fitz, who was frozen in some kind of trance, to our gargoyle waiter, who was hovering awkwardly with one grey hand flung out in panicked reaction to the glass we'd knocked over.

His expression was as bewildered as mine.

"Here, got it." Fitz smiled, holding out the undamaged glass like nothing else had happened.

The waiter took the glass warily and set it beside the other before filling them from his water pitcher.

I leaned toward Fitz. "Uh . . . Where'd you go just then?"

"Oh, um . . ." He rubbed the back of his neck. Was that a *blush*? "My magic does that sometimes."

"Sparks out spontaneously and puts you into a trance?"

"Not quite." He shifted his glass closer, the ice clinking. "It's hard to explain."

"If it's personal or something . . ."

"No, it's fine. It's just my quirk."

Most everyone with magic had one unique thing they could do—their quirk. Mine was the ink-shifting. His . . .

"I see connections. Basically, when I touch something . . ." He paused.

"Oh, are you one of those people who can see the whole history of something when you touch it?"

"Nothing that useful, I'm afraid." He smiled wryly. "No, it's more ephemeral. Like . . ." His eyes darted around, landing on a black stone sculpture that branched like coral in the alcove beside our table. He brushed it with the tip of one finger.

That same golden sheen raced outward before disappearing.

Fitz shook himself. "Like this. A woman in a blue raincoat once sat beside this statue, smoking a chocolate-flavored cigarette, the smoke curling around the stone. I just get little snippets like that. Completely random."

I blinked. "A chocolate-flavored cigarette?"

He shrugged. "Just reporting the facts, ma'am."

I laughed, then jabbed a finger at him. "No ma'ams."

"Yes, Madam Tour Guide."

"That might be worse."

He grinned.

"So you pick up scents, or tastes, not just visuals? What about sou—"

Our waiter reappeared beside our table, wings folded tidily behind him. "Have we decided on drinks? Appetizers?"

Oh. I met Fitz's eyes; his dismay matched mine. "Not quite yet, sorry. Give us a few more minutes?" I smiled up at the waiter sheepishly.

"Of course." He smiled back, pointy teeth glinting in the restaurant's soft light.

We picked up our menus as he bustled away.

My perennial problem was everything looked good, and I couldn't eat—or afford—it all. Not that affording it was a consideration tonight, but one measly potential sightseeing escapade was hardly worth seventeen dishes of amazing food.

Plus Fitz'd only agreed to buy me one dinner.

So far.

I skimmed past snow crab, hamachi carpaccio, oysters, and five kinds of ramen, settling on my old standby: pork belly bao buns.

Mucho delicioso.

Wrong language for this restaurant, but hey.

I tapped my phone for any new messages from Bracchius, but the screen was empty. Maybe he *had* gone for that lava bath.

When I looked up, Fitz's gaze was on my phone rather than his menu. "I thought you said your phone was broken?"

"Oh, it was. Is. This is a new one."

He leaned over. "What is that, the latest model from Obsidian? Nice. Saskia Skies must pay you well."

I scoffed. "Not so much. This was a gift from a friend. Well, my roommate, actually. Bracchius. You met him earlier."

Wow, lips, just keep flappin', why doncha.

Fitz chuckled. "You could say that." He pulled out his own phone. "Since you have a working phone again, mind if we exchange numbers? That way if I get hopelessly lost in the middle of some ridiculous series of one-way streets, maybe I'll have someone who can rescue me."

It was my turn to grin. "So I'm supposed to rescue the dude in distress? I can get behind that."

He barked a laugh, then clamped his lips shut, glancing around guiltily at the startled patrons nearby.

I held out grabby hands. "Here, gimme your phone."

He handed it over, and I added my number to his contacts under 'Lady Knight in Shining Armor.'

Might as well jump on Cucumber's bandwagon and ride it for all it was worth, right?

The whole name didn't display at once, but I didn't give a flying hoot.

I tapped 'call' beside my number, then handed Fitz's phone back as my own rang. 'Fitz Greymoore' popped up on the screen, and I put him in my contacts as 'Dude in Distress' for kicks and giggles.

Life's no fun without 'em, after all.

Fitz unlocked his phone, which was still on my contact page—my self-inflicted appellation marqueeing across the top. He cracked up. "I think we're going to get along just fine."

"Good, because I'm kinda hoping for more tour-guide dinners in my future."

Our waiter must have supersonic hearing, because he popped up a scant second after the word 'dinners' left my mouth. "Ready to order?"

I locked eyes with Fitz, who nodded. "Yup!"

"For the lady?"

"Knight," Fitz mumbled. I covered my laugh with a cough.

The waiter looked perplexed, but kept his head cocked toward me.

"Uh, yes." I scooted my chair in, consulting my menu. "I'll have peach lychee juice, pork belly bao buns—main course, not the appetizer—and a side salad."

"And for the gentleman?"

"Melon soda and tonkotsu ramen, please."

I tilted my head. It wasn't often I encountered someone who also wasn't drinking. Was he being polite because I hadn't ordered alcohol, or?

"Wonderful. Your drinks will be out momentarily." The gargoyle collected our menus, topped off our waters, and strode away.

"No sake?" I asked casually.

Fitz shrugged. "Got a lot of alcoholics in the family. Decided as a teen I was better off not taking after my dad."

"Oh. Sorry."

"S'okay. You?"

"Alcohol doesn't really jive with my system."

Fitz nodded. We stared at each other in silence, then he plunked his book on the table.

Great. Was I so boring that he was going to read while we waited for food?

He opened the book, pursed his lips, glanced around, then twisted in his chair and rummaged through his fanny pack. "Here we go." He whipped out a wet wipe in its little paper packet, and swapped it out for the brochure marking his page.

The brochure crackled as he unfolded it. "Okay, Lady Knight Tour Guide of Excellence—any of these actually worth seeing?" He laid it to one side so we could both read it.

It actually wasn't a bad list. Though, if his magical quirk triggered every time he touched something, some of these might not be real fun for him.

"The touchy-feely thing." I pointed at his fingers. "Does that happen only with your hands, or any skin contact?"

He flexed his fingers. "Just my hands. Gloves are my go-to if I'm worried about getting overwhelmed."

"'Kay. Then I'd rule out the water park, since you can't really wear gloves there, and it's always crowded."

"Got it. What about the springs?"

They were the first item on the list—Saskia Springs, which the city was named for. There were actually multiple springs in the area, but my favorite were further away from the city center.

"They're nice, usually pretty chill. I mean, they're hot springs, but the *atmosphere's* chill. But they're a little ways outside the city, more like a day trip."

Fitz bobbed his head. "Okay, so maybe not a first choice."

I scanned the list for an easy introduction to the city. Netherworld was kind of a labyrinthine combo of an escape room, a kids' play center, and a hands-on science museum. If he wore gloves, he'd have a blast.

Pegasus Point was one of the taller skyscrapers, and they offered pegasus rides from the roof. Not for the faint of heart, but a great view of the city. Most pegasi wouldn't stoop to such a, quote, unquote, demeaning activity, but everybody had to pay the bills, and the occasional pegasus was a bit more down to earth.

Crème de la Crème usually had a line out the door. While unicorns were just as hoity-toity as pegasi, they were more interested in capitalizing on their superiority; their bottled water, Pure Bliss, was their most famous brand, but not their only venture. Crème de la Crème was a small-batch unicorn fromagerie that made prize-winning cheeses from unicorn milk—and led tours of the cheesemaking process.

Wyvern Way . . . I rested my finger on the title. "Wyvern Way is actually really close. We could walk over after dinner. It's more of a Pentagram photo op than anything, but it's pretty."

"I'd love that." His eyes were still fixed on the brochure, though. "What about Pegasus Point? It says it has the best views of the city?"

I explained the pegasus rides, and his eyes lit up. I chuckled. "You're not afraid of heights, then?"

"Not even a little. But if you are . . ."

"Nah, I'm good. Only afraid of the actual falling part." I winked.

Really, Immy, *winking*? Get ahold of yourself, girl.

"Would you be down for doing that sometime?" Fitz asked. "In exchange for another free dinner, that is."

I chewed my lip. Two people going on a pegasus ride, even on separate mounts, was more like a romantic date. And that was *not* happening. But . . .

"Actually, my friend Samaire and I have been wanting to do that forever but haven't gotten around to it. The three of us could go, if that's okay? She doesn't need a free dinner, though." I grinned.

Ugh, why had I said that? It wasn't like Samaire didn't enjoy tasty food as much as me.

Way to throw your girl under the bus.

At least Fitz didn't seem to find my proposal odd. "That sounds great! Are they open Saturdays? Are you both free? Maybe around noon?"

"Um . . . I'll double-check with her, but that should wo—"

An echoing clang had me whipping around in my seat, butter knife in hand. After the last couple days of near-constant chases and ambushes, my nervous system was ready and rarin' to go.

And if the bad guys had figured out our dupe this fast, then I was *more* than happy to skewer someone.

My gaze landed on the tangle of limbs—and metal prep bowls—being walloped by the swinging kitchen door.

Not an attacker. Just some poor waiter and sous chef covered in salad dressing.

With a deep breath, I turned back to our table.

"You okay?" Fitz looked pointedly at the butter knife clasped in my fist.

I tucked it back beside my fork and chopsticks. Probably looked like I'd lost my marbles. "Yeah, just a bit jumpy. I've had some . . . stalkers the last couple days. Shouldn't be an issue anymore."

"Stalkers?" His expression was alarmed, to say the least.

"Not the creeper kind of stalkers." I sighed. "It's a long story."

"Uh, what other kind of stalkers *are* there?"

I didn't really want to say 'the murdery, hunt-you-down-for-not-exactly-stolen-goods kind,' so I settled for, "The wanting-to-rob-me kind. But I think we sorted things out."

For now. Hopefully they wouldn't figure out we'd stuck them with a dupe before we could offload the real thing.

"That does sound like a long story. Maybe for our second . . . tourist outing?"

"Maybe."

Not wanting to wander further down this conversational path, I made a blatant topic change. "So your magic . . . your quirk, I mean. Is it uncomfortable to touch things?"

Fitz shrugged. "Not really uncomfortable. Just more . . . inconvenient. Kind of distracting to get interrupted every time you brush something with your hand. That's why I've usually got gloves with me." He patted the fanny pack clipped to the back of his chair.

Just how much information did his ability give him? He acted like it was a fleeting glance, but was he holding back?

Maybe he'd known everything about me from our first handshake.

Our gargoyle waiter popped up beside us, looking smug; *he* hadn't been one of the swinging-door casualties. "Your drinks."

He slid the melon soda in front of Fitz, but I took my peach lychee juice right from his hand. "Thanks." I slurped from the straw, and the fresh, mellow sweetness hit the spot.

Fitz drank as well, not seeming to pick up anything from the glass. Maybe it was new?

More info about his ability would be good, if only so I wouldn't spiral into another paranoid tizzy.

I set my damp glass on a paper coaster and nodded at Fitz. "Would you do it again, with something I choose?"

"You mean touch something? Sure, I guess. As long as it's not gross." He wrinkled his nose.

I grinned. "Don't worry, I won't make you stick your finger in ghoulplasm." I rummaged in my purse under the table, contemplating my options. Most everything in here was boring: keys, wallet, lip balm, gum . . .

Ooh, yes.

Out came Jumpin' Jemima, looking more like a rainbow pom-pom of ball-bead chains than an electrified flail.

I plunked her on the table—safety lock on, of course.

Fitz's brows rose. "That's not a sex toy, is it?"

I laughed. "Nope."

"Self-defense weapon for cheerleaders?"

"Closer. It won't hurt you." I nudged Jemima toward him. "Why don't you touch it and see what it tells you?"

Fitz narrowed his eyes. "All right, but only if you tell me about *your* quirk first."

"Sure." It wasn't like my ink shifting was some big secret. "What's your favorite kind of pet?"

"Pet? A fuzzwarg." He smiled, probably thinking of some childhood pet. Or current one. Heck, he might have a whole menagerie at home for all I knew.

I laid my arm on the table, palm up, showing off the black-ink tattoo on my wrist: a rib cage with poppies.

"Nice tattoo?" Fitz remarked.

"Just watch."

Tongue between my teeth, I focused on the ink beneath my skin. I pictured a fuzzwarg, with its rounded ears, fluffzilla torso, flat tail, curving teeth.

The black lines on my wrist bled in a diffuse haze, then concentrated, reforming into a simple stylized fuzzwarg, line by line, detail by detail.

"There. That's my quirk."

Fitz leaned in and squinted at the tattoo. "That's amazing."

I shrugged. "It comes in handy sometimes."

"Can you do that with any ink? Or just tattoos? And only your tattoos, or . . ."

"Just tattoos, and mine." So far, anyway. I had done some testing after my quirk had manifested, but you could never cover *all* the bases.

His gaze lifted to me, roaming over the rest of my bare skin—arms, face, neck.

I helped him out and tapped the tiny design behind my right ear. "Another one here, not that I really ever change it."

Not being able to see the tattoo made it way harder to shift, and why bother? The tat—the word 'astray' trailing behind a will-o'-wisp—was one of my favorites.

I took a sip of my peach lychee juice as he kept staring at me, probably wondering where else I had hidden tattoos.

Like I was going to tell him.

"'Kay, your turn." I shoved Jumpin' Jemima further across the table toward him, the colorful metal chains tinkling against my silverware.

Fitz straightened in his chair. "And you say this thing isn't going to shock me?"

"Pinkie promise."

He tentatively stretched out his pointer finger and gave Jemima the barest brush. He blinked rapid fire, then sat back. "Huh."

I propped my chin in my hand. "So why do some of your touches zone you out longer than others? These last two, it's like they didn't affect you at all, but when you caught the glass earlier you went dopey for a while."

Fitz shifted in his seat. "It depends on whether it's intentional or not. If I'm prepared for a glimpse, it doesn't usually faze me. But if it's an unexpected touch, sometimes it'll take me a second to snap back to reality."

"More like *twenty* seconds."

His head jerked back. "Wait, seriously?"

I nodded. "Enough time to scribble a silly mustache on your face, if you're a quick draw with a pen."

His hand rose to his upper lip, his eyes widening.

"Don't worry—only occurred to me after. You're Sharpie-free." I waved at Jumpin' Jemima. "So what did you see?"

Fitz opened his mouth, closed it, then opened it again. "I think it was . . ." He squinted. "A barghast getting hog-tied by pink magic and toppling into the bed of a pickup truck?"

A grin spread over my face. Right, the barghast who'd tried to steal a brand-new Chevy Dreadnought. That had been fun. Lasso Lainey worked like a dream, even with my disaster magic.

Yes, we *had* given dorky names to most of our customer disservice gadgets.

Fitz adjusted his glasses. "What are you, some kind of bounty hunter on the side?"

I chuckled. "Career goals, maybe, but no, just another day on the job."

Not that I really wanted to become a bounty hunter—long hours, always sweaty, not many opportunities for kicking back in your sweats with popcorn and a cheesy movie. But it was pretty kickass.

"Your current job?"

"Yep."

"Someone took down a barghast at a rental car place?"

"Not someone." I jabbed a thumb at my chest. "Little ol' me."

"Wow." Fitz scooted the weapon back toward me with his elbow. What, he didn't want to risk seeing any more of my adventures on the lot?

Oh well.

I put Jumpin' Jemima away as Fitz took a long gulp of his melon soda. "So, tell me more about your job. Not much barghast wrangling involved?"

Fitz choked, nearly doing a spit take.

Whoops. Bad timing on my part.

"Not quite, no. It's more like—"

"Here we are." Our gargoyle waiter hefted a large tray beside our table. "Two orders of bao buns for the lady"—he clanked a wide plate before me, expertly avoiding our glasses and silverware—"as well as the side salad."

Sweet. I stripped the paper off my chopsticks and broke them apart as he turned to Fitz.

"And the tonkotsu ramen for the gentleman. Enjoy!"

My eyes were only for my food now; Fitz could entertain himself for a minute while I dove in. The real question was bao bun first, or salad?

Who was I kidding?

I gathered up—you guessed it—*not* the salad. The pillowy softness of the doughy white bun disappeared into my mouth, and I slumped back in my chair in pure bliss with the first bite.

The caramelized crust of the pork belly yielded to tender, savory juiciness. Then came the tart bite of the pickled carrot, radish, and red cabbage.

A sweet soy aioli coated the meat and veggies, silky and creamy, melding everything together.

"You look happy."

I opened my eyes. Fitz smirked across from me.

"Lemme guess, the happy dance in my chair clued you in?" I grinned.

"That would be it. Glad you're enjoying it." Fitz reeled up a massive spool of ramen noodles, along with some enoki mushrooms and pork. He wasn't going to just—

Oh no. I raised a hand in warning. "Wait—"

I blanched as he shoved the whole shebang in his mouth.

Too late.

WYVERN WAY

Mouth full of hot ramen, Fitz gaped, face reddening, his gaze latching on to his glass of ice water. He snatched it up and guzzled, water runneling down his chin.

Poor guy—the ramen here always came out of the kitchen hot as the three hells. I pressed my lips together against a smile. "You gonna make it?"

He waved a reassuring hand as he continued chugging.

And chugging.

Glass empty, he clunked it down.

"Give my condolences to the roof of your mouth."

He winced. "I'll survive."

Our waiter bustled over and refilled his glass. "Enjoying your meals so far?"

I beamed up at him. "*I* am."

"Wonderful."

Fitz wedged one half of his soy egg between his chopsticks and started blowing on it.

Lesson learned.

I speared some salad and shoveled it in. The subtle tang of the milky mayo dressing brightened the crisp lettuce, and I munched contentedly.

Fitz eyed his egg, steam still rising off it. "To answer your question, mostly it's a lot of research and paperwork."

I furrowed my brow, mouth cram-packed with salad. What was he talking about?

Oh, right—work. I'd asked him about his work.

Good job, brain.

I swallowed. "But this time seems like it's a lot more than research and paperwork."

"Yeah, this case is unique. If I don't find who I'm looking for, there could be some pretty serious consequences." He risked the egg, popping it into his mouth, and didn't immediately lunge for his ice water again.

"For you? Like you'd lose your job?"

He bobbed his head from side to side as he chewed. "Probably not. But . . ."

"But what?"

His lips tightened. "I'm not really supposed to go into specifics."

I just stared at him inquisitively.

"Sorry. It's too important to gossip about." His gaze shifted to his bowl, an uncomfortable tension between us.

I grimaced. "No, it's my bad, sorry. Curiosity killed the charybdis, right?"

He chuckled. "Suppose so."

"So what *can* you tell me about your job?" I scooped up another bao bun.

"At this point it's really just going back over everything with a fine-tooth comb. I've got someone scrubbing through the security footage, trying to enhance it, but I don't have much hope of turning up anything useful."

I took another bite of bao bun to hide my sudden anxiety. They were enhancing it?

Not like the grainy footage would give up much in the way of detail, but what if it was enough to see me scooping up the artifact, or even that fifty-dollar bill?

Keeping abandoned car contents was a rental-car tradition, but it probably didn't look too good to an outsider.

I was half tempted to just get the artifact back from Bracchius and dump it in the lost-and-found box after all—wash my hands of it completely.

So what if some scary dudes got ahold of the even scarier demigod or whatever trapped inside?

Yeah, right.

I clamped my lips together. *Please* let Cynna know of someone who could take this magical menace off my hands.

Well, off Bracchius's hands— Out of Bracchius's bu—

Never mind.

I smiled up at Fitz. "So do you ever just give up on a job, call it quits and go home?"

"Oh, no, all the insurance investigators at my company are highly motivated to get the property back."

"How's that? Bonuses? Extra vacation time?" Both of which I could only drool over.

He gave me an evaluating look. "We do get those, but that's not why I've never quit until I've repossessed the property." He looked down, toying with his chopsticks. "Not a lot of people know this, but Gravis-Witherspoon is owned by a dragon."

"Yeah?"

He continued without looking up. "All the excess money from insurance premiums—after employee salaries, business costs, et cetera—goes into her hoard." He swallowed. "If we can't repossess, or can't prove the claim doesn't have merit, we have to take the client reimbursement . . . from her dragon hoard. *Nobody* wants to do that."

I narrowed my eyes. "You're joking."

His eyes glinted with mischief. "Maybe, maybe not."

I mock glared at him and tucked in to another bao bun.

My last bao bun.

Sniff.

I could admit it—after an hour of chatting over tasty food, I was starting to like Fitz.

But I didn't know him yet. Like, at all. He could be genuine or putting on a sweet front. Hardly anybody ever showed their true self on a first . . . not-date.

And Bracchius was right—I deserved better than another Tucker.

Way better.

And I was perfectly happy to become friends—and stay friends—until the end of time.

Or until he showed his true colors.

I stared down at my empty plate, picking up one sad scrap of pickled carrot. I'd forgotten just how small these bao buns were.

Fitz jerked his chin toward my plate. "Still hungry?"

"Maybe."

"Then order something else."

"Really?"

He nodded, ramen noodles hanging out of his mouth, a bead of broth dripping down his chin.

I couldn't help but laugh. "Okay, thanks." I flagged down our waiter as Fitz nabbed his napkin.

"What can I do for you, miss?" The gargoyle collected my barren plates.

"Could I see the menu again?"

His stony fangs peeked out with his smile. "Certainly, one moment."

He returned with a menu, then strode off to deal with another table.

Fitz watched me studying the menu, my eyes bouncing between a zillion different options. He leaned in. "We could share an order of snow crab if you like."

I blinked up at him. "Crab? That's so expensive."

"So are tour guides—and down payments for the services of lady knights in shining armor."

I rolled my eyes, smiling. "Maybe not the tour guides, but yeah, I hear lady knights go for a premium."

"Absolutely. Do you like crab?"

"Yeah . . ."

He waved at our waiter and placed the order.

"Thanks."

"My pleasure."

I ended up hogging most of the crab, but since he was still finishing off his ramen, I didn't feel too bad. Our waiter brought the bill, and I rested a hand on it before Fitz could grab it.

"Now, I'm only letting you pay because you're taking shameless advantage of my local knowledge, and I deserve to be compensated accordingly."

Fitz laughed and shook his head. "I get it. This *isn't* a date."

Maybe I was belaboring the point a bit. I retracted my hand, and he slipped his card inside the small folder with the bill.

Fitz stoically buckled on his fanny pack. "Still up for stopping by that . . . What was it?" He picked up the brochure.

"Wyvern Way?"

"That's it. You're not ready to run away screaming yet?"

"Not *quite* yet." I held up two pinched fingers as I shrugged my purse over my shoulder.

We walked the few blocks to Wyvern Way, glowing devas overhead drowning out the stars, the buzz of neon lights competing with the rush of traffic.

I couldn't help peering down every dark alley and glancing over my shoulder at every scrape of a footstep behind us. I wasn't exactly a shrinking violet, but the last couple days of nonsense had really put me on edge.

Hopefully it would take the goon gang a while to figure out we'd tricked them.

Fitz slowed. "You okay? You seem a bit twitchy."

"I'm fine."

"I wouldn't let anything happen to you, you know."

I put on a fierce grin, raising my chin. "Yeah? Well, I wouldn't let anything happen to *you* either."

"I don't doubt it."

I pulled up short at a small gap between buildings.

Fitz trudged a couple steps further before hitting the brakes. "Oh, this is it?"

"Yupperoo." I pointed up the narrow stairs.

He peered up into the dark—they weren't exactly well lit at night. "What's so special about this?"

"One sec." I scrounged my phone out of my purse and flicked on the flashlight. The beam played across the steps, and Fitz drew in a startled breath.

Every one of the seventy-seven steps was paved with wyvern scales, arrayed so the spectrum of colors blended into one another seamlessly. Each scale shimmered with a hidden iridescence like labradorite, the brilliant color only showing from just the right angle.

"Whoa." He knelt and traced a finger half an inch above the surface of the first step. "That must've taken forev—"

Fitz slapped a hand to his pants, and I raised my brows before I heard the buzzing.

He pulled out his phone. "Ah, that's work. Gotta get back to the grind."

"At this time of night? Man, your boss must be a hardass."

Fitz smiled. "It's not too bad. Anyway, I've got to take this. Can I walk you to the subway or anywhere?"

"Nah, I'm good, but thanks."

We did an awkward dance of 'should we wave or hug or shake hands,' and ended up in a one-armed hug as I gritted my teeth in a smile.

He pulled back, looking as flustered as I felt. "See you Saturday." He answered his phone on what had to be the final ring and walked off. "Fitz."

I headed toward the closest subway station, his voice fading behind me. The last thing I caught was "I thought she left the city?"

Hopefully he'd find his mystery woman before he got me into trouble.

The sidewalks filled as the nocturnal denizens of the city started their nights; headed to work, out on errands, or just enjoying the fresh—ish—air. It was bizarrely refreshing not to have anyone leaping out of the darkness to accost me.

Smiling at a shadowsylph family leaving a McDonald's, I turned the corner onto Jefferson Street.

And smacked face-first into something warm, dark, and *definitely* alive.

INNER FIERY PARADISE

"Oof."

I bounced back from whomever I'd bumped into, hoping for a duskmallow rather than a Nalustrak night terror.

Instead, a familiar demon faced me.

"Wha—? Kor, what are you doing here?" I narrowed my eyes. "Were you following me this whole time?"

Kor groused, "Bracchius was worried about leaving you, but he also forgot Sparkles at home and was becoming anxious, so I told him to return home and I would watch over you."

"You? Watch over *me*?"

"I'm sure that is what I said, yes."

"That was . . . nice of you . . ." I poked him in the gut, which felt spongy and warm like normal. "Are you really Kor? You're not some doppelgänger filling in for him—badly—while he's up to some evil plot?"

"I am me."

"Prove it."

"You have a demonmark just above your right kidney in the shape of one of those strange goldfish crackers."

I sputtered. "First off, I thought you made a point of *not* looking when I'm—"

Kor's red flickers went wild as he cringed away. "Don't say it! The sight is already burned into my consciousness for all of time, Immaline—don't make me relive it!"

"Hmph." I crossed my arms. "And second, it's a *birthmark*, not a demonmark."

Kor muttered, "That's what you think."

This was more like the Kor I knew. It didn't explain his behavior of the last twenty-four hours, though.

"All right, Kor, spill it. What's up, that you're being so bizarrely helpful all of a sudden?"

"I'm lulling you into a false sense of security!"

"And then telling me about it? Nuh-uh, I don't buy it."

"I'm . . . testing out a new 'kill them with kindness' regimen for the contract cabal?"

"You don't sound so sure about that, buddy."

He hemmed and hawed a bit, pacing in midair.

"You know I'm just gonna keep bringing it up."

Kor drooped a few inches. "And your stubbornness rivals that of a demon."

I grinned. "Rivals? Try *outstrips*. Come on, tell me, Kor."

"Urgh, if I must. Immy . . . demons are extremely good at getting exactly what we want. I have my own domain, imps and demonlings at my beck and call, magic beyond compare, and I've struck fear into the hearts of my enemies. And yet . . ." He pulsed in a shrug. "Things could be better, somehow. Only I don't *know* how. And Bracchius, who flouts nearly all demon traditions and is just . . . just *weird*, seems to be . . ."

He trailed off, his internal crimson flickers spasming.

"Happy?" I suggested.

"Happy," Kor grumbled. "So I talked to my therapist and—"

I came this close to toppling right off the sidewalk in shock, my eyebrows shooting for my hairline. "Your—Your therapist?"

"Yes, of course, Doctor Sondra. She's been instrumental in helping me cope with the chaos *you* inflicted upon my domain, Immy." He huffed. "Do I not deserve formidable mental health as much as the next demon?"

"I— Of course, obviously, I just—" I pressed my lips together to shut off the stuttering faucet my mouth had become. "I'm just surprised is all."

"Well, Doctor Sondra asked me if there would be anything so wrong with me mimicking some of Bracchius's coping methods to try to find my own inner peace—er, my own inner fiery paradise. And I couldn't come up with a rebuttal she was satisfied with, so here we are."

Who'da thunk? Now the real question was . . . "So exactly *which* of Bracchius's coping methods have you been trying?"

"That's classified."

"Classified?"

"Yes. Between me and my therapist. Now buzz off."

Clearly the therapy hadn't robbed him of his customary charm yet.

"You're the one following me, buster." I jabbed both thumbs at myself as I backed up in the direction of the subway station. "I have a couple places I have to go, so . . . Do you wa— Are you gonna tag along?" I quirked an eyebrow at him.

"If I must."

"I mean, you *don't*, actually . . ."

Kor squirmed. "If Bracchius hears I abandoned you when he entrusted you to my care, he can take me up before the demon council."

My steps faltered. "I'm sorry, *what*? If he could do that every time you annoyed him, wouldn't he have done it long since?"

"This is different."

"How?"

"Well . . . Bracchius didn't believe me when I promised to watch over you. So . . . he made me sign a contract."

I almost choked. "You made a demon contract . . . with *Bracchius*?" Hells below, Bracchius was wilier than I'd given him credit for.

"Indeed. And if I break its terms, he can drag me in front of the council."

"But I thought the whole point of demon contracts was to try to trick the other party? To *technically* fulfill the terms while making their life miserable? Wouldn't the council be impressed if you managed to get out of it?"

Kor swiveled from side to side in a pitying gesture. "Oh, Immaline, your naïveté is on full display this evening. While that *is* true for contracts with *lesser* beings, interdemon contracts are a whole nother matter. Breach a contract with another demon and . . ." He shuddered.

Huh. Good to know.

"So, you *are* tagging along?"

Kor sighed. "Unfortunately."

"Well, this way, then." I headed down the street, Kor bobbing alongside me.

He broke the silence as we entered the subway station. "How was your . . . dinner?" He sounded like gritting out the question was worse than chewing glass.

"Tasty."

Kor halted with a retching cough. "Immaline, tell me you *didn't* sample your date. It's bad enough you're consorting with another foul human, but *tasting* one?" He convulsed. "Really, you *must* broaden your horizons. Take up with a devious ghoul, or even a succubus. Just . . . don't bring another human home, I beg of you."

"Wasn't planning on it. And I was talking about the *food*, you utter buffoon, not Fitz."

"Ah. I was inquiring about dinner, the event, not dinner, the comestibles."

"Yeah, got that." I rolled my eyes. "For future reference, I'm not a cannibal."

"My estimation of your taste just rose several degrees, Immaline."

"Imogen."

"You're changing your name?"

I glared at him as the train pulled in. "No. Imogen has *always* been my name."

"Then why did you previously wish to be called Immaline?"

If he'd had a throat, I would've strangled him.

My smile was as sweet as toxic hydra sugars. "How about we stick with Immy? No Imogen, no Immaline. Just Immy."

"Very well. But if you insist on changing it every few months, I cannot guarantee I won't slip up from time to time."

"Whatever." At least I'd tried.

I stepped onto the train, whose lights were dimmed a bit for the nocturnal crowd. The black light car was my favorite to ride, but this one was jam-packed with lepidopterafae and scorpiofae.

No way was I tangling with *that* many pincers and stingers.

Kor tucked in close to me to avoid a shopping golem bedecked with grocery bags. I swatted an intrusive pixie out of my face and leaned into the demon. "So, while you were following me, notice any more of our stalkers lurking?"

Kor about-faced. "Of course not. Why on earth would they follow us now? My replica of the artifact was a perfect dupe. I would be surprised if they *ever* returned to harry us."

"Until they open the artifact, that is, and find out it's not what they thought." Assuming opening it was what they wanted with the thing.

Didn't seem too likely they just needed a fancy knickknack for their bookshelves.

"Oh. I suppose until then, yes. Hrm." He rose past the level of my shoulder, giving the train car a cursory inspection. "I'll keep an eye out, just to be safe."

"Appreciate it."

We got off at the stop closest to Samaire's nightclub slash cocktail lounge—Croon. Near the entrance, we approached a line of hoity-toity people waiting to get in, dressed in tuxes, gowns, and tuxedo dresses, tail suspenders and sequin-studded wing wraps.

I marched past every last one, right up to the massive cerberogre bouncer, who glowered down at me with all three heads.

Kor tugged at my sleeve. "Immy, don't be dense. The line starts back there."

The cerberogre bouncer peered closer at me, then pulled a pair of glasses out of his breast pocket and shoved them on his middle head.

I waved my fingers. "Hey, Lex."

"It *is* you!" He beamed. "Good to see ya, Immy! You here for Samaire?"

"Yup. Mind if my roommate here joins me?"

"Not at all." He speared Kor with a nearsighted glare. "But no pestering our guests into demon contracts, or you'll have me to answer to."

Kor floated back a few inches. "As though I would need to arrange contracts with such—"

Lex growled.

"I mean, of course, sir. No problem, sir."

Lex tossed another smile my way as he raised the velvet rope.

Kor muttered, "I could take him even with my hellfire trapped in Rokonor."

"I wouldn't count on it." Lex was big and half-blind, but he was far from stupid.

We entered Croon.

The place was packed, a given with the line down the block. It smelled like pricey perfume and wine, and aside from the stage, the lights were dim.

A bar ran the length of the wall to our right, stopping just short of the stage. Tables dotted the floor, those for macrofae closest to the door, then human-sized, then microfae tables bordering the stage. Servers wove between tables, delivering food and drinks and whisking away plates.

Under the spotlight, Samaire, appropriately, crooned a jazz number, "'Round Midnight," her siren voice impossibly alluring. Her floor-length golden gown sparkled against the plush red velvet curtain behind her, rivaling the gold feathers in her long brown hair.

"This way." I elbowed Kor, and led the way to an empty table near the sweeping steps down from the stage on the left. The 'Reserved' placard didn't put me off; this table was for the singers on their breaks— and for their guests.

Ergo, moi.

I sat. Kor drifted between the other chairs and the place settings, and finally came to rest on a gold charger.

"What are we doing here? This place reeks of mortal," he grumbled.

"I gotta talk to Samaire." I pointed toward the stage. They'd met before, but Kor usually hung out in his mirror when she dropped by. "She'll be on break soon."

It was just a few minutes before eight, when she usually took one of her breaks.

Sure enough, after one more number, the spotlight faded to uproarious applause, and Samaire coasted down the stairs to our table.

"Heya." She wrangled her gown to take the seat beside me as a waiter dropped off water and a couple plates of appetizers. Samaire gestured toward them, but I shook my head, not hungry.

"What'd you think?" Her voice was lower than usual, with a not-so-subtle rasp.

"Gorgeous, like always. But what's with your voice?" I pushed a glass of water her way, along with the fifty bucks I owed her.

"Double thanks." She guzzled half the glass in one go. "Remember how I told you this week is variety week?"

"Like I'd forget."

"Well, yesterday was screamo redcap death metal day. Thank Demeter that today is sultry jazz—at least my current state of throat gravel works okay for that. I've really gotta kick back with a nymph honey tea when I get home tonight."

I winced. "Ouch, sorry. Want me to stuff the comments box with notes that variety week sucks and we the customers want the same-old, same-old?"

She cocked her head. "That . . . might just work."

"A diabolical deception," Kor declared. "I approve."

"Great." I dug in my purse for a pen. "Then you won't mind getting us the paper?"

"I suppose not." Kor's crimson center flashed, and a thick scroll of parchment materialized on the table in front of him—the kind demons used for contracts, of course. He spooled off a foot of paper before severing it with a tight line of hellfire.

"Thanks, Kor."

The paper's charred edges glowed with embers, smoke trailing toward the ceiling, and I patted a heavy napkin across it before anything else could catch fire.

Samaire and I took turns writing disgruntled notes in varied handwriting as we caught up on the last couple days—what'd happened after I left her at the restaurant, my dinner with Fitz, all the zaniness of my ill-advised adventures. I left out the bulk of the details about my little trip into Kor's domain, since he was listening in.

No need to piss the demon off even further.

"That's so wild. So you think those whackjobs will leave you alone now?"

"At least long enough for us to get rid of the real thing, hopefully." If I didn't hear from Cynna soon about someone to ditch the artifact with, I'd have to bug her. "So how'd that 'protect you from the elements' sigil work out for you in the dragon storm?"

She squirmed in her seat. "Yeah, I might've misread the description. Apparently it protects you from the dangerous elements on the *periodic* table . . . Not the weather elements."

"So . . ."

"So I was impervious to plutonium for twelve hours, which, like, sure, that'll be good to have around in a nuclear crisis, but . . ."

I grinned. "You got drenched too, huh?"

"Totally drowned, yeah. It's a good thing I wasn't working, 'cause about the only thing I could've pulled off was a mermaid act. But . . ." She bit her lip on a smile.

"But what?"

"I met a girl."

"While you looked like a drowned rat?"

Samaire laughed. "Yeah, well, we both did. Actually, I already kinda knew her—she comes in here sometimes, but we've never really talked before."

"And . . . ?"

"Annnd I like her. And she likes me. And we're gonna see where it goes." She toyed with her hair, smiling.

"That's so great!" I nudged her under the table with my knee. "Is she cute? What's her name?"

"Nadine, and she's drop-dead gorgeous. And apparently pretty well-off, which doesn't hurt."

"Right? That's awesome. You'll have to let me know how it goes."

"Totally." A waiter stopped by and muttered something to Samaire before striding off again. "They want me back on stage in five minutes, so if there's anything else . . ." She popped a teeny tartlet into her mouth.

"Yes!" I sat up. "This weekend's your weekend off, right?"

"Yeah, Delia is singing this weekend. Why? You got something fun planned?"

"Maybe." I explained Fitz's invitation to Pegasus Point on Saturday. "But you've gotta promise not to make a liar of me. I told him we've been wanting to go pegasus riding forever, so it won't just be me and him on Saturday."

Samaire laughed. "Pegasus riding? Girl, it's a good thing I don't have a fear of heights."

I rolled my eyes. "I *know* you don't have a fear of heights. I wouldn't have volunteered you if he'd wanted to go jump in the eel tank at the aquarium or something."

Samaire shuddered.

"But you're free? We were thinking noon." I wrinkled my nose. I did *not* like the way saying 'we' felt. I'd have to stick with 'Fitz and I' or 'Fitz and me.'

Ugh, that wasn't much better. Maybe just keep it separate entirely: '*I* was thinking noon.'

"Noon works for me. Meet there?"

"Probably. I'll text you the deets when I know."

I sucked on my lip as Samaire finished the last of her snack. There was something else, wasn't there? Um . . .

Brow furrowed, I stared into space as I racked my brain. Saturday, Samaire, something . . .

Aster! Aster had wanted to go to the Comet club with us.

"Are you free later on Saturday too?"

"Yeah . . ."

"One sec." I sent a text off to Aster to double-check if Saturday would work.

Her reply popped up almost immediately: YES!!

I chuckled as I replied, then tucked my phone away. "Wanna go to Comet? Caveat that Damarion's vampire friend, Aster, wants to make a girls' night of it."

"Um, yes I want to go to Comet! I still haven't seen it since they remodeled, and it's supposed to be a-maaa-zing." She stood, draping her gown around her just right. "Would she mind if *I* brought a friend too?"

I grinned. "You could probably bring twelve, and she'd be stoked."

"Awesome. But yeah, just the one—Nadine." She swooped in for a hug. "Gotta get back to work. Love ya!"

"Love you too. Good luck!"

She raised a hand to her throat. "Thanks, I'll need it."

The spotlight bloomed back to life as she ascended the stairs and resumed her place at the microphone.

"All right, Kor, next stop is—" I glanced at the gold charger he'd been sitting on, only to find it bare. "Kor?"

I turned full-circle, gaze sweeping fruitlessly over the nearby patrons. Where had that little ball of evil incarnate gone? It wasn't like he needed to use the restroom.

Purse in hand, I slunk along the wall, scanning the more distant tables. He wasn't at the microfae tables, or the human-sized ones . . .

My heart thudded in my chest when I spotted him at a macrofae table, bothering one of the patrons.

Ravens and revenants, was he *trying* to get us killed?

KEEP YOUR VILLAINESS CLOSER

At the back of the room, Kor was cozied up to a massive typhon in a tuxedo dress, their hair snakes hissing at him.

I stomped closer, ready to tuck Kor under my arm like a football and make a break for it.

Typhons in polite society were only slightly less likely to suffocate you like a python, slice you up, and snack on you throughout the rest of the day—especially if you annoyed them.

Kor was gushing a mile a minute. "Strong, fierce, capable . . . You would be *perfect* for the job. It does require relocation—expenses paid— but comes with excellent benefits. My demonlings will polish your scales daily, and they even make a good hors d'oeuvre in a pinch."

"Kor!" My vicious stage whisper cut across the room, but he ignored me.

"And it's an illustrious position, being charged with keeping such powerful creatures contained—though none as powerful as yourself, of course."

The typhon's head lowered toward Kor, fanged maw opening.

Yup, he was a goner. I sprinted up right as the typhon—

Spoke.

"And precisssely what," the typhon hissed, "happened to the previousss holder of the posssition?"

I gulped, but Kor steamrolled right on. "Tragically, he died of natural causes."

My snort skirted dangerously close to being too loud.

"Skar had been with me a long time, you understand. Absolute ages. *Devastated* to see him go."

Aggravation tinged his last line, and I eased away a few inches. Was I imagining the frenzied swarming of his crimson flickers in my direction?

Nope.

"Here is my card." Kor produced a blank black card, which the typhon took between two slicey-dicey claws. "If you're interested, simply hold it and say my name—Kor Fatescorcher—and you'll be teleported to my domain to go over the particulars."

More like to be trapped and enslaved, by my guess, but I wasn't about to say anything. I'm happy not being human sushi, thanks.

"Nice meeting you," I chirped to the looming typhon. "But we've really gotta be going."

I wrapped an arm around Kor and steered him away at top speed. "Seriously? Trying to hire *another* typhon?"

"It's only necessary because you *murdered* my last one! For which I will never forgive you. Ever."

"Might wanna keep your voice down—this one might hear you."

"Hmph."

Kor grumbled dire threats under his breath as I surreptitiously jammed all our 'variety week is terrible' notes into the comments box, then we slipped out a side door.

"Can we finally end this tedious outing and return home, Immy? Gallivanting about with you is exhausting."

"I'm not stopping you. But I've got one more errand to run."

Kor heaved a sigh worthy of a banshee.

We took the subway to the Garden City District and walked over to Ruby's tattoo parlor, the red neon sign flashing above the glass doors.

Kor screeched to a halt. "Don't tell me you're decorating your disgusting human flesh with even more tawdry decorations. They really don't make your form any less repugnant, you know. Wasted effort."

I glared down at him. "Gee, thanks for the tip." I flung the doors open with a clang of the Stymphalian feathers overhead.

A few people dotted the space—a salamander waiting on the black leather sofa, a faun and a goat-faced capricorn poring over the tat designs on the walls, Ruby washing up at the sink. She glanced over her shoulder and smiled, her lipstick matching her red eyes. "Hi, Immy. And a friend?"

I cast a glower at Kor, who'd followed me in. "I wouldn't go that far."

Kor sniffed haughtily and floated over to another wall plastered with designs.

Stepping up to the counter, I raised two fingers with a fifty folded between them. "Just dropping by 'cause I've got some of what I owe you."

"Wonderful." Ruby strode over and took the bill from me. "Let me check on your ink while you're here. Come on back."

We slipped through a dark curtain to a private room. I took a seat in the chair and rolled up my sleeve, exposing my wrist.

Ruby wiped it down, then examined it under her light. "Whoa, this is healing up fast. I expected my new formula to help *some*, but this is unbelievable."

I bit my lip. "About that . . . It might not've been your serum stuff. At least not completely."

She met my eyes. "No? Then what?"

"They were called"—I scrunched my eyebrows—"Negalopes? Nergentraps?" I pictured Cucumber waving at them enthusiastically as he explained. "No, wait. *Negentropes.*"

"Interesting. I haven't heard of those, I'll have to do some research. You think you could bring me some?"

"Maybe? Not sure if they're down for going on field trips."

Ruby laughed. "Either way, there's nothing to worry about here. I'd say you only have a few days of healing left, tops. Did it work for what you wanted?"

"Yes and no. But I figured it out." I stood and tugged my sleeve back down. "I'll get you the rest of the cash as soon as I can."

She smiled. "I know you will. Though, if you can get me some of those negentropes, I'll happily waive the rest."

My money-grubbing radar went *ping!* Maybe I could ask Cucumber to round a few up for me. I grinned. "I'll see what I can do."

Ruby walked me back out to the lobby, and we said our goodbyes.

"Come on, Kor, *now* we can go home."

"At last." He swiveled away from the wall, and I gaped.

Instead of his usual flickers, the crimson at his center had formed an intricate design of a dragon skull engulfed in flames.

The flames were even dancing.

He froze as I stared. "Oh—" In a flash, the design vanished, everything back to normal. "You didn't see that, did you?"

"Totally did."

"Erm, I . . . was only exercising my abilities out of *extreme* boredom. Can't afford to get rusty!"

"Yeah, right. You were trying out different badass tattoos, weren't ya."

"Immy, I am more 'badass' than you could possibly conceive, without needing a pathetic crutch like—"

My phone buzzed, and I pulled it out as Kor droned on. A call, not a text, and the caller read *Cynna Baudelaire.*

I picked up. "Hey, Cynna. I got your gift, that was . . ." Ridiculous? Over the top? " . . . generous."

She purred over the phone. "Immy, my lamb, it was the least I could do for a new friend. But I'm calling because I have something you'll adore even more."

My grip on the phone tightened. Please let there not be an express package of a bloody head wending its way to my front door at this very moment.

Not that I was at my front door to sign for any bloody heads, but tripping over one when I got home wouldn't be a picnic, either.

What else would Cynna think I'd adore more than a trillion flannels?

I cleared my throat. "You do?"

She chuckled on the other end of the phone. "Of course, darling.

Courtship hardly ends with one simple gift, and Damarion informed me you needed something very particular."

Hope rose in my chest. "You know someone who can take my Dreyelian device?"

"You didn't doubt it, did you?" A pout colored her tone. "I number a vast host of delightful beings among my acquaintance, poppet. Of *course* I know someone who can handle a problem as trifling as yours. It was just a matter of scrounging up someone altruistic enough to be bothered."

"But you found someone? That's amazing!" Relief flooded me, washing away the anxieties of the last few days.

"Hardly, but I appreciate the flattery, darling. She's a sorceress by the name of Elena Cordova. She won't be able to take possession until Saturday evening, as she's out of the country, but I'll send you her address and the meeting time."

"And she can handle this thing if it goes boom? Or if anyone comes looking for it?"

Cynna tittered. "Immy, Elena wouldn't flinch if she was juggling three of these devices and an archdemon knocked down her door. You're in excellent hands. I'd hardly recommend her to you otherwise."

I closed my eyes on an ecstatic sigh. Even if the bad guys realized they had a dupe, we'd be home free. Though maybe I should take a video of me handing over the artifact and post it everywhere.

Too bad I didn't have the goon gang's phone numbers to send it to.

And now I wouldn't have to worry about this thing going nuclear inside Bracchius either, or even about handling the owner if she ever got back to me. I could point her—or the baddies, if they came calling again—straight at this sorceress, and it would be *her* problem.

Damn, but it'd be nice to have enough power to brush off jerks and bullies like flies.

Would she be willing to give me tips?

Cynna continued. "Now, I do need some more details so she can prepare appropriately. Damarion said it's a caladrian artifact?"

"No, the creepy dude on the phone said 'Calamandrian.' Extra 'man' in the middle."

"How delightfully odd. So no relation to a caladrius."

"Don't think so." I'd be way less worried about this thing if all it contained was a big ol' glob of bodily fluids with healing powers. The birds were pretty chill, overall.

Kor drifted into my field of view, bobbing between me and the door of Ruby's tattoo parlor, sending a clear message. I held up a 'wait one sec' finger as Cynna kept talking.

"And the configuration of the Dreyelian device suggests it contains a nova-class being, yes?"

I licked my lips. "Unfortunately."

"Perfect. Well, I believe that is all she'll need to know. I'll message you the details for the meeting. And since this is hardly a diverting gift, I'll send my next soon to make up for it. Then perhaps we can get together for a little tête-à-tête and have some fun together."

Cynna's idea of fun was probably bathing in the blood of her enemies, but who was I to turn her down when she'd just solved all my problems in one fell swoop?

"Totally. Maybe next week?"

"I look forward to it. Ta, my delicious darling!"

"Bye."

Keep your friends close, keep the people who might just suck the marrow out of your bones even closer?

"Finally." Kor buzzed with irritation. "Really, how long does it take to arrange a drop-off? Let's go."

I followed him to the door. "You heard?"

"Obviously, Immy. I may not have alarming auricular protrusions like you do, flapping in the breeze, but my hearing is excellent. Better than yours, certainly."

"Ears. They're called ears."

"Either way, they're unsightly."

"*You're* unsightly."

"Well, now you're just being rude."

"Turnabout's fair play, jerkwad."

We rode back to our subway stop in silence, Kor inscribing some demonic language on his parchment scroll with a quill made of fire. Well, burning rather than inscribing, I guess.

I gave in as we headed up the stairs to our street. "What are you writing?"

"Notes for Doctor Sondra for our next session. They're about *you*." His quill sizzled through the paper with his vehement jab.

Welp. Was I one of the reasons he was in therapy? Maybe I *should* be nicer to him.

"I, uh . . . sorry."

"Sorry?" He glanced up from his notes.

"Yeah."

"Hmm." He went back to scribbling. "I'll still feel better about it once I've burned you in effigy."

My brows shot up. "Once you've— *What?*"

"Burned you in effigy. Doctor Sondra cuts out a little paper person and colors it like you, and I blast it with hellfire. Sometimes we need a whole paper chain of Immys before I feel demonically serene again."

A car honked—I'd stopped in the middle of the crosswalk. I raised an apologetic hand and jogged to the sidewalk, Kor bobbing beside me.

What kind of therapist *was* this?

At least he wasn't lighting the *real* me on fire.

I chuckled nervously as we reached our yard. "Wow, uh, yup. Super sorry about that. How about we have a movie night soon, or something? We could watch, uh . . ." I scanned my brain for movies a black-blooded demon would like.

Not that they have blood, but you know what I mean.

"Drag Me to Hell?" I finished lamely.

Kor rolled up his scroll and stashed it. "Definitely not."

I nearly toppled as my foot stuck to the walkway leading up to the door. What the—?

Peeling my shoe away from the concrete, I peered down at whatever muck I'd stepped on.

Bright blue, with flimsy threads stretching away from it.

Gum? It didn't look right.

I yanked off my shoe and sniffed the sole.

Laffy Taffy—the last remnants of ChromaSlayer, no doubt.

I felt a little bad that I'd made Bracchius get rid of the giant candy skeleton, but the last thing we and our rental deposit needed was fifty pounds of Laffy Taffy oozing into the carpet.

Brownie cleaning services notwithstanding.

Keys in hand, I paused at the door. Were those *wails* coming from the other side?

"Do you hear that?" I whispered.

"Undoubtedly just Bracchius crying over a lost speck of glitter or some such."

I pressed my ear to the door. If that wasn't despondent warbling, then someone was drowning a seagull on live television.

Fumbling with my keys, I managed to unlock the door, and swung it open.

Bracchius sat on the sofa in the dark, only his despondent *blue* flickers lighting the space around him as he clutched Sparkles with two nubby arms, blubbering.

GOT THE BLUES

"Bracchius! Whoa, my dude, what's wrong?!" I rushed into the apartment, dread weighing in my gut.

Was the artifact inside him hurting him, causing the blue glow? It had been surprisingly placid since Bracchius had subsumed it, especially considering all the flashy ice-and-darkness spurts it'd been giving off before.

Could it be icing him from the inside out?

With a snotworthy snurfle, Bracchius tilted back to look at me, his newly blue flickers flashing into a frenzy. "Immy!! You're alive!" Clinging to Sparkles, he shot up to face level, doing a 360 as if to make sure I was real.

I cocked my head, mouth half-open. "Uh . . . Yeah. You thought I wasn't?"

"Yes! I was sure you were dead or dying or trapped or kidnapped or murdered or chopped up into itty-bitty pieces and fed to the garbage goats!"

I decided against pointing out the overlap between half of those. "But why?"

Bracchius sniffed. "After I made sure Sparkles was okay, I had that spa treatment—which was amazing—and then I came back to check on you. But you weren't at the restaurant, or at home, or anywhere between, and I couldn't find that dastard Fitz either, and I looked *everywhere*. And then I couldn't find Kor *either* either, and if Fitz managed to kill *Kor*, then *you* were *definitely* dead, and . . ." His voice ended on a quaver.

"Whoa, whoa, buddy, c'mere." I scooped Bracchius up and squished him close, plushie unicorn and all. "I'm fine. Kor and I just ran a couple errands after my dinner with Fitz."

A muffled hitch of breath came from within my arms, and he nuzzled closer to my collarbone, his body toasty enough that I'd be overheating before long.

"Good grief." Kor bowled past us on the way to the bathroom and his mirror. "And I thought *I* needed ther— er, *thermal* . . . urgenblurgh." With that incomprehensible garble, he darted out of sight.

I rolled my eyes, then nestled my chin against Bracchius.

"You *do* seem okay," he confirmed, voice muffled as well.

"I promise I am."

He pulled back enough to see my face, his flickers cheered up to magenta. "I was so worried. I even tried tracking your phone, but it didn't work."

"You can—" Nope, really shouldn't be surprised that Bracchius would want to keep tabs on me. I should just be glad he hadn't made me swallow an AirTag. "Never mind."

The rest of his statement percolated, and I frowned. "Wait, it didn't work?" I dug out my phone.

Which was dead as a doornail. Cynna's call must've used up the last of its juice.

I winced. "Forgot to charge it at work, sorry." I dropped it back in my purse. "So you got home just before we did?"

His whole body rocked in a nod.

At least he hadn't had too much time to wallow in despair. I tried to think of something to cheer him up.

Kor going to therapy would do it, but I wasn't comfortable spilling those beans before Kor did . . .

What else?

Oh, duh.

"I've got some good news, by the way." I steered him toward the couch and curled up on a cushion.

"Yeah?"

"Yup. We're getting that gizmo out of you on Saturday." I explained about Cynna's sorceress.

"Oh good. Not that I don't like helping, Immy, but . . ." He squirmed. "It's starting to get a teensy bit uncomfortable."

Panic flirted with my heart rate again, and I sat up straight. "Is it hurting you? Giving off magic? We can find another way to—"

"Nothing like that." He rolled up onto my lap. "It's like . . . well . . . I think humans call it a wedgie."

A startled laugh bubbled out of me, and I slapped a hand over my mouth. "Sorry. I mean, that's a relief. Uncomfortable, obviously, but, y'know, better than it exploding inside you."

"I guess that *would* be worse." He shifted on my legs, canting to one side and jiggling.

I suppressed a smirk. "Trying to fix the wedgie?"

"It's hard to do!"

"Lemme know if you want me to shake you around like a snow globe or something."

"Okie."

My stomach grumbled as Bracchius kept fidgeting.

Seriously? It hadn't been *that* long since dinner, had it? I poked at my stomach disconsolately.

Gurgle.

Whatever. Shaking my head, I set Bracchius aside, planting Sparkles upright beside him, then tore apart the kitchen, looking for a snack that actually sounded tasty.

In the end, I smeared peanut butter across a tortilla and called it good.

A yawn snuck up on me. I *should* go to bed soonish.

Wasn't there something else I had to do first?

I stared blankly at my kitchen counters, then the living room. My work shirt sticking out of my purse sparked a brainwave.

Laundry! I had to switch over my laundry.

Something else tickled at the back of my mind too, and I scanned back through my day. Flannels, laundry, typhon, Ruby, sorceress lady, Cynna . . .

Hmm.

Bracchius held Sparkles aloft, wiggling her like she was galloping along, and it clicked—pegasus riding.

I hung over the back of the couch, swallowing the last of my peanut butter tortilla roll-up. "Hey, you wanna go pegasus riding with Samaire and me on Saturday?"

Fitz was probably still a touchy subject, so I left him off my list.

Bracchius scoffed. "Immy, why in the charred hells would I want to go pegasus riding? You know I can fly, right?" He hummed. "I . . . thought you'd noticed."

I laughed through my nose. "Yeah, I've noticed. Just didn't want to leave you out if you wanted to go."

"Oh, thanks, but no." He bolted to attention, a ripple rolling across his inky surface. "But if you ever go *unicorn* riding, I'm *absolutely* coming along!"

"Deal."

"Shake on it!"

I blinked down at his proffered nub of an arm. "How about a fist bump instead?"

"Okay."

Promissory fist bump out of the way, I headed to the bathroom. About to launch head-first into Kor's mirror, I paused.

What was I doing? He was *in* there. I didn't want him stumbling across me mid laundry load and incinerating every stitch of clothing I owned in petty revenge for my typhon slaying and tower demolishing.

Therapy couldn't have helped him *that* much. It'd only been two days.

Not that I really wanted my laundry sitting there wet overnight, either, collecting whatever hellish mildew hangs out in a demon domain.

Foo.

I bobbed my head, contemplating, still standing on the toilet seat.

Oh, what the hells.

Gripping the ornate frame of Kor's mirror, I took a deep breath and plunged *just* my head in.

TWO-EYED ONE-BRAINED HOPPING DORKY DEMONLING

Oof, but it still smelled awful in here.

"Cucumber?" I whisper-shouted. "Is Kor around?"

As long as he wasn't in the vicinity of the laundromat, I should be fine. I could be in and out in two minutes, tops. Just had to heave my wet laundry into the dryers, start 'em up, and book it.

A slorp-slorp grew louder, until Cucumber hopped into view, a pouf of bubble-bath bubbles adorning his misshapen head and jouncing with every hop. "Lady Immy, please hurry through! It's not safe to remain in the portal for protracted periods! There have been . . . accidents."

Visions of my head popping right off my body made their cheery selves known. "Crud, okay, hold on one sec."

Facing down Kor in his own domain was at *least* a mite better than being decapitated.

Assuming he didn't do any decapitating himself.

Unable to see what my body was doing back in Bathroom Land, I braced myself on the frame of Kor's mirror with both hands, gave an experimental bounce on the toilet seat, and then vaulted through.

What's a little skinned shin and stubbed toe compared to imminent death?

I tumbled onto the laundromat floor and cradled my poor abused leg. Yowza, but you'd think such a disproportionately minuscule part of your body wouldn't be able to dish out this much pain.

Stupid toes.

I sat up, relieved to find I hadn't created Cucumber mashed potatoes with my graceful splat on the linoleum. "Kor's not around?"

Cucumber shook his head. "The Master is rebuilding his Baleful Tower at present. Of course, it will be branded with a new name—what do you think of the Pinnacle of Perfidy? That was my suggestion." He propped his toothpick arms on his . . . well, not really hips proudly.

"It's, um, a definite improvement over the original. Wait, does that mean Kor is building it himself?"

Kor had never seemed like that much of a hands-on go-getter to me.

"Oh, milady, of course not! One of such an elevated status as the Master would not sully his own ha— er, self with such menial concerns! He's simply overseeing the construction."

"So . . . who's building it, then?"

"Who else? My fellow demonlings."

My brain conjured an image of a long chain of teetering demonlings placing bricks one at a time a la the Great Pyramids. After about three seconds, cinder blocks and demonlings were spilling all over the place.

Talk about mental carnage. I shook my head. "How did *you* get out of construction duty?"

"I obscured myself in the suds, my lady."

Sneaky devil. Demonling.

I clambered to my feet, favoring my stubbed toe. My shirt was already clinging to my skin with how sweltering it was in here. "You've clearly got more brains than the rest of them, Cuke."

He blinked up at me. "Milady . . . as far as I'm aware, I only have one brain, like any other demonling. Unless you have information to the contrary?"

I clasped my hands to avoid face-palming. "No, no. I'm sure you're right, Cucumber. My mistake."

"Oh, what a relief. For a moment I wondered if I might have a second head I wasn't aware of." He craned his neck around as if looking for his nonexistent Siamese twin.

Jiggle-jiggle went his bubble-bath hat.

Once positive I wouldn't bust up laughing, I hazarded, "Nope, looks like just the one head."

His sigh whistled on the way out. "Thank you, Lady Immy. I am greatly reassured."

"Glad I could help. All right, I'm just here to switch over my laundry real quick and then get out of your hair, so I'll just be over here." I hooked a thumb toward the washers.

Cucumber peered up at me with his manifestly bald head, and I waited for the inevitable protestation of his hairlessness. Instead, he deflated. "Oh, if you have to leave so soon . . . that's fine."

Uh-oh. Lonely demonling alert.

"Well, I could stay a *little* longer. As long as you don't think Kor will be back right away."

After all, time in the real world wasn't passing while I was in here, so a short chat with the Cukester wouldn't cost me any shut-eye.

My sense of smell, maybe.

Cucumber nodded eagerly. "Master Kor is determined to complete at least the first three stories of the tower before returning to the shadowmurk to convalesce. It will be an arduous task, to be sure."

"Fab." I flipped open the two dryers furthest from Cucumber's still-looming mountain of suds in the corner—and the stench coming off them. At least it'd had some time to disperse.

Slightly.

Both washer cycles were long since done, so I dumped the soggy loads into the dryers and cranked the timers to the max. Low heat, obviously.

Granted, the ambient temperature might take its revenge on my delicates.

When I turned away from the dryers, my favorite demonling stared up at me, hope of some quality conversation shimmering in his gloopy eyes.

And my brain went blank.

What *do* you make small talk about with a demonling? We'd covered Kor, the new tower, Cucumber's braininess . . . And there wasn't much left on the topic of odiferous bubble baths.

I peered around the dark, hot, smelly environs and latched on to the first thing I could think of. "So tell me, Cucumber: why is the entrance to Kor's domain a laundromat, anyway?"

Cucumber leaned in like the gossip granny at Friday-night bingo. "Lady Immy, you must swear on the rotting graves of your most villainous ancestors never to divulge what *I* am about to divulge." He glanced around furtively.

Now *this* could be interesting.

"I solemnly swear on the— what was it?"

"The rotting graves of your most villainous ancestors."

Why he thought *that* would guarantee my silence, I couldn't begin to guess. I didn't even know which of my ancestors might've been villainous.

But what the hey.

I thwapped a hand over my heart and intoned, "I solemnly swear on the rotting graves of my most villainous ancestors not to blab."

Cucumber eyed me solemnly. "And you most especially must not blab to Master Kor, milady."

I slapped my hand over my heart one more time for good measure. "And I even more solemnly swear not to narc on you to Kor."

"Ever."

I suppressed an eye roll. "Ever."

Something started clanking in one of the dryers, but I ignored it. Cucumber's lure was way too tantalizing for distractions.

Cucumber hopped closer and tugged on my sleeve. "Please, Lady Immy, place me beside your ear so I may tell you, and you alone."

I glanced around the patently empty laundromat and back down to him. "Cucumber, we *are* alone."

"Master Kor has spies everywhere," he proudly declared, fists on hips.

"All right, all right." I wrapped a hand around the leathery demonling and plucked him off the floor with a suctiony smack as his slug foot released. I deposited him on my shoulder.

He nestled deeper into my wild curls and gripped my ear with both puny hands.

I did my best not to flinch. What was he gonna do, climb inside and tell his secret to my eardrum?

Thankfully, he didn't go that far.

In a whisper not even a camazotz could hear—at least not without being *this* up close and personal—Cucumber revealed, "Master Kor is not the first of the Dark Ones to rule this domain. Its previous lord had the laundromat constructed for their own devices."

No. Way.

I craned my neck to goggle down at the sucker who just made my day, and failed miserably. "Wait, so this is a *secondhand* demon domain? What did Kor do, buy it at a rummage sale?"

That didn't even address what sort of demonly 'devices' would require a laundromat. I had been puzzling over that one the last couple of days already.

Was it a torture room? Had the former owner needed to wash sinister substances out of absolute mountains of laundry?

Clank, clank went the dryer, but I focused on Cucumber.

"I do not believe it was a rummage sale, milady."

"So . . . what?"

"I believe the master won it at auction, and for quite a hefty sum at that. It *is* a redoubtable domain."

I smacked my lips. "Unredoubtably."

Despite my tease, my mind reeled. Were demon domains a whole area of commerce for the Dark Ones? Who made them? Was there a black market? Were they status symbols you upgraded, like buying the latest Mercedes?

Had Kor not been able to afford better than secondhand? Had he *imported* his lowly subjects?

Master of all he surveys, my foot.

But the real question was . . .

"Why didn't Kor get rid of the laundromat after he bought it?"

Cucumber tightened his grip on my ear and squeaked, "Master Kor has been frustrated to no end trying to rid himself of it, milady. But it was imbued with the mightiest of archdemon magic, beyond his reckoning, and seemingly impervious even to the most fearsome destruction."

I smirked. "So he's stuck with it, eh?"

"I believe he has resigned himself to it at long last." Cucumber squirmed on my shoulder and lowered his voice further. "To *my* great pleasure!"

The little demonling sure did love his wailing whirlpool extravaganzas.

So Kor's vaunted domain was the next best thing to a hand-me-down. Glee bubbled inside me. I may not be able to lord this over Kor verbally, per my solemn oath to the Cuke, but that didn't mean I couldn't chortle deep in my soul every time Kor bragged about the prestige of ruling over his own domain.

If you buy a kingdom, are you *really* a king?

Ugh, I really wished I hadn't promised Cucumber my silence. Now I couldn't even make snide comments.

The clanking in the dryer became too much for me to stand without losing my mind. "One sec."

Cucumber held on for dear life as I flounced over to the dryer. I yanked open the door and fished around in the hot, damp laundry for the culprit. Too noisy for sweatshirt aglets, too quiet for spare change.

Got it—a pen.

I slammed the door and started the load up again. "Sorry. Any more secrets?"

My hair twisted with his headshake.

I really wanted to see the little bugger. "Here." I detached him from my ear, curls, and shoulder and plopped him atop the dryer.

He pulled a stray hair—mine—out of his mouth and let it flutter to the floor. "Did the information please you, milady?" He clasped his hands earnestly. "You'll keep it secret?"

"I swore, didn't I?" I grinned. "And yes, your info *totally* pleased me, Cuke. In fact . . . I think I'll have to knight you for this."

"Knight me?" Cucumber's eyes welled over. "Oh, Lady Immy, that would be an honor to surpass all honors!" Trembling, he flopped face-first onto the washer, arms raised.

Was the whole prostration thing gratitude? Or did he expect me to knight him post-haste?

Better play it safe.

Dredging up my hazy memories of *A Knight in Camelot* and *The Court Jester*, I went all in.

"For valorous deeds far beyond the bounds of your duty, I, Lady Immy, do solemnly declare thee, Cucumber the demonling, a knight of my court, with all the honors and privileges that title entails."

'Solemnly' was my word of the day, clearly.

I lowered my freshly scavenged pen to each of his dinky shoulders. "Rise, Sir Cucumber."

Now I really *would* have to get him a plastic cocktail sword.

Cucumber sproinged back up jack-in-the-box style. His voice wavered. "Th-Thank you, milady. It is the earnest truth when I say I never in my dread existence anticipated receiving such distinction from anyone, never mind from one such as yourself. I will serve you however I can, and—"

His next words were lost as he dissolved into tearful burbles.

I smiled down at him, but the warm glow faded as another thought surfaced.

He was vowing to serve me, Lady Immy. I had knighted him as a knight of my—totally real—court.

Mine.

Had I just usurped him from Kor? Was he *my* demonling now?

Was he going to want to live in my apartment?

Uh-oh.

KISS THE CUKE

"There, there, Cucumber." I tucked the pen behind my ear, then patted him with a sweaty hand as he recovered from the great honor of being fake-knighted. "I'd, uh, like you to keep serving me here in Kor's domain, if that's okay?"

My apartment was small enough already with me, Bracchius, and Kor. I didn't really want to add a fourth occupant to the one-bedroom.

Not that Cucumber exactly took up much space—physically, anyway.

He had quite the *auditory* presence when he wanted to, though.

I winced. My ears were still recovering from all the panicked wailing he'd subjected them to on our recent adventure to retrieve Sparkles.

Cucumber wiped his streaming eyes. "But of course, Lady Immy. This is my home, though I'm ready to abandon it in your service should you require."

"Great, but totally not necessary. And I don't have any specific, y'know, quests or anything for you to complete just now." I gave him a stern look. "But I expect you to be knightly in the meantime."

How he'd interpret that, I had no idea. It gave me an out, though, so he wouldn't be waiting with bated breath for orders I might not ever bother coming up with.

Cucumber flopped around in a half salute, half bow, nearly taking out an eye. "My conduct will be knightly in the extreme, milady!"

I smiled down at him, about to make my excuses and leave this stenchdom before I dissolved into a puddle of sweat, when a potential quest occurred to me.

"Oh, actually, Cuke . . ."

He perked up. "Yes, Lady Immy?"

"Those negen . . . thwaps? traps?" I scrunched my face, trying to remember.

"Negentropes!"

"Yeah, those. Do you think I could take a couple with me? Doesn't have to be today," I rushed to add, "but at some point?"

"You wish to remove them from Kor's domain?"

"Just a couple."

Cucumber glanced up at me nervously. "I do not wish to deny you such a simple request, milady, but I must consult the negentropes first.

Please, I mean no offense." He shook in his not-shoes.

Sheesh, what did Kor do to these poor demonlings when they disappointed him?

I held up both hands, palms out, and soothed, "No offense taken. If you have the chance to talk to them soon, maybe lemme know what they think when I come back for my laundry?" I tilted my head toward the rumbling dryers.

"Yes, milady, that will—"

A blaring foghorn rattled the building, drowning Cucumber out and nearly toppling him from the dryer.

"What in the three hells was *that*?"

Cucumber waved frantically. "Lady Immy, you must return to your own domain! The Horn of Heinousness signals a halt in work on the tower. Master Kor might arrive at any moment!"

Not like I'd been planning to stick around and watch my laundry dry anyway. "Thanks, Sir Cuke. See ya soon!"

I planted a chaste kiss on his tiny greyish scalp, then booked it for the portal.

It was much more intimidating on this side, the swirling vortex like the inky maw of a black hole. At least the chill coming off it was a relief in this sweltering heat.

Considering the drop from the mirror in my bathroom, feet-first was definitely the way to go. I took it more cautiously than last time—left foot in, and shake it all about . . . until I found what had to be the toilet tank.

Then I eased the rest of me through.

Much good it did me. I stumbled off the toilet, taking the paper-roll stand and plunger with me, and coming *this* close to braining myself on the baseboard heater.

Lying dazedly on the linoleum, I glared up at the stupid mirror. Why had I hung it there anyway? Talk about a genius decision.

It *had* done a good job hiding the ugly patch of warped paint behind it . . .

When Kor moved in, he hadn't been picky about his mirror placement; he'd just wanted somewhere safe to keep it, off the street and away from vandals—me excluded. *I'd* been the one to decide on the bathroom, and its current ill-thought home above the toilet.

What? It looked decorative. I never really anticipated wanting to lark through it on a regular basis.

But now that I'd be sneaking my laundry in and out, it was a tad inconvenient.

Should I move it? Not breaking my neck *would* be ideal.

Granted, the thing weighed like a hundred pounds, but I didn't have to hang it somewhere else. I could just lean it against the wall like some avant-garde dude too lazy to buy nails.

As long as I could get it off the wall without crushing myself beneath it, that is.

The other consideration was Kor. The mirror was his, and he'd gotten used to it hanging here. But would he really care?

As long as I didn't hide it in a closet or shut it inside the oven, probably not.

I could tell him I was feng-shuiing the place.

I clambered to my feet and frowned at the mirror. Come to think of it . . . "How is it you *haven't* fallen yet?" I'd done the whole 'find a stud' thing, and used fancy-schmancy picture frame wire, but still. This apartment's walls weren't that sturdy.

Believe me, I know. Between the cerberats gnawing their way through, and the oopsie dent in the wall by my bed, I've had plenty of proof.

The longer I stared at the mirror, the more determined I became. Why not? This *was* my place; I could damn well move anything inside.

Kor would just have to lump it if he didn't like it.

I glanced down at my feet. Shoes on or off? Off gave me a better toe-grip on the toilet, but a higher likelihood of bones crushed to dust if I dropped the mirror.

On. Definitely on.

Hip braced against the wall, one leg up on the tank to take the initial load, I wove my fingers through the gold curlicues for a—fingers crossed—firm grip on the frame.

"Please don't kill me," I whispered to the mirror, and heaved.

Hernia, here I come.

Kor's mirror lifted away from the wall like a styrofoam prop, and I nearly toppled backwards at the startling weightlessness.

What the—?

I stepped off the toilet and examined the mirror from both sides. It looked the same as always, but I could swing it around like a Frisbee.

"Seriously, you couldn't have lightened up when I was dragging your hundred-pound ass across the apartment when Kor moved in?"

Woulda saved me a week of sore muscles, plus three stubbed toes.

Shockingly, the mirror didn't respond.

"I'm keeping my eye on you, buster." It *was* a magical dimension-porting mirror. Guess I shouldn't be too surprised.

I tucked the mirror under my arm. Now, where to put it instead? In here was a no-go; my bathroom was cramped enough without me having to worry about stomping on the mirror as I got in and out of the shower.

Kitchen, no . . .

My bedroom, hells no. Like I wanted Kor interrupting my fugly sleep any more than he already did.

That left the living room and the hall. I tested out a few places: propped up against the back of the sofa, on the floor beside my shabby-not-chic credenza, at the corner into the hall like a low-hanging safety mirror.

Eh.

This puppy needed room to grow, and for me to maneuver my hamper up to it. Plus, I didn't want to tumble out and smack schnoz-first into a wall.

Hmm . . . It'd be harder for Kor to spy on Bracchius and me from the hall. *And* I'd be less likely to knock the mirror over, or spill food on it or something, riling up Kor.

I leaned it against the wall between my bedroom door and the hall closet. Whaddya know, it actually made the hall look bigger.

I dusted my hands of it, got ready for bed, and flopped face-first into my pillow.

Didn't even have to count golden sheep.

I slapped my alarm into submission and groaned. Why didn't I ever give myself a break and go to bed on time?

Unplugging my phone, I sat up. At least it was Friday. If I got through today, I had two blissful days to sleep in before getting back to the grind.

The bare patch of wall above the toilet threw me for a sec. Right, I carted the mirror off last night. I peeked back into the hall to make sure it hadn't vanished.

Nope, exactly where I left it.

Mouth full of toothpaste, I was scrubbing the morning breath from my tongue when Kor barged into the bathroom.

"As if it isn't bad enough that you murdered my typhon, absconded with my prisoners, and *burned* down my tower, but—"

"Mmphle." I flapped a hand at him and spat in the sink.

"Eurggh." Kor disappeared back out the door.

I rinsed, spat again, and started the process of taming my hair.

Kor edged around the doorframe. He must've decided hair-wrangling was less offensive than toothpaste spit, because he resumed his tirade like he'd never left off.

"Immy, how *dare* you wrest my mirror from its rightful location and—"

I fibbed at lightning speed. "We had an earthquake. Didn't want it to fall." I headed into the kitchen to rummage up lunch for work.

Kor's red flickers churned as he followed me. "An earthquake?"

"Yup. While you were in your mirror."

Bracchius rolled out from under the sofa. "I missed the earthquake?! Aw, murk! They're so fun to bounce along to . . ."

I blinked down at him. "Aw, *murk*?"

He gathered up Sparkles. "It's not like I wanna say 'Aw, *man*,' Immy. I'm a demon! You . . . don't like it?"

"You can do better, bud."

Kor sizzled up at me. "We were *talking* about my *mirror*. If this earthquake has passed, then why haven't you replaced my mirror?"

"Aftershocks. Could go on for *days*." I tried my luck a little further. "Y'know, we might want to leave your mirror down permanently. Never know when an earthquake will hit, and it'd only take a small one to shatter that thing to smithereens. What if I'm at work? I wouldn't be able to rescue your mirror then."

"Hmph." Kor buzzed around the mirror's new home down the hall. "It does bring a certain . . . darksome ambiance to this space. And I imagine there's less chance I'll witness your ghastly form unclad . . ."

I nodded enthusiastically. "Yup, *way* less chance."

"Very well. I deem it a sufficient location, as long as you do not see fit to decorate my mirror with your offcast garments, as you seem wont to do with everything else in this abode."

I rolled my eyes at his increasingly pompous tone. "I won't turn it into a pile of clothes, don't worry."

"If so much as a foot garment desecrates my mirror, Immy, I will bathe it in unholy flame until it departs this plane of existence."

"Sock, Kor. They're called socks."

"Whatever." He dove back into the mirror with an inky ripple across its surface.

I was just slapping together a sandwich for lunch when the doorbell rang. I paused, totally nutritious plasticky cheese slice in hand, and glanced between the dark window and the oven clock: 4:13 a.m.

What kind of lunatic would ring my doorbell at four in the morning? I grabbed my sword and wrenched open the door.

Damarion. The 'never sleeps' kind of lunatic.

Of course, he looked his usual perfect self—three-piece suit, suave salt-and-pepper hair—while I looked like I'd been mauled by a dustdevil in my sleep.

"Good morning, my dear Immy." He bustled inside, handing me a paper sack and steaming to-go cup.

I sniffed the cup suspiciously. "Hot cocoa?"

"Of course, and with hazelnut whipped cream, just the way you like it."

"Don't tell me this is from Cynna." I sipped it hesitantly, not wanting to turn my tongue into burnt leather.

Perfect temperature, and delicious. I slugged down a bigger gulp.

"From Cynna? Why— Oh, her absurd *courtship*, that's right." He held a hand to his no-longer-beating heart. "No, this is my gift to you, Immy, to brighten a dreary morning."

I eyed him over the cup. "And?"

"And what?"

I shook the paper sack, which was heavy enough to have at least two tasty somethings inside. "And what are you bribing me for?"

"Bribery? Me? Your most winsome friend?"

"Yup, you."

He grinned. "You know me too well."

"Gee whiz." I opened the sack to find three fresh-baked pastries, the homey scent of flaky, buttery goodness drifting out. I crammed the end of one in my mouth. Tangy cheese and pesto burst through the warm pastry. "So spiwu."

Damarion's eyebrows rose. "Spiwu?"

I tucked the big bite of pastry in my cheek—it was too good to swallow in a hurry. "Spill."

"Ah. Well, I was hoping to . . . how do you say it . . . Vent." He nodded firmly. "I would like to vent."

PERISH THE THOUGHT

I reluctantly swallowed my bite of pastry. "You want to vent?"

Damarion cocked his head. "That is what I said, yes. Are you amenable?"

"I mean, yeah, but I've gotta keep getting ready for work. You mind if I listen on the move?"

"Not at all. Please, don't let me interrupt your preparations. And I have Paolo waiting, if I can drop you at work as well."

Me not having to take the smelly subway to work for once—*and* not risk missing the train?

"Count me in. Vent away."

"Much obliged. So, Immy, do you remember Ambrose, the vampire we happened upon at Vein & Vice earlier this week?"

"Your archnemesis? The wrinkly old dude? Yeah . . ." I finished assembling my sad lunch sandwich. Maybe I should save one of Damarion's pastries for lunch instead?

Nah, they'd never survive that long. These suckers were delish.

Damarion dubiously contemplated my sofa. He flipped over one couch cushion and found the curry stain on the backside. He righted it and unfurled a handkerchief across the cushion instead before collapsing onto the sofa with a sigh. "I haven't been able to stop thinking about him."

My latest bite of pastry almost tumbled out of my mouth. "Like . . . romantically?" I wrinkled my nose.

Damarion bolted upright. "Immy, *no*! Ambrose?! Perish the thought."

Oh good. If *that* had been Damarion's taste in dates, I'da seriously worried about his sanity.

"Then why can't you stop thinking about him?" I stared longingly at Kor's mirror in the hall. All my clean clothes were in there, but somehow I didn't think I could convince Damarion to hop through the mirror with me to continue his venting.

Yesterday's work shirt would just have to do. It was Friday, nobody would care.

"I— He—" Damarion raked a hand through his already tousled hair.

"He infuriates me. He does his utmost to give my kind a bad name, what with all his scheming and illicit activities."

I popped my head up from my search for my work shirt. "Say what?"

"His scheming and—"

"No, I meant what's he up to? Is he trying to give vamps a bum rap on purpose?"

"I can't imagine, no. It's just an unfortunate consequence of his disgraceful behavior."

Getting Damarion to give me the deets was like wrestling a pretzel from a pigeon. I marched in front of the sofa and leaned down nose to nose with him. "Get to the juicy stuff already."

Damarion quirked a smile. "If you insist. Ambrose has . . . Well, I told you he wasn't content with a mortal life after seeing my transformation, and he wouldn't leave well enough alone despite my warnings."

I nodded, grabbing yesterday's jeans and one of Cynna's flannels.

"Obviously he found another vampire to grant him immortality long after we parted ways."

"*Really* long." The dude could beat out a naked mole rat in the wrinkles department.

He inclined his head. "And that, of course, is part and parcel of the problem. Ever since he turned, he's been obsessed with finding a way to revitalize himself, to add youth to his immortality."

"Gee, he's not happy to be a shar-pei for all of time?"

Damarion stifled a laugh. "I suppose I would not be either."

"And Botox isn't doing it for him, I'm guessing."

"It seems not."

I frowned. "But how does this make vamps look bad? All us wimpy mortals already know a healthy dose of vanity gets injected along with that immortality stuff."

"Piffle."

I ducked into the hall and changed out of my PJs in ten seconds flat. "Pretty sure it's a side effect of the venom, actually," I called.

Damarion was mock glaring at me when I rounded the corner, dressed for the day.

"But seriously, what gives? What's Ambrose doing that's so bad?"

Damarion fiddled with his tie. "Let us say Fountains of Youth are hard to come by."

"Meaning?" I widened my eyes in exasperation.

"Meaning Ambrose continues to resort to less-than-savory methods to acquire these promised Fountains. Last year, he even went so far as to hire a thief to purloin a potion of soulsprite essence from the private collection of Makemo Firemaw. Believe you me, Makemo was *not* best pleased. I'm surprised Ambrose even survived that particular peccadillo."

I raised an eyebrow at *that* tongue twister. "So he's loaded and hires criminals to get him what he wants. Sounds pretty typical for the rich and famous to me."

"He's hardly famous."

"Then you shouldn't have to worry about his *peccadilloes*, right?"

Damarion pursed his lips. "I might not, if he weren't in town. Last I heard, he was living in Massachusetts. He's undoubtedly up to something."

"Didn't they just open that new caladrius wellness spa downtown? Maybe he's booked in for some treatments."

"If a caladrius could ameliorate his puckered visage, he'd've stopped looking for a solution long since."

I smirked. I wasn't exactly skint in the vocab department, but Damarion had me beat by a mile.

Well, by a few hundred years, I guess.

The sofa skirt lifted, and Bracchius emerged from beneath the sofa. "What about reaper blood, has he tried that?"

Damarion peered down at the pudgy demon. "Oh, hello, Bracchius. Have you been listening this whole time?"

"Duh. You were sitting on top of me. It's not like I could ignore you."

"Apologies. I had no intention of disturbing you. To answer your question, I haven't the faintest. It's not as though I'm managing Ambrose's sordid thievery and experiments for him. I just know his presence in our fair city is no favorable omen."

"Ohh, he's a bad guy, huh?" Bracchius whirled toward me. "Do you think he's one of *our* bad guys?"

I shook my head. "He's like a hundred and two, twice my height, and a vamp. Definitely not one of our thugs."

"Maybe they're just hired guns!"

Damarion glanced between us. "You mean the incompetent hoodlums who have been harassing you the past few days?"

Bracchius bobbed. "Yes, exactly! The *hoodlums*!" He caressed the word like it was his new favorite.

Guess I know what I'll be hearing for the next two weeks.

Damarion shook his head contemplatively. "Ambrose is not above hiring out his dirty work, obviously. But he at least has the cunning to hire competent talent. If he were behind this, you'd be facing off against a master thief, or an elite team of former soldiers, mercenaries. Not . . ." He waved his hand. ". . . flounderers."

I huffed a laugh.

"Maybe it's that Cynna person!"

Man, Bracchius really was nursing a grudge for her. Maybe I'd better keep any future gifts from her on the down-low.

Damarion chuckled. "Hardly. If Cynna were the culprit, you would have never even seen her—or her operatives—coming. Your troublesome gadget would have simply disappeared in the night."

"Whoa." Bracchius rocked back.

I smiled. "Sounds like we'll have to keep looking, Bracchius."

"Not after Saturday!"

"True." I downed the last drops of my hot cocoa and grabbed my purse. "You still up for driving me to work?"

Damarion stood. "Of course, Immy. It's that time?"

"Yup." I waggled my fingers at Bracchius. "See ya later. Have fun without me!"

Bracchius swiveled deeper into the long-since-flattened carpet. "It's never as fun without you."

"Aw, same. But I'm sure you and Sparkles will manage. Have a tea party or something."

Bracchius's flickers bloomed brighter. "Ooh, a tea party! Did you hear that, Sparkles?"

He zipped back under the couch.

Damarion and I stepped outside, and I locked the door behind us. Sure enough, Damarion's car was parked at the curb, Paolo a silhouette in the driver's seat.

I almost tripped over a couple goodies the crows had left me. "Oh, the crows! Sorry, I've gotta feed them. One sec."

Good thing Damarion was driving me—I could spare the extra time and still not be late to work.

I scooped up some kibble and scattered it across the walk, not bothering to shake the container like usual. The crows would figure out the food was here eventually, and I really didn't want them tugging at Damarion's hair or shoelaces.

"Okay, we're good to go."

"Quite." Damarion skirted some kibble bits and took my arm as we strolled toward his car. A shadow shifted in the backseat.

I nudged him. "Brought a friend?"

He frowned. "What? No, I came alone aside from Pao—"

The back door swung open, and someone barreled out.

MAIL TIME

A blonde streak rammed into me at waist height in a miniature linebacker tackle. "Immy!"

I pulled back to contemplate my pint-size hug-attacker. "Aster?"

"Aster?" Damarion said sharply. "How is it you're here? I left you at home."

She let go and beamed up at me, diminutive fangs glinting. "I called Paolo to pick me up, but he wouldn't leave you, so I walked over. It's only a few blocks."

"And *why* are you here?"

Her smile fell. "Cynna was being mean. I—"

I wrapped an arm around each of them and steered them toward the car. "I'm gonna be late for work if we stand around any longer. Let's finish this chat inside, yeah?"

"Oh, sorry, Immy!" Aster hopped into the car and crawled across the leather bench seat.

I slid in beside her and closed the door. Damarion took the front passenger seat, and Paolo slipped the car away from the curb with a purr of its overpriced engine.

Aster scooted close as I buckled in. "Damarion, can we go to the mall after we drop off Immy?"

"Of course."

"Yay, thanks!" She tugged my arm. "You work at the airport, yeah? One of the rental car places?"

"Yup. Here, why don't you put on your seat belt."

I reached for the strap, but she rolled her eyes. "Like a car accident would kill me."

"Still might not be fun to fly through the windshield at fifty miles an hour."

"Fiiine." She strapped in, then drummed her short legs against the seat. "Are you totally excited for Saturday? It's going to be *so* awesome! As long as Cynna's not coming. She's not, right?" Aster peered up at me with beseeching eyes, her silvery freckles stark against her rosy cheeks.

Was the kid gonna change topics every ten seconds? "Well, *I* didn't invite her. Did you?"

"Nope! And I'm not gonna."

I poked her snub nose. "Then it's just you, me, Samaire, and her friend. Don't forget your ID."

Vampire or no, the bouncers would have enough qualms letting in someone who looked like Aster even *with* proof of her age.

Kindergarteners aren't exactly your usual scene at nightclubs.

"I won't. And *no* inviting Cynna." Aster crossed her arms in a huff.

Sheesh, musta been some fight. "Pixie promise."

"What about your roommates? Damarion says you live with *demons*?" Her eyes widened dramatically.

I smirked. "I don't think they'd wanna come. Besides, you wanted a girls' night, right? They're both dudes."

Not that Bracchius wouldn't fit in just fine, but a demon trying to smuggle a plushie unicorn into a nightclub might look a bit sus.

Last thing we needed was security ripping Sparkles apart into tufts of stuffing, thinking she was an inanimate drug mule.

Drug unicorn?

Aster bobbed her head. "True. But I totally wanna meet them sometime! Living with demons sounds fun."

"You and Bracchius would probably get along." Kor, I suspected, was more Cynna's speed—though *way* less classy.

Damarion turned in his seat. "So, Immy, what's this you said earlier, about having no worries after Saturday? Something about this outing?"

"No . . . Didn't, um . . . Cynna tell you?" I winced, hesitant to bring up the *C* word again with Aster right here.

"I don't believe so." He blinked. "Oh, does this have to do with your troublesome trinket?"

"That, yeah. There's apparently a sorceress who'll take it off my hands."

I filled him in on the details as we drove. Aster wanted to coordinate outfits for Comet on Saturday, and promised to send pics.

We pulled around to the rental car lots at the airport, and I got out. "Thanks for the ride!" I waved from the curb as Paolo pulled away.

Aster's tiny hand smeared against the dark window in a wave, and I chuckled.

I headed into work, changed, and got settled at my booth before clearing the line of cars that'd piled up overnight. Ready for the weekend—and giddy at the prospect of finally ditching the dumb artifact—I was in a pretty good mood.

My work day was shockingly uneventful, and flew by at top speed. I finished *Hellbound Guilds & Other Misdirections* and even got halfway through the sequel.

A fan-freaking-tastic Friday, in my book.

With a few more of Cynna's flannels tied around my waist, I took the subway home, ready to kick back and relax. Tomorrow would be a bit crazy, what with pegasus riding, clubbing, and meeting up with that sorceress, but tonight and Sunday I could be a total lazy potato.

Digging out my keys, I scooped up the couple crow goodies I'd ignored this morning—a lone stud earring and a shiny penny—and shoved them into my front pants pocket.

My fingers tangled in something stringy, and I grimaced. "What the—?"

I pulled out a ropey clump of hair.

Not mine.

"Eww!" I flapped my hand, flinging off the random-person hair bits. They slowly drifted to the concrete.

Wait . . .

I unearthed an old gum wrapper from the bottom of my purse, and used it to pinch the hairs off the walkway. These were from one of the jerks who'd been stalking me, the hairs I'd saved in case I ever wanted to track *them* down in return.

I was lucky they hadn't ended up in the wash with the rest of my clothes.

Better find a safer place for these.

The foil gum wrapper folded nicely around the greasy hairs—ick— and I palmed it until I could find a suitable hidey-hole. I unlocked the door and stepped inside.

"Immy!" Bracchius swooped out from under the couch and hovered over a single envelope on the coffee table. "You actually got a piece of mail that isn't junk!"

I dumped my purse. "Whoa, really?"

Bracchius usually checked our mail. As he explained anytime I said something about the lack of mail, his reasons were threefold:

One, if he left it for me to grab, the crows would crap on it, or just steal it outright, while I was at work.

Two, he didn't want me to waste any of my limited mortality skimming through pegasus religious mailers and political postcards from the People's Prosperity, Neo Alliance, and Equus Elevatur Parties. He'd sort through it for me, and incinerate the junk mail—which was all of it, most days.

Kor, of course, emerged to participate in the carnage every now and then.

Unsurprisingly, he found it highly cathartic.

And three, to keep me from scalding my skin off. The first time a piece of demon mail arrived, I blithely picked it up—and instantly regretted it.

I'm *still* missing the fingerprint on my right thumb.

Turns out, demons magic their snail mail so any interlopers suffer dire consequences for daring to touch their precious envelopes. Postal workers have to wear a special charm to keep the demon mail dormant until delivery.

Bracchius inspected the simple envelope from multiple angles. "Yup! So weird. Who would want to send *you* a letter?"

"Gee, thanks, buddy."

His crimson flickers went into a panicked flurry. "I mean . . . Everyone who loves you lives really close, right? So we don't *need* to send letters. We all just talk to you."

"Nice save."

"I try."

He did have a point, though. Nobody really ever sent *me* mail. It all came to 'Resident' or 'Respected Voter' or 'Valued Customer.' Even if it said 'Imogen Cordell' on the front, it wasn't exactly personal.

This envelope was hand-addressed—not even that fake printed handwriting—and had no return address. My address, a stamp, and that was it.

Intriguing.

Bracchius bounced beside it on the coffee table. "Can I open it? Whaddya think it is?"

"No idea. But yeah, go ahead."

A tight laser line of fire sizzled along the envelope's top, then Bracchius tugged out the contents. "Here you go!"

I took the letter and unfolded it.

The letter was handwritten too, in a spidery script.

> To Immy Cordell, fortuitous and gracious deliverer of these humble beings,
>
> This missive is to inform you of Sharn and Arghbargle's new living situation, so you are able to collect on their debt if and when needed.

I faltered after the first line—had this letter been drafted by a lawyer? *Was* the necrowraith or the chupacabra a lawyer?

It wasn't like I'd ever quizzed my monster posse about their day jobs from before Kor had kidnapped them.

Or was Sharn—presumably the writer out of the two of them, since I didn't see a chupacabra being able to handle a pen, never mind write legibly—talking about themself in the third person?

I kept reading.

> Sharn and Arghbargle now reside at Morning Glory Hospice Center. (Do not fear, they are not patients of the facility. They are, in fact, flourishing.) You can find them in the staff apartment known as Rose Resplendence.
>
> Sharn and Arghbargle honor their debts, and are very grateful for your timely rescue. Particularly Arghbargle (he

instructed Sharn to write this). He could have escaped the demon's tower at any time, but did not wish to leave his friend Sharn behind.

(Sharn is also very grateful. The typhon did not make for an enjoyable companion, and consuming only the soul energy of the few shadow vermin who ventured close was not satisfying in the least.)

It is difficult to discern proper recompense for a deed such as yours, but Sharn and Arghbargle are at your service. Do not hesitate to call upon them if you require assistance with anything they might be useful with—including hauntings, vengeance, and goat infestations.

Be well in life and death, 
Sharn & Arghbargle

A smudgy pawprint accompanied the signature. I grinned. I had my doubts about Arghbargle's claims of being able to escape, but still.

"Who's it from, who's it from?" Bracchius hovered at my elbow.

"The necrowraith and chupacabra I rescued from Kor." I folded the letter and pinned it to the crumbling corkboard above the credenza.

Doubtful I'd ever get myself into the kind of trouble *those* two could get me out of—goat infestations, really? That just seemed like wishful thinking on Arghbargle's part. But hey, it might be fun to visit sometime.

I could bring ChupaChews.

"They know our address?" Bracchius sounded a tad concerned.

"Guess they paid attention on the way out." I patted his dark orb form. "Don't worry, they seem nice. Plus they owe me big-time."

Although . . .

"Maybe keep Sparkles out of sight of the chupacabra if they ever stop by, just in case."

Bracchius gasped in horror and dove under the couch. "That chupacabra is never coming back here, oh no it isn't. Never fear, Sparkles, you're safe with me!"

The mumbly sounds of a cuddle session ensued.

A whiff of sweat drifted up from my purse, and I tugged out my now rank work shirt. Next up, laundry retrieval. Or rescue, maybe. Hopefully stewing in Kor's domain for an extra twelve hours hadn't permanently imbued my clothes with The Stench.

I cringed. My poor clothes deserved better than that horrible of a fate.

Something skittered across the floor as I stood from the couch, and I looked down. Right, the gum wrapper with the gross hairs. Must've let go of it during the whole letter-reading thing.

I should put it in a safe place—though not the kind of place *so* safe that I'd never remember or find it ever again.

Been there, done that. Only like a million times.

The battered, leaning credenza beside the door was kinda my command center for the apartment; I'd think to look there first even if I couldn't remember where I'd stashed the hairs.

But if I put them in one of the drawers, they'd probably disappear pronto—squirreled away by the inklings I was pretty sure were still haunting this place.

Bracchius assures me they've been successfully banished, but I seriously doubt he or Kor are the ones stealing my bobby pins.

Chip-bag clips, totally, especially with Kor's hankering for Cheetos.

Bobby pins, not so much.

I rummaged through the credenza drawers until I found an empty old sunglasses case with a predilection for snapping onto fingers alligator-style. In went the gum wrapper, and I gingerly tapped the lid, ready to jump out of harm's way.

The case snapped shut so violently it flipped itself over and nearly toppled off the crooked credenza.

Brutal little bugger.

I settled it more securely amongst the other paraphernalia cluttering the credenza, then headed toward the bathroom to grab my hopefully-not-stinkified laundry. The marred patch of bathroom wall stared back at me from ten feet away, and I slowed in momentary confusion.

Right, Kor's mirror lived in the hall now. Good for my knees, elbows, and future bruise-free state, bad for the aesthetic appeal of my bathroom. Not that it was exactly show-home worthy.

I *really* needed to find something else to disguise that ugly spot. That was a problem for later, though.

I course-corrected toward the hall and sighed in annoyance.

The bulb halfway down the hall—the only one up there—was burned out. And I'd used my last spare bulb when Bracchius's literal sprinkle explosion had shattered the one in the kitchen last month.

I was picking rainbow sprinkles out of the living room carpet for *weeks*. Don't ask.

"Bracchius? Can you remind me to buy lightbulbs?"

"Sure!" He was still under the sofa, but sounded chipper enough not to be stressing about potential chupacabra attacks.

If Sparkles were a plushie *goat*, I'd be more worried.

"Thanks!"

Granted, with Bracchius's non-sense of time, he might remind me about the lightbulbs in three years or three minutes, but he still had a better chance of remembering than I did.

Yup, even with the active reminder of the dead bulb above my head—knowing my brain, I'd become completely oblivious to it in about seven minutes.

I stepped toward Kor's mirror, glanced down . . .

And my heart nearly jumped out of my chest.

COCKTAIL SWORD

Glowing red eyes gleamed from the mirror's surface, eerier than usual thanks to the darkened hall.

I took a second to let my pounding heart come back down from the stratosphere. "Hi, Kor."

"Hello, Immy. You don't have designs upon my mirror, do you?"

"Nope. Just heading to the hall closet."

The mirror rippled, and Kor emerged, sans sinister eyes. One of these days I'd figure out how he did that; maybe he just assumed a more humanoid form to peer through the mirror?

Cucumber might know.

"Good. Did I hear something about mail? I could really use a nice conflagration to soothe my soul before my appointment with my ther—" He cut off with a strangled growl.

"You're *really* not good at keeping your own secrets, are you?" I jabbed a thumb over my shoulder at the sofa. "Take it up with Bracchius. If you're lucky, there might be some junk mail left. Better hurry."

Kor zipped into the living room. If he was heading off to therapy soon, I wouldn't have to worry about dodging him to get my laundry. I peeked around the corner to watch.

Bracchius was back out from under the sofa, bobbing beside Kor—who'd settled atop the illustrious pillar-candle plinth.

"I saved one for you . . ." Bracchius held out an oversized postcard, cringing like he thought Kor might incinerate him along with it.

But Kor took the card. "My favorite kind." He sounded surprised. "These cherubim charity drives are pernicious, and I revel in the destruction of their propaganda. Die, foul drivel!"

The mailer glowed at one corner, a line of ember-light eating across the surface, leaving filmy, charred wisps in its wake. A thin trail of smoke curled toward the ceiling—and the smoke detector.

Don't worry, I took the batteries out *years* ago.

C'mon, if two demons can't handle a simple house fire, they'd shrivel in embarrassment and cloister themselves in the nearest numenery.

Not like Kor wants his mirror melting into slag any more than I want to find a new apartment.

Junk mail handily dispatched, Kor spiraled up off his pedestal. "I, uh, thank you, Bracchius." With that, he vanished with a 'pop' and a swirl of flames, teleporting off to therapy, presumably.

Laundromat, here I come.

One foot into the mirror, I about-faced, thinking of the recently knighted Cucumber. I could swear I had one of those kitschy plastic cocktail swords kicking around somewhere, and if I could present it to him, he'd be over the moon.

The question was, where?

I searched the credenza without success, then made for the junk drawer in the kitchen. No luck there either.

Rude.

Hand on the drawer's lip as I closed it, I paused, leaning in.

"Hey, you—inklings. I know you're hanging out here somewhere. If you borrowed my cocktail sword, I'd like to trade you for it."

I was about to tell them they were welcome to anything in the drawer, but that would be like telling a raccoon it could eat anything in the trash can it'd just climbed into. I'd better offer something new.

"How about . . . an earring? Or a penny?" I dug deeper into my pockets. "Erm . . . Incubus Anonymous sobriety chip?" I'd picked one up off the asphalt at work the other day and forgotten all about it.

Something inside the drawer rustled.

I grinned. I *knew* those sneaky suckers were still lurking around.

"Awesome, one sobriety chip coming right up!"

I dropped the hot-pink token in the drawer and shut it. A few shuffles and slithers later, the drawer went silent again.

Cautiously, I slid it open.

Presto change-o: a purple cocktail sword lying right on top of the jumble.

"Sweet, thanks!" I plucked it out and headed to the mirror.

This time, I entered feet-first. They found solid ground through the mirror immediately, but I had the disconcerting experience of watching the mirror stretch and ripple around me as my face plummeted toward the surface.

No banged-up shins: 1.

Getting sucked into a morphing magical mirror like quicksand on steroids: 0.

Gurgle glug.

Thankfully drowning in liquid silver wasn't in the cards for me today.

Cucumber's wails filled the sweltering laundromat, and I could just make out the quivering tower of bubbles at the other end of the room. Turning on my phone's flashlight, I opened the first dryer and pulled out a wad of dry clothes.

I shoved my nose in the still-warm laundry and sniffed.

It . . . smelled fine, actually. Come to think of it, the whole laundromat smelled fine.

That, or Cucumber's bubble bath had finally cauterized all my scent receptors.

Yeah, probably the latter.

I'd have to ask Bracchius to give my clothes his own sniff test.

The wails died out, followed by a splash-thwack. "Lady Immy? Is that you?"

"Hi, Cuke. Didn't wanna interrupt your me-time over there." I dumped more clean laundry into my hamper. "If you're taking a break, though, I brought a gift for you."

"*Another* gift?" he piped. "Milady, you are too generous. What is the occasion?"

"You becoming a knight, obvi. Stay there, I'm coming over."

"As you command, milady!"

I crammed the last of my laundry in the hamper and flapped the lid shut. Mostly. I closed my hand around the purple cocktail sword and joined Cucumber at his bubble tower.

Which was bumping up against the freaking *ceiling*. I'd really have to leave that basilisk's store a five-star review.

Cucumber squinted up at me from the top of the neighboring washer, one hand raised to shield his eyes. "The light, milady . . ."

"Sorry." I shut off the flashlight and waited for my eyes to adjust to the darkness, lit only by the washer lights and an exit sign. Then I presented the translucent plastic sword on my palm.

Cucumber rocked back, saucer eyes going even wider somehow. "Milady . . ." he breathed. "For me, truly?"

"Yup, just for you."

He delicately gripped the hilt and lifted the sword. I'd guessed right—it was the perfect size for him.

Not like it could do much damage, but he'd probably just be slaying bubbles most days.

Cucumber gave it an experimental swipe, then cradled it in both hands. "To honor me not once, but twice in such a short span, and with a *sword*—!" His voice went supersonic with his excitement.

He kept babbling, a squeaky garbled streak I couldn't make heads or tails of.

Smile and nod, smile and nod.

Eventually his monologue came back into my hearing range. "—and here I thought you'd merely returned to inquire as to my negotiations with the negentropes, but instead, to confer upon me *such* a boon—"

His pitch was rising again. Better cut him off before I went deaf.

"Actually, I'd love to hear about that too."

Cucumber lowered the sword. "The negentropes?"

"Yup. What'd they say?" Assuming they *could* say anything. They'd seemed more like bugs or nanobots than something you could sit down and chat with.

"The negentropes are in deliberations regarding your request. I planned to notify you once they'd reached a decision."

"Oh, great, thanks." Guess they could communicate.

"You're very welcome, milady."

I stared down at Cucumber in the dim green light. Wasn't there something else I'd wanted to ask him? Uh . . . Something to do with Kor . . .

Right, Kor's eyes!

"Hey, Cuke, have you ever seen Kor looking through the portal from in here? Sometimes he'll watch me with these red eyes that are creepy as all get out, and—"

"Immy?"

I blinked down at the Cukester, but the whisper hadn't come from him.

"Immy, are you there?"

Was that *Bracchius*? How had he come through the portal without me noticing?

Scratch that, how had he come through at all? Kor had keyed the mirror to let me through, but no way would he want Bracchius wandering into his domain willy-nilly.

I glanced around, but didn't see him anywhere.

Cucumber tugged at the hem of my shirt. "The voice comes from without the portal, milady."

Oh. Duh.

I walked over to the swirling maw of the portal. "Bracchius? You out there? What's up?"

"Immy . . ." Bracchius's voice wavered. "Something's wrong."

STUBBORN AS A DEMON

Bracchius's voice didn't make it sound like an 'Oops, I smeared glitter glue on the sofa' or even 'One of the pipes has burst' kind of problem.

He sounded worried.

Scared.

Bracchius didn't really do scared, except where Sparkles was concerned—or me. And I was pretty sure both of us were fine.

That left Bracchius himself.

Anxiety roiled through me.

"Coming!" I raced back for my hamper and rolled it toward the portal. "Gotta go, Cuke!"

"Farewell, milady!"

I was facing the wrong way, but safe to say Cucumber was waving his shiny new cocktail sword in parting.

I hit the portal at a full jog, hamper first. The swirling black vortex was replaced by the wall of the hallway a foot and a half away as Kor's mirror ejected me into the real world.

Well, the not-a-demon-domain world.

The hamper crashed into the wall, but I let it go flying and whirled, searching for Bracchius. "What's wrong? Bracchius?"

"Over here." His voice trembled.

I dashed toward the sofa and skidded onto my elbows and stomach on the floor. Sofa flap up, I searched the dusty under-the-couch landscape for my little demon.

Bracchius huddled in a corner, his crimson flickers listless and sporadic. It was more like looking at a lava lamp than his usual plasma-ball self.

"Immy . . ."

"What's the matter?" I stretched an arm into the dust, and Bracchius rolled forward jerkily until he was leaning against my palm.

"I . . . hurt," he whispered. "Inside."

Panicked, I scooped him up and settled on the sofa with him on my lap. I didn't even bother asking whether he'd subsumed a gallon of Pop Rocks or gotten trapped in the freezer again.

Whatever was wrong, it had to be because of the artifact.

"Spit out that gizmo right now."

Bracchius shrank on my lap. "But if I release it, the bad guys will know we tricked them!"

"I don't care. I want that thing out of you right now."

"But you entrusted it to me. I promised to keep it safe for you."

"Damn it, right now I'm more worried about keeping *you* safe, Bracchius. What if that thing's going supernova inside you? I have to check it."

"If it was exploding, I'd know, Immy. This is more like . . ." He squirmed. "What do humans call it? A tummy ache?"

Could I trust him to know what that actually meant on the pain scale? He hadn't even had a tummy ache after eating ten whole pounds of candy last Halloween. In one sitting.

"Are you sure?" I leaned in. "Uncomfortable but not awful?"

He quirked into more of a lopsided squash shape. "Yes? But I don't like it."

"Then give me the freaking thing already!" I flung a hand in front of him, palm up.

"I don't want the bad guys to start chasing you again, Immy. You could get hurt."

I half growled in frustration, fists clenched. "But *you're* getting hurt right now!"

"It's not that bad."

A burst of flames erupted above the coffee table, and I jerked back right as Kor popped into existence atop his pedestal.

I tucked Bracchius closer, protectively. "What are you doing back already?" Surely his therapy took longer than, what, fifteen minutes?

Kor swiveled between us. "One of my ward spells tripped. Did Bracchius dare to enter my domain?" He floated closer, flames gathering around him like the rings of Saturn.

"No!" I shoved Kor back with one hand, the flames licking at my fingers but not burning. "I . . . ducked in to make sure the mirror portal was still working in its new home, and Bracchius called through for me, that's all."

That gave me an idea, though.

I cradled Bracchius on my lap, peering down at him. "What if we went into Kor's domain for you to get rid of it? Shouldn't it be safe from scrying there?"

Kor squawked. "He's not befouling my domain! And get rid of what?"

I glared at him. "The Dreyelian device. It's hurting Bracchius."

"Oh." He settled back down. "Immali— Immy, do you really think I would not have whisked that trinket away to the deepest recesses of my domain if that would've prevented these ingrates from pestering us? I have better things to do with my time than swat such mosquitoes."

I sagged. "Your domain's not safe from scrying?"

"Unfortunately, no," he grumbled. "Let us just say I am . . . still upgrading the security measures. Including ones to keep *intruders* from wreaking havoc."

His glower in my direction was obvious despite his lack of eyes.

"However . . ." Kor sounded reluctant. "I may be able to assist in another manner."

I perked up. "How?"

"Yeah, how?" Bracchius spun toward him.

Kor puffed up. "I am hardly surprised that Bracchius is too weak to keep such a powerful being subdued, despite the protections of its cage. I, on the other hand, am more than skilled enough to handle such a paltry matter."

Bracchius hmphed, and I patted him reassuringly. "Meaning what, exactly?"

"I can safeguard the device until such time as my services are no longer needed."

The word 'services' got me instantly suspicious. "And just what do these services of yours cost?"

"Unfettered use of the fridge, a more illustrious pedestal—I've seen you besmirching this one, Bracchius—and to be addressed as Master Kor at all times."

"Done." Those were easy asks compared to watching Bracchius suffer, even if I would roll my eyes every time I called him 'master.'

Kor reared back, startled. "O-Oh, wonderful." He paused, probably thinking he should've asked for more. Too late. "In that case, let us proceed."

He drifted closer to Bracchius, who I scooted forward on my lap despite him trying to roll backwards.

"Bracchius, on the count of three, spit out the artifact, and, Kor, you suck it in pronto. That gives us the best chance of it not being detected by the bad guys."

Kor twitched in a nod. "Very well, Immy. I am prepared."

"One . . ." My hands tightened around Bracchius. "Two . . ."

Hopefully this would do the trick.

Kor was poised and ready. I prepared for a sputtering orb of dark, icy magic to come shooting out of my little demon buddy. "Three!"

"No!" Bracchius squashed himself down on my lap.

"No?" I gaped. "What? Why not?"

Bracchius swiveled to look up at me. "I can handle it, Immy, I promise."

I groaned. "I'm sure you can, but I don't *want* you to. Let Kor deal with the artifact for a while, please."

"No," he insisted stubbornly. "I'm just as strong a demon as Kor is. And we're getting rid of it tomorrow anyway, right, Immy?"

"Yes, but . . ." That was still a whole twenty-four hours away. My stomach clenched at the thought of something awful happening to Bracchius. "I at least need to see it, to make sure it's not about to blast you to smithereens."

I flashed a glance to Kor, hoping he could read my mind. If Bracchius was willing to let me take a peek at the artifact, Kor damn well better snatch that thing up lickety-split while it was out in the open.

Otherwise I'd be lobbing it straight into his stomach.

"If you wanna see it, Immy, that's easy. Here."

Bracchius's black orb form flickered, instantly going clear, translucent. He might as well have been a giant soap bubble sitting on my sofa.

Huh. New trick.

And floating at the center of the demon soap bubble was the artifact—interconnected gold rings encompassing that creepy ebony core.

The occasional dark glimmer of energy raced along the rings, but the device looked intact. No wires bent or broken, no sinister creature bits poking out.

Maybe the device's inhabitant was just getting antsy, flexing its magical muscles.

I still only felt a smidgen better.

Bracchius shifted a few degrees in each direction. "How's it look? Is it bad?"

I stopped chewing on my lip. "There's some magic skittering along the outside, but it seems okay. Not like it's breaking or anything."

"Oh good. Then I'm definitely hanging on to it for now." Bracchius darkened to his usual solid midnight with red accents.

Stubborn, sensitive, doesn't-know-what's-good-for-him demon.

"Okay, but anytime—and I mean *any*time—I want to see that thing, you show it to me immediately."

"All right."

"And if I think it looks too dangerous, you'll unsubsume it without a second thought when I tell you to, or so help me, I'll squeeze you like a tube of toothpaste and pop it out, you hear me?"

Bracchius gulped. "Yes, Immy."

I raised a stern brow. "Do I need to make you sign a contract?"

"No, I-I'll listen. Promise."

Kor scoffed. "Well, if you do need me after all, please knock on my mirror." He wandered off, grumbling about fridges and pedestals.

At least I wouldn't have to be calling him Master Kor for the time being.

I didn't really want to let Bracchius out of my sight, considering. I'd planned a peaceful evening anyway, so once Kor had vanished, I nestled Bracchius in a wadded-up blanket beside me, and turned topsy-turvy to pluck Sparkles out from under the couch.

"Here." I snuggled the plushie unicorn up to Bracchius. "How about a movie night? We can watch whatever you want, and if you need any snacks to help you feel better, just let me know."

"Can you check if there's any Rainbow Turds left?" He shimmied deeper into the blanket, drawing Sparkles close.

"Sure." I upended myself again to peer into the murk under the couch. I rustled up his snack basket—really just a dollar-store plastic bin—and teased out the crumpled-up bag of Rainbow Turds.

A firm shake confirmed the presence of at least a few turds.

I rolled open the bag and propped it beside Bracchius. "There you go. Now, whaddya wanna watch?"

Bracchius popped one of the multicolor marshmallow swirls out of the bag as I got off the couch. I'd long since lost the remote, so I had to feel up the back of the cracked-screen TV to turn it on.

"Um . . . I know! The newest *My Little Unicorn* movie!"

I should've known.

Pulling up KidCast on my phone—yes, I have a subscription purely for Bracchius, I'm a good roomie that way—I settled back against the sofa cushion with a smile.

There were worse ways to spend an evening.

I woke up in the middle of *My Little Unicorn 23: Shimmering Secret*. Bracchius was still watching avidly, whispering to Sparkles not to worry, that Iri Glitterwind would defeat the evil farrier and be just fine.

Considering we'd started at number 17, he'd been at it a while. I squinted at the grubby windows, daylight streaming through them. Well, weak morning light, anyway.

"You're awake!" Bracchius cozied closer to me. "You missed the best part! Should I start over?"

I smacked my dry mouth until I had enough saliva going to contemplate speech. "That's okay, you two keep watching without me. I've gotta go do human things."

"Okie." He faced Sparkles toward the TV and resumed his reassuring whispers.

I nearly tripped over Kor's mirror on my way to the bathroom. I went to nudge it out of the way, but it was back to its astronomically heavy self.

Rude.

At least I hadn't stubbed my toes.

Brushing my teeth, I heard Kor emerge from his mirror, midrant—

the demonlings weren't constructing his replacement tower fast enough. But for the first time, I had the bathroom to myself.

No irate demon buzzing out of the mirror straight into a cloud of hairspray, only to curse me with a plague of frogs for daring to fumigate him. No appearing halfway through my shower, to both our horror.

A little ranting from the other side of the door, I could deal with.

I was teasing my curls into some semblance of order when I remembered Bracchius's situation: the Dreyelian device acting up inside him. Anxiety balled up my insides.

He'd seemed okay last night during our uni-thon. At least, he hadn't complained.

And today was the day we were meeting up with that sorceress, after which neither I nor Bracchius would ever have to worry about that troublemaking trinket again.

We just had to make it until seven o'clock tonight.

I checked the time on my phone: seven thirty. I could have a lazy morning before pegasus riding at noon, then clubbing with Aster and Samaire, and then finally ditching the Dreyelian device.

Today was gonna be a good day.

The doorbell rang as I was changing into fresh clothes. I'd done another sniff test, but either my nose was still cauterized, or they really hadn't soaked up any of the stench of Kor's domain—or Cucumber's bubble bath.

I checked the peep hole just in time to catch a delivery griffin winging away into the cloudless morning sky.

Weird. My packages tended to come on the slow boat from China—literally or metaphorically—and I wasn't expecting anything.

An innocent white box the size of a donut sat on my stoop.

"Bracchius, you mind doing a package check for me?" Not like anyone would be mailing me package bombs, especially by pricey griffin delivery, but he could make sure it wasn't gonna spring me with any nasty magical surprises.

"Coming!" He zoomed over at top speed, probably not wanting to miss more than a second of his movie. One tornado whirl around the package, and he was zipping back toward the couch. "All clear!"

I dumped the package in the kitchen and scrounged up my junk scissors—the ones with divots in the blades, scraps of tape stuck everywhere, and a janky screw. I sliced open the packaging tape and lifted the lid.

Inside lay a weird greyish nubbin on a red cushion. What the—

I peered closer and almost hurled.

It was a bloody severed *toe*, pillowed on velvet like an engagement ring.

MONDO CONCERNING

"Gahh!" I only avoided dropping the box because my hands had spasmed around it in horror.

"What is it?" Bracchius pried his attention away from his movie.

"A dismembered human toe."

Bracchius gasped. "One of yours?!"

I blinked. "Uh . . . no. Pretty sure I'd notice if someone lopped off one of my toes in the middle of the night." Or anytime, really.

To be safe, I wiggled all ten within my socks.

Yup, still there.

Hey, you never know.

"Then why would someone send you a toe?"

Bracchius was clearly gonna be distracted for a while, so I paused the *My Little Unicorn* movie from my phone—easier than going back to find his spot in ten minutes.

I grimaced. "Well, sometimes it's a threat. Sometimes it's proof they're serious if they just kidnapped someone you care about. But it's usually a finger, or an ear."

Bracchius shuddered. "You mean humans do this *often*?"

"Not really. Mostly on TV." I flicked a glanced at the stubby digit, my nose wrinkling. That better be actual red velvet it was resting on, and not only red because it was blood-soaked. Eurgh. "But seriously, a toe? What am I gonna do with a toe?"

Bracchius bobbed closer. "What were you going to do with a finger or ear?" he asked in horrified fascination.

"Nothing!" I threw my head back, exasperated.

"Does it say who it's from? Did they kidnap someone? Thank darkness it's not Sparkles!" He squished the unicorn against him.

A weight settled in my gut. Was that what this was? Kidnapping? The toe was clearly humanish, which narrowed down the possibilities. Samaire, Damarion . . .

But who would be dumb enough to hit *me* up for a ransom? I wasn't even rolling in pennies, never mind legit cash.

Reluctantly, I glanced back at the box and raised the lid again. A folded note fluttered from the underside of the lid. I flipped the paper open, and as soon as I saw the handwriting, I knew.

> Sadly, it isn't a head as I promised, but I do hope you can forgive me, Immy dearest. I simply couldn't bring myself to part with the rest.
> Yours,
> Cynna

Of *course* it was from Cynna.

I contemplated the greyish toe in disgust. "It seems to be the toe of one of our enemies."

Bracchius clasped Sparkles tighter. "Why are they mailing you their toes?"

A breathy laugh escaped me. "They're not. Cynna must have found one of them—the bad guys, not their toes. It's from her."

"Cynna," Bracchius grumbled. "Why does she keep giving you gifts? That's *my* job."

"To be fair, it's a pretty terrible gift."

Bracchius brightened.

"Immy . . ." Suddenly I realized I had two demons chumming up to my elbows.

"Yeah, Kor?"

His attention was fixed on the box. "If you don't want it, *I'll* take it."

Say what? "I thought all things human disgusted you."

"You are a foul species, to be sure, Immali— Immy, but a gruesome trophy of a vanquished foe? That would make an excellent display piece in my new tower, to strike fear into the hearts of my enem—"

"A foe's toe," I muttered, unable to stop myself.

"Hmph." He bristled at the interruption at the height of his villainous tirade. "Can I have it or not?"

"Go for it." I presented him with the box, which he reverently took between two blobby appendages. Cynna and Kor would probably get along like a house on fire.

Maybe I should set up a villain tea party for the two of them.

But did I really want to risk them teaming up?

I shuddered.

"Thank you, Immy. This almost makes up for the insufferable smell emanating from your room this morning."

My mind flashed to the laundry I'd lugged back through the mirror last night.

Oh no.

"However, it doesn't even come close to making up for my—"

I scooped Kor up with one hand like a basketball I was about to dribble, and dashed into my room as he cursed in protest.

"Is this the smell?" I snatched a sock off the top of the clean hamper and flapped it in his face. Well, in front of him, anyway.

"Ack! Yes, get it away!" He sputtered, and I let him go, raising the sock to my nose. Nothing. I *still* couldn't smell anything.

But if *Kor* thought it smelled bad . . .

"Wait."

He paused by the door, spinning back toward me but keeping a wary distance.

I waved the sock. "What does it smell like to you?"

"Some foul flower or fruit or other saccharine human nonsense. Disgusting."

I smiled. How it was possible, I had no idea. But if my laundry didn't reek like Kor's sulfurous demon domain, or Cucumber's gag-worthy bubble bath, then life was grand.

"All right, I'm getting dressed, so shoo. Go enjoy your creepy toe."

Kor zipped out at top speed, still cradling the awful little box. Maybe Cynna and I needed to have a chat about appropriate gifts. Send me chocolate, books, take-out sushi, straight-up cash or jewels even . . .

But not body parts, pretty please.

My stomach growled, and I wrinkled my nose. I swear, it was a reaction to the thought of sushi, *not* the toe.

Never the toe.

I shuddered. Time to think of something else.

Breakfast time!

I got busy in the kitchen, and halfway through pouring milk on my cereal, a whimper sounded behind me. I whirled.

Bracchius and Sparkles were finishing the movie, but Bracchius looked more squished than usual, huddled up in the corner of the sofa. Another whimper squeaked out.

Crud. And here I'd thought he might be doing better.

"Bracchius, you okay?"

"Mmhm!"

Convincing. I stalked over to the sofa. "Lemme see."

He grudgingly went clear, showing off the artifact. It looked the same as last night—a few glimmers of magic along its rings, but nothing *too* sinister.

"Stay put." I raced back to my room and unearthed the whopper of a book about Dreyelian devices—*Dreyelian Design: Theory, Creation, and Use.*

Plopping back on the couch beside Bracchius, I flipped through to the 'use' section. How to activate it, how to release the contents, maintenance while it was occupied . . . Troubleshooting, that was probably my best bet.

I skimmed the troubleshooting tables, which included things like 'The device won't close,' 'The device won't open,' 'The stasis malfunctioned and the contents died,' 'The device melted into a ball of slag and ate through my floorboards.'

I eyeballed that last one dubiously. That that was even a *possibility* was mondo concerning.

Nothing about the 'contents' reaching out into the world with little zaps of magic.

Helpful.

Disgruntled, I tossed the book onto the opposite end of the sofa and grabbed my phone.

My first text was to Cynna: Got your delivery. Thanks for the thought, but please no more people bits. Any chance we can see your sorceress friend before tonight?

My second was to Fitz, after I scrolled through my contacts, trying to remember what dorky name I'd listed him under.

Right: Dude in Distress.

I let him know I'd be bringing not one, but two friends pegasus riding. I felt a little bad outnumbering him by that many people, but I wasn't risking leaving Bracchius on the other side of the city while I ran around having fun.

"Immy, can I go back to normal yet?"

I glanced down at Bracchius's translucent self. "Oh. Sorry. Yeah, go ahead."

He gave a little shake, and red flickers and darkness filled him once more. "Thanks. You find anything?"

"Not so much. Which means you're coming with me everywhere today, no ifs, ands, or buts, okay?"

"Okay. Can Sparkles come too?"

"C'mon, like I'd ask you to abandon her."

"Yay, thanks!" He squeezed her close. "Wait, where *are* you going today?"

My phone buzzed with an incoming text. "Pegasus riding, and—"

The text was from Cynna: *pout* I am sorry my gift didn't meet your expectations. The next one will surpass them, I assure you. And I'm afraid I must disappoint you a second time, darling. Elena's flight doesn't arrive until this afternoon, so an earlier meeting is out of the question.

I didn't bother texting back. That did remind me, though . . .

One more text went off to Aster: How would you feel about meeting one of my demon roommates today after all? The nice one. Okay if he comes with?

Bracchius nudged me. "Pegasus riding and?"

"Oh, sorry for leaving you hanging. And Comet."

An excited ripple bounced across Bracchius's surface. "The club??"

"Uh, yeah. I guess you've heard of it?"

"Heard of it? Immy, it's only the—"

My phone started up with the buzzing again. This time it was Damarion, on a video call.

I meant to let Bracchius finish, really I did, but my phone slipped, and I answered the call.

'FIT CHECK

Damarion popped up on my phone screen, dressed immaculately as always in one of his three-piece suits.

When we first met, I'd worried he just wore the same suit 24/365—they all looked pretty much alike. I'd had the audacity to mention that, and he'd changed up his collection but quick. In the years since, he'd even added some flamboyant options to his rotation—including a natty sky blue number covered in parrots.

Okay, that one was all me. Thrift store finds for the win. But he's actually humored me and worn it once.

Once.

"Hey, Damarion, what's up?"

He didn't look aggravated this time, so hopefully he and his archnemesis hadn't bumped into each other again.

"Good morning, Immy! Aster somehow managed to turn on the childproof features on her phone, and can't get it to video call or even send photos any longer, so it is my solemn duty to send you her choice of club outfits for consultation."

He swung the phone over and way down to Aster, who was gleefully waving faster than the camera's frame rate. "Hi, Immy!!"

Bracchius nosed in on the screen. "Who's she?" His voice tightened with suspicion. "Is that Cynna?"

"That's *Aster*. Bracchius, meet Aster. Aster, Bracchius."

Aster stole the phone from Damarion, judging by the jostle and sudden closeup of her. "It's *so* nice to meet you! You're cute for a demon."

"Er, um, thanks." Bracchius's ebony form suffused with the slightest soft pink glow.

Was he . . . *blushing*? Wonders never cease.

I angled the phone more toward me. "Is it okay if he comes to Comet with us after all?"

"And Sparkles too!" Bracchius interjected.

"*And* Sparkles, his little unicorn buddy?" I clarified.

I shouldn't have bothered—Bracchius waved the plushie unicorn in front of my face, showing her off very thoroughly.

"You can both totally come! Ooh, this'll be so fun." The camera angle went way up again. "Okay, Damarion, hold the camera while I change. Immy, grab your outfits too! Be right back!"

My outfits, right. Good thing I'd just done my laundry.

Damarion appeared onscreen again as I hurried to my room. "She won't take my advice, so I do hope you can talk her out of the tutu outfit."

I half choked. "Tutu?"

"Tutu?" Bracchius's tone was much more excited than mine. Thank goodness we didn't have any tutus in the house, or I could just see him leaving in one.

"I'm afraid so." Damarion pursed his lips.

"I'll see what I can do." I rummaged through my hamper, flinging clean clothes every which way.

What? I'd pick them up later.

Sometime.

I tossed some candidates on my bed—graphic tees, crop tops, faux leather leggings, a strappy halter thing that should *not* be worn on its own. The pile grew until Aster's voice piped out of my phone speakers from somewhere within.

"Here's the first one!"

"One sec." I clawed through the pile until I unearthed the phone. Aster wore an ultraclassy outfit, sleek, neutral, with surprisingly long lines on her kid-size body. It looked like something Audrey Hepburn would've worn in third grade.

"What do you think?" She twirled for the camera.

"Nice, but way too classy for Comet. Plus, if we're trying to coordinate, I'd look like your hillbilly cousin."

Aster covered her minuscule fangs with a hand as she erupted into giggles. "'Kay, next one!"

Damarion switched back to the selfie camera. "I believe she only has three outfits picked out at the moment, if that's any consolation."

"Nah, this is fun. If she had three *hundred*, though . . ."

He chuckled. "We might get there, if you don't approve one of these."

"Not happening."

Damarion stepped away for a moment, and I took the opportunity to sort out a couple good options from my pile. Bracchius tugged at a hot-pink-and-purple tie-dye tee, and I smirked. *That* was more dreamweaver-rave appropriate, but I added it to make him happy.

"Outfit two!" Aster declared, and I picked up my phone again.

Ah, the tutu had come into play. She was decked out in pastels and sparkles, and unsurprisingly, Bracchius gasped in delight.

He came by it honestly, given his career before he retired.

I hummed, pretending to at least consider this outfit. "A little too cotton candy fairy."

Aster cocked her head, silver-blonde curls bobbing. "I *am* sweet."

"But you've also got bite."

This time she didn't hide her fangs as she giggled. "The next outfit *is* a little more bitey."

"Lemme see!"

She vanished from the screen again. Bracchius cradled Sparkles and whispered, "What's that, Sparkles? You need a tutu? Hmm, your birthday *is* pretty soon . . ."

Yup, shoulda seen this coming.

"Why don't you go look up tutus on my laptop?" I suggested. "That way Sparkles can see them too, and you can bookmark her faves."

It wasn't safe to close my laptop anymore, but it still worked—mostly.

"Annnd three!" Aster popped back up on the screen, and I grinned.

This was the one.

She looked like a pint-size punk, with a black choker, dangly neon pink lightning earrings, and an oversized stonewashed Grateful Dead tee tucked into dark jeans.

She'd even pinned her silvery curls up into a fauxhawk.

Adorable.

"What do you think?" She flicked one of the earrings, with a mischievous-and-yet-cherubic smile.

"Winner winner, phoenix dinner."

"Yeah?"

"It's perfect."

"Yay!" She bounced on her toes. "Okay, now yours!" Her face got alarmingly close to the camera—I could've counted her silvery freckles.

"Lemme change, one sec." I flipped my phone over in case she didn't take the hint. I grabbed my 'Danger to Society' tee, dark tights, and ripped jeans, then topped it off with a chunky necklace made of chains and neon cords.

Dressed, I grabbed my phone again and propped it against the clothes pile so Aster could see most of my outfit.

"Ooh, I love it!" She clapped. "We're gonna look *fab*."

Fab, and I wouldn't have to wear a tutu. Score.

She backed up from the camera. "Okay, I got us on the VIP list for two o'clock, and I just added Bracchius too. Should we meet here? Or your place?" She glanced up as the view jostled again.

"Wherever." I wasn't sure how long pegasus riding would take, but my place and Damarion's were so close to each other that it really didn't matter which.

Damarion filled the screen. "Paolo will be driving you. For simplicity's sake, why don't he and Aster collect you at your home, then proceed to the club?"

"Sounds good." I tapped out a quick text to Samaire to give her a heads-up. We could come back here together after pegasus riding, but she'd probably want to change first. And collect her friend Nadine.

"You're not wearing *that* pegasus riding, are you?" Bracchius bobbed in my bedroom doorway, taking in my outfit.

Damarion quirked an eyebrow. "Pegasus riding?"

"Oops." Bracchius shot over. "Uh, do you want to come, Damarion?"

I covered the microphone and whispered, "We can't invite *everyone!*"

Not that I had anything against Damarion, but I really had to stop shoehorning extra people into what poor Fitz had thought would be a simple sightseeing shindig.

Besides, they couldn't have *that* many pegasi willing to cart us bipeds around.

Bracchius potatoed, looking sheepish. "Sorry."

"S'okay." I uncovered the mic.

Damarion ran his thumb across his dark stubble. "A very kind offer, which I will gratefully decline. When I ingest blood, it is to sustain me, not to have it splattered all over the pavement from fifty stories up when I topple off a flighty pegasus."

I stifled a laugh. "Afraid of heights?"

"Afraid of being immortal in a pulverized body, more like."

I winced. Fair. There weren't many ways you could kill a vamp.

Bracchius tugged at my sleeve. "Immy, it's almost eleven. Shouldn't we get ready to go?"

Banshees and barnacles, it was eleven *already?*

Damarion smiled. "Don't let me keep you. And, Bracchius, try to ensure our Immy doesn't do any toppling of her own, yes?"

Bracchius gasped. "Sparkles and I would *never* let Immy become a sidewalk pancake!"

I broke out into helpless laughter. Today was gonna be interesting, that was for sure.

PEGASUS POINT

Bracchius, Sparkles, and I got off the subway at Pegasus Point, the tallest building in Saskia Springs. It really wasn't possible to crane your neck far enough back to see the top of the building from this close.

Well, *I* couldn't, anyway. Bracchius just swiveled backwards into a slow 360. "Whoa . . ."

"You've never been over here?"

He swiveled from side to side as we headed across the street. I guess he *was* mostly a homebody.

My phone buzzed, and I checked the screen. A text from Dude in Distress: Meet at the top or the bottom?

Good question. Um . . . I texted back: The bottom?

Bracchius bobbed closer. "Is that Samaire?"

"Fitz." I should text Samaire too, though.

"Fitz?" Bracchius slowed. "You said it was you and Samaire going pegasus riding."

I stared down at him. I . . . had, hadn't I?

"I, uh, yeah. Sorry, buddy. Didn't mean to keep that from you."

"So he *is* coming?" Bracchius puffed up a couple inches. "If we're doing this with him instead of Samaire, I wanna go ho—"

"Samaire's coming too! I just forgot to mention Fitz." I fired off that text to Samaire while Bracchius engaged in dire grumblings in Sparkles's ear.

"You didn't have to text me, you know," Samaire called from behind me, and I spun. She was twenty feet down the sidewalk, her dark brown hair trailing in the breeze, the sunlight glinting off the gold feathers tangled in the strands.

"Samaire!" Bracchius darted over and cannonballed into her stomach.

She wrapped an arm around him and Sparkles with a grin. "Hey there, Bracchius. Good to see you too. I didn't know you were coming." She glanced up at me. "So we're just waiting on Fitzy boy, then?"

"You knew?" Bracchius slipped out of her arms, sounding betrayed. "I thought you'd be on my side! Immy shouldn't be going out with weirdo humans she doesn't even know. I haven't even had a chance to vet him yet!"

I quirked an eyebrow at him. "Say what? Fitz and I went to dinner two nights ago. That was a whole lotta time you coulda been vetting."

"I didn't know you were going to see him *again!*" He turned to Samaire. "She kept it completely hush-hush. She didn't even tell me until just now! It's not like her to keep secrets from me. See? He's already corrupting her. She's gotta find someone worthier!"

Samaire patted Bracchius with one hand. "Don't worry, we can both keep an eye on him today."

Bracchius whispered, "We don't want another Tucker."

Samaire smirked. "You never even *met* Tucker."

"But I heard the horror stories! The crows told me all about—"

"Hey." A deep voice came from behind me.

What was it with everybody sneaking up on me today? I turned and looked up at Fitz. "You made it!"

"Just have to follow the current of tourists." He nodded toward the line starting at the main doors into Pegasus Point.

Ugh, why hadn't I thought about tourists? This was prime time for sightseeing. Of course there would be a line.

Hopefully it didn't wind all the way through the gazillion floors to the top.

"Mind introducing us?" Fitz's gaze bounced between me, Bracchius, and Samaire.

Samaire scooped up Bracchius and Sparkles. "Better get in line before it gets any longer. Then we can take care of introductions."

She marched toward the end of the line as Bracchius swiveled within her arms and peered over her shoulder. The mental daggers flying toward Fitz were palpable.

Fitz leaned into me as we followed Samaire. "He still doesn't like me, huh?"

"That may be a permanent problem."

He shrugged. "I get it. I'll deal."

A cordon kept the line of tourists from taking up the whole sidewalk. We slipped in at the end, behind a selkie. Samaire let go of Bracchius and nudged me as she faced Fitz.

Right, introductions. "Samaire, this is Fitz. Fitz, Samaire—the best singer in Saskia Springs."

He dipped his head. "I'd love to hear you sometime."

She smiled. "That can be arranged."

The heat coming off Bracchius beside me was amping up. Better get this over with.

Even though they'd traded banter—and barbs, in Bracchius's case— outside Nozomi Nosh the other night, they hadn't really been introduced. Maybe a formal introduction would soothe Bracchius a touch.

"Bracchius, this is Fitz Greymoore. Fitz, Bracchius Doommonger.

And Sparkles." I pointed to the unicorn.

Bracchius clutched her tighter. "Neither of us are shaking your hand."

Fitz raised both of his. "No problem. I like your last name. Doommonger is much cooler than Greymoore."

Bracchius hmphed.

Samaire hooked arms with me as the line inched forward. "Let's give them a little space."

I glanced at her in disbelief. "Them? Seriously? You wanna end up with corpses in the street?"

"You'll get those anyway if they don't work this out sooner than later."

She had a point. But I couldn't help nervously peeking over my shoulder every couple minutes as Fitz tried his darnedest to make small talk with Bracchius.

Bracchius just grumpily ignored him.

After about ten minutes, with me filling Samaire in on the latest with the artifact, and more details about our club outing later, Fitz's tone changed. The casual, polite nothings morphed into more earnest undertones.

"I just want you to know, Immy and I aren't dating. I'm new to the city, and she's nice enough to be my friend."

Bracchius interrupted. "But she's already got so many friends! And now there's you, and Cynna, and Aster, and—"

"And you're her best friend, right?"

"Absolute best!"

"And you're worried that if she gets too many friends, you'll lose her?"

Bracchius stayed quiet.

The tiny tinkle of bells broke the silence, and I risked a peek over my shoulder.

Fitz was jostling one of Sparkles's hooves with a finger. "But I'm betting Sparkles is your other best friend, yeah?"

Bracchius gripped Sparkles tighter. "Yeah . . ."

"And do you love Sparkles any less because you and Immy are friends? Or Immy any less because you and Sparkles are friends?"

Bracchius listed slowly to one side. "Oh . . ." For the first time since Fitz had shown up, he didn't sound sullen.

Fitz kept facing Bracchius as we all shuffled forward with the line, close to the doors now. "I promise I'm not gonna take Immy away from you. I'm pretty sure I couldn't even if I wanted to."

Bracchius brandished Sparkles with a jingle. "You couldn't!"

"Then what are you worried about?" Fitz smiled.

Bracchius mumbled, "I don't want you to hurt her either. I don't know *anything* about you, and you might be a really bad guy. We've got a whole bunch of those right now."

Fitz bobbed his head. "Then how about we get to know each other too? After the pegasus rides today, I promise I won't go anywhere with

Immy until you're sure about me, however long that takes."

Samaire leaned in. "Um . . . where did you find *him*?"

"Hush." I elbowed her, not wanting to miss any of this convo.

"Really? You'd do that?" Bracchius drifted a couple inches closer to Fitz.

"Absolutely." Fitz held out his phone. "Let's trade numbers, and you can let me know when and where you'd like to meet. Anytime this weekend is fine. After that, we'll have to fit it in around my work schedule."

"Okay." Bracchius's phone materialized opposite Sparkles.

The line started moving again as they exchanged numbers. The doorman was counting off people. "Three, four, five . . ."

Samaire was six, me seven, eight and nine for Bracchius and Fitz, and then one lone tourist behind them for ten. The doorman ushered us through, latching the heavy velvet rope back into place once we passed.

Pegasus rides, here we come.

Now if I could just keep Bracchius from shoving Fitz off his feathery steed . . .

Twelve feet inside the doors of Pegasus Point was a bank of employees waiting behind a counter with cheery smiles. The usher inside directed our group of ten toward the counter, and we splintered into twos and threes—well, four or five counting Bracchius and Sparkles.

"Welcome to Pegasus Point!" The closest employee, a hydra with three heads and blue-purple scales, beckoned us closer.

I hit the counter first. "How much is one adult ticket?"

"Fifty dollars," the hydra's center head said soothingly with a plastic but toothy smile. The other heads looked like they were napping.

Fifty?! I made an effort not to grind my teeth. Yowza.

I was about to back up in horror when I remembered all the cash I'd conned the Man Cave's manager guy out of. Well, in that case, I could pay for me and Bracchius, but Samaire and Fitz were on their own.

Temporary windfall or not, I was still broke.

Fitz pulled his credit card out of his wallet and held it out toward the hydra. "Charge the tickets to this, please."

Whoa, wait a minute. I'd agreed to let him pay for ramen, but this was too much. I stepped forward, raising a hand, but Fitz continued.

"Three adults and a . . ." He cocked his head at Bracchius. ". . . demon and unicorn combo."

The hydra blinked down at Bracchius, who had snuggled up to Samaire's elbow again. Sparkles's multicolor pizzazz in the arms of a demon—usually rather sinister types—seemed to bring the hydra's brain to a screeching halt.

At least the middle brain, anyway.

She recovered after a second, saying sweetly, "And will that be a child ticket?"

Bracchius rocketed up. "One child ticket for my friend Sparkles, and one adult ticket for me! And he"—Bracchius wiggled Sparkles in Fitz's direction—"isn't paying for me *or* Sparkles!" He spun toward me. "Or Immy!"

He zipped up beside my ear and whispered, "He's maybe not that bad, but you definitely shouldn't let him pay for you! Who *knows* what he'll expect. And you don't owe him anything!"

Flashbacks of my mother muttering similar things before my first dates back in high school gave me a little unwanted jolt from the past. I shook it off.

The hydra's center head glanced between the four of us dubiously.

Samaire pushed Fitz's hand closer to the hydra's scaly face. "*I'm* happy to be paid for, thank you very much." She beamed at Fitz. "That's so nice of you, thanks!"

The hydra snatched the card, probably thinking it was her best chance at getting paid, but Bracchius buzzed back toward the counter and started spilling out spare change, Dubble Bubble gum, rainbow Nerds, and a puff of glitter.

"How much is it for me and Sparkles?" He shoved the jingling pile across the counter. "I have lots more pennies if you need them!"

The racket woke the hydra's other two heads, and all three peered down at the mess in dismay.

"Um . . . uh . . . respectfully, O Dark One, w-we," the main head stuttered, "aren't really equipped to handle change or . . . or bubble gum or . . ."

Fitz swept the hodgepodge back toward Bracchius with one arm. "Hey, Bracchius, why don't I pay the nice lady for all of us, and then you can reimburse *me*." He flashed the hydra a nervous smile. "I don't think she'll have time to count all your pennies."

"They," I muttered. Who knew what genders the other two heads were.

Bracchius contemplated his pile of coins for a moment. "Yeah, okay. Do you want me to pay you now? Or later?"

Fitz swayed back from the coins. "Later. Definitely."

"Okie." Bracchius stretched out two dark arms over the pile and squirreled it away.

I tossed Fitz a half-grateful, half-'hope you know what you just got yourself into' look, and he grimaced playfully.

The hydra handed over five colorful tickets, including a mini one for Sparkles. "And don't forget your complimentary experience guides!" She pointed a claw at a display stuffed with brochures.

Complimentary, my ass. Those things probably accounted for ten bucks out of the fifty.

"Just follow the arrows to the elevators on your left. Enjoy your tour of the skies!"

We stepped away from the counter just as a massive troll lumbered up to the next check-in over. The cherub behind the counter piped, "I'm sorry, sir, but we have a height limit. We won't be able to accommodate a pegasus flight for you today."

"Oh. Really? Bummer." The troll hovered for a moment before dejectedly clomping out.

Poor guy. But yeah, just a *little* overkill for a pegasus.

As we strode toward the elevator, the next counter agent stage-whispered, "Not until we can recruit one of those Hyperion pegasi, anyway."

Samaire snorted, and I nudged her with a grin. Good luck with *that*—the Hyperions took their privacy to almost cultlike levels.

We squeezed onto the elevator with a sphinx, and the doors slid shut. Fitz and I each reached for the bank of buttons, arms colliding, only to find that both panels beside the doors were button free aside from the emergency stop and assistance button.

My stomach dropped as the elevator cruised upward, apparently automated.

The fluorosprites glowing above the door flashed the number of each floor as we ascended: seven . . . eleven . . . thirty-two . . . eighty-eight . . .

Until finally we lost a touch of gravity as the elevator coasted to a stop. Whoo, head rush.

The doors opened with a pleasant chime.

We emerged into a glass-walled vestibule on the roof with a gorgeous view of the city in three directions: skyscrapers, parks, Ponderosa Lake glittering in the sunlight.

"Whoa." Samaire traipsed forward, all eyes, and I followed, equally awed. Sure, I've been pretty high up in some of the other buildings, but *this* was something else.

The sphinx pushed politely past us, seemingly less impressed with her surroundings, and headed for one of the staff members waiting before us with clasped hands and his own hospitable smile.

Thank goodness I didn't work in this kind of customer service. I wouldn't last a *day*.

Nobody really cared if I looked grumpy while checking in cars.

While Fitz and Samaire stepped forward, I tugged Bracchius back by one blobby appendage.

"You feeling any better?" I kept my voice low.

"About Fitz? Or . . . the other thing?"

"The other thing."

Bracchius twitched in a shrug. "Well, it's not any worse . . ."

I grimaced. "You let me know the *second* it does get worse, yeah?" I was still hoping it wouldn't, but that might be a pipe dream.

"I will, Immy." He hugged Sparkles close.

With a sigh, I slung an arm around him, and we joined Fitz and

Samaire at a bar-height table with another creepily cheerful employee. No sign of any pegasi yet.

The dude clapped his hands once. "All right, let's get you folks ready for the ride of your life!"

A WINGED HORSE OF MANY COLORS

"I'm Kai, and I'm thrilled to help you out today." Our helper dude fixed his gaze on Bracchius and Sparkles. "Demon? And comfortable with heights?"

"Yup and yup! And a unicorn, but she's not afraid of heights either!" Bracchius tossed Sparkles half a foot in the air to demonstrate.

"Great. Okay, let me just arrange you . . ." Kai grabbed my shoulders and steered me left of Samaire and Fitz. "There, now we're in height order. Everyone stand straight, let me get a good look atcha . . ."

We awkwardly complied, Bracchius hovering to one side.

"And relax, thank you." Kai whisked a piece of paper in front of each of us on the table, near a jumble of pens. "If you'll all just fill out these liability waivers, I'll grab your gear."

I glanced back as he jogged over to the elevator wall, which was covered in saddles and harnesses of all shapes and sizes. Kai perused the most boring section—we didn't have tails or extra sets of legs to worry about, after all—and started slinging equipment over his shoulder.

After a quick scan of the waiver to make sure I wasn't signing away my soul, I scribbled my name across the bottom. Bracchius read his much more thoroughly—even a 'bad' demon has contract know-how drilled into their very being.

Kai thudded the heavy load of gear onto the long table, followed by some vibrant peachy-pink-and-lavender jackets with baseball-style script that read *Pegasus Point*.

Samaire raised both brows. "Are the jackets optional?"

"Nope!" Kai beamed. "And believe me, when you get out there, you'll want 'em. The wind chill is *wicked*. If you can please put them on now so I can fit your harnesses."

He passed out the jackets, including a pint-size one for Sparkles that Bracchius bundled her into immediately.

"Can't have you turning into a popsicle, Sparkles! Plus, this looks *fab* on you."

Bracchius's own jacket looked more like an upside-down shower cap with fins for arms. I caught Samaire's gaze, and we both stifled a laugh.

Kai collected the paperwork as we dressed, glancing over each waiver before stacking them in a tidy pile.

Next came the harnesses, which buckled over the shoulders, around the waist, and under the arms. Fitz watched me getting strapped in, a half-puzzled, half-concerned look on his face. "These seem less secure than the climbing harnesses I've used. Shouldn't there be straps around the, er, leg area?" He scuffed a hand across the back of his head, eyes on the ground.

Kai cinched one of my shoulder straps as I held my arms out to the sides. "Nope! You'd be sitting on leg straps, which is uncomfy to the max. And climbing harnesses keep you from falling out the bottom, but we've got pegasi for that." He slapped a saddle. "Our goal is to keep you from toppling off the sides."

"No harness for me, nuh-uh!" Bracchius swiveled in a whole-body negation. "I trust my flying skills way more than those pegasi. I'm not gonna be tethered to one as it plummets to our death!"

"You could always teleport out," I murmured.

"I guess, but still. No harness for this demon!"

A flash of sunlight and the drum of hooves drew my gaze to the roof outside. Three pegasi landed one after the other, feathered wings majestically spread.

The sun glared off the white coat of the first one, a stark contrast to the ebony horse who landed next.

Pegasus number three was a whole nother story, though, and I bounced on the balls of my feet, grinning.

It *had* to be a dye job. Pegasi come in a lot of colors, but lilac with deep purple cheetah spots and a bright turquoise mane and tail definitely isn't on the list.

Kai tightened my last strap. "That's Zane. Want him to be your chauffeur to the skies today?"

"Absolutely."

"Me too!" Bracchius hovered at my elbow, reverently watching the multicolor pegasus. Zane even had his feathers dyed in a gradient from purple to teal.

Kai bobbed his head side to side. "Normally we only allow one rider per steed, but considering . . ."

The riders unclipped their harnesses from the saddles and dismounted with varying degrees of clumsiness. The last one . . . Was that a voidling?

The dark figure almost sucked in visible light, its edges hazy like a mirage off asphalt.

I strode to the glass walls and peered around at the moonless sky. "Is today the new moon?"

Fitz and Samaire shrugged, but a tourist at another table nodded. "Sure is. New moon in Cancer—the perfect day for activation, initiation!"

"Uh, yeah, great." *So* not why I'd been asking. Voidlings only came out at the new moon, and even then, it was pretty unusual to see one.

This one must've had a real hankering for a pegasus ride.

Another few pegasi came in for a landing as the first set of riders filed in from the roof, chatting boisterously—the voidling included.

Kai clapped again. "All right, folks, you're all geared up! Let's head outside, and I'll introduce you to your pegasi."

"No helmets?" Fitz muttered as we stepped onto the roof, the wind instantly tugging at us.

The nearest pegasus whinnied, a dappled grey with charms tied into their mane and tail. "Helmets are for certifiable optimists. You take a nosedive from up here, you're road jam, helmet or no."

Fitz shuddered as Bracchius whispered, *"I'd* be fine."

I bumped him with my hip. "Yeah, but you're the only one."

Bracchius bumped me back. "You're safe with me!"

Kai stopped in front of three pegasi: the dappled grey, the ebony, and Zane, with his explosion of color. "These'll be your flight partners today. Flitter, Samaire. Moondark, Fitz. Zane, Immy and Bracchius."

I blinked at his use of our names, then relaxed. He must've memorized them real quick from the waivers we'd filled out.

"And Sparkles!" Bracchius held the plushie aloft.

Zane clopped forward and lowered his nose to Sparkles. "Nice to meet you, Sparkles."

I developed an instalike for the guy. Not everybody's kind to Bracchius—one of the reasons he moved in with me in the first place.

Bracchius cozied Sparkles up to Zane's muzzle. "You too! I . . . thought pegasi were too proud to let people ride them?"

Zane whickered. "You're not wrong for most of us. In fact, our little crew's been a target of pegasus terrorist attacks before—that's how affronted some of us are at the concept of any pegasus 'lowering itself to be used as a beast of burden.'" He twitched his wings in obvious air quotes.

"But *you* don't mind?" Bracchius whispered.

"Me? I love it! I see it like I'm a rollercoaster. Who doesn't want to make people ooh and ahh and scream in sheer delight and terror all at the same time?"

Flitter tossed their dark grey mane, charms tinkling. "Besides, if anyone gets too entitled, we can just lose them and feel much better about our day."

Safe to say all our eyes widened in horror, and Fitz even inched away from the pegasus.

"I'm joking!" Flitter pranced in place.

Zane whapped Flitter with a teal and purple wing. "Gotta work on your delivery, girl."

"Yeah, yeah."

The pegasi trotted into place beside little staircases, and Kai swapped out their saddles. Each of us mounted, and he helped clip our harnesses onto several attachment points around the saddle.

He tugged at one of my straps, testing the connection, but it held firm. "Good to go!"

I nodded gratefully as I zipped up my jacket the last two inches, nearly catching my neck in the zipper teeth. He hadn't been kidding about the wind chill up here, even with the blazing summer sun. Pretty soon I'd have to retract turtle-style into the jacket collar.

Samaire shimmied on her saddle. "The harness does make me feel a lot better about this."

Flitter flicked her tail. "Yeah, after we lost the first few tourists, OSHA really came down on our asses. Guess it's for the best."

"Cut it out!" I lurched as Zane butted Flitter. "Ignore her, she has the absolute *worst* sense of humor."

Bracchius perched behind me on the saddle, Sparkles squished between us.

With all of us strapped in, Kai stood in front of us, hands clasped. "All right, everyone, enjoy your tour of the skies! And don't worry, I'll be here at the end of your tour to help you get your land legs back."

"Ready or not, here we go!" Zane hollered.

"Or not?" I squeaked, holding on to the pommel for dear life.

Too late—Zane galloped toward the roofline, massive wings pumping, and flung us off the edge.

PEGASUS IN THE SKY, I CAN FLY TWICE AS HIGH

The buffeting wind and the plummet toward the street literally stole my breath, my chest tightening as I struggled to breathe.

Bracchius didn't have the same problem.

"WahOO!" His cheerful bellow gave me a mini heart attack, and I thanked Finéa I was so thoroughly strapped down to the saddle beneath me.

Zane's purple and teal wings snapped out to either side, and our sidewalk-pancake plunge did a hairpin turn—along with my stomach—as we shot back toward the cloudless blue sky.

"Having fun yet?" Zane called back, his deep voice clear despite the whistle of his wings.

"Absopositively!" Bracchius chirped. "Look, Sparkles, that's Fablefern Park! Maybe we can see some of your unicorn cousins!"

Teeth gritted, I chanced peering over. Maybe focusing on the far distance would make this a touch less terrifying?

The private unicorn park was a huge swath of greens, pinks, oranges, and reds—must be poppy season. Idyllic ponds dotted the fairy tale forest that covered half the park. Bracchius was gonna be disappointed, though—no way would we spot a unicorn from this high up, even if an overpolished horn caught the sunlight.

Just as I flexed my aching fingers around the saddle pommel—white-knuckling isn't the comfiest, shocker—Zane's wings stopped pumping. The flutter of panic in my chest eased, and I finally sucked down a deep breath.

We coasted above even Pegasus Point, the roofs of the skyscrapers at least a hundred feet below us, the sun warm on my skin, and the wind winding with us instead of against.

This was . . . actually pretty peaceful.

The whole city was laid out beneath us, the bustle at street level transformed into a tranquil stillness at a bajillion feet up. No honking horns, cursing pedestrians, buzz of neon lights, rumbling bass beat of the minotaur in the lowrider down the block.

"Whoa . . ." Bracchius mumbled. "I've never been this high before."

"Me neither."

"You're not shaking anymore. Is that a good thing?"

I croaked a laugh. "Yeah, that's a good thing. You still got Sparkles back there?"

"Of course! I'd never let Sparkles fall. Or you, Immy!"

"Please don't mention falling." I fought not to tighten into an anxious corkscrew again.

"Sorry." Bracchius wiggled at my back, and I craned around, trying to see what he was up to. A moment later, Sparkles's head popped up over my shoulder, her plush horn nearly going right up my nose. "You might be the *only* unicorn to go this high, Sparkles. Except on airplanes, obviously, but that doesn't count. Isn't it pretty?"

He was right. Sunshine sparkled off Ponderosa Lake and a smattering of windows across the cityscape, making Saskia Springs glitter even by day. Traffic snaked along the highways like leaves drifting along a lazy creek. The wind in my ears and through Zane's feathers was the only sound.

Until Samaire started belting out 'A Whole New World' in the distance, that is—melodious enough to rival the original singers.

I mean, she *is* part siren. What do you expect?

She came to the end of a stanza right as her pegasus steed, Flitter, flew past us, grumbling, "Really, woman? I'm not a damn magic carpet."

I didn't bother to stifle my laugh.

Samaire's fading strains reminded me, though—it wasn't just us up here. Where was Fitz, anyway? Hands tight on Zane's pommel, I peered around, trying to find him.

A delighted whoop clued me in—he was down amongst the skyscrapers, his black steed, Moondark, really leaning in to the whole rollercoaster vibe with sharp banking turns, corkscrews and loop the loops past the mirrored glass.

Damn, I'd never thought pegasi were *that* aerodynamic.

I squeezed Zane with my legs. "Can all pegasi do loop the loops?"

"Nah, just those of us with real talent." He gave his wings a hearty flap, the jostle like hitting a pothole on our graceful glide. "Wanna do one?"

"No!" I cleared my throat and eased off my death grip. "I mean, no thanks. I'm enjoying this just fine as it is. Peaceful. Calm. Nice view."

Give me a rollercoaster any day—something about being attached to a bunch of steel rails made the whirling and plummeting seem a lot more secure than riding a lone feathered horse frolicking through the skies.

My lower back got real toasty as Bracchius scooted closer. "This isn't *that* amazing. I could fly this high or even do loop the loops anytime I want, y'know. I'm just usually doing more important things. Like snuggling Sparkles."

I chuckled. "That *is* pretty important. You gotta admit, though, a pegasus has a couple legs up on you—they're a teensy bit more majestic."

"More majestic, eh?" Bracchius shifted with a nudge at my back, and suddenly my butt was cold.

"Bracchius??" I cracked my back trying to see behind me.

Zane whinnied a laugh. "Not bad, little demon."

I whipped forward again. A chubby black pegasus the size of a beagle was fluttering its wings beside Zane's head, a plushie unicorn clamped in its—his—mouth.

"Arnks! Hrrz aah ver mawdresskik?"

Oh boy. "Didn't catch that, buddy."

"Mmphle omnommin." Bracchius the pegasus twisted around and carefully spat Sparkles onto his back, between his wings. "I said, how's that for majestic?"

I tapped a mock thoughtful finger against my lip. "Hmm . . . It does definitely amp you up in the majesty department, but who's going to ride you? Kobolds and gremlins? I don't think they're the biggest fans of heights."

Bracchius's tiny wings approached hummingbird speed. "I could carry anybody! I'm *way* stronger than I look." He flapped right up beside me, wingtip tickling my thigh. "Hop on, I'll show you. Just don't sit on Sparkles!"

"Uh, thanks but no thanks. Maybe another time. Closer to the ground. Like, a foot off the ground. Inside a bouncy castle."

"Come on, really! I can do it!" Bracchius flicked his black tail and gave a cute little encouraging buck.

Which propelled Sparkles off his back in a tumbling, bell-tinkling arc toward the pavement below.

Very far below.

My hubcap-wide eyes as Sparkles tumbled to earth must've clued Bracchius in.

Or it could've been me pointing in horror and gasping, "Sparkles!"

Bracchius, in miniature chubby pegasus form, meeped à la Beaker the electroshocked Muppet, then took a nosedive after Sparkles.

My stomach leapt into my throat as Zane followed suit. Ever plunged toward the sidewalk face-first at mach speeds from a thousand feet up? No?

Let's just say my face looked like one of those dog versus blowdryer videos, and there might've been gibbering.

Scratch skydiving off the bucket list—check.

Zane's massive multicolor wings gusted us ahead of Bracchius, who was screeing, "*Sparklesparklesparkles!!*"

While my hindbrain was petrified, my rational brain did a little out-of-body musing: I obviously understood Bracchius booking it after

Sparkles, but why was our pegasus steed so gung ho? Worst-case, if no one caught Sparkles, we'd have to cram a little stuffing back inside her.

Well, and probably get the name of Kor's therapist for Bracchius, to cope with his shiny new PTSD. But still.

Zane didn't think Sparkles was real, did he? Nah. Maybe he was just really nice, or loved freaking out tourists.

I came back to reality as Zane passed Sparkles, only a hundred feet from the busy street below, and bellowed back to me, "Get ready!"

Get ready? For what?? Imminent death? Becoming one with the lemon yellow minivan toodling along beneath us? Making a feathery crater in the middle of downtown?

The universe was kind enough not to let me wonder any further— Zane's folded wings unfurled, and gravity plastered me to the saddle as he swooped parallel to the street.

Just in time for Sparkles to *piff* right into my open mouth, tail-first.

Ah. He'd meant for me to catch her. Too bad I'd lost every 'think fast' bottle toss anyone had ever lobbed at me.

Choke, cough, a panicked hand-slap to my face, and I just barely kept Sparkles from flitting away with the wind again, her squishy golden horn tenuously trapped between my pinkie and ring finger.

Then, of course, my friendly neighborhood demon barreled into my chest. "Sparkles! I can't believe you caught her, Immy!! You saved her life!"

Back in his regular orb form, Bracchius wedged between my legs and the pommel, Sparkles half enveloped within him like a unicorn being consumed by The Blob. Sweet nothings drifted up from the megahug.

"Safe and sound, I take it?" Zane called back.

My first attempt at a response was more like the croak of a dehydrated amphibifae. I cleared my throat and tried again. "All good!"

As we circled back up to the top of Pegasus Point, I studied Zane's wings. How had they not ripped out of the sockets with that last maneuver? What was he, the Arnold Schwarzenegger of winged beasties? Could pegasi even lift weights?

The utterly ridiculous image of a musclebound pegasus loaded up with barbell plates hit me.

Yup, time to bail on this train of thought.

"Immy?" Bracchius asked, like it wasn't the first time he had.

"Huh? Sorry."

"Sparkles wants to say thank you for saving her." Clearly reluctant to let go of her, he only raised her far enough to nuzzle my belly button with her horn.

"You're very welcome, Sparkles. But really you should thank Zane— he did all the hard work."

Bracchius scooted around in the tight space on the saddle, then poked Zane's neck with Sparkles's horn. "Thanks, Zane!"

"My pleasure. Couldn't let a beautiful lady unicorn like Sparkles come to any harm, now could I?"

"Did you hear that?" Bracchius whispered. "I think he has a crush on you, Sparkles."

I shook with a suppressed laugh, then winced. *Ow.* My muscles were sore from all the clenching in panic.

We flew another couple lazy spirals above Pegasus Point, then Zane swept in for a graceful landing.

I heaved a deep, shuddering sigh. Solid ground. Halle-freaking-lujah.

Not that it had all been bad. But next time I wanted to go skybound, I'd settle for something nice and peaceful, like a hot-air balloon.

Tethered to the ground.

Bracchius popped out of his hidey-hole and drifted away as Zane trotted toward the mounting steps. In no time at all, I had pried my fingers off the pommel—the seams permanently imprinted on my fingers—and was sliding off his back.

"Thanks for a, uh, exhilarating ride. Though I gotta say, I liked the peaceful part better." I patted him twice on the neck, his coat warm in the sun despite the constant wind.

Zane whinnied. "Not like your friend over there, eh?"

Fitz was just coming in for a landing on his own steed, Moondark, the widest possible grin on his face.

I huffed a laugh. "Not so much."

Zane folded his wings as I climbed down the steps, and one cockeyed purple feather caught my gaze. "Oh, you've got a wonky feather here. Should I smooth it?"

The pegasus craned his neck to look. "Nah, that one's a loosey. Would you mind grabbing it for me? I've got a nasty crick in the neck from sleeping funny last night, and that one's just far enough out of reach that I just *know* it would tweak it."

"Sure." I carefully tugged the feather from amongst the others and offered it to Zane.

"Keep it, golden girl. Nice souvenir for ya."

I smiled, twiddling it between my fingers. "Thanks." I'd have to add it to my collection of crow feathers.

Fitz dismounted beside me, his glasses somehow still on his face. "That was amazing! I—"

He slapped his pants pocket and pulled out his phone as Samaire's pegasus in the distance swung toward the roof as well.

"Work?" I guessed.

"Yeah. Perfect timing, really." He smiled at me, the exuberance of a moment ago replaced with a focused intensity. "Thank you for proposing this—I had a blast. You too?"

I chuckled. "Mostly."

He started shucking out of his harness and branded jacket. "Forgive me for the lack of ramen this time?"

"I mean, you paid a ridiculous amount of money to send me careening around the sky, so . . ."

"True." He adjusted his glasses with a smirk. "Thanks again, Immy. I'll text you, but I gotta run."

And he literally did, jogging across the roof and disappearing inside the glass walls.

"He leaving to hurl?" Samaire asked, as her pegasus, Flitter, trotted over.

"Work." I glanced around for Bracchius.

"Ah, a workaholic. Gotta watch out for those."

"Yeah, yeah." I swatted a playful hand at her as she passed.

There. Bracchius sat beside Sparkles on the roof, his dark form splooted a bit. I thought he was mumbling to the plushie again, but I frowned as I approached.

Those weren't mutters.

I raced forward and crouched in front of him. "Bracchius, what's the matter?"

"Immy . . ." A pained grunt escaped him. "I think changing shapes might've . . . made things worse."

COSMIC LULLABY

Ravens and revenants.

I hovered my hands around Bracchius, hesitant to touch him in case that made the pain worse.

It was still hours until our meeting with the sorceress, but we'd have to risk it—I'd rather be fighting off dastards all day than have some superpowered magical monstrosity explode Bracchius. "Get rid of it, now."

Bracchius shrank back. "But then we'll be too busy battling the bad guys to go to Comet with Aster!"

"You really think you're gonna have any fun at the club with whatever you've got going on in there?" I eyeballed his tummy sternly.

Bracchius moaned—because of the pain or the prospect of missing out on the club, I really wasn't sure.

A waft of sandalwood and vanilla wrapped around me as Samaire stopped beside us. "What's his problem? Demon gas?"

Bracchius sputtered. "You think demons are gross like humans? Nuh-uh!"

I stood up beside Samaire. "You remember that . . . shiny bobble I picked up the other day?"

"Ooh, yeah, the supersecret powerful one?" She glanced down at Bracchius, then up to me again, eyes widening. "Wait, it's—"

"Inside him, yeah. It was the only way to keep those jerks from tracking it."

"Demon as antidivination safety deposit box . . . Never would've thought of that." But then her brow creased. "It's hurting him?"

"It's acting up, like it did at the bar." Or worse, I thought to myself, hoping the universe wasn't taking its cue from me. "And he's too stubborn to hand it over like he promised, because he doesn't want to miss going to Comet."

I glowered at the blobby demon. "Not like we couldn't go any other day."

"But I promised Sparkles we would go today!" Bracchius wailed.

Samaire sank to her knees in front of him. "It's hurting you because it's leaking magic?"

He rolled with a whole-body nod. "But it's not *that* bad. If Kor could handle it, I can handle it!"

I closed my eyes in exasperation. This again. I thought *I* was stubborn.

Samaire tugged at my hand, drawing me to a crouch again. "We're thinking whatever's in there is alive, yeah?"

"Definitely." Nothing on that list of nova class beings had been anything but. The word 'being' being the operative word. I mentally rolled my eyes.

The English language, folks.

Samaire chewed at her lip. "I might be able to help. Let me try something."

"Please, anything to keep Sparkles from becoming an orphan." I eyed Bracchius, hoping that statement alone might be enough to get him to eject the doohickey.

Bracchius gasped. "But you agreed to be her darkmother! It's in my will and everything!"

Samaire rocked back. "Demons have *wills*? I thought you guys were immortal."

"It's a complicated subject," I muttered. Bracchius's flickers had gone more turbulent than I'd ever seen them, so I gave in. "And yes, Bracchius, of course I'll take care of Sparkles. Do your thing, Samaire."

Whatever it was.

"May I?" Samaire held both hands toward Bracchius, and he gave another nod. She gathered him into her lap, pressed against her stomach, and began to sing.

Whoa.

This song wasn't like her jazz croons, pop covers, or any other song I'd heard.

It was like the lullaby of the universe, soothing but primal, soft but endless. Overtones added an eerie, beautiful lilt to the wordless melody.

My whole being relaxed, her voice sinking deep into my bones, my soul sighing.

Good bet this was what'd happened to Rip van Winkle before he took that zillion-year snooze.

I ripped out a lip-cracking yawn.

Sirens weren't allowed to use the full effect of their powers without consent, and never in public. Sluggish, I glanced over my shoulder, but the pegasi, the other riders, and staff were far enough away to hopefully not be caught in Samaire's spell.

The last thing we needed was a pegasus going off the roof into Dreamland.

Just in case, I nudged Samaire and made a hand alligator, closing the mouth halfway. She lowered her voice, but kept singing.

I always wondered just how much power she'd inherited, given she was only part siren, but I'd never had a chance to find out before today.

Her lullaby had to be a 10 on the seismic scale.

Okay, yeah, I'm sure that's *not* how they measure levels of siren whammy, but your girl is pretty much drooling facedown on a roof. Gimme some slack.

Another yawn assaulted me.

Demons don't sleep, but Bracchius sure was doing a great imitation—his chubby orb form relaxed into more like a midnight Ditto.

I giggled, sleep-drunk. I had never thought of Bracchius as a Pokémon before, but I couldn't get rid of the mental image now—both amorphous blobs that could transform into pretty much whatever.

Bracchius probably wouldn't even mind being pink.

A shake of my shoulder had me blinking up at the blue sky, Samaire's smiling face swimming in and out of focus.

"Don't think the staff will love it if I let you stay snoozing. Come on." She offered a hand, and I groggily got to my feet, reorienting myself from the weird-ass dream of lunar cows I'd been enjoying.

Right, we were at Pegasus Point. And Bracchius—

Bracchius!

I whipped around, but he was floating to my left, no longer Dittoed, but definitely more relaxed than usual.

I lurched over. "Did it work? Or are you still hurting?"

"Samaire defeated the tummy monster!" he crowed.

She shook her head, smirking. "More like Samaire gave the tummy monster some magical Valium. But that won't keep it quiet forever."

I sighed in relief. "We only need to make it to 7 o'clock." Panic hit me. How long had I been asleep? Had we missed our meeting with the sorceress? "What time is it?!" I scrabbled for my phone.

"About 1:15." Samaire showed me her watch.

Phew. But also, bummer. I'd kind of hoped we'd slept till 6:30 and this was almost over.

At least Bracchius could fulfill his promise to Sparkles this way, about going to the club.

I smiled. And if I didn't have to worry about Bracchius blowing up, *I* could enjoy myself too. "You're really sure you're okay?"

Bracchius zipped over. "Really really. Let's go to Comet!" He jiggled Sparkles in excitement, her fairy bells making a racket.

"All right, all right. But first we've gotta go home to change."

"Me too." Samaire opened the door into the building, and held it while Bracchius drifted through.

We dropped off our gear, and took the elevator back down. At the front doors, Samaire leaned in for a cheek kiss. "I'm grabbing Nadine too. I can't wait for you to meet her." She grinned, a slight blush warming her cheeks.

"Ooh, look at you, all smitten!" I squeezed her hand. "See you there?"

"Definitely."

Bracchius and I engaged in some more yawning on the subway ride home. Well, I did the yawning, but he was pretty blissed out. We were gonna need some kind of pick-me-up if we were gonna survive the club.

Granted, Aster's personality alone might do it. The little vamp was like cotton candy on steroids.

A package sat on the stoop at home. Bracchius drifted ahead of my lackadaisical trudge and peered at it. "It's for you, Immy!" He floated it back over to me.

I groaned. If it was another body part from Cynna, I was calling it quits on this week.

Then I saw the sender—Sequinrama—and I perked up.

"Actually, Bracchius . . ." I dug into the overkill packaging tape, immediately breaking an already-short fingernail. Scissors it is.

"Yeah? What?"

Smiling, I tucked the box under my arm and unlocked the door. "It's for *you*."

"For me??" Bracchius bumped my elbow as he followed me inside our apartment. "What is it?"

"Guess you'll have to find out." I grabbed scissors from my junk drawer and went to town on the package.

"You don't know what it is?" He hovered dangerously close to scissor-range. Not that you could exactly cut a demon to ribbons.

"Oh, I know. But I'm not gonna spoil the surprise." I wrenched the top open, popping the last bit of packaging tape, and passed Bracchius the box, swapping it for Sparkles.

He glommed into the box face-first, the rest of him muffin-topping out of the cardboard. "Ooh!"

Demon darksight for the win.

He pulled back, but the box went with him, stuck. I held one flap long enough for him to tug back out—complete with the pastel rainbow sequin scarf I'd bought him.

Gripping one end, Bracchius flapped it, and the fabric unfurled, glittering in the dim light of the living room.

"Whoa . . ." He floated beneath it, staring up at the swath of sequins, and the scarf parachuted slowly down until it draped over his orb form.

I snickered. He looked like a ghost who just came back from a pride parade.

He twirled, the scarf twisting around him. "I love it!"

I shook the box. "You missed one."

"Whaa?" Bracchius zipped out from under the scarf, snagging it behind him with one nubby arm.

He peered inside the box, then pulled out the similarly besequined black scarf. "Immy, this is the best idea ever! Sparkles can wear the black one to match me, and I can wear the rainbow one to match her! Twinsies!"

I nodded and smiled. No harm in pretending that was the idea all along, right? "You wanna wear them to the club?"

There was no way I could convince him to leave Sparkles behind, so she might as well look the part. And if anyone thought she was a drug mulicorn, well . . . Hopefully Comet had drug-sniffing dragons instead of hepped-up stuffie-shredding security guys.

"Absolutely!" Bracchius snatched Sparkles back from me and wound the black scarf loosely around her neck. "Whaddya think?"

"She's one classy lady." I fluffed out her mane where the scarf had squashed it, then set her on the back of the couch.

"Me next!" He held the rainbow scarf out, then swiveled left and right. "Hmm . . . Where . . . How . . . ?"

Maybe I hadn't thought this through—a floating orb isn't exactly the easiest to style. Assuming he *didn't* want to go to the club as a kaleidoghost, that is.

"Lemme see." I took the scarf and stretched it between my hands, angling it as I considered Bracchius. "How about . . ."

I slung it around his bottom and knotted it at the top, then stepped back. "Nope, too Rosie the Riveter."

"Maybe around my tummy?" Bracchius tipped forward to demonstrate.

"Here, gimme." I unknotted the scarf, looped it around his equator as he straightened, and did a simple over-and-under tie.

He bobbed past me with catwalk attitude, the ends of the scarf swaying. "Better?"

I pursed my lips. It looked like he should be trying out for the genie in a local production of *Aladdin*. "Not yet."

"Aw, midnight." He drooped.

I shook my head, smiling. "You still trying to come up with a demonly replacement for 'Aw, man'?"

"Yeah . . ."

"You're getting warmer, but keep trying." I untucked the scarf from around him. "Stick out your arms."

He blooped out two nubbins from his orb form. "Now what?"

I flicked the multicolor scarf behind him and draped one end over each arm, like a shawl. "There. Academy Awards worthy."

"Really?" He spun, the shawl rippling but staying put.

"Yupperoo. Now, if you pull your arms back in, you'll lose the scarf, so be careful."

Bracchius rolled in a nod. "Okie." He collected Sparkles and hugged her close. "Let's go!"

"Hold your unicorns—I've gotta get dressed too."

"Oh, right. Well, hurry up!"

I stuck my tongue out at him, then headed for my room to change into the outfit I'd picked out with Aster: ripped jeans, neon necklace, 'Danger to Society' tee.

The doorbell rang just as I was tugging on my combat boots—all the better not to get your toes crushed by a hydra on the dance floor.

"Bracchius, can you get that?"

A high-pitched squeal from the living room had me tripping over myself, half-shoed, into the hall.

Whew. Just Aster hug-strangling Bracchius in delight.

The minuscule blonde released him, beaming. "I've never hugged a demon before! You're squishy!"

Bracchius pushed Sparkles toward her. "You've gotta hug Sparkles too. She gets jealous."

I finished tying my shoe as Sparkles took her turn being squished into submission.

"Immy!" Still clutching Sparkles, Aster thudded into me, hugging my legs just below my butt.

"Hiya, Aster. Ready to hit the club?" She looked it, all kitted up in her kindergarten-punk outfit.

"I've been ready for *days*!" She let go, then skipped out the open door. "Are we picking up your friend? Samaire?"

"She said she'd meet us there." I grabbed the essentials—ID, chapstick, cash, brass knuckles—and stuffed them in a clutch before locking the door.

Paolo waited at the curb in Damarion's sleek black car. Aster scooted into the back, and with Bracchius strapping in Sparkles in the middle of the bench seat, I climbed into the front with Paolo.

"Miss Immy." He nodded politely, his bottle-green suit the perfect complement to his russet fur.

"Thanks for the ride, Paolo."

"But of course."

I'd known Paolo for years, but had yet to figure out what magic he worked with traffic. Weekend traffic was no joke in Saskia Springs, and Comet was at the heart of downtown, miles away, yet we somehow peacefully coasted there in under ten minutes.

Talk about your major miracles.

We piled out of the car at the curb in front of a converted warehouse.

A line of hopeful clubgoers stretched from the front door around the block, but Aster tugged us the opposite direction, down a narrow alley to a service entrance with only a slot marring the blank steel door.

She reached for a buzzer two feet above her head with a little hop. "Drat."

"I've got it." I pushed the buzzer, to no effect. Was it busted? Nah, probably just keyed to nonhuman ears.

A few seconds later, metal scraped, and the slot slid open. Golden cat eyes peered through.

Aster stood on tiptoe. "Aster Baudelaire and guests, on the VIP list for two o'clock!"

The eyes gave a slow blink, and a gravelly voice rumbled, "What echoes when it speaks and when it seeks?"

"What?" Aster frowned. "Check the list—Aster Baudelaire."

Another blink over slit pupils. "Incorrect. What echoes when it speaks and when it seeks?"

I groaned. "What genius hired a sphinx to be the doorman?"

"Incorrect. What echoes when it speaks and when it seeks?"

Cheeks reddening, Aster opened her mouth, but I clapped a hand over it and dragged her and Bracchius a few feet from the door.

Once you engaged with a sphinx on duty, walking away was no longer an option—not one you survived, anyway. Leaving now to wait in line was a no go.

We had to go through that door.

And we only had *one* chance left to answer the riddle.

SPHINX'S RIDDLE

Crouched on the alley floor, I put a hushing finger to my lips and gave Aster a stern look before removing my hand from her mouth. She nodded, eyes wide, lips zipped. Bracchius bobbed beside us, quiet as he clutched Sparkles.

I grabbed my phone, opened a new note, and typed: Sphinx guarding the door. Anything we say = answer to its riddle. One chance left!!

Aster's mouth formed an *O*, and Bracchius reached out a stubby arm to cover Sparkles's mouth.

A puff of air escaped my lips as I fought down a laugh. The plushie unicorn was the person I was *least* worried about prompting a sphinx attack here.

I glanced over my shoulder. The sphinx's golden eyes still watched us from the door slit.

Thank Finéa that sphinxes were patient—as long as we didn't leave, and didn't speak, we could sit here forever trying to puzzle out the answer to its riddle.

Not that I wanted to starve to death in this alley any more than being eaten by a sphinx.

Quick, brutal death or slow, uncomfortable one?

I shook the thought off. We could solve this. It might take a few hours, but . . .

Oh. We *did* have a hard deadline: our appointment with the sorceress, to finally ditch the stupid whackadoodle causing Bracchius so much trouble. No way were we missing that. Samaire might not be around the next time the gizmo got frisky, and—

Samaire. I couldn't let her get tangled up in this same situation.

I closed out of the notes app and sent her a text: We're stuck with a sphinx. Go in the front at Comet, and we'll see you inside.

Hopefully.

Back in the notes app, I erased the text and started typing again: The riddle is—

Heh. Um, what was it again? Seek, speak, repeat, something?

I closed my eyes to concentrate. Echoes! The sphinx had definitely said something about echoes.

A tug at my phone slipped it out of my fingers, and I snapped my eyes open. Bracchius had taken it and was typing, the sequins on his shawl sparkling with his movement.

He handed my phone back, new words on the screen: What echoes when it speaks and when it seeks?

I sagged in relief and mouthed, "Thank you."

First things first, I copied the riddle and pasted it into Google in quotes. No exact matches.

I removed the quotes. Thirty-five million results popped up, and I started scrolling.

The first few pages of results were only marginally related to half the words in the riddle, and it got worse from there. I blew a curl out of my face in frustration.

For once, cheating wasn't gonna work for me.

The riddle back up on the screen, I set the phone on the asphalt between the three of us. We peered at it in silence.

Aster hovered a hand over the keyboard, then tapped out a few words with pauses to think. The screen dwarfed her tiny fingers as they flew over the keys.

Man, it must be *way* easier to type on these tiny keyboards with kindergartener hands.

She sat back, and I read the screen: 'Speak' could be metaphorical, like it could be anything that makes sound instead of something alive, but with 'seek' . . . I bet it *is* alive. Objects don't look for things.

I nodded. The kid—er, wise and ancient vamp—had a point.

Although, *magic* could seek, like tracking spells . . . but even if it made noise too, it wouldn't echo every time it went off.

And sphinxes didn't go in for sketchy riddles. Whatever the answer was, it was something that always echoed, without fail.

Echoing speech, and echoing seeking.

A fluorosprite flicked on in my brain. Could it—? It had to be.

I typed in my idea. Aster beamed, and Bracchius bobbed in silent excitement. If this wasn't the answer, I'd eat a manticore's left socks.

Scooping up my phone, I stood and marched toward the door.

The sphinx's slit-pupil eyes gave another lazy blink. "What echoes when it speaks and when it seeks?"

I took a deep breath, really hoping I wasn't about to become sphinx chow. "A camazo—"

"What—?" A man's voice cut across my answer, and the sphinx's eyes disappeared from the door slot. "Ah man, Toby, I leave you alone for one minute and you're already harassing customers?"

A pair of blue human eyes appeared in the slot. "Sorry about the sphinx, ma'am. Can I help you?"

Aster rose on tiptoe again. "Aster Baudelaire and guests, on the VIP list for two o'clock!"

I gave the guy my best smile. "I swear, we were on time before Toby started with the riddles."

He muttered a curse under his breath—something anatomically impossible, even for a sphinx. "Come on in, and my apologies again."

As Aster thanked him graciously, I shot off another text to Samaire: JK, sphinx averted. Skip the line and head to the alley door. VIP pass under Aster Baudelaire.

Clank, rattle, and the steel door swung open on a darkened hallway.

A beefy bouncer stood sheepishly beside the door, casting the occasional glare at Toby the sphinx pouting in the corner.

Just to be safe, I faced Toby and finished. "A camazotz."

Toby's slit pupils rounded out, and he smiled with the teeth of a predator. "Correct."

The bouncer rolled his eyes, but they landed on Aster. "Whoa, wait a minute. I'm gonna need some ID, little girl."

Aster's eyes narrowed.

I hurried to assure the guy before she decided he looked tasty on top of being annoying. "Believe me, she's at least a hundred years older than any of us." In a stage whisper, a la Bella Swan, I added, "Vampire."

Aster flashed her kitten-size fangs.

"Still gonna need some ID." He held out a whopper of a hand, palm up, then glanced between me and Bracchius. "From everyone."

Bracchius grumbled. "Really? Do I look like a freshly blazeborn demon?"

The demanding hand didn't budge.

I passed him my ID, and handed Aster's up. Bracchius slapped *two* IDs onto the man's palm—his own, and the one that had come with Sparkles courtesy of Build-A-Beastie.

"Uh . . ." The bouncer zeroed in on the very fake ID, and the plushie unicorn it belonged to. "I don't—"

I leaned in. "Look, we've got kind of a Calvin & Hobbes sitch going on here, understand? Just roll with it. Don't need to shatter any demon hearts today, right?" I glanced meaningfully toward Bracchius and Sparkles.

Bouncer Guy did *not* look convinced. "The toy's gotta stay here. Lemme check the rest of these."

"But Sparkles . . ." Bracchius sank toward the ground as the bouncer examined the rest of our IDs.

A fire lit in my chest at Bracchius's despondence. Getting a plushie unicorn into a club might be the silliest hill to die on, but *nobody* was ruining my demon's day today.

I squared off with the bouncer, lips firming. Come hells or wightwater, Sparkles was going clubbing.

I faced down the bouncer, equally ready to charm the socks off him or badger him so persistently he'd eventually give in.

"Immy, I . . . I can go home with Sparkles," Bracchius mumbled sadly. "I don't want to leave her here by herself."

"You—" My protest was cut off by an arm snaking past me, holding another couple IDs.

"Sorry we're late." Samaire gave the cards to the bouncer, and her voice took on a charismatic lilt. "It's okay, really. Let the demon keep his unicorn friend, please."

The bouncer smiled dazedly. "Of course, sweetheart. Anything else I can do for you, just let me know." He passed back our IDs.

Bracchius became a limpet at Samaire's side as the bouncer waved us down the hall toward the bass beat thudding in the distance. "You're Sparkles's hero! . . . Heroine?" Bracchius shook himself. "Whatever. Thank you!"

Aster beamed. "That was *so* cool."

I elbowed Samaire. "That was *so* illegal."

"You're one to talk." She smirked. "Here, hold on a second." She slowed, and the rest of us turned back. "Introductions while we can still hear each other?"

Oh, right. I was notorious for forgetting who knew whom.

"Aster, this is my friend Samaire." I waved between the siren and the mini vamp. "Samaire, this is Aster."

Samaire smiled down at her. "I love your outfit."

"I love your voice!" Aster clasped her tiny hands. "Have you ever done blood chants?"

"Uh . . ." Samaire's gaze flicked to me, and I shrugged dubiously. "Nope."

"I am *totally* stealing you later. Ooh, sorry, but first—who's your friend?"

"This is Nadine." Samaire drew her hand forward, and a woman stepped out of the shadows.

How had I not noticed her before? I wasn't usually *this* oblivious.

She was taller than Samaire, her wavy red-brown hair braided back on one side in a faux undercut. She was pretty, but in a disconcerting way. She wouldn't turn heads walking across a room—you might not notice her at all—but once you looked, she had a quiet allure, something indefinable that drew you in.

Literally—Bracchius drifted toward her, and Aster swayed forward.

I'd have to pick her brain later about her quirk, if Samaire didn't hog her the whole time.

I leaned in to my friend. "She *is* cute."

"Told you so." Samaire pointed to each of us. "Nadine, I'm sure you caught this is Aster. Then we have Bracchius and his friend Sparkles, and Immy."

Nadine blinked rapidly and gave me the once-over. Weird. She recognized my name, which made sense since Samaire had probably mentioned me . . . But then why did Nadine seem surprised?

Had we met before? I didn't recognize her. And it wasn't like I was famous—or even infamous, really.

Outside my little circle, anyway.

She recovered quickly, but still threw me the occasional glance as Bracchius had her shake hands—well, hand and hoof—with Sparkles.

Maybe she was staring at me for some other reason? "Do I have a big sriracha stain or something?" I craned around to check my outfit.

Aster orbited me. "All good."

"Thanks."

Nadine released Sparkles. "Lovely to meet you." Her warm voice was whisper-soft but not hushed. Some people just talk quietly, I guess.

I'm not one of them.

I kept an eye on Nadine as we approached the door at the end of the hall, with another bouncer station. Something was up with her, but hells if I knew what.

"Welcome to Comet." A short musclebound troll lady lounged behind a hostess podium. She kicked off the wall and pulled out several small black boxes. "Ready for your full VIP experience?"

"Are we ever?!" Bracchius bolted forward. "Me first!"

The woman inked a stamp on a neon pad, then surveyed Bracchius. "Hand or other appendage?"

Bracchius presented her with one arm nubbin, and she stamped it with the neon-orange comet. "Sparkles too!" He thrust Sparkles forward.

The lady gamely stamped one of Sparkles's hooves, then the rest of our hands. "These are for you. Please let me know if you have any questions before you begin your experience."

She passed us each a box. I opened mine. Inside lay a black velvet clutch, a dozen bendy glow sticks, and . . . several bottles of fabric paint?

I picked one up, looking it over. "What are these for?"

"Our Comet Colors are for play and creative expression within Comet. They are UV paints safe for skin, scale, feather, fur, and fabric. Use them to decorate yourselves, your friends, and your environment."

What a bland way to say we were just about to enter a giant paint party bonanza.

"Define 'safe.'" Samaire held up one of her paint bottles. "This's gotta be a gremlin to get out of hair and clothes, right? Especially blond hair?" She glanced between me and Aster.

My hand automatically went to my curls. Not that I was fussy about my hair—I'd dyed it all kinds of colors over the years—but I'd rather not come out of this wearing a rainbow clown wig.

"Sigils that will remove the paint are placed at each exit. Simply activate the sigil before you leave." The lady squirted a line of lime-green paint across her forearm and smeared it in.

I didn't noticed the huge sigil embedded in the rubber floor until she stepped within it. She stomped a boot on the closest line, powder blue magic sparking through the sole and racing along the design.

When the sigil closed, the green smear of paint disappeared from her skin.

"Nifty." I grinned. Paint war, here we come.

"I wanna try!" Bracchius extruded a third arm. He gripped Sparkles with one, and doused her in duochrome with the other two. He zipped over the sigil, sent a red beam of magic arcing down, and voilà: in an instant, Sparkles transformed from dripping green-and-purple nightmare fuel to her usual fluffy self.

Bracchius held up the two paint bottles. "I think I need refills."

The troll woman grumbled, but swapped out his bottles as I crammed all my paints and glow sticks into the velvety clutch provided.

Well, except one. I cracked a glow stick, breaking the seal between the dormant fluorosprites and the goo they feed on. It glimmered to life, a vibrant purple, and I looped it into a bracelet.

Aster was already decked out in her own glow sticks, and Samaire had looped a couple together to keep her and Nadine attached at the wrist.

Good idea. I snagged Sparkles and fashioned something similar to keep her attached to Bracchius—assuming he kept his arms about him like I'd suggested.

After all, the last thing we needed was Sparkles getting lost in the chaos of the club, and Bracchius burning half the place down trying to find her.

The troll bouncer stashed Bracchius's empty bottles inside the podium. "Other sigils are placed throughout the club for your entertainment. If at any point you need to leave, simply show your stamp upon your return today, and you'll be readmitted immediately. Enjoy your play!"

With that, she swung open the door behind her, and we stepped into the mayhem.

CHA-CHA SLIDE

The rumble through my shoes and the sheer wall of sound hit me first. That door must be magically soundproofed, because wow—them's some *major* bass beats.

Pretty sure that was 'Anti-Hero' hidden somewhere under all the techno whomps.

Second was the smell: the sweat of skin, the musk of fur, the bite of alcohol and the pungent drinks favored by other species.

The hallway had been dim, but my eyes still had to adjust to the darkness of the club, lit only by black lights and the scattered reflections from mirror golems roaming the girders above our heads like giant disco balls.

Glowing jolts of neon broke up the darkness: paint streaks, glow sticks, clothing and more made bright by the black light—which emanated from glass columns buzzing with black-light fluorosprites.

A kappa dude nearby had a lemon-lime UV-paint handprint across his face, like an Uruk-hai who got 'rave' and 'raid' mixed up. Every third scale on a seadragon shimmered blue—those not hidden by her cyberpunk Hello Kitty tank, also glowing.

The main floor teemed with humanoids, while raised platforms kept the microfae out of harm's way as they danced their little hearts out. Sunken mosh pits, on the other hand, let the big guys go nuts without trampling the rest of us.

Was that a Naga and a moose shifter having a dance-off?

Cool.

Above, in the rafters of the converted warehouse, flitted the winged clubgoers: fairies, harpies, dragons, griffins, gargoyles, and bird shifters diving and rolling to the beat. Even one rogue pegasus.

Maybe this was where the Pegasus Point employees came to blow off steam.

A bar to one side was packed with row upon row of bottles of alcohol, nectar, venom, blood, you name it. A leprechaun at one end sipped blue syrup from a shot glass, while a hydra nursed a pint of bubbling green acid.

No thanks.

The dance floor was surrounded by a couple dozen seating areas for all shapes and sizes, each raised a few steps off the ground—a good place to crash with your drink or snacks, kick off your heels.

Ten feet of clear floor created a buffer between the raised seating and the walls, a calmer place untouched by the frenzy of the dance floor. And maybe something else . . .

A glowing sigil marked out in smears of UV paint peeked above a couch to my left. There was no door nearby, so . . . "I bet that's one of the sigils the bouncer lady mentioned," I hollered over the music, pointing.

Aster hopped, facing the same way. "No fair, I can't see!"

Before I knew it, she was charging toward the wall on her bitty legs, disappearing between dancers two and three times her size.

I jogged after her.

Not that I didn't trust a vamp of *any* size to take care of herself, but I'd never forgive myself if she got trampled by a titan.

Bracchius and Samaire crowded my elbows as I caught up with Aster at the giant sigil, Nadine not far behind. The music was quieter here somehow, less overpowering. Probably some kind of ward set up for the lounge areas—only so long you can stand your innards vibrating with the beat, especially while you're eating.

Most of the sigil swirled way above Aster's head, but the base of the circle was only a foot off the ground. She tapped it with a finger, and sunshine-yellow magic infused the lines.

Bubbles spawned to life around us, pink and purple, as small as a cherry pit to the size of Aster's head.

I blew one out of my face as Aster started in on a gleeful popping frenzy. "Bubbles! This is awesome!"

"Wow, little girl's easily impressed."

I glanced over. A goth teenage girl perched on the edge of one of the raised lounge areas, kicking her heels against the wall below.

She rolled her eyes when she saw us looking. "This is only the *lamest* of all the sigils in here. I bet you can't even find the cool ones, loser."

Aster pouted, and my 'protect the cute cherubic vampire' instincts kicked in. "You're what, like, fifteen? Should you even be in here?"

"Right back atcha, loser mom. Your kid is what, like, five?" She mimicked my tone, swaying her head aggressively to punctuate each word.

"Definitely not my kid." It was my turn to roll my eyes.

Aster bared her fangs, only this time it was *not* a cutesy look. Her teeth gleamed in the black lights, and her red eyes glowed as she glared up at the teen.

"Oh sh—" The girl lost her balance and slipped off the ledge, then tried to book it.

Aster was faster. She popped up in front of the goth girl, still looking like the star of a horror flick.

Goth Girl flailed back. "Please don't hurt me! I'm sorry!"

Cue the third eye roll of the evening. It definitely brought Aster's intimidation factor down a notch—not that she'd had a ton to begin with.

"Hmm . . ." Aster tapped a finger to one fang. "I accept your apology. But only if you tell me what you meant about finding the cool sigils."

Goth Girl unfolded from her defensive hunch. "Oh. That? Really? Sure, kid." Aster's eyes flashed again. "I mean, um, sure, you. They have a few lame-o sigils around that anybody can find, but the really good sigils you have to go looking for. They hide 'em in all kinds of weird spots."

Bracchius chimed in. "Like a scavenger hunt?!"

"I guess. Anyway, can I go now?" Goth Girl's eyes flicked toward the closest escape, and Aster stepped out of her way. The teen vanished posthaste.

Aster whirled on Bracchius. "We've totally gotta find all the sigils! Wanna help?"

"Duh." Bracchius guided one of Sparkles's hooves to pop a bubble. "But let's pop all the bubbles first!"

I turned to give Samaire a knowing look, and laughed instead. She and Nadine had gotten busy with the UV paint, with smears and smooches across almost every inch of bare skin.

"Think you missed a spot." I waggled a finger at Samaire's hairline.

Nadine tilted her head toward me and murmured, "She's like a blank canvas."

"Not for long." Samaire grinned, then puckered her purple-painted lips.

She lunged, and I grabbed Bracchius and whipped him in front of me as a shield.

"Hey!" Bracchius swiveled, trying to see his new smudged purple badge of honor.

I let him go and scrounged up one of my paint bottles, and all-out war ensued. Suffice it to say, by the time we found another—totally obvious and not hidden—sigil, every last one of us was our own personal mural.

As we gulped down gasping breaths, Bracchius activated the sigil.

Annnd the floor dropped out from under us.

I'll admit, I screamed.

We dropped six feet into a foam pit beneath the floor. Bracchius landed in a gap between foam cubes, and vanished from sight along with Sparkles. Panicked adrenaline gave way to helpless giggles, then snorts and side-stitches.

It was a full five minutes before we recovered enough to find the stairs back up.

Aster and Bracchius found two more sigils before Samaire called for a break for food and drinks. One morphed the sound of the music around us for a few minutes, and the other instantly cocooned us in cotton candy.

Eating our way out just whet our appetites.

We claimed one of the empty lounges, and Samaire returned with a tray in short order.

"Comet Dust." Samaire passed everyone a drink. "No alcohol, but apparently a nice buzz anyway. Figured that was the easiest between all of us. And"—she set the tray on the low table between couches—"snacks for days . . ."

She wasn't kidding. Nuts, popcorn, fries, pretzels with dipping sauces, chips and queso, mac and cheese bites, candy like red Gushers . . .

Health food, basically.

Samaire pushed the little dish of Gushers toward Aster. "These are just for you."

Ah, *blood* Gushers. I left her to them, and ripped into a soft pretzel as everyone chowed down.

Bracchius and Aster were in the middle of a cheerful gripefest about Cynna when my gaze fastened on a voidling a few lounges over. *This* was more the type of place I expected to see our new-moon pals.

Not so much in the bright sunshine atop Pegasus Point.

The voidling was, shockingly, pretty much just a humanoid void on the sofa, indistinct around the edges like a heat mirage. It was enjoying some snacks of its own—little globules of light—and talking to a really old dude on the couch opposite.

A really tall wrinkly old dude who looked vaguely familiar.

I squinted. That wasn't . . . No, it couldn't be.

Could it?

I stood. "I'm gonna go get some more mustard. Be right back."

Nomming on another pretzel, I danced my way through the crush of the crowd, closer to the voidling's lounge area.

I was right—the old guy seated across from the voidling really was Damarion's nemesis.

Ambrose.

Dude was hitting all the clubs in the city, apparently. Not that he seemed to be enjoying himself—not eating, drinking, dancing, or even blood sucking.

Damarion had said the guy was no good. So what was he up to with a voidling?

I pressed close to the wall, but the music was way too loud to catch anything. At least on this side . . .

Cha-cha sliding through the crowd, I looped around to the walkway along the walls. The music quieted, and I slunk up to the same lounge, keeping my head down.

"—bargain. I would make it more than worth your time and effort."

That was Ambrose, the conniving creep. I slid to the floor, my back against the short wall, and listened.

"There's no good use for what you ask." The voidling's voice was deep, velvety. "No amount would make me feel comfortable giving that to you."

"I'll double it." A heavy thud and rattle made me twitch. Definitely not cash—maybe coins? I had a hard time imagining anyone would thunk down a bag of quarters to bribe someone, though.

Gold? Jewels?

What the hells was Ambrose asking for?

"You won't change my mind, or that of any voidling. Good moon."

Footsteps thumped toward me—toward the stairs to my left. Crud.

I scrabbled back into the shallow alcove between lounges just as the voidling's inky feet touched the floor. It stalked past, not glancing my way.

A moment later, Ambrose passed as well, but swift and silent—impressive for a towering octogenarian. I held my breath, motionless, waiting for the coast to clear.

It didn't.

Instead, Ambrose lunged forward and socked the voidling right on the chin. The voidling slumped, and Ambrose heaved it over his shoulder, glanced both ways—luckily neither of which were *my* way—and skulked toward the nearest exit.

TOE-TO-TOE WITH A FREAKY OLD VAMPIRE

I sat there in shock. Damarion had said Ambrose was sketchy, but to kidnap someone in the middle of a club . . .

Not that anyone had seen him do it but me.

Ambrose skirted the wall, head on a swivel, but he still didn't spot me in my alcove.

Nobody paid him any attention as he hit the push bar of an 'Employees Only' door and slipped through.

My stunned paralysis broke, and I shot to my feet, taking off after the dirtbag.

Was I the best person to go toe-to-toe with a freaky old vampire criminal?

Nada.

But if I raced back for any of my more-competent friends, he and his voidling victim would be long gone.

So, me it was.

Of course, I really should be calling the cops, but with the noise of the club, they wouldn't hear a word I hollered.

I hit the door just as it clicked shut, and I slammed it open. Beyond was a dim hallway giving on to bathrooms, storage, and a break room.

At the opposite end, another door eased closed, daylight visible through the narrowing gap.

I dashed down the hall and managed to sashay through the opening before the door shut.

Daylight blinded me after the darkness of the club, and I backed up to the building wall, blinking to try to speed up the process. Hopefully Ambrose wasn't about to clobber me with some magic—I'd never see it coming.

Just in case, I summoned a handful of my own magenta magic, cupped in the palm of my hand so it wouldn't be too obvious. It tickled my fingers as it sputtered and sparked, and I willed it to cooperate for once, to tighten into a tidy ball.

No such luck.

Now, out here, it was quiet enough to call the cops, but if I opened my mouth, Ambrose would spot me real quick.

Oh. Plastered against the wall, hoping not to be noticed, I suddenly felt incredibly stupid. I shifted my hand to my new white ink tattoo and let one spark ignite the lines of the sigil.

It wouldn't keep Ambrose from hearing me if I made a racket, and wouldn't hide me in broad daylight. But for the purposes of being sneaky while blinking around an alley, trying to spot where he'd gone, it was better than nothing.

My eyes finally adjusted as a scrape of gravel came from my right. I peered down the alley—this wasn't the one with the VIP entrance.

Ambrose lurked near the corner onto the main road, looking both ways as though contemplating darting into traffic.

He slunk back into the shadows as a pair of salamanders passed the end of the alley, happily chatting.

With a grunt, Ambrose lowered the unconscious voidling to the ground, then raised a phone to his ear.

"Where are you? I have to get out of sight before some helpful citizen notices me."

As he spoke, I crept along the alley wall, heel to toe, watching out for noisy litter and keeping to the shadows myself.

"Cops?" He glanced up and down the main street again. "Well, where did you park?"

He had a ride, who probably wasn't far away. If I was going to keep him from taking off with the voidling to who knows where, I had to do something ASAP.

I kept inching toward Ambrose as he spoke, only pausing when he listened to the person on the other end. When I came within range of where I trusted my aim, I tucked my hand behind my back and fed the blob of magic between my fingers, building it to a whopper of a magical charge.

Now or never.

I flung my hand forward as the crackle of magenta sparks grew too loud to ignore. My magic shot out as Ambrose glanced back.

He only had time to yelp, eyes widening, and drop his phone before my missile whammied him in the chest.

Thankfully—or not?—it didn't jellify him like it had the door in Kor's domain.

Not that I really cared what happened to a slimeball like Ambrose, but at least this way, I wouldn't be answering super awkward questions at a police station for the rest of the day.

My magic sucker punch did, however, knock him back, his head cracking against the brick.

He slumped, dazed. I rushed forward and slung the dead weight of the voidling's ice-cold arm over my shoulder.

For such a small person, its weight was *astronomical*.

I heaved, barely managing a half crouch as I supported the voidling's limp form, and stumbled back toward the club.

"You!" Something tugged at my curls and yanked me back. The voidling's weight overbalanced me, and we collapsed to the ground in a painful heap.

More of me landed on top of the voidling than vice versa, so not *all* of me was ground into the asphalt.

Ambrose hoisted the voidling over his shoulder again, saving me the trouble of extricating myself from our tangle. I slung another gob of magic at his ankles as I jumped to my feet, trying to ignore the sting of the asphalt burn on my forearms.

My magic hit, and his pants caught on freaking *fire*.

Ambrose dropped the voidling with another yelp before batting uselessly at the pink flames with both hands. I rushed forward and hooked my arms under the voidling's armpits and dragged it back down the alley as Ambrose wised up enough to do the stop, drop, and roll.

I actually made it to the club door—definitely scraping up the back of the voidling's legs something fierce—before Ambrose finally extinguished the flames.

I released the voidling with one hand to grapple for the door handle.

Oh. Slight flaw in my plan.

There *was* no door handle. Only a keypad beside the door.

As Ambrose hobbled toward me, I desperately punched in the no-brainer codes: 1234, 0000, 1212, 7777.

No go.

I jabbed random buttons at top speed, each set of four punctuated by an angry red light and the disapproving boop of rejection.

Giving up with a snarl, I summoned more magic to my fist and whirled.

I'd meant to fling the magic at Ambrose, who had to be close . . . but he was even closer than I'd thought.

I walloped him right in the face with a crunch.

Yep. At least half that crunch was my poor fingers.

We both reeled back, Ambrose clutching his face, and me cursing over my fist.

I'd taken three weeks of kickboxing classes once, so I didn't punch like a newbie, but in the 'human fist meets vampire face' equation, I still lost out.

Lips pressed together against the pain, I entered more random combinations—with my *left* hand. One glance at Ambrose's face had me reassessing who had come out the winner, though.

Between his fingers, his skin looked like broken glass, jagged translucent shards over a bed of crimson—*not* what damaged vampire flesh usually looks like.

Had my magic done that? Yikes. I almost felt bad for the guy.

Random code-punching wasn't getting me anywhere, and my magic was clearly in destructo mode, so what the hells. The club could afford to replace the stupid thing, right?

At least there weren't any security cameras out here, for them to hunt me down to pay up.

Though I was almost wiped out on the magic front—What? Not like I get much practice, considering I don't usually want to turn my surroundings into slag—I mustered up enough pink juju to douse the door.

It splashed across the steel in a chaotic wave and dissipated, leaving behind . . .

A pristine steel door. Well, no worse than it started off, anyway.

Damn, must be quite the protective ward to brush off my disaster magic.

I spun at a groan behind me. Ambrose crouched a few feet away, nursing his creepy face. The voidling stirred at my feet, but it wouldn't be in good shape anytime soon.

Then a car turned in at the mouth of the alley with a flash of its headlights.

Help for me?

Not likely. No one even knew I was out here.

Time to solve that problem. I wasn't getting in this door, and I wasn't making it away on foot with the voidling—not with Ambrose so determined, and with his friend waiting with wheels at the end of the alley.

Ambrose looked like he might be recovering, so I kicked him in the gut, pulled out my phone, and called the five-O.

The emergency operator answered, but I spoke right over her soothing tones. "Yes, hi, I'm just outside Comet, the club, and there's a man trying to kidnap a voidling."

Ambrose hadn't noticed the car flashing its lights at the end of the alley, curled up in a moaning ball as he was. But it was only a matter of time before the driver got out.

I tucked the phone between my ear and shoulder, and gathered magic with my uninjured hand.

"An attempted kidnapping in progress at Comet," the operator repeated. "I'm letting the authorities know now. And who am I speaking to?"

I lobbed an—admittedly small—ball of magic at the sedan with my best pitcher's throw to hopefully deter the new arrival from budging their ass quite yet. I was close to running on vapors, and they probably had a full tank.

The longer I could keep them hunkered down in that car, the better.

"Immy, but that's not important." My magic burst across the driver's door with no visible effect. "You need to send someone right away to help. I'm not gonna be able to stop him on my own."

"On your— Immy, I need you to stay calm and not try to interfere in the kidnapping. The authorities are on their way, and there's no need for you to put yourself in harm's—"

"I am fine, and I *am* calm, thank you very much."

She must have taken that to mean I'd behave—fat chance—as she switched to more questions instead of scolding. "And what part of the club can I direct the authorities to?"

"It's an alley behind . . . or beside? . . . the club." I spun, trying to find some landmark that would give her a better idea, but no luck, and I was hopeless with directions. "One end is a dead end, and the other lets out on a busy street."

"Thank you, Immy. And do you have a description of the suspect?"

"A tall ugly old vampire named Ambrose. White. Minimal hair."

The culprit himself was finally getting back to his feet from my gut kick, glaring crimson daggers at me. Probably should have kick-stomped him a few times while he was down, but it's pretty much impossible to pummel a vampire into permanent submission.

"Wrinkly. Terrible taste in suits," I added, perfectly happy to tack on insult to injury.

"And how do you know this vampire?"

Ope. Still-soothing tone aside, that was my cue to hang up.

"Ah—stay back!" I half yelled into the phone, then gave it a couple of love taps against the door for dramatic effect before hanging up.

Probably shouldn't have given her my real name. Oh well. Not like I wouldn't be talking to the cops in thirty seconds anyway.

The voidling behind me had recovered enough to rise to his feet, slumped against the alley wall beyond the steel door. "Thank you," he rasped.

"Don't thank me yet." I nodded at Ambrose. "Still got the vampire and his getaway car between us and the exit."

Hopefully cops between the *vamp* and the exit any moment now.

The voidling glanced at the door into the club.

"Door's a no go, sorry. Tried that already."

The voidling slipped a couple more inches down the wall, then jerked. "Behind you!"

I whipped around, keeping my injured fist well away from any potential collisions. Ambrose was almost on top of me, fangs bared, and I backed the hell up.

No way was I getting drained—or turned—by this bozo.

Why was I the only one slinging magic here? Sure, vampires were pretty formidable in the fangs and fisticuffs department, but magic gave you a long-range attack, and he just kept closing with me. My magic was borked, and even *I* was using mine.

Was he still recharging from some major use earlier today? I couldn't think of any other reason he wouldn't be dishing it out as good as he got.

Fangs notwithstanding, he went for my neck with those long arms of his, and I almost tripped backpedaling as I gathered my last few crumbs of magic to my defense.

Whoosh.

I blinked in shock as a dark miasma shot past me and engulfed one of Ambrose's arms, clinging like napalm.

Okay, no, I've never seen napalm in real life, but go along with me, all right?

Ambrose bellowed, his arm falling limp to his side, but he kept right on coming. I shoved my last scraps of magic at his eyes, but he reared his head back. The pink sparks rammed into his nose instead.

Instant. Bloodbath.

I jumped back again, almost pulverizing the voidling between me and the wall. Who knew vampires had explosive nosebleeds? Majorly gross.

Sirens wailed in the near distance—finally. What's it take to get the cops to show up in under five minutes? I should've told them the mayor's purse got snatched or something.

Ambrose whirled toward the mouth of the alley just as the passenger door of the car opened and the driver crawled out headfirst.

Heh. I must've done some damage to the driver's door after all.

"Get over here!" Ambrose's voice was a bit gargly around the nosebleed.

Crud. It was hard enough playing keep-away with Ambrose alone, never mind with fresh blood—not that the new guy looked like a vampire.

He did look vaguely familiar . . .

Before I could place him, Ambrose was coming at me again. I summoned my magic, but it sputtered and choked, out of commission.

It'd take me at least an hour to get enough of it back to do any damage.

Half my body aching, I squared up to Ambrose, reluctantly ready to try to fend him off with just little ol' me. Three feet away, he dodged right and barreled past me.

Straight for the voidling.

Shoulda seen that one coming. I rounded on him, only to come nose to Nelly with another dark glob of the voidling's magic that'd missed Ambrose. I ducked, the chill mass skating across the top of my curls.

Close call.

Wham. A blow to my back knocked me forward, and my clumsy somersault across the asphalt was . . . not pretty. On a lot of counts.

Roadburned, stunned, and gasping for breath, I sprawled faceup on the alley floor as the sirens blared closer. As the driver of Ambrose's getaway car stomped up, another charge of magic ready at his palm in case I was feeling frisky.

I wasn't.

New Guy disappeared from sight, then lurched past with the voidling over one shoulder, and Ambrose leaning on his other side.

Groaning, I pushed myself painfully onto my elbows, then side, then knees. New Guy bundled Ambrose and the voidling into the car too far away.

I stumbled to my feet as the car backed up. I managed a jog as they swung out onto the street. I hit the sidewalk as they disappeared into traffic.

Standing at the curb, I searched the street for a cab, rideshare, motorcycle—heck, even a centaur I could commandeer.

A cop car pulled up, lights blinding, siren deafening.

That would do.

I waved my banged-up arms frantically after Ambrose's car, but the police officer, a barghast, just climbed out of the cruiser and approached, uselessly.

"They went that way! Just twenty seconds ago! A dark red sedan." Why hadn't I paid attention to the plates?

That at least gave the cop pause. He considered me from behind his mirrored blue sunglasses, then reached back to his radio and said something indecipherable. A second set of flashing lights down the street pulled a U-ey and headed in the right direction.

I spent the next ten minutes repeating myself a zillion times as more cops showed up, and cops' bosses, and a firetruck and ambulance and crime-scene techs, and . . . Woof.

"Immy!"

The voice was actually one I knew. I turned toward Aster gratefully. Maybe she could extricate me from this mess.

Only . . . she looked panicked, her red-brown eyes wide and her cherubic face drawn as she raced toward me on tiny legs.

"What? What is it?" I interrupted another cop halfway through his sentence, giving my full attention to Aster.

She latched on to my hand and tugged. "You've gotta come quick—it's Bracchius."

I ditched the milling cops without so much as a glance back.

OFF TO SEE THE SORCERESS

The cops in my wake weren't thrilled with my disappearing act.

"Miss—"

"Excuse me, we're not—"

I didn't stop.

Aster, definitely the smart one out of the two of us, had propped open the club door with a little trash can. She pushed me inside and plucked the can back up.

The dim employee hallway might as well have been a lightless cave once the door shut behind us. I froze, not wanting to face-plant into a wall—especially after all the pummeling I'd taken in my fight with Ambrose.

"Immy, what— Right, you have silly human eyes. This way!"

The healer with the paramedics had patched up my obvious injuries—road burn, cuts, blooming bruises—as the cops interviewed me. But, scintillating example of brilliance I am, I'd forgotten my beat-up hand.

Until Aster grabbed it, that is.

I hissed in a breath and yanked my hand back.

"Oh no!" She brushed against me in the dark. "Did I squeeze too tight? Sometimes it's hard to tell . . ."

"No, it's not you," I said through gritted teeth. "I hurt my hand punching Ambrose."

"Ambrose?" She whirled on me as my eyes adjusted. "Like, *Damarion's* Ambrose?"

"I'll tell you on the way. Where's Bracchius?"

She gingerly took my other hand and led me forward as I explained everything that had gone down. I had to yell most of it as we raced past dancing clubgoers.

"But what does he want with a voidling?" Aster shouted back.

I shrugged. "What does *anyone* want with a voidling?"

Like any species, they had their own powers, but aside from hibernating the majority of the month, voidlings weren't anything special.

"There!" Aster pointed at the door to a bathroom ahead. "We took Bracchius inside to try to help him . . ."

I shoulder-checked some faun as I fought toward the door. "Sorry!"

Aster piped behind me. "Our friend's in trouble."

I grabbed the handle with my good hand and yanked, but the door thudded within its frame. Push, not pull? I shoved into it, but it still didn't budge.

Three hammers of my fist and one frustrated kick for good measure later, I was assessing my magic reserves. It had been maybe twenty minutes since I ran dry—did I have enough to chaotify this door into submission?

I was just summoning the first pitiful spark when the lock clicked and the door swung open.

Nadine stood on the other side, asleep on her feet. She waved us inside with a languid hand. "Oh, good. You're here."

Eerie music echoed off the tile walls, swelling into a discordant chorus. Samaire sat on the grimy floor, Bracchius cradled in her lap, as she sang the same lullaby she had on Pegasus Point this morning.

Bracchius had gone all melted ice cream in her lap again, but crackles of frost crept over his black surface, and a hazy dark corona radiated off him.

"Samaire's been singing for fifteen minutes. But she doesn't think it's working this time," Nadine explained sluggishly as I struggled not to succumb to the soporific melody myself. "What's wrong with him, anyw—"

I stumbled forward and fell to my knees beside Samaire and Bracchius. My knee bumped something soft—Sparkles, flopped over by herself on the bathroom floor, discarded like trash.

My eyes flicked to Bracchius in horror. If he'd let her go, let her tumble across the floor amidst tampon wrappers and suspicious smears on the tile, then—

"Immy?" Bracchius shifted within Samaire's arms, and my heart started beating again.

"Hey." I lay a comforting hand on my little demon buddy, but almost jerked back. He was cold, colder than any demon should be.

A new fern frond of ice crackled across him. "I'm sorry, I accidentally woke it up with one of the club's cool sigils, and I don't think it wants to go back to sleep."

"It's okay." I swallowed, fighting back tears at the deepening chill beneath my fingers. I nestled Sparkles in beside him, my lids heavy. "You can stop, Samaire, thanks." The argument I was about to have with Bracchius would be easier if I wasn't half-unconscious.

Samaire sang a few more unknowable words before drifting into silence, looking defeated.

I shifted my hand from Bracchius to hers for a moment and squeezed tight. "Thank you for trying. But Bracchius is the only one who can fix this now."

"M-Me?"

"You." Despite my terror for his well-being, I put some iron into my voice and thrust out my hand. "It's officially time to cough it up."

He balked. "But then the bad guys might realize we gave them a fake!"

"I don't care."

"But they might come after it!"

"Still don't care."

"But—"

"Bracchius." I jiggled him with one insistent hand. "I care about YOU."

"And I care about you," he whispered, "and they might hurt you."

Aster piped up. "Not if *I* have anything to say about it."

"Or me." Though Samaire smiled, her eyes were troubled.

But Bracchius wasn't done being stubborn. "M-Maybe we can go home first, and then I can give it to Kor!"

"That'll take too long, and who knows if he's even home." I'd never thought I'd actually *wish* Kor were at my elbow.

Bracchius perked up slightly, the frost across his surface shifting and crackling. "I could teleport us there!"

"I don't want you teleporting with that thing inside you. Who knows what'll happen?" I ground my teeth in frustration. "Just. Give. It." I skewered him with my best death glare. "Before I start squishing my hands through you like Play-Doh, trying to find it."

A minuscule "meep!" squeaked out of Bracchius, and at *last*, he gave up the goods.

Nadine and Aster had gathered around, but jerked back when the artifact plopped out of Bracchius and clattered across the tile floor.

It had gotten a bit more lively since the last time I saw it. Its interlocking gold rings were in motion, orbiting the black core at its center. Ice rimed the rings just like Bracchius, and dark plumes lashed out like inverse sun flares.

"Whoa . . ." Astor took another step back.

"That's—" Eyes wide, Nadine went even further, plastering herself against the bathroom wall.

Probably not a bad idea.

I, on the other hand, ripped a handful of scratchy brown paper towels off the dispenser and scooped up the whirligig like a pile of dog poop.

Not really trusting the paper towels for long-term protection, I glanced around for a better container. Samaire offered my clutch, which I had abandoned in my quest for pretzel mustard—finding Ambrose and the voidling instead.

Eh. Better than nothing.

I rammed the wad into my probably doomed clutch and snapped the clasp shut.

Bracchius was already looking a million miles better: reforming into his pudgy orb, his red flickers revving back up and sloughing the half-melted ice off his surface.

He clutched Sparkles again as he groggily took to the air and bobbed toward me. "Now what?"

We could waste time trying to hunt down Kor, but then he'd just be in the same state Bracchius had been, and we really needed a long-term fix. It was only a few hours until we were supposed to meet Cynna's sorceress lady, so . . .

"We're gonna start spamming that sorceress's doorbell a little early."

"Sorceress?" Samaire asked.

I sighed. "Yeah, Cynna dug up this lady who should be powerful enough to put this thing in lockdown and keep it from being tracked. Plus enough of a do-gooder that she theoretically won't take advantage of it herself."

"*Cynna.*" Bracchius uttered it like a curse.

Aster flicked him a curious glance, but I got my question in before she could voice hers. "Do you mind if we borrow Paolo to drive us over there? I'll send him right back here so he's ready for you whenever you guys decide you're done with clubbing for the night."

Aster and Samaire traded looks, then both turned back to me, Samaire's gaze steely and Aster's chin jutting stubbornly.

"What? What's that look about?"

Samaire pursed her lips. "We're definitely going with you, Immy. Except . . ." She eyed Nadine uneasily and reached out a hand. "You can stay here if you want. Or we can drop you somewhere on the way?"

"I . . ." Nadine's eyes had hardly left my clutch, which now had its own dark corona and frost coating. I pinched it between two fingers and held it at arm's length. "Thanks, but . . . I think I'd better come with you."

Samaire's brow furrowed. "You sure? It really wouldn't be a problem to drop you off anywhere you want."

Nadine gummed her lips, then straightened. "I'm coming."

Huh. She sure looked like she wanted to get the hells out of Dodge, so why come along? She must be worried about Samaire cozying up to this disaster nugget.

I couldn't blame her.

The bathroom door thumped, then rattled beneath a pounding fist. "Come on, open up!" A chorus of giggles made it past the door and the bass beat outside. "We gotta, like, *go!*" More giggles.

I glanced down at Aster. "Can you call Paolo to meet us?"

She nodded and retrieved her phone from a pocket.

Unlocking the door, I put on my best 'just one of the girls' voice, hiding the clutch of doom behind my back. "Oh my gosh, so sorry! Little bit of a girl emergency!" I opened the door.

The four gals outside collapsed into another fit of giggles before one bolted past me and slammed a stall door behind her.

"Us too." The shortest girl laughed. "Thanks!"

The rest of them rushed past. My gang followed Aster toward the VIP door as I held my clutch like a revolting piece of garbage.

Thankfully, the overzealous sphinx was nowhere in sight—not that they're usually very territorial about people *leaving* their domain.

But you never know.

A new bouncer mumbled some polite parting comment as we left. Paolo waited in the black sedan at the end of the alley, engine—and hopefully AC—running.

We did an awkward dance at the curb, trying to figure out who should sit where. I was used to sitting in the back, but Samaire and Nadine wanted to stick together, obviously, and Aster insisted she was too short to ride shotgun.

I slipped into the passenger seat. "Flying Spaghetti Monster bless you, Paolo." After the press of the club, and my fight with Ambrose and police interviews under the hot summer sun, the blasting cool air was the cat's pajamas. "Mind if I borrow your glove box?"

"Please do, Miss Immy."

I popped the glove box open and crammed the clutch inside with the biggest user manual I've ever seen. My knee rammed it shut with minimal effort.

One layer of plastic might not give me much extra protection from the demigod getting antsy inside that thing, but I'd take anything I could get.

Fingers crossed it wouldn't bust the engine—or, perish the thought, my beloved AC.

Paolo shifted his hands on the steering wheel. "Where to, Miss Immy?"

"Uh . . ." I dug out my phone and opened my texts with Cynna. The address was in here somewhere . . .

Found it. I rattled off the address to Paolo, and the sedan purred away from the curb.

Where was this place, anyway? I pulled up the map. Morningstar Heights? At four o'clock on a Saturday, it was gonna take us at least half an hour to get over there.

Not like we were in a rush, though. Our official appointment wasn't until seven, and the wheels of Sorceress Lady's plane might not even be on the ground yet.

Probably would be good to *know* her name before we showed up on her front step . . . I scrolled further up Cynna's texts.

Elena Cordova. I repeated it a few times in my head to try to cement it.

Samaire sat in the middle of the backseat, with Nadine on her left, alternating between gazing out the window, and glancing nervously at the glove box. Aster sat at the other window, with Bracchius bobbing on her lap.

What *were* those two muttering?

"Cynna is the worst!" Aster flopped her head back against the seat. "Just be glad *you* haven't had to deal with her for cennnturies!"

"That sounds terrible!" Bracchius was aghast. "Would you believe—"

Smiling, I left them to their gripefest and focused on Paolo. "So, how's little Hela doing?"

Paolo had put up a good effort at being the silent professional driver when I first met him, but it hadn't taken long for him to crack beneath my onslaught of nosiness.

The world's tiniest smile tugged at the corner of his mouth. "We found cottage cheese in her shoes yesterday, but on the plus side, she's having a wonderful time in kindergarten."

I went on to bug him about his horror story podcast, his wife's bonsai collection, and even wrested out a promise to pass along her recipe for chow chow relish—I'd been a convert after one hot dog at the family barbecue.

Despite the stop-and-go traffic, we made it to Morningstar Heights before too long. We pulled up in front of a fancy one-story house set way back from the road, with a flagstone driveway and manicured garden leading up.

Now we just had to wait for Elena Cordova, sorceress extraordinaire, to show up—and hope our friendly neighborhood crew of thugs wouldn't beat her to it.

ABANDON SHIP—ER, SEDAN

"So . . . do we just wait in the car until she gets here?" Samaire glanced between Nadine, and Aster and Bracchius on her other side. Damarion's car was pretty roomy for a sedan, but cram four somebodies in the backseat, and it's still not gonna be the comfiest.

Her hand already on the door handle, Nadine muttered, "I don't love the idea of staying stuck in a car with a Dreyelian device about to go bust."

I whipped around in my seat. "You know what a Dreyelian device is?" Nobody in my circle, including the demons, had recognized the gadget . . .

"Well, of course, uh . . ."

Did I imagine that nervous flicker before the doe-eyed innocence?

Samaire laid a hand on Nadine's knee. "Nadine works for the Athinia Archive, verifying and acquiring artifacts."

Oh. Clearly, my—justified—paranoia from this week was spilling over a bit.

"That's so cool!" Aster bounced in her seat. "Maybe you could help me track down a watch I lost last century. I've never found another one like it!"

Nadine blinked down at the pint-sized vampire. "Sorry, you'll have to talk to Theodosius in Historical Lost & Appropriated Property."

It was my turn to blink. "That's a thing?"

Nadine nodded. "The Archive does try to keep it fairly quiet, though. They don't really want to be bogged down with requests to find every fountain pen, ring, or cravat pin misplaced over the last thousand years."

"I . . . Yeah." That job would be a little less *Indiana Jones, Artifact Hunter*, and a lot more *Poor Harassed Kevin* juggling three hundred peeved customers at an empty baggage claim.

Nadine shook herself. "Anyway." She opened the door and climbed out. "I'm getting out of the blast radius. I really recommend you do too."

Samaire clambered after her. Paolo looked dubiously at the glove box, hands tightening on the wheel.

I sighed. "Go on, Paolo. You know full well Damarion values you way above any car, and if it doesn't explode, no one's going to steal it in this neighborhood anyway."

Bracchius bobbed beside my headrest, hugging Sparkles. "*We'll* stay with you, Immy, if you're not getting out."

The click of the door behind me signaled Aster was booking it too. Loath as I was to leave the chill embrace of the AC, Nadine probably knew what she was talking about.

"Nah, let's beat it, buddy."

I hauled myself out of the low seat, and Bracchius followed in my wake.

We trailed up the long driveway after Nadine. I figured halfway up would be good, but she just kept truckin'. She finally nodded, satisfied, once she reached the flagstone steps up to the huge porch.

Paolo hit the key fob as I squinted at the car in the distance. The chirp announced the doors had successfully locked.

I tickled Bracchius with one finger. "Can you lob your fireballs that far, if the bad guys show up before Elena?"

"Hells yeah!"

Paolo blanched, and I patted his arm soothingly. "Make sure to aim for the gas tank, Bracchius."

With a gulp, Paolo resigned himself to the car's probable fate. "It's . . . The tank is on the opposite side, just behind the backseat."

"Got it!"

Silence descended upon us as we—or at least I—contemplated the firestorm we might be unleashing in a little while. That would be enough to fry whatever was in the whirligig, right? Nova-class being or not?

Nadine might know, but I was honestly a bit afraid to find out.

She spoke up, her voice just as quiet as ever, though she wasn't whispering. "Is it true, what you said earlier? That this Elena person can secure the Dreyelian device?"

"Yeah, why?" I ran my tongue over my teeth, trying to figure out Samaire's new flame. "Why would I lie about that?"

Everyone focused on Nadine, who shrugged. "It's valuable, yeah? Some people might wanna sell it, or use it themselves. No offense—I bump up against the black market a lot in my work."

Bracchius puffed up. "Immy's been *protecting* it from people like that! She's not—"

I tugged him back midtirade using one of Sparkles's dangling legs. "Chill, it's okay. She has a good point."

Bracchius deflated and settled on the step beside me.

Nadine wasn't done with her questions yet, though. "Someone's come after it? They can track it? Is that why you hid it inside the demon?"

"Yup. And why we're worried they're going to show up now. We palmed a fake off on them, but with the real deal out in the open, they'll probably realize."

Paolo shucked out of his suit jacket beside me. Must be getting hot, what with all his fur.

"And you trust this Elena person?" Nadine glanced behind us at the fancy near-mansion.

"Not yet. But the person who recommended her seems . . ." How to sum up Cynna in one word? Probably impossible. ". . . Reliable?"

My eyes flashed to Aster, who bobbed her head side to side. "She says lying is for simpletons, and she *does* seem to like you a lot."

"There you go." I beamed at Nadine like that was all the reassurance anyone could need.

Hey, it wasn't like I had much to work with.

Nadine didn't look sure whether to take us seriously. Samaire bumped shoulders with her. "It'll be fine, really. Immy's heart is in the right place."

She softened. "And . . . if 'they' show up before the sorceress does?"

I gave myself a fist bump, complete with exploding hands. "Kaboom."

Nadine's leg bounced against the flagstones. "Great."

Bracchius drifted toward my ear and whispered, "Does she mean that? Because it doesn't sound like she—"

I shook my head. "Nope."

"'Kay. Thought so."

I waved at Nadine. "You really *can* leave, you know. This isn't your problem."

A laugh burst out of her, startling in contrast to her quiet voice. "Right." She intertwined her fingers with Samaire's. "Like I'm gonna ditch Samaire. Besides, strength in numbers, yeah?"

"Yeah." Samaire smiled and kissed their joined hands, teasing a smile out of Nadine as well.

Nadine looked back over at me. "How did it become *your* problem?"

I stretched my legs out and leaned back on my elbows. "Poor impulse control."

Samaire sputtered a laugh, and Aster giggled.

I couldn't hold back a grin. Not really wanting to admit to my half-theft to a relative stranger, I hedged, "Seriously, though, I . . . kind of stumbled upon it. Didn't think it was a good idea to leave it lying around. Also didn't plan on keeping it long term, but the owner never called me back, so . . ."

"But we figured it out!" Bracchius chimed in. "Mostly. Except for what's inside."

I expected a 'You know who the owner is?' Instead, Nadine blurted, "Wait, you don't even know what's insi—"

Aster interrupted. "Look! Someone's coming."

I followed Aster's finger to the crest of the hill, where a dark SUV with tinted windows was creeping along—slower than someone familiar with the neighborhood would realistically be driving.

Maybe Elena had only recently moved here? Maybe she was low on gas? Ooh, texting—*please* let her be texting and driving.

Heat at my side had me glancing at Bracchius, his hellfireball at the ready. Aster's fangs were bared, and Samaire and Nadine had shot to their feet, hands clasped.

As the car rolled to a stop ten feet from ours, I gave my magic reserves a tentative nudge.

Not even enough to barbecue a hamster.

Caskets and *capricorns*.

IN SAFE HANDS

Not that I *would* barbecue a hamster. Just an expression, promise.

My heart in my throat, I stared at the car idling at the curb. The sorceress would've pulled into the driveway, right?

Then again, if this was the thugs, wouldn't they have started slinging magic already? Or rammed our car with theirs?

Bracchius was whispering, "Gas tank's on the other side, behind the seat. Onnn the other side, behind the seat. Riiight there . . ."

I thrust an arm in front of him, singeing a few hairs on his burgeoning fireball. "Don't toss it yet."

"I'm not! Just getting ready."

Paolo started mumbling a prayer under his breath.

The driver's door of the new car opened, and we held a collective breath.

It wasn't a concrete ogre who stepped out, or the guy who'd stolen my blood for their tracker, or any of the other thugs I'd seen.

It was a woman—and not one who looked like she'd gang up with our baddies. She closed the door behind her, giving our sedan a perplexed, then suspicious, once-over.

Our relieved chuckles must've been loud enough to carry, because her head snapped in our direction.

I'd been expecting some elegant lady in a white pantsuit, at least a little holier than thou. The woman stomping toward us was a short, wide Hispanic woman with curly hair in a braid down to the small of her back. Her outfit was super bohemian, but not the fashionista type.

No, hers said, 'I don't give a rat's ass what you think about me. I wear what I like.'

Gotta respect that attitude.

Wasn't gonna keep me from grilling her before we handed anything over, though.

Down to earth or not, she still didn't look thrilled about having a bunch of randos on her porch. She gave our car a wide berth and stalked up the driveway.

"Who are you? How did you get past my property wards?"

Wards? I frowned. We hadn't hit anything like—

"Sorry . . ." Bracchius shifted closer to my side. "I took them down so we could walk up here."

"Demons," the woman muttered, stopping in front of us. She carried a beaded purse and had a marker tucked behind her ear. "That doesn't tell me who you are, though. Trespassers don't usually fare well here."

"I'm Immy," I rushed to say. "We're supposed to meet you later, about our Dreyelian device, but things kind of snowballed, and . . ."

The severe look in her eyes eased. "Immy, yes. At seven. What do you mean by 'snowballed'?"

Bracchius seemed to have forgotten about the hellfire blazing at his side, so I elbowed him before answering the sorceress. "Put that away before you catch one of us on fire."

"Oops." The ball of flame compressed to a single flicker, then sparked out of existence.

I met the sorceress's eyes again. "Elena, right?" She nodded. "The dirtbags who are after this thing have a tracking spell or something on it, which was fine as long as my demon friend here had it hidden inside him, but it started acting up—"

"More like going *bonkers*!" Aster helpfully supplied.

"—and we took it out before it could hurt him anymore than it already did."

Bracchius rolled in a whole-body nod. "It wasn't super fun."

Elena's gaze roved between all six of us. "Going bonkers how? And where is it now?"

"The car, in—"

Bracchius talked over me. "The rings started spinning, and it was making all this ice and darkness glowing around it. I mean, not *glowing*, but . . . Anyway. And it gave me *such* a tummyache, and—"

Elena raised a hand, her eyes fluttering shut. "That's enough. It sounds like the power of this Calamandrian being Cynna mentioned is beyond the scope of the device containing it."

I half shrugged. "Safe bet."

"And do I understand correctly it's a *Nova*-class being?"

Bracchius and I nodded.

Her eyes narrowed. "What fool would want to . . . Never mind. Do you know what grade of device it is?"

Hey, something I actually knew for sure! Only thanks to my brand-new textbook at home, but still. "Grade Triple-X."

Her eyes narrowed further, into literal slits. "No, that can't be right. A Triple-X device wouldn't be failing to contain its inhabitant's powers like that. Do you . . . know much about Dreyelian devices?"

My shoulders sagged. "Only what I could dig up in a book."

Elena looked reassured. Maybe I *was* wrong. Or the book was wrong. If this wasn't the biggest, baddest type of Dreyelian device after all, that meant she could swap the being inside into a better prison, rather than trying to hide it away in her house while it was oozing out all kinds of weird magic.

That got me thinking, though . . . Should it even be imprisoned? Shouldn't we figure out what it is, and let it get back to living its überpowerful life in peace somewhere?

Somewhere *else*, that is.

Elena shook herself. "If these people are after it, probably not sensible to keep standing around out here, lollygagging about. Can someone show me where exactly the device is?"

"Me." I headed back down the driveway, the sorceress at my heels.

The softest grumble reached my ears. "So much for my nice, relaxing bath."

Oops. I guess my day wasn't the *only* one being ruined around here lately.

I slowed down to walk side by side with her. "So how do you know Cynna? Old friends?"

"Not exactly." She frowned. "Let's just say I dissuaded her from enacting horrifying violence on someone—who probably deserved it—in the eighties. And you?"

"Friend of a friend." I waved a dismissive hand.

So Elena probably had a conscience. Spiffy. Even decent people can get power-hungry, though . . .

"And what would you say you want from life? Any goals?"

"I *like* to be left in peace to just sit quietly in my house, drink tea, work through my record collection, and peruse my books." The look she leveled at me was irritated at best.

"So . . . no big ambitions for power? Subjugate the city? Rule the world?"

No, I really wasn't expecting an honest answer, but even a simple reaction can give a girl something to go on.

Elena sighed as we stopped beside the car. "In my experience, power just brings trouble. And I've really been enjoying a life free of trouble these last few years. It's . . . soothing."

The chirp of the car unlocking almost gave me a heart attack, but I waved gratefully back at Paolo. Hadn't thought about that.

It wasn't likely I'd find anyone better to offload this thing on—especially in the little time we had before the thug squad inevitably showed up—so I opened the passenger door.

I struggled with the catch on the glove box for a sec before prying it open with my good hand. Man, this thing really was jampacked.

Annnnd shimmering with dark energy.

I reached forward to wrestle my clutch out, but the sorceress gently took my hand and lowered it to my side.

"Let me. You've likely had too much exposure already."

I speared her with an alarmed glance. "What, like radiation? Is that thing gonna give me cancer?"

She seesawed one hand. "*Not* like radiation, and not cancer. But not good either."

"Fabulous."

And if she was worried about me, that meant Bracchius—

Nope, didn't want to think about it. Maybe Elena could give us both a thorough check-up once she had this thing tidied away.

She retrieved the marker from behind her ear, and I did a double take. It was a wet-erase marker, like the ones they used on overheads when I was in school.

They still made those? Pretty sure nobody was still using those janky lightbulb contraptions in schools anymore.

With a familiar pop, she uncapped the green marker and started scribbling on the back of her hand—a sigil.

I tried to memorize the design, but she finished it in three seconds flat, activated it with a spark of tangerine magic from her other hand, and then it was out of sight as she wriggled my clutch out of the maws of its bear trap.

Damn. A protection sigil she trusted against something as hairy as the nastiness coming off a demigod would be nice to get my grubby hands on.

Couldn't hurt to ask, right? "Any chance I could nab the design for that sigil from you?"

"Later." Once the clutch was free, she moved in slow motion, like she was shifting a bomb.

Woof. If she was taking it this seriously, I felt like a total noob for all the hijinks I'd gotten up to with it in the last week.

Should I really still have all my fingers and toes?

Maybe all the luck in my whole life had been compressed into these last few days. Not that it *really* seemed like that, looking back, but . . .

It was slow going rejoining everybody else at the top of the driveway. What better way to pass the time than pester her with more questions?

"Shouldn't we be finding out what's inside? And letting it go if it's safe?"

Elena gave me a flat stare. "Does it *seem* safe to you?"

"Well, uh, not exactly, no. But it could be a perfectly harmless, law-abiding citizen under normal circumstances, for all we know, and just using its powers to try to escape. You'd go full-out trying to get out of a cell too, wouldn't you?"

She nodded consideringly. "Fair enough."

"So? Whaddya say?"

Her sigh made it quite clear *I* was the self-same trouble she'd been blissfully free of the last few years. "Once I have it safely contained, I'll do my due diligence to determine what's locked inside and whether it should be freed."

"Sweet, thanks."

Samaire, Nadine, Aster, and Paolo made way as we approached the porch. Bracchius darted toward the front door. "Let me get that for you!"

"No, stop!" Elena's eyes went wide in panic, and I whirled, heart pounding.

Bracchius screeched to a halt at the top of the steps. "Uh . . . Okay?"

Elena blew out a relieved breath. "Not *all* my wards react well to demon prying. Or proximity."

"Oh." Bracchius's flickers churned faster as he drifted backwards down the steps. My pulse slowed with every foot he put between him and whatever danger he'd just avoided.

If Elena thought these wards were demonproof, I believed her. Sorceresses—and sorcerers, sorcerex—were like the PhDs and mechanical engineers of the magisphere: Most people just used their own magic and quirks, plus sigils. Sorceresses were the ones devising *new* magic, and new ways to use it.

It was probably one of them who invented Dreyelian devices in the first place.

With everyone else frozen, afraid to move and set off the wards, Elena glanced between my clutch in her hand and her front door.

"I . . . don't feel comfortable working any extra magic while I'm holding this device." She dragged her lower lip through her teeth. "Would you be willing, Immy?"

What, to take down her *wards*? I boggled.

Oh. No, the easier part of the equation.

I held out my unscathed hand, but instead of passing me the clutch, she uncapped her marker again and took a moment to write out the sigil on the back of my hand. I grinned.

Sigil acquired.

I was pretty much out of juice, but I at least had enough for this. I tapped one of the thick green lines with a morsel of my magic—of course, a morsel was the whole shebang—and the sigil lit up magenta.

A weird, cool pillowyness enveloped my hand, like I'd just plunged it into a bowl of the world's fluffiest whipped cream.

Cozy.

I nodded to Elena, and she settled my clutch on my open palm with utmost care. "Only for a moment," she assured me, then scurried up the steps.

On the top step, she mumbled something under her breath. Brilliant golden lines flared to life all along the porch: up columns, along railings and floorboards, framing the doors and windows, and even traversing midair.

Some alarming combo of wards and tripwires?

The glowing lines dimmed as she mumbled a few more words, but they didn't vanish until her key turned in the lock. "It's safe now. Please come inside."

I nodded everyone ahead of me, then traipsed up last with my icy clutch shrouded in darkness.

I paused on the fancy doormat. Closing the door probably reactivated all those intricate wards, and I really didn't want to get stuck in here if things went haywire. I stepped inside, but only leaned the door to, not letting it latch.

Better safe than sorry.

The room inside had tall, sweeping ceilings, sunlight spilling in the huge windows. The furniture was nice, classy, but also looked like it wouldn't be a literal pain in the ass to sit on.

"Immy, over here please." Elena crouched at the edge of a single smooth piece of pale grey stone inlaid in the hardwood floor, about four feet across.

Marker still in hand, she was sketching out the design of a much larger and more complex sigil. She pointed. "Place it at the center, please."

I toed off my shoes and pussyfooted over the lines she'd already drawn, the stone cool against my socked feet.

At the center, I snapped open my clutch and carefully upended it. The glitching gizmo rolled a little too far, and I nudged it back into place with the other end of my clutch before collecting all the random crap that spilled out with it.

Then I backed the hells out of there.

The rest of the gang was huddled by the empty fireplace on the other side of the room, and I joined them.

Paolo whispered, "Miss Immy, we can leave now, yes? Since the object in question is in safe hands?"

"You all can go." I shifted my weight. "I just wanna make absolutely sure this thing gets locked away for good."

Bracchius cuddled up to my elbow with Sparkles. "Me too. It's caused *way* too much trouble."

Paolo and Aster glanced at each other, and Samaire and Nadine as well.

I made a shooing motion with both hands. "Go on. Really, it's fine."

Out of the four, Paolo was the only one who moved toward the door. He stopped when he realized no one was following him.

Rounding on Aster, he propped furry hands on his suit-jacketed hips. "Master Damarion won't be happy if you get yourself blown up for no good reason, Miss Aster."

She rolled her red-brown eyes. "No one is getting blown up, Paolo. And it *would* be for a good reason—I don't like ditching my friends."

Paolo looked conflicted. Stay and possibly get blown up, or 'ditch' us and head to safety? Not like he had any obligation to stick around—especially with a wife and kid at home.

Aster softened. "But we really could use a getaway driver ready to floor it. Know anyone like that?"

Paolo smiled. "At your service, miss. The car will be standing by." He headed out, leaving the door leaned to just as he'd found it.

"That was nice of you." Samaire smiled down at Aster.

"And we really *could* use a getaway driver, just in case." I traded glances with Bracchius. Out of all of us, he and I knew best how persistent our personal gang of punks was.

If there was any way to speed this process along . . .

"Anything we can help with?" I called over to Elena, who was still scrawling out the massive sigil.

"Quiet would be nice."

Samaire snickered, giving me a knowing look. Quiet wasn't really in my wheelhouse.

I kept my mouth shut for a whole ten seconds. "Is a sigil really going to be enough to keep that thing from causing problems?"

Elena's lips tightened. "Long enough for me to design and construct a more powerful Dreyelian device, yes."

"Just let her get on with it." Nadine glared daggers at me. "This is delicate work."

The sorceress glanced at Nadine appreciatively, and I shut my trap.

Furious honking erupted outside. I shot up from my surly slouch against the mantle. "You think that's—"

"*Paolo.*" Aster dashed toward the closest window.

Crap. There was only one reason Paolo would be honking up a storm. I sprinted for the unlatched door.

Gotta close that thing gotta close that thing gotta—

Fingers outstretched, six inches from the handle, I got smacked to the side as the door burst inward.

NO SWORDS, BUT SORCERY

Being batted aside by the door was actually an *excellent* turn of events—considering the wave of black and purple magic that I effectively limboed under on my way to the floor.

Surprise, surprise. Mr. Minotaur towered above me as I lay sprawled on the sorceress's floor, my freshly banged-up elbows grumbling.

"How—?" The sorceress whirled, startled.

"YOU!" Bracchius rounded on the thugs filing in the door. "My fireballs weren't enough for you before, huh?! Geronimo!"

He flung one of said fireballs, and the intruders scattered—some in the door, some back outside. Fury in her eyes, Elena immediately followed up his attack with a gout of magic far more impressive than anything I've ever managed.

Maybe I could take a nap down here while the heavies battled it out.

Instead of tossing more magic, however, Elena returned to her incomplete sigil. The gizmo inside shifted on the stone as its rings orbited the dark core, more lashes of darkness flicking out.

Elena fingered a crystal pendant on a long chain as she put her marker back to the stone. Suddenly I was hearing her voice in my mind.

Nifty trick.

"I have to rework the sigil to include a physical barrier, and finish drawing it. I need you to hold these men off for five more minutes."

Who, little ol' me, all by myself? Against one, two, three . . . was that *nine* jerkwads clustered at the door?

Gulp.

Except, Samaire, Aster, and Nadine were getting back to their feet, facing off with the newcomers, and Bracchius was amping up his fireballs.

Elena's message hadn't been for *just* me, then. Phew.

Still babying my possibly broken hand, I clambered back to my feet. Without magic, I had to find other ways to make a menace of myself.

As I scanned the room for impromptu weapons and projectiles, the goon squad paired off. Two brutes each for Bracchius, Aster, Samaire, and me. Only one for the sorceress, who, truth be told, was looking pretty nonthreatening crawling around on hands and knees on the floor and paying none of us any mind.

Unfortunately, they were right on that front—she probably wouldn't be helping us out for the next few minutes as she rushed to rework and finish the sigil.

But . . . no assailants squared off with Nadine.

Did she just look like that little of a threat? If they were going to underestimate anyone, I would have thought it would be our fun-size vampire. No, Nadine looked no less threatening than Samaire—two midtwenties humanish gals in club outfits, no fangs or claws or creepy eyes. But why else—

A voice rose from behind the wall of muscle, the speaker out of sight. "*Attack them!* We're running out of time!"

Great, they had someone in charge. *Just* what we needed.

I snatched up an iron poker from a fancy stand beside the fireplace and raised it menacingly.

Thankfully, each bruiser fired up a ball of magic rather than charging forward for a physical brawl. They definitely had us beat on brawn, but when you're not sure who exactly you're up against—maybe a succubus who can ensnare with a touch, or a rotwraith who can disintegrate with the same—staying the heck away is the better part of valor.

Or however that saying goes.

Elena's back was turned to the burgeoning attack from her self-assigned thug—the concrete ogre. I feinted left, throwing my own bad guys off kilter, then sprinted toward him.

He had to be the same ogre I'd fended off with the face-eating plastic bag—better known as a drifter—although his mug looked fine now.

Mineral surgery? Or was he one of those ogres who could reform their body at will? Maybe he'd just found an elemental healer.

Hope he'd kept their number.

I swung my poker like I was Babe Ruth and his face was a home run.

Elena glanced back in alarm at the shower of gravel that pattered her shoulders, then returned to working on the sigil. I took a quick sec to scan the room.

My two toughs had been temporarily stymied by Bracchius, who was gleefully lobbing more fireballs and turning planks of the floor into booby traps.

Aster had just sunk her fangs into one dude's leg, and he was clearly headed to loopy, drunk-on-venom happy land.

Closest to me, Samaire shot a stream of gold magic, her aim not the best.

I stepped within stage-whisper range. "Can't you just put your lullaby whammy on all of them?"

She shook her head. "Not a good idea. Siren song doesn't affect every species, and we don't know what some of these guys are. Plus, it probably *would* affect Elena, especially if she doesn't know it's coming . . ."

". . . and if we warn her, then *everybody* will know." I nodded in chagrin. Too bad Elena was the only one with a telepathic amulet, or whatever that was around her neck.

My personal plug-uglies finally broke past Bracchius's volley and stomped my way, magic gathering threateningly at their fists.

I broke from Samaire and waved my poker menacingly, but they halted way out of stabbing range. Crud.

Gingerly switching the weapon to my injured hand, I summoned a wimpy spark of my own magic with my good hand—the one Elena had sigiled up.

A single attack I could probably dodge, but two? That was pushing it. But if I could focus this little pink fizzle into a precision strike, bullet style, then maybe I'd only have one dude to deal with.

Tongue between my teeth, I was just raising my hand when both goons unleashed their magic at once.

Leftie's green missile went wide as I jinked right. But the second attack was more like a slo-mo lightning bolt—and even if I managed to dodge, it would lance right into Elena.

In desperation, I flung out my sigiled hand between me and the incoming magic. If Elena trusted this sigil to ward off demigod magic, then hopefully it would deflect the much less intimidating salvo of an everyday scoundrel.

Failing that, maybe my little dribble of disaster magic would turn it into jelly beans or something.

The grey magic zapped into my palm with an electric jolt, all the hairs on my arm rising in a flash. Instantly, my hand was engulfed in a massive ball of magenta magic—all mine, and under my control.

My magic . . . had *eaten* his?

I grinned. I could get down with that.

Time to get into the fray with more than a poker. I unleashed my brand-new magic orb at Bad Guy #2, not sure *what* it would do, but sure it would do *something*.

So what if it turned him into French toast?

It wasn't like he was *my* buddy.

My magic hit, and the guy careened upward, arms pinwheeling.

No . . . he *fell* upward, face-first, plummeting up and up toward the sorceress's very high ceiling.

Crunch.

Ouch.

Wincing, I glanced away, only for my gaze to fall on Nadine slinking up behind Samaire.

My earlier concerns came crashing back. Nadine *still* didn't have her own pair of ruffians, and there was only one reason I could think of for that.

She was their inside woman.

And she was sneaking up on Samaire.

I booked it toward her, my remaining bodyguard giving chase along with the finally recovering concrete ogre. My sights on Nadine's knees, I wound up with my poker as she summoned a mass of copper magic at her fingertips, still lurking behind Samaire.

No way in Rokonor was that conniving bimbo taking out my friend on the sly.

I swung just as Nadine released her magic, which soared forward, *past* Samaire . . .

I blinked, faltering.

. . . and right into the gut of one of the dudes attacking Samaire.

What?

My ferocious swing had petered out into a confused fumble of the poker, allowing Nadine to skate out of knee-breaking range in the nick of time.

I caught a glance of her alarmed expression as I spun a 180, sweeping the poker back up and slamming the closest numbskull in the 'nads.

Squeak, topple, thud.

Not *exactly* where I'd been aiming, but if it did the trick . . .

"What was *that*?" Nadine hissed, eyes still wide. My bizarre behavior didn't keep her from lobbing another fistful of magic toward the first dude, sending him somersaulting backwards through the open door.

I slashed menacingly at the gravelly concrete ogre, forcing him back enough that I could answer Nadine. "We each got two brawlers ready to take us on—except *you*. And no offense, but you don't exactly look like a challenge to take out, so . . ."

Her jaw firmed as she ducked around to Samaire's other side and tossed another attack. "You thought I was *with* them?"

She went back-to-back with Samaire, who glanced over her shoulder for half a sec before continuing with her own magical barrage. Nadine met my eyes insistently, not blinking. "Look. Again."

"Yeah, yeah, I saw you attacking them. It's—" I stopped as I *did* actually look at her with more than just a passing glance.

My eyes kept wanting to slide off her, to focus on Samaire, or Bracchius, or the nearby thugs.

Nadine wasn't invisible, but she was . . . insignificant.

Not worth noticing.

Whoa.

I refocused on bashing baddies. "Your quirk?"

"Yeah. Comes in handy in situations like this."

I scoffed. Pretty sure *I* had the monopoly on situations like this. "And just how often do you—"

My brain screeched to a halt as the punks facing us shifted enough to reveal the commander guy behind them.

No. Freaking. *Way.*

LEADER OF THE HENCHDUDES

Ambrose's pants were no longer cinders from the knees down, but half his face still looked like broken glass. He stood in the doorway, speaking into a phone, not watching the fight.

I backed away from the others, swinging my poker wildly to deter any attacks as I lost myself in my cascading thoughts.

Ambrose?? *Ambrose* was behind this. *He* wanted the Dreyelian device. He'd been the one sending the thugs after me. And he'd wanted—and gotten—a voidling too.

Why would an ugly old vampire want some unknown demigod and a voidling?

What did Ambrose want?

My inner snarkologue erupted forth: a new face, hair plugs, Botox . . .

For once, it probably wasn't far off. Damarion had said Ambrose was bitter about not being turned when he was still young. The fangy geezer probably wanted to wind back the clock, but vampires were stuck with the face they had when they were bitten.

No caladrius rejuvenating treatments or unicorn serums had ever helped them out in the looks department. Even plastic surgery didn't tend to stick for vamps, with their bodies rejecting it as an injury and healing it right back to normal.

But how did a voidling and some trapped being of ice and darkness get you the Fountain of Youth?

A tug at my hand broke me from my thoughts. Aster peered up at me, licking blood from her pointy teeth. "C'mon, don't freeze up! The new guy's not that scary. I could take out most of these guys on my own, but you gotta handle at *least* that concrete guy for me. I hate going to the dentist."

I blinked down at her. "You . . . don't recognize him? That's Ambrose."

Aster's red-brown eyes flashed up to the older vamp in the doorway, her expression torn between shock and indignation. Then it settled into a smile. "You did *that* to his face earlier? You've *gotta* tell Damarion. It'll make his whole month!"

That sparked a memory. "Didn't Damarion say Ambrose was too smart to hire thugs this incompetent?"

Aster pursed her lips. "Maybe someone else hired all the talented guys in town, and he had to settle?"

"Man, I hope not." This was bad enough. If some other crook was beefing up their forces, it better be way on the other side of the city from me.

My latest victim finally recovered enough to prop himself up and think about leaving the floor. Before I could whack him with my poker again, Samaire darted over.

She whispered in his ear, her tone melodic and persuasive. "Your boss wants a twelve-layer salad. Go to the kitchen and make it for him, perfectly, before he decides you look tastier."

The chump bolted to attention and limped toward the hallway leading deeper into the house.

"Nice one!" I grinned.

Sirens couldn't *really* make you do something you didn't want to, like throw around friendly fire. But pleasing the boss?

Absopositively.

Only, I found *myself* heading toward the kitchen too.

"Not you." Samaire pulled me up short by my elbow, and the compulsion snapped. "Don't stand so close next time."

"Oops."

Ambrose pocketed his phone, taking in the room with building annoyance: The five of us, giving it all we were worth. His minions, a couple of whom were on the floor or in Aster's venom la-la land.

One of Bracchius's fireballs scorched past us, and a ne'er-do-well jerked up the next best thing to a freaking wok. He swung it toward the roiling ball of flame, which careened off . . .

Straight for Aster and me.

I snatched the little vampire under the arms and whirled her out of the way. My shoulder wasn't *quite* out of the danger zone—my shirtsleeve caught flame.

"Immy!" Across the room, Bracchius twitched in panic, and the flames snuffed instantly.

Left my shoulder a little roasty, but could be worse.

"Thanks, buddy!"

When I looked up, Ambrose's gaze was fixed on me. A smirk overtook the half of his face that wasn't aquarium gravel as he waved off one of my attackers.

Ambrose reached into a pocket and pulled out . . . a Dreyelian device.

I almost flashed a glance at the sigil Elena was drawing. If *that* device wasn't still lurking creepily at the center, she for sure would've said something.

Ambrose was holding our fake.

He chucked it at my feet contemptuously, shaking his head. "You really thought you could fool me with such an infantile trinket?"

"Seems like I did for a while, Grandpa."

Ambrose was *not* best pleased by the grandpa comment. He snarled, baring his fangs, and— Was that a chipped tooth? Had I chipped his fang with my inadvertent face punch outside the club?

Almost made my probably broken hand worth it.

I groaned at myself. *Why* hadn't I asked Elena if she could heal my hand while things were still bumping along peacefully? She probably had a whole arsenal of top-tier healing spells at her disposal.

Maybe once we knocked out these boneheads.

I tossed my short curls and scooped up the gizmo at my feet. It might only hold a little nubbin of Kor's substance, but if he and Bracchius were to be believed, it *was* a fully functioning Dreyelian device. Never know when you'll need one of those.

Besides, Kor probably wanted his kidney—or whatever was in here— back at some point.

I unfastened my necklace and slipped one of the neon cords through the rings of the orb, Ambrose watching my movements—which gave me an idea. As long as he was focused on *me*, he wasn't noticing Elena.

Or how close she was to completing the sigil.

I marched toward him, adopting the same expression I'd given Bracchius when I discovered he'd filled my showerhead with glitter as a 'special surprise.'

Just keep looking at me, dirtbag. We only need like a minute more . . .

Okay, I really had no idea how much time was left on our ticking clock, but a girl can hope.

I cupped my hand low at my side like I was secretly summoning magic, although my reserves were sucked dryer than a dune leech's last meal.

Ambrose retreated half a step, still not summoning any of his own magic either. He glanced around—for a weapon?

Nope. A minion.

"Stavros, get over here and deal with this—"

One of his henchdudes backed toward us, fielding a hellfireball from Bracchius. But Ambrose's questing eyes had landed on Elena, then the sigil, and finally, the real Dreyelian device pulsing with darkness at the center.

Oh well. I tried.

"Morons!" Ambrose stabbed a finger in Elena's direction. "Stop trifling with these amateurs and get my Calamandrian artifact!"

Every thug still left in the fight disengaged, dodging bursts of magic and flame and tiny vampire teeth, and rushed Elena. The five of us exchanged a panicked glance, then followed suit, trying to stay between the sorceress and the scoundrels.

A redcap was in the lead, on track to reach Elena before any of the rest of us. Bloodmist swirling at his fist, he raised his arm to strike.

Another shadowy tendril flicked out from the Dreyelian device, longer and thicker than those before. The tip extended past the incomplete sigil . . . and touched the redcap.

He didn't even have time to scream. One second, he was running. The next, his body sheared into desiccating strands stretched across the floor.

Everyone froze in horror for a second, even Elena, sweat beading her forehead.

Um . . . were Bracchius and I just *insanely* lucky that it hadn't pasta-machined us too?

Or was this thing on our side?

I recovered first—probably more used to terrifying and nonsensical things happening around me on a regular basis—and charged ahead.

A volley of attacks chased me: the bad guys trying to stop me, and my gang fighting back. Magic collided, and the resulting explosion blasted me the last few feet toward Elena.

Unfortunately the concrete ogre was along for the ride as well.

We both bowled right into Elena, toppling in a groaning heap of knees, elbows, and concrete a few feet from the sigil.

Ugh. I was going to be one *ginormous* bruise tomorrow.

Still looming by the door, Ambrose decided to get a head start on his villainous monologuing. "You really think your pathetic little group can put a stop to my plans?"

As I untangled myself, I tried to push Elena toward the sigil and Sidewalk Bod the opposite direction.

Let's just say that when you're made out of concrete, you're not that easy to budge.

Nadine ducked out from sneak-attacking in Samaire's shadow, and helped me wrestle the ogre away from Elena. Once I got myself between the concrete ogre and the sorceress, I waved Nadine back to the fighting.

Ambrose wasn't finished. "You're merely irksome gnats, made to be squa—"

Hoping Ambrose had been engulfed in hellfire or something, I glanced over to see what'd stopped his mouth flapping.

His face rigid with shock, he was staring at . . . Nadine.

ABOUT TO BITE IT

Ambrose's gaze fluttered side to side like all his Tetris blocks were toppling together into one perfect square. I wished I were in on the game.

Instead, I was ducking a heavy swing from a concrete arm sweeping toward my noggin.

Nadine stood frozen a moment, pinned by Ambrose's scowl.

He stepped toward her. "I was sure you'd been killed, with the artifact falling into the hands of this girl by chance. But entrusting something so valuable, so volatile to a bumbling girl like this? I really thought more highly of you, Nardi."

I gaped. It— *Nardi*— But—

There was so much to unpack there . . . But first things first: *bumbling girl??*

"I'll show *you* who's bumbling, jerkwad," I muttered.

So I didn't have my act all together. So what? I'd kept this gizmo out of his clutches this long—I could hold out a bit longer.

Assuming I didn't get clobbered by this ogre first.

The concrete ogre growled, like boulders careening down a mountain. "I've been waiting for this."

"Sorry to disappoint, but—" I jumped back from his vicious kick, but his booted foot still caught the edge of my shin.

Yow. Za.

Half collapsing, I stumbled to the side. Across the room, Nadine—Nardi?—recovered with a scowl of her own, and started raining magic on Ambrose with a vengeance.

He ducked out the open door with not a second to spare, the copper cascade pummeling the walls and windows to no effect.

Of course not. We were in a freaking *sorceress's* house. You could probably douse the place in gasoline and set a phoenix on it without so much as smudging the pristine white walls.

Glowing magic whipped toward my face, and I barely raised my sigiled hand in time to intercept the attack. Grey sparks arced off my palm, spraying back at the ogre, who dove out of the way.

His own magic shouldn't hurt him, but after the nonsense I'd been up to, he was probably right to play it safe.

I sized him up as he got back to his feet. I was the only thing between him and Elena, but my fireplace poker was lost in the melee somewhere, my magic was still guttering at best, and punching a concrete ogre in the, well, *anywhere* was a laughable idea.

All it would take was one of those gravelly arms crashing down on me to send me broken to the floor.

Ergo, my chances were even worse than usual.

I danced left and right, trying to keep him from committing to an attack quite yet, and searched the room for potential allies.

Nadine and Samaire were back-to-back, each facing off against a thug of their own and looking worn out.

Bracchius shielded Sparkles against a spray of acid from a half-form snake shifter.

Aster was pinned in the corner by two colossal dudes, a nasty gash across her cheek.

And Elena was furiously scribbling behind me.

Guess I was on my own.

The concrete ogre got tired of my lightfootedness and slammed forward with a dual attack—uppercut on the left, another slash of magic on the right.

I reeled back, but his mottled grey fist scraped across my cheek, stinging something fierce, and lodged in my hair with a sharp yank.

The magic, at least, sizzled past without touching me.

A half squeak, half growl left me as the ogre hauled me forward by my curls. Ow ow ow ow—

"Why. Won't. You. Stay. Down?" he rumbled.

Desperate to get out of his grip, I rammed both hands forward, fingers out, and jabbed straight for his eyes. I wasn't sure if his eyes would be made of concrete too, but safe to say *nobody* likes a finger in their eye regardless.

I clawed at his face, my injured hand smarting, and he released me with a grunt. A few ripped-out blonde curls scattered to the floor as he jerked his hand back.

My throbbing scalp didn't feel any better, but at least I could put a little distance between us.

I frantically searched the walls and furniture within reach, hoping for anything even remotely of the bad-guy-bashing persuasion.

Canvas prints and throw pillows weren't gonna cut it.

Focusing inward, I scraped deep for any fledgling flickers of magic that might've quivered to life in the last few minutes, but there wasn't enough to even latch on to.

I'd just have to keep dodging and weaving, and hope this guy didn't beat me to a pulp before Elena completed the sigil.

Ogre Dude lashed out with another hard kick, and I dropped like a puppet with its strings cut, his foot rustling my curls as it sailed overhead—one advantage of being so much shorter than the goon gang.

I thrust out and grabbed his ankle with my good hand, throwing him off-balance.

He made a valiant effort to stay upright with a couple awkward one-footed hops, but my heave as I stood sent him keeling over with a monstrous thud on the floor.

I took the split second to peer back at Elena's progress. Sweat-matted wisps of hair clung to her forehead as she furiously scribbled across the stone. The sigil sprawled out before her was more complex than any I'd ever seen—no wonder it was taking so long.

But it *did* look nearly complete.

Elena caught me staring and tried to blow a damp strand out of her face. "Almost there. Another minute at most."

On her last word, the artifact's dark corona pulsed. A shadowy flare swelled toward her, and she lifted her own sigiled hand.

Darkness embraced her fingers, but she didn't dissolve into freaky ribbons like the other guy had.

Phew—her protective sigil really *was* hot stuff.

Elena hissed and yanked her arm back as the darkness receded into the orb. She cradled her arm for a moment, a patch of skin just past her wrist crumbling into black dust.

Gremlins and graveyards.

The disintegration didn't spread, though, and with a clenched jaw, she snatched the marker back up and resumed drawing the sigil.

The concrete ogre, pushing back to his feet, had missed the show—all over in a matter of seconds. This time, he lobbed another magical attack before advancing, and it barreled into my shoulder before I could slip out of the way.

Pain burst across my shoulder like I'd been punched, and the force thrust me back. Arms pinwheeling, I teetered on the edge of Elena's sigil, not wanting to scuff the intricate marks by stomping across them—or fall back within range of the hellspawn lurking at the center.

I regained my balance just as the concrete ogre closed.

Movement over his pitted shoulder swayed my focus. An absolutely massive cannonball of swirling yellow torpedoed toward Bracchius, who was all in on a fight with the minotaur in front of him.

"Bracchius!" I hollered, but it was too late. The magic blasted into my demon buddy.

No—into *Sparkles*.

The sizzling yellow glob smacked right into the plushie unicorn and tore her out of Bracchius's grip, sending her tumbling across the room.

Was that a little fluffy white stuffing flying ceilingward?

Oh no.

The thug who'd flung the attack looked annoyed that he hadn't hit his target. Bracchius rounded on him, his red flickers blazing so violently that the pudgy demon didn't look black anymore, but like a crimson ball of rage.

His voice, less dorky than usual, boomed across the room. "How *dare* you attack Sparkles?!"

I got an amazing view of Bracchius's bombardment as I—thoroughly distracted—was bodily hurled aside by the concrete ogre.

Whoops.

The half of my body I landed on flared with the aching pain of smacking into the floor. But my eyes were still glued to Bracchius and the onslaught he was unleashing on the misguided thug.

Poor guy was engulfed in a howling vortex of glitter. I finally peeled my eyes away, scrambling to my feet.

The ogre was just six feet from Elena, whose gaze was flashing between him and her linework.

Two new punks had joined him, flanking him shoulder to shoulder— a desert troll and a hulking human.

Where had these guys come from? Maybe Ambrose had kept a couple guys outside with him.

I unleashed my best manic battle cry and launched myself into the closest thug. He stumbled back, dominoing into the other two.

I rode the doggy pile to the floor and rolled off the thugs on the other side. I still wasn't between them and Elena, so while they were down, I reached deep inside me, hoping against hope.

No magic greeted me.

I almost gave up, but it wasn't like my magic was *gone* gone, right? New magic would seep out from *somewhere* given enough time.

Maybe if I . . .

Raking anguish seared through me as I gouged deep into the dry well of my magic, scouring the merest dregs from somewhere I probably shouldn't be messing with.

I'm a stubborn witch, what can I say?

Magic glimmered at my fingertips, and I forced the teensy spark into the thinnest line possible. One sling of my hand, and the flickering pink thread flung toward the three thugs.

The desert troll ducked, the concrete ogre didn't, and the human flailed up a domed metal shield like the one I'd seen earlier.

My magic sank into the concrete ogre's chest. Fast-growing weeds burst from fresh cracks in the concrete and sprouted like . . . well . . .

Weeds.

But I didn't stare long, because the far end of the shimmering pink thread whipped across the surface of the last dude's weird shield, and caromed off at the opposite angle.

Lancing right into Elena's back before I could get out even half the word "Duck!"

Dark pink light flashed out from her like a firework, searing my eyes.

When I blinked my vision back into focus, Elena was gone.

Dread seized my gut.

Had I teleported Elena? Obliterated her? Erased her from existence like all those guys in *Doctor Who*?

I'd thought, surely, if anyone could fend off my stupid magic, it was her.

Guilt and horror gnawed at me. I'd killed our one freaking chance at—

Wait. I squinted. *Something* tiny sat in her place on the hardwood, pastel purple and maybe four inches across.

A glance at my pile of thugs eased my worry that they were about to pummel me. Their alarmed gazes were shifting between me and what remained of Elena.

So I risked scrambling over.

A shinnystar huddled on the floor, its five limbs protruding from its cute chubby form. A few pieces of Elena's jewelry lay scattered around it—enchanted items that had shrugged off my disaster magic. And her green marker too, somehow.

The star was Elena, all right.

One sizzling thread of my magenta magic had struck the vaunted Elena Cordova, high sorceress of the whatever, capable of fielding magic beyond comprehension and subduing whatever bonkers-class megafreak was lurking in the artifact.

And I'd turned her into the next best thing to a toad??

I hesitantly poked the shinnystar, and its short limbs twitched, retracting half an inch.

It was Elena, *and* she was alive.

Though about as far from human as you can get. I cringed.

Shinnystars are harmless little creatures that pepper the city, scooting along the vertical planes of skyscrapers, billboards, and even buses, with bitty suction cups on the underside of their limbs, a lot like sea stars.

Everybody loves them, since these guys *adore* slurping up all the grime that coats walls and windows over time—dirt, rust, splattered bugs, streaks of harpy poop.

Rumor had it they hadn't always been fun pastel colors, but once civilization declared them a protected species—purely for being such helpful buggers—most of their natural predators left them alone, and evolution steered them away from the dingy greys and browns they'd camouflaged themselves with before.

That said, they were still super vulnerable squishy little things.

I plucked up Elena the shinnystar, not willing to see her get trampled. But where would be safer?

I glanced down at my ripped jeans.

Screw the women's fashion industry and their useless tiny pockets—if I tried to shove her in one of mine, she'd become star jam in three seconds flat.

"Bracchius!" I yelled.

He spun toward me amidst the chaos, still more red than black.

"I need you to subsume something on the fly!"

Literally.

"Aye-aye, Imm—!" he started, but I'd already lobbed Elena the shinnystar, and he cut off as she smacked into him, suckers first.

Thank Finéa, she didn't bounce right off. Bracchius enfolded the chubby purple star within his darkness, and she disappeared from sight in an instant.

The hit squad still looked shell-shocked, but one bellow from Ambrose peeking in the door had them back on their feet. Even the concrete ogre, who'd combed his new chest full of weeds out of his face and seemed as rarin' to go as ever.

They all rushed me at once, and I cursed.

I raced right back at them, like I was just as much of a threat as they were. The concrete ogre stalled, the human raised his shield thing, and the desert troll whipped up a miniature sandstorm between his palms.

Fabulous.

At least only one was attacking.

The troll thrust forward, unleashing the swirling sand, and I squeezed my eyes shut. Sharp particles dashed across my face and arms, scraping my skin, and I spun to put my back against the torrent. Luckily, it only lasted a second.

I dashed the grains from my eyes and gave my curls a firm shake as I faced the three again.

They'd taken the moment I was blinded not to attack, but to put their heads together in a hushed conference.

Planning my demise?

Indubitably.

I grazed a cupped hand along the floor and scooped up a small heap of sand. One hurl scattered it right for their eyes.

I nailed the human guy, but the concrete ogre shielded his face. The desert troll took control of the grains pattering over his sepia skin.

His next sandstorm was a wee bit bigger than the first.

A howling brown vortex swallowed me, and it was all I could do to keep breathing. Hands over my nose and mouth, one ear tucked against my shoulder, every inch of me was pummeled by the stinging sand.

It scoured my skin, burrowed into my clothes, clogged my unprotected ear, and scratched at my eyes.

I tried not to sink into despair as I huddled within the whirlwind, but it was tough. I was trapped in a maelstrom, enemies just waiting for their chance at me.

Elena wasn't here to finish the sigil, and it wasn't like any of us knew the design, since she'd come up with it on the fly.

The demigod whatsit was getting stronger by the minute.

And—

A fist met my side with a solid thud. I yelped, my hands dropping from my face and the sand worming its way into my nose and mouth.

I erupted into violent coughs and sneezes as my body tried to evict the sand. A powerful kick slammed into my hip with a burst of agony.

On the plus side, the blow knocked me out of the column of raging sand.

On the downside, once I clawed the grit from my eyes, I had a front-row seat to exactly how hopeless our situation was.

Aster was nowhere to be seen, and my heart plummeted at the little vampire's chances.

Nadine glared down at her open hand and shook it, like she was trying to summon magic but had run dry.

The faint strains of Samaire's latest song cut off with a cry as sparks exploded across her torso with devastating force. She sailed backwards and crunched against the wall, her head lolling.

Bracchius hovered despondently over Sparkles, his smoldering red inferno faded to a hopeless blue.

I could try calling someone—Damarion? Cynna?—for help, but who could even get here in time? I slapped my back pocket, but my phone was gone anyway—lost somewhere in the fight.

The sandstorm dissipated, revealing my attackers only feet away with triumphant smiles, their gazes fixed . . . at my feet?

My eyes flicked down with my worry of an unseen attacker. But they weren't smiling about one of their buddies tying my shoelaces together.

I was standing just beyond the verge of Elena's sigil. And the doohickey's dark corona had swelled to a full two feet in diameter.

I looked up right as the concrete ogre lunged to sock me again, clearly hoping to drive me deeper into the danger zone.

Not ready to take up macramé with my maker quite yet, I leapt forward within the swing of the ogre's furious punch and clung to the verdant patch of weeds on his chest.

Both handfuls tore right out of him, dumping me on my ass on the much-too-solid floor.

My tailbone joined the rest of my body in wailing in outrage.

"Shut up," I growled.

Sadly, *none* of my aches and pains listened.

At least I hadn't dropped right on the globe of deathiness.

Yowling, the concrete ogre was doubled over in front of me, clutching his chest.

Huh. Those weeds must've been rooted in nerve bundles or something.

The preposterousness of nerves inside concrete threw me for a second, but not enough to keep me from lashing out with a kick to his knee. He toppled with a harsh cry and a *wham* that shook the floorboards beneath me.

My do-si-doeing burst of satisfaction was cut short by a firm grip around my ankle as I pulled my leg back. The human thug glowered down at me and hefted.

"Hey, we're both humans, how about we—"

He didn't wait to hear my offer, hurling me toward my doom at the center of the sigil.

Y'know all those old yarns about time slowing down and life flashing before your eyes and all that nonsense? I always thought that was sentimental tripe, until I was five feet off the ground, lurching through the air toward that lovely little ball of evil.

No, the Hallmark Channel of my life didn't start streaming across my eyelids, and no god of time made a convenient appearance to get me out of my jam.

But things *did* become just molasses enough for my mind to do a little racing.

This was it. The end.

If I bit it here—and that seemed like a guarantee—these scumbags would get their demigod, wipe out my friends, and probably level the city.

Or at least give Ambrose exactly what he wanted.

And I wasn't even a *teensy* bit cool with that.

But what other option was there?

As I flailed through the air, one of my desperate clawing hands swam into view. The one with the sigil scrawled across the back in green marker.

The lines were growing a little hazy with the sweat rolling off my body, but it was still whole.

And *maybe* still working.

I was one hundred percent headed for the great sushi bar in the sky. Unless . . .

THE TRAMBLE TERROR

Mentally chanting 'Please don't zap me' on a loop, I aimed my hand for the undulating black globe I was about to face-plant in. My fingers disappeared within the inky shroud and gnarled between the cold rings deep inside.

Tucking my head the instant before my shoulder slammed into the floor, I focused on keeping the gizmo of destruction as far from the rest of me as I could.

I *didn't* let go, though.

My breath exploded out of me as I flopped forward onto my back in a heaving mess.

I gasped, but my lungs were taking a sick day. Strangled rasps escaped me as the scuzzball squad broke out into whispers somewhere behind me.

"Is she—"

"Don't think so. Look."

"Why isn't her arm—"

"Keep back!"

I sucked down air with my best banshee croak as my lungs finally got with the groove again.

The whispers morphed to curses.

I'd staved off the Reaper for now, but I doubted he'd larked away quite yet. One dedicated blow from any of these chumps, and I'd be outta here.

There was only one thing I could do.

One thing I've never *wanted* to do.

My ace in the terrifying, this-is-really-a-lousy-idea hole.

And it might not even work if I couldn't scrape up one more particle of magic somehow.

But before I could try, I needed the bad guys to hang back for another second. *That* would be the easy part.

The Dreyelian device still clutched in my hopefully-not-disintegrating fingers, I brandished the darkness-seeping doodad at the looming trio.

It would be too much to ask that it lash out with one of its random strikes right now when I could use it, but they staggered back anyway. Its murky corona was plenty threatening all on its own.

While they were busy evading my wild swings, I reached back into my core. Instant raw pain assaulted me.

That had never happened before.

Not a good sign. I'd definitely damaged something with my desperate gouging earlier, but this was my only chance.

I clawed my way past the pain, still feeling it but too determined to let it stop me. I just needed *one* more itty-bitty speck of magic to answer my summons.

My wellspring ached, empty and hollow. But I wasn't taking no for an answer. I mentally punched at it, tore at it, anything to get it to give up just one final drop.

Okay, I know I said that the last time. But seriously, *this* would be the for-reals final spark.

Especially if doing this knocked me out.

Or worse.

My whole body wrenched in a disconcerting, twisting pain. Pretty sure that was *me* screaming my head off as I strangled the wellspring of my magic to within an inch of its life—and probably my life too.

Just when I was about to pass out from the pain, one dewy drop of pink bloomed at my core.

I seized it before it could change its mind, and tugged it, burning, through me until it twinkled to life at the tip of my finger, barely visible.

Success. Sucky success, but still.

The trio of chuckleheads had backed off at my tortured screams, probably afraid the shadowy prisoner in my clutches was eating me alive.

Couldn't blame 'em, but I *could* take the extra seconds it bought me.

My palm facing me, I held up the hand clutching the orb and focused on the white-ink tattoo on the inside of my wrist. Shifting the ink around had always been a bit of a process, but I didn't have time for a struggle today.

I bore my will down on the pale ink, picturing the secret sigil handed down my mother's side of the family over generations.

And with steely determination, I *commanded* the ink to reform.

To my shocked delight, the ink beneath my skin snapped into place in the shape of the sigil I envisioned.

A pounding headache erupted along with it, but hey. I'll take whatever little victories I can scrape up.

My three thugs, who'd started stomping forward at my inaction, paused as I grinned up at them devilishly and lowered the mite of magic to my new tattoo.

The ink flared to life with a magenta glow. If I'd thought the wrench of drawing out my very last inkling of magic was bad, I was kidding myself.

My entire being fragmented with the sharp agony of muscles tearing, bones crunching, and skin shredding. My gaze rose toward the ceiling, until the thugs before me looked Aster's size.

Thankfully, the transformation stopped well before I hit my head.

The ghost of the harrowing pain lingered within me, but the worst was over. The schmoes stared up at me in horror, actually clutching each other for support.

One yelped and glared at the concrete ogre, wrenching his nearly crushed arm away, before his gaze refastened on me.

Or, more accurately, on the Tramble Terror.

I'd never seen anyone in my family actually use this sigil, or had any desire to use it myself. My dad had warned that my Uncle Gerald used it too many times for Halloween pranks, and that was why he looked the way he did—fugly as the backside of a squonk.

He claimed the more you used it, the more you embodied the creature, and I've never quite been sure whether he was joking or not—or brave enough to find out.

My grandma had scared us all with stories of how her mother had been trapped in the Terror's form for six full months, hunted by townsfolk and having to live deep in the woods until the magic left her.

Not even pictures or drawings were passed down, so my curiosity was rampant.

I couldn't get a great look at my body, but I felt long, and way more limbs were reporting in than I was used to. I peered over my shoulder, along my spine.

Yep, a *lot* of limbs.

They spiraled around my elongated torso like nails in a rain stick, but that was the only pattern to them. Each limb was different—a leathery wing, a hairy human arm, a slick tentacle, a three-toed talon nearly buried beneath feathers, and on and on.

Could I—?

Yep. I rolled, settling my weight onto new limbs and freeing others as they came off the ground.

The most disturbing part was that my head didn't swivel with my body, but stayed parallel to the floor without any twisting of my neck.

Was my head . . . not actually fixed to my body? Just kind of plugged into a loose socket and free to roll around?

A shudder racked through me at the thought.

Not loving this.

Neither was anyone else, apparently.

I had way more than the attention of my most recent thugs. The whole room was staring at me, petrified. Even the dudes Aster had juiced up on venom earlier, who'd been slumped, giggling, against the wall.

Samaire huddled where she'd fallen, her groggy gaze taking me in. Nadine crouched over her, one hand cradling Samaire's face, but my transformation had her gaping my way.

Bracchius was halfway through pulling Aster out of a pile of henchdudes. Aster's ruddy cheeks paled, and Bracchius drifted backwards in shock.

"Holy harpies," one flunky uttered.

Somehow, I was still holding the Dreyelian device in one, well, *hand* was being way too generous.

Better put it back.

Not that returning it to the sigil would do any good, but I *really* didn't want to hang on to it any longer than necessary.

My monster eyes took in the sigil as I set the orb at its center. It was *so* close to being complete. If only I'd bought Elena three more seconds instead of mutating her, it would be done.

Suddenly Ambrose snarled, "Take that abomination down!" Some of our clowns had been pussyfooting toward the door, but at his command, they about-faced and converged on me with the rest of the brotherhood.

Did I want to tussle with all of them at once?

Nope.

Was I scary enough to just send them all running with one aggressive move?

Worth a shot.

I opened my mouth to show off whatever horror of fangs and gross awaited inside, and—

Whoa, wait, *what*?

Eurgh.

My jaw unfurled like one of those creepy flower-faces from *Stranger Things*, and it felt like my face was falling apart.

Only, y'know, intentionally.

One segment flapped in front of my eyes, and I almost lost it.

Definitely *never* doing this again.

Ambrose's henchdudes did scatter, but Bracchius swelled up to twice his usual size and zoomed over.

Why on earth would he be coming to my defense? I was the person *least* in trouble now that I'd—

"Give her *back*!" Bracchius was back in beast mode, hellfire blooming to life above him like his own molten halo.

He thought the bad guys had Sparkles? Or me?

An inferno roared toward me, and it clicked.

Wuh-oh.

MONSTER YODEL

Bracchius thought *I* had me. I the monster. Me, Immy.

I was too big to duck his attack, so the burning wave crashed over me, scalding my skin. Feathers crisped, tentacles writhed, and the dark hair on the manly arm sticking out of me charred away.

Hey, cheaper than laser. *More* painful than wax, though.

I hollered, "Bracchius, it's me! I just transformed!"

Except no intelligible words were issuing from this mouth. Just something between a dragon's roar and an alpine yodel.

As I spat out garbled nonsense, a glob of magic rose from the criminal contingent and soared toward Bracchius.

A deep voice protested, "Wha—? Don't attack *him*, he's helping!"

Bracchius barely dodged the missile, ripping his attention away from me to hail more flames down at the speaker. "Help you?! I would *never* help the dastards who maimed my poor Sparkles and unleashed the monster that— that *ate* Immy!"

With a strangled sob, he plunged into the group like a hellish meteor.

I needed some way to get through to him before he refocused on me. If I couldn't speak . . .

Elena had spoken to us telepathically earlier with some kind of charm. What if—

One of the goons flung himself onto my monstrous torso with a growl, and a sting like a mosquito bite pricked at my shoulder.

I snarled. Was this maniac *biting* me? What the actual hells?

I shook him off and unleashed a hair-raising roar toward the other baddies arrayed against me. They stumbled back from the sheer force of the sound, and I whipped toward the sigil, hoping against hope that Elena's telepathy amulet would be amongst the jewelry scattered on the ground.

My gaze snagged on the sigil itself. It was complex enough that I'd never stand a chance at memorizing it, but it had symmetry, a logic to the lines. And everything looked perfect . . .

Except for a six-inch gap in one quadrant that didn't match the other three.

A shimmer at the corner of my eye got me back on track. I scanned the jewelry. A ring, a bangle . . .

The crystal pendant.

Gotcha.

Inky shadow furled out from the artifact as I grabbed the pendant, but it fell short of my various limbs and dissipated.

Thank my lucky stars.

I lifted my head just as Bracchius burst from the groaning throng—all a bit toastier than a minute before. Red hot and filled with righteous—wicked?—fury, he rounded on me again.

Fumbling the crystal pendant between two claw tips, I pushed my magical awareness toward it. Gotta figure out how it worked, pronto, or I'd be maaany slices of monster toast in short order.

One energetic facet of the crystal beckoned to me, and I focused on it.

Next thing I knew, my mind was being sucked through a much too narrow winding channel, like someone had slorped my consciousness through a crazy straw.

It hurt like the dickens, but it worked. I could sense the others in the room—not their thoughts, but their mental . . . presence?

As fire washed toward me, I prodded the one that felt like glitter and marshmallows engulfed in flames.

"Bracchius! The monster's me! Immy! I'm the monster!"

The fire scorching my toes winked out.

"Immy?"

I pried an eye open. Gosh, I hoped I still had only two eyes. I didn't *feel* like my vision had changed.

Bracchius hovered before my face, anxious. "Immy, is that really you?"

I nodded my big monster head and confirmed with a telepathic "Yup."

He splatted against my face and hugged part of it—possibly the floppy fanged part, but if he didn't mind . . .

"Bad guys," I squeaked out before I had to release my mental hold on the crystal. Being contorted like that wasn't my fave.

"Oh!" He pivoted and blasted the poor guy who'd just worked up the courage to approach big scary ol' me.

Ambrose's heavies momentarily distracted, I glanced back at the sigil.

And that *one* missing line.

This might not work, but my instincts told me that one little squiggle was all that stood between us and the finished, functional sigil.

I snatched up the tiny pen between furry fingers as three thugs made it past Bracchius. I snapped my freaky jaws mere inches from one guy's face, and all three lurched back.

When I uncapped the pen, Ambrose's eyes widened.

"Stop that fiend! Everyone hit it *now!*"

And here I'd thought things would be easier as a huge creepy monster.

Guess my problems only multiplied with size and power.

Rude.

I curled my alarming body around to shield the arm closest to my eyeballs. Whacks and jabs and stinging sparks assaulted me, but they really weren't as pesky as in my human form.

Forked tongue between my teeth, I lowered the green marker to the stone.

A particularly vicious jab pierced what was probably my butt at present, but I fought back a snarl and the instinct to whirl and savage my attacker.

Instead, I traced one short curving line across the gap in the sigil to match the others.

No Hallelujah chorus materialized, not that I was expecting one. Besides, the sigil might still be incomplete for all I knew.

One roughneck with distinctly singed hair clambered over my freaky torso, but I pinned him with several arms and legs. Next step was to test the sigil, see if it activated.

Could I—?

Nope. My monster form hadn't sped up my magic regeneration one bit. At least my wellspring wasn't quite as raw, but it was still pretty peeved at me.

Unable to trust my mangled jaw to get the message across, I concentrated once more on the crystal clutched in one of my palms.

Back through the contortionist's water slide my mind went, complete with all the same lovely squashing and tortuous shenanigans.

Unsure which of my gang was closest—or had any of their *own* magic left—I felt around for each of their mental signatures.

The glittery marshmallow one was Bracchius, though less engulfed in flames than last time.

A warm, kind knot of humor suffused with throbbing pain: Samaire. A strangely bland, indistinct consciousness giving off hints of worry: Nadine?

Or *Nardi*, apparently. I frowned. I'd be getting back to *that* as soon as we'd soundly defeated Ambrose and company, and I was back out of monster form.

Hopefully less than six months from now.

If I got stuck this way for long, it might not be quite so dire as for my great-grandma. Bracchius, at least, would do what he could to take care of me, though I had the sneaking suspicion I'd lose my job at Saskia Skies.

I might not fit in my apartment either.

Shaking myself, I refocused on my mental questing. The last nonthuggish presence was a larger pool that felt bubbly and bright, but also . . . old.

Very old.

Whoa.

Aster? I couldn't be mistaking her for Ambrose—no one in their right mind would describe him as bubbly and bright.

Burning agony ripped me from my mental focus, and my eyes flashed open. Bracchius was busy with at least half the doofuses at once, while the rest had ganged up to channel their magic into one powerful gout streaming into my side.

This time I didn't hold back the snarling roar and instinctive attack.

Most of them dove out of the way in time, but I bashed one aside with my snout and clamped down on another's arm.

Something shifted toward the back of my throat as the thug I had bitten fell forward.

I froze.

No, no, no.

Had I—?

Canker and cannibals.

I gagged and evicted—yep—a freaking *arm* from my mouth, then spent a little more time gagging.

Safe to say this monster gig was not my cup of tea.

I thrashed my lower half violently, sending my contingent of cads tumbling across the room. Then I plunged back into 'ouch my brain hurts' land and focused on my friends.

Really not wanting to do this again to answer follow-up questions, I tried to cover the deets in one fell swoop.

"I think I completed the sigil! But I don't have any magic left. If any of you do, get your asses over here and activate the damn thing so we can get the hells out of here and take a nap!"

Worried negation bloomed from both Nadine and Samaire before I broke contact with the crystal's power. They must be just as out of juice as I was.

Well, *they* probably hadn't ravaged their minds like me the imbecile, but still.

That left Aster and Bracchius.

If Bracchius broke from his collection of thugs, he could zip over me and light up the sigil. But I'd probably get mobbed by every bad guy in the room, so that might not be his first choice.

As for Aster, I couldn't spot her in the hubbub. She might be at the opposite end of the room or fangs deep in someone's leg in the thinning crowd before me.

I swatted a couple ambitious rogues away from the artifact. One sailed over the heads of the rest just as a white-blonde mop of curls appeared between the legs of the desert troll.

Aster raced toward me, and I shifted my body to form a little arc for her to dart under.

She mustered an exhausted smile as she ducked through. "Pretty sure I'm down to my last spark, but this is better than wasting it on another of these jokers!"

I let my body slump to close off the mini passage. Aster crouched at the sigil's edge and summoned a sunshine-yellow glimmer at the tip of one bitty finger.

Magic met marker, and a glowing yellow cascade washed across the sigil, tracing every line until the complete design flashed.

Activated.

Relief and pride swelled in my chest, but the sigil wasn't done throwing fireworks *quite* yet.

A translucent sheet of dazzling gold rose from the outer circle of the sigil, curving inward like a dome, inch by inch.

As I stared, transfixed, the concrete ogre hurtled past me and launched toward the closing gap at the top.

PHANTOM LIMBS

The golden dome forming around the Dreyelian device was only halfway up and climbing as the concrete ogre's jump carried him toward the apex.

I shot out a tentacle—the longest and stretchiest of my hodgepodge of limbs at present—to try to stop him, but he was already out of reach.

Fingers crossed he'd topple inside just in time to get trapped as the dome closed.

But either he'd misjudged the leap, or the extra weight of the weeds growing out of his chest threw off his equilibrium. Instead of sailing through the gap, he struck the top edge of the ascending energy field and—

WHAM.

—rebounded with at least as much force and speed as he'd come in with.

And, of course, hammered right into my monster gut. Or a portion of it, anyway.

I belted out an explosive breath, jaws flapping, but kept my eyes fastened on the rising dome. Two feet to go, one foot, six inches . . .

When only the barest breath of an opening was left at the zenith, a shadowy whiplash flew up from the spinning rings of the Dreyelian device. The darkness speared through the gap, colliding with the edges of the golden ward.

Which stuttered, blinked in a haze of furious sparks . . .

And collapsed.

An irritated roar burst from me, and I flopped three assorted limbs between Aster and the dull green sigil.

She got the message. Her face scrunched up, turning red with effort, but no sunshine yellow magic erupted from her hands. She shook her head in frustration, then whirled toward the diminishing chaos beyond my blockade of a body.

"Bracchius! Help!"

Not a moment too soon, my favorite demon hurdled my back half and sped toward us. "What?! What's the matter!"

Aster jabbed a peremptory finger at the inert lines. "Activate the sigil, quick!"

"Yessirree!" Way more than the needed spark gushed from

Bracchius's nubby arm, the glittering red exploding against the lines of the sigil and filling them to brimming in an instant.

The sigil flashed, activating.

Annnnd that was it.

No dome. No rising golden curtain. Not so much as a spark before the red glare of Bracchius's magic faded away to nothing.

Had he overpowered it? Blown the fuse, as it were?

I waggled several limbs frantically to get his and Aster's attention, then squished one tentacle and one wing close together.

Aster's eyes narrowed. "You think it was too much?" She snatched Bracchius's arm urgently. "Try again with just a teeny bit of magic!"

A single glimmer like a red shooting star popped from his other arm and landed on the sigil. It trickled along the design much slower, and we waited with bated breath.

"Immy!"

That was Samaire's voice. I twisted to look across the room behind me, but Nadine was waving her arms in a warding gesture.

Samaire pointed back toward the sigil, yelling, "No, over there!"

I wheeled back around; Aster and Bracchius had looked the wrong way too. The human thug I'd clashed with earlier was just settling a strange grey cloth over the device at the center of the half-lit sigil, like a magician about to make a dove disappear.

We stumbled over each other rushing over, my big unwieldy body doing more harm than good in such close quarters.

Bracchius accidentally bowled Aster over, and in my attempt not to pulverize her, one of my errant limbs batted Bracchius aside. Then, predictably, I tripped over my own weird feet and crashed to the ground in a tangled heap.

The large square of cloth was the flattest grey I've ever seen, almost taking light into itself rather than reflecting it. As it settled over the orb, the shape beneath was weirdly tiny, like the Dreyelian device had shrunk.

No, not shrunk—that was the original size, without the dark corona and bursts of shadow.

The cloth was *suppressing* the escaping magic.

Dang. Wish we'd had something like that.

I finally untangled my feet as the thug snatched up the corners of the cloth and twisted the whole shebang together into the next best thing to a Gordian knot.

All the better to take it away from you, my dear.

I twitched. I was starting to sound like Cynna.

Not really life goals.

Unleashing another heart-stopping roar, I lunged for the poor sap.

Only to find my body no longer responding to commands, limbs writhing and my torso compressing slinky-style.

Humanity, here I come?

I tried to bellow to Bracchius and Aster to stop the dude, but I couldn't find the crystal, and my contorting monster mouth was exactly as nonhelpful as before. I couldn't even see the two of them, and sent up a prayer to all the various divine beings and beasties that I wasn't trampling them underfoot at this very moment.

Bracchius would survive that, but vampires were only so tough.

I wrenched my mind away from the pain of transformation as someone yelled. I ordered at least my ears to cooperate with me as the rest of me worked on figuring out how to become human again.

"Should I teleport out, boss?" That had to be the thug with the cloth.

"What, are you *mad*?" Ambrose shrieked. "Not with the artifact!"

"But, boss, it was fine when we did earlier this week."

"With the replica they conned you with, you mean?" Ambrose scoffed. "If you tried that with the genuine article, we'd be lucky if it only killed you. Just get over here!"

I was human again by the time Ambrose's minion hurried forward, cloth satchel in hand. Unfortunately, I wasn't in fighting shape quite yet.

More like flopped on the floor, gasping.

"Immy! Are you okay??" Bracchius hovered over me, Sparkles tucked back under his arm but dirty, torn, and shedding stuffing.

I could only reply with a groan.

Every time I tried to stand, my brain sent the impulses to phantom limbs rather than my newly reacquired human ones. I glared at my body, trying to convince my brain I really was back down to just two arms, two legs, and to get in gear.

My clothes didn't seem to have survived my transformation, hanging off me in scraps.

Great.

Aster was being held upside down at arm's length by one of the few thugs still standing, way out of biting range.

Nadine was helping Samaire back to her feet with a pained wince, but neither of them were going anywhere fast.

Most of the baddies were taking a breather, nursing their wounds, or just out like a light. One guy was dashing between the worst off, touching them, and lighting up a sigil on a chunky ring on his finger.

Poof. Off they teleported.

A second later he'd flash back into existence and grab the next couple guys.

My brain finally located one of my actual arms, and I flailed it past Bracchius. "'M fine. Stob tha guy . . ."

"You don't *sound* fine!" Bracchius pulled a 360. "Which guy?"

Antimagic cloth dude had just jogged past Ambrose and out the front door.

"Nermind. Help me up." Bracchius darted behind me and pushed me to my unsteady feet, my brain and body finally syncing up better.

"Boss?"

Ambrose spun back, looking annoyed. "What now?"

I peered toward the speaker behind me.

One of the baddies stood at the entrance to the hall, proudly holding up a massive glass bowl filled with layer upon layer of salad fixings. At least a couple of the layers looked suspect.

Were those *Twinkies*?

"I've got that salad you wanted! Isn't she a beaut?"

Figuring Salad Boy wasn't much of a threat, I chanced a glance back at Ambrose.

Who looked *absolutely* flabbergasted.

"Revin, what are you—?" Ambrose shook himself. "Get over here. We're leaving, *now*."

Salad Boy obeyed, bringing the masterpiece along for the ride.

With Bracchius's support, I limped over to the open door, my right leg half-asleep. A grinding crash echoed up the drive just as we stumbled onto the porch.

Paolo had moved our car to the end of the drive, blocking the bad guys' escape. The picturesque stone retaining wall lined the drive on either side, with Elena's tasteful landscaping above, so taking off across the lawn hadn't been an option for Ambrose and crew.

But they hadn't given in that easily.

Paolo's trunk was a crumpled wreck, smashed in from the side and thrust out into the road amidst crumbles of auto glass. Ambrose's own car sped out of sight down the hill.

"Toss her, and let's go!" a deep voice hissed behind us.

The hulk holding Aster chucked her toward Nadine and Samaire, then teleported away with the last two crooks. Nadine somehow caught Aster and lowered her to the ground, Samaire wobbling without her support.

Aster looked between us, red-brown eyes wide. "Now what?"

My gaze flitted between Aster, Samaire, Bracchius, Nadine, and the pulverized car at the bottom of the drive. Only one of us was in good enough shape to chase Ambrose's car, and Nadine and Aster were the next most mobile.

"Bracchius, follow the bad guys. Aster, go see if Paolo is hurt. Nadine, can you"—I fluttered a hand over the tattered remains of my outfit—"steal some clothes from Elena's closet for me?"

Aster and Nadine nodded and dashed off. Samaire slowly followed Aster out the door.

Bracchius didn't. "Immy, I can't take all of them on by myself . . ."

"You don't need to. Do you have enough magic left to teleport?"

"Yeah, but—"

"Follow Ambrose's car, but don't let them see you. Once they get wherever they're going, teleport back here. We can try to find a healer, grab a few other people for help, and then head to Ambrose's base or lair or whatever."

Bracchius tilted sideways. "Why don't you all just come with me now?"

"What do you mean?" Maybe he'd gotten pummeled harder than I'd thought . . .

"I can teleport everybody!"

The knowledge sank in one word at a time. "Wait . . . You mean this *whole* time you could've been teleporting me places?! Why didn't you mention it before?"

Some demons—typically the most powerful ones—could teleport more than themselves, but it was a fairly rare ability. I'd never considered Bracchius could.

Okay, yeah, he teleported Sparkles sometimes, but *that* didn't count.

Could I go like this? I wasn't really fussed about showing skin when big scary magic was at stake, but if the remaining scraps of my clothes fell off, I might be arrested for public indecency.

Or break a leg tripping on the blasted bits.

But Aster and Nadine weren't back, and I still didn't know if Paolo was okay, or—

My jaw firmed. "Go without us. If you don't go now, we'll lose them."

"But—"

"Go!"

Bracchius wobbled in surprise, then buzzed away at top speed, trailing specks of fluff all along the way from Sparkles's torn leg.

With a sigh, I crouched and collected the fluff within reach, my body protesting.

Ambrose had a decent head start on Bracchius, but their car would be in rough shape after smashing into Paolo's. Easy to spot when you can fly way up in the sky and dart across the neighborhood.

Fluff clasped in one hand, I took a quick survey of myself.

Clothes—in scraps. Busted hand—still busted. Sigil on my other hand—smudged beyond belief. Phone—who knows where.

I patted my collarbone. Necklace with the Dreyelian dupe—gone.

Better start hunting.

While Elena's walls and floor still looked pristine, her furniture and belongings had come out of the fight even worse off than we had.

On hands and knees, I reached through shredded couch cushions, checked beneath splintered, overturned end tables, and peered through the mess of shattered picture frames and broken floor lamps.

I turned up a phone that *wasn't* mine, the screen cracked. Judging by the black, pink, and purple sticky jewels plastered across the case, this had to be Aster's.

No wonder she and Bracchius got along.

The dupe of the artifact had rolled behind a couch. The clasp of my necklace had snapped, but I tied it into a rough knot at the back of my neck, and it held.

I was just considering how to retrieve my own phone from the middle of a glass debris field when Nadine shuffled in, half-hidden behind a mass of clothes on hangers.

"I wasn't sure what would fit or be comfortable, so I brought some options." She dropped the heap on the desecrated couch. "And shoes." Her gaze flashed to my feet.

I'd kicked off the pathetic scraps first thing.

She dumped a few pairs of shoes beside the clothes. Most looked too small, but the house slippers were promising.

I stepped out of the remnants of my clothing and rummaged through the pile. Nadine had even brought socks and underwear. Almost made me feel bad that I was about to grill her about her part in all this.

But not quite.

Nadine averted her gaze as I pulled on underwear and a sports bra. "Okay, time to fess up. How are you involved in all this? And if I don't like your answers . . ."

I lifted my arm with the Tramble Terror sigil tattoo. "I might just go all monster on your ass."

Yep, a total lie. I'd rather cannonball into a hydra acid bath than try *that* stunt again.

But Nadine didn't need to know that.

She blanched and held up her hands. "Look, I would've told you earlier if I had known what all was going on here. I didn't know what the artifact was when I stole it, or who I was stealing it for. Ambrose is bad news. When I found out *he'd* hired me, I left the device in the hands of fate and took off."

She'd stolen it herself? Interesting.

And I guess *I* was the 'hands of fate.' Harhar. But Nadine didn't look anything like the girl on the camera footage, the one I only vaguely remembered—long silver-blonde bob, classy, flashy.

My mind flicked back to when I'd left work that day, stopping by the bathroom to change clothes and check the bite mark from that feisty little beastie. Someone *had* dropped a wad of hair in the trash . . .

Silver-blonde hair.

A wig.

I glared at Nadine. "And you thought leaving it at the bottom of a cup holder on *my* car rental lot was the best place?" I got stuck pulling a too-small T-shirt over the top of my head, but rebuffed Nadine's help.

I'd wriggle out on my own, thank you very much.

Nadine tugged at her red-brown waves. "In retrospect, no. But I was in a rush, and half the reviews on Yelp for Saskia Skies Car Rental mentioned new customers finding gross things in their cup holders when they picked up their cars. And—"

I interrupted, my professional pride injured. "Excuse me? Did you check the dates on those reviews? Because I promise you, those were *all* posted before I started working there."

Nadine stared at me dubiously. "No. I was just hoping it would get thrown out, or at least go unnoticed for a few days, until after the new moon. I figured people would think it was a rearview mirror ornament I didn't bother taking on my flight, or some kitschy souvenir."

"The new moon?" I yanked on a bigger shirt, then dug for pants. "*That's* why Ambrose was all panicked? His big whizbang whatever is going down today?"

Not that there was much of today left. Crud.

Nadine nodded. "Otherwise he has to wait another forty years and—"

Aster burst through the front door. "Paolo's okay! Mostly. He'll live. I think."

"You realize that's not actually encouraging, right?" I eased into a pair of cargo pants one leg at a time, wincing at my sore muscles.

Aster rolled her eyes. "Then come see for yourself!" She darted back out the door.

I clawed through the mess I'd made and unearthed the shoes. The legit shoes were way too small for me and my big toes, so I plopped the thin house slippers on the floor and shuffled into them.

Snug, but workable.

I followed Aster outside. Samaire and Paolo were both seated at the bottom of the porch steps. I drummed down the stairs and crouched in front of him. "Aster says you'll probably live?"

He chuckled, holding a folded handkerchief to a cut marring the fur above one eye. "The crash threw me into the steering wheel, so I've got this and some bruised ribs, but nothing serious."

I yanked him into a hug, with a grunted "oof" on his part.

"Thank Finéa." I straightened. "You've got the longest arms of any of us—think you could do me a favor?"

He eyed me suspiciously. "That would depend . . ."

I dragged him up the steps and back inside. "Reach past the glass moat and get my phone for me?" I pointed across the glittering shards.

"*That* I can do." He stepped to the edge of the debris, tiny specks of glass crunching beneath his shiny loafers. One bend at the waist and swoop of his arm, and he secured my phone, passing it to me.

"Thanks." I blew off the remaining glass dust. The case wasn't so much as scratched, never mind any cracks on the screen.

Freakishly expensive phone for the win.

I faced the others and handed Aster the phone I had found.

"Yours, I assume?"

"Yes!" Beaming, she snatched it. "It even works! I thought it was a goner for sure."

I glanced between the other three. "Everyone else got theirs?"

Nadine patted her pocket reassuringly. Paolo raised his phone, on which he was currently texting.

Samaire fished hers out of her back pocket with a groan—it was definitely toast, the cracked screen like ten cobwebs overlaying each other, and smashed plastic parts clinging to the edges for dear life.

"Okay, it'll probably be a while before Bracchius comes back. He's following Ambrose's car to wherever they end up, and then he'll report back. In the meantime, we should find a healer for at least Samaire—"

"You too, moron," Samaire muttered with a smirk and a pointed look.

"Fine, me too, and Paolo's ribs, and— Anyway. Then, since we're in no shape to do *that* song and dance again, we really need—"

With a pop, Bracchius reappeared two inches in front of my face.

I jerked, stumbling back half a step, adrenaline rocketing. "Th-That was fast. Ambrose's car stopped already?"

"No time!" Bracchius flew to the center of our little huddle. "They're just stuck in construction! Quick, everyone touch me!"

"But—" I looked around the room for anything we might be forgetting. Everyone else had already touched a wary hand to Bracchius, except Aster below, who he'd extended a longer-than-usual ebony arm toward.

"Immy, *now*!" Another amorphous arm thrust out and wrapped around my wrist.

And the world twisted away in a haze of purple glitter.

TOPSY-TURVY TELEPORTATION

Though Bracchius's teleportation took maybe a second, that was apparently enough time to squeeze in a healthy dose of vertigo—or maybe we really *were* tumbling head over heels, left, right, and backwards at top speed.

And what tasted like lemonade?

My stolen house slippers hit the sidewalk with a disconcerting lurch, and the nearby pedestrians jumped aside with cries of surprise as the six of us popped into existence.

I doubled over, fighting nausea. To top it off, sand—finally dislodged by the teleportation?—rained out of my curls. Half the grains went straight down my new shirt to get lodged in my bra and underwear.

Fabulous.

"This doesn't look like a construction zone," Nadine grumbled.

I cautiously straightened, not wanting to upchuck all over everyone's shoes. Was I the *only* one feeling nauseous?

Guess I wasn't *that* annoyed after all about Bracchius never mentioning group teleportation before. I'd walk to the grocery store any day over dealing with this stomach-churning.

Bracchius peered around and drooped. "It's harder teleporting everybody than I thought. But we're almost there—grab me!"

We all demonhandled Bracchius once more.

My vision went purple and sparkly, then I went somersaulting through the lemony funpark of interspace again.

Joy.

This time we materialized on the rough gravel of a partly paved road, surrounded by orange cones and noisy construction equipment.

"See! *Now* we're here." Bracchius floated a little lower to the ground despite his triumph.

A few startled construction workers meerkatted in our direction, and one stomped over, looking pissed off.

With a sweeping arm, Paolo ushered us out of the construction zone toward the bordering parking lot. "Maybe not the best time to tussle with the authorities, even those of the construction persuasion."

The foreman slowed to a disgruntled halt as we booked it.

"Is Ambrose still here?" Aster stood on tiptoe, studying the stalled line of cars skirting the roadwork.

"That's his car up there!" Bracchius poked one arm toward the head of the line.

Good—the car was facing away from us. Hopefully none of the thugs inside would have their heads on a swivel.

I tugged our little group beneath the shade tree at the edge of the parking lot just in case.

The orange-vested dude hefting the stop sign at the head of the line of cars didn't look like he was budging anytime soon, so I collapsed back against the tree trunk.

"Was it easier to teleport us the second time?" Samaire asked.

"No . . ." Bracchius wriggled sheepishly.

"And here I thought demons had phenomenal cosmic power," I teased, hoping a little snark would get my mind off the nausea.

Bracchius squished Sparkles to him. "I'm *retired!*"

"That is a pretty good excuse." Another tuft of Sparkles's fluff caught the breeze and drifted past me. I nabbed it out of the air and crammed it in a pocket of my cargo pants with the rest I'd collected.

If teleporting was this much work for him, it was no wonder he hadn't brought it up before. Though it might not be *this* much work for all demons.

A while back, some real ambitious startup had tried to bargain with the demons, collectively, to create worldwide teleportation services.

Not only had they not wanted to trade their souls, they'd wanted to stick the *demons* with the day-to-day operations of teleporting people, like glorified bus drivers—understandable since it really couldn't work any other way, though maybe not the best proposal.

Let's just say the demons laughed their asses off, right before teleporting the whole startup to the middle of the Mojave Desert.

Lucky for the entrepreneurs, there's cell service even *there* nowadays.

"Ambrose is on the move." Nadine jerked her chin at the line of cars. The construction guy had flipped his sign to 'slow,' and the line was creeping forward.

"Even *I* could keep up with him in sight at that speed." Aster snickered.

Bracchius scooted into the middle of our group again. "I'm ready!"

I didn't leave my slump against the tree. "Give them a minute. We don't want to get too close."

The leading cars picked up speed, and when Ambrose's sedan turned on their blinker, almost out of sight, I clapped a hand onto Bracchius. "Now."

I was coming to enjoy the swirling purple and taste of lemonade. I yelled an experimental "Wooooo!" as I tumbled around. Maybe I could trick my brain—and stomach—into thinking this was a roller coaster ride.

"Oooo!" The last half of my energetic holler came out after we returned to earth beside a chapel of the Followers of Skarn.

A zebra centaur almost jumped into the road at the dual shock of us all appearing and me hollering in their face.

Whoops.

I didn't even have time to apologize before Bracchius was collecting all our hands again. "Wow, they're going really fast!"

And poof, we were gone.

We materialized a block away from a red light, which Ambrose's car was just rolling to a stop at. It wasn't a smooth landing, though—we dropped a few inches to the pavement.

Bracchius immediately sagged almost to the ground, looking pooped, and I stumbled face-first into Nadine.

"Oops, sorry, Na—" My eyes narrowed as I reminded myself we weren't exactly best buddies. "Do we call you Nadine, or Nardi?"

She pressed her lips together. "Nadine. That's my real name. Nardi is just an alias—a burned one, now."

I scoffed. "So you have *multiple*? What are you, some criminal mastermind?" I glanced to Samaire, worried about who she'd gotten herself tangled up with. At least the relationship was new.

Plenty of time to break it off without breaking hearts too.

Nadine rolled her eyes. "Hardly. I just meant I need a new one if . . ." She trailed off.

"If you wanna commit more crimes? Wow."

She turned away from me in a huff, raking her fingers through the ends of her hair. Samaire looked conflicted, clinging to Paolo for support.

But I was on a roll. "And what kind of alias is *Nardi* when your real name is Nadine? Not like people won't put two and two together there."

She whipped back around, glaring. "An alias close to your name is one of the best kinds, actually. People expect you to choose one as different from your real name as possible, so they don't even usually look at the ones similar. And it's easier to instinctively respond to a name like yours when someone catches you by surprise. If you're meeting a contact at a crowded café and the barista calls out your order for Allisia, chances are you won't react, and you'll give yourself away."

That . . . actually *did* make sense.

Rude.

But now I was leaning more toward international spy than criminal mastermind.

Though, why would a spy steal an überpowerful disaster ball for some egotistic vampire moron? They'd be stealing stuff like that for their government or whoever.

I reluctantly admitted chances were low I was in a Bond movie.

Life's just one disappointment after another.

The tinted backseat window of Ambrose's car rolled down, and one of his cronies hung out the opening like a dog.

Luckily he was looking ahead of the car, not—

Crap!

I clotheslined our group with my arm, turning us away from the roving eyes of Ambrose's lookout to blend into—well, sprawl into, really—a pack of tourists mincing by.

The few cries from stubbed toes, barked shins, and jostled camera phones were masked by the general cheerful clamor of the group, and the meadow dragon tour guide's booming voice.

Samaire staggered away from an irate elderly couple, brushing melting specks of sno-cone off her shirt. "What was *that* for?"

"Bad guy was leering in this direction." I glanced between two heads of a hydra tourist to check on the car, but the window was rolling back up.

"Time to go . . ." Way less chipper, Bracchius wobbled up from the sidewalk, putting himself within reach for teleporting.

Poor little guy. Most of the rest of us had run out of juice, so why not him too? I'd just never seen a demon hit the end of their road.

Please let Ambrose's hideout or mansion or Batcave be close.

The cars streamed through the green light. Ambrose's car kept straight this time, and when it disappeared over the curve at the top of the hill, we made like a wraith and vanished.

We appeared just shy of the crest of the hill, smack in a mound of prickly bushes.

Bracchius was definitely losing his edge.

We squawked and scrambled to get out of the bushes with minimum pokage as Ambrose's car toodled down the hill.

I'd expected this to be more of a frenzied car chase, with Ambrose racing for his destination, careening around corners on two wheels, and us struggling to keep up.

Not that I was complaining.

I'd just forgotten about things like traffic, red lights and construction. And driving like a grandpa definitely had its advantages in the 'don't get pulled over with an illicit object and a bunch of criminals in the car' department.

It *was* nice knowing that if—when—we stopped him today, even if he got away afterwards somehow, we wouldn't be starting this whole rigamarole over again in a month at the next new moon. Forty years from now was plenty long enough for me to worry about.

If I even survived that long—if not, it'd be someone else's problem.

That actually cheered me up.

It did get me curious, though . . .

I sidled up to Nadine as I plucked bush bits out of my newly acquired clothing and fought digging into what had to be a sand wedgie.

"So . . . if the ritual has to happen on the new moon, why is Ambrose's next shot not for another forty years?"

Nadine blinked, tossing aside her own handful of bush debris. "It's not *just* the new moon. His ritual requires one of the darkest nights possible—new moon, with most of the brighter stars and planets aligned behind it. Venus, Jupiter, Mars . . ."

"And that only happens every forty years." I was surprised it was that often.

"Give or take." Nadine nodded.

"But . . . we're in the middle of a city." I gestured at the towering buildings. In smaller towns with less diverse residents it might be darker at night, but Saskia Springs way outdid the stars at night. "Shouldn't he be doing his ritual in, like, Antarctica?"

Nadine shrugged. "Apparently it's more like metaphysical darkness? The darkest night's sky, not the darkest place on the planet."

So chances were, a flashlight or blast of hellfire wouldn't ruin the ritual.

I sighed. Elena probably would've better understood all that, but she was still a skyscraper starfish in Bracchius's belly.

Guilt twinged through me. Hopefully she was finding something to eat in there.

Maybe cleaning all the grime off his hoard of coins?

Checking on her—and seeing if anyone could fix my mess—was a problem for tomorrow. One day as a peaceful chubby little critter shouldn't be *too* traumatizing.

Fingers crossed.

Samaire nestled up to Nadine. "Useful info. I'm glad we have you around, even if you weren't exactly honest with me." She gave Nadine a reproving look, and Nadine flushed.

Wait a minute. Something in my mind clicked together at Samaire's words, and my brow did its best impression of the backside of an elephant.

How did Nadine know all this junk about the alignment of planets and the requirements of Ambrose's ritual?

She'd said when she was hired she didn't know what exactly she was stealing, or who for, then she hightailed it out of there when she found out it was Ambrose.

And she'd assumed I knew what was inside—probably thinking at first I was in cahoots with Ambrose myself.

But how would she know the exact dates he could do his ritual if she didn't know more than the simple fact he'd been her employer? She'd cut and run, not reached out for more details.

What was it she'd asked me? *"Wait, you don't even know what's insi—"*

Anxious pixies fluttered in my stomach. That panicked look in her eyes, her disbelieving tone . . . I'd been distracted at the time, but . . .

She hadn't just been concerned about what *might* be inside.

She'd been horrified that I didn't *know* what was inside. That I wasn't aware of just how scary a monster was hiding in there.

Because *she knew*.

Wights and witches.

But if she knew, why hadn't she said something? Was she afraid if *we* knew, we'd want the demigod thing for ourselves?

Or was it so terrifying that she worried we'd take off the moment we found out, rather than trying to stop Ambrose—like she had?

But if we knew what it was—scarier than I was already imagining or not—we'd know what to do about it, right?

More information just meant better strategies for stopping Ambrose.

My head spun.

The others gathered around in a tight circle as I stood frozen in shock, staring at Nadine.

Bracchius mumbled, "Okay, here goes . . ."

Paolo snatched up Aster and balanced her on his hip, the sudden movement breaking my trance. What—?

I glanced over as Paolo placed his hand with the others'. Bracchius had extended part of his dark form down for Aster, but not far enough.

He would've missed taking her along.

Nadine cleared her throat, and I met her gaze. "Nadine . . . Do you know what's inside the Dreyelian device?"

Her eyes widened, lashes fluttering.

But Bracchius started phasing out, rather than his previous instantaneous *pops*, jolting my attention back to him.

Crud—I wasn't touching him yet.

I frantically slapped my hand onto the worn-out demon before he could leave *me* behind. That was why Nadine had coughed—hinting for me to get a move on and grab on, as the only person not touching Bracchius yet.

My hand went translucent in front of me, and then the world disappeared again.

CANDY CONVALESCENCE

We phased back in on asphalt—in the middle of the street.

A dozen feet from the hood of Ambrose's oncoming car.

The blare of horns and squeal of brakes drowned out everything else as I shoved Samaire into a clear lane and tucked Bracchius under my arm football-style to dive aside.

Paolo, still holding Aster, leapt the other way, narrowly dodging a truck as it whipped past, the driver spewing expletives.

Nadine stumbled after Samaire and me, a split second before Ambrose's slowing car screeched through the space we'd been standing in.

The face of the driver—not Ambrose—was locked in a rictus of panic, but the passenger windows rolled down as Ambrose bellowed, "It's them!"

Crud.

Glimmering orbs of magic shot from the dark interior of the car and blasted our way. Paolo shielded Aster, one magical strike grazing his arm and spinning him further across the road.

More oncoming cars slammed to a halt at the chaos of magical attacks, giving Paolo the chance to make a break for the sidewalk, Aster cradled against his chest.

I threw myself over Bracchius and Samaire, Nadine trying to shield Samaire too.

A multicolor barrage crackled right for us.

I ducked.

Nadine didn't.

The magic flung Nadine off our dogpile right as the car's tires burned rubber. They rocketed down the road, no longer worried about the speed limit.

"Nadine!" Samaire struggled to sit up, and I gave her a helping hand.

Our redheaded thief was sprawled on the asphalt, eyes closed.

Oh no.

We both raced over and crouched at her side. Samaire already had a hand to her pulse point.

"She's alive! Just unconscious." She glanced over her shoulder at the rest of our scattered group. "I'll take care of her. Go, follow them!"

"You sure?" I didn't want to leave them vulnerable, especially Samaire.

"I know a good healer near here." Samaire tugged Nadine's phone out of her pocket. "We'll be fine, go!"

I hurried over to Bracchius, who hadn't left the road after Ambrose took off. The cars that'd stopped at the eruption of magic hesitantly pulled forward again, merging into the far left lane and skirting us—and the new divots in the asphalt.

Unlike Nadine, Bracchius *was* conscious, but looked utterly exhausted. I scooped him up and dashed toward Paolo and Aster on the sidewalk.

"You up for one more teleport?"

"Maybe . . ." He shifted in my arms, accidentally squishing another blob of fluff out of Sparkles. "Will you hold Sparkles for me? I'm worried I'll drop her."

It was *that* bad? Yikes.

"Of course I will." I wedged the plushie unicorn under one arm and pocketed the errant fluff.

As Paolo and Aster reached out to touch Bracchius, I glanced back at Samaire, worried.

Someone had stopped their car just short of her and Nadine, their emergency lights flashing. They'd be okay.

Or at least Samaire would be.

I swallowed another dose of guilt at prioritizing my friend over her girlfriend as the world faded away like purple molasses.

We fell way short of Ambrose's car, but at least it was in sight— barely—when we landed a foot up from a grassy verge.

Paolo and I both avoided sprained ankles, but it was a near thing.

Bracchius glooped right between my arms to splat on the grass like a quivering lump of black jelly.

"Oh no!" Aster leapt from Paolo's arms as I dropped to the grass, aghast.

I'd *never* seen Bracchius like this.

Maybe he'd feel a little better cuddled up to Sparkles. I nestled the noticeably less puffy unicorn beside him, but he didn't so much as react, even when the breeze teased more stuffing out.

I caught the fluff and picked Sparkles back up. "Paolo, can you hold Sparkles? Keep her from . . . disintegrating more, at least?"

"Gladly." He took the stuffed unicorn into one arm, his other hand inside the breast of his suit. "You've been collecting the stuffing?"

"Yeah . . ." Distractedly, I handed him the whole poofy wad. We were never catching up to Ambrose now, but that was the least of my concerns.

Bracchius had gone through way too much already over the last couple days, with the Dreyelian device acting up inside him. And now I'd run him *literally* into the ground.

He deserved better.

Any more teleportation was out of the question. He didn't even have enough oomph to levitate, never mind teleport.

And by the looks of him, I'd better fix that, *fast*.

I cupped his side with one hand, his substance barely warmer than my own fingers, and the flickers deep inside him muted and sluggish.

"Bracchius?" He twitched at his name, but didn't respond. "You've gotta eat something. You used up too much of your magic. Can you spit out some of your candy hoard to eat?"

Demons didn't strictly need to eat to survive, but food gave them energy—both physical and magical—just like any of the rest of us. And he could use all the energy he could get right now.

His too relaxed form wobbled like he was trying, but no sugary sweets spilled out of him.

I stroked a thumb over his surface, managing to suppress most of my own anxious trembling. "It's okay, buddy. Don't strain yourself. We'll get you something." I glanced around the part of town we'd landed in.

A strip mall veered off into the distance on our right, with a gas station and a dollar store across the street.

I met Aster's worried gaze. "Do you have money? Cash, card?" I'd either left my clutch with my wallet at Elena's, or it'd been completely obliterated in the fight.

With my luck, probably the latter.

She nodded and hopped to her feet. "I'll max out my credit on candy if I have to!" She dashed for the nearest sidewalk.

"Don't buy more than you can carry!" I hollered after her. "And hurry!"

With a tight smile, I glanced up at Paolo and blinked in surprise.

He had Sparkles in one hand and a needle and thread in the other, a little leather case like a nail kit clamped between his lips.

Sparkles was back to almost her usual level of chub, with the rip by her leg already stitched halfway shut.

My heart nearly melted.

"Paolo . . ." I teared up. "You— How did you—?"

He pulled the case out of his mouth. "I always keep a small sewing kit in my suit pocket for when Master Damarion loses a button or such. I thought having his friend shipshape might cheer Bracchius up."

I nodded, fluttering my lashes to try to get the stupid tears to evaporate. "It definitely will. Thank you so much. Don't let me stop you."

He slipped the kit into his inner breast pocket and resumed stitching.

I dug in every pocket in these cargo pants on the off chance Elena hung her clothes back in her closet with forgotten granola bars or Pop-Tarts.

No such luck.

Didn't even find any money.

The cars at the nearest intersection slowed to a halt. Aster hustled across the zebra stripes, totally overloaded with two grocery bags bursting with candy.

She didn't drop a single piece, though.

Now *that* takes skill.

"I got it!" she piped. "Hold on, Bracchie!"

Even in such dire circumstances, I couldn't help but snort at the nickname. She upended the bags around Bracchius like a protective circle, except six inches high. I grabbed a Laffy Taffy and viciously ripped the wrapper off.

Aster got the idea and started denuding candy too.

I pressed the pink Laffy Taffy against Bracchius. He twitched. A second later, the candy was sinking into him and disappeared in his dark depths.

I could only hope he was actually eating it instead of just subsuming it.

Not that I really understood the difference. Demons have a habit of torching any info on their anatomy that gets out.

Never been sure if it's a privacy thing, or they just like remaining mysterious.

Bracchius absorbed piece after piece of candy—Reese's, M&M's, gummy unicorns—slowly shifting from a molten blob with blades of grass poking through to more of a rotund orb.

We went through the whole two bags, until all that was left was a giant box of rainbow Nerds. Aster shredded one end and rained the pellets down over Bracchius like a gaudy, sugary hailstorm.

Each Nerd vanished within him with a ripple.

Was even *that* much not enough? He definitely looked perkier, but he still hadn't said a word.

Not that any amount of candy would do much for his magical reserves. Food helps recover magic a *little* faster, but you could eat a whole elephant centaur and not even get back to half-full from empty.

It's more of a helpful factor than a fuel source when it comes to magic.

And demons are more magical than most. If Bracchius's magic was still too low, he might not even be able to recover physically. Not until his magic replenished naturally, anyway, and that could take hours.

Days.

Paolo stretched out his white thread and snipped it with the tiniest pair of scissors I'd ever seen. "There." He tucked away the needle, thread, and scissors, and lowered Sparkles in front of Bracchius. "Good as new."

He wasn't wrong. Sparkles looked much better without the gaping hole. Paolo's stitching was tidy, and—

Damn. He'd even switched thread colors—purple to white—to match Sparkles's fabric. Talk about attention to detail.

I held my breath and nudged Sparkles closer to Bracchius. If anything could make him feel better, this was it.

Nothing . . .

I shifted the plushie unicorn to show off the mending.

A jiggle. And then . . .

Bracchius reached out two nubby arms to envelop Sparkles.

I heaved an enormous sigh of relief that Bracchius was recovering. Aster hugged me around the neck with a "squee!"

"Sparkles?" Bracchius's voice was hoarse. "You're healed! How—?"

I tugged Paolo down by his tie to crouch beside us. "Bet you didn't know Paolo is secretly an emergency unicorn surgeon."

Paolo waggled his furry fingers hesitantly.

Bracchius swayed up off the ground. Sparkles squished between them, he pressed against Paolo's chest in a hug. "I can't believe you saved Sparkles! I'm gonna have to get you a huuuge gift! And have you over for *dinner*, and when's your birthday? Your kids' birthdays? What's your favorite color?"

Paolo laughed helplessly and patted Bracchius's backside. "Don't worry about it. It was the least I could do."

"I *will* worry about it! In fact—" A frisson panged through Bracchius. "Oh no!" He spun like a globe in the hands of a five-year-old. "Ambrose! Where'd he go?!"

Aster pointed down the road, and I yanked her hand down in alarm. But Bracchius had already spotted it, and was off like a shot.

Well, more like a wobbly arrow that would only make it halfway to the target, but still.

"Bracchius, don't!"

There was no way he'd ever catch up with the car. It had been at least ten minutes since Ambrose's taillights disappeared into the distance.

I flumped back on the grass, noticing for the first time the nausea from all the teleporting had finally eased up.

At least I had *one* thing going for me.

More sand cascaded out of my curls, and I groaned.

Aster flopped onto her stomach beside me, propped on her elbows. "Think he'll be okay?"

"With that amount of sugar churning through his system, he better be." I scrubbed at the sand trying to make inroads between my eyelashes, then took turns blowing out either side of my mouth to puff away the grains.

I was going to need a whole ass bath tonight, not just a shower.

Maybe both.

The cold metal of the Dreyelian dupe slid across my neck as I shook out more sand. I touched the knotted strands of the necklace—they were coming loose. I freed it with a couple tugs and slipped it into a cargo pocket.

It was a few minutes before Bracchius came idling back. Triumph number one: he hadn't lost Sparkles along the way.

"No luck?" I called.

He drifted down to roll across the grass, and stopped beside us.

"No . . . If only I'd grabbed that one guy's arm you spat out, then we could track them."

I shuddered again at that memory, and at the same time the perfect plan formed in my mind.

Energized, I sat up with a jolt. We didn't have an arm, but we did have *hairs.*

Going back to get them would slow us down even further, but it wasn't like we were catching up to Ambrose any other way at this point.

"I got this. Let's go to my place."

Bracchius rolled closer to me. "Immy, this is no time to take a nap at home! We can't give up!"

A nap was his first assumption? I'd say rude, but . . . Eh, fair enough.

"I'm not giving up, silly. Don't you remember, I accidentally ripped some hairs off that one bozo when they attacked us on the subway? I've still got those!"

Aster glanced between my hands like she was expecting me to be toting someone's scalp. "Where?"

"At my place. We can use that to pin down Ambrose!"

Aster didn't look convinced. "Was that same guy with him today?"

"Oh . . . Maybe?" It wasn't like I'd memorized the faces of every thug we'd come across. Although there was a special vengeful place in my heart for a few of them.

"Either way, it's our best shot. If it leads us to a liquor store on the north side of town, then we'll know he didn't stick with Ambrose. But even then, he might tell us *something.*"

I eyeballed Bracchius skeptically. "Safe to say you don't have enough magic yet for another group teleport?"

He swiveled side to side. "No way. Maybe in an hour . . ."

Paolo was texting again, which gave me the bright idea of calling an Uber. I fished out my phone from a cargo pocket.

The screen lit up with notifications: seven missed calls and three voicemails.

All from Fitz.

Hadn't pegged him as *that* desperate. Had he gotten lost? Mugged?

Cornered by an amorous titan skunk?

I shook myself. Whatever it was, it could wait. He was a grown dude, and I was not the only person who could solve his problems. Not by a long shot.

I *was* the only person who could solve *this* problem, though.

Aster squirmed as I searched for the Uber app in my cluttered folders. "Maybe I could help out?"

I paused. "How so?" No vampire I've ever heard of had teleportation abilities, and you'd've thunk she'd've said something by now if so.

She grinned, though it didn't look cheery. "My venom." She pointed at her fangs. "Vampire venom has a soporific effect on most species, but on demons . . ."

Bracchius chimed in. "It's like LivingDead Energizer! Except . . ." He looked dubious. "Don't you humanoids have teeth covered in the poop of some kind of parasite?" He shuddered. "Not exactly sanitary."

I bumped Aster with a knee. "Yeah, when's the last time you brushed, Aster?"

She unleashed the most adorable little growl.

Bracchius wriggled. "Could you maybe . . . bite something that's *not* me? And then I can just take in the venom?"

Paolo reached into a pocket and presented a blinding white handkerchief folded into a perfect square.

Bracchius perked up. "That would work."

"Fiiine." Aster's face scrunched up as she crumpled the fabric against her fangs.

At our stares, she shielded her mouth with her other hand. "'S not powite tah staow, y'know."

After a minute, she passed the damp wad to Bracchius. "There you go. The very last drops of my venom. Plahh." She stuck out her tongue and wiped it with a flurry of fingers. "Tastes like Moonlight Breeze detergent, and now my mouth is coated in lint!"

Paolo's lips pursed. "There wasn't a speck of lint on that."

Bracchius held the handkerchief by the absolute corner. "Yick. Here goes nothing . . ." He draped the handkerchief over top of him like some weird 1800s nurse's cap.

The fabric clung tighter to him, slowly drying before our eyes.

No, not drying—he was sucking the venom in, minus the handkerchief.

Once it was fully dry, he spasmed, shaking it off. Paolo plucked it from the grass and secreted it in his pants pocket.

Clearly *he* had no squicks about vampire teeth, venom, or plaque—probably a requirement of working for a vampire.

Aster peered at him. "Is it working yet?"

Bracchius shimmied. "It's . . . tingling."

"How long *should* it take?" I looked up at Aster as I stuffed a few escaped candy wrappers into the grocery bags.

"I dunno. Never bitten a demon before."

"You still haven't."

"Same diff!"

Bracchius raised one of Sparkles's plush hooves into the air, and we all quieted, looking down at him.

"Yeah, Bracchius?"

"There might be a teensy problem with this plan to find the bad guys."

I waited for him to explain, but he kept mum. "And that would be?"

He hemmed and hawed before getting to the point. "You're . . . not planning on doing the tracking spell *yourself*, are you?"

I laughed. "Me? Hells no. We'd probably end up at the center of the Earth. I was figuring you would do it."

Bracchius turned to Aster and Paolo. "Do either of you know how to do one?"

They both shook their heads.

"All right, what's up?" I crumpled the grocery bags and rammed them in my roomy pockets. "Why can't *you* do one for us? You should have enough magic again for a spell that small."

"I do . . ." He wiggled self-consciously, burrowing a couple inches into the dirt. "It's just . . . that was one of the few things I could never get right. I am great at all sorts of other magic! Just not tracking spells."

"Really? But I've seen you do way more complicated magic."

"Really-dilly. I tried to track down one of my friends once, and found a will-o'-wisp instead, and I thought for *days* that she had been cursed and transformed, and I was trying to find someone who would help—"

"Annnd it wasn't your friend," I concluded.

He nodded morosely.

"No problem. So, we just find someone else who can do the tracking spell for us." I screwed up my lips. "Like . . ."

"Kor can do them really well," Bracchius grudgingly admitted.

Oh. Fan-freaking-tastic.

Just what I needed—to owe Kor a favor.

Actually . . . I tilted my head consideringly. Kor *was* at least as pissed at Ambrose's guys as we were. Not that he knew they were Ambrose's guys yet.

But if I presented this as an opportunity for vengeance . . .

He *might* just do it with no favors owed.

Bracchius suddenly gave a "whoop!" and burst up from the ground. "Ack! That feels so strange! Is this what it's like for mortals to drink carbonation?"

Aster giggled. "We call it the venom tickle. You think you can teleport now?"

"Definitely!" Bracchius gave a little twirl.

I crossed my arms. "You think you can teleport *and* not immediately collapse again? Because I don't want you ending up in that bad of shape again. Ever."

He rolled in a nod. "Me neither. I feel like a new demon!"

"If you say so . . ." Not like I had any way to find out for sure. Just had to believe him and hope.

Paolo, Aster, and I formed a little triangle with Bracchius at the center. We laid hands on him like the most mismatched, short-handed sports team ever, about to say "Go team!"

And for hopefully the last time for a while, Bracchius teleported us.

We popped right onto my front lawn in a swirl of purple, and scared the living daylights out of someone on the stoop.

Not just someone.

Fitz.

Who did *not* look happy.

TRAITOROUS TRESPASSER

Seriously? Fitz hadn't gotten an answer from me on the phone, so he had the gall to show up at my *place*?

I'd really misjudged him.

But . . . My brow furrowed. How did he know where I lived? I'd given him my phone number, not my address.

Insurance investigator, my foot. There was only one way he could be here. And it wasn't a good one.

"What is *he* doing here?" Bracchius sputtered. He whirled on me. "Did you invite him without telling me?"

"Weirdly, no. I didn't even tell him where we live." I glared daggers at Fitz.

"Stalker!!" Bracchius must not have been too affected by the teleportation, because he raged over to Fitz with astounding speed . . .

Just as Fitz stomped down our dilapidated concrete walkway toward me. "I actually believed you!"

Their collision rivaled the Big Bang, and just might have thrown a new baby universe off into the wild somewhere.

Fitz toppled over backwards, his head unfortunately landing on patchy grass instead of jagged concrete. Darn.

He was mumbling something about, "You played me, and I can't believe I fell for it . . ."

Which just made it even easier to believe the truth: he had been working for Ambrose all along, just another crony sent to track down Ambrose's precious bauble—by sweet-talking me instead of hunting me down and attacking me like the others.

I didn't hear any of the rest of what Fitz had to say. Bracchius was too busy cursing him out with every expletive known to unicorns—surprisingly many—and metamorphizing the yard to create impromptu shackles for Fitz's wrists and ankles.

Paolo and Aster watched agape.

I marched toward my front door. "Thank you, Bracchius. That should hold him, if you want to help me get ready for our tracking spell."

"Anything to get away from this dastard! I *told* you he was no good!"

I sighed. "You did . . ."

And he'd never let me forget it either.

Fitz kept hollering as I tramped past him to the door. "I know Nardi Seabrook passed the device off to you! And—"

His next words were garbled as my flock of crows descended, battering him in the face with their wings. Jekyll perched right on Fitz's chin and held on despite his violent head jerks.

"Ow! Get off!"

Front door unlocked, I grabbed the kibble bin and gave it a noisy shake. The crows fluttered my way, Flirt depositing an insult in a long messy streak across Fitz's business suit.

I scattered kibble like I didn't have a care in the world.

Fitz struggled against his restraints—the tree roots and hard-packed earth weren't budging anytime soon. "And here I was going to give you a chance to explain yourself before I called the cops. I guess I'll be adding unlawful imprisonment to my report instead."

"You were gonna call the *cops* on me?!" I flung my next handful of kibble with unintended violence, pelting the crows.

They squawked and hopped away.

Oops. "Sorry, my feathered frenemies." I aimed my next handful at Fitz's face. "I should've been smart enough to call the cops on *you*!"

Sure, I could do it now, but I had other priorities. Plus, they'd ask questions I didn't really want to answer.

I'd had enough of Fitz's nonsense. I stomped into the house, Paolo and Aster scrambling after me.

Fitz got one more shout in before I slammed the door with righteous fury. "*You're* the one colluding with the thief!"

Slam.

I bolted the lock, but hollered back for good measure. "You're the one working for a deranged vampire *criminal*! And good luck calling the cops in that position!!"

In any other neighborhood, I'd worry about the neighbors doing the job for us with this racket. But my neighbors were well used to the insanity Kor, Bracchius, and I got up to by this point.

I'd be astounded if they called the cops for anything short of my whole building going up in a mushroom cloud.

Hopefully Fitz hadn't noticed the part where I didn't deny colluding with a thief. I hadn't, really . . .

Not to start with.

He probably couldn't hear me through the door anyway.

Bracchius buzzed around me anxiously. "What do we do now?"

"We get those hairs, get Kor, and make the tracking spell." I went to ram the kibble tub home in the credenza by the door, but my hand was empty.

I stared at it blankly for a second. Must've left the tub outside.

The crows would have a heyday.

Muffled yells came from the yard, but—shocker—my walls were actually thick enough to garble whatever Fitz was spewing. Paolo and Aster were still hovering awkwardly by the door.

Aster stepped forward. "Who was that?"

I grunted as I ripped open the drawer of the credenza. "Just another of Ambrose's henchguys, I guess."

Where *were* those hairs? I couldn't remember exactly where I'd stashed them, but the credenza was a safe bet.

I rummaged through the random junk lining the drawer, shunting aside loose Tic Tacs, old keys, balled-up receipts, and more pens and pencils than anyone could possibly use in their lifetime.

Sunglasses case—right!

Cautiously, I pried open the hungry case, not wanting to sacrifice a finger to keep it happy. It snapped open with a clack, revealing the little twisty wad of hairs I'd hidden inside.

"Paolo, Aster, why don't you guys make yourselves comfy while Bracchius and I find Kor?" I waved an expansive arm at the saggy sofa and . . .

And nothing. That was the sum total of my living room seating right now, other than a stool—missing one leg—that did a bad impression of a desk chair.

Aster happily hopped onto the sofa. Paolo checked the wall behind him before leaning back. And here we just had a brownie cleaning crew come through, what? Three days ago? Maybe this place was hopeless without a complete makeover.

Not happening anytime soon.

Gross hairs in hand—well, still in the glasses case if I'm being honest—I headed toward the hallway and Kor's mirror. But a spotty banana on the kitchen counter drew my eye, and my stomach rip-roared a furious protest.

Oh. Food.

Hadn't had a chance to think about *that* in a hot minute.

I glanced between Aster and Paolo. Who was more likely to be a deft hand in the kitchen?

I chuckled at myself. Dumb question.

Aster might be thirty times older than Paolo for all I knew, but could she even reach a drawer, never mind the counter? The fridge handle?

Nope.

And Paolo was married, with kids. Even if he wasn't a chef at heart, surely his wife would've recruited him into cooking long since.

Paolo it was.

"Hey, Paolo? Think you could whip up some fast food for us?"

At his concerned frown, I hurried to clarify. "Not, like, greasy fast food. Like, five-minutes-or-less food. Burritos. Sandwiches. A milkshake. Something."

Yeah, Immy, good job on not making it sound like fast food. But it wasn't like I could say salad—the only lettuce in my fridge had withered an agonizing death long ago.

His brows lifted. "Oh, a quick lunch? Or . . ." He checked his watch with a grimace. "Dinner?"

"Yes!" I pointed at him in relief. "That."

"I'll see what I can do."

Munchies in the offing, I ducked into the hall and lowered a finger to Kor's mirror.

I should have at least a *little* magic back by now . . .

Only, I didn't.

Zip.

Zilch.

Zero.

Heh. That couldn't be good.

I glanced at Bracchius, who'd followed in my wake. *He* had magic, but it wouldn't do me any good. I was the only one aside from Kor who had permission to access the mirror.

Which required my magic . . .

I chewed on that for a second before proceeding with the only reasonable plan.

I crouched on the floor and hammered the mirror with both fists like a gorilla shifter on a bad batch of Domin8.

"KOOOOOOOR! KOR! KOR! KOOOR!"

Bracchius gleefully joined in, and I swear the building shook.

Just another demon-induced earthquake for the neighbors to add to their logbooks.

No biggie.

It only took a minute of our ruckus before sinister red eyes bloomed on the surface of the mirror.

"*What?!*" Kor snarled. "I'm busy with a prisoner!"

I really hoped his prisoner was the thug he'd captured, rather than a new monster he'd collected for who knows what reason.

Too bad I hadn't gotten cell phone numbers for my monster posse before I unleashed them on the city. Not that they'd had phones, granted . . .

But it *would* be nice to check in. See how the gang was doing.

Kor's second snarl snapped me back to reality.

Time to get crafty. "Well, if you're gonna be rude about it, maybe we *won't* let you in on this prime opportunity for vengeance against the crew who tried to steal your mirror."

Kor slowly emerged from said mirror, those red eyes vanishing. "I'm listening . . ."

I gave him the fastest possible rundown of our clash at Elena's, and the aftermath, then held up the hairs. "These belong to one of Ambrose's goons. If we're lucky, a tracking spell on them will lead us right to them."

If we were *extra* lucky, it would lead us to wherever they were setting up the ritual Ambrose had planned.

A glance toward the windows showed it was starting to get dark, but how dark did it have to be for him to get started?

Kor considered the hairs. "A childishly simple plan. I detect Bracchius's involvement." He cast a scathing look at Bracchius, who didn't flinch or even try to hide Sparkles behind his back.

That was a new development.

Kor released an aggrieved sigh, scorching air washing over me. "But I suppose even the least devious plans occasionally succeed. And I'd love to whoop their—" He coughed. "I mean, I would direly *loathe* if those upstart ingrates were allowed to proceed unhindered."

I was getting better at suppressing snickers by the day.

"So you're in? Because we're counting on you for the tracking spell part of this thing."

Kor puffed himself up majestically. "I will aid your fiendish endeavors this once, Immy."

"Thanks. So where do you want the hairs?"

He looked a little disappointed I hadn't prostrated myself before him in sobbing gratitude, but he should know better by now.

A crimson glow surrounded the hairs stuck to the inside of my sunglasses case. They levitated up and floated closer to Kor.

"Now, let's see, shall I do a Tardisian tracking spell, or a Winchesterian? The Tardisian certainly has its disadvantages, however—"

The front door shuddered beneath pounding fists.

Ugh, what now?

I jogged toward the door, calling back, "Whatever you pick, make it snappy!"

The voice yelling through the door told me this was an old problem, not a new one.

Fitz had escaped his restraints.

"If you tell me where the device is, maybe we can work out a deal! We don't have to get the cops involved if you cooperate with me!"

The gears in my mind reversed direction, whirring furiously.

As one of Ambrose's team, Fitz should know *exactly* where the Dreyelian device was. And yet . . . he didn't seem to know.

Why *wouldn't* he know?

The obvious answer presented itself to me: Because he wasn't working for Ambrose after all. Because he really *was* some insurance investigator looking for a stolen insured item—the Dreyelian device.

And if he recovered it without having to go to the cops? He

guaranteed got a bigger bonus on his next paycheck, I bet.

I wrenched the door open. Fitz almost stumbled right into me, helped along by the fact Darth the crow was busy tying his shoelaces together.

"Why do you think I was working with the thief?" I demanded.

An awful squelch erupted behind me, followed by the wail of damned souls if I ever heard it.

Fitz's eyes shifted over my shoulder and widened, but I resisted the temptation to look. Whatever it was, knowing Kor, it wouldn't be good.

At least we should have a tracking spell lickety-split.

Fitz recovered quickly. "I don't think. I *know*."

I rolled my eyes, but decided to humor him—though protecting my completely unfairly maligned character with the judicious use of air quotes. "Fine, how do you 'know'?"

"The same way I know . . ." He looked around, then crouched to touch the doormat beneath him. His face froze, eyes glazing over.

When he came back to earth, his expression shifted from anger to bafflement. "The same way I know . . . a vampire gave you this doormat specifically so you would . . . *have* to invite him in?"

I smiled at the memory, then focused. I'd completely forgotten about Fitz's magic fingers— Er, touch.

No, that wasn't any better—

His quirk! That worked. It was even the official term.

My stuttering brain finally latched on to the significance of what he'd said. His quirk had told him that Nadine had given me the artifact. Only, she hadn't. So . . .

Oh, that text he'd gotten from work after pegasus riding. He must've gone back to the rental lot and felt up the cup holder of the car Nadine had rented.

The car I'd snagged that pesky doodad from.

Saskia Skies must've rented the car right back out again, with it only being returned today, for Fitz not to have figured this out sooner. His quirk had shown Nadine dropping the device in, then me helping myself to it.

Sure would look like collusion to anybody with eyes.

I gulped. "Actually . . ."

Tires screeched from the road, and I immediately went on alert. What *now*?

I ducked under Fitz's arm, ready to dig up clods of dying sod if I had to, to chuck at whatever new threat had just pulled up.

A short midnight red sedan idled at the curb, windows oh-so-helpfully tinted to hide the occupants.

The back passenger window rolled down, and I braced for another magical assault.

Instead, Cynna poked her head out the window, white-blonde locks in an immaculate updo, and grinned with perfect pointy teeth. "The cavalry has arrived, darling."

WAR UNICORN

"How did you—?" I shook my head and made for the car with Cynna inside.

Fitz sputtered. "Where are you going? This isn't over y—"

Cthulhu grant me patience.

I rounded on Fitz and speared his chest with a finger. "Believe what you want, but I didn't help steal that artifact. In fact, my friends and I are off to try to get it away from a vain vampire with a god complex, so you can either leave me alone and get the hells out of here, or come along and help."

"But—"

I jerked the finger up to his face. Good thing he was wearing glasses, or I might've scratched his cornea. "Those are your options—get in the car, or buh-bye. Now shut it."

Shockingly, he shut it. I left him trying to rub my fingerprint off his hipster glasses.

"So commanding and quarrelsome . . . I love it," Cynna crooned.

"Thanks. I think." I peered through her open window at the driver's seat. As I suspected, Damarion was watching me from behind the wheel, pleased as punch. "Are you suddenly telepathic? How did you know to show up?"

He rolled his window down as well. "Paolo was kind enough to keep me informed of your hijinks. Admittedly, we had to alter course a few times, but no matter."

I could've hugged Paolo. Despite his venom high, Bracchius would be too pooped to keep teleporting for much longer, and I hardly trusted Kor to beam us around the city.

This was perfect.

The crows agreed. Flirt fluttered up to perch on the door. Jekyll landed on the roof before rolling down the windshield in an awkward sprawl of feathers, cackling all the way.

"Crows, what a delightful omen! I have a feeling this evening will be positively *medieval.*" Grinning, Cynna scooted to the middle of the backseat with her hands. "I am sorry Elena wasn't of more help to you, but I'm happy to remedy her failings. Shall we depart?"

Should I tell her Elena was even worse off than she thought? Maybe a convo better saved for a less hectic day.

"Uh . . . let me grab some stuff. And let the others know."

I was halfway to my front door when Paolo trudged out, discouraged. He held a jar of peanut butter and a plate with a dozen apple slices.

"I'm afraid I couldn't conjure up much from your kitchen, Miss Immy, but—" He blinked at the car—or more specifically, Damarion in the driver's seat—and paled.

"Master Damarion! That you had to drive yourself— Please, let me!"

He unconsciously passed off the apples and peanut butter to Kor of all people, who'd just drifted out behind him.

Paolo dashed over as Damarion unfolded himself from the front seat and smoothed out his suit.

"Quite enjoyable, really. My skills are perhaps a little rusty, but it's been ages since I was behind the wheel. Rather a treat."

Cynna thunked a massive cooler perched on the center console with a thud that definitely wasn't hollow. "And we have much more suitable refreshment than some paltry slices of fruit."

Kor unscrewed the peanut butter jar and peered inside. "What an appalling substance." He ditched the container wholesale, but a new orangey smear marred his dark surface.

"You've got something, riiight . . . there." I pointed.

"Ack!" He rubbed at it with one of the stubby arms he'd protruded. "Appalling and *pernicious*!"

It took him another thirty seconds of panicked rubbing before he summoned hellfire to the end of his arm and set the offending peanut butter streak ablaze.

Tiny crumbles of soot meandered to the ground.

I gave them a wide berth on my way into the house. "Aster, Bracchius! Ride's here!"

Giggling came from behind the closed door to the bathroom.

Did I want to know what those two were up to?

Probably not.

Instead, I ducked into my room and retrieved my sword. If I was gonna be low on magic—or completely out—for the next few hours, I needed an alternate strategy for bashing baddies.

I took the chance to change into my own clothes too, during which process every ache and pain cheerfully reintroduced itself. I kept Elena's cargo pants, though.

Something to be said for massive pockets, and plenty of 'em.

Speaking of Elena . . .

"Bracchius?" I rapped a knuckle on the bathroom door. "Maybe we should—"

The door whipped inward, revealing a beaming Aster and ecstatic Bracchius. He held out Sparkles, who'd gotten a makeover—Roman military style.

"We made Sparkles some battle armor!" he crowed.

Yup. The plushie unicorn was bedecked in cut-up metallic plastic pieces of an old Halloween costume, strung together in a horsey suit of armor.

Complete with a helmet that gathered her fluffy mane into a rainbow plume.

"Wow. You really did."

Aster patted Sparkles. "Now she'll be safe when we find Ambrose and whoop his ass."

"Good. And about that: Damarion's here with a car, and I think Kor has the tracking spell ready, so we better hit the road."

Staring down at Aster and Bracchius, I realized the pink flush of her cheeks wasn't just from excitement. "But first, missy, sunscreen."

She raised a hand to her cheek as I rummaged in my drawers for my heavy-duty sunblock. Her hops didn't get her in range of the mirror, so I hefted her to let her see her rosy face.

"But I put some on before the club . . ."

"That was more than two hours, plus a vigorous fight and car chase ago. Here." I coated her in the stuff like frosting and let her rub it in, then ousted the two of them from the bathroom.

Last thing a girl needs heading into battle is a full bladder.

I grabbed my sword again and chased down Bracchius, who was showing Sparkles her reflection in Kor's mirror in the hall. "Yes, you are a fierce war unicorn! Hmm . . . maybe we should get razor shoes for your hooves . . ."

"Hey you, warlord." I poked him, and he drifted up to my level. "Can you put Elena in the terrarium under the sink? I think she'll be happier there than inside you."

With any luck, she'd even devour the crusted-on grime.

Bracchius rubbed his tummy. "She does feel pretty weird moving around in here. Okie!" He bolted for the bathroom.

"Just leave the cabinet door cracked!" I was *not* adding 'suffocated a sorceress to death' to my résumé.

Not today.

Sorceress happily glomming across dirty glass, I ordered Bracchius to the car, then locked the front door behind me.

Fitz was nowhere to be seen, but Aster, Paolo, Bracchius, Kor, and Damarion waited by the car, along with the crows. Paolo had the hood up, muttering over various engine parts.

Kor lugged a Tupperware with something bobbing inside.

"Whatcha got there?" I nodded at it.

He tucked it behind him. "The physical component of my tracking spell."

"Then why are you hiding it?"

"No reason you should concern yourself with."

Not suspicious at all.

I acted like I didn't care—no narrowed eyes, no raised brow. I casually inspected my nails, then lurched behind Kor to get a look at the thing.

The Tupperware was half-filled with murky water.

And a hot dog wobbled inside.

I just stared. "The physical component of your tracking spell is an old *hot dog* floating in greasy water?"

Kor harrumphed. "If I'd had better tools at my disposal, I would've used them, Imogen. However, *someone* burned down half my domain, leaving me bereft of my most prized possessions, so—"

I raised both hands. "I get it, I get it. Sorry."

At least, if he was going to punish me with my full name anyway, he was using my *actual* name for once. Not that I'd put it past him to revert to Immaline if I really pissed him off.

Seemingly satisfied, Paolo dropped the hood into place and climbed in the driver's seat. I opened the back door and stood aside, but nobody else moved.

I turned to the others. "Well, what are we waiting for?"

Damarion glanced between Aster and Bracchius. "We . . . seem to have a dustup over the seating arrangements."

Bracchius puffed up. "Immy, you can't make me sit next to Cynna! Or Kor. Or especially Fitz!"

Fitz? Frowning, I ducked to see inside the car.

Sure enough, Fitz was seated—nervously—next to Cynna in the backseat. Oh boy.

EVIL OVERLORD LOVEFEST

Guess Fitz had decided to join the club after all. Whether he was here to help or harangue me further was another question.

I asked it. "You actually want to help us?"

He glowered. "I don't want to let you out of my sight."

My fingers itched with exasperation, seeking something to strangle. "I *told* you, I didn't steal i—"

"I saw you take it! And you didn't tell me about it when I was questioning everyone at your work. If you were innocent—"

Cynna's jaguar smile lost all its cheer as she trapped his lips beneath a hushing finger. "Our Immy is not anything so banal as innocent, young man, but I will not have you taking that tone with her."

Fitz shrank against the seat. "Yes, ma'am."

She sighed, her silver eyes world-weary. "Why does no one understand proper forms of address any longer? For me to rate a drab 'ma'am' . . . Whatever happened to 'Your Maleficence' and 'Her Heinousness'?"

Kor ducked under my elbow, nearly scorching me. "I absolutely agree, my depraved queen. And may I say, it's a darksome delight to make your acquaintance."

Oh no. I needed to interrupt this evil overlord lovefest but quick.

I clapped loud enough to burst eardrums. "All right, peeps, we've got a ticking clock! Listen up!"

Everyone dutifully blinked at me.

We had a grand total of eight beings and one sardine can of a sedan to squeeze into. Nine if you counted Sparkles, though she was sure to be the least fussy about seating arrangements.

I slid my sheathed sword into the back window well. "Damarion, you have the longest legs, so you sit in the other bucket seat up front with Paolo. Kor, you and your hot dog keep Damarion company—you need to give Paolo directions from your tracking spell."

Kor grumbled but obeyed, hovering a few inches above Damarion's pressed suit pants.

Fitz and Cynna were already in the backseat, leaving one official seat left.

And three people.

Cynna smoothed her dark skirt. "You're welcome to sit on my lap, Immy dearest. I do so enjoy getting cozy with those I'm courting."

I almost said 'Hard pass,' but she was looking a bit too voracious to risk being rude. "Thanks, but I'm sweaty, gross, and shedding sand. Don't want to ruin your nice outfit."

Aster huffed. "Well, *I'm* not sitting on her lap!" She shoved me into the open seat, then plopped on my lap.

Which left Bracchius hovering awkwardly outside. His only reasonable options were beside his archnemeses: Kor, Fitz, and Cynna.

"Um . . ." He fidgeted. "I can ride in the trunk?"

Cynna tittered. "I'm afraid that is already well occupied by my wheelchair, dear demon."

Wait, what?

Startled, I still managed not to give her the once-over. I *had* only ever seen her sitting . . . I'd just never put it together. So she was a badass bitch on wheels?

Yep. That suited her one hundred percent.

"I'm *not* your dear demon!" Bracchius's indignation didn't last long as he swiveled between the open doors. "Um, then . . ."

Him deciding the least of all evils might take a week, so I yanked him inside with my good hand and slammed the door, to his squawk.

"You can float, Bracchius, get over it. We'll figure out where to put you. Paolo, drive."

"Buckle up, darlings," Cynna crooned. "Best to be vanquished by our enemies, not mangled by a tin can."

I nearly strangled Aster in the process, but we got strapped in.

As Paolo pulled away from the curb, Bracchius glommed to the ceiling like a nascent stalactite, keeping as far from Cynna and Fitz as possible without blocking Paolo's view. Sparkles dangled precariously in front of Cynna's face.

"Aster . . ." Bracchius whispered. "Can you switch seats so I can sit with Immy? Please?"

She scrunched up her face. "Well, I'm not sitting with someone I don't even know, *and* who's stalking my friend." She cast a sizzling glare at Fitz, and Cynna turned toward him with a dire raised eyebrow.

Fitz quailed.

"And I'm not sitting on my sister's lap either! But . . . I could sit with Damarion!"

He glanced over the seat back. "I'm afraid, Aster, between your juvenile appearance and the illegality of stacking multiple bodies onto one seat, we would be accosted by law enforcement, which I assume we can hardly afford. Best to stay back there, where the tinted windows afford you privacy."

She shifted on my lap. "Sorry, Bracchie."

Bracchius drooped into a longer stalactite, almost touching Cynna's hair before sucking back up in a panic.

This was going to be a wild ride.

As Kor watched his bobbing hair-wrapped hot dog and barked directions to Paolo, Fitz leaned past Cynna to see me.

"Speaking of the authorities . . . Say you're telling the truth about not stealing the device, and about chasing down this vampire who supposedly has it. Then why aren't you calling the authorities?"

A laugh burst from me. "And tell them what? Some bad dudes have an unknown ball of terrifying magic and are taking it to an also unknown location, but that's okay because we're tracking them with a hot dog and a few hairs I ripped off a guy in the subway? Unless . . ."

I narrowed my eyes. "Do *you* know what it is? Or where they'd be taking it?"

"I don't know where they'd take it. And . . ." His glasses shifted with a wriggle of his nose. "No. Not exactly."

My lips firmed. "Not exactly? Or not at all?"

"I know it's dangerous. But what it specifically is . . ." He raked a hand through his hair. "I wasn't entrusted with that information."

"Great. So you're useless to me." I slumped.

"He's useless to *everyone*," Bracchius groused.

Cynna smirked. "If you're still seeking more suitable seating, demon, I *could* let this delicious, insolent young man sit on my lap, freeing up his seat for your use."

She'd still have to scoot over to put me and Aster between Bracchius and them, but it wasn't a bad idea . . .

Maybe she'd eat Fitz for me.

Fitz coughed, plastered as far into the door as possible. "No thank you."

Paolo turned left, squishing us passengers even further together, as Kor bleated, "Not left, straight!"

"This car can't phase through buildings, regrettably," Paolo muttered. "We'll have to zigzag left and right for a while to maintain your 'straight.'"

Kor gave the Tupperware an aggravated shake. "None of this would be an issue if you pathetic mortals would just learn how to levitate already."

I kept my eyes trained on the front window, trying not to get carsick.

A centaur-swallowing pothole jounced the car, and Bracchius plummeted from the ceiling.

Right onto Cynna's lap.

Cynna cupped Bracchius as he quivered in shock on her lap. "Well, hello, Dark One. We haven't been properly introduced."

With a yelp, Bracchius slorped up off her lap like a slinky making for orbit. He mashed into the back window well, buddying up to my sword and forming a long black roll with Sparkles at one end.

Put a tail and a pair of floppy ears on 'im, and he'd make the perfect doxie.

I leaned in to Cynna. "That's Bracchius. You're one of his mortal"—immortal?—"enemies."

"As I gathered. I'll be sure to add him to my address book with the rest. Now, enough squabbling, my tasty morsels. I came to assist, and assist I shall."

She shoved the top off the cooler wedged between the front seats, then dove in with both hands in a clatter of ice cubes. "As the adoring younger sister—"

Aster scoffed.

"—I of course must take care of my dear older sister first, so the rest of you will have to forgive the wait for your victuals."

Cynna lifted two plastic pouches of blood out of the ice. But not standard IV pouches—these were shaped like a dinosaur and a puffy star, respectively.

"I even got the kids pack, just for you!" Beaming, she offered the pouches to Aster.

I genuinely couldn't tell whether she was trying to be nice or ragging on her. Even with as little as I knew Cynna, the latter was probably *always* the safer bet.

Aster didn't let the potential taunt stand between her and her dinner, though. She snatched both packets in her little hands and punctured the dinosaur like her fangs were her own personal Capri Sun straw.

"And for my intended . . ." Cynna reached back in as I fought a flurry of alarm.

Her *intended*? Please let that not be me.

Would anyone else here qualify?

Maybe she and Damarion were getting hitched on the sly.

But nope, she turned to me with an open carton of poke—salmon, tuna, edamame, carrots, sweet corn, cucumber, avocado, watermelon radish, brown rice, furikake . . .

Yum.

I took the carton and chopsticks gingerly. "Intended *friend*, right?"

"Of course, darling. Whatever else could you possibly imagine I mean?"

I swear a devious red gleam lit up those silver eyes of hers.

Oh, I was in *so* much trouble.

But in trouble with poke, I could handle. My stomach roared louder than a storm dragon as I snarfed the first shovelful of goodness.

Bright citrus sauce lit up my mouth with the freshness of the veggies, the saltiness of the soy, and the buttery texture of the tuna.

Maybe being her intended—*whatever* that meant—wouldn't be *so* bad.

"And for our beloved Paolo . . ." Cynna retrieved a platter of sashimi and raw steak cubes, which she handed off to Damarian with another pair of chopsticks. "As I rightly assumed you would insist on resuming your cherished driving duties, Paolo, I procured something Damarion can easily feed you. A carnivore's meal seemed fitting."

Damarion took the news in stride, already pinching one slice of fish between the chopsticks, but Paolo was rattled.

"Really, sir, that's not necess—"

Damarion shut him up with sashimi to the face.

I really wanted to savor my poke, but we might be screeching to a halt at Ambrose's door in the next two minutes.

"Kor?" I piped, not bothering to swallow first. "Can you tell how much further it is?"

He spun, the murky water sloshing violently inside the Tupperware as he glared at me. "I'm using a *months-old* hot dog, Immy, and you expect me to—" He stopped with a rumble. "I mean, er, it's unlikely we're close, as my . . . tracking spindle . . . is still fairly sedate in its motions."

I couldn't help myself. "Ya mean the hot dog will start barking when we're almost there?"

If Kor had teeth, they'd have ground into bone dust in an instant. "The *tracking spindle's* movements will become exaggerated, yes. But there will be NO barking."

Cynna interrupted our spat with another crunch of ice. "And although I only anticipated one demon on this excursion, this should be enough to share . . ." She held out some weird black crystalline chunks with glowing golden embers inside. "Rock candy phoenix briquettes."

Kor eagerly snatched half, but Bracchius impossibly retreated further into the window well.

Rolling my eyes, I took the remaining briquettes from Cynna, the sugar crystals hot in my hand.

If ever I'd laid eyes on demon crack, this was it.

I jammed the rocks in beside Bracchius, indenting his tummy or butt or— I really couldn't tell with him squashed into a zucchini. "Sparkles needs you to keep your strength up to defend her in battle. So eat up, buster."

"Oh. Right!" Bracchius devoured the candy in one go. His demonly efforts not to sound like he was on cloud nine failed miserably.

"I also didn't anticipate our rude human guest, so I'm afraid he will have to go without refreshments." Cynna threw a haughty look at Fitz.

He loosened his tie nervously. He wasn't becoming immune to Cynna's intimidation tactics anytime soon.

Kor barked a lane change at Paolo, who did his best to comply. I was too busy happily stuffing my face to care about anything else.

Aster peered into the cooler. "Hey, Bracchie, you could fit in here now!"

"And give my enemies the chance to trap me inside? Nuh-uh!"

"You could just teleport right out . . ."

"But I'd still be the demon who got lured into a cooler and trapped!

Kor would bring it up every day for the rest of forever!"

Kor turned away from his hot dog. "I would, and you would deserve it."

"See??" Bracchius wiggled Sparkles, the rainbow plume on her battle helmet tickling my neck.

I was just tipping my last heaping bite into my mouth when Cynna fastened her eerie stare on me again. "By your battered appearance, I assume some of your foes got the better of you all."

Mouth full, I nodded.

"Who would we say has the most grievous injuries?" She glanced between us.

I poked at my ribs. Samaire had probably been the worst off of all of us, but hopefully she was seeing a healer right now. Paolo didn't seem too dinged up, and it was hard to tell with Aster, thanks to her perpetual pep.

We'd solved Bracchius's exhaustion for now, and I never could quite figure out how injuries showed up on a demon anyway. It wasn't like bruises bloomed to the surface of their ebony forms, and if they had bones to break, I'd sure never heard of 'em.

"Immy, I think." Aster patted my knee, then resumed shoving her tongue into the crevices of the dinosaur pouch to get the last possible molecules of blood.

"Excellent. Then I will begin with you, darling." Cynna reached for me, *not* into the cooler for first aid supplies.

Why wasn't she reaching into the cooler for first aid supplies?

"What exactly are you—"

"Hush now."

She didn't so much as blink as she took my hands—awkward around Aster on my lap—and squeezed my fingers between her own.

Ouch. My abused hand kicked up a stink at this latest mistreatment.

"My, you did engage in some mischief today, didn't you? Broken metacarpals, bruised ribs and tibia, burnt shoulder, abraded skin, posttransformative strain to your muscles and organs, extensive soft tissue bruising . . ."

How did she know all that? I tried to jerk my hands away, but her grip was firm as faeglass. "How—?"

"Now, I did say hush." She punctuated the last word with a bounce of our joined hands, and suddenly my lips were sealed.

No, like, really—*sealed.*

I mraowed a protest angry-cat style, but my lips were stuck together worse than the time I forgot to drink for three days.

"Cheeky of me, I know, but this will only take a minute, and incessant questions do ruin my concentration so."

I didn't let up on my muffled mewling, but it didn't stop her.

Something *inside* me twitched.

UNTWIST YOUR BOXERS ALREADY

I jolted, legitimately afraid for my life, but I still couldn't get any further away or reclaim my hands from Cynna's grip. My insides quaked like jiggling Jell-O.

What in the name of all that's unholy was she *doing* to me? Nightmare visions danced through my mind: implanting me with giant maggots, stealing my spleen, turning me into a human protein shake she could slurp down—

My flesh shifted.

Visibly.

Bones twinged and bruises ran through the color spectrum. My injured hand fluxed, knuckles and tendons shifting.

After today, I'd pay a million bucks for my body to never rearrange itself again.

Just gotta get rich first.

"What *are* you?" Fitz goggled at Cynna in horror.

"Now, haven't you already committed enough improprieties for one evening, young man? You should know there are several questions one never asks a lady: her age, her species, her secrets . . . There."

Cynna released me, and my lips started working again. The first noise out of them was a whimpering caterwaul.

She patted my cheek. "Isn't that much better? Most everything back in order."

I touched my face to make sure I still felt like me. Nose—the right level of perky. Lips—dry, but the right shape. Acne scars along my jaw—check.

Yup, still me.

Bonus: neither hand hurt as I poked and prodded. Actually, I felt way better overall. But that wasn't like *any* healing I'd ever had.

"I . . . I think so. How did you do that?" I scanned Cynna, but her silver eyes, pointy teeth, and normal humanoid appearance didn't clue me in to how in the hells she'd patched me up.

Cynna crooked a finger and whispered in my ear. "Just a little flesh manipulation, darling. It's not often I've used it for beneficent purposes."

I gulped at that implication. She could shift flesh and bone with a touch, and she *didn't* usually use it for healing?

Yep, I was officially never doing anything to piss her off.

I summoned a smile. "Neat trick."

She fluffed her sleek updo with a hand. "Why, thank you. You know, we haven't even had the pleasure of being acquainted for a week, and here I am, already revealing my secrets to you."

Hopefully she considered that a good thing, and not a reason to dispose of my corpse in the most alarming way possible? "Isn't . . . that what friends do?"

Her smile was positively devilish. "Touché."

My phone buzzed under Aster's butt, and she scooted to let me grab it.

"Your turn, dear sister." Cynna extended a hand toward Aster.

Nope, didn't wanna watch *that* process from the outside. I glued my eyes to my phone.

An unknown number had texted.

The message said: Done with the healer! We're both okay, but Nadine has a concussion, so they're keeping her for observation. Did you stop Ambrose?? Do you need any help? Can I meet you somewhere?

It had to be Samaire, using Nadine's phone. My heart unclenched at hearing she was all right.

"Samaire and Nadine are okay," I announced, to relieved murmurs and smiles from the others.

I texted back: Where are you? Damarion picked us up and we're tracking Ambrose down. Maybe we can get you along the way.

Samaire: Right by Sizzle & Saltado.

That wasn't too far from where we'd left her. I peered out the windows at the streets and buildings rolling by. Where were we, anyway? I didn't recognize this neighborhood.

Further afield, Hoof Heights poked above the shorter buildings, its shallow stairstep silhouette and large grassy balconies easy to pick out among the more boring skyscrapers. And we were heading east . . .

As long as Kor's hot dog didn't send us for a loop, we'd be a few blocks from Samaire in five minutes or so.

"Paolo, we need to swing by Sizzle & Saltado to pick up Samaire. That shouldn't take us too far off course, right?"

"Not at all, Miss Immy." He glanced dubiously at Kor's Tupperware, though.

I texted Samaire back: Wait outside? We'll be there soon. *hug* Glad you're okay!!

Aster wriggled on my lap as Cynna released her hand. "You didn't mess with my brain again, did you? Because I *don't* need to act more mature."

My hand lifted to my head of its own volition as Cynna chuckled. "Don't worry, I gave up on that centuries ago."

"Um, you didn't rearrange *my* brain either, right?" I didn't feel any different . . . But would I?

"No, darling, I won't be muddling with any brains today. At least not any of *yours*."

Yikes. The bad guys had no idea what was coming.

I shifted to help Aster get comfortable again, but yelped as something hard and angular jabbed into my leg. I almost tipped Aster face-first into the window, but caught her just in time.

"Sorry."

"What is it?" She peered at my burrowing hand.

I dug out the offending whatnot as we coasted to a stop at a red light. Right—the dupe we'd made of the Dreyelian device, with the piece of Kor inside.

Cynna leaned forward over the cooler. "And now let me attend to our dear Paolo, while I won't distract you from the road." She touched his shoulder.

He went rigid, hands clenching on the steering wheel, but thankfully the car didn't budge into the intersection.

To distract myself from the horror show going on under his skin, I twiddled the metal orb in my fingers, trying to remember what I'd read in that chonk of a book on how to open these things. You had to shift the rings a certain way . . .

Tip of my tongue between my lips, I slid one ring, then another. No, that wasn't it. How about this way . . . ?

"There. All better?" Cynna released Paolo.

He cracked his neck and stretched his furry fingers. "I suppose so."

"Excellent." Cynna sat back, no longer blocking Fitz's view, and his eyes landed right on the gizmo in my hands.

He snapped forward so quick his seat belt almost bisected him as it drew him up short with a clunk. "You— That—!"

Cynna shoved him back with a single finger as we gals talked over each other. "Do try to compose yourself, young ma—"

"Untwist your boxers already, it's a fake." I rotated a few more rings. "Hey, Kor, want your liver back?"

Kor almost dropped the Tupperware. "My *what*? I don't have anything as foul as a liver, Immy!" Shuddering, he caught sight of the device, with the dark blob trapped inside—way less sinister than its counterpart.

Not that I'd be telling Kor he didn't measure up in the intimidation department.

I have enough trouble with him as it is.

"Oh, that! Yes, I *absolutely* want that back!" He lurched forward just as I slid the last ring into the right configuration.

The orb opened like a flower made of miniature gold hoops, the little glob of Kor's substance floating at the center.

Fitz flinched as the device opened. "Don't—"

"Give me that!" Kor snatched the blob and reabsorbed it.

Fitz blinked, then narrowed his eyes at me. "You've got a *lot* of explaining to—"

With an aggrieved sigh, Cynna rested a hand on his knee, and his lips clamped together.

Heh. Maybe that trick wasn't so bad after all.

Completely ignoring Fitz's bugged-out eyes and grunts of protest, Cynna turned in her seat to look at Bracchius in the window well. "And are either of our demon friends in need of repair?"

"No!" Bracchius squeaked.

I pinned him with a stern stare. "Bracchius did get pretty pummeled, and basically passed out on us earlier. Kor wasn't with us, though."

Cynna lifted a hand toward Bracchius, but didn't touch him as he squirmed into an even tighter log at the base of the window.

Sheesh. If he compacted any further, he might become his own black hole at this rate.

Cynna flexed her fingers. "I don't know what quarrel you have with me, Dark Lord Bracchius, but I only wish to aid Immy and her allies."

Dark Lord? That was a new one on me. Maybe some formal demon honorific? Pretty sure Bracchius would rather be Rainbow Lord.

Cynna flicked me a mischievous glance. "And surely your unicorn companion would want you at nothing less than your best before engaging in such a *harrowing* battle as we are about to face."

Oh, she was taking a leaf out of my book.

Devious.

Bracchius pulsed. "I . . . suppose that might be a good i—"

"*Right*, mortal fool!" Kor bellowed, shaking his waterlogged hot dog like a maraca as Paolo turned left a block beyond the light.

Paolo blithely ignored him.

"May I?" Cynna pressed, still studying Bracchius.

He hesitated, then whispered, "Okay."

She lowered her hand with a toothy smile. "What a treat! I've never had occasion to work on a demon before."

That didn't inspire confidence.

Bracchius's surface rippled like he'd been struck by raindrops from all angles. "RAWCHOO!"

I ducked at his explosion of a sneeze, anticipating a gout of hellfire like the last time Kor had stuck his metaphorical nose in my shaker of Everything Bagel seasoning.

But no. Instead, Bracchius's sneeze blasted glitter all over the backseat. And me.

Just when I'd finally gotten rid of the last of the sand—I think. To be fair, I *really* should've expected this.

I pinched glitter out of my eyelashes and wiped my face, but it didn't help. The glitter just spread.

Aster giggled as she drew patterns in the glitter coating her own skin, and Cynna looked shell-shocked for a moment before erupting in a belly laugh. "It's not often I'm surprised! Bravo."

Fitz spewed and sputtered, swiping his hands together like the glitter was cooties.

Not that it was much better . . .

But his grumpitude cheered me right up.

"No fair!" Bracchius pouted. "Everyone's shimmery but me!"

"I can fix that." Grinning evilly, I smeared my hands all over Bracchius and Sparkles both.

The car swerved and pulled to a stop, swaying me dangerously close to Cynna's pointy teeth. I blinked up from my glitter attack. "Are we there? We found Ambrose?"

"No, Miss Immy." Paolo rolled down his window and lifted a hand at Samaire, who stood on the sidewalk, hugging herself.

Samaire's face brightened at his wave, and she rushed over.

Her healer had done a bang-up job—she moved quick and sure, no sign of the pain or limping from earlier, or the bruises and general weariness.

Hopefully we could punch Ambrose's ticket before his muscle beat us to a pulp this time.

Fitz's door opened, and Samaire stalled, her grin freezing. "Oh . . . Hello, *lots* of people." She peered around the inside of the car. "And Fitz, right? Can I . . . sit with you?"

Cynna took pity on him and unsealed his lips, but I answered before he could get a word out.

"We *hates* him," I hissed in my best malnourished creepy hobbit voice.

Samaire's eyebrow rose in her signature 'challenge accepted' look. "All the more reason to crush him and make him feel awkward, then." She climbed onto his lap with a maximum of elbow jabbing and stomping on his toes.

I could've shed a tear. *This* is what best friends are for.

Clambering half-under Aster and over Cynna, I crushed Samaire in a hug. "Don't get hurt like that again, okay?"

"I'll try. Don't go monster again either."

"Deal." We shared a smile as we untangled.

Kor hadn't let up on a steady muttered chorus of "*right, right, right, right, right*" since Paulo had detoured to get Samaire. She slammed the door, and as Paolo pulled back into traffic, Kor blurted, "FINALLY!"

Samaire rubbed glitter between her fingers. "So, are we celebrating? Or is this camouflage? I'll admit, I didn't think Ambrose would retreat to a glitter factory."

"I sneezed," Bracchius confessed. "But isn't it great?!"

He rolled in the window well, kicking up plumes of glitter. I snorted out my nose to keep from sucking the stuff straight into my lungs.

Glitter pneumonia was *not* how I wanted to die, thanks.

"It's very you." Samaire smirked.

"Hungry?" Cynna pulled something out of the cooler and blew the worst of the glitter off before offering it to Samaire—a carton of potstickers. "Perhaps one of our demons would be kind enough to reheat it?"

Kor ignored us, but Bracchius coughed, and steam rose from the carton.

"Oh wow, thanks." Samaire snatched it and dug in.

Fitz's jaw dropped. "Wait, but you said there wasn't any more food!"

"Not for you, there wasn't." Cynna stared him down.

"Remind me why I'm here again?" he grumbled, flopping back against the seat.

We all talked over each other in an irritated chorus.

"An excellent question."

"Because you're a jerk!" Aster glared.

"S'all your own fault, my dude."

"You should just leave!" Bracchius snapped.

I *almost* felt sorry for the guy.

Samaire stomped on Fitz's foot again as she found a more comfy position. "Wait, is that a *hot dog*? Why do we have a hot dog?"

Kor puffed up. "It's actually a highly sophisticated—"

"Tracking spindle," half the car monotoned in chorus.

"O . . . kay." Samaire fought a smile.

"It's how we're tracking Ambrose," I explained. "Best Kor could come up with on the fly."

Kor bloomed a brighter red. "It's not *my* fault that—"

Cynna reached forward, probably to shut him up like she had Fitz, but I caught her hand. "We'll never find the place if all he can do is shake the hot dog at us furiously."

She grunted. "A pity."

Samaire swallowed a bite. "So catch me up, guys. Did I miss anything exciting?"

I yawned. "Not much. Bracchius got tired, we gave him a sugar high, made the tracking spell, and hitched a ride with these two." I jerked my thumbs at Cynna and Damarion.

Samaire focused on me. "Did anyone finally get up the courage to ask you about what in the actual hells happened back there? Y'know, when you turned into a literal cryptid and stripped ten years off our lives from pure terror?"

Cynna quirked an eyebrow, intrigued.

It was my turn to smirk. "Just you. Everybody else must be too chicken."

"So what was that about, anyway?" Samaire took another bite, supremely unconcerned.

We'd been friends long enough for her to know I really should come with my own liability waiver.

I shrugged. "Family sigil handed down from way back when. Never felt desperate enough to use it before. Ya want a copy?"

She choked, and Fitz pounded her half-heartedly on the back. "That might be the only one I ever say no to. But no. Very much no."

"Kk."

Cynna's eyes sparkled. "*I'd* be interested in learning more . . ."

She was already terrifying. Did I really want to let *her* turn into the Tramble Terror?

Hells to the naw.

"Maaaybe another day."

Kor gave Paolo more directions, which he followed the best he could with the layout of the city. Skyscrapers popped up around us as we headed into the most recently built section of downtown.

We passed the infamous abandoned lot of the never-built Silver Spires, then the shimmering pink glass tower of the Scintilla Center.

Aster leaned toward Samaire. "I'm sorry your girlfriend turned out to be a thief. Are you okay?"

My shoulders tightened with guilt. I'd been so focused on Nadine's lies that I hadn't even asked Samaire how *she* felt about it.

Great friend I was.

With a sigh, Samaire brushed her dark hair behind her shoulders—into Fitz's face. "I will be, I think. It sucks finding out she isn't who I thought she was, but . . . I do still like her. I guess I just have to reconcile that with—"

"STOP!" Kor boomed, and the car screeched to a halt, jerking us forward.

"Me? Or Paolo?" Samaire asked hesitantly.

"What?" Kor faced us, the hot dog spinning propeller style inside the Tupperware. Damn, it was creating its own whirlpool in there. "No, not *you*. We've arrived!"

TRICKED-OUT WHEELS

We'd stopped beside the lot of a brand-spanking-new skyscraper, with a few scaffolds still in place and plastic sheeting flapping in the breeze. Baby trees and bushes dotted some uninspired landscaping of grass and concrete, bordering a minuscule parking lot with fresh asphalt.

The construction crew was clearly gone for the night, their equipment parked and empty. No sign of Ambrose either . . .

Only the dregs of daytime still touched the horizon as Paolo turned into the lot and parked beside a row of the pitiful trees.

I reached for the door handle. "All right, let's get goi—"

The locks all clunked. "We are *not* dashing into danger without a proper briefing of the situation." Damarion caught my eyes in the rearview mirror.

I pulled the handle experimentally, but the door didn't open. "Fine, but two minutes tops."

"Well?"

Oh. I *was* probably the logical person to run down the situation. "Ambrose is doing some big scary ritual with a big scary Nova-class being, probably to fix his face, or become all powerful, or who knows. Plus he has a lot of thugs and isn't afraid to use them."

"And we're here to *smite* them!" Kor chuckled evilly.

"That's about the gist. Now can we go?" I tugged at the handle uselessly.

"Not quite." Damarion turned in his seat to see us all. "Is everyone in fighting shape? I don't want to risk anyone who would be better left here. Sound off on your status and capabilities, if you would."

Aster piped up. "I have venom and magic again! Not full on either, but maybe half? And if I suck on a few bad guys, I won't run out."

Samaire grimaced. "My magic reserves are still low, but I can rely on my siren powers. As long as I'm not too close to any of you." She gave me a playful knowing look.

I stuck out my tongue. "Yeah, my bad—I won't listen in to your songs out of curiosity."

Pointing at the window well, I added, "I've got my sword, and . . ." I checked my own reserves.

Still nothing.

Crud. I'd really messed up, hadn't I? Hopefully I hadn't murdered the seed of my magic or something.

"Annnd my dazzling charisma. I'll be fine."

Damarion didn't look convinced. "No magic?"

"Not yet, but you know how much of a disaster it is even when I do have it. I'm used to thinking on my feet."

Bracchius hmphed. "That's not fair. How come we all ran out of magic but the bad guys didn't?"

"I'd imagine they train their magic on a daily basis, increasing their reserve." Cynna surveyed us. "Not a practice amongst present company, I take it?"

Awkward coughs and shuffles filled the car.

"Well, I assure you *I* am well equipped for battle. And happy to suggest a training regimen for whoever survives the day."

"I'm well equipped too!" Bracchius actually plumped back up to his orb form, getting surprisingly close to Cynna. "My magic is almost back to full, and I'll make those scallywags regret the day they hurt Sparkles!"

"That's today, just FYI." I winked. "You'll make them regret today?"

"Duh. And as for Sparkles, she's protected by her battle armor, and can channel magic through her horn to attack our enemies!"

We all blinked down at the plushie unicorn.

Had Bracchius finally cracked for real? He couldn't think Sparkles would actually blast the baddies . . . Could he?

Guess we'd find out.

Fitz sighed. "My magical reserves are full, and I'm fairly well trained. Not that I'll be fighting anyone until I verify whether a word you've all said is true."

Big shocker.

Kor took his turn. "My magic is vastly superior to *all* yours, so I suppose I'll be carrying the day—er, night. I will ensure these foul fiends will be charred to cinders and scattered upon the wind, but only after a thorough evisceration and—"

Damarion cut in. "And I'm *also* more than fit to fight. Excellent. I do believe that's everyone?"

Paolo cleared his throat nervously. "I can help, Master Damarion."

Damarion gripped his shoulder. "Brave soul, but I must insist you stay with the car for your own safety. Your wife would readily behead me and pour napalm over my dismembered corpse if I were to let anything happen to you."

Paolo smiled, sitting up straighter. "Yes, sir. I think she would."

Damarion raised a censuring finger. "And this time, no matter how tempting it may be, do not put yourself between these villains and their escape. You are worth more than a few errant miscreants. Am I clear?"

"Yes, sir."

Damarion straightened his tie. "I suppose our fates await us, then." He unlocked the doors and stepped out.

The rest of us piled out, doing some serious detangling of limbs in the process. I retrieved my sword, and Damarion unfolded Cynna's wheelchair from the trunk.

It was the highest-class wheelchair I'd ever seen, all chrome and gold—that couldn't be *actual* gold, right?—with a contoured seat like a throne, upholstered in plush emerald velvet. The bedazzled wheel rims sparkled as the chair shifted, the crystals placed points out like spikes.

If those were real diamonds, I was gonna pass right out on the asphalt.

He and Paolo helped Cynna into the wheelchair like a queen. She stroked the armrests covered in tiny sigils. A few gleamed black, and the chair rolled around the back of the car.

"Do you like it?" Cynna grinned up at me.

"It's *amazing*." My fingers itched to feel up some probably-diamonds.

"So . . . sparkly . . ." If Bracchius had eyes, they'd be the size of those golden hubcaps.

Raucous cawing stole my attention. Overhead, a dozen dark feathery forms were barely visible against the patchy clouds of the night sky.

Crows.

They dove, and fluttered to a landing on the car.

My crows.

"What are you doing here?!" I waved my arms—and sword. "Scram! Get out of here! It's not safe!"

No way did I want a whole murder of dead crows on my conscience.

They scrammed, but only as far as a newly planted wimp of a tree, which sagged almost to the ground beneath their weight.

I sighed. They never listened. "Fine, but you won't be getting any kibble in the afterlife! So you better not get yourselves killed."

Amused croaks bounced through the flock.

Other than the crows, and us, it was quiet. I turned a suspicious look on Kor. "Are we sure your hot dog actually worked? This place seems abandoned."

Kor gasped. "You dare insult me? My tracking spells have *never* failed! Not once!"

"Then lead us to Ambrose, will you?" I swept an arm out to encompass the lot and skyscraper.

He drifted back a few inches. "I already did. He's here."

"Could ya narrow that down a skosh?"

"Well . . . no."

My mouth fell open. "Whaddya mean, *no*?"

Kor stared down at the hot dog, which was still spinning in a frenzied whirlpool. "This is as specific as a Tardisian tracking spell gets."

"Seriously?"

He rolled in a nod, and as he tilted, so did the whirlpool.

Oh crap. "Kor—"

Too late. The lid burst off with a goosh of water, and the hot dog flopped limply to the pavement.

I wiped drops of greasy meat water off my face.

Delightful.

"Didn't we still need that?" Aster whispered.

"Apparently not." I raised my voice. "All right, the tracking spell got us as far as it was gonna. Let's get inside and start looking for Ambrose."

I swallowed a moan as I peered up at the building. This place had to be seventy stories. How the hells were we supposed to find him in there? It'd take a couple days to search every floor, every suite.

Damarion reached the doors into the building first. "Locked."

Of course they were. "Anyone have a lockpicking sigil?"

Silence.

I vowed to add those BrownieBasics lockpicking videos to my watchlist the instant I got home. "Kor? Bracchius? Can you teleport inside?"

The two demons swiveled toward each other, then back to me. "Sorry, Immy." Bracchius rippled apologetically.

"The building's interior is warded against teleportation. Impressively done, actually."

Nothing could ever be easy, could it. "Okay, then Samaire, Fitz, split up and circle the building to check for other doors. Please."

They nodded and took off.

"Kor." I waved him over. "Can you tell if the glass is warded?"

He floated along the doors and walls for a minute. "Yes, but . . ." He bobbed skyward. "Only the first floor."

"Immy!" Samaire called, jogging back. "There's an underground parking garage, and I took a quick peek. Ambrose's car is down there."

"And Ambrose?" My hope and anxiety spiked.

She shook her head. "Not unless he went into the building from there, but the doors to the stairs are locked too, and the elevator's not responding."

"Okay, keep checking around the building for now." I squeezed her hand. "Be safe."

"You too."

"Only the one car?" Damarion asked. "Perhaps Ambrose is overconfident. He couldn't have brought more than a few lackeys with one vehicle."

I grimaced. "He's got a teleportation sigil too."

"Oh. That is unfortunate."

A sizzle overhead had me glancing up. Kor was emitting a tight line of hellfire, slicing a small circle into the glass on the second floor.

No alarms yet . . .

Light flashed in the night sky. Lightning? There hadn't been a storm on the forecast. I looked up.

Not lightning. The streaks of clouds above the skyscraper—and *only* above the skyscraper—were glowing a sickly green.

I grinned. Gotcha.

475

A KINK FOR ARCANE SYMBOLS

I sent a text to Samaire and—ugh—Fitz to head back, then waved the others over. "Found 'em." I pointed toward the night sky.

Damarion, Aster, Cynna, and the demons peered up at the green-tinged clouds.

"I should have guessed." Cynna rolled her wheelchair back with the tap of a sigil. "An ideal location."

Kor and Bracchius floated to either side of me, so I took shameless advantage and elbowed them both. "You up for a little reconnaissance?"

They faced each other.

"Totally, Immy!"

"*Both* of us? Surely I'm the better candidate."

"Are not!" Bracchius gored Kor with Sparkles's squishy horn, to zero effect.

I raised both hands. "Why don't you each take one end of the roof?"

"Okie."

"Fine."

"Just don't get spotted!" I leveled my best commanding stare.

"Imogen, we are demons, lords of darkness. You cannot really think we'd be spotted at night like simpletons—amateurs!"

I flapped a hand at Kor. "But you've got the glowy nonsense going on. I could spot you from half a mile away."

His red flickers faded, leaving him looking oddly empty. "And now?"

"Much better."

Bracchius followed suit as Fitz and Samaire jogged over. "I guess Sparkles isn't camouflaged very well . . . Can you hold her?"

"Sure." I tucked her butt into a cargo pocket, letting her enjoy the view and keeping my hands free. "Now git."

The two demons buzzed up the glass walls of the building, disappearing in the darkness. Hopefully the glitter coating Bracchius wouldn't be *too* much of a giveaway.

Damarion gripped his lapels. "There's still the problem of attaining the roof."

"Bracchius and Kor can both teleport." Though I wasn't positive Kor could take others with him, but if even Bracchius could, it was a safe bet.

"That's a looong way up." Aster craned her neck and stumbled back, but Samaire steadied her.

"No kidding . . ."

I didn't have a good sense of how far Bracchius had been teleporting us before—and we had even *more* people now.

And while Kor clearly was looking forward to smiting his foes on the roof, I wasn't sure if that outweighed his enthusiasm for avenging my destruction of his Baleful Tower . . .

Given the chance, he might just teleport me right into whatever new prison he'd installed in his domain and throw away the key.

"Boo!" The voice behind me threw me into a panic.

Luckily I karate chopped Bracchius with a hand instead of bisecting him into semispheres with my sword.

"Ouch!"

I gave him a flat stare. "Ouch? Really? You're second cousin to a squishy stress ball."

"It's an *emotional* wound. You whacked me!"

"*You* scared the crap out of me!"

Kor sniffed. "Since Imogen is embroiled in a childish skirmish, who shall I report my findings to?"

I glared at him. "Just spill it."

"The villains have constructed an elaborate sigil upon a helicopter pad on the roof, which—"

"Is glowing this *really* gross green, just like the clouds! And—"

"One of the brigands has enclosed himself inside the sigil, with what I can only imagine are his minions standing guard by—"

"The door to the stairs! Immy, like half the roof is clear of bad guys, they must be *so* bad at planni—"

Kor spun on Bracchius. "It's perfectly reasonable to guard the only conventional means of ascension, but yes, it does leave us an opening that—"

"STOP." I smeared both hands down my face, probably leaving marks in the glitter like the facepaint of the Uruk-hai. "How many minions?"

"A lot."

"Eighteen."

Eighteen? Rack and ruin—I'd thought we were in trouble at Elena's.

Where did Ambrose get all these guys?? Thugs 'R' Us?

That was more than two thugs for each of us. Plus we had to contend with Ambrose and the demigod he was about to unleash.

Right, about that . . .

I sucked down a deep breath. "Everybody ready?" I met everyone's eyes—or equivalent—to make sure. Chins firmed; tight smiles and nods were exchanged.

Cynna and Kor were the only ones who looked downright excited.

I gripped my sword hilt, the weapon still sheathed. "All right,

Bracchius—think you can teleport us to the opposite side of the roof from the bad guys?"

He tipped back, assessing the distance. "Pretty sure."

Kor zipped beside him. "*I* definitely can!"

Maybe we could split the load? As long as I wasn't in Kor's group, he'd probably behave himself.

"'Kay, Cynna, Fitz, and Damarion, you're with Kor." He was neutral toward Damarion, liked Cynna, and had a common enemy with Fitz—me.

Hopefully that was enough for him to see those three safely to the roof.

"Aster and Samaire, you're with me and Bracchius."

"And Sparkles!"

"Obviously." I plucked the plushie unicorn from my pocket and returned her to Bracchius.

We formed two little groups each centered on a demon.

I took another deep breath to try to calm my racing heart. "Get ready to fight in three, two, one . . ."

Shimmering purple haze enveloped my vision, and we tumbled through nothingness.

Only to pop back into reality forty stories up, hovering midair for a second à la Wile E. Coyote.

I had enough time to see my dim, glittery reflection in the glass a foot away, my shoes dangling over nothing, before gravity came back from its smoke break.

Bye-bye, whacky world. Nice knowin' ya.

"Yipe!" Bracchius blasted out a glowing web of red that caught us after only falling a couple of—nail-biting, heart-stopping—feet.

Gibbering, we drifted left along the glass, my vision tinted crimson, until the top level of scaffolding appeared under our toes. Bracchius lowered us to the planks of wood, then released his telekinesis.

Samaire and I clung to the railing, gasping, and Aster hugged our legs in a death grip.

"*Pretty sure?*" I squeaked. "Next time you're pretty sure, Bracchius, I'm running the opposite direction!"

"I'm sorry, Immy!! Only the best demons got elite training on stuff like this! All my education was in the under-the-bed demon department . . ."

"*There* you are, cowards!" Kor thundered, dive-bombing us. "This is no time to run away from the fight!"

"We're no—"

Before I could finish, Kor had whipped out four black tentacles, ensnared us, and—

Poof. We vanished in a swirl of flames.

Pale concrete appeared beneath our feet. I glanced up at the twinkling cityscape laid out before us in the darkness, then whirled.

We stood at the edge of the roof with the others, a fogbank of shadow suspended before us. It rose just high enough to hide us, without blocking our view.

Well, except Aster's. I hefted her onto the opposite hip from my sword.

"Your work, Kor?" I breathed.

He bobbed.

No one had noticed us yet. Or, at least, if they had, they weren't hollering or throwing magic yet.

"Don't draw their attention until we have to," I murmured to Kor and Samaire. "Pass it along."

I'd somehow ended up close to Fitz, and I leaned in. "Believe me now?"

He fiddled with his glasses. "I . . . think I'll have to."

The roof was bigger than I'd imagined. There was probably a good fifty feet between us and the painted circle of the helipad, with the thugs arrayed near the door to the stairs on the other side.

Utility boxes, antennae, dishes, and massive ventilation units littered the edges of the roof, providing potential cover.

And a nasty surprise for the developer and construction crew when we'd inevitably obliterate them.

Sorry not sorry?

But the real star of the show was the massive sigil, its blazing lines casting everything in a noxious green light.

Its circumference was just smaller than the helipad, with arcing lines and complex shapes filling it. Seven smaller circles dotted the perimeter, each enclosing a different sigil of their own—and a being.

Five of the subsigils were already lit, creating glowing green columns. I couldn't tell what—who—was inside the furthest two, but those closer held . . .

My friend, the voidling . . .

An angry naiad propped up in an overflowing metal drum, her beautiful chubby form translucent and giving off steam . . .

A firefox curled up in a sad ball, the flame of its tail dim . . .

I squinted. In the fourth sigil, a tattered black cloak dripped red from each tendril, and matching gory driblets marred its chest beneath the obscuring hood. Plumes of darkness flowed from beneath the shredded hem.

Was that a *bloodwraith*? Unholy hells, please let me not have to deal with *that* one . . .

And fifth, some kind of giant jellyfish suspended in the column of air, blue-purple tentacles curtaining the frilly pink arms curling down from its matching cap.

It was twice as big as Damarion—and probably deadly.

Yowza.

Shadows darker than the night flashed toward us from the left, and I braced—until I recognized them. On silent wings, the crows swooped in to land on my shoulders and the closest piping.

Without so much as a caw or click.

"You sly scamps," I whispered to Flirt and Darth, their talons pinching my skin, but only just.

Darth ruffled his feathers proudly, and Flirt leaned in to stroke his beak along my ear.

Movement inside the larger sigil drew my gaze. Ambrose approached the naiad, whose sigil was still dull.

She spewed boiling water at him, but he dodged and lit the sigil with his magic—the same sickly green as the rest.

This was why he'd been saving his magic earlier. Sigils this large, this complex, took a *lot* of zing.

And he wasn't even done yet.

Another chartreuse column flickered to life around the naiad, and Ambrose moved to the final one—the firefox.

Was one of these the Nova-class being from inside the device? Maybe the jellyfish, or the bloodwraith? I didn't know the wraith's class, but they were scary as all get-out.

Or it could be one of the two beings I couldn't make out . . .

Dragging my gaze back from the far columns of light, I snagged on yet *another* smaller sigil at the center of the helipad.

This man had a kink for arcane symbols, that was for sure.

Within the anchoring sigil sat a familiar little orb of golden rings.

It looked just like when I'd found it at the bottom of that freaking cup holder. No ice, no lashing darkness.

And still closed, with a dark core.

Ambrose hadn't opened it yet. But I had a feeling he was about to.

Behind Kor's dark shroud, I waved my arms to get the others' attention. "Time to make a nuisance of ourselves."

A wicked smile slunk across Cynna's face. "Oh, I do so love a good spot of mayhem."

I clasped my sword, sucked down some oxygen . . . and stepped forward through Kor's shadow.

DISAPPOINTING LACK OF SIX-SHOOTERS

Our mad dash out of the dark fogbank caught the bad guys' eyes within seconds. Cynna's racing wheelchair outpaced us all, and Bracchius dropped back to stay with Aster, whose short legs weren't a match for the rest of us.

Ambrose finished activating the sigil beneath the firefox, and green light sprang up around it.

That sparked an idea. Would the ritual still work without the trapped beings?

Only one way to find out.

I dashed toward the voidling as Ambrose spotted us, but he only smiled and strolled toward the central sigil holding the Dreyelian device.

Clearly *someone* didn't understand the ass-whooping they were about to get.

The columns of magic kept the beings inside from escaping, but most wards like that were one-way: keep things in, but not out; or keep things out, but not in.

If I was lucky, I could reach in and haul the voidling out—or at least disrupt the sigil.

I burned rubber stopping my sprint beside his prison. "Me again. Immy. Don't think I introduced myself earlier."

"Twi . . ." He sounded dumbfounded.

Reaching for Twi, my hands bounced off the barrier. So this was a more sophisticated imprisonment sigil.

How dare.

My magic could probably end it like the heat death of the universe, if it had reared its ugly magenta head again.

Nope.

Stillll no beans.

The *one* day I actually *wanted* my disaster magic . . .

"Sorry, sword." With a wince, I unsheathed it and dragged the point along the concrete toward the outer line of the sigil. If I could just interrupt the design—

My sword shrieked to a stop at the bounds of the ward.

So much for that.

I stroked the hilt. "I promise I'll get you patched up and sharpened as soon as this is over." I'd have to wheedle the favor out of my local steelsmith, a Highland cow minotaur, but she was used to it—and my unhinged bartering—by now.

Globes of magic streaked across the roof, and Kor reflected them easily. The goon squad scrambled to get out of the way of their rebounded missiles.

Kor zoomed over to me. "Immy, where are the machine guns?! I thought for sure there'd be machine guns, or six-shooters, or *something*! Aren't mortals supposed to use firearms? How else can I show off my boundless talents against a barrage of bullets?!"

I just stared at him. "You've been reading too many Westerns. Or . . . secondary world thrillers?"

"But I wanna hail of bullets! These magical attacks are *pathetic*! Smiting piteous foes is much less fun."

I shook my head. "Only morons use bullets." Sure, bullets were still good for hunting deer and pheasants—

But no one in their right mind would bring a *gun* to a *magic* fight.

"Bullets don't get past that bio . . . magic . . . membrane . . . whatsit." I almost sprained an eyebrow, scrunching up my face to remember long-past biology classes.

The magic that naturally infused your body did a good job of rebuffing mundane projectiles—not that they wouldn't still wallop you like a slug from a baseball bat. They just wouldn't blast right *through* you.

Wielded weapons were a whole nother story. Magic had a habit of enveloping anything you held on to, for as long as you touched it. Magic-engulfed knife meets magic-infused mortal became a slicey-dicey proposition real fast.

A harrowing thought surfaced. With the way I'd brutalized my wellspring, did I even still have that helpful ambient magic strolling around my system?

My sneaking suspicion said no.

Kor groaned. "Oh, *please* don't give me more horrifying mortal anatomy lessons."

I glanced up, his whine startling me back to the here and now. Disembarking *that* train of thought . . .

"Then help me free this voidling." I pointed at the glowing column.

"Anything to shut you up." Kor unleashed a blast of red magic, and Twi flinched back from the ward.

It stayed strong.

"Hmm." Kor upgraded to hellfire.

Nothing.

Kor spewed some garble of syllables like the death rattle of a formless evil, the words quivering with power.

My ears might've started bleeding, but the ward held.

Hot damn.

A baddie's attack sizzled past us, and Kor twitched in a shrug. "You're on your own, Imogen. I have more wastrels to work vengeance upon!"

And off he rocketed.

"Sorry." I grimaced at the voidling. Without another potential solution jumping to mind, the surrounding chaos stole my attention.

Fitz, Samaire, and Aster had taken my cue, each trying to free their own captured being, with similar luck.

Damarion was fangs deep in a slumped brute, and spat on the concrete when he released his bite.

He really *was* picky about his blood.

Kor was cackling and raining blue hellfire on a cluster of thugs sheltering behind a massive air-conditioner, which was quickly melting to slag.

Bracchius and Sparkles bobbed way up, testing the apex of the ward, but it rebounded every spurt of magic, fire, and glitter he threw at it.

The crows dove with gleeful snickering caws, aiming for eyes and fleshy bits with beaks and talons. Enemy magic blazed their way, but the wily birds dodged it easily.

Cynna perched in her wheelchair beside one twitching dude on the ground, her hand on another's arm as his flesh quaked.

Annnd looking away now . . .

Ambrose crouched over the Dreyelian device, knotted fingers shifting the rings with confidence. He'd have that thing open in a jiffy, and I did *not* want to know what would happen then.

"Everybody!" I bellowed. "Concentrate your magic on the same spot! It's our only chance!"

I demonstratively jabbed the perimeter of the big sigil with my sword, then skated.

No need to get crisped for the cause by the coming onslaught.

Streams of magic shot from Samaire, Fitz, and the two vamps. Bracchius and Kor contributed raging hellfire.

Cynna was another matter entirely.

Silver eyes alight with glee, she raised both hands, spread fingers grasping air. Black lightning laced with crimson arced from each fingertip with a crackle that stole the breath from my lungs.

One bolt flashed past a thug, just grazing him, and he puffed into a cloud of dust.

Holy. Crap.

What *was* she, Empress Palpatine?

I backed up another few steps along the curve of the helipad as all my friends' attacks struck the ward.

The green dome blazed to life like a kryptonite sun. Fingers crossed it was reacting to the barrage of magic, not absorbing it.

Cuz it *totally* needed to be even stronger.

The ward flashed and sputtered, putting on a light show to rival the phoenixes' at the Rebirth Revelry every year.

But aside from the pyrotechnics, it seemed unaffected.

I scissored two negating arms to get everyone to stop. If the ward hadn't failed by now, it wouldn't, and wasting all their magic on this would almost be worth a Darwin Award.

Their magic and fire guttered.

The ward still stood.

I blinked away the bright streaks across my vision. Inside the dome, Ambrose triumphantly held the Dreyelian device aloft as its rings unfolded.

Crappity crap crap crap.

Everyone, thugs included, stopped to stare as the Dreyelian device opened. Darkness bloomed from within the gold rings, a black so complete it swallowed the light fuzzing off the sigils, the only thing on the roof not tainted green.

The sphere unfurled, growing impossibly large, an ebony fringe like feathers fanning out from the tight ball.

A bright pulse whisked along the main sigil's perimeter, strengthening with each of the seven creatures it passed through. At number seven, it dispersed into the intricate lines beneath Ambrose's feet and flowed up into him—and the dark Nova-class being.

Ambrose raised his arms, welcoming the power, the connection. The pulse faded, but I had no doubt the link remained.

"What do you think it is?" Samaire whispered, her coppery face gone bloodless.

"No idea."

My eyes widened as streamers of translucent green stretched inward from the glowing wards and sigil lines like drawn-out taffy—not the magic this time, but its luminescence.

Ambrose's new pet was *sucking in* the light?

It was already his size, and still burgeoning.

I shivered, clasping my arms instinctively. For summer, even after dark, it sure was getting cold fast.

When my breath puffed out in a white cloud in front of me, I realized.

This thing wasn't *only* sucking in light.

"C-Cold," Aster stuttered.

I rubbed her arms absently. "Best way to keep warm is to keep moving." And right now, fighting was the best kind of moving. Even if we couldn't get through the wards, we could still take down the thugs.

And Ambrose would have to come out *some*time.

Right?

"Or I could just steal warmer blood." Aster eyeballed the nearest of Ambrose's minions. None of them looked interested in budging, or fighting—too fixated on the main event.

"Go for it, girl."

I wasn't quite cold enough yet to unpeel my own eyes from the nightmare unfolding in front of us. How did something so huge cram into such a tiny package?

Yup, those were wings spreading left and right, inky feathers riffling into place. The tips brushed either edge of the helipad, dimming the green glow with a touch.

Was this some kind of titan *crow*?

Hopefully my personal murder of feathered friends wouldn't switch allegiances.

"Whoa," Bracchius breathed beside me. "You were right, Immy. That void phoenix would've turned me into demon jam, spread me on toast, and eaten me for breakfast."

"That *what* now? Did you say *void phoenix*?" I gawped.

"Yup."

"Are they . . . friendly, by any chance?" I crossed four pairs of fingers.

"Nooope."

"Fabulous." Why was I not surprised? "So Ambrose is trying to become what? A voidpire? Vampnix? Phoevamp? Nope, none of those are marketable crossbreeds."

"Is she rambling again?" Kor asked.

I nodded. "Yep."

The void phoenix, apparently, raised its jet-black head. I couldn't even make out any features—eyes, beak, feathers—beyond its silhouette. It hung above the ground, wings spread but not doing any work to hold it aloft.

Was this what a starless, moonless sky would look like? I shuddered.

No thank you.

An onyx wisp snaked from its fanned tail and caressed Ambrose, twining around him. He inhaled, and the darkness wound inside him with his breath.

Yeesh. All this for a facelift? Not on my life.

I'd guessed right—as soon as the murk filled him, he screamed, black rays of nothingness beaming from his eyes, ears, nose, mouth . . . And the jagged glass I'd so kindly bestowed upon his face began morphing.

His wrinkles slowly softened, his drooping skin tightening.

Talk about your Fountain of Youth.

On the plus side, at least he didn't seem to be enjoying his makeover.

"Misguided fool," Cynna muttered.

Darkness flooded Ambrose in a steady stream, leaking from the phoenix. He was healing, de-ageing, but it would be a while yet before he was a strapping twenty-year-old—or whatever the goal here was.

Slow process, apparently.

I eyed the thugs. The thugs eyed me back, probably not wanting to look like total slackers in front of their about-to-be-revitalized boss.

Magic gathered at their hands. I hefted my sword, ready to warble my best battle cry.

But the void phoenix beat me to it.

It raised its beak and screeched. Well, I only say that because my brain *expected* a screech, y'know, like other big scary birds. Eagles. Falcons. Griffins.

Really what rang out was the deep toll of a bell forged at the center of the earth.

Like the death knell of freaking creation.

Maybe the void phoenix had been in shock, or hibernation, and only just fully came to. Maybe Ambrose's spell had kept it subdued until he lost his focus. Whatever the case, the void phoenix gave up on the whole peaceful floating vibe and *revolted.*

Its wings beat violently against the green dome, leaching the light with every battering contact. One taloned foot struck Ambrose, dashing him into the column containing the jellyfish, which surged upward, limbs trailing.

Suddenly I wasn't so unhappy about the super strong barrier between me and it.

A flurried gust of wind pummeled my back, a couple crows tumbling past with vexed croaks. A commotion of thuds echoed on the roof as I turned in alarm.

Various winged peeps—a griffin, gargoyle, really buff camazotz, and more I couldn't see—deposited a pack of fighters armed to the teeth. Some armed *with* teeth.

More heavies? They had to be late to the party—Ambrose was in no state to call in backup right now.

These guys sure looked tougher than the current bunch. Maybe they were the actually decent muscle who'd been tied up elsewhere.

Till now.

They shifted, revealing more of their group. Was that a *llama* pegasus? I rubbed my eyes and checked again.

Yep, furry brown llama pegasus at six o'clock.

Well, maybe an alpaca. I never could tell the difference.

The fighters I could see included several humanoids, complete with a couple badass women; the griffin, judging by the bandolier strapped across her chest; and a pygmy unicorn with a blue-green mane and tail.

I'd have to keep Bracchius *far* away from that one, or he might defect.

Grey magic whizzed past my face—from the original batch of hoodlums, not the newcomers. I pivoted to keep both groups in sight.

And ogled as one of the newbies, a brunette with hot-pink extensions, lobbed her own attack.

But *not* at me.

Her roiling orb of turquoise magic arced overhead . . . to land in a tight cluster of Ambrose's flunkies. More blasts followed from her companions, headed the same way.

Huh.

That was, no lie, the exact last thing I'd expected. I surveyed the literal blow-ins with fresh eyes. Were they . . . here to help?

We couldn't be that lucky, could we?

The universe must've heard my thought and laughed and laughed, because next thing I knew, a hells-cursed *storm dragon* launched above the roofline, massive wings billowing, and scattered all the winged beasts right off the edge in a whirlwind of panic.

SUPERNATURAL SURPRISES

The storm dragon's eyes glowed the white-blue of a lightning strike, and tiny bolts of static raced across its form. Its scales were the perfect camouflage for a creature that hunts within thunderheads: an ever-shifting miasma of blues, teals, greens, greys, blacks, and even purples roiling across the contours from wing to wing, scale to scale.

Its wings were sleek, elegant, but powerful, and nascent storm clouds gathered at the tip of its tail, the dark plumes lit from within by hidden flashes of electricity.

Please let the storm dragon be here to face off with the void phoenix.

Oh so pretty please.

But the new fighters looked just as alarmed by it as I was, so unless it had been drawn here on its own, wanting to defend its territory . . .

It might just wreak more havoc.

At least it wasn't spewing hail or lightning yet. Although, the cloud cover overhead was thickening, darkening, as humidity rolled in, energizing the air.

Can't have a storm dragon without a storm.

The dragon touched down amidst the morass of our potential allies, who looked torn between facing off with it and skedaddling at top speed.

Another booming peal rang out from the void phoenix, shaking the roof. I couldn't keep eyes on it, the dragon, *and* Ambrose's bootlickers all at once. The dragon was further away, so I faced the green dome to make sure Ambrose wasn't about to unleash his monstrous bird on us.

The void phoenix had kept growing while I was distracted, its wings curving along the inside of the dome—which was more like a flickering plasma ball now than a translucent wall.

Ambrose was back on his feet, nursing the arm he'd landed on when the phoenix threw him. The magic of the ritual continued changing him; he looked closer to sixty than eighty now.

The massive phoenix lashed out with both taloned feet, but Ambrose dodged.

Heh—trouble in paradise.

But that got me worried . . . Once Ambrose was all youthified again, did he have a game plan for the phoenix?

Unleash it on the city and frolic off?

Or would he be nice and put it back in the Dreyelian device?

Not likely.

Shivering, I patted my pocket with the unfolded metal rings of our dupe. It *was* a fully functioning device, and the exact same kind . . .

Could *I* put the phoenix back in the proverbial box?

Magic hissed behind my head, and I whirled.

Just in time to get walloped in the gut by the follow-up blast as more thugs streamed from the door to the stairs.

Yow yow yow . . . The force of the blow hurtled me back, and I hit the roof spine-first, but managed to turn it into enough of a pained roll that I kept my breath. Half crouched, half sprawled, I pushed down the throbbing of my back and looked for threats.

Void phoenix, still thrashing. Sigils, still active. The dragon didn't seem to have eaten anyone—

The dragon. It was *gone*.

But where? Why? Had it dropped someone off and just left again? Had it transformed?

Lightning flashed in the seething storm clouds overhead, followed by a bellow of thunder.

With any luck, it was skylarking around up there.

I shook my head. Bigger issues at hand, Immy. Focus.

I'd released my sword instinctively as I rolled—good thing too, or I might've impaled myself. Luckily, my surprise flight had thrown me clear of any immediate danger.

Not that there weren't a dozen dazzling streaks of power spiraling across the roof.

I just had more time to dodge.

Snatching up my sword, I ducked a glob of liquid—venom?—sailing straight for my face. My gang and the new fighters were in all-out war with Ambrose's yes-men, bandying sparks, hellfire, crackling voltage, cascades of rock, and who knew what else . . .

And with my magic still borked, I couldn't contribute.

Except with my blade.

I darted into the pandemonium, sword at the ready.

I wasn't alone with my weapon, though. Damarion had pulled a matching pair of slender daggers from somewhere, wielding them in tight quarters when his fangs wouldn't do.

A cockatoo griffin was raking bad guys from above with her claws and talons before sailing back out of the danger zone.

The brunette fighter had pulled her hair up, the pink tip of her ponytail flying as she lobbed magic and thrust with her own sword in turn.

I spotted Bracchius in the melee. A chimaera—top half lion, bottom half faun—was sneaking up on him from behind. With a lunge, I sandwiched myself and my bare blade between my friend and those monstrous teeth.

The chimaera roared, golden mane shaking and jaws wide enough to swallow my head in one gulp.

"Sorry, pal, but after what I've seen today, one little kitty growl isn't up to snuff on fear factor."

I stabbed, chipping a feline fang and nicking his tongue before he jerked out of range with a spitting howl. Another couple thrusts, and I had him turning tail—a nice lithe tail with an *impressive* tuft of fluff on the end.

My back was heating up as Bracchius belched hellfire. Had to be the cool blue kind, based on the awful sulfurous stench invading my nostrils.

Squelching a gag, I raised my voice above the cacophony. "How ya doin', buddy?"

"Awesome!" he chirped behind me. "I think we're winning!"

"That would be nice . . . Know who these new players are?"

"Nope! You?"

"Nada."

Opponent-free for a moment, I fingered the cold rings in my pocket. "You read that book I got on Dreyelian devices, right?"

"Yup!" Bracchius blasted blue hellfire at an incoming whirlwind of sand.

That damn concrete ogre stampeded up on my right, his new crop of wildflowers tamed with hair ties. I snickered until I realized he was barreling toward *me*.

Not easy to turn a hunk of cement into a pincushion.

I readied to weed-whack his chest meadow, hoping that would hurt him enough to make him vamoose.

Alas, my sword never fulfilled its scything potential. Instead, crimson-laced dark lightning bolted past me in branching veins . . .

And blasted him into nothing but rubble and fertilizer.

Rest in pieces, my persistent gravelly dude.

I waved a grateful arm toward the source of the shuddersome lightning.

"You're welcome, darling!" Cynna called from somewhere in the hubbub. I turned back to Bracchius and helped him stave off a harpy in full-on blitzkrieg mode.

Why couldn't we get more of the run-of-the-mill human thugs over here? Humans usually considered a live sword more of a threat than these bozos did.

I Zorroed my blade, giving one of the harpy's wings a stylish feathercut. "Did you read the part on how to put things *inside* the gizmo, Bracchius?" I wasn't sure if he or Kor had handled that part of the operation.

"Double yup!" He paused, his gout of hellfire stuttering. "Ooh, that's a fantabulous idea, Immy!! You kept the one we made?"

"Right here." I patted my pocket with one hand, whacked the harpy upside the head with the other.

Mr. Mean and Feathery *didn't* like that.

Big shocker.

"Except . . ." Bracchius hemmed as I kept furious talons at bay. "For it to work, it has to touch what you want to trap."

"Kinda figured that." It would've been too easy—too improbable—to suck the phoenix in from fifty feet away, genie-in-the-lamp style.

But it was a plan, even if we couldn't use it till Ambrose left the safety of his sigil.

The harpy winged way up into the sky, then took a nosedive right for us.

"Oh no you don't!" Bracchius growled. "Sparkles, show 'em what you've got!"

Say *what* now?

Bracchius hoisted Sparkles, spiral horn pointed skyward . . .

And I wigged the freak out as a jet of *rainbow* magic blazed into the sky.

From.

Her.

Horn.

WONDER WOMAN PARAMEDIC

I gawked as Sparkles's rainbow magic blistered right into the swooping harpy.

Not only was it not a hallucination, it was damn powerful. I swear that harpy twinkled as it shot for the horizon like Jessie, James, and Meowth.

Bracchius hugged the plushie unicorn tight, disarraying her battle armor. "You did it, Sparkles!! I told you you could! That was AMAZING!!"

"How— What— I—"

"Isn't she amazing?! Tell her, Immy!" Bracchius turned Sparkles's helmeted head toward me.

I could stand here, useless and gibbering, or I could accept that I'd just seen the demon equivalent of a miracle, and keep from getting skewered by a minotaur or frozen by a void phoenix.

I chose the latter.

Not that I wouldn't be giving Bracchius a thorough interrogation about all this later.

Very thorough.

I looked the unicorn in her embroidered black eyes. "Sparkles, you're a showstopper. Just . . . unbelievable."

"See?!" Bracchius bobbled, crushing Sparkles within his nubby arms. "You're the best! Oh, Immy, watch out!"

A chunk of ice smashed into my arm, burning and biting. I wheeled, searching for the attacker, but couldn't pick them out amidst the madness.

That didn't stop whoever from flinging more icy shards my way.

Dodge. Deflect. Duck. The rocketing ice and I did a frenzied dance, until the deluge finally slacked.

As I smashed one last flying icicle into smithereens, a chorus of hisses drew my gaze.

The brunette fighter from earlier was facing down a miniature hydra. But even at half-height, its five heads were *more* than a match for one gal.

I bopped Bracchius with an elbow. "You good here?"

"Sparkles and I are *conquering!*"

"Good," I laughed. "Keep it that way. I'm gonna help someone else out."

Wary of the gal's sword, I stepped up on her opposite side.

"Need a hand?"

She barely flinched at my sudden appearance—and her sword didn't falter as it fended off two heads at once. "Might be nice."

Elbow to elbow, we duked it out with the hydra's heads. Needle-teeth raked, steel flashed, long necks weaved and writhed.

The sweep of my blade kept two heads back, but a third made a break for my ally's arm. I kick-stomped it, almost swaying back too far, but regained my balance.

Shoulda worn cleats for maximum bad-guy quashing.

Maybe next time.

"Thanks." The brunette flashed me a grateful glance. She was older than me—late thirties, early forties?

I grinned. "No prob. Can I ask—how did you know to attack these guys and not us? We could've been Team Ambrose too, y'know. Er, Team The-Megalomaniac-Over-There."

She huffed a laugh as her sword grazed one undulating neck. "Watched you as we flew in. Plus, you don't exactly look like hired muscle. No offense."

It was my turn to rasp a breathy chuckle. What, little ol' me, a guy in a suit, lady in a wheelchair, two twentysomethings, and a vampire the size of a minifridge didn't look impressive?

Kor and Bracchius didn't count—impressive or not, *no* demon was demeaning themselves with gruntwork like that for pay.

She parried another head. "Can *I* ask . . . Why are you encrusted in glitter?"

I'd almost forgotten. "Demon sneeze."

She faltered worse at that than when I'd popped up beside her. "*Demon* sneeze?"

"He's a very special demon."

"I'll bet."

I whacked one toothy head back with the flat of my blade, then carved a furrow in the hydra's chest on the way down. It squalled in pain, heads thrashing.

"Where'd you learn to fight with a sword?" Fighter Chick panted, taking the opening, but the heads snapped forward to defend the hydra's vulnerable chest.

Chopping off heads—bad. Skewering vital organs—good.

"Videos, lessons with a steelsmith, and loooots of training with my roommate. You?"

"My daughter"—thrust, jab—"needed a sparring partner!"

Two heads reared back, the classic sign of an acid attack, and I yanked my new friend down by the elbow with a startled cry.

The sizzling stream of acid arced overhead, and I jammed us in closer to the hydra's toes. Better getting poked by claws than dissolved by the drops raining down.

I scooted further back. "How'd you know to be here?"

"It was the only night in—" Fight Chick thrust up with her sword, piercing the hydra's scales toward its lungs with a grunt of effort. "In forty years he could do this."

How did everybody know that but me?

The jet of acid faltered as the hydra gasped and wheezed, all four feet stomping. We scrambled back in a frantic crab-walk, skirting the bubbling acid-drenched concrete.

"Think you got the lung," I puffed. "I'm Immy, by the way."

"I did." She grinned. "And Gemma."

We shook hands as the hydra toppled with a thud.

"Just a second." Gemma launched to her feet, sheathing her sword and grappling with the body armor she wore. She peeled a thin floppy black tube off the back, then wound it around all the hydra's necks and connected it.

One aqua spark of her magic lit the world's tiniest sigil along the tube, and the flailing hydra calmed.

Whoa.

"Sedating collar," she explained, climbing atop the hydra's bulky chest.

Snazzy. Maybe I could get my hands on some of those? Pretty sure my eyes were gleaming greedily.

I glanced around. Aster was back-to-back with a bodybuilder of a dude, and Samaire fought alongside the pygmy unicorn. The griffin lofted Fitz to safety, dragging him from the clutches of a powerful dust devil, while a lithe older Asian woman sparred with the offending desert troll.

Kor was thoroughly engaged in raucous smiting, and Damarion had buddied up with a raccoon of all things.

But the fight was dwindling, with maybe two-thirds of the thugs maimed, fleeing, or taking forty winks, with those same black tubes tied around them.

We *might* just win this thing.

Especially if Gemma and her crew had some idea how to stop Ambrose.

She pulled out a medkit, then slammed something pointy into the hydra's chest. The scaly critter gasped with all five heads, sucking in air.

Who *was* this chick? Some Lara Croft–Wonder Woman hybrid paramedic?

Hydra subdued and breathing again, she helped me to my feet. "What were we talking about?"

Hells if I knew. That whole display of dazzling competence had completely derailed my train of thought.

"Dunno." The chill air on my sweaty skin was making for a frigid combo. I shivered, looking around for a new fight, a new way to keep warm.

"Oh, right—how we got here." Gemma dodged a double whammy of magical torrents, tugging me with her, and drew her sword again. "We weren't sure exactly where he'd be, or if he even had all the components. That voidling was a tossup, and I didn't know about the bloodwraith or—"

"Wait, you know what all these are?" I brandished my sword and stared down a ruffian who looked like he was getting ideas.

"Well, yeah. He's been collecting them for a while. He designed the ritual to—"

I didn't catch the rest.

A third clanging *bong* tolled out from the void phoenix, who'd ballooned to fill the entire dome.

A dome that was just the barest whisper of green now.

Scratch that—the ward *vanished* with a whimpering crackle of power. The void phoenix exploded upward with a scree of pure delight, instantly swelling to twice the size and dimming the lights of the nearest buildings.

I'd expected a cold front to wash over us, but the reality was way more unnerving. Instead of chill air enveloping me, my body heat siphoned away, lured in by the phoenix's pull.

Brr freaking brrrr.

And for the clincher, one space-black wing grazed the roof's tallest antenna on the way up. When the wing shifted, the metal spire was just *gone*.

Not bent, or smashed, or knocked off the edge.

Gone gone. Into the literal void.

I gulped.

Roast me on a dragon spit and feed me to the manticores—we just might be doomed.

NEFARIOUS PLANS

We stared up in horror at the vast black bird blocking out the sky. Lightning lanced from the rumbling storm clouds, but it disappeared within the phoenix's wings, gobbled up as surely as all the heat and light it was devouring.

Safe to say this was its final boss form.

Beside me, Gemma cursed, "Fraggle Rock."

That was enough to shake me out of my awestruck stupor. "I'm sorry, *what*?" I blinked at her.

Her eyes didn't leave the void phoenix as she absently muttered, "Old habits die hard."

Because that explained it.

She shook herself out of her own daze. With trembling fingers, she teased her phone out of her vest pocket, tapped the screen, and raised it to her ear.

"Son of a bagel. Of course there's no reception." She waved the phone around, seeking bars.

Said bars were probably all getting slurped up by the void phoenix too, but I might as well offer. "Wanna try mine?" I held out my fancy-schmancy phone.

"Thanks." Consulting her screen, she typed a number into mine. She put it to her ear, and her eyes widened. "Wow, it's ringing."

That Obsidian phone really *was* worth its weight in gold.

As she talked to someone named Cherise, some of Gemma's buddies raced over to steer the newly freed beings away from the busted sigil. A few hotfooted it out of here, mounting the griffin or heading for the stairs, but others joined the fight.

I waited for the void phoenix to fly off into the night, but despite its flapping wings, it didn't go any further, swaying back and forth like a kite on a string.

Narrowing my eyes, I peered down at the fulcrum of its wavering course. Ambrose.

He was tethering the phoenix.

Now a perky forty-five or so, he stood at the center of the

extinguished sigil. Darkness rimed his skin like creeping frost crystals, but he didn't seem to notice.

Even with the sigil dead, the connection between him and the monster bird was alive and well.

Or deadly and dire?

But if the void phoenix was trapped, this was my chance. "Bracchius!" I hissed. "I need you!"

He heard me, spinning away from his fight with a humdrum human. "Coming!" He and Sparkles zipped over. "What is it, Immy?"

I held out the linked rings of the inert Dreyelian device. "Can you set it up to catch that big flying freak?"

Bracchius plopped onto my palm, and the metal tickled my skin as he shifted it. "Like this, and then over here, and . . . Ta-da!"

He breezed up off my hand, revealing the rings arranged like a little basket—open and ready to receive a new tenant. Red glimmers of his magic frisked along the gold bands.

"It's good to go?"

"Yupper-do!"

"Okay. Here goes nothing."

I gave it my best windup, all the magic firing around the roof a nice facsimile of anime bokeh. I lobbed the doodad with every ounce of oomph in me, and yelled, "Pokéball, go!!"

In retrospect, knowing how often those flimsy little money pits bite the dust in the games, I should've known what would happen.

Or I should've yelled, "*Master*ball, go!"

Either way, my aim was good, and the gadget went the distance, but when it struck the void phoenix, it simply vanished.

Sigh.

On the plus side, the phoenix didn't seem to notice the puny assault, too busy straining at the limits of its tether.

The original Dreyelian device had to be around here somewhere, but was it even worth looking? Whoever had trapped the void phoenix the first time around probably had a trick up their sleeve that we didn't know.

But if that birdie started raining down basketball hail or void juice, I'd kick off a scavenger hunt like a shot.

A fresh bout of evil cackles harbingered half the damn roof catching on fire.

Kor. *Of* course.

Luckily that 'half' was patchy, the flames only leaping around the remaining thugs—annnd a couple of our surprise allies.

Gemma surged over, and—

Wow. She clobbered Kor right in the face with the hilt of her sword.

He dropped like a rock. A cursing, sputtering rock.

I couldn't help but grin. She had spunk, that one. Wouldn't be surprised if she wrestled Kor the rest of the way down and doped him like the others.

Maybe even took him in for public endangerment.

I got pulled from my little joyfest at Kor's expense by a flash of movement near Ambrose.

Damarion approached him, daggers drawn and suit somehow still impeccable—and glittery. "Ambrose!" he bellowed. "Face me like the leech you are!"

Ouch. 'Leech' ranked pretty high on the list of vampire insults.

Though I wasn't sure his fighting words actually held up. Did leeches even *have* faces? And wouldn't you expect a coward to bolt, not stay and fight?

Thankfully the sudden cloudburst put an end to my deranged musings.

"Ack!" This was no sedate sprinkle tinkling down. We were all instantly drenched, practically drowning on dry land.

Well, it definitely wasn't dry anymore.

Water runneling off my nose, and glitter streaming off my body, I just thanked Poseidon—no, not Zeus, he's a jackass—that it wasn't a full dragon storm.

The downpour was so thick I could hardly see what was going on aside from occasional spurts of magic.

But guaranteed that void phoenix was still lurking up there, slowly darkening the city and turning us all into cryogenic popsicles.

And *somebody* had to do something about it.

Might as well be me.

But how? My proven prison gizmo had failed miserably, and it wasn't like I had anywhere else I could stash a titanic raptor of doom.

. . . Or did I?

A mischievous chortle snuck out of me as I examined my epiphany from all sides.

That . . . actually might work.

I sidled up to Kor—okay, slipped and skidded across the wet concrete until I crashed onto my butt beside him in a frigid puddle.

He wasn't wrapped up like a tranquilized Christmas tree, surprisingly, but he was grousing about the rain.

I cheerfully interrupted him. "Hey, Kor . . ." Now how should I word this so I didn't set off his spidey senses?

"What is it, Immy?" Incomprehensibly, he sniveled, like demons could actually catch a cold.

"Since I visited, I've been wondering . . . how big is your domain, exactly?"

"Twelve thousand three hundred and nineteen gloams."

That . . . *sure* was exact. Not that I had any inkling what in tarnation a 'gloam' was.

"So, pretty big?" I clasped my hands to keep from drumming my fingers together like a movie villain.

"Immense."

I was veering into dangerous territory here, but I had to know. "And if you'd known *someone* was going to scamper in and pull a prison break, do you have a way to temporarily seal off your portal from the inside? Keep them from escaping?"

His red flickers burned brighter at the reminder of my perfidy, but he didn't crisp me to a pillar of ash, so he couldn't be *too* angry.

"Of course!" he growled. "You can't imagine every demon wants mortals waltzing in and out of their domains at will. And thank you for reminding me. I will have to implement that upon my return."

"Great, thanks!" I launched back to my feet, then sobered. "Will you . . . keep an eye on our little throng? Protect them? That void phoenix scares the soul out of me."

"I . . . suppose. Where are you going?"

That was the best assurance I could hope to get out of him. "It's a secret!" I yelled as I sashayed my sopping way over to Bracchius.

Hopefully Cucumber would know how to set the portal to Do Not Pass. If not, and *if* my plan actually worked, it'd be easier to beg forgiveness after the fact—asking Kor to activate that handy little feature once it was too late for him to stop me—than to tip him off by asking for the deets now.

I passed Gemma, paused, and shuffled back. She was guzzling water amidst the downpour, one of her fellow fighters watching her back. She lowered the bottle at my shoulder tap.

"So . . . I've got an idea for how to handle the void phoenix, but I've gotta leave to do it. Don't die while I'm gone, yeah?" I quirked a smile.

"As if." She coughed. "Er, as my daughter would say, that is. Um, good luck?"

"I'll need it, thanks."

After a few more sloshes, I poked Bracchius in the derriere as he adjusted Sparkles's armor. The plushie was bedraggled to say the least.

"Who—" Bracchius pirouetted, flinging droplets into my face. "Oh, Immy! What's up?"

"Can—" We both ducked a stray surge of sickly green magic, and I glanced, worried, toward Damarion.

Yep, that was Ambrose's magic, all right. He already held another bright ball at his fist, not shy to use his power now that he was done with the hungry sigils.

He'd de-aged another five years, but those traceries of darkness were creeping further across his skin. The green light of his magic glinted off Damarion's daggers as he slashed.

"Can I what, Immy?" Bracchius tugged at my sleeve.

I pulled my gaze away from the fight. "Sorry. Do you have enough pep for another few teleports? With just me, though."

We both winced as a few hailstones joined the deluge, courtesy of the void phoenix.

"Just you?" Bracchius wriggled in midair, rain sheeting off him and hail bouncing. "I can manage that!"

"For sure? Because I've seen your 'pretty sure.'"

He heaved an aggrieved sigh. "Yes, Immy, for *sure* sure. Where are we going?"

"Home. But then right back."

"Okay . . ."

I glanced over my shoulder as Bracchius reached for my arm. Damarion and Ambrose were still fighting, neither having a clear advantage. I couldn't make out much between the rain and the dark, but I *did* see when a green bolt ripped through the night and slammed into Damarion's chest.

He tumbled across the roof to lie crumpled in the rain.

No! I had to check on him! I had to help—

Shimmering violet clouded my vision, and we were gone.

A QUEST FOR CUKE

We appeared halfway across town, but not quite as far as our place. I sagged against Bracchius, aflutter with worry for Damarion. "We have to go back! Damarion's hurt and—"

Bracchius enfolded my shoulders in his warm black self. "Shh, he's a vampire, Immy, he'll be fine. It takes *way* more than one blast of magic to stop them!"

I sniffled against Sparkles's butt. "I guess that's true . . ." Damarion had probably popped right back up and dusted off his drenched suit.

I couldn't kick the anxiety gnawing at my bones, though.

Straightening from our hug, I drew a deep breath. Damarion had a whole swarm of people to take care of him if he *had* scraped a knuckle, knocked out a fang—or worse.

I shoved the 'worse' into a deep dark hole in my brain.

Besides, if I hurried, we'd be back in no time.

"Okay." I nodded. "Let's get home."

"Aye-aye!"

One more swish of purple and tumble through nothingness, and we popped right into the living room.

"Peachy. I'm impressed." I frowned. "This doesn't mean any old slimeball can teleport into my bedroom, does it?"

"Of course not! But *I* know how to get through the wards."

"Right. Good." I trooped toward Kor's mirror.

Bracchius trailed after me. "Why are we here, anyway?"

"To make Kor's life absolutely miserable. Hopefully."

"Uh-huh . . ." He swiveled as I stopped in front of the mirror. "While I like that idea, should . . . that really be our priority right now? You know, with the big doomsday bird and all the explody stuff back there?"

"If we're lucky, this'll ruin Kor's day *and* take care of the big doomsday bird."

Though I'll admit, the former was dwindling as a motivating factor. Kor had been really helpful today, and actually not completely unpleasant to be around.

Wonders never cease.

But no matter how I felt about Kor, this was happening. I was desecrating his domain once and for all, in the most permanent way possible. Assuming it worked, that is.

Please let it work.

I lowered a finger to the mirror, and promptly remembered I was a dry husk when it came to magic. Unless . . . ?

Nope. No glimmers, no gleams.

Maybe this was my life now.

I *really* hoped not. As unruly as my magic was, I still liked having it around.

But, magic or no, I had to get into this mirror.

And so I started howling into the mirror for the second time today.

"Cucumber! *Sir* Cucumber!! Can you please, with a smelly soap bubble on top, activate the portal for me?" Pause. "Cuke?"

If he was eyeballs deep in his favorite wailing whirlpool pastime, he might not even hear me.

Granted, if he did, it'd take him a while to hop and squelch across the laundromat.

"Immy, what's going on? Should I . . . get you a cucumber?" Bracchius was clearly concerned for my sanity.

"I'm hoping the cucumber will get itself for me," I muttered. "*Him*self."

Bracchius nodded jerkily and drifted slowly backwards from the crazy woman.

Just as the silvery maw of the portal roared to life.

Sweet.

"Be right back!"

One foot raised, I about-faced, darted into my bedroom, and grabbed a drawstring bag.

Then I stepped through the mirror into the gloomy laundromat— and almost right on top of poor Cucumber.

"Milady!" he chirped, springing out of the way. "This is highly irregular, but it's an honor to be in your presence again so soon!"

I tried to close off every one of my airways against the wretched reek in here, but I unfortunately needed one for speaking. "Same to you, Cuke. And it's about to get even more irregular, so brace yourself."

The squishy little demonling thrust his cocktail sword into the air with vigor. "I'm braced, Lady Immy!"

"Point me toward your most prized possessions, Sir Cuke. We're clearing out of this joint, and pronto."

"Oh my!" He looked conflicted for a sec, then jabbed the purple plastic sword toward his washer.

And the bottle of bubblebath perched beside it.

Aww. My rascally heart melted a little, despite the fact I'd be lugging the source of the stench into my home.

Hopefully he didn't want the washer too.

I rushed over, tipped the—yes, closed—bottle into my bag, and rejoined Cucumber. "Anything else?"

He pointed toward a trinket box on a shelf. "Why are you moving so quickly, Lady Immy? Is there danger?"

My feet stuttered to a stop. Why *was* I scrambling like my life depended on it? Sure, things were grim outside, but in here . . .

In here time stood still.

I grinned. "Because I'm a forgetful joker, Cuke, that's why." I'd been planning to bustle Cucumber to safety and skip out with the mirror, but if I had the luxury of time . . .

Well, of lack of time— No. Absence of time?

Never mind.

"Sir Cucumber, I have a solemn task for you. A quest, if you will."

He nearabout keeled over in rapture. "My first quest!" he gasped. "Milady, I'm overcome!"

Should I start fanning him? Even if there were smelling salts in here somewhere—*not* likely—I couldn't imagine they'd work on *this* scragglebutt, with all the huffing of noxious fumes he did on the daily.

If he hadn't passed out yet . . .

"Yup, your first official quest," I hazarded. "I seek to evacuate all the, um, *not* irksome beings from this domain before it's invaded by a terror of the highest order. And I need your help."

Cucumber quaked. "A being more terrible than Master Kor?"

"*Oh* yeah. I mean . . . Verily, my knight. Much more terrible."

He squeaked. "It must be fearsome indeed! Of course I will aid you, Lady Immy!" He sheathed his sword in a makeshift getup crafted out of . . . gum wrappers?

Looked like.

He tugged at the hem of my cargo pants, and I offered him my hand. He hopped on and suctioned himself to my palm.

One demonling, going up.

"A safe haven is prepared for us through the portal?"

Oh. Um.

Hmm.

I hadn't thought this through quite that far. Anyone I evacuated from Kor's domain would just be . . . chilling in my apartment.

Well, that was a problem for Future Immy. Right Now Immy had a plan for at least the next five minutes.

"A, uh, temporary waystation, yup." Visions of all the ways this could go wrong danced through my head. "Kor didn't hire a new typhon to guard his latest tower, did he? Or anybody else?"

"Nope, no typhon!"

Phew.

"But Master Kor *did* conscript a dusk kraken!" Cucumber announced with pride.

My eyebrows rose for my hairline—if only to scurry up into it and hide, whimpering.

"A— A dusk *kraken*?"

"Yes, milady!"

Why me? Could I get away with leaving it behind to duke it out with the void phoenix?

"Her name is Umbrannia Shadowvale the Destroyer of Souls, but she lets me call her Umbra! She makes a *delicious* cup of tenebrous murk."

I closed my eyes in defeat. The Destroyer of Souls was gonna be my new roommate, wasn't she.

"Are you unwell, Lady Immy?" Concern laced Cucumber's voice.

"I'm . . . fine." I opened my eyes and gave him my best reassuring grimace. "All right, Cuke, here's the plan: I need you to drum up your fellow demonlings, Umbra, the negentropes . . ."

Who else lived in here? The shadelurk, but under no circumstances was I inviting that Slenderman wannabe into my house.

Oh, the imps.

I cringed. "Should we save the imps?"

Cucumber quailed, goopy eyes bugging out. "*Nononononononono—*"

I touched a finger to his mouth to stop the avalanche of panic. "I get it, that's a pretty firm no. Not best buds with them?"

He shuddered, hugging himself. "Imps *eat* demonlings, Lady Immy."

Oh. "Well, to hells with them, then."

Cucumber cheered up. "My sentiment exactly, milady!"

We spent the next fifteen minutes gathering up the far-flung demonlings, notifying Umbrannia Shadowvale the Destroyer of Souls of our impending departure, and whistling up the negentropes.

The other demonlings I stashed in the bathtub. Of course, that was *after* they screeched about the absurd levels of light in the hall, and the bathroom, and the unfathomable arctic temperatures.

I lunged for the light switches, then cranked the bathroom baseboard heater to max, and left them with firm instructions not to let the place burn down.

"It'd be warmer if we did," one griped, shivering.

I thrust a stern finger in their face. "*No.* Just no. If I come back and you're luxuriating in the scorching ashes of my apartment, I'm feeding you to the void phoenix."

The demonling meeped and huddled closer to their compatriots.

And no, Cucumber wasn't around to hear my ghastly threats. I returned to the mirror, and Kor's domain, where he was giving the negentropes a stern talking-to.

I plugged my nose. "What's the matter?"

He flung both toothpick arms into the air. "Some of them wish to stay! They insist their work here isn't finished."

For creatures bent on tidying everything up, I could see the appeal of Kor's domain. But given the circumstances . . .

"You explained about the void phoenix?"

"Yes, milady. They understand perfectly, and still wish to remain."

If Cuke couldn't convince them, *I* sure couldn't. I didn't even know if they had ears. "All right, then, anyone who *is* fleeing the premises, head through the portal."

Most of the symmetrical cloud of negentropes buzzed through the churning portal in a dead-straight line, leaving me, Cuke, and the Destroyer of Souls in the laundromat.

What was left of the laundromat, that is. Turns out dusk krakens are exactly as big as you'd think.

Didn't bode well for my apartment.

"One last thing before we leave, Cuke—once we're on the other side, can you activate whatever function locks the portal shut?"

"Erm . . . no. Only from this side. But . . ." He puffed out his chest and gripped his sword hilt valiantly. "I will gladly sacrifice myself to aid in your escape, milady!"

Yeah, *not* happening. "I roundly reject your selfless offer, Sir Cucumber. You're too important to sacrifice."

But how else could we trap the void phoenix in here?

One of the remaining negentropes zizzed over to Cucumber and bobbed in frantic hexagons.

"Really?" Cuke mumbled. "You can?" He peered up at me with a malformed smile. "The negentropes will deactivate the portal upon the arrival of the void phoenix."

I was tempted to sweep the whole horde into a relieved hug, but the sheer disorder would probably send them into a tizzy. "That's amazing, thanks."

The little swarm bobbed in unison.

"'Kay, Sir Cucumber, let me get you settled, and then I'll be back for Her Unholiness." Cuke might be friends with the gargantuan squid of shadows, but I was under strict instructions not to utter so much as a syllable of her given name.

A command I had *zero* intention of disobeying.

I ferried Cuke through the mirror into the dark hall. "Cucumber, welcome to your vacation Airbnb. Let me show you to your room. It's lined with lava rocks, has a heat lamp feature, which . . ."

Oh. Heat, good. Lamp, not so much.

"Which you may *not* want to use, but is available for your convenience. And it comes prestocked with a roommate I think you'll get along with great. Elena, this is Cucumber. Cuke, Elena."

I tucked the demonling in at the opposite end of the tank from the shinnystar and former sorceress. "She might try to suck on you, but she's just looking for grit to eat. Don't kill her if you can avoid it, yeah?"

"Yes, milady," he said dubiously, gripping his cocktail sword. He gave Elena's blobby form an exploratory poke, with no reaction.

"You'll be fine, don't worry."

Me, though, I had my doubts about. I shut the bathroom door behind me and faced the mirror, bolstering my courage for my next task.

Then I stepped through the portal to invite an actual eldritch horror into my parlor.

DESTROYERS OF SOULS

The dusk kraken waited for me, her eyes darker globes against her bulbous head. Way too many shadowy tentacles writhed out from her, curling and twisting to fit in the limited space of the laundromat.

"Ready, Your Unholiness?"

She slithered forward, the mouthing tooth-lined suckers on a couple tentacles getting much too close for comfort.

I'd take that as a yes.

"Then follow me." I threw in a flamboyant bow, then hopped back through the portal.

Lights were off, though I couldn't do anything about the daylight sneaking in past the blinds on the windows. I whipped the bathroom door open again to allow room for all the tentacles.

I'd warned Bracchius to wait outside, and it seemed he'd actually listened. Not sure how fragile the mirror was, I laid it flat on the carpet as the first squirming limb poked through.

In the mere semidark of my apartment, I got a better look at Her Unholiness, Umbrannia Shadowvale the Destroyer of Souls. She was a little see-through, with the darkest concentration of shadow matter behind her eyes and within each pulsing sucker.

Her tentacles were different lengths and shapes, and her head elongated with a fin at the top, more like a squid than an octopus.

And she was *humongous*.

As her arms flailed down the hall, into my room, and into the bathroom, the demonlings ensconced in the tub peeped in panic like a brood of baby chicks.

I was lifted on a tidal wave of tentacles in short order as more limbs rippled toward the living room. One of my hands slipped into a toothy sucker, and I blanched . . . but the fangs didn't chomp down.

Whaddya know—I might actually have a polite houseguest.

"THIS ABODE IS INSUFFICIENT FOR MY CURRENT SIZE."

"Sorry about that."

But instead of griping, or trying to leave, Her Unholiness . . . shrank.

Well, not quite. Her head was just as ginormous, but suddenly there were fewer tentacles to contend with.

Nifty. "How'd you do that? Where'd your tentacles go?"

"THEY LIVE IN THE SHADOWS NOW."

Huh. "Why didn't you do that back in the laundromat?"

"ANY PART OF ME ANCHORED IN SHADOW WOULD NOT HAVE PASSED THROUGH THE PORTAL."

Gotcha. Amputation was a no-go in my book too.

Her Unholiness swarmed into the living room and spat globules of sticky black across the window blinds. The room plunged into darkness.

Guess that was one alternative to blackout curtains.

Hopefully my landlord didn't pop a surprise inspection on me this weekend. Even with twenty-four hours' notice, this place would send him screaming.

My leggy houseguest settled across the living room, withdrawing her visible tentacles from the rest of the apartment. That left the mirror nice and accessible on the hall floor, shrunken to its normal size, the surface once again glass instead of howling vortex.

Now that I was back in the mortal world, time was ticking.

I strode to the mirror and glared down at it. "You, bratty mirror. We're going on a trip, so you'd better stay lightweight as a feather for the foreseeable future, or I'm gonna drop you from a height you won't survive. Crack, shatter, and in the trash you go. If you want to keep existing as a pretty little mirror, you better cooperate."

Hands on hips, I paused, like the thing might actually respond.

No dice. I did feel like it was laughing at me, though.

"And if you're magical enough to be shatterproof, believe you me, I *will* find a way. I'll throw you under a street leviathan. Feed you to a magma dragon. Drop you over the Mariana Trench and let the water pressure do its thing. Savvy?"

The glass gave the tiniest ripple . . .

And then the mirror shrank to the size of an avocado.

Well, slap a pixie and call me Alice in Wonderland. How . . . strangely helpful.

Maybe my threats had struck home.

I slipped the mirror into a pocket and nervously checked my magic reserves again.

Still nothing—I was starting to feel like a broken record.

I chewed my lip. As unlikely as this was to work anyway, I wouldn't get very far if I couldn't trigger the portal into Kor's domain. Cucumber wasn't inside anymore to help me out, and the only other person I knew who could activate it was Kor himself.

Because *that* was totally happening. Hey, Kor, can you rev up your portal for me so I can trap a huge terrifying monster inside and ruin all your evil plans?

Guess I'd just have to hope I got lucky.

I could practically hear the demonlings' teeth chattering, so I closed the bathroom door again to trap the heat.

Then I ghosted.

JK, I clambered over and under the dusk kraken's multitudinous limbs, wriggling my way toward the front door.

Success.

Outside, Bracchius was busy trying to peer in the blackened windows. "Oh, Immy! I only caught a glimpse of the kraken before—" He prodded the window. "Did you take a picture?!"

"Uh . . . no. C'mon, we gotta go. Plenty of time to see her later, okay?"

"All right . . ." He shimmied dejectedly, but drifted over to teleport us.

Kor's mirror burning a hole in my pocket, a new concern whammied me. I shied back from Bracchius's outstretched arm. "Wait, wait!" I ran my fingers over my pocket, feeling the curlicues of the mirror's frame. "Think it's actually safe to teleport the mirror?"

Bracchius jolted. "Oh. Um . . . Maybe?"

Bussing it across the city would definitely be the safer option—for me and Bracchius—but at that speed, the void phoenix would've fridged the rest of my friends long before we got back.

They were worth the risk.

But *another* concern loomed large. "Think you even *can* teleport the mirror?"

It was a whole nother realm, however many 'gloams' wide, and might be as easy to move as the Rocky Mountains.

Unless the mirror only was the gateway, not the contents too?

Dunno.

"If you can carry it, I'm pretty sure I can teleport it."

I groaned. Again with the 'pretty sures.'

But I gritted my teeth and held out my hand. "Let's do it."

For once, my worries didn't come true. We traveled the Purple Glitter Highway with one rest stop, then materialized on the roof, with the mirror still in my pocket.

Of course, we arrived at the crumbling edge of a brand-new sinkhole in the roof.

Can you still call it a sinkhole if the ground is falling *up*?

Bit by bit, the roof beneath the void phoenix was disintegrating, the particles streaming up toward its form before being engulfed.

Greeeeat.

Rain pelted up my nose, also on its merry way into the pitch-black bird.

Bracchius proved himself the more sensible of us two by seizing my collar and hauling ass away from the crater.

If it'd started sucking up matter in addition to energy, we were seriously screwed.

Oh no.

I whirled and scanned the crowd at the far end of the roof, counting off everyone I recognized. Samaire, Kor, Aster, Cynna, Gemma, Fitz, a slew of crows, the griffin and that oversized dude, the raccoon and the pygmy unicorn, plus—

My brow furrowed. There were several more kitted-up fighters than before.

But no Damarion.

Nausea sank its nasty claws in. "Damarion?! *Damarion!*"

Samaire rushed over, darting around the three remaining fights. "Immy, he's hurt, but they think he'll pull through." She'd infused her voice with melodic calm, but I fought against it.

"Is that just doctor speak for 'He's dying but we don't want to freak you out?'" I snarled.

She pulled me into a stiff hug—stiff because I was clenched like a board. "I don't think so. The mercs seemed optimistic."

I swallowed, the slightest relief creeping into my veins. If he didn't make it and I found out they'd been sugarcoating things . . .

It would *not* be pretty.

A feverish ruckus of caws and croaks rose above the drumming of the rain, and I jerked back from Samaire.

Flirt, the smallest crow of the murder, was tumbling through the air, wings spasming as he fought the pull of the void phoenix.

I lurched forward with a cry, but he was too high up even if I sprinted across the roof in time. I seriously considered becoming the Tramble Terror again just to extend my reach, but the transformation might take too long, even if I had a spark of magic to trigger it.

Kor, of all beings, rocketed into the sky and grabbed the frantic corvid, towing him back to earth.

The rain masked my tears as I dashed over and threw my arms around the pair—to squawks from both bird and demon. "*Thank you!*"

Kor wriggled out of my grip, still clasping Flirt against his orb form. "If *that's* my reward, I'll think twice next time!" He harrumphed, convulsing. "*Humans . . .*"

I gentled the crow out of his grasp, then turned to the others, all perched much further along the roof.

Flirt must've been coming to say hi to me.

"Stupid, *reckless*, sweet floozy, you," I muttered. "Don't *ever* do that again."

I released him with the others at the roof's edge and scolded the crows. "You need to leave, *now*. You're brave and smart and I love that you helped today, but you *have* to go. You've earned a bucketload of bologna, but I can't give it to you if you die."

A clamor of caws drowned out the storm, and in one fell swoop, the crows dove off the edge and flapped down into the city.

Thank the Morrigan.

My feathered friends safe, it was time to do what I could for everyone else too, before bigger things than crows got sucked up by this black hole of a bird.

"Bracchius!" I yelled. "It's showtime!"

I faced the void phoenix, my demon pal at my side, and patted the mirror in my pocket.

Please let me live to regret this.

ALICORNS & APOPLEXIES

Seemingly unable to get too far from the void phoenix, Ambrose was battling several mercs, and Cynna, near the edge of the crumbling pit. The light of their battle—what wasn't getting sucked up—was bright enough to see by.

The phoenix above thrashed at the end of its tether, the center of an imploding maelstrom of rain and debris.

And I had to get up there.

While Bracchius could drag me around with his telekinesis, it would be slow going, and wouldn't leave me much room for maneuverability.

"Bracchius, I need you to turn into a pegasus again."

"Not a unicorn?" he asked hopefully.

"How about a *unicorn* pegasus?"

"That's called an alicorn, Immy."

"Whatever. Just do it."

"Okay . . . but why?"

I hadn't exactly clued him in to the whole plan yet.

"We're gonna fly up there, catch the void phoenix, and try not to get slurped up like soda through a straw in the process."

"*What?*" Bracchius squeaked, nearly strangling Sparkles. Speaking of whom . . .

"But first I need you to give Sparkles to Samaire for safekeeping." Neither of us would ever forgive me if the plushie unicorn got sucked into the void.

"O-Okie."

He whirred over to Samaire and nestled Sparkles into her arms. "Take good care of Samaire, Sparkles. I'll . . . I'll be back soon."

Back at my side, he exhaled a few steadying—hyperventilating?—breaths, then began to transform.

It was too much to hope for that Bracchius would become a full-size alicorn, seeing as he wasn't much for the harvesting of souls to let him twist-tie the laws of physics.

For which I *was* grateful.

I just could've used a bigger steed than the one before me.

Bracchius the blobby black alicorn was no bigger than the pygmy unicorn with the mercs—maybe two feet at the withers, with shrimpy legs, and wings like a cherub's.

Thankfully he didn't need to rely on wing power to get us airborne.

To wrap up the aesthetic, Bracchius's floofy mane and tail were purple, and his stubby spiral horn all the colors of the rainbow.

"How do I look?" He chased his tail trying to get a glimpse of himself.

"I think you'd win best in show." *What* show wasn't important.

"Really??" He whinnied in delight, and a spurt of multicolor sparks cascaded from his horn.

I started getting suspicions about just where Sparkles's astounding burst of magic had come from . . .

"Really." Channeling one of my personal heroes, I added, "Now let's take chances, make mistakes, and—"

A huge chunk of roof cracked apocalyptically and bobbed up toward the phoenix.

"And hurry the hells up. Giddyup, Bracchius."

The demon alicorn launched into the air, and I swung a leg over his puny back.

Here we go . . .

Bracchius ascended no problemo despite my weight and his minuscule size. We did look *utterly* ridiculous winging off into the night sky, though.

My butt threatened to slip off his back end, and I'd somehow caught both his mane *and* tail beneath me. My legs dangled below my, well— below my *hips*, really.

Rain and gravel pelted us from behind as we approached the void phoenix. A single crow feather darted by, then a hair tie, a stray shoe . . .

We were navigating the weirdest asteroid field ever.

A crunch behind us had me glancing back—at another mega chunk of helipad. "Left, left, *left*!"

Bracchius fluttered thataway, and the jagged chunk narrowly missed scraping us to ribbons.

I patted Bracchius's equine neck. "How you doing? Is the phoenix's pull affecting you?"

"A little. It's getting more powerful."

All the more reason to hurry this up. Unfortunately, the void phoenix wasn't making it easy. It careened in a wild arc, testing the limits of its tether—but hopefully wearing itself out, too.

Anytime we thought we were getting close, it hared off in a new direction, battering us with debris from a different angle as the bits and bobs changed course to follow.

I slapped a pebble growing a single buttercup out of my face as Bracchius veered for the third time, racing along in the phoenix's wake.

"Whoa!" Bracchius swerved around a bloody knife toppling point over hilt, cherub wings flittering and tickling my thighs.

"Yaah!" I instinctively jerked back from the tickle, and plumb near toppled right to my doom. Bracchius wasn't the biggest fan of my save—I snatched his tail with both hands and hauled myself back up.

"Owowow!" Bracchius bucked, I held on for dear life, and we both recovered within a few seconds.

Right as the void phoenix zigged straight for us.

"Crap!" I fumbled in my pocket for the mirror, not having wanted to wave it blithely around this whole time with the drifting debris to knock it free.

Bracchius jinked left as black nothingness swam before us, closer, closer—

"Got it!" I whipped out the tiny mirror. One stark wing swept forward, curving, and Bracchius damn near rode it like a wave, surfing mere feet above the sinister surface in a desperate bid not to get ensnared.

Begging every arcane nightmare and deity out there to take pity on me, I delved into the barren well of my magic.

Please, even if all you blighters make the rest of my life a living hell, just give me this one thing . . .

A single lonely spark sat waiting for me.

Just one, but that was enough.

Booyah!

I collected it with care—and hellafreaking urgency—and infused it into the surface of the mirror.

One portal, incoming.

We rocketed toward the tip of the netherdark wing, and I hollered, "*Stop!!*"

Bracchius slammed on his flight brakes, but he was gonna overshoot. I unclamped my legs from his sides, twisting to touch the mirror's surface to the absolute edge of the longest feather.

Geronimo—

Except, I didn't plummet. The void phoenix's . . . magnetism? vacuum? event horizon? whatever . . . was just the right amount of force to counter gravity, and I *floated*.

I slammed that bitty mirror into the feather like there was no tomorrow. I mean, there might not be, for me.

The portal engulfed the feather's tip, the mirror's gold frame ballooning to take it in. Just as I wondered where to go from here, suspended awkwardly beside the vacuum of nothingness, Bracchius flashed back beneath me.

"You *scared* the hellfire out of me!" he shrilled.

"I'll apologize later! Fly!"

He fluttered forward in a breakneck corkscrew as the massive black wing flapped, the void phoenix on the move again.

Guiding the bloating mirror across the feathers, I expected each inch of the wing to simply disappear.

Boy was I wrong.

Instead, a silver film stretched out from the back of the mirror, coating every groove in the feathers like a second skin, actually letting me see what the phoenix looked like beyond just the dark void.

This film was a lot like when the shadelurk had chowed down on Kor's typhon.

I was already gaping to rival a starving whale, but when the mirror *wrenched itself out of my hands* and swept further across the phoenix's expanse *on its own . . .*

My brain abdicated and left the building.

How— But—

Silver rippled across the phoenix as the mirror swelled to epic proportions. Within moments, the whole wing was encased in a steely sheen.

The mirror *had* to be more than just a magical object. Was it some sort of being?? Or was this just an effect spelled into it by someone more powerful than I ever wanted to meet?

"IMOGEN!! What have you *DONE*?!!"

I flinched. Here came my consequences.

Kor screeched into sight. He flitted between me, the mirror, and the shiny film over the wing like a Ping-Pong of rage and disbelief.

Ding-ding-ding, you're not a winner!

Teeth gritted, I waggled my fingers apprehensively. "Hi, Kor. I'll make this up to you, promise."

An incomprehensible garble of vitriol spewed from him. Had I just been officially cursed?

Guess I'd know when all my organs started failing or something.

Literally incandescent with rage, he howled another blue streak of hostility, then scorched off into the distance.

Probably to burn down my apartment in revenge.

If so, he might get an unpleasant surprise from Her Unholiness, conscripted or not.

The mirror continued gulping down the void phoenix, despite the bird's berserk thrashing once it realized what was going on.

Within the span of a minute, it was totally coated in silver.

As the last scrap of darkness disappeared beneath the metallic membrane, the phoenix stilled.

A roar like the end of worlds deafened me, a much louder version of the usual caterwaul of the portal. And then . . .

Pop! The phoenix was gone.

There went my in-home laundromat.

A different howl of rage rose from the roof. I peered down at Ambrose, who'd made it to a chiseled thirty-three or so. The blackness encroaching on his skin fizzled out as the bond between him and the bird broke.

He stopped repelling attacks from the surrounding fighters and bolted across the roof, perilously close to the disintegrating edge.

Where was he going? He wasn't fleeing—he clearly had a destination, his eyes locked on something high above.

I followed his gaze. The mirror, swiftly shrinking, tumbled from the sky. Its surface was back to the smooth silver-backed glass, reflecting flashes of Cynna's red-laced lightning as it spun end over end.

Ambrose was trying to catch it.

Oh hells no.

"Bracchius, dive for that mirror!"

We swooped in a harrowing tailspin, faster and faster, with me barely clinging to Bracchius's neck. Good thing he didn't actually rely on a throat to breathe, because I was flat-out throttling him.

If we got to the mirror first, maybe I'd give Ambrose exactly what he wanted and scoop him through the portal too.

Probably a bad plan.

My face flapping in the gale-force wind, I gritted out a few words. "I. Can't. Catch. *It.*"

If I let go, I'd be worse than toast.

The mirror sparkled just feet from Ambrose. He lunged, arm outstretched.

Bracchius pulled up in a hairpin turn with the crushing gravity of the sun, his muzzle coming within inches of Ambrose's fingers.

Plastered to Bracchius's back, I was dying of anticipation. "D-Did. You get it?"

He threw his head to the side—the once-again puny mirror clenched between his teeth.

"Woohoo!!"

At least those syllables were suited to my wind-rippling lips.

As Bracchius slowed, I peered back for Ambrose's reaction to being foiled once again.

Oops.

The youthified vamp was plunging into the depths of the reverse sinkhole, his last leap for the mirror perhaps a bit misguided.

Toodle-oo. Not nice knowing ya, jerkwad.

We landed, to raucous applause. Bracchius beamed and sought out Sparkles. I collapsed in a worn-out heap, cradling the little mirror in my lap.

Who would win out—the void phoenix or the negentropes? I could just see them locked in an eternal war of chaos and order, the phoenix trying to black-hole everything while the negentropes put it all back together like Lego sets. Not a fun time for anything stuck in the middle—the imps, for instance.

Cucumber would be thrilled.

All my buds and most of the mercs crowded around me. "That was astounding!" "Are you okay?" "We'll need to debrief you." "Can I get you anything?"

Ignoring everyone, I wiggled the mirror at Samaire. "What do we do with this thing now?? Can we ship it into space? Do we know any astronauts? Do you think the inferno of Rokonor would be enough to—"

Cynna snatched the mirror from my hand. "Never mind your darling head about it. I'll handle everything."

Why did that *not* sound like a good thing?

"Uh . . . okay?" I didn't have the energy to argue. "But no unleashing it on your enemies. Or friends. Or anyone between."

She sighed. "If you insist."

My vitals were taken, and a bottle of water slapped into my hand along with some protein bars. The conversations around me smeared into a blur, and I nodded absently whenever it seemed that was expected of me.

"Leave her alone! And bring that over here!" Bracchius, back in demon form, plopped into my lap.

Someone settled us on a stretcher, and I leaned back to a soothing lullaby in my ear.

Bracchius snuggled Sparkles against my cheek. "It's okay, Immy, you take a nap. We've got it from here."

Smiling, surrounded by my friends, I conked right out for the best-deserved sleep ever.

Halle-freaking-lujah.

SWAN (SHIFTER) SONG

Her Unholiness, Umbrannia Shadowvale the Destroyer of Souls, moved in with a bewitching barrow-wight, but she'd dropped by for tea—well, a cup of tenebrous murk—with Cucumber once already.

The crows got their bucket of shredded bologna, and Gemma gave me her number for future emergencies. Fitz skulked off to report to his boss, Samaire dumped Nadine, and Paolo didn't try any more vehicular heroics.

Aster made friends with the pygmy unicorn, Krissy, and had a girls' night planned.

Cynna did I don't even *want* to know what with that mirror.

And Damarion *was* okay.

Turns out even vampires can have heart attacks when slammed with magic amped up by a void phoenix. But considering vamps' nontraditional relationship with mortality, he pulled through just fine after a few agonizing hours.

Kor, on the other hand, was less fine.

And living on my sofa; Bracchius and Sparkles had moved back under my bed for the time being.

I pulled half a bagel out of my ancient thrift-store toaster, only for Kor to engulf it in hellfire.

That was the third scorched bagel this week.

"Where's my new domain, Immy?!"

I dropped the smoldering hunk of charcoal to the kitchen floor. "I'm looking for one, I swear!" The linoleum started to bubble. "It can't be that hard to replace a secondhand *laundromat* domain with something equally stupid, right?"

Kor huffed. "It may have been stupid, but it was mine!"

Oops. Had I said that out loud?

I softened. Nobody deserved to lose their home, despot demon or not.

"I know. And I'm sorry I wrecked your domain, really. But it was either that or have all of us be obliterated, so . . ."

We'd only had some variation of this argument seventy-seven times already.

The negentropes descended on the smoking baked good, and hey presto—they returned the linoleum to its former state, before presenting me with a glob of raw bagel dough.

Let's just say they didn't quite get the nuances when it came to 'fixing' food.

My house was sparkling, but they were driving me *bonkers*.

I'd thought I'd like having my own team of housemaids buzzing around the house, but they took everything way too far.

I no longer had left and right shoes—just perfectly symmetrical ones, for very unsymmetrical feet.

In the same vein, my microwave was a mirror image, with no buttons to get it working.

Not even my Swiss cheese had holes.

And the whole place reeked of that damn peaches-and-marshmallows smell—including my salt, and pepper, and sriracha.

Turns out chaos has its uses.

At least they'd steered clear of *me* since I bought a tennis racket bug zapper.

Though, I did appreciate how quickly they destinkified the bathroom when Cucumber used the tub for his foul bubblebath adventures.

"Lady Immy, may I have my own domain too?" Cuke squeaked from behind me, his voice muffled *and* echoing.

Where the dickens had he clambered now?

"Maybe," I hedged, checking my kitchen cabinet for skulking demonlings. I had already been thinking about finding *Bracchius* a domain too, while I was at it.

Not that any existing dark and gloomy demon domain would suit him.

Demon domains had to come from somewhere, right? Was there some dude out there I could pester about making custom domains?

Wasn't exactly the kind of thing you could look up in the three-ton slab of scrap paper they called a phone book, that *still* got religiously dumped on my stoop once a year.

Not that my phone book didn't always get donated for lining for crow nests anyway.

And the internet was no help. Demons made a habit of scrubbing any mention of themselves off the interwebs, probably to the ire of the exact same domain creators—architects?—I was hoping to hunt down.

Pausing in my search of the cabinetry, I cocked an ear.

Was that *chanting*?

I yanked open the oven, only to be confronted with a whole coven of demonlings arrayed in a pentagram on a baking sheet.

Giggles kept interrupting their sinister chanting.

Staring, I licked dry lips and said the only thing I could think of. "Do you . . . want the door closed?"

"Yes please!" Cucumber, the ringleader, piped.

Okay, then.

Bracchius whirred into the room as I shut the oven on the budding cult. "Practice time!" He was toting a broom handle along with my sword.

Not like I was eating my bagel anyway . . .

"Gimme that." I grabbed my sword and unsheathed it.

Demons really were the ideal sparring partners. They could move lightning-quick in any direction, and wouldn't be harmed by any blow I could land.

Not that I *had* landed one yet, in our several years of practice.

I danced out of the way as Bracchius half-heartedly tried to wallop me with his stick. No matter how many times I insisted he should put more oomph into his attacks, he still went easy on me.

Probably 'cause I get grumpy when I'm bruised and battered.

And yeah, 'cause he likes me, duh.

I whipped my sword out, and Bracchius teleported with a *pop*. My sword tip stuck in the wall. "That's cheating!"

"Yup!"

Cheating was totally allowed—if you only practice against Goody Two-Shoes, you're really setting yourself up for an epic fail.

Doesn't mean I can't *gripe* about the cheating, though.

I pried my sword out of the drywall and admired the deep slice left behind, right beside the dent from attacking a direghast with my umbrella.

Long story.

The negentropes swarmed over, but I held up a forbidding finger. "Nope, not that one either. We gotta leave *some* memories in this place."

And I fully intended to make a lot more.

Especially the good ones.

THE END

AUTHOR'S NOTE

Thanks so much for reading! While you're waiting for your next dose of snark, magic, and mayhem, if you'd be SO amazing as to leave a review for this book—no spoilers, please!—it would abso-freaking-lutely make my day.

Want to know the instant Immy, Bracchius, and the gang get up to more mischief? Join the Snark Squad at NiaQuinn.com for sneak peeks, exclusive goodies, unicorn glitter, and other magical nonsense!

And if you managed to tease out any typos in this book, I'd love to hear from you directly! Some things always sneak through despite Herculean efforts, and I can fix them fastest if you email me at nia@niaquinn.com – please report any errors with either a page number, the surrounding paragraph text, and/or a screenshot.

ACKNOWLEDGEMENTS

This was a new adventure in writing for me—publishing chapter by chapter for serial readers before the full book release—and I found so much joy along the way, both from my hilarious and endlessly kind readers, and from my characters, who absolutely like to have their own way (and make their stories all the better for it—despite my occasional outbursts of 'You want to do what now?!')

Thank you to my fantabulous snarksters for your jokes, love and support, including Gaius, Chuck, Cynna, LL, Katie, Jillian, Kirsty, Sandy, and Elisha.

Thank you to my narrator, Amy Hall, for your boundless talent, humor, magic, and kindness—you have such a gift for bringing stories to life, and will definitely be making a lot of folks snort and cackle with this one!

Thank you to Ravyn for all your amazing help—this book (and my life these last few months!) would've been much messier without you.

Thank you to Malcolm Acan, Nate Gillick, and everyone else at Laterpress, who were among the first to love this story and help it take its place in the world.

Thank you to all my wonderful author friends who have helped me along on this journey.

And thank YOU, my amazing reader, for riding along on this dorky, shenanigan-filled pegasus flight with me—demons, unicorn plushies, Laffy Taffy skeletons, and all <3

                – Nia

Nia Quinn grew up devouring fantasy about powerful girls with magic and swords, humor and kindness (and let's be honest, that's still the majority of what she reads . . . and writes . . .)

She spends her spare time chasing after every fuzzy animal that will allow her to pet it, and will hurl any book where the dog dies across the room with righteous fury. And then possibly burn it. And toast marshmallows over it. And make s'mores.

Delicious.

When she's not enjoying s'mores, you can find her worshipping the sun, geeking out over a game, or frantically scribbling down a conversation between two characters in her head. (Yes, she is crazy, but she doesn't mind.)

CONNECT ONLINE

NiaQuinn.com

NiaQuinnWrites

PRONUNCIATION GUIDE

animafae	ANN-uh-muh-FAY
axolotlae	AXE-uh-LOT-ull-ay
Bracchius	BRACK-ee-uhs
Calamandrian	cal-ah-man-dree-an
camazotz	camm-uh-ZAWTS
cerberat	SIR-burr-ratt
cerberogre	sir-burr-oh-ger
corvidae	CORE-vuh-day
Cynna	SINN-uh
Damarion	duh-MARE-ee-in
Dreyelian	dray-YELL-ee-in
Echendia	ee-KEN-dee-uh
Eldevarian	ell-deh-VARE-ee-enn
Emendelmiria	EMM-en-dell-MEER-ee-uh
enraenra	en-RAIN-rah
Enthilia	enn-THEE-lee-uh
Faina	FAY-nuh
feefal	FEE-full
ferromites	FAIR-oh-mights
Finéa	feh-NAY-uh
fluorosprites	FLURE-oh-sprites
Immy	IMM-ee
kerfluffle	curr-FLUFF-ull
Kor	CORE
lepidopterafae	lep-uh-DOP-ter-uh-fay
Meraki	murr-AH-key
merbrine	MURR-brine

mycofae	MY-koh-fae
Nalustrak	NAL-iss-track
Nardi	NARR-dee
necrowraith	NECK-row-raith
negentropes	NEGG-in-tropes
orrax	OAR-RACKS
pixious	PICKS-ee-iss
polymerae	PAUL-uh-murr-AY
Rajaki	rah-ZHAK-ee
Reinhuf	RINE-hoof
Rokonor	ROE-kuh-nore
Salamandrine	sal-uh-man-DREEN
Samaire	Suh-MARE
Sanguinsation	SANG-gwin-SAY-shen
Saskia	SASS-key-uh
somnubus	SAWM-nuh-bus
Stymphalian	stimm-FAIL-ee-enn
Totine	toe-TEEN
Vicente	vee-CHEN-tay

These Imperfect Reflections: Short Stories by Merc Fenn Wolfmoor

What's the price of revolution backed by artificial intelligence? Can you change the past to free ghosts trapped in endless loops? Do fairy tales always end the same way? Witness the last documentary about alien whales; travel with the Wolf prophesied to eat the sun as they look for alternatives to their fate. These eleven fantasy and science fiction stories will take you on otherworldly adventures tethered to the heart.

The Transcendent Green by Mati Ocha

Magic tears through an unsuspecting human planet, bringing mythology and monsters to life—and giving humanity a chance to prove their mettle. Calum Green wants to reach what remains of his family. He does not want to make the 99-mile trek through the the Scottish Highlands with his cheating ex-girlfriend's bestie at his side. Eilidh MacIntosh has always disliked Calum, and now she's armed with a bloody claymore on top of her haughty disdain. But the ascension directive is clear: humans cannot survive this new world alone—and this pair makes an annoyingly good team.

Liquid City by Andi C. Buchanan

Casp works transporting cargo through the ancient tunnels beneath Liquid City. It's a dirty, dangerous game but affords them the independence they always longed for. But the offer of a lucrative contract persuades Casp to journey into the unexplored parts of the tunnel network, deep underground. Accompanied by an ill-tempered cephalopod and the scientist daughter of their wealthy sponsor, Casp quickly finds success means an end to the livelihoods of the tunnel folk who have become their family—and a discovery that will shift the balance of power in Liquid City forever

To Catch a Flieff by Julia Rios

Alessia is an engineer who just wants a smooth trip home to celebrate Mizzentide with her family, but what are those pawprints leading into the Astral Dancer's engine room? Darmanda didn't mean to let an arctic flieff loose aboard a spaceship, but once she has, her only choice is to go after it. Now the two women must work together to find the flieff, AND pretend to be dating so the ship's captain doesn't suspect anything. Fake dating, only one bed, awkward lesbians, and a fluffy agent of chaos add up to a holiday romance that is truly out of this world!

You Fed Us To the Roses
by Carlie St. George

Final girls who team up. Dead boys still breathing. Ghosts who whisper secrets. Angels beyond the grave, yet not of heaven. Wolves who wear human skins. Ten disturbing, visceral, stories no horror fan will want to miss.

Hollow King by Dante O. Greene

Five years ago, Barridur Sharrow deserted the army rather than commit war crimes. Now a well-liked mason raising his adopted child, everything falls apart when his former commanding officer discovers him—and Barridur is executed as a deserter. Barridur finds himself in Hell, where he meets the fabled Hollow King. A cruel and capricious god, the Hollow King offers Barridur a chance to return to the living world. All Barridur has to do is defeat the Nine Champions of Hell. How hard can it be, really? If he fails, the Hollow King will devour his soul and Barridur will become part of the wraith army, enslaved for all eternity. No pressure.

TRIGGER WARNINGS

Some of these topics are only mentioned or
discussed in passing. Any topics actually shown on the
page are marked with an asterisk.

amputation*
animal attack*
assault*
attempted murder*
banishment
blood*
bodies/corpses*
bones*
car accident*
cheating
death*
demons*
drug use (illicit)
drug use (prescription)
explosions*
forced captivity*
hostages*

imprisonment*
kidnapping*
occult*
physical injuries*
serious injury*
skeletons*
smoking*
snakes*
spiders*
storms*
violence*
weapons*

www.ingramcontent.com/pod-product-compliance
Lightning Source LLC
Chambersburg PA
CBHW061533190726
48289CB00004B/1027